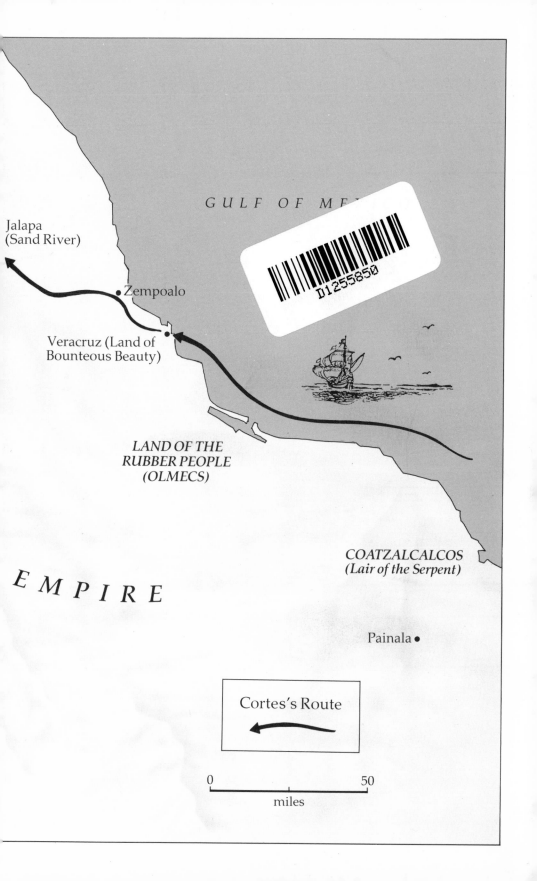

GULF OF ME[...]

Jalapa
(Sand River)

• Zempoalo

Veracruz (Land of
Bounteous Beauty)

LAND OF THE
RUBBER PEOPLE
(OLMECS)

COATZALCALCOS
(Lair of the Serpent)

E M P I R E

Painala •

Cortes's Route
⟵

0   50
miles

Death of the
Fifth Sun

DEATH
OF THE
FIFTH SUN

Robert Somerlott

VIKING

VIKING
Viking Penguin Inc., 40 West 23rd Street, New York, New York 10010, U.S.A.
Penguin Books Ltd, Harmondsworth, Middlesex, England
Penguin Books Australia Ltd, Ringwood, Victoria, Australia
Penguin Books Canada Limited, 2801 John Street, Markham, Ontario, Canada L3R 1B4
Penguin Books (N.Z.) Ltd, 182–190 Wairau Road, Auckland 10, New Zealand

First published in 1987 by Viking Penguin Inc.
Published simultaneously in Canada

LIBRARY OF CONGRESS CATALOGING IN PUBLICATION DATA
Somerlott, Robert.
Death of the fifth sun.
I. Title.
PS3569.06516D4   1987   813'.54   86–40260
ISBN 0–670–81377–X

Printed in the United States of America by
R. R. Donnelley & Sons Company, Harrisonburg, Virginia
Set in Bembo
Designed by Ann Gold
Map by Paul Pugliese, General Cartography, Inc.

For T.B.S.

"Behold the atom . . ."

Lansing, 1946   San Miguel, 1982

Part One
"ONE GRASS OF PENANCE . . ."

1

The City of Mexico—April 25, 1564 —The Feast of St. Mark

Yesterday noon at the end of the Watch of the Fifth Ruler of the Day my lord the Captain came home to this his city—if the arrival of a box of dry bones from Spain can be called a homecoming. But "homecoming" is the word the archbishop used later that day when he was shouting and sweating behind those bones in the cathedral. I heard it myself, just barely, from His Grace's blessed but liverish lips.

That was about all I caught of his harangue. I was more fascinated by watching him tie a mask of pleasure over his rage. The archbishop was cornered and he knew it. If he had not led the wild paean to the Captain, the mob might have gutted him alive at his own altar. His Grace is not seeking the palm branch of a martyr—not he! Such stuff is not in him.

The uproar in the church—the yells, cheers, hammering of drums and shriek of whistles—so deafened me that His Grace seemed to be performing a dumb show, mouthing and gesticulating like the comic hunchback mimes of Cholula. I watched him through a dark veil— I wore the habit of a nun yesterday—but I heard little even though I stood so close I could see the gray ring of dirt above his collar. His Grace does not splash water below his chin, he is so holy.

I heard him cry, "Oh, glorious homecoming . . . triumphant return of the beloved . . . the obedient, yes, obedient child of God and our Most Catholic Sovereign."

3

"Thy mother, priest!" I cursed him from behind the nun's veil. "I dirty thy mother's milk! I piss on her grave!"

". . . humble soldier of the Faith brought home today . . ."

"Thy dead balls, Archbishop! My dog spits them out!"

I learned my Spanish from soldiers; they speak it plainer than priests.

His Grace could not hear me, of course. But saying the familiar words I have not used in a long time gave me satisfaction. And at about that time a riot began.

I have not enjoyed myself so much in ten years. No, forty.

But I am far ahead of my story—I suppose it is a sign of my approaching senility. Let me go back; let me explain.

For two weeks I have been lodging at the Convent of the Holy Child in this city where nobody realizes I am still alive. Convents for women are a great novelty in New Spain, although I expect they will soon spring up like toadstools. They are residences for ladies who have never been screwed or never much liked it, plus a few lecherous relicts like me. A very strange idea. Of course, in the old days we had the House of the Virgins but that was quite different and certainly more amusing. Ah, yes!

At any rate, I engaged quarters in this new convent where Mother Superior, the Lady Maria Monica, knows me only as Señora Xamarillo, the Christianized Aztec widow of a Spanish knight and sea captain who was lost on a voyage many years ago. She also knows I am owner of plantations far to the south. Such is my true condition and even my name. Of course if she knew my other name, Malinche, she would gape at me speechless with disbelief and then consternation. No one, least of all Mother Superior, would know how to behave in the presence of such an inconvenient ghost.

My living beyond my time has been impertinent; I know I am vestigial and should have had the decency to die in obscurity long ago. Yet in living on, I am typical of this land where time defies arrangement. Here the dead centuries do not obligingly glide into the night but remain listening and watchful, only half-blind and half-dead, like village elders who have been pushed aside but will not quite relinquish seats at the council fire. Like them, I cling to my place in the shadows.

The convent has been a comfortable enough place to stay while I awaited the return of my lord's bones, but yesterday morning just after dawn it seemed to have turned into a prison, and I was the only inmate who had run of the corridors. The nuns had retreated to their domestic chapel to pray for deliverance from any devils who might be arriving later in the day with the captain's cortege. Hiding with them were the faded, papery gentlewomen boarders, all spinsters or widows cast off by their families. Some, instead of praying, were simply cowering in their beds—or under them. Poor creatures! Elderly, timorous children whom propriety has so shriveled that it is hard to believe they are human, that they would bleed if slashed.

I sat alone in the courtyard near the grille in the gate, awaiting any messenger who might tell me news. Would the procession arrive in the city today? Would it make a detour and not be seen here at all? I had heard both rumors.

A troop of the viceroy's cavalry pounded past, helmets flashing, pennants whipping the dusty cloud that moved with them. Besides swords and lances, I saw three harquebuses strapped to saddles. They expect trouble.

The horses almost trampled a street singer, a blind boy who seemed dressed in nothing but European patches and who was groping his way along the walls. After the troops had passed, he coughed until his throat was clear of dust, then began to serenade the deserted street in a thin falsetto like the quivering voice of a clay flute, his tone not sweet yet almost beautiful in its pain and loneliness.

His boyish face seemed not chiseled enough to be Aztec, yet there was highland strength in his cheekbones and chin. He sang in the old tongue, mourning and lamenting as they always do nowadays, casting his grief into images of scattered plumes and petals ripped from flowers. In his song a hummingbird died.

When he finished, he hesitated for applause that did not come, but since he was not aware the street was deserted, he began a more popular number. By the third note I knew what was coming and thought of covering my ears. This was another of those songs that are supposed to be about me but are only about my name, since I am nothing like the person the foolish, romantic words depict and never have been. When I hear these grotesque ballads—and they are sung everywhere—I wonder what peyote eater could have invented such unlikely dreams. Worse, so many lies! The boy's ballad was just like the others and just as bad. The words are so much the same that I almost knew the lyrics before he uttered them.

"She weeps in darkness, Lady Malinche,
above the dying lakes
above the broken altars.
Are hers the tears of evil, as old men say?
Ah, her body knew the plumes' embrace,
the serpent's tongue caressing . . .
Young men weep in darkness for Lady Malinche."

What's this rubbish of embracing plumes? I have known only embraces of flesh—but of those I knew considerable. Such songs cannot move me because they are not about me. They are like the remarks I overhear in the streets. "My mother was as beautiful as Malinche." Or a market wife will cluck, "My son's betrothed is as clever as Malinche—and as treacherous!"

What can they matter, the praise or the slanders? Malinche is dead. It merely happens that quiet Señora Xamarillo now inhabits the decrepit body that was once Malinche's.

Yet I really know that the other lives I lived are not quite entombed. For instance, my name on the lips of a singer can sometimes bring back the day in girlhood when I, bound with wet rawhide and gagged with cotton, heard my name lamented in my own funeral chant as it was sung by paid mourners. At such a memory I can still feel myself struggling against the wrist thongs, trying to scream against the wadding.

"Come over here, boy!" I called, impatient with the ballad. When he fumbled his way to the grille, I gave him a coin, pressing it into his thin hand, not using the bamboo tongs that hang inside the gate so the nuns may give alms without touching flesh that might be leprous.

"What news of the city, boy?"

"People are arriving from everywhere. They say the box with the god inside it might pass through the city on the way to its burial in Texcoco." His chest swelled a little. "I am to be among the singers at the burial if I can learn the barbarous Latin words in time."

I thanked him. Then, looking at that fine face, I asked if his people were Aztec.

"No, my lady. I am of an older tree. My family came from Culhuacan, bride of the lakes, the city that kept the seed of the Toltecs."

"My father's people were also from there! Not many of us are left. Are you a Christian, my nephew?"

He answered quickly, much too quickly. "Yes, of course, my lady! We worship the Virgin Goddess and her white Son-in-the-Wafer."

Then he added a bit of truth because, I hope, Culhuas have a habit of straight speaking. "We also revere the Earth Mother and Plumed Serpent—his bright face, not the dark."

"So do I, nephew. We cannot be too cautious about gods." *Nor about men,* I thought, hoping he was not always so forthright. Spies of the Holy Office are everywhere, and I would not like to hear the blind boy's voice cry out among the purifying flames in the plaza. I gave him another coin and sent him on his way.

No one passed for another hour. The sun was turning molten on the distant snows of the volcanoes, the Smoking Man and his wife the Sleeping Woman. The city seemed unnaturally silent, and I realized it was the portentous watch before midday when the sun sweeps along escorted by the burnished souls of fallen soldiers.

Then a charcoal burner, a soot-stained old fellow full of gossip and excitement, came to deliver fuel for the convent's braziers. From him I learned how my lord the Captain, instead of avoiding the capital, was going to make an unexpected return—coming back in state to this city we destroyed street by street and even stone by stone a lifetime ago . . .

Much of what the old charcoal burner told me I already knew. It has been no secret, of course, that the Captain's bones made port a month ago at Veracruz after moldering for fifteen years in a Spanish monastery. The world has been astir for weeks while the sacred cortege has inched over the mountain trails, pausing at every cornpatch altar to receive reverence—which looked suspiciously like worship—from folk along the way.

Don Martin, the Marques del Valle, my lord's son and heir by his second Spanish wife, had ordered the bones returned. So he rode at the head of the march on a black charger caparisoned with blue-black plumes and velvet, looking somewhat like a mourner but rather more like a future king of New Spain.

My own son, Tepi, the son I bore my lord the Captain and who was also christened Martin in honor of my lord's father, rode somewhere in the long procession. I have been hoping he was shrewd enough to stay well behind the coffin. Would he be cautious? I know next to nothing about this middle-aged son of mine.

Along the route, sometimes ahead of the march and sometimes behind, moved the two Avila brothers, pious expressions on their weasel faces. Their father, who now groans in purgatory if he is not screaming in hell, was a thug and rapist. The sons, smoother and more devious, were born with their father's claws. God alone knows what they are up to.

"Two miracles have been reported on the road," said the charcoal burner, wide-eyed. "Near Tlaxcala a golden hawk, a spirit of the Sun, swooped low over the coffin. Its talons actually brushed the velvet. Then it hovered above the marques, uttering a cry so fierce that they say the echoes rang like a clash of swords. That same night a shower of fire was flung across the heavens."

I had heard this, too. Fire streaked the Cloud River where the stars drift in clusters and Lady Moon feeds upon them.

The viceroy, Don Luis de Velasco, learned these things and scented sedition. He ordered the marques—and my son?—to withdraw from the march. The Avila brothers were seized and shackled, the procession from Veracruz was secretly ordered to follow an unlikely route. Naturally the whole world knew everything within a day.

"The marchers were warned to stay far from the capital," the charcoal burner continued. "His Excellency is frantic that the people may gather. They say he has even tried sorcery to make the marchers and the coffin as invisible as water goblins."

I doubted this. The viceroy is superstitious as a nun and trembles at the thought of demons. He has decreed that magicians will be fastened to a pillar in the new park and burned alive along with heretics. Yet I felt sure he mentioned the cortege in his prayers and implored its disappearance. He is forever praying; His Excellency knows only two positions: on horseback and on his knees. They say his wife has adjusted to both postures.

"Three days ago a mingy honor guard was dispatched," the charcoal burner told me. "Old veterans on starvation pay."

I knew of these men, so poor they had long since pawned their armor and now wore bark paper imitations.

These soldiers were to meet the procession and lead it away from the main road, bypassing the capital, following a trail through the swamps where the lakes are retreating, a track so obscure that only scorpions and rattlesnakes know it. The final destination was the shabby monastery among the ruins of Texcoco. In other words, nowhere.

"Ah, yes. Texcoco," I said. The charcoal burner nodded, and for a moment we were both silent, two old relics remembering a place of their youth.

Texcoco, although it once had greater glories, used to be praised as "the city of ten thousand whores with a hundred thousand ways." I remember being taken there as a child to visit my beautiful cousin who had been chosen Unblemished Youth for sacrifice that year. When we walked from the boat landing toward the holy precinct, I saw the pretty ladies, their teeth painted bright pink with cinnabar. They lolled in the shade of the junipers in the plaza, they petted and groomed one another, tickling each other's necks and ears with tips of dyed turkey feathers, their voices like twittering songbirds. Clusters of tiny silver bells were stitched to their clothing, so they never walked without music—a cloud of music and incense. They wore pure white robes embroidered with petals, and I thought them as exquisite as guava blossoms. I was so enchanted that I gasped aloud in amazement.

My mother cuffed me and pinched my arm. "Keep your gaze downward, Mali!" she ordered. "Stop making owl's eyes at everything. People will take us for clods from the backcountry."

Which was, of course, exactly what we were. I pretended to look down, but I missed none of the charms of Texcoco.

Now coyotes and ocelots hunt in the ruined courts where the pretty ladies once worshiped the Flower Prince and performed his rites with such voluptuous art. The thousand fountains lie broken; lizards make nests in them. Plague carried off half the people, and slavers did for the rest. Now there remain only ruins and a few skeletal survivors who dwell in holes, like foxes. In this bleak desert stands the raw monastery where my lord the Captain's bones are to be entombed in obscurity beside the remains of his first wife, that whey-faced bitch he strangled. Afterward he ordered her buried in a place he could forget, a spot he never need visit.

Now it seems that an unintended visit will be made after all . . .

Again I am showing my age. I have strayed from the news the charcoal burner told me at the grille of the convent gate yesterday morning.

He said, "The procession with the bones was winding down the slope near the Valley of Mexico. Suddenly a mob that had been hiding in a ravine swept upon the marchers. They engulfed the viceroy's guards—in fact, some of the guards helped plan the ambush."

Yelling and singing, exalting the coffin above their heads, two thousand celebrants danced across the plain. "Right now the whole world is at the edge of the city," the charcoal burner murmured in awe. "They say there are wizards in feather capes—things I have not seen since I was a boy. There are Zapotecs from the south painted like demons, giants from Jalisco. Even Chichimecs wearing dog-skin breechclouts!"

"They are going to enter the city!" I exclaimed. "When? How do you know?"

"Some horsemen raced ahead and spread the news. The whole crowd will be here soon! What a noise it will be, what a show!"

Then, even as he spoke, I caught the sound of music far away. The charcoal burner listened, then gave a shout and tossed his sooty bag over his shoulder. "They are coming now!" Waving me farewell, he ran down the street to join the celebrants.

Excited families emerged from the adobe huts that huddle against the convent wall. They, too, had heard the distant clamor.

"Malintzin! Malintzin!" they cried, which means Malinche's lord in the old tongue. "He is coming back! Malinche's lord is returning!"

Suddenly, as I hesitated at the convent gate, I found tears running down my cheeks. It was odd; I could not remember my own tears and they had a strange taste. Neither could I remember when anything had clutched at my heart and made it pound so—for a moment I had the strong heart of a girl.

Then I hurried as best I could toward the cathedral, knowing that the procession could end nowhere but at the high altar. To ease my way over the rubble that always blocks some streets nowadays, I carried two canes, and I was wearing, as I have said, the veil, habit and outsize rosary of a nun, although not from piety. Such dress has lately become fashionable in New Spain, especially among widows, and I am a widow—although I have a perfectly serviceable young man to warm my sleeping mat back home. I am grateful for the veil I can lower to cover my face in harsh daylight. For myself, I care nothing about the wrinkles and pouches of age; they are honest battle scars. But in the unlikely event I should be recognized, I could not bear to overhear anyone say, "What? That crone is Doña Marina? Malinche? He took that hag for a bedmate?"

My body, except for the arthritis, has served me better than my face. Even today my shadow is almost that of a girl.

So, in fashionable and pious disguise, I arrived at the broad plaza. At that same moment the whole world poured into it from the opposite side, a human cascade. The vanguard, besides the acrobats, jugglers and fire dancers, now had ten thousand screaming Chichimec savages, their bodies tattooed yellow and green. They leapt into the air, whooping for joy as they brandished war clubs and lilies. Behind them the air burst with an eruption of flowers, thousands of handfuls of blossoms tossed not only for joy but to make a flower carpet for the feet of the coffin bearers. A haze of scented smoke drifted around me.

They marched with drums and flutes and cymbals. A troupe of acrobats, male and female, formed a guard of honor for the coffin, sashaying as they strutted on their hands doing flips and cartwheels, naked except for their flowers and bells. As at festivals in the old days, men and women coupled and joined in astonishing combinations while they moved forward like gigantic caterpillars or inchworms.

I would have had no chance for a place inside the church except for a strange event that delayed the marchers. A new palace, two stories high, stands on the western side of the plaza, and a small tower rises from one of its corners. Suddenly a grotesque old woman, monstrously fat, appeared on the roof of the tower, and behind her were two trumpeters blowing for all they were worth. But it was not the trumpets that arrested the march, it was the woman herself—so obese, so enormous, that I was sure the roof, perhaps the whole tower, would give way beneath her. Long ago the Emperor Moctezuma kept a collection of human freaks in the royal zoo, and now I stood marveling that one of them had escaped and survived all these years into old age.

She was utterly naked, wearing not a stitch except for two red funerary swathings at her wrists and a little stone burial mask of jade bound to her forehead. Her hair, which must have been white, had been dipped in solemn crimson.

"I am his wife!" she screamed. "I was an earthly bride of Plumed Serpent! Bride of Quetzalcoatl!"

She pointed toward the coffin, the soft ham that was her forearm jiggling, and the pendulous breasts, red streaked, swung like wineskins from a saddle. As she swayed, I saw a glint of light from her spread crotch and realized that the lips of her monstrous cunt were gilded and bejeweled.

This spectacle halted the Chichimecs in their tracks, and they held their ground against the crush behind them, ogling her, agape, never having seen a living mound of female flesh before. Whether they longed to fondle it or devour it I cannot guess.

"His wife, his bride!" she cried again, this time in Spanish to make sure no one in the world failed to understand. Enraged, I looked around for a loose cobblestone to hurl at this blaspheming monster, but there is never such a thing handy when you need it.

Then suddenly I was as agape as the Chichimecs. I recognized the woman, although I had not seen her for forty years! She had been a princess given to the Captain by her uncle, and even then we joked about her girth. But the Captain did not laugh. He received her with gentleness and grace, and—at least once—he gave her more pleasure than formality demanded. He understood courtesy; he could be kind.

I stood dazed, for a moment no longer in the great plaza of Mexico but in a clearing in the hotland jungles. My lord the Captain stood beside me, and not far away was the Fat Princess beside her uncle the Fat Chief. Decked in bridal finery, she looked like a whole meadow of glorybush in blossom; she pouted and simpered, she waggled her fat fingers in a way that was at once childish and obscene.

My lord the Captain spoke gravely, acknowledging her as a gift, and I translated. "Tell her uncle that he has just given me the largest jewel in the world. His generosity is boundless, beyond measure."

The Captain turned toward me and suddenly, secretly, he winked. Struggling against laughter, I solemnly translated his words into . . . what language? Where were we? What did they speak? I have forgotten.

Now standing on the tower the brief and long-ago bride shrieked in ecstasy. "I join my lord now! Now I come!" She popped something into her mouth; it must have been a carved heart of jade for the Narrow Passage. Then she raised those ugly arms high and hurled herself from the roof while the watchers screamed and leapt to save themselves from being squashed on the paving.

I could not see the body. They crowded around her, most of them not having seen a self-sacrifice in years. A sharp rat-a-tat on the paving beside me broke the spell, my own cane rattling as my right hand trembled. My senses came back, and I made for the cathedral doors, still marveling at the long survival and now the death of the Fat Princess.

They say our fate is set by our own rabbit, an invisible creature born with each of us; our feet must unknowingly follow the rabbit's tortuous, random course. What an odd track the Fat Princess had pursued to reach her public suicide. But of course she could not have died earlier or privately; she had been touched by a god, and her extinction had to be performed nobly in the god's service.

But if that plunge toward the astonished faces and the stones below was her ordained sacrifice, how much stranger my own must be, how beyond my imagining. We follow the rabbit; we do not see the cliff at the end of the path.

Inside the church I found consternation as priests and acolytes scurried about removing valuables, snatching up golden candlesticks, hauling away embroidered chairs used by important worshipers. Terrified, not knowing what the next hour might bring, they raced this way and that, wildly flapping their full-sleeved arms like sacrificed turkeys.

A young priest with a Castillian lisp tried to bar my way, crying, "Go home, Reverend Lady, go home and lock your door. No masses today, no confessions!"

He was determined to save me, to halt me, so I raised the two canes, crossing them, and thrust them at his face as though exorcising a demon. I uttered a snarl as I rapped him hard on the shoulder.

"Fuck you, devil's spawn!"

He fled in panic, and I moved quickly down the aisle past the tapestry of the woman saint called Judith who holds a sword in one hand, a severed head in the other. I nodded at her in admiration. Near the chancel rail I found a quiet place where I had a column at my back for protection.

Then, as the mob burst in with the coffin, all thirty-four bells in the towers began to clang at once in a violent but hollow welcome.

I have already described the archbishop's performance, and will add only that I found it wonderful how he could pretend not to see the rites the acrobats were performing in a side chapel. A dozen dwarfs had formed a human pyramid at the altar of St. Christopher the Giant, the smallest dwarf gyrating at the top, blessing the multitude, waving fertility upon them with his swollen cock, a member so enormous on such a small man that no one knew which was the appendage of the other. My lord the Captain would have found him hilarious.

Meanwhile His Grace was orating, and when he spoke of the "homecoming," I cursed him for dishonoring the word he uttered. A man with no reverence for words can have no reverence for magic, so he must never be trusted. All my life words have been my good tools—some say my evil weapons—and I try to honor them as a Toltec honors his paints and brushes.

Homecoming! My lord's home was nowhere and everywhere— no place could claim him, although he claimed all places. And the oak coffin, now on a stand behind the chancel rail, could no more hold my lord the Captain than the veiled box on the altar can encapsule the Almighty God of the Universe. Preposterous! Wherever the Captain might be, in whatever reach of the heavens or depth of the Nether Valley, he was not present in the Cathedral of Mexico! The coffin did not radiate; it glowed with no heat of his spirit, no sweetness of his breath. *I* would have known, would have felt it. The box contained . . . nothing.

But the people believed otherwise. Suddenly, as if at a signal, the basilica rang with a vast unison chant, the hymn of death before battle, the ancient song of passage through the Narrow Way, the paean that welcomes the soul to Mictlan where the withered branch one carries bursts into blossom. The song became a roar. It spread from the church to the throngs in the atrium, past the palaces and towers, ringing over the waters of the dying lakes until the volcanoes themselves must have sounded the echoes.

The crowd surged forward to touch the coffin, to seize threads of velvet as relics of the god. On the floor they dropped little hearts of stone and glass cut like jade for the journey of the dead Lord. The acolytes fighting to hold back the mob were brushed aside; shouting priests were pinned to the walls, there to be buffeted, elbowed and punched.

"Oh, my children! Be calm, my children! This place is holy!"

the archbishop cried. But his words were flung against the thunder. I
have stood in the middle of battlefields that were quieter.

"Rejoice in this homecoming, but do not be deceived by evil men
who would use it for wicked ends!" he implored them at the top of
his lungs. "Even now those who would mislead you have been seized
and await punishment."

I thought, *Could he mean Tepi? Could he mean my son?*

Then I was caught up in the power, the exultation around me.
I clung to my pillar while the chancel rail split and was trodden under
bare feet. His Grace fled to the vestry as the people, triumphant,
claimed the cathedral and the newly returned god as their own.

And so, for the second time, Captain General Hernan Cortes
conquered Mexico.

2

The Jalisco Frontier—
1499–1508

My birth name—which Spaniards could never pronounce, much less understand—is Ce Malinalli. It means One Grass of Penance, a name so unlucky that it can truly be called disastrous. Certainly it is not what my parents would willingly have chosen, but in this matter there is no human choice; a birth name is ordained by the positions of the stars, of Lord Sun and his sister Lady Moon at the hour one enters the world. The name is selected by Time itself and so cannot be changed.

Even an amateur astrologer can recognize Ce Malinalli as a confluence of heavenly signs too dangerous to be tolerated. Because of this, I suppose, no other living woman shares my name although other girl babies must have been born at almost the same time. None of them can have survived more than a day or two. As soon as their horoscopes were revealed, these babies, my little star-sisters, were drowned or burned or beheaded by their parents to keep them from their ordained destiny. Here and there one may have lived because the mother concealed the true hour of birth and gave the baby an alias. In the long run I doubt it did much good. Trying to deceive the gods is a losing game.

My own mother, a pious woman, intended a quick death for me, and it is no sin of hers that I was spared a cradle of lake water.

My father, Prince Chimal, was then serving on the frontier as governor of part of the wild region called Jalisco, vast lands that the

Aztec monarch claimed but did not control. Nobody ruled there, except farther west the bald Tarascans, cousins of the Dog People. It was the brink of the civilized world.

My father's position amounted to polite banishment. Prince Chimal was not Aztec; neither was he a lord from any of the three cities of the powerful Triple Alliance that dominated the world. He came from the royal house of the ancient city of Culhuacan, daughter of the lakes, once a mighty state but now a minor Aztec vassal. But the Aztecs, like many upstarts and climbers, felt awe of older races, so my father gained a position of honor, if not of power, in the empire that the Aztecs unblushingly called a confederacy.

As a youth, Prince Chimal had been taken to the capital to study at the great academy, where he was looked upon partly as an honored guest, partly as a hostage, even though the wars had ended long ago and rebellion by a nearby city had become unthinkable. He won honors in combat with the short sword and in use of the spear thrower.

Outstanding though he was in war, Prince Chimal's great talent was for astrology. This would be his distinction—and later his undoing.

The prince was given an Aztec noblewoman as a wife, the Lady Iztac, called that because of her pale complexion. An old woman carried the bride on her back to the groom's quarters, where, after ritual bathing and drinking, their mantles were tied for life. Then my father went off to stay with friends for several nights while my mother's male relatives initiated her into the rites of the Flower Prince. Everything was done properly and respectably.

My father began his public service in the reign of King Ahuizotl, that mad ruler still known as the Wrathful, and before long some of that sea of royal wrath splashed onto my father. I suppose it was some trouble about religious observance, but it could have been anything. "The Wrathful" exiled Prince Chimal to Jalisco as a mock governor.

The prince took with him his widowed mother, his wife, two concubines, all their slaves, and a handful of soldiers with their families—about three hundred people—to establish a village as his capital.

My father's prospects for a great career were not dead, since Aztec rulers must one day die like all men even though this fact could not be admitted aloud. What the family needed now were strong sons who would distinguish themselves early by both courage and intelligence. Perhaps also by piety, but piety was a silently disputed subject and even a dangerous one in our household.

During the first three years while the new colony built houses and fortified a hillside overlooking a lake, no males or even females came forth from my mother's womb except one puny boy who was strangled by his own birth cord. Lady Iztac, desperate, tried to bargain for a son with the goddess Five Flower. She pressed nettles into her armpits, she pierced her nipples with cactus spines. The goddess accepted the pain and blood drops with a mute smile and gave no repayment.

Then at last my mother became pregnant again. Rejoicing, she went back to the thorns and nettles, paying no attention to my grandmother who called her a fool. Lady Flint Knife, my father's mother, had her own religious views—and it was this that saved my life.

When I think of my birth I always remember a faint perfume of trumpet blossoms, because a trumpet tree grew near my grandmother's door, and she used to strap the crossbar of her loom to its trunk. She told me stories while she wove the finest cotton cloth I have ever seen, and a favorite story, repeated over and over, was the tale of my birth and my narrow escape from the water goddess.

"It was winter, and your mother's time was so close that you were hammering at the door. Your father was called away to deal with a caravan of merchants who were evading the tax collectors. But he left certain warnings with your mother."

Since a child was about to be born, the heavens had been read and everyone knew that the next day would be a dangerous time for a birth, especially if my mother should be so unlucky as to bear a girl child—the signs on the female horizon were especially forbidding. Nothing could be determined exactly until the circumstances of a birth became known, but the risks were great.

"That morning your mother, Lady Iztac, stayed on her mat and would not stir, hoping to delay her hour at least until the rising of Lady Moon, when the aspects would change. She was so fearful she would not lift a gourd to her own mouth, but kept a midwife beside her to moisten her lips with wet cotton.

"A wind swept down from the high mesa, a wind as cold as the drafts of hell, so a second blanket was brought to your mother, and her little dog placed across her ankles as a foot warmer. It was a lovely dog, not a hair on his body, skin smooth as a lizard's.

"Your mother and the midwife fell asleep in the dim room, but soon Lady Iztac was aroused by the dog's wiggling. It had inched over her knees and she felt its little head touch her thigh. Then she opened her eyes and saw that the dog was across the room, sitting in a corner grinning at her. What then could be crawling beneath the blankets?"

This was the dramatic and horrible moment of the tale, and my grandmother always paused to tighten the weft of her loom and blow away imagined dust motes, prolonging the suspense.

"Yes, yes! What was it, *citli*?" I demanded, knowing exactly what came next since I had memorized her words.

"The thing between her thighs moved again, and unable to bear more, your mother threw back the covers. The eyes of a great snake stared into her own, a deadly singing snake with diamonds on his back. The serpent, or the demon that had taken that form, must have crept in through the thatch walls and slipped into the warm bedding. When your mother saw the fanged mouth and its split tongue darting at her, she was so gripped by horror she could make no sound. But the midwife had awakened, and she screamed so wildly that the snake turned from your mother and struck the shrieking woman in the heart. She died with her screams still on her lips while your mother fled the house. Lady Iztac hurled herself on the ground outside, writhing and choking, her labor begun.

"The slaves and your father's lesser wives came running, but they dared not touch her, so they stood in a circle, wailing, until I arrived."

My grandmother's back straightened at her loom; a small but proud smile came to her lips.

"So I, who knew nothing of the proper spells and prayers, delivered you alone, child! I dragged you into life with my hands while your mother lay like a corpse. But you helped me—oh, how you fought to live! To struggle is in your blood, Mali."

So my cord was severed at a moment when Lord Sun stood high and there was no Lady Moon, not even a beheaded and dead one rising over the horizon. And all the while, as my grandmother fought for me, only a few steps away the wood and thatch house roared in flames, for Lady Flint Knife had ordered it burned, thinking it defiled past any purifying. The midwife was cremated where she had fallen; later the snake's charred skull was found among her bones.

Because of the flames my grandmother could not enter the house to bury my cut cord in the hearth, a rite to keep me from straying far, to hold me near home and family, which is the destiny decreed for females. For this omission my mother later reproached my grandmother, but I myself think nothing could have changed what was to come. My path was already determined, the rabbit set running, and I would follow it, sometimes unwillingly and often with the illusion that its turnings were choices of my own.

My grandmother, Lady Flint Knife, was as unyielding as her name. The roof beams of the house were still smoldering when I was given the triple baptism of pure water to banish thievery, untruth and dishonor. Meanwhile my mother's spirit fluttered between life and death.

Since I was female, house implements—borrowed, since ours were burned—were brought to my cradle: a broom, a grinder, a spindle. My baby hands were pressed to these, the ancient ceremony to tie a girl to her future tasks. But I have hardly touched such objects since, and those tools remain unnatural to my hands. My fingers, though once nimble at other tasks, could never easily thread a needle.

The haste of my baptism was calculated. Lady Flint Knife admired my struggle to live, the boldness of my squalling, and hoped to establish me as a daughter of the family before the priest came to reveal a horoscope. But by the third morning my mother was recovered enough to demand, with her Aztec imperiousness, a reading of the signs that would determine my name. She had been warned of evil; the appearance of the serpent seemed to confirm the worst, for although a snake is not a demonic creature in itself—quite the contrary—the behavior of this one seemed to show that nature's intentions were hostile. So there was no staving off the time of a religious pronouncement.

By luck my father returned home just before the priest's arrival, so when the holy books were unfolded and the charts studied, I lay nestled in my father's arms, placed there by Lady Flint Knife. My mother declined to touch me for fear of defilement.

The priest, wearing the double mask of the Lord and Lady of the Night, spoke through a cloud of burning copal incense. "Ce Malinalli, one grass of penance, is her name. She brings strife and destruction. Death surrounds her—death and the destruction of ancient houses. This child is a stranger."

I do not know if those assembled hid their horror or not; surely my presence filled them with fear and revulsion. Neither do I know what thoughts warred in my father's mind at that moment. Perhaps he remembered Lady Iztac's ungenerous womb and that except for me, he was still childless after seven years of marriage; perhaps he was moved by something else—some pleading in my grandmother's face. Maybe it is true that I uttered an angry cry, a protest and a demand for life at a moment when a doorway to my father's kindness stood ajar.

It is even possible that he believed his own words when he said, "I, too, know the stars, and they can be read in many ways. The serpent was a god who has already claimed his sacrifice and needs none other. We will rear my daughter, Ce Malinalli."

In most households that would have been the end of the matter.

My parents shared some religious beliefs, as all the world did in those days; but my mother was nevertheless an Aztec, and Aztecs have never been like other people. Years ago when they first came creeping into the civilized Valley of Anahuac, poor and bony-tough as wild turkeys, they carried their own bloody gods with them in medicine pouches. They gave much to those gods, and the gods in turn gave them mastery of most of the Only World. But Aztecs have a blindness; they cannot see that two differing truths may both be possible. In my life I have given far too many religious speeches, and I do not intend to deliver another one now. But unless one understands how stiff-necked and self-righteous Aztecs have always been, it is impossible to understand what my mother did at two crucial times in my life.

A bride, when the mantles are tied, naturally accepts her husband's religion—at least outwardly. No other way is practical. I myself have shown such acceptance in circumstances somewhat like marriage, and found it made no difference at all. I exchanged one set of outward joys and evils for another; I lost some old sins and gained some new ones. My own spirit, my *self*, stayed untouched. My deepest soul has been utterly impervious to conversion, but I have kept a pliant mind and taken no foolish chances.

Lady Iztac, having accepted my father's beliefs at marriage, should have also accepted his decision about my survival. But she was an Aztec . . .

· ·

I was now my father's daughter; I had a right to Lady Iztac's breast, and she faced her duty with courage, even though it meant giving suck to a demon. Yet try as she would, the touch of my gums on her nipples filled her with such revulsion that she could not stop shuddering. Her own food would not stay in her stomach. On the second day Lady Flint Knife, who had watched closely, ended the torment by handing me over to a wet nurse despite my mother's tears and protests. Lady Iztac *wanted* to do her duty, but her body betrayed her. She found the shame of her failure hard to endure.

My nurse was a young slave named Vitsa whose first child had just died at birth. Vitsa came from one of those villages in the northern wilderness where they know so little of religion that they actually devour holy creatures such as hummingbirds and butterflies. They hardly know enough of the heavens to be able to determine planting season. So Vitsa, being a pagan, simply looked upon me as a baby to relieve the fullness of her breasts. She felt no danger. It is said that nursing is a double nourishment, since as the milk flows out, love of the child flows into the woman. The saying must be true; otherwise I cannot explain why Vitsa did what she did.

After nursing and taking care of me for perhaps ten days, Vitsa appeared unexpectedly at my grandmother's loom one morning, carrying me tucked in her mantle. She made an awkward sign of courtesy, as she had been taught, but when she spoke she was bold as a parrot.

"I have taken the little one to visit her mother each day as you ordered, Lady." Something in Vitsa's tone made my grandmother stop working.

"Yes, Vitsa, that is proper." Lady Flint Knife gave the girl an encouraging smile. "The mother should have time alone with her child —to play and grow acquainted."

"No, they should not be alone," said Vitsa flatly, the rudest contradiction imaginable, although she seemed to mean no insolence.

"What are you saying, girl?" my grandmother demanded, sensing danger.

"This morning I left the baby with her in her room as usual, but I returned a little early, and Lady Iztac did not hear me coming. I saw . . . something strange. Lady Iztac is not well. Since the birth she has been—" Vitsa used one of her northern words that did not precisely mean mad but perhaps entranced, like someone who has eaten peyote at a rite.

"What did you see? Tell me everything."

On approaching the door curtain Vitsa heard weeping—not a baby crying, but hoarse sobbing. She edged the cloth aside and saw that my basket cradle had been moved from the floor and placed on the stone altar that my mother had retrieved from the ruins of our burned house and had put in the new one. It was a pretty little altar dedicated to the changing gods of the seasons and garlanded now, because it was early autumn, with those brown marigolds that are also the flowers of dead children.

Lady Iztac kneeled nearby, sobbing, and she stared with fixed eyes at an obsidian knife that lay before her. Her hair and clothing were in disarray; she had bitten her own lips and drawn blood. Vitsa, alarmed by my mother's god-intoxication, still kept her good sense. She went quickly into the room, murmured a courteous word or two that my mother seemed not to hear, and carried me to safety.

Most mistresses would have had a slave beaten, at least, for telling such an indiscreet story so bluntly. Servants were expected only to hint at awkward matters. But Lady Flint Knife valued loyalty above custom or family embarrassment.

"You behaved well, Vitsa," she said, calmly resuming her weaving. "The god who is distressing Lady Iztac will no doubt leave soon. But until he does, the baby will see her mother only here at my loom while I am working. I will give orders."

Although Lady Flint Knife believed Vitsa and sensed danger, she did not know what to make of the scene that had been reported. It seemed incredible that Lady Iztac would defy her husband—which in this case would be outright murder. Unthinkable, and yet . . .

Each morning the mother and baby were together near the loom, and Lady Flint Knife watched from under lowered lids, pretending to puzzle over designs in her fabric. Usually Lady Iztac seemed affectionate toward her little daughter, even though it was a sad affection and not without fear. Forgetting herself at times, she would become almost playful. Then her gaze would wander, the black eyes clouded, and she would fall silent, as though painfully weighing one sin against another. Gradually such moments became less frequent, and Lady Flint Knife finally believed that my mother had reconciled herself. She relaxed her guard. By then it was late autumn, the fifteenth month of the year and time for the Feast of the Flags.

When I remember that rowdy holiday as I knew it in later years on the frontier, a little tingle of childhood excitement still comes to me. I remember men and women running together through the four streets of our settlement-fort, shouting and laughing as they doused each other with jugs of water. When every garment was soaked, they threw off all cloth covering to reveal arms and legs newly decorated with blue paint. Then they donned special festival clothes made of tough fig bark paper, the paper from which officers make battle crowns. Attired in painted paper, they danced. Then the Aztec troops went off to their special altar to sacrifice whatever Tarascan captives were on hand, the human offerings also costumed gaily in patterned paper. Sometimes the allied troops, about half the men at the fort, joined the Aztec ritual and feast; sometimes not. I myself never thought of the Feast of the Flags as a time for sacrifice. I was too occupied with the feats of the acrobats and jugglers, who must have been backwoods amateurs, although to me they outdid the storied marvels of Tula as they flew in circles from high poles, truly bird-gods.

The feast must have brought memories of childhood lessons and duties to my mother, and I understand this. The beating of the great four-tone drums, the trumpets and flutes, the chattering rattles and deep-voiced conch horns can cast a spell that numbs the brain even while the heart is pounding.

Important in the festival are the four Cold Nights when men must sleep apart from their wives and other women and are left with no amusements except those they may choose to have with each other.

And so my mother lay alone during the late watches, and no one suspected her torment. Perhaps she had been fevered by the sacrifices she had witnessed at sunset, and I am sure copal incense and other herbs smoldered on the altar in her room, their fragrance mingling with the aroma of roasted human flesh that drifted from the silent barracks nearby. At some moment a god must have whispered to her in that smoky darkness, telling her what she must do.

She rose; she smeared her face with the pigments of sacrifice and put on her long tunic of holiday paper. It was near dawn when she slipped into a street now deserted by the revelers and made her way silently to my grandmother's house. Everyone—guards, slaves, nurse and mistress—lay sleeping so heavily that had the Tarascans attacked, they could have cut off every head in the settlement without a single outcry of alarm.

She gently took my basket and carried me outside into the fading moonlight, and I, feeling the sudden chill of the last watch of the night, cried fitfully, but she soothed my crying as she hurried away from the houses toward the lake at the bottom of the hill. She intended, of course, to deliver us both mercifully to the heaven of the Rain Bringer, a happy meadow where those who die by water will play forever among the butterflies and blossoms.

Lady Iztac would certainly have succeeded had she not been betrayed by a lingering tenderness she felt for me. She had already decided on the most painless death she could think of, and looked forward to the sweetest eternity; I was her own flesh, she meant me good, not harm. When, in the first glimmer of dawn, she saw purple and yellow straw flowers growing near the shore, she paused to make me a garland to wear through the Narrow Passage and to adorn the cradle with green moss, the color of life.

Finished, she moved calmly toward the water. But her sandals had not touched it when she heard a great shout behind her and turned to see my father and other men racing down the slope. Vitsa had heard my faint crying outside the house, but had been so deep in sleep that time passed before she roused herself, saw that I was missing and raised an alarm.

Even so my mother would have had time to send me through the Passage before anyone reached us; my basket was already weighted with a heavy stone. But instead of plunging ahead into the water, at the sound of my father's voice her deep sense of obedience halted her, and she collapsed on the shore weeping. A moment later the men carried us home, our hair still decked with funeral flowers.

3

As soon as I was old enough to understand a little of the world around me, Lady Flint Knife told me about the unlucky circumstances of my birth and my mother's belief that I should not have been allowed to live, that I was marked as a bringer of calamity. She did not tell me this because of malice—although she hated her daughter-in-law—but for my own protection. Lady Iztac appeared reconciled to my existence, but who knew when the god that had seized her might return? Who knew what feelings some of the more devout soldiers might harbor? It was safer for me to know everything.

"We know the astrologer spoke nonsense, of course!" She always tacked this reassuring ending onto the tale. "What can a backwoods yokel know compared to your father? Not even the wizards of Tenochtitlan know the stars as well as Prince Chimal."

Her voice made me believe her, although later I realized that her conduct belied her words. Like all children, I trusted what I saw far more than what I heard.

I became aware that girls, even those of high birth, were broken early to the loom, spindle and corn grinder. A rich wife might seldom use these skills, but she must know them. Besides, hard training from infancy forms a wifely mind, a dedication to the details and routines of life.

Lady Flint Knife, in charge of my rearing, never set me to such tasks, and except for Vitsa's easy supervision, I was left to run as free as a fawn. I waded in the shallows of the lake and learned to swim so early that I cannot remember when I did not know how. I shinnied up trees to gather fruits and blossoms, threw rocks and sticks to bring down what I could not reach. Vitsa, being a northern barbarian, did not find these pursuits unfeminine. I suppose the neighbors were scandalized, but no one complained too loudly about Prince Chimal's daughter.

Only a few things were forbidden. During a shower of rain I took shelter beneath a lone tree that stood on a hilltop near the shore. Vitsa found me and dragged me away, cuffing me to aid my memory.

"A tree that grows high and alone defies the gods," she warned me. "Sooner or later they will strike it down with lightning. When the sky is dark, stay away from such trees."

"It defies the gods?" I asked, awed.

"Of course. A tree should grow with other trees. The gods single out a lone one and consume it with fire."

Until then I had often played in the tree's cool shade, but now I avoided that single patch of shadow on the hill. Yet I studied it from a safe distance, sensing that there was something perilous and magical in the tree's power to invoke the gods.

The gods I knew in those days were not wrathful, not like the ferocious deities I would meet later. Childhood was the time when gods were more real than persons. They were close at hand, always within calling distance. In the hills and forests of Jalisco the gods were my daily companions. A water goddess lived in a stream only a bow shot from my grandmother's door, a cold-fingered goddess whose power and voice swelled with the summer rains.

"The butterflies are returned souls," Lady Flint Knife told me. "That's why they have celestial clothing. Your brother who died during birth is among them."

Vitsa explained that the jade-colored hummingbirds darted back and forth carrying messages among the gods; they brought news to deities disguised as hyacinths or lilies. Every breeze that stirred was the breath of a god, unless its rustle was the wake of the god's unseen passing. Plumed Serpent, best and wisest of the gods, often took the form of a wind. So when the soldiers built a stone base for his little temple, they made it oval-shape and without sharp corners so the Wind could flow where it would.

Besides being warned away from the tree on the hill, I was forbidden the ridge to the south because jaguars hunted there, and I was not allowed to approach the river gorge to the west, the most dangerous place of all. The river was the border of the Tarascan kingdom, and Tarascan warriors often crossed it to spy on the outpost or to steal peppers and gourds from our gardens.

"They would cut your heart out with pleasure," Vitsa told me. "Their knives are quick as a lizard's tongue."

Since the Tarascans were so cruel, it was right that our soldiers brought any they captured to the altars of Smoking Mirror or Hummingbird of the Left, where they were sacrificed by the priests. I believed what I heard about the savagery of the Tarascans, and in little more than a year I would learn with my own eyes how true those tales were.

I loved my freedom, the days of playing and exploring, and by the time I reached my eighth winter I was far stronger, quicker and taller than girls my age who spent their hours hovering near cook pots or griddles or fire pits. My shoulders were never hunched from a day spent grinding corn, the eternal and binding task of women.

Yet I began to wonder why my life was different from the lives of other children.

"Why would Prince Chimal's daughter work scraping rabbit skins and scaling fish?" Lady Flint Knife replied haughtily.

Certainly I did not do much scraping or scaling. Yet my mother, with four household slaves at her command, did such things. Lying on my belly in a weed patch, I spied shamelessly on Lady Iztac's house, watching her swift, graceful hands as she combed cotton, embroidered mantles for my father and compounded incense of flowers and herbs. My father's two concubines, who occupied a separate house suitably far away yet conveniently nearby, did much the same work. These were the natural tasks of women.

At this time I had begun to think seriously about becoming my father's wife, so my lack of domestic skills worried me.

Brooding on the problem, I wondered if Lady Flint Knife, despite her words, really believed I was very different from other girl children. Perhaps I was given no wifely training because she did not expect me to become a wife, although no other future was imaginable. In time I despaired of reading my grandmother's mind, although I no longer felt easy when she assured me that I had been a beautiful, natural baby and was clearly blessed by the gods who had saved both me and my mother from the serpent's fangs. I smiled and nodded, but I had begun to doubt.

Whatever my grandmother believed, the soldiers and settlers at the outpost obviously took a dark view of my birth. They avoided me, stepping from paths, changing directions. I was inspected from afar, men looking at me narrowly as they might have observed new smoke from a volcano. None of the children of the settlement approached me; they had been warned. But until the next summer I did not fully understand that they watched me as the source of some unknown danger. I supposed they were wary of my rank; no other noble family lived at the outpost, so it had not yet dawned on me that I was simply an alien and would remain one. That knowledge was soon brought home to me in a manner I would not forget.

My grandmother never told me what punishment my father inflicted on Lady Iztac for her defiance of him when she tried to kill me in the lake. Such matters are private between husbands and wives, but I suspected the penalty must have been severe. Prince Chimal had been flouted, he was disgraced, so despite his kindly nature, he could not have spared her pain. I supposed he had beaten her. Often enough I heard the howls of women being flailed with switches by their soldier husbands or owners.

I hoped it had been something more dramatic than a mere switching, yet I could hardly imagine my mother locked in a cramped wooden cage without food or water, her lips and tongue smeared with burning chili—a common enough punishment in tales my grandmother told.

Sometimes I glanced at the scourge my father wore coiled at his belt when he acted as a judge in legal cases. Perhaps he had used that? No, the scourge was too cruel, almost murderous. Then I learned the truth.

I can recall every detail of that night, the shadows luminous with cloudy moonlight, the images of the gods on the twin altars shimmering in the smoke of incense. The trees surrounding the open ceremonial circle seemed like watching giants. It was the festival for the Birth of Flowers, and until this year I had seen only the daytime rites. Now I sat beside my father on a low earthen platform where a log served as a rustic throne. I occupied what should have been a boy's place, the seat of honor where my father's son should have sat. But if Prince Chimal chose to perch his daughter in an inappropriate spot, no one dared complain. I suppose there were mutterings, raised eyebrows.

After the scattering of jasmine had been performed, my mother swept from the shadows leading the other young matrons in the formal dance to the Lords of the Night. She was, of course, naked except for the usual garlands, and although I must have seen her unclothed before, to me this seemed the first time.

Her lithe body, slender and strong as a sapling, amazed and enchanted me; more than beautiful, she radiated a woman-mystery, some female power still unknown to me. I marveled at her smooth thighs, the firm breasts that rode so high, their nipples tipped with silver for the festival. She stood proud and regal, a moon goddess.

Clay flutes sighed and whispered, then the drums beat a commandment: the moment for the passing of the Flower Wand, the carved and painted phallus that emerged from the opened bell of a huge lily. The women slowly and lovingly passed it hand to hand, each one dancing her own brief reverence to the symbol, pivoting to speak the sacred words into the darkness—words that could be spoken only between women and the Flower Prince himself.

At last the phallus reached my mother in the center of the line. She received it with both hands, swaying as she pressed it to her thighs, her belly, her breasts. She let her hair cascade over it, a black perfumed veil. Then she turned away, a swift, sharp movement, and her back was revealed by the moon and the torches. What I saw made me gasp aloud.

Lady Iztac's skin, otherwise unblemished, was disfigured by terrible scars, lash marks crisscrossing her back and shoulders, weals such as I had seen only on the bodies of the most rebellious and dangerous criminals. I knew such wounds were made by scourges of thongs tipped with sharp stones, whips that tear the flesh like fangs.

Again she turned to face the worshipers, and the horror vanished. She was again the moon goddess, flawless and cool, her head lifted proudly as though she had just displayed badges of honor.

Now I knew what her punishment had been—and the realization so startled and sickened me that I blurted a question at my father. How had this happened? Had his whip really left those scars?

For an instant he seemed unable to believe I had asked such things. Then he struck me full in the face with his open hand so hard that I crumpled, head ringing, too stunned to scream.

Until that moment I had never known anything but gentleness from him, and the next morning, when Vitsa treated my swollen cheek and eye with toad's grass compresses, I complained of my father's abuse.

"What do you expect when you remind him of that time?" she demanded, her voice as rough as her big hands. "I suppose the years have blinded him a little to her scars. Last night you made him see them afresh."

"But I only asked if he—"

"A fool's question, Mali. Would Prince Chimal destroy his wife's beauty? Harm his own property?"

"But then who—" Suddenly I saw an explanation and cried out, "Tarascans! She was captured by the Tarascans in the gorge and they—"

"Nonsense! If you must know, Lady Iztac laid open her own back the day after you were saved from the Water Goddess. I saw her hardly an hour later, I helped carry her home from the shrine in the forest where she had gone to lash herself in secret. It is a miracle she lived —the bones of her left shoulder showed bare."

"She did that to *herself*? How could she? She would have fainted, she would—"

"I have just told you. And, no, the Lady Iztac did not faint. Not until she had struck herself at least three or four times. Faint, hah! The Lady Iztac?"

Vitsa ended the conversation by pressing the hot compress so hard that I clenched my jaw not to cry. The strength of her hands hurt, but I realized I knew nothing whatever about pain. But my mother knew! I was horrified by what she had done, yet something in my blood responded to the deed—I was old enough to recognize the gleam of nobility. Even Vitsa's tone had betrayed unwilling admiration.

Now I knew what my grandmother meant when she said, grudgingly, "Your mother has great strength." And I felt a sudden pride in that half of my ancestry that Lady Flint Knife usually disparaged or dismissed. I knew, of course—how many times had she told me?—that only a few generations ago the Aztecs had slipped into the Valley of Mexico carrying their northern gods in buckskin pouches. The people of the ancient cities regarded them as thieves and savages.

"They were stealthy as weasels," said my grandmother. "And just as bloodthirsty—although no one knew it at first. One king in the valley made the mistake of befriending them. He sent his daughter as a bride for their chief, and in a few days went to their camp to attend the wedding. Child, you cannot believe what happened! Instead of a wedding, it was a feast, with the bride as the main course, roasted nicely and served up with peppers!"

Savages they may have been, yet in a single sheaf of years they had conquered most of the Only World, sweeping great states and older religions before them like dead leaves. Thinking of my mother's scars, I knew how they had done it. No, how *we* had done it, I told myself. My mother was Aztec, my father's people were subject allies. But the "we" was not really the truth, and my longing to be as courageous as my mother could not change me into an Aztec.

Late that night I lay wakeful on my straw mat listening to the unlucky voices of owls and wondering if those eerie calls were made by real birds. Tarascan raiders, stalking a village, used such signals. But it was neither owls nor Tarascans that kept me from sleeping. Some meaning, some important implication of the scars on my mother's body taunted me, eluded me.

Near dawn, when I was half-asleep, the truth came to me suddenly, clearly and—a moment later—with an upsurge of joy. Why had Lady Iztac inflicted such punishment on herself? Because she felt remorse—guilt for what she had tried to do to me. She had realized the wickedness of her attempt and then wielded the fanged whip without mercy, inflicting pain to drive out the god that had possessed her.

In recognizing her sin, had she not admitted my right to live? I had never suspected she felt this way, and my discovery was like finding a jadestone, a jewel I could fondle, turn in my hand, treasure to myself.

The severity of her penance still surprised me, although I was accustomed to seeing self-punishment. It was an Aztec specialty, although I later learned that other peoples such as the Zapotecs, Mixtecs and pious Spaniards also hunger for it from time to time. Some universal god whispers, "Attack yourself! Punish your body, for it is wicked and unclean. Purify it by pain." I myself have always been deaf to this god's promptings, so my impurities must be incalculable and encrusted on me like invisible barnacles even though I never notice them.

Soldiers at our outpost frequently jabbed thorns into their own tongues to pay for ill-considered words such as blasphemies or unlucky wishes. To relieve other sins they nestled burrs or even burning coals in the softness of their armpits and crotches. A few men were always limping or hobbling because they had pierced their cocks with cactus spikes and wore these skewers until their sins were cleansed or their unseemly desires were quenched. Such penitents could be recognized by the dark streaks on their legs where blood had dripped and dried.

But familiar though I was with penitential scars, I had never seen any worse than the stripes on my mother's back. Now I looked upon her with new eyes and considered the shame that had driven her to such punishment. Shame so powerful that it still kept her from approaching me, from taking me into her house.

I knew my discovery would not change my daily life. I must continue living with my grandmother, and I would see Lady Iztac only at a little distance. I sensed that we must still avoid speaking more than formal greetings. Even so the marks of repentance on my mother's back formed a cord between us. I had become her daughter.

During the next weeks I longed to show Lady Iztac that at last I understood, and that her pain had more than repaid any wrong she had done, anything she owed me. When she made courtesy calls on Lady Flint Knife, I now lingered nearby, hoping to convey my new understanding to her, to confirm the bond. My shapeless feelings could never be fitted into words, but I imagined myself smiling at her, a secret smile full of meaning. Or I would make some subtle gesture— I did not quite know what—to reach across the silence, a signal she could not fail to recognize and return.

But never once in those weeks could I catch her eye. She looked above me, past me, through me. I remained as invisible as a water goblin. When I coughed loudly, she did not hear.

Then one day during one of the courtesy visits an opportunity came. It was a gusty afternoon; clouds were piling up on the eastern horizon as the first summer storm of the year gathered. Lady Flint Knife excused herself to command the slaves.

"Take in my loom, but don't tangle the yarn! Are the lashings tight on the rafters? Cover the dye pots!"

While my grandmother bustled about, I found myself standing unnoticed behind Lady Iztac. She had dressed that day in a *huipil*, a long tunic, of such sheer cotton that the scars showed faintly but lividly through the cloth. I stared at them wide-eyed, studying their twistings, my gaze finding patterns that looked like the wavering reflections of willows in the water at the lake shore, thin trunks etched on her shoulders, then branches that spread and intertwined down her back, horrible yet fascinating. Compelled, I reached out and gently touched my mother's neck where a broad scar protruded above her collar, and I was startled because the skin felt dead—rough as the bark of a tree, yet scaly. I remembered the snake that had entered her bed, crept between her legs and thighs.

She was unaware of my touch, the cautious tracing of my fingers, and made a vague gesture as though brushing away a fly. Perhaps the scar flesh had no sense of feeling, was truly dead. Then, from the edge of her eye, she saw me and realized what was happening.

Choking back a cry, Lady Iztac recoiled as from fire. She whirled toward me, and when our eyes met I saw her fear and revulsion. She clapped a hand over the spot I had touched as though to shield it from filth. I stared at her, unable to move or speak, and the image of the snake came to me again. I felt its scales, its flicking tongue.

Lady Iztac, mute with fear, made the sign against evil, her lips forming unspoken words, and somehow the gesture broke the spell holding me. I turned from her, my hands over my face, shuddering. Then I fled in panic.

I ran blindly down the long slope, stumbling toward the lake and my secret shelter among the reeds. Rain began to pelt me, cactus and mesquite thorns clawed my bare arms and legs, but I did not know I was bleeding, nor did I hear the storm breaking overhead as I reached my hiding place where I could crouch unseen, sobbing and shaking.

Looking into my mother's face, I had understood the real meaning of her scars, her penance. She had scourged herself, ripped open her back, not because she had tried to destroy me but because she had failed. Evil had grown in her womb; she was foul; she deserved pain as I deserved death. Now I knew the truth and I knew that nothing could change or soften it. I was what I was.

With no tears left, I gazed dumbly at the falling rain, still haunted by my mother's eyes, by the scaly touch of the snake. I thought of the soldiers and women who left the path when I approached, averting their eyes, and of the old slave woman who would not drink from a gourd I had touched.

Nearby, only a bow shot away, the shoulder of the hill jutted into the lake and on it stood the lone tree Vitsa had warned me against, perilous and solitary in the storm, a target for the gods. Vaguely I understood my mother's fear, the fears of others, that I would draw disaster just as the tree would draw lightning and death to those who stood in its shelter.

Desolation swept over me, a grief so powerful that I could not bear to think anymore, could not endure what I knew of myself.

During that hour—or during the next or the next—something happened to me. It looms over my life, but I do not know what it was.

When I grope backward in my memory, those next hours flicker beyond reach. I can feel rain striking my arms like hailstones; water streams down my cheeks, and the wind whips my hair. I hear Vitsa far away shouting my name, and I want to answer but I cannot because the name fills me with dread, chokes me.

Then I am hiding among the reeds, watching the lone tree on the hilltop. Even though the rain is heavy, I can see every gnarl and furrow of its bark, the twigs and matted leaves of its branches.

Hearing voices, I crouch lower and see three figures approaching, two soldiers and a woman, and at first I think the men are Tarascans, enemies, and I feel a chill. Then I recognize them as Aztecs, men of our outpost, but strangely this does not lessen my fear. They splash through puddles, shielding their faces with their hands as they run to seek the shelter of the tree, passing so close to me that I could almost touch the muddy hem of the woman's robe. I see embroidered pink flowers and know she is a whore.

The taller soldier—he is an Aztec jaguar knight wearing a bedraggled cloak of spotted fur—hoists the woman to his shoulders and she straddles his neck. Squealing, she kicks her little painted feet.

When they reach the tree, she dismounts and they huddle close under the leafy branches. Soon the soldiers begin to fondle the whore's breasts—high, pointed breasts like Lady Iztac's. The nipples flash in the gray light and I see they are tipped with silver although it is not the time of year for this ornamenting; the Birth of Flowers is long past.

As they caress her, she squeals again and cowers, pretending to be terrified of the thunder, then she sinks prettily to the ground, opening her robe, lifting and spreading her legs. Her hairless cunt is garlanded with tattooed flowers. The tall soldier kneels, then covers her while his companion urges him on. "Hurry, hurry! I can't wait till sunset!" They have forgotten the rain, the thunder.

Gathering courage, I stand up and shout to them, warn them that the lone tree is dangerous in a storm, but they pay no attention. Gradually my anger grows. They will not hear me, and I realize how obscene they are, performing the rites of the Flower Prince like animals, like the caged monkeys whose rutting amuses my father's concubines. I wait quietly now, knowing what will come. Then clenching my hands and gazing up at the sky, I wish the lightning down.

It splits the tree. The ground under my feet shakes with the thunder while the yellow brilliance of the fire blinds my eyes for a moment. When I can see again, the trunk of the tree is blazing, a hissing column of flame; blackened branches have been lopped off and smolder on the wet ground. I remember that our house was burning when I was born.

Soon I smell wood smoke, and mingled with it is the sweetish odor of flesh charring, the smell that pervades the outpost on days when captives have been sacrificed on the altar of the war god, Hummingbird of the Left. Afterward the soldiers roast the thighs and liver and other tender parts and feast on them. "Sacrilege!" my grandmother says. "Only priests may eat human flesh. Aztec sacrilege!"

Slowly I climb the hill, moving toward the fire where the three corpses lie blackening. Their limbs look broken, contorted; eyelids and brows have been burned away, the sockets gape at me. I am sorry they were destroyed, but not horrified. What happened could not be helped and is not my doing, although I know that somehow I am the instrument of their destruction, that I am both the tree and the lightning that struck it down. But nothing could have saved these three people who lie twisted and seared at my feet.

Then, because there is nothing to be done and I have grieved enough, I turn away from the corpses and start for home.

I wonder if this happened the way I have said. I am sure there was a burned tree on the hillside; later that year my beautiful boy cousin and I decorated each other's bodies with charcoal we found there. Also I remember that at about that time two or three people from the outpost were destroyed by a lightning bolt and it made a great stir. One of the victims was blamed for carrying a mirror of polished obsidian; when storm gods catch sight of their own faces, they obliterate the ugly image they have seen.

So I must be resigned to not knowing what happened that day when I hid among the reeds; I must satisfy myself with fragments, uncertainties. But I am sure I returned home and that I left much of my childhood behind me. I had changed.

That same year and I suppose only a few nights later the bloodstone that is now so infamous first appeared in the night sky.

The commotion began as dusk was fading into darkness. I lay on my mat, already asleep because I had been ill ever since being chilled at the lake shore. My throat had closed; I could neither speak nor take food. I awoke to the booming of the signal drum. People were running outside, their voices loud and excited.

In the next room I heard Vitsa speaking to Lady Flint Knife, and I sat up in alarm at her shrillness. "Oh, my lady, it is the end of the World of the Fifth Sun! The gods destroyed everything four times before, and this is the fifth! They say—"

"Hush! All my life people have said the world would end the next moment, but it goes on."

I heard them leave the house, so I rose quickly, wrapped my blanket around me and followed, staying far enough behind so Lady Flint Knife would not see me and order me home. Everyone was hurrying toward the little plaza where the main altars stood: the war god, Hummingbird of the Left, terrible on his blue throne; and Smoking Mirror, the sky ruler, black and vengeful. Long ago one of Smoking Mirror's legs was bitten off by Earth Monster who is his own sister. They had a fierce quarrel about dividing the earth and sky, and she seized his leg in her mighty jaws, snapped it off and swallowed it. I supposed this mutilation left him permanently wrathful, like the raging Aztec emperor who had exiled my father but was now safely dead.

The whole outpost had gathered in the plaza—soldiers and slaves, artisans, priests, women who clasped little children close as they gazed and gestured at the eastern sky. Babies squalled and shrieked as I stood on tiptoe vainly trying to see over the crowd. Then, in the middle of the babbling, gesticulating mob, I found my father, who silently took my hand. He stood quietly, calm himself but not trying to calm those around him, and he gave no orders, simply stood transfixed as he stared at the horizon, not in fear but in wonder and awe.

The Chief Priest, a fat man with glittery little eyes, shouted,

"Pray! Pray, all of you! Beg deliverance of the Lords of the Night!"
He was terribly frightened, and the loose wattles under his chin trembled.

Around us people dropped to their knees or fell prostrate in
supplication. Then above the crowd, I too beheld the strange light in
the darkness to the east. It shone just above the horizon, a tongue of
silver fire or a flaming arrow aimed at the very arch of the heavens.
The tip gleamed like a cold white jewel, pale as a thin Lady Moon.
As I gazed, it seemed less like an arrowhead and more like a huge eye
watching us, an eye that streamed light as it stared unblinking and
baleful.

An old slave woman kneeled near us, a hag with bird-claw hands
and a white bird's nest of hair. It was said she had been a priestess in
some faraway land, and even her owner feared her as a witch. "A
bloodstone!" she wailed suddenly. "A bloodstone of death!"

"Yes, a bloodstone!" A soldier echoed her, naming the unluckiest
of all gems. Then the whole crowd was shouting the word.

I knew what a bloodstone was. Lady Flint Knife kept one hidden
among her skeins of unmatched yarns. It was for use in invoking
demons and for pronouncing curses against enemies, a beautiful but
sinister object, dangerous to look at, worse to touch. Lady Flint Knife
treasured it like a concealed dagger. Now I saw that the fire in the sky
was indeed like a bloodstone, and this resemblance added to the terror
and strangeness of the night.

"Fiery death!" the slave woman chanted, seeming to implore the
fate she dreaded. I saw a line of foam trickle down her chin.

The Chief Priest with two acolytes carrying torches had mounted
the steps at the altar of Smoking Mirror and was invoking the Lords,
waving his arms, crying and gesticulating, but I could not catch the
words because of the wailing all around me. Then he lifted both arms
to the sky and I realized, still without hearing, that he was chanting
the rite of penance before sacrifice.

> *"Mother of the gods, Father of the gods,*
> *God of the belly of the earth*
> *And, oh, ye old God of Fire!*
> *Behold one who comes weeping,*
> *One who comes bleeding . . ."*

"Death, death, death," chanted the slave woman, her hands clawing her hair.

Suddenly my father scooped me up in his arms and, holding the blanket around me, carried me through the crowd toward home, his stride so rapid that Lady Flint Knife, who had seen us, was panting to keep up.

"I want to stay!" I protested. "Let me stay."

"Hush, Mali!" He squeezed me tight in the blanket—a command to keep silent.

"I thought she was asleep," Lady Flint Knife whispered. "I never dreamed she would come here by herself." I had never before heard fear in her voice, and I realized it was not fear of the presence in the sky but of the people around us—our neighbors and my father's troops. "I will keep Mali indoors for a few days until things are quiet. This frenzy cannot last."

"I hope not. Keep her out of sight until we know more," my father said.

We had left the plaza and were halfway to my grandmother's house when I heard a great clamor, the shouting of hundreds of voices behind us. They were no longer wailing; this was a chorus of exultation. Edging aside the blanket covering my face, I looked over my father's shoulder and saw that the plaza had suddenly become a forest of burning torches, and a new fire blazed up before the altar of Smoking Mirror. In the midst of the torches the old slave woman was being borne high above the mob, passed from hand to hand, shrieking as she neared the altar and its fire. Then the shrieks were muffled as they slathered her body with oil and pitch. Then I saw her long hair burst into flame.

A little later, although I did not see it, they lifted her alive from the fire so the Chief Priest could tear out her heart and offer it still beating to the Sky Lord. Then, through the night, her body fed the Old God of fire.

But the demon in the eastern sky, the bloodstone, returned each evening to watch us for five more nights, lingering through the hours of every House of Darkness until dawn when the sun, as they say, beheaded it. On the sixth evening the demon did not appear. We welcomed the familiar stars in the east, and they had never looked so friendly and comforting.

The next morning I was allowed to play outdoors again. Lady Flint Knife decided that there was no more danger that some pious person would be inspired to kill me as the probable bringer of the bloodstone to our horizon. After all, this was the sort of calamity predicted at my birth.

No one spoke of the demon, except once I heard my father remark that the sight had been one of the three most beautiful things he had ever seen in the sky. I could not understand this at all; I often could not understand my father who was so different from other people.

We forgot the bloodstone, and it was only long afterward I learned it was but the first of eight evil omens marking the death of the Only World, and that it had been seen everywhere. At the outpost, once panic subsided and the sky was again itself, no one suspected that our world was doomed. How could anyone? Who can imagine what happens after the end of the world?

4

Jalisco, 1508–1509

As a young man, my father fell in love with the stars, and I think the perfection he found in the heavens diminished all other experiences for him. He did not expect much from people, and so he was seldom surprised.

Since Prince Chimal drew the rhythm of his life from the poetry of constellations, he enjoyed a serenity of soul that I early resolved to imitate but have never achieved for any three consecutive waking hours. My father appeared to be exactly what he was: peaceable but not passive, self-sufficient but neither cold nor aloof. Ah, enviable man!

I suppose his features were too sharp to be handsome, but I was only aware of this when he dressed in the regalia of a Jaguar Knight commander. Elaborate uniforms did not become him; simplicity was his style.

He stood taller than most men, just as I would grow taller than most women. His eyes were unusual—bright jet on pure white. Their gaze, which people found arresting, was clear as rock crystal, and this gave him a look of penetrating honesty. He appeared discerning but sincere. I have been told that I inherited this straightforward, open expression, although in my case it has usually been described as a mask of candor. I suppose that is accurate enough. In my father's case the disarming smile was honest—and I know what his honesty earned him.

On the frontier my father had no companions to share his interests. The soldiers, even had there not been the unbridgeable gap in rank, were mostly louts who had not been bright enough to wangle better assignments. Border outposts are everywhere the same: garrisoned by tough men who are a little stupid. Our troops were even more doltish than usual because the Aztec empire, vast though it was, did not maintain a regular standing army. When need arose—rebellion or conquest—a huge force was convoked from among the military orders of citizens and allies. Our situation as a frontier outpost with a professional battalion was a rare and novel experiment.

The officers who served under the prince spent their free hours gambling, playing three-stone for high stakes in almonds or cocoa beans, shells and quetzal plumes. Even jade ornaments, quills of gold dust and slaves changed hands at a single throw of the painted pebbles. Probably they never settled the most costly bets, for the games went on and on with none of the players gambling himself into slavery, which usually happens in such cases.

I knew from spying on them that every night they got as drunk as four hundred rabbits. A less wise commander would have charged them with drinking pulque; blood would have run. But Prince Chimal pretended not to know. He told my grandmother that as long as they were sober on duty, it was best they stay drunk the rest of the time. It kept them out of worse mischief, such as hunting Tarascans in the gorge. "The only serious duty of an army is to stay peaceable," he said.

So my father had no friend with whom he could talk about the stars. Even had such a thing been proper, his wives would have blanched at the thought of venturing into the demon-haunted night. So, again taking the place of an absent son, I became Prince Chimal's devoted pupil and so learned a little about the heavens and much more about the darkness itself, which, it turned out, was not aswarm with goblins as people thought.

Most of the year the night skies of Jalisco are the clearest in the world. The stars are closer to the earth there. I often felt a drowsy illusion that I could throw a stone and hit one.

"Yes," my father said, smiling. "They are almost within bow shot tonight."

I quickly learned to recognize the patterns of the sky, the ocelot and deer, the silver river, the Torch of the North. The Torch is a pale fire kept burning by Guiding Lord, protector of caravans. Also through my father I came to know Plumed Serpent, most beautiful of all the lights in the sky.

"Plumed Serpent is the Morning Star, the star of fair weather and kept promises. Of the stars that wander, he keeps the truest path in the sky."

Long ago, my father explained, Plumed Serpent was a man and a king, ruler of the great city of Tula, long before the Aztecs came. In those days the wild birds would perch on your shoulder and sing to you, often several birds singing in harmony. Cotton grew in a hundred colors—no need for the trouble of dyeing or the worry of fading! Gourds grew so big that a single one fed a family for a week.

Plumed Serpent, tall and fair and bearded, was the wisest of all kings. He taught the people to grow corn, to tame dogs and turkeys, to make painted books.

"And he is now there in the sky, Father?"

"No. What we see are the fires of his temple. It was given to him by Lord Sun. His own heart lives in the center of the fires and shines with pure goodness.

"Plumed Serpent, when he was a young man, was so gentle that he would not pick a flower for fear of taking life, or slay any creature."

But this good king had jealous rivals, and the worst of these was Smoking Mirror, who tricked Plumed Serpent into drunkenness and incest with his sister. When the king realized what he had done in his stupor, he was so stricken by remorse that he lay four days and nights in a stone coffin taking neither food nor drink. Then he commanded his followers to carry him to the shore of the eastern sea. A great fire was built on the sands, and Plumed Serpent, knowing his own unworthiness, flung himself upon it.

His ashes rose as a flock of white birds carrying his heart to his mother, She of the Serpent Skirt, queen of the heavens, mother of gods. At the same time Plumed Serpent himself stepped whole from the fire. He commanded the serpents of the earth to weave themselves into a raft, and on this raft he floated across the sea into the red dawn of the east.

"One day he will return to rule us," said my father. He gazed up at the lovely, luminous temple sailing in the sky and smiled quietly, at peace with himself.

I did not ask how Plumed Serpent could be both ashes and flesh, how his heart could rest among the blue flames in the sky while he

himself waited in the land of the red dawn until the time came for his
return. In those days such things were sensible; we understood the
marvelous. I already knew enough of Plumed Serpent to realize that
he took many forms at once and had been at different times various
gods and priests of gods. He was the wind, the deep waters of the earth
known only to serpents, the sky eagle, the bringer of wisdom to
scholars. He was all these things, yet no single form contained him. I
understood that he was gone, yet appeared everywhere.

A different question bothered me. "If Plumed Serpent is so good,
Father, and Smoking Mirror so wicked and treacherous, why do we
have such an important altar to Smoking Mirror? Why give sacrifices
and prayers to the evil god instead of the good one?"

We had been lying on our backs on the thin grass of the hilltop
studying the sky. Now he sat up and turned toward me, his face grave.
"Men worship Smoking Mirror *because* he is evil and must be placated.
The same with Hummingbird. The worse a god is, the more dangerous
it becomes to neglect him. Often the priests pretend that worship is
love or some sort of gratitude. But fear is the heart of it all, Mali.

"Someday when you are older you will see Tenochtitlan. The
city is the capital of the Only World and in its heart the greatest
temples are always to the fiercest gods."

Hearing me sigh, he took my hand and spoke gently. "But there
are also temples to Plumed Serpent—he has shrines everywhere. But
just because he once took the form of a good king, Mali, do not count
on him as a kindly god. Gods are unknowable; they do not answer to
laws or customs.

"They say Plumed Serpent is peaceable, yet his voice rang the
whole length of a great valley. Once, when he was thwarted, he called
up a whole army of moles, so many that the mountainsides seemed
covered with a coat of fur, and they burrowed into the depths of the
earth at his command to rescue the bones of his father. Who could trust
such a being? When it comes to gods, Mali, *all* gods, do not think of
good and evil. It is enough to be careful of their power."

He gazed up at the starry beauty of the sky, but when he spoke
it was with sadness. "This world is doomed—like the worlds that came
before it and those that come after, if any do. In worship of the gods
we may delay the catastrophe; we cannot prevent it."

Then, because he felt he had made me too serious, he told me of
the birth of Plumed Serpent. The goddess She of the Serpent Skirt was

sweeping among the stars, trying to sweep the night away, when she found a beautiful white feather, so lovely that she pressed it to her breast. She began to weep at the hopelessness of cleansing the sky of darkness; then she smiled and laughed, for she felt a baby quickening within her and knew that the feather had given her a child who would be called Plumed Serpent.

"She had a child without being with a man, Father?" I asked, wonderingly.

"Certainly. Several goddesses have." He riffled my hair. "Among the gods, Mali, we males are quite dispensable. Only mothers are essential."

That night and many other nights I fell asleep outdoors at my father's side, and I often dreamed that Plumed Serpent himself climbed down the star ladder to visit our hilltop, looking as he did in drawings and statues: tall and bearded, very fair, wearing a pointed cap. His eyes were startling, like my father's, but they shone with the blue of the Morning Star but turned more to pale amber as dawn drew near.

Usually Prince Chimal carried me home without my knowing it, but at other times, when he was lost in contemplation, I would be awakened by the howling of ocelots in the gorge, and this was natural after my dreams because the ocelot is sacred to Plumed Serpent, Lord of the Dawn, and the servant ocelots cry to greet his coming when he appears as the first pale light, shimmering and silver, from the red land of the east.

The time was approaching for another celebration of the Feast of the Flags, the last time I would see that festival on the frontier. Most mornings I sat in the shade in front of my grandmother's house helping her and her friend Sparrow Woman make bark paper clothing the revelers would wear.

Sparrow Woman was Otomi, the race said to be the oldest of all people in the Only World, more ancient than the grasshoppers and born of the earth itself. Sparrow Woman seemed the living proof of their antiquity, the oldest person I had ever seen, nothing but bones, beak and feathery hair white at the roots but dyed sparrow brown and gray. She had come to the frontier with her half-Aztec husband and their son, both of whom had since died of old age. She earned a good living as a color maker, blending or creating the most beautiful dyes and paints, which seemed advertised on her own skin. Her cheeks were tattooed as the two wings of a monarch butterfly, her nose its body, and on her forehead was a purple net that might have trapped the creature.

While she worked, Sparrow Woman told stories or related history, making Lady Flint Knife complain that little was done because the slaves lolled about listening. But Lady Flint Knife enjoyed the tales as much as the rest of us.

Once I asked her if the butterflies on her cheeks were Toltec symbols, because my father had mentioned that warriors of that long-vanished race carried shields shaped like butterflies.

"Toltec!" she exclaimed with contempt. "My designs are sheaves of years older than the grandfather of the first Toltec! I saw such butterflies when I was a child. They were painted on the walls of a dead city, the Place Where the Gods Gathered. Once its people were without number, like hives of bees. All gone! Gathered up with the years and now scorpions live in their palaces."

As Sparrow Woman talked, I began to glimpse Time in a new way, not as hours or years or even generations, but Time as my father knew it from the stars. Sparrow Woman, with a tiny bird's gesture, dispelled great nations to oblivion; their all-conquering armies were no more than cornfields, tall and flowering one season, blackened ashes the next.

"But the Only World remains," she said softly. "The rulers of the Gods' Gathering Place who were once lords of all the land between the oceans are gone. No one knows their names or their songs. No one knows how many other proud ones went before them. The Toltecs are ghosts, and in a summer or two the Aztecs will follow them into the house of the fleshless, the house of no memory. Who comes then?"

For a moment I thought she was uttering prophecy, a treasonous prediction that would be punished by the most painful death the priests could devise—slow flaying, roasting over the coals of the Old God. Lady Flint Knife studied a piece of bark paper, pretending not to hear.

But no, Sparrow Woman was not uttering sedition, although it could have been misunderstood as such. She meant only that Time is an invisible fire consuming everything. The world was, I thought, like the dead logs or fallen tree trunks that crumble slowly to ashes without flame or heat.

Usually Sparrow Woman delivered livelier tales than sermons on history. I remember that on the day that first the heralds and then the caravan arrived from Moctezuma's court, she was repeating for the hundredth time my favorite legend, the story of the Warrior Princess, Lady Six Monkey, who, after the deaths of her three brothers, took to the field, sword in hand, to defend her right to the throne of a kingdom in the southern mountains, the cool green kingdom of the Cloud People.

"A priestess in the Town of Skull warned Six Monkey to learn the arts of war, to wield a sword and lance, to hurl darts and aim arrows. The princess mastered these male skills, then went into battle and destroyed the usurpers, slashing a red path through the heart of the enemy lines. She was invincible! So great was her courage that the bird lords of the skies, the hawk, the eagle, swooped down shrieking and clawing to join the struggle at her side. When her human followers heard her battle song, they drew courage from her and triumphed!"

My grandmother nodded approval, eyes glowing as though she herself had led the victorious charge. I wondered how Lady Flint Knife could so admire the Warrior Princess, yet be so annoyed when I proposed to learn the same skills that won Six Monkey fame and a kingdom. The feats of women in legends were noble, everyone applauded them, but when I borrowed a small bow and a few arrows that had belonged to my father in childhood, Lady Flint Knife seemed to think I had desecrated them.

At any rate, we were gathered that morning with three or four slaves painting the festival clothing and listening to Sparrow Woman when the signal drum in the plaza sounded the four long, even strokes that meant the arrival of messengers from the capital, a rare event in our village at the edge of the world. A distant horn replied with four solemn notes.

There was a flurry as the men ran to put on proper regalia. Priests who had been on errands raced toward the temple storehouse to fill the censers and light incense for greeting visitors. I saw Prince Chimal emerge from Lady Iztac's house, and his retinue began to gather around him. He held an obsidian-toothed sword in one hand, a lily in the other.

Suddenly Lady Flint Knife squeezed my arm. "Ay, Mali! Good news is coming at last! For two nights I've dreamed the same dream. Your grandfather—you never knew him, child—calls my name four times in the darkness, then his face appears as bright as Lady Moon. He tells me I have been patient long enough and soon I will journey to another land. Now you see? The four drum strokes are his calling. The Revered Speaker must be honoring your father! Yes, that's it. Moctezuma is raising Chimal to some high position. We will leave here."

At this I was astonished, because Lady Flint Knife distrusted all dreams, but there was no doubt she believed this one. To another land? To Tenochtitlan? Or to my father's estates in the south at Coatzacoalcos, Lair of the Serpent?

A sudden hope flashed through me. I imagined living in a place where no one knew the story of my birth, where no one would stare or glance away too quickly. My unlucky name would still be with me, but I could bear that. Few people were even amateur astrologers. Not everyone would remember the evil confluence of signs. Yes, I thought, on the family lands in far-away Lair of the Serpent I would be unknown and happy.

As the first arriving visitors, two running heralds, appeared on the path bearing the standards of Moctezuma, I seized my grandmother's hand and pressed it to my cheek. I believed her omen.

The officials from Tenochtitlan delayed their entrance, giving us plenty of time to spruce up ourselves and our village, and to prepare a welcome of such elegance as our isolation would permit. Flowers were scattered in abundance, although being autumn, the blossoms looked a bit funereal. Turkeys being fattened for the approaching holidays were promptly killed, plucked and put to roast; two or three dogs were slain and dressed. Canoes plied the lake in hope of fresh fish, and from the shore slaves brought clean sand to make a white corridor in the street.

By now, of course, we knew from the running heralds who was arriving. The leader of the party, an Aztec noble sent here by Moctezuma himself, was called Lord Five Deer Hawk Lancer—although I later came to know him simply as Lord Lancer. Some of the outpost soldiers thought they had heard of him, that he had been a young hero in one of the Flower Wars. The Flower Wars were raids the Aztecs launched against their Tlaxcalan neighbors in order to take captives who would later feed the sun with their hearts on the altars of Tenochtitlan. One of the officers said, "Yes, he was famous in a Flower War. I'm sure of it."

"Flower War? Nowadays Thorn War might be a better name," said Lady Flint Knife. She was calling attention to the sharp defeats the army of Tlaxcala had recently inflicted on the Aztecs. The officer glared at her.

Lady Iztac, standing nearby, said, "This lord did win honor fighting the Tlaxcalan barbarians. No doubt he was chosen to come here because he is our cousin." Pride swelled in her voice.

I glanced at Lady Flint Knife, who seemed as surprised as I was. Of course, she had never bothered to learn the names of all Lady Iztac's clan cousins who would probably number several hundred. Lady Iztac, being Aztec, would know all the details of kinship even if the connection was almost prehistoric. Now she was eager and a little flushed, which was odd because her public face always appeared impassive.

In the Fourth Watch of the Day the official party arrived with a vanguard of loud musicians, and since the military musicians of the outpost were also playing a salute, there was a clash of sound, a battle of flutes and rattles, until my father signaled the local band to surrender.

They arrived in magnificence, a dazzling panoply with sunlight flashing on silver and gold, glittering on burnished shields adorned with feather mosaic—designs of life, of nobility, and the stern crest of Moctezuma. Green standards ornamented with tinkling bells waved and fluttered.

All this color was merely background to set off the splendor of Lord Lancer himself. He wore a simple enough mantle, dark red with yellow piping, and a plain headdress, a knot of blossoms that did not hide his glossy hair. A five-tiered necklace like a rainbow almost covered his broad chest: turquoise, garnets, coral, opals and pearls; his earlobes and lower lip had been pierced to hold heavy golden ornaments, and a golden serpent seemed coiled around his left arm. To me he seemed one of the handsomer and richer gods—perhaps Xochipilli, lord of flowers and goldsmiths.

Lady Flint Knife heard my admiring sigh. She pinched me to stop my gaping and muttered, "A mountain of gold, yes. But not a scrap of silver or jade. This lord is flashy but second-rate."

The ceremonies of greeting began—the kissing of the ground, the incensing and presentation of bouquets. I watched agog.

"Our Lord First Speaker the great Moctezuma sends health and blessings to his beloved servant Prince Chimalpopoca," Lord Lancer announced, and I was startled to hear my father's full, formal name of "Smoking Crest" because it was used so seldom. I was sorry my father had chosen to wear a plain white tunic and a cape with a single ornament, a jade pectoral of the Morning Star.

Lord Lancer was flanked by two black-clad priests hovering close to him like a pair of bedraggled crows, their hair matted and kinky with dried blood. They made a startling and, I think, not accidental contrast to Lord Lancer's elegance—like the black edgings artists give royal figures in the painted books.

Then, when the priests kneeled to kiss the ground, I caught sight of a youth standing a little away, a youth so beautiful that Lord Lancer, for all his glitter, faded from the scene. This boy was, as ballad singers say, a child of the Sun.

Neither in that first moment of surprise nor in the years afterward could I ever decide exactly what made my cousin Lark Singer so beautiful. I remember high cheekbones too sharply arched, a skin almost translucent that made his lips and cheeks vivid. Beyond that, when I try to recall Lark's face, the sculpted countenance of Yum Kaax, young god of corn, always imposes itself over my cousin's features. No artist ever made a statue of Lark, yet I feel his face looks down from the friezes of a hundred Maya temples. The boyish god is grave and gentle, long lids half-lowered over almond eyes; his full lips seem sensuous, yet their touch and taste are not to be imagined. His smile is gracious, but he himself remains as cool and elusive as moonlight.

Perhaps Lark was too pretty. I do not know what the man, the warrior, might have become. Perhaps he would have grown more like his father, Lord Lancer, whose handsome face was weak at the edges. When I first saw Lark standing in the Jalisco sunlight, he was only on the verge of manhood, about two years older than I, so still a boy.

That first day, amid the music and rejoicing and incense, I somehow sensed that Lark was doomed, though like my grandmother I am little given to discovering omens in every frog that croaks or fox that yelps. But they say some special children are born neither in the light of the sun nor the light of the stars; they come forth in the shadow of a god, and afterward they can no more elude that shadow than shed their own. When I saw Lark and was astonished by his beauty, from the edge of my eye I glimpsed the god's shadow.

When the official salutation was ended and the crowd began to mill and mix, my father suddenly shouted and rushed toward a young man, rather plainly dressed, who stood to one side smiling shyly. They embraced with a warmth, an eager enthusiasm my father never displayed; so, bold as a boy, I went over to see who the newcomer might be.

"Mali, I wish to present you to your uncle," Prince Chimal said, still holding the stranger's hand. "This is Lord Two House Willow Rod, son of my father and a beautiful lady of the Cloud People."

Uncle Willow, as I was to call him, was frail and round-shouldered, with eyes so big and lively that I thought of a pet squirrel I once had. But I was too dazzled by Lark Singer to pay much attention to anyone else, even a new uncle whom my father so obviously loved.

That night at the feast of welcome I greeted my young cousin formally, eyes properly lowered, and I poured chocolate into his cup, for although slaves served the meal, the ladies of Prince Chimal's household were expected to make gestures of hospitality and display domestic grace. I learned that Lord Lancer was only distantly related to Lady Iztac. But Lady Iztac, an orphan, had been reared by Lord Lancer's aunt so they had known each other from childhood. Even so, I thought he was too familiar, almost disrespectful when he complimented her.

That was only one of the things I disliked about Lord Lancer. I resented his calling our outpost the world's farthest-flung shit pile, even though he said it complaining about my father's banishment. His voice was too loud and his laughter seemed too hearty to be sincere. Lady Flint Knife, refilling the chocolate pitcher, muttered, "The hollower the drum, the bigger the booming."

Uncle Willow sat as silent and attentive as the squirrel he reminded me of, seeming to regard Lord Lancer as an exotic example of plant or animal life who deserved scrutiny but not, perhaps, approval.

But Lady Iztac appeared delighted by Lancer's every word and gesture. At the end of the banquet, just before we were dismissed, she passed the bowl of perfumed water so the men might dip their fingers. Floating on the surface were blossoms from Lady Flint Knife's trumpet tree, the last before winter, and Lord Lancer held up one of the pink, bell-shape flowers, then made a joke so unseemly that my father pretended not to hear. But Lady Iztac, who should have been deaf as a mallet to such allusions, actually blushed and her eyelashes gave a hint of a girlish flutter.

This from Lady Iztac? I could hardly believe my eyes, but then it crossed my mind that even tigresses are at one time kittens. By what magic did Lord Lancer so declaw and tame my mother? I could not understand it—neither then nor later.

As we women were making our obeisance and starting to withdraw, there came a sudden commotion from the darkness just beyond the torchlight—footfalls and murmurings, one voice wailing and another babbling gibberish. Earlier Lord Lancer had asked to see the captives who would be sacrificed for the Feast of the Flags, which he would stay to celebrate with us, so now they were being brought in their cages by guards and slaves.

There were three of them, two men and a woman, elderly worked-out slaves purchased for the festival from some northern tribe. Not understanding our language, they apparently believed they had been carried here to face the knife at once, for the woman screamed and tore at the wooden bars while one of the men implored some sky god to save him. The other man crouched like an animal in its den, uttering little yelps, almost laughter. I suppose he was mad—probably all three were.

Seizing a torch, Lord Lancer approached the cages. The old man who was like an animal hissed and spat.

"By the Ruler of the Night Sky, what have we here?" Lord Lancer peered into the cages, astonished. "My dear Prince Chimal, are these creatures the best your men have taken? Surely these bone-bags aren't the Beloved Sons for the festival?"

"These offerings were bought, not captured," my father said, unruffled. "There is a truce here. We have no Flower Wars with the Tarascans."

Lord Lancer shrugged. "Our revered Lord Moctezuma is less respectful of the Bald Buzzards than you seem to be, cousin." He called the Tarascans this because among them both men and women shave their heads.

My father's brother had said nothing, but now when he spoke the quiet strength of his voice compelled attention, and I thought, the brothers are not really so different as they appear.

"Perhaps Lord Moctezuma will be more respectful this year than he was last in dealing with Tarascans."

Lord Lancer bristled. "What we suffered was not a real defeat. It was only trickery!"

"Tell that to the dead at Cedar Valley. You will have a large audience."

"What has happened?" my father asked.

"Moctezuma's forces put a Tarascan army to flight, or so it appeared," said Uncle Willow.

"The old ambush trick? I suppose a larger army lay in wait, hidden under straw or in cornfields."

"No, a different trick. It appeared that the Tarascans had abandoned their camp when they fled. They left behind roast game, squash stuffed with mushrooms and countless big jars of strongly brewed pulque. Our victorious army halted to gorge themselves on food, which was bad enough—and on drink, which was worse."

Lord Lancer interrupted. "Well, they had just won a victory, so they had a feast. Only pagans neglect to honor the gods of victory with a feast."

Two House Willow Rod gave him a glance that mixed patience with pity. "Ah, yes, the army did its religious duty at this abandoned camp in a place called Cedar Valley. But the Tarascans had only feigned defeat. When Moctezuma's army lay bleary from food and drink, the Tarascans swept back—like the death wind. Today Cedar Valley is heaped with skulls and bleaching bones."

"Trickery, stinking trickery!" said Lord Lancer so angrily that the captives in the cages began to cry again. He glanced at them and saw a chance to change the subject. "Well, I did not mean to belittle your offerings for the feast. I suppose living off the land is the way of the frontier. At least my men and I can bring in some venison for the holidays. I take it there is no truce with the deer?"

Vitsa, who had been set to watch me, tugged at my elbow; I had no excuse for lingering. But before I left I saw a strange thing.

Lark Singer had followed his father to inspect the captives and now stood near the cage of the old man, who was again hissing and snarling. Lark kneeled beside the bars, and even in the dimness of the torchlight I could see compassion in his eyes, and I thought again that his was the gentlest face I had ever known. He whispered to the prisoner, words I could not hear, and the old man, although he did not know our language, fell silent and nodded as if some subtle understanding had passed between them.

The next morning was unusually warm for so late in the year. A hot wind blew from the Jalisco plain and, evading work on festival clothes in the dusty yard, I went to the lake to swim alone. I stripped and waded through the shallows, pushing aside tangles of lilies, then plunged ahead, swimming as free as a trout, diving into the dim world of the Water Goddess, then sweeping up to burst into the sunshine.

An hour later I returned to the shore and was picking up my clothes when I heard a pair of birds—I thought they were jacanas, whistling and quarreling in a nearby thicket. Now the voices of jacanas are anything but melodious, but I was always curious about their language. Most birds utter only a few words; jacanas speak at least a hundred, a whole list of insults and complaints. I stood perfectly still listening, not wanting to intrude upon the argument.

But apparently an intruder had already arrived, for suddenly the jacanas were hushed by the insistent trill of a red-throat. For a moment longer I listened, charmed; then I became puzzled. Red-throats, I had thought, came here only in spring. I moved cautiously toward the thicket, peering among the pine boughs for any telltale flash of crimson. Then, just as I reached the tips of the branches, the angry scream of a hawk burst upon me and I leapt back, throwing up my hands to shield my eyes.

But no hawk exploded into the air from the foliage. Instead the branches parted and Lark Singer stepped out, eyes twinkling, holding back laughter. "Good morning, cousin," he said.

"You?" I gasped, amazed. "It was you—not the birds?"

"How do you think I earned my name last year?" Then he imitated a red-throat's call, the arguing jacanas and then the rippling voice of a lark.

In my awe it did not strike me for a moment that I was naked. Then it did, and I knew I was much too old to stand nude in front of a boy. Long ago Lady Flint Knife had warned me sternly about such things, and Vitsa lectured on the perils of bareness before soldiers. ("It inflames them," she said. For an hour afterward I studied my flat, pole-shaped body, wondering how it would inflame anybody.)

I was holding my tunic in one hand, my wrap-around skirt in the other, and now I fumbled to put them on quickly, managing to drop the skirt and to get my head poked through one of the armholes of the *huipilli*. Lark Singer came gracefully to the rescue, straightening my clothes, knotting the skirt as if he did such things all the time. In the face of such naturalness, I could no longer be embarrassed, and obviously I had not inflamed Lark Singer. He gave me a comradely smile. But what a lovely smile! There was light in it.

We sat in the shade of a jacaranda, leaning our backs against its trunk, and I felt more at ease sitting because, when we stood, I was a little taller than Lark even though he was older. It seemed wrong for a girl to be taller, and I thought it might not please him—a sort of thing I had never considered before.

Lark imitated other birds for me. Some I knew; many I had never heard. "Those birds are not from our part of the world," he explained. "Lord Moctezuma has an aviary at the royal zoo—every bird in the Only World. I go there to listen."

Perhaps Lark's performance was less marvelous than I thought; even then I knew there were soldiers at the outpost, especially among the scouts, who were skillful at echoing at least the common birds. Perhaps I was entranced more by the singer than the song. And part of my delight came from the joy he found in his own art. He seemed to say, without vanity, "I am Lark Singer, and it is glorious to be alive and to be me."

"Could you teach me the bird voices?" I asked eagerly. "I could never do the songs. But the calls and whistles—maybe those."

"Yes." Lightly he took my hand. "And you will teach me to swim."

"You can't swim?" I was astonished that anyone so remarkable could lack such a simple accomplishment. Just as surprising was Lark's asking a girl to teach him anything. I knew little about boys, but I was sure this was not their usual way. Boys had to worry about dignity.

He said, "I hope we stay awhile. We traveled a hundred days."

"A hundred days? So long to come from Tenochtitlan?"

"Oh, no. We were first in the Otomi country checking the tax rolls. Then Lord Moctezuma's swift-messengers caught up with us and told my father to come here to speak with Prince Chimal. Then your uncle, who is on a different errand, joined us a few days ago."

I longed to ask what business Lord Lancer had with my father. So far nothing had been revealed, but we already knew there was no chance of hearing the good news Lady Flint Knife had dreamed of. We had known almost immediately that no promotion was being given my father. None of Lord Lancer's party had worn the full green mantle of good tidings or had braided his hair to show royal pleasure. Concerned though I was about the purpose of the official visit, I did not dare to pry.

"It must be exciting to travel," I remarked, hoping he would drop some hint. "And an honor to act for the great Moctezuma."

"I suppose it is an honor for my father. For me, I love seeing new places, different peoples. I had never been farther than two long-runs from the city before, and I didn't expect to be taken on this journey. My father awakened me in the middle of the night and said I must be ready to leave before dawn. I had known he was going, but I never thought I was. Do you suppose a god came to him in a dream and commanded it?"

"Probably." I was disappointed to have learned nothing important. "Was your mother worried about your going?"

Was this a proper question to ask a boy Lark's age? Was it demeaning? He took no offense. His mother, he explained, had died a year ago trying to birth a child who also died. "She was very fortunate. The baby who died was a male, so my mother is now a hero and among the great chiefs and warriors."

He said it gravely, but with no sadness. Yet I think he felt her loss, and I hoped the lady was indeed happy in all that military company. Was such a heaven really designed for mothers of future warriors? It sounded to me like an eternity of serving chocolate and perfumed water to deathless officials. But when I glanced at Lark's face, serene in perfect faith, I rebuked my own thoughts.

As he spoke of the lands he had visited, the valleys and rivers, I began to understand that poets and artists see the world through special eyes. I think colors were more vivid to him than to me, his hearing keener and perhaps attuned to voices whose overtones eluded my ears. I knew no deeper pleasure than listening to him speak, noticing the curve of his slender fingers as he gestured, the turn of his lips when he laughed. The morning passed too quickly.

We agreed to begin our lessons—swimming and bird language —the next day. Then Lark, remembering, shook his head. "My father is leading a hunting party tomorrow, going before dawn. I suppose I must attend him. But if he doesn't need me, I'll meet you here at the Second Watch."

We raced each other up the hill, from the shore to the log watchtower, laughing and panting. Halfway there I realized I was swifter, had better wind. I could have beaten him, but I let him win.

I have known many men in my life, but only two for whom I would do that.

. .

When the swallows and sparrows twittered at dawn, I awakened, imagining that Lark Singer was outside playing a game of birdcalls. I dressed quickly and silently, then tried to slip past Vitsa without making a sound, but she raised herself on one elbow, gave me a baleful look, then went back to sleep. I almost tripped over Lady Flint Knife's pet dog who was tethered inside these days, lest some soldier steal him and roast him for the holidays.

It was not quite daylight. Only the east was gray as I ran down the hill, not really expecting that Lark would meet me but hoping at least to catch sight of him as the hunting party left. Probably they would follow the shore to the gorge, the usual route.

I soon realized I was too late. The tracks of a dozen men who had crossed the sand were now blurred by the wind; they had gone an hour before. I turned to trudge back up the hill and then, to my delight, I saw Lark himself standing where I had stood yesterday near the pine thicket. I raised my arm in greeting, was about to hail him, when he motioned for me to be still, to watch quietly.

"A bird, a strange one," he whispered when I reached him. We waited motionless, listening, standing back to back so we could see in all directions like the twin statues of Life and Death or two-headed carvings of the Doorwatcher. For what seemed an endless time there was no sound but the chatter of swallows and the stirring of a few waterfowl. In the gorge the ocelots howled for Plumed Serpent at Lord Sun. Then a call came, ringing across the lake.

"Aaaaaaiiiiiahhhh!"

It came lonely and lost, yet so beautiful that it made my heart tremble. We stood not breathing, waiting. Then something burst from the reeds, swept low over the gray water toward the west, not really a bird but a flash of silver. Then it was gone, vanished in the trees of the far shore.

I clasped Lark's hands, excited. "Oh, it was so beautiful. Sad, and yet— Can you do that song? Did you learn it?"

He was pale as he turned from me, shaking his head. "No, I have no voice for it." Then he said, sighing, "I think when gods weep, they sound like that."

Lark learned to swim that day, at least to paddle and float a little. But I failed to master the language of the birds except for a whistle or two. At noon we lay in the sun drying our hair and decorating each other, drawing with bits of charcoal we found on the ridge where a tree had burned. On Lark's chin I sketched a beard such as Plumed Serpent wore but, of course, it was black, not fair or golden as it should have been.

"It might well be black," he said when I apologized. "I have seen painted books with the god having a black beard. Or at least it was dark brown. There is such a picture in the library of the great school in Texcoco."

"A school? For young warriors?"

"No. For scribes and scholars and astrologers. Someday I will go there to learn everything about birds. That is my hope. One day maybe I can know as much about birds as your father knows about the stars —or your uncle knows about plants."

"Uncle Willow? He is a scholar?" Of course he looked like one, dressed in careless clothes that seemed to be afterthoughts.

"Of course. He has studied and taught at Texcoco. He came on this trip in search of a marvelous plant, a flowering tree. But I suppose he will tell you all about it himself."

I drew lightning symbols on Lark's back and arms, because somehow I kept thinking of lightning that day. His skin was the tone of the smoothest dark copper, the color of my mother's throat and breasts. I enjoyed touching him, but it was a quiet pleasure and nothing at all like Vitsa's descriptions of the joys of fondling a man.

"I'm glad your father did not need you for the hunt today," I told him.

"I, too." But there was no happiness in his voice. The weeping of the bird among the reeds had cast a melancholy over him. I sensed that he heard its call again and again in his mind. We were so different. I would recognize the bird's voice if ever I heard it again, but I had already forgotten its timbre, the shape of the song. It did not haunt me.

At the shore we admired our own reflections in the water, then washed away our handiwork. I wondered how Lark would look wearing real decorations for a festival, designs the Sparrow Woman might paint. Then, of course, he would not have the loincloth he had worn swimming. We had just finished ridding ourselves of the charcoal when we heard voices shouting in the distance, and drums.

"The hunters are coming back," said Lark, and started toward the sound, but I caught his arm and held him back.

"No, Lark! They are singing in a language not ours!"

Tarascans, I thought. They had come at last. And since there was no time to flee to the outpost, we crouched among the reeds. So they had broken the peace; my father's hopes were destroyed.

I was mistaken—at least in part. The men who emerged from the pine woods near the ridge were led by Lord Lancer, and they were indeed the dozen hunters who had set out that morning. But in their midst, bound by thongs and held on poles by nooses, were four men with shaven heads and peculiar clothing. Tarascans, of course, and they were the ones singing. I could not understand the words, but I knew it was a song of death and defiance, both a war chant and a threnody.

Something strange about the advancing party occurred to me. The Tarascans, although they were now weaponless, were dressed in what seemed to be clothes of hunters, while the Aztec troops, who had supposedly been on a hunting expedition, wore quilted armor and battle dress.

"So they went to raid the Tarascans," I said. "They weren't after deer at all."

Lark Singer looked away, not answering, ashamed that his father had deceived Prince Chimal but too loyal to admit this.

The two priests Lord Lancer had brought with him, the chaplains of his company, were running from the outpost, holding their black mantles off the ground and trying not to trip on their own tatters. Before I had thought of them as crows or grackles; now they looked like descending vultures. They had been waiting for this arrival, of course, waiting hopefully, for they had brushes and paint pots tied to their belts, and when they reached the captives they began to mark them with the stripes of sacrifice, not even waiting to catch their breath. Once they were marked, they belonged to the altars; there was no reprieve, no appeal to my father possible. The gods had seen their consecration, and Prince Chimal would be helpless to free them, to mend the breaking of the truce.

I pressed my fist against my mouth to hold back a shout of rage. Lord Lancer had betrayed my father. Lord Lancer's tongue should be pierced and forked for lying. I did not hear Lark slip away, but a moment later I was alone, which, in my helpless anger, was what I needed.

I saw nothing of the Feast of the Flags that year. I was confined to my grandmother's house and Vitsa never left my side. "You're lucky

Lady Flint Knife is just making you stay in. It could have been worse
—it *should* have been worse."

While Lark and I had been enjoying ourselves, swimming, doing
birdcalls, a busybody guard had been spying on us from the watchtower. He must have been one of those soldiers who frequently skew-
ered their cocks with thorns to tame impurity, because there was
something foul in his mind. He told his whore that Lark and I had
been "disporting ourselves" in the water, then hidden ourselves among
the reeds secretly to indulge our nasty passions. His whore told the
slave who dressed the hair of my father's concubines, and the second
concubine, a simpering bitch called Honey Nipple, made sure the tale,
with juicy embellishments, reached my grandmother in an hour.
Honey Nipple was so eager to malign me, since I was Lady Iztac's
daughter, that she came running to the house and, as the saying goes,
stuck her tongue in Lady Flint Knife's ear.

Vitsa and my grandmother seized me, dragged me into bright
sunshine and bent me backward over a log, Vitsa gripping my hair.
Lady Flint Knife opened my lower lips, then probed, poked, and
finally exclaimed, "At least the seal is unbroken! Probably not from
want of trying. Or maybe neither of the young scoundrels knew which
hole to use."

"What is it?" I cried. "What am I supposed to have done?"

Instead of answering, Lady Flint Knife suddenly slapped my face,
a stinging blow. Then to my shock she crumpled to the ground,
weeping.

"Citli, Citli," I wailed, calling her "star" as I always did when
I was hurt or troubled. I kneeled beside her, trying to put my arms
around her.

"I have hurt you," she said, drying her eyes. "How could I have
done such a thing?"

Until I saw her weeping I never knew how much I loved her.

She recovered herself quickly, and the three of us, shaken, went
into the house where, amid recriminations, the story was more or less
straightened out.

"From this learn discretion!" exclaimed Lady Flint Knife. "I
believe your innocence, but it is hard to forgive your stupidity. You
have let yourself get the reputation of a ruined slave girl."

Then she pronounced sentence: imprisonment in the house or

dooryard for the entire festival; no meetings alone with Lark Singer during his stay.

"But we are friends! I have never met anyone I felt so close to."

"That is precisely the trouble," said Lady Flint Knife. Then she marched out of the house, and Vitsa stopped me from following to plead further. To my mortification, she went straight to Lord Lancer and told him to keep a tighter tether on his son. She minced no words; Lord Lancer's scene with my father over the seizing of the Tarascans must have seemed friendly by comparison.

There was nothing I could do but sulk and glare at Vitsa. At my first chance, when she went out to the garden, I quickly got out my grandmother's bloodstone and pronounced a curse on the gossiping guard, invoking Tlaloc, Lord of Waters, to swell the man's ankles with dropsy, one of Tlaloc's specialties; then I implored the Flower Prince to send his particular vengeance, which is a gift of hemorrhoids. I considered including Lord Lancer in the curse, but decided his was a different case; besides, Vitsa might return at any moment and catch me with the bloodstone.

Although I saw nothing of the festival, I heard a great deal: the joyful shrieks as the men and women doused each other with water, the cheers for the bird-dancers and, more solemn, the temple drums announcing sacrifice of the prisoners to Hummingbird of the Left, bringer of victory. Two of the Tarascans were slain in gladiatorial sacrifice where they each fought a fully armed warrior while themselves having only wooden weapons and no armor, besides being restricted by a short tether. Such a contest has little more equality than the sacrificial stone. I understand the Tarascans died bravely; they always do.

That afternoon while the air was still heavy and faintly sweet with the smoke of cooking fires, an unseasonable rain began to fall, so Lady Flint Knife and Sparrow Woman, bored with the festivities, sat just inside the doorway near the pale light, drinking ash-leaf tea to help their rheumatism and smoking tiny clay pipes to honor the holiday. Since I was making a show of suffering, I did not join them, although I listened to every word as I languished on my mat in the next room, sighing audibly from time to time and watching to see if this had any effect.

They chatted of domestic matters; then Sparrow Woman, with

an old lady's bluntness, asked the question that was in most people's minds. "What does your son think about the sacrifice of the Tarascan hunters? Will it bring an army down upon us?"

"I cannot read the mind of Prince Chimal," replied Lady Flint Knife haughtily; then she relented. "But I may tell you he is sending a runner tomorrow morning to the Place of the Hummingbirds."

There was no need to say more. The message to the Tarascan capital could only be an apology and an explanation that a mistake had been made by green troops, men ignorant of the truce. Doubtless the apology would be sweetened with a bribe. The Tarascans had no cotton or access to the lands where it was grown, so they lacked fine garments for ceremonies. People marveled that the gods so often blessed the Tarascans in war, considering how shabbily they dressed for it.

"I think they might settle for a gift of mantles and sashes," I said, trying to sound adult and judicious.

"Perhaps it would be tactless to offer them clothes," Lady Flint Knife remarked, putting me neatly in my place. The endless wars between Tarascans and Aztecs, storytellers said, had started centuries ago when the two peoples were one, or at least they were related closely enough to travel together. During their wanderings they reached the shores of Lake Patzcuaro, where a goddess commanded the Tarascans to swim in the cool waters. While they were performing this religious duty, their Aztec friends stole all their clothing and everything else they had left on the shore and made off. The Tarascans, naked, remained in the neighborhood of the lake, where they are to this day, and they never forgave their Aztec allies. A gift of clothing, as Lady Flint Knife suggested, might indeed be tactless.

Sparrow Woman considered the situation, drew on her pipe and released a puff of smoke. "Let us hope the Tarascan lords do not think too much about the morsels of Tarascan flesh the messenger will still be digesting in his belly."

"We can hope." Lady Flint Knife was trying to control her rage. These had been difficult days—her good news had not arrived, I had lost my reputation and risked my virginity, her son's authority had been flouted by a man she considered a coxcomb. She tilted her head toward the barracks yard, where the feast was in progress amid a din of flutes, horns and rattles. "Listen to them gorging on human flesh!

For all their rich clothes and fancy airs and talk of culture, they are savages."

"Well, there have always been some people who ate human flesh," said Sparrow Woman, trying to calm my grandmother.

"Yes, but never before did cannibals conquer the world! What are the subject peoples but herds of tame deer for the Aztecs to feed on? Flocks of turkeys for a fine feast."

"My dear Lady Flint Knife," exclaimed Sparrow Woman, not really as shocked as she pretended. "The gods demand sacrifice. We must give life for life now and then."

"Of course! Do you think I'm an atheist? Hard times and droughts always demand a victim or two—and what better way to get rid of criminals? In my mother's time they always gave a life for the crops at planting season, another at harvest and when prophecy was needed. But not these public feasts! And never this daily feeding of hearts to Lord Sun! *My* people fed the sun only when the sheaf of fifty-two years was bound up. Yet the sun shone brighter for the Culhuas than for Aztecs!"

"*And* for the Otomi," Sparrow Woman added, not letting her ancient people be forgotten. "In the old days people were religious and made pious sacrifices. But there were no excesses."

Lady Flint Knife nodded. "Common sense tells us when a time comes to placate the gods, and only a fool would object on principle to the priests eating flesh at a rite." She glared through the wall in the direction of the Aztecs. "I am no theologian, but I know where piety ends and gluttony starts."

I had never heard her talk with such open bitterness. Young as I was, I sensed the strangeness of the scene: two elderly, rich and respectable women speaking treason and blasphemy while they quietly puffed their pipes and sipped tea within bow shot—maybe within earshot—of Lord Moctezuma's own messengers.

"Lord Lancer went hunting because he hungered for flesh. His religion is as false as his jewelry." Lady Flint Knife ended the discussion.

They smoked in silence for a moment. Sparrow Woman studied her hands, which were splotched with paints and dyes she had used for festival decorations. One palm was bloody red, the death color, and there were ugly splatters she had not been able to wash from her hair.

She said, "Dear lady, I have been thinking about that shade of vermil-ion you asked for. Perhaps if we took cochineal and boiled it with a little cinnabar . . ."

Outside a loud cheer went up for Lord Lancer.

That evening when quiet fell on the outpost and even the hardiest celebrants were exhausted, Prince Chimal came to see me. Unfortu-nately he did not offer me parole for tomorrow morning when our visitors, except Uncle Willow, would be leaving for Tenochtitlan.

"I have brought a festival gift," he said. "A special gift for a special daughter." This was his way of saying that although I might have behaved foolishly, he did not believe Honey Nipple's lurid story.

The gift was indeed unusual: a knife with a wooden handle and a dark gray blade about as long as my hand. I could not recognize the lusterless stone used to make the blade. It seemed very heavy.

"Run your fingers over it," said my father.

I did, then exclaimed, "Silver! But so dark. What is it?"

"That question is what the great Lord Moctezuma should be asking. Only a few smiths who work in the forges in the Land of the Fishermen can tell, and it is not likely they will."

He meant Tarascan country. Their kingdom is rich with lakes full of fish. So Tarascans had forged this knife from a strange metal known only to them. Years later I would learn that it was the alloy bronze, unknown to the rest of the Only World then.

"They use it only to make weapons, I believe. Someday, Mali, weapons this sharp and hard could conquer all the Only World. To wield a powerful new weapon is to have a god on your side, Mali."

Because he had awarded military honors earlier, he was still wearing his sword as a decoration. It was a fearful weapon made for both clubbing and hacking, longer than his arm, a hand span wide. Although it was made of wood, both edges were set with obsidian blades sharp as cat's claws. The little knife just given me, even imagin-ing it grown to sword size, looked harmless by comparison.

Prince Chimal saw my doubts. "Remember, your small knife can cut the wood of my sword, but the heaviest blow I can strike is powerless to slash through your knife blade. Wood and even obsidian will simply shatter on that metal."

I studied the knife with new respect, feeling it, touching it with my tongue—I thought it had a sharp taste. Few things in life are so amazing as encountering a new metal. I had seen silver and gold and a few pieces of copper, but no others, and I cannot describe the feelings that later in life swept over me when I discovered the new world of metals: iron, steel, tin and brass. Each one is a miracle.

My father talked a little about the power of the new weapons, how long ago the Toltecs poured into the Only World from Nowhere North to vanquish powerful kingdoms. "Not because they were stronger or braver, but because they had bows and arrows. No one else knew of such things. Today we think of Toltecs as almost gods. But it was the arrows that won their divinity, Mali."

I thanked him for the gift, promising to keep it near me. Now it seemed not a knife but a sword, and I was suddenly the Warrior Princess herself.

"Another gift is coming. Did you notice that my wife Honey Nipple did not dance at the festival?"

"No." How could I notice anything? I had been a prisoner.

"She is with child. I hope for a son, but a daughter like yourself would be welcome."

My heart leapt. Hating the mother, I instantly hated the unborn child. Lowering my head so he could not see my face, I said the formal prayer of joy and blessing. All the while I was thinking, Is this child really my father's? Honey Nipple looks like a slut, probably is one. I have seen her raise her eyes when men walk by.

While such thoughts were churning, I felt shame that I did not rejoice for my father, that I was pretending happiness. He had three wives, yet his only child was a girl. What did other men say about this? What did they think that they dared not say?

Prince Chimal rose to leave, then hesitated. He turned to me, his face gentle, and said, "You and I will watch the stars together soon, Mali. It seems my star-watching has become interesting even to the great Moctezuma."

"It has, father?"

"That is why Lord Lancer was sent here. He brought charts drawn by scholars in Tenochtitlan and Texcoco. They, too, saw the bloodstone in the sky. What is the omen? Does it mean that Plumed Serpent is coming back? Moctezuma asked me—as he has asked a dozen others—for an answer."

"What did you say, father?"

Prince Chimal seemed surprised by my question. "Naturally I

said that Plumed Serpent will come. Of course he is coming."

"Is he?" Excitement kindled in me. I forgot Honey Nipple. "When? Tell me when!"

"When?" My father's left eyebrow twitched ever so slightly, as it always did when he held back a smile. "Now that, my daughter, is a much harder question." He gave me a quick, affectionate embrace, and before leaving he said, "Tonight I am entertaining a few of our guests before they leave us. I think my favorite daughter should help serve them."

To my disappointment Lark was considered too young to be invited, and the real guest of honor that night was a strange one: a young tree, hardly more than a seedling, which Uncle Willow had found growing in a sheltered valley.

"Yes, it is the Tree of Achiotla," said Uncle Willow, proud of himself but awed by his discovery. "I have searched all summer and fall for this, and to think I came across it by accident!"

The tree looked quite insignificant and puny in its big earthen pot, but it was one of the few things in the world that Lord Moctezuma desired and did not already possess.

"It began a few years ago when Moctezuma had just risen to the throne and the rank of First Speaker. He learned that far away in Oaxaca the ruler of Achiotla had a tree whose beauty and fragrance surpassed anything on earth or in heaven. Moctezuma demanded it for his own garden. When the Achiotlans refused to yield it, he sent a huge army against them. When they stormed the city, they killed most of the young defenders, then Moctezuma ordered every person over fifty put to the sword or stretched on the altar."

"Quite right, too," said Lord Lancer. "The old codgers urged the defiance, so Moctezuma got rid of them like so many farts."

The subject turned to military matters, and as I offered clover water for my uncle to dip his fingers, I whispered, "What happened to the tree?"

He whispered back, "It died from being uprooted. Everybody lost that war." I turned away, smiling. It was the sort of unpatriotic and irreverent remark my father often made in private.

The guests stayed for hours, telling the histories of old campaigns, debating military tactics and rituals. I had often heard such talk when my father entertained his officers; I knew about feints and false retreats and ways of carrying enemies off the field alive for sacrifice. But, staying in the shadows, I absorbed every word while I imagined myself as the Warrior Princess or the Soldier Queen of the south who long ago led great armies to victory.

The next day our visitors from Tenochtitlan departed with less pomp than they had displayed when they arrived. Vitsa said they were offended because Prince Chimal would not appear to make a formal, public farewell. Instead he sent word that he was occupied designing new fortifications for the outpost and had no time for more ceremonies.

I was not allowed to see Lark, but I consoled myself that some of the birdcalls I heard that morning were actually his farewells to me. Try as I would, I could not manage a whistle in reply, and only when the party was well on its way was I granted freedom from the yard. While I was lingering near the street, a slave woman I did not know strolled by, quickly thrust something into my hand, then hurried on without glancing back. I gazed down at a little ring of clear rock crystal, the purest of stones. Tied to the ring with a thread was a tiny feather, bright yellow. Blinking and swallowing hard, I tucked the ring and feather into the sheath that held the Tarascan knife. I would wear it under my tunic, a talisman.

My uncle, before setting out to find a replacement for the dead Tree of Achiotla, had been promised that success would be rewarded. Lord Woman Snake, who ranked only behind Moctezuma himself, had offered a post among the royal tutors. Lord Willow Rod would teach Moctezuma's sons and nephews the nature and uses of all benevolent plants in the world—that is, all except those that are for the making of poisons. The royal wizards held that lore secret. For Lord Willow Rod, a bastard with no inheritance who was called lord only by stretching courtesy, this was a fine opportunity, and now he was eager to return to the capital and claim it.

"But I can wait until tomorrow," he told my father. "I will not risk the tree or myself traveling along the frontier with Lancer's party. Not after what has happened with the Tarascans. I prefer to look like a harmless scholar with not enough meat on my bones to roast."

So that night he joined my father and me on the hill for starwatching. But since the heavens were screened by clouds, the brothers talked of other things.

"How does the capital look these days?" my father asked.

"Swollen with tribute, richer than ever. I have a friend who is chief clerk of the royal tax inventories. It is astonishing what he tells me. Every year a quarter of a million cotton mantles come in and just as many embroidered skirts, ten thousand shields, enough corn and beans to make two mountains. I've seen the storehouses—huge jars of liquid amber, heaps of jade. One man does nothing all day but count and list the jewelry arriving."

"Rich, indeed," said my father.

"More than rich. Engorged with wealth, wallowing in useless tribute. Everything is done to excess—styles, wars, religion. You'll be shocked when you return, brother."

"Yet a city so rich must be a place of opportunity for a bright young man like yourself."

Uncle Willow suddenly spat in disgust. He lowered his voice before he spoke, although the whole broad hill was open and empty. It was as though he suspected even the bats and owls of being spies. "Everything has changed since Lord Moctezuma rose to power. Only the high-born have a voice or any respect now. Now the question is not what can you do, but who was your grandfather. Moctezuma despises anyone who is not at least a third cousin of royalty. If a common man rises too far, Moctezuma will cut him down fast."

"Really?" My father frowned, shook his head. "I remember Moctezuma from our days in the army. He seemed modest. I thought him too pious and too deferential to be a ruler."

"That used to be his mask—humility, fear of the gods. Now he shows his real face."

"Forgive me, brother, but you yourself are what you call a common man. Will you really be appointed a tutor?"

"Lord Woman Snake—and the Woman Snake is still powerful —has promised." Uncle Willow laughed, a chuckle as dry as the dead hillside grass. "To think my future is guaranteed not because of my knowledge or skill, but because I have found a frail little seedling of a tree that will quickly perish in the cold of Tenochtitlan. Well, let us hope my career outlasts the tree."

"Yes," said my father. "Let us hope so." He was not smiling.

5

During the next days I felt lonely and troubled. Some mornings I went to the shore to listen for the call of the god-bird in the reeds, but he never returned. I often wondered about my new sister or brother who would be born soon; I worried about the baby's horoscope, yet my jealousy flared when I caught sight of Honey Nipple, swollen as ripe as Lady Moon, and always a moonlike simper on her mouth.

My father's messenger arrived back safely from the Place of Hummingbirds, a cause for astonishment since most people had never expected to see him again, except perhaps delivered in several pieces. Sparrow Woman darkly recalled how the Aztecs used to cook up a dish they very appropriately called ambassador stew to send back to enemy kings in lieu of their envoys.

The swift-messenger brought good news. The Tarascan lords said they understood how a mistake might be made; the peace and love between the Land of the Fishermen and the great Lord Moctezuma were too sacred to be broken by a misunderstanding. And would Prince Chimal accept a trifling gift from the Tarascan ruler? The gift turned out to be a panache of dyed heron feathers. It looked cheap.

"We have received the response of a generous lord and a noble people," my father proclaimed. Then he ordered extra shifts to work on the new palisades.

. .

Winter crept down from the western mountains, bright days but cold nights. The visitors from the capital had brought me a glimpse of horizons, of people and cities I had known only from legends. Suddenly the world beyond the outpost had become real and I longed to see it, to be part of it. I felt restless; my life had mysteriously changed.

A shabby little merchant caravan, on no particular route but following wherever the Guiding Lord might lead them for profit, brought a message from Uncle Willow. He had received his appointment, he was thriving, but the precious tree looked puny. My father did not like the omen.

Slowly I realized I had learned something important. My meeting with Lark Singer had made me realize that I was, after all, a girl, no matter that I could outrun him. He had not actually treated me like a girl but like a comrade, and this was pleasing yet disturbing. So I began to change, to mature a little. Not that I gave up my freedom and started grinding corn flour; but I no longer felt content to dress in a torn and usually muddy *huipilli* too short for me, or to let my hair hang lank like a rabbit skin.

Lady Flint Knife understood my new feelings and began to teach me. As she showed me how to comb and bind my hair, how to shape my nails, I glimpsed another woman behind her wrinkled face—a woman young and lovely, deft in all the subtle arts of femininity.

From watching Lady Iztac, whose gestures had the grace of a dahlia, I learned how to move my hands, to nod, to tilt my head. One day I discovered that Vitsa, who had no other physical beauty, moved like a queen. Perhaps it was no more than her years of bearing water jugs and other burdens on her head that had given her such carriage, but when she glided down a path, Vitsa floated like a moon goddess. I lifted my chin and straightened my thin shoulders, imitating her.

The five unlucky days before the new year passed, those days that will fit no month of a perfect calendar and so must be left dangling at the end, dangerous because they have no place and misfits are not to be trusted.

Early in the new year a messenger arrived, a runner such as merchants use, and indeed his loincloth was painted with the mask of the trader's god, the long-toothed Guiding Lord whose fangs, Lady Flint Knife said, were especially sharpened the better to bite you. All merchants were wolves. Usually such messengers were on errands that did not interest me—inquiries about politics at the frontier or the flooding of rivers.

This time the message was a reminder to Prince Chimal that four months ago he had accepted an invitation to a wedding feast at a trading and pilgrimage place called Boiling Springs, a short journey from the outpost. Lord Hot Hammer, the local chieftain whose son was being married, had built a stronghold on the main trail to the capital, so he deserved courtesy as an ally—even though people said he was a part-time bandit and a full-time barbarian. Now Lord Hot Hammer was making final arrangements for the feast and revels.

"My master hopes Prince Chimal will honor him by bringing a large party," the messenger said, humbly kissing the ground for the third or fourth time—really too much. "Lord Hot Hammer respectfully suggests a company of one hundred and four guests from here." That was a lucky number, being twice fifty-two, the number of years to make a sheaf. It was an astonishingly extravagant invitation.

"No," my father replied. "There will be twenty-six of us, plus a few slaves. That is half fifty-two and just as sacred."

The messenger, as far as he dared, wheedled for a larger attendance, but Prince Chimal held firm, not intending to leave the outpost undermanned. The Tarascans' words had been friendly and scouts reported no unusual activity along the border, but Prince Chimal remained suspicious. "I mistrust people who forgive a wrong that has never been righted," he said. "I may next see them emerging from ambush."

Besides this worry, my father liked to travel simply and without fuss; that was his style. Lady Iztac would accompany him, but of the lesser wives, Honey Nipple was too swollen to travel and Night Jasmine would remain at home to pamper Honey Nipple. Lady Flint Knife, with her stiff joints, would not think of going.

At the last moment it was decided that I should join the party because of Lady Flint Knife's urging. "Any journey, even to a dunghill like Boiling Springs, will help educate her. Mali has never been anywhere. And she must be more with her mother in public. They must get used to each other. Think of the future, my son."

We set out the next morning while the stars were still uneaten, walking toward the false dawn, my parents and I with twenty-three soldiers as an honor guard. Ten slaves carried baggage and wedding gifts, but Vitsa had been left behind, which pleased me because I felt unwatched and grown-up.

"You must get used to being without her," Lady Flint Knife told me. "This summer Vitsa will have saved enough to buy her freedom. Then she will marry and take care of her own children."

I knew that such a day would come. Slavery was very seldom a permanent condition for anyone. But I did not like the thought of Vitsa's having children she would love more than me. Now the excitement of the journey swept away any sadness about Vitsa.

To please our host, Prince Chimal had chosen soldiers and even slaves who could play drums, rattles and flutes. We would make up in noise what we lacked in numbers. Some of the men played as we marched, and as a breeze fluttered the emblems we carried, I thought we were an impressive sight.

Within two hours we stepped beyond the limits of my world. Everything—trees, gullies, even cactus—struck me as utterly different, although they must have been exactly the same as those I had always known. We climbed a steep, wooded ridge, and at the crest I turned back, gazing in wonder at the small corner of the view that had been my whole universe. How tiny the outpost seemed with its little watchtower and toy palisade. Even the lake had become a frog pond! This, I decided, was only a beginning. I would see all of the world, not just what lay beyond this ridge, but beyond the mountains that loomed faint and cloudy on the horizon.

Except for the moment on the ridge, the day's travel was without adventure except for the oddity of walking for so long beside Lady Iztac, and even that lost its novelty after a few hours. From time to time she actually looked at me and once she nodded. I nodded back, not too awkwardly; we were getting used to each other. At sunset we camped, spreading out mats, unrolling cotton blankets and building a fire to ward off animals and demons. I discovered that Lady Iztac, who was so brave, felt uneasy being outdoors at night. This pleased me because I was unafraid of darkness and used to having the stars for company.

Again we began walking before daylight, now moving through tall grasses and among low-branched trees too sparse to be called a forest. I thought, *Tiger country,* and enjoyed a little thrill of fear. Jaguars loved tall grasses, I had been told. Late that afternoon we reached the settlement.

Boiling Springs was exactly what my grandmother had said it was—a dunghill, fetid and flyblown. But we entered with great clatter and array. The gaping, slack-jawed inhabitants, even more ignorant of the world than I was, stood goggling at us. Our feathered banners trimmed with bells made a sensation.

Lord Hot Hammer kissed the ground before my father so awkwardly that I thought of a pet monkey doing a new trick and wondered if he had been coached in the ceremony only that morning. After a lengthy exchange of grins and praises and incense, the bride was unexpectedly trotted out naked. This was for my father's, and everybody else's, inspection. Lady Iztac looked thunderstruck, but Prince Chimal lauded the girl politely. She was nothing but tattoos and bones. The points of her teats and buttocks looked sharp enough to stab you.

The villagers crowding around were an odd assortment in both appearance and languages. I recognized the savage Chichimecs in their dog-skin finery. They wore human bones through their pierced noses, and I was thankful that the stench of their unwashed bodies would make it impossible for them to sneak up on anybody. Some of the others spoke with Otomi accents, like Sparrow Woman's; still others were Huastecs with foreheads molded into a slope in infancy. The place seemed less a village than a collection of several hundred huts and people who had simply been swept up in corners of the world by a random gale and then dropped here. Among the droppings were a good many cutthroats with hungry, calculating eyes. I should not have been surprised; but it was the first border town I had ever seen.

I felt no fear of the men who ogled us; they were weasels, not jaguars. We walked among them surrounded and protected by the might of Tenochtitlan, the power of the Triple Alliance that hovered over us like a flock of invisible eagles. The shields of our honor guard were emblazoned with the face of the War-Bringer, and he was inexorable, dealing death to rebels. I felt assurance and pride.

"That is our new fort," said Lord Hot Hammer, gesturing to a stockade set in stone and mud foundations. "Tomorrow I hope you will inspect it, Highness. Today it is being decorated for the feast."

"I shall be honored," murmured the prince, stepping around turkey shit as we made our way through the swarm of wattle huts.

"Here are your pavilions, Highness," our host announced proudly. "So new that the rushes are still green. Not a flea in them yet, I swear. Not a tick!"

"Very nice, very fresh."

"Thank you, Highness. This pavilion is for you and your beautiful wife and daughter. Ten of your men can be quartered next door,
and the rest have quarters over there beyond the temple. You will not
be crowded."

The two-room pavilion was clean, dry and prettily decorated
with pine branches. But there were no flowers, which surprised me.
Then I realized I had not seen a blossom anywhere in the village. These
were indeed strange people, to live without flowers.

A little later the bridegroom, a squat youth called Ce Atl, came
to greet us and guide us to the hot springs from which the village took
its name.

"They are a wonder, Highnesses. Very sacred, very potent."

It turned out they were also foul-smelling and brackish. True to
their name, a few springs boiled at moments, and a cloud of perpetual
steam hung over them. It made a rainbow in the sunset. Three old men
were sitting in a shallow puddle, pouring water over each other with
gourds. The chief's son reeled off a list of medical miracles the waters
had wrought.

"Their greatest power lies in unlocking the wombs of women.
They never fail to yield the gift of fertility."

Lady Iztac looked at the bubbling waters with sudden interest,
then shrugged her shoulders. "If they do that, why aren't the waters
crowded with women? They would be thick as fish in a net if what
you say is true."

"Ah, not in daylight, Highness. The waters work for women
with the help of Lady Moon. When her light touches the springs, the
waters draw life from her."

He went on explaining that the goddesses of the springs were
moon children, but I needed to hear no more. This night Lady Moon
would be full and ripe. Lady Iztac might be wary of darkness, but not
Smoking Mirror himself could keep her from bathing in these springs.
She would be here every night we spent in the village; it glowed in
her eyes.

On the way back to our pavilion my father said to me privately,
"Tonight I will read the stars, a horoscope for the wedding couple.
Would you like to help me?"

"Yes, Father."

"Good." He did not smile, but his left eyebrow twitched. "We

will go to that hilltop over there as soon as your mother leaves for
the springs."

That night during the Second Watch a heavy meal was brought
to our pavilion. We were served chocolate with it, but the soldiers
must have been treated to gourds of forbidden pulque. Their laughter
grew raucous, and someone started singing a barracks ballad. "There
is a rich whore of Tenochtitlan who has a double cunt."

My father went to pay a visit to the barracks and what was left
of the pulque was poured on the ground. A little later the men were
snoring, not singing.

When the village seemed fully asleep, I heard my parents whispering to each other; then Lady Iztac rose from her mat and quietly
left.

My father said to me, "Come now. Bring a blanket; the night's
cold."

I took not only a blanket but also the sheath that contained my
three treasured possessions—the Tarascan knife, the ring from Lark
Singer and a bit of carved jade Lady Flint Knife had given me as a
parting gift. I certainly would not leave them unwatched in this nest
of thieves, and the slave who was supposed to be on guard snored
louder than the soldiers.

As we moved through the turkey runs that passed as streets, the
silence seemed oppressive, unnatural. What was wrong? Then it struck
me that no dogs barked at our passing. Most of them, of course, had
already been slaughtered for tomorrow's feast. But all? Was there not
even one spared as a pet or foot warmer? No flowers and no pets—
what dismal people!

Leaving the huts and garbage heaps, we climbed a hillside path,
and as we passed the boiling springs, my father waved a greeting to
a figure shrouded in steam. Lady Iztac was bathing alone.

The brilliant moon had devoured most of the stars; only a few
patterns could be discerned. My father made a note or two on bark
paper, then abandoned the effort.

"The stars promise the bridal couple health, happiness and riches.
But less of all these and for less time than they hope for and expect."
He looked at me solemnly. "Is that a safe prediction?" We laughed
together, partners in blasphemy.

From this height we could see part of the interior of Lord Hot
Hammer's new stockade, clearly lighted by the moon. We watched

several men move across the open area, then disappear. "They seem to have finished decorating," I said. "The big gates are opening now." Even as I spoke, I became aware of other activity in the village below, figures moving quietly among the huts. "Is there some ceremony tonight?"

Then I heard soft footsteps running toward us. "My lord! My husband!" Lady Iztac's voice was hushed but urgent as she hurried up the hill, her bathing robe wet, her hair dripping.

"Tarascan soldiers!" she gasped out the words. "They are in the town—I heard their language."

Prince Chimal stood undecided for a second, then he whispered, "Quick! Stay low to the ground, but run!"

A coppice of piñons stood nearby and, crouching, we fled for its cover. I suddenly noticed that my father was wearing his sword, which he now drew, and this was strange since he had gone out only to see the stars. He had been suspicious, I realized. But not suspicious enough.

A terrible clamor, yells and shrieks, now burst from the village, a boom of drums, the wail of shell trumpets. Torches flared inside the stockade and companies of men, Tarascan soldiers, charged from the fort into the streets—not attacking the fort but coming from it, where they had been lurking concealed. I gasped to see the big pavilion where we might have been sleeping blaze like a bonfire—no, not a bonfire, a torch, for it exploded into a roaring cloud of fire as though its mats had been stuffed with tinder, shooting sparks to the sky. In the melee one thing was clear: Tarascans and the villagers had united to butcher our honor guard.

My father watched in horror. Once he took a step forward, raising his sword as though to charge down the hill, but Lady Iztac grasped his arm. "No, my lord! The slaughter is already done."

She was wrong—although her words halted my father. Only the fighting was over; the slaughter had just begun. Lord Hot Hammer had treacherously divided our men into two camps for sleeping, the easier to surround and murder them. The Aztec soldiers had been seized and bound or disabled before they could even lay hands on their weapons. Now the bloodbath began.

Some men were disemboweled where they lay, others dragged to the temple for sacrifice. A few were simply torn to pieces by the mob.

A child with a shrill voice screamed, "Death for the Aztecs! Death, death!" Then he shrieked in mindless laughter.

Lady Iztac whispered a reply. "We will see Hot Hammer's heart ripped from his chest. His children will watch it roast before their own time comes!" Her fists were clenched, and she trembled and bit her knuckles.

A strange and hollow singing rose from the town, the chant I had heard from the Tarascan hunters Lord Lancer had captured for sacrifice. It trembled in the air above the yells of the killers and the screams of the dying. Huts near the pavilions had now taken fire from the shooting sparks, and the scene of horror was now eerily bathed in flames and moonlight.

I saw one of our soldiers, the only one still standing, lift his arm to hurl a spear, but a Tarascan sword slashed the air and suddenly the man had no arm, no spear, and a fountain of blood spurted from his shoulder. He stared at the blood, astonished; then the mob swept over him.

Although the slaughter and torture took place in front of my own eyes and only a few bow shots away, it seemed unreal to me— it was a dance, a performance, mimes acting out a legend. I could not comprehend the horror.

Two figures were stumbling up the path from the springs, and my father, recognizing them, cupped his hands and gave the signal call of a nightjar. Then he spoke their names, as loudly as he dared. "Cholol! Miztli! Over here in the trees!"

A moment later they collapsed beside us, two young soldiers. One of them, a dark-faced youth called Cholol, was badly wounded, open slashes running across his chest and right shoulder. Lady Iztac quickly ripped cloth from her robe for bandages. Cholol was silent but the other soldier, Miztli, who seemed unhurt and had kept his sword and shield, could not stop cursing and weeping. Spittle ran from the corners of his mouth. "We must get away from here! They'll hunt us down soon."

"Yes, Miztli, little son. We will go." Prince Chimal put a calming hand on the warrior's shoulder, his voice gentle. "We go as soon as those clouds in the east cover Lady Moon. The village will be busy a little longer."

So it was. The mob's attention had now shifted from murder to the salvage of possessions from the burning huts—the rescue of their own goods or the stealing of their neighbors'. Others were yelling and belaboring each other as they fought over clothing from our soldiers' bodies. The Tarascan troops stood about uncertainly, waiting for orders, but a few had begun a shuffling victory dance, and those watching them cheered and clapped and shouted over and over, "Death to Tenochtitlan!"

Then a cloud bank swept over Lady Moon, darkening the hillside, and we fled like rabbits, darting from shadow to shadow, dodging behind rocks and bushes, knowing what would happen if we did not reach the country of the tall grass before daybreak.

All the next day we lay in the grass unmoving while search parties scoured the country. My father and Miztli had swords; Cholol had found a broken branch to use as a club. They would not, they swore, be taken captive alive.

Neither would Lady Iztac—or at least she would not remain a living captive long. I watched her break the string of the necklace she was wearing, detach the gold ornaments and hide them in her hair. She would swallow them if she became a prisoner. It was a sure but painful way to die, and the gold of her death could be offered up to the sun god along with her suffering. Noticing that I watched, she held out her hand to offer three beaten ornaments, small but heavy, shaped like arrowheads with sharp tips and edges.

"I do not need them," I said. "Thank you. I have a knife. I will use it one way or another if the time comes."

She nodded, then returned to her own prayers and preparations. I think my refusal of such an excruciating death made her own resolve feel more noble; at any rate, she did not repeat the offer.

A flock of crows had established a colony in a tree near our hiding place, and when they flapped or scolded, we dared not whisper, hardly dared breathe. When the crows fell silent, the men talked in low tones about what had befallen us.

"At least, my lord, you saved many lives by refusing that traitor's generous invitation. A hundred and four guests he wanted! I'll bet a month's pay he would have divided that large a party into four camps instead of two. Cowards!"

"I was thinking of the strength of the outpost," said my father. "I thought the attack would come there. I did not suspect Hot Hammer would betray us."

"Bribes! Tarascan bribes!"

"Perhaps," my father said cautiously.

No doubt bribes. And I think the barbarians of Boiling Springs would have dismembered us for the clothes on our backs. But I remembered the cries of death to the Aztecs. It sprang not just from greed, but from rage and hate. I remembered, too, that Lord Lancer's party had passed through Boiling Springs not long ago. They were tax collectors; had they plucked the villagers down to their very pin-feathers?

I now realized why every dog in the village had been killed, even dogs they should have kept to breed new litters. The Tarascans were strangers; the dogs would have raised an alarm when they moved through the dark streets.

The silence of the dogs . . . the divided quarters for our troops . . . the stockade we could not enter. These were lessons I would remember. One day, I think, I would remember them too well.

We moved at dusk, crawling through the grass like five lizards. Later, because the night was again cloudy, we took the risk of walking, taking turns helping Cholol, whose breath came so hoarsely that it was alarming. Suddenly he spoke in a loud voice. "Miztli, old friend, are we almost to Texcoco? I think I'm drunk. Are we near the lake?"

He believed he was back in his own land, near home. We tried to silence him with whispered words, then we gagged him with leaves and thongs, but behind the gag he cursed and shouted loudly enough to put us all in danger. Prince Chimal nodded to Miztli, who moved behind his friend, sword in hand, ready to kill him at the next outburst. I kept my eyes on the ground, thinking I could not bear to see another man die, although he would die for all our sakes.

Praying that Cholol would keep quiet, willing him to do so with all the force of our minds, we did not realize we had stepped into a little clearing until I almost stepped on a smudged fire.

Four men muffled in blankets slept near the fire; a fifth, who must have been a sentinel, slept soundly hunched against the trunk of a tree. The man supposed to be on guard wore Tarascan quilted armor. A metal Tarascan sword lay on the ground near his hand.

Perhaps we could have slipped away undetected, for no one woke although the man nearest me grumbled and turned over, jerking his blanket over his face. Prince Chimal gestured to us to be silent, to move away softly. But Cholol, walking in his fever dream, saw the metal sword, the guard's decorations, and must have thought he was back at

Boiling Springs in the thick of battle. Ripping the gag from his mouth, he gave a war yell and leapt across the clearing to bring his club down on the skull of the sleeping sentinal. I heard the blow strike, the dull popping as the man's skull caved in.

Shouting, tripping over blankets, fumbling for weapons, the startled Tarascans leapt to their feet. If they had pulled back, grouped together, the four men with their heavy weapons would have cut us down like corn. But thinking they were attacked in force, they panicked, striking out in the darkness, each fighting for his own life.

I saw Miztli slash at a warrior who had not yet found his weapons, hacking him with the obsidian-toothed blade. Two men had set upon Cholol, cutting his club from his hands, doing him to death in seconds, and he fell across the fire where I stood. Smoke and steam sizzled from the hot embers.

Leaping back, I almost stumbled over Lady Iztac, who had withdrawn to the edge of the clearing and kneeled there impassively, hands folded, head slightly bowed. She neither fought nor ran; she simply waited.

Before I had a chance to think what I should do, I was seized by the hair and thrust violently into the fight, suddenly finding myself facing my own father's sword. The Tarascan who had caught me used me as a shield. His right hand gripped a long metal sword, and over my shoulder he thrust and slashed at Prince Chimal. In the moonlight I saw my father's face and knew it was all over for us even before the two swords clashed and my father's wooden blade was shattered.

I do not know what I did then; I only know what happened. I have no memory of drawing the knife from its sheath, of reaching behind me and striking upward with all my force, of striking again and again until the beast that was tearing my scalp from my head loosened his grip, sank to his knees and died, covering my legs with his blood.

My father seized the Tarascan's sword, sprang to Miztli's aid. Before I had caught my breath the fight was over. Four Tarascans lay dead in the clearing; a fifth had escaped into the woods. Cholol, of course, was dead. Miztli appeared to have come through the struggle untouched; he took a step toward Prince Chimal, a twisted grin on his face, lifted his hand in salute to the victory, then crumpled to the ground, lifeless. I saw a dagger that had been plunged hilt-deep in his back.

Lady Iztac rose quietly, searched the dead until she found two bits of jade to place in the silent mouths of Cholol and Miztli, jade to pay their fare through the Narrow Passage. The Tarascan corpses she spurned.

All the rest of that night and most of the next day we fled toward the safety of the outpost, no longer hiding, counting on speed now instead of stealth. My scalp burned and throbbed. I longed for Vitsa to hold me, for Lady Flint Knife to comfort me with words of love and pride.

I wept only once, and that was not because of the pain in my scalp or the throbbing of my bruised feet. When I discovered that the ring and the feather Lark Singer had given me were stained with blood, I burst into tears. It seemed an omen, and I could not stop crying until Lady Iztac spoke to me firmly. "Enough, Mali. Your tears add to your father's burden, and he is already carrying the deaths of twenty men." I thought there was a faint note of sympathy in her voice. I kept quiet.

We did not dare climb the ridge that separated us from the outpost; it was too open, too obvious a place for a Tarascan ambush, so we skirted it, approaching home from the north, moving through forest. Now I could think of nothing but honey cakes, thick bean soup and steaming lake trout. I kept smelling cooking fires, which was nonsense for we were much too far away.

At last the odor could not be denied. There was smoke in the air, curls of thin smoke floating in the sky wherever we came to a break in the trees. We exchanged uneasy glances, and no one spoke. Then we heard in the distance an unlikely sound, a clamor heard only at night and seldom then: the angry barking of a pack of coyotes quarreling and fighting among themselves, a coyote tribe disputing a feeding ground. Footsore though we were, we began to run, suddenly suspecting what we had not dared think about before. A moment later we broke from the forest onto the path at the shore of the lake. There we halted, gasping, pressing our knuckles to our mouths, unwilling to believe what we saw.

The smoking ruins of the outpost lay just above us, darkly shadowed and tinged with red by the late sun. The heaviest beams and pillars of the watchtower still stood, charred bones of a skeleton, but the palisades had been leveled and burned, the houses had crumbled to ash heaps. In the sky ravens and vultures wheeled and shrieked, disputing the remains with the scavenger coyotes who now held the village.

"Gone," whispered Lady Iztac. "All gone. All dead." Quietly she began to weep.

"Grandmother! Oh, Citli!" I cried, suddenly realizing the full meaning of the burned houses. Then I darted ahead, climbing the steep path I had used all my life, running now as I had run so often to answer Vitsa's summons or Lady Flint Knife's. But now the path led to nothing, to no one. Halfway there my father overtook me, with Lady Iztac hurrying not far behind.

"Wait, Mali! There are too many coyotes. We must stay together, stay close."

There might have been Tarascans, too; enemy soldiers still lurking among the ruins. If there had been, we would have been cut down in our tracks, for we were far past any thought of caution. But the desolation, the boldness of the scavengers, told us that the invaders had gone, their work finished. Only the carrion eaters remained to feast on the dead. I stopped running. I knew what I would find—only corpses, only ghosts.

The outpost had been taken by surprise, overwhelmed in the dawn with apparently little resistance. The three chief officers had died together just outside the hut where they spent the nights getting drunk and gambling. They lay almost touching each other, faces down as though kissing the earth, sprawled and naked except for a living blanket of crows swarming over them so thickly that the bodies might have been clothed in the black feather capes of priests.

Most of the inhabitants had not been slain here. The victors had killed only the very young and very old, the sick or crippled, pregnant women and those soldiers who resisted until death. The others had been led away for sacrifice or slavery in the Land of the Fishermen. Lady Flint Knife was a weaver, I thought wildly. They could use her, they would spare her to weave for them, they would spare her . . .

My father's youngest wife, Night Jasmine, must have been taken; she was a pretty little thing. But Honey Nipple lay dead on her back, her hands crossed over her belly as though trying to defend the child inside her even as they hacked her with their swords. Prince Chimal drove away a coyote who had been tearing at her. For a moment he turned away from us. I did not see his grief for the unborn son.

Vitsa must have been taken. We did not find her body, and although I shouted her name again and again, there was no reply but the hateful shrieks of the birds.

The priests lay mangled at their own altars, their hearts torn out. The stone temples would not burn, but layers of blood dried on the walls and floors did, blackening the smashed images of Smoking Mirror and Hummingbird.

In the field of rubble and ashes and half-burned bodies I recognized the ruins of our house only because the trumpet tree stood untouched, gaudy with blossoms.

As I picked my way, stepping over fallen roof beams and smashed crockery, I was hardly aware of Prince Chimal walking behind me. Both of us knew what we would find; both were as ready as one can be at such a time. I paused to fling a useless stone at coyotes who were dragging Sparrow Woman's corpse through what had been our garden. Her throat had been slashed in the shape of a hideous grin. The coyotes paid no attention—when I screamed and waved my arms at them, they glanced up, then went on eating. The garden belonged to them now. I walked toward the gutted house.

Her severed head lay at the foot of the trumpet tree, near the charred loom, in the place where she had spent so many of her days. I was thankful that the birds had not plucked her eyes. The horror on every side—hacked limbs aswarm with flies, devouring ants, the unblinking birds perched and waiting in branches above—these could not defile her. Her face in death kept the unflinching dignity of her life. Her hair, though stained, was neat and freshly bound. Somehow she had found time and composure to put on a funeral garland of dried marigolds. Her bearing must have awed even the man who murdered her, for he had not ripped away her little jade earrings. I knew she had met death as she met life, unafraid and on equal terms. And in dying she had given me a final gift: the strength not to weep for her.

For three days we lived like foxes, hiding in the forest, venturing from the thicket only to find food, alert to the snap of a twig, the rustle of a branch. We watched the ruins for survivors or the return of escaped prisoners. No one came. We killed two coyotes, made soup from their bones and smoked the meat to carry on our journey.

On the fourth morning we realized that even the crows had abandoned the outpost. We would linger no more. So, dressed in rags and coyote skins, we set out on the long trek through hostile country, the journey to Tenochtitlan.

I remember trudging along the path that led to the crest of the eastern ridge, and we paused to rest at the top. This was the place where only a few days ago, yet a lifetime ago, I had turned to gaze at the village, the lake, surveying the whole of my universe from horizon to horizon.

"We must hurry on now," my father said.

I followed him, not glancing back, putting behind me the naked hillside where picked bones now bleached in the sun, the place where Lady Flint Knife, and with her the girl-child who had been myself, had died together.

Part Two

"EAGLES IN THE SUN..."

6

The City of Mexico—April 29, 1564 —The Feast of Saint Catalina

There are fewer troops in the streets today. The high authorities, perhaps too sanguine, think the five-day uproar is over now that the sacred bones are stowed away in a slapped-together tomb in Texcoco, haunt of locusts and lizards. In his written will my lord the Captain asked to be buried in Coyoacan, Place of the Wolf, but this has been denied him—a final humiliation.

The mob that stormed the cathedral to worship his coffin has dispersed: the hotter the fire, the sooner the ashes. Many of them have turned their fervor toward Tepeyac Hill, where only yesterday the Virgin of Guadalupe performed another timely miracle, thus distracting everyone's attention from the bones. Virgins are notoriously unaccommodating; Guadalupe is the exception.

Yesterday I bought a bloodstone and invoked a formal curse against the king of Spain, his wife and his puny heir. I threw in the names of the archbishop and the viceroy for good measure. The stone, now heavy and soaked with my prayers for revenge, is hidden behind the altar of the domestic chapel here in the convent, so the chants and *aves* of the nuns will reinforce my supplications. The notion that the ladies are unknowingly beseeching Smoking Mirror (or Whomever) to put fire in the royal bowels of His Most Catholic Majesty comforts me a little.

I am not usually so religious, but what else can I do? There is no news of my son, Tepi, or of his half-brother Martin Cortes, Marques del Valle. Rumor says they have indeed been caught in the same net as the Avila brothers and will be charged with treason any day.

My son trying to overthrow a government? I suppose it runs in my side of his family. What should I expect?

Naturally I shunned the burial ceremonies. At my age it is dangerous to expose oneself to sermons and other drafts of wind. But early this morning, after a night made sleepless by curiosity, I decided to inspect the grave site . . . No, that is not the truth. Some feeling stronger than curiosity nagged at me, kept me staring into the darkness of my chamber while the interminable Watches of the Night dragged along as slow as the stars. A yearning stirred in me, a wish that is futile and cannot be examined closely. But I knew I would have no peace until I visited the tomb.

The boatman I hired put me ashore at a landing near the ruins of Texcoco, helping me over the crumbling blocks of what had once been a wharf for pleasure craft. Then he carried me on his back through the mud where the lake is withdrawing. Flower-decked canoes and barges, bells tinkling, bobbed in my memory. I heard the music of dead flute players; skeletons played tambourines. I tried to distract myself by concentrating on the strength and beauty of the boatman's shoulders. He was a fine, husky man, golden brown as toasted cinnamon.

"Shall I wait, my lady?" he asked, letting me dismount. Despite my long sleeves and heavy veil, he had guessed I was not Spanish and addressed me in the old tongue. Then I realized he had inspected my ankles while I straddled his hips. My ankles are still shapely; almost every day I see young girls with thicker ones and it always makes me feel better.

"Wait, by all means!" I told him, having no wish to be stranded in such a forlorn place.

I went the rest of the way on foot, meeting no one because plague still rages among the wretched survivors in this town. Plague is everywhere, always, or else on the way. One disease wanes while a new one waxes. That is the chief difference between our old world and the new. We used to suffer slavery, oppression and torture. Now we have all those blessings plus the plagues.

No, it is not that bad. Of course, the new world has not turned out as I had once hoped, once dreamed. Yet the dream has not become a nightmare—it simply became life. And life, I suspect, is much the same among all peoples. Only the disguises change.

I had no trouble finding my way. The Monastery of St. Francis, gaunt and humpbacked, rises above the desolation of the town's crumbled roofs and fallen walls. Even without that landmark I had only to follow the muddy tracks of yesterday's mourners who had littered the way with gnawed corncobs, peanut shells, husks of tamales. Led by these and by balls of horseshit dropped by the viceroy's mount— yes, he had the gall to *ride* here, and ahead of the coffin!—I easily reached the sacred spot, passing through a broken gate and crossing a yard strewn with the rubble of construction. Several brownish cypress trees were keeping a death watch there—poisoned, I suppose, by the lime dust that whitened the ground.

The bones have been deposited in a cobbled wall of the monastery, a shoddy burial except for one thing: the slab sealing my lord in the wall must be twice as heavy as the stone that, they tell us, an angel rolled from the entrance of the Holy Sepulcher. I know little of angels, but it would strain a team of oxen to budge that stone at Texcoco. It seems proof against resurrection; they are taking no chances. I suppose they will post a guard lest something embarrassing should happen on the third day. My lord the Captain had a talent for doing the unexpected. After all, he *was* a god.

Ugly as it all was—the raw new stone, the heap of Castillian roses rotting in the sun—I should have turned my back and put the whole scene from my mind forever. Instead I found myself almost running as I hobbled toward the sepulcher, trying not to stumble as I kicked aside the dead flowers and placed my hands on the slab. I stood there trembling, eyes closed, and waited. Something (Oh, God!) must come now, something must happen—a sign of his presence, some touch of the god or spirit or whatever Being resides in such a place.

There was nothing. It will always be nothing. I am a fool.

I stepped back, blinking, then let my eyes wander to the adjacent crypts while I calmed myself. A daughter of his, a sickly child, is sealed up in the wall next to him. What was the name of the poor whey-faced girl? Of course, Doña Catalina Pizarro, after his lady mother. He bought the daughter a husband; she was an embarrassment to the country; just as his lady mother, I am told, was an embarrassment in

Spain. They say she was a provincial housewife thrust among the nobility, awkward in new silk clothes, agog at her own jewels, talking forever of prices and recipes.

"She is common," the noble ladies whispered of her behind their fans. "Common as a mule shoe!"

So she was. For that matter, my lord the Captain had not a drop of royal blood. He came from a province so poor that it still exports nothing except its sons. His father was a petty squire not even addressed as "don," and my lord himself told me his father differed from other men of his rural tribe only in owning an old lance and a leather shield, and he could afford to eat ham and eggs once a week on Sunday.

My lord the Captain was always apologizing for this. Yet he himself became a god, brought down an empire, conquered a world. No other man of common birth had done such things before, neither in our world nor theirs. No common man is allowed to! It is presumptuous, dangerous. Questions might arise in the minds of other common men.

Looking at the crude tomb, I realized that the viceroy and the archbishop have accomplished in his death what they could not quite manage during his life: the upstart conqueror and his family have been brought to suitably humble compartments. The order of the universe is no longer threatened; the country squire's son is in his lowly place.

I turned away, my eyes cloudy, and found an uncomfortable seat on a stack of squared building stones. I should have left; there was nothing for me there. But, regardless of the emptiness of the tomb, it seemed wrong to go without pausing to meditate. I had to say a prayer to Somebody.

The day was warm, flies buzzed lazily over the horse droppings, and I promptly fell asleep. Perhaps half an hour went by, perhaps more, when suddenly I was brought wide awake by a voice mumbling my name.

"Marina . . ."

My eyelids flew open, and glancing quickly over my shoulder, I saw the speaker: a Franciscan monk garbed in a brown habit so dusty that he blended into the gray of the cypress tree behind him. He sat on a low, flat rock and huddled against the tree trunk, shivering in the hot sun, his robes drawn tightly around him so only his bare toes, his hands and just the edge of his profile emerged from the cowled habit. His fingers twitched strangely in his lap.

He mumbled again, but I caught no words except my own name. "Marina . . ."

Who was he? How could he have known me through the veils I wore? If he came from the Inquisition and had followed me here, a score of armed men must be waiting for me outside the gate.

I glanced furtively at his hands, half-expecting to see a ring with the green cross of the Holy Office, but the gnarled fingers, hardly more than bones strung together, were bare. Then I saw that his fingers were silvery, and he had lost his thumb up to the first joint on his left hand. There was the dread cast of silver on his bare feet, too, and a little toe was missing. I gazed at him with revulsion and relief. He could not be from the Inquisition. He was a leper; the silver tint of his skin marked him out as a meal for the gods. Now they were nibbling his fingers and toes, tasting and savoring. Soon they would devour him entirely. A scrawny victim for a feast, I thought.

"Marina . . ." he mumbled once more, the fingers twisting convulsively.

Then I knew him, although I was not sure if he was a man or a ghost. "Aguilar! Is it you?"

Jeronimo de Aguilar. All those years ago when I first knew my lord's army, Aguilar had been the only man among the Spaniards who knew a civilized language, for he had been captive for years among the Maya after coming ashore on their steamy coast, cast away in a shipwreck. He was my first acquaintance in the army, the only man I could talk to with words. But not my friend. How could we have been friends when we so despised each other behind our masks of politeness?

He was jealous of me, of course. Jealous of my knowledge, my mind and my endurance. Jealous also, I was sure, that I spent nights clasped by the Captain's thighs, circled by his arms, pinioned by him, sharing the joy of his passion. In other words, I was in exactly the position Aguilar longed to occupy, although he did not really know his desire and would have died of self-loathing had others suspected. Naturally I knew; such things were understood in the Only World. I understood and pitied him, even when I became the target of his helpless anger. I kept my mouth shut.

"I thought you were dead, Aguilar," I said. "Someone told me you died at least twenty years ago."

Instead of answering he drew his mutilated fingers into the full sleeves, hiding his deformity. The feet with the missing toe vanished under his robe. It was, I thought, the gesture one would expect. He spent his life hiding behind clerical vestments. That is understandable in the young, tolerable in the middle-aged, but insufferable for a man long past seventy. I found myself detesting him again—at the very moment when our years and memories should have brought us close.

I looked away, studying the stone slab of the new tomb. "So we meet after all these years in this place! The three of us together again. Well, that is as it should be. You and I, Aguilar, were the only ones who loved him." I heard him stir, knew he was about to interrupt me, so I hurried on.

"Oh, he was worshiped and admired and desired. But only you and I, Aguilar, gave him love. I remember that night after we fought at Otumba—what a day that was!—how you helped him take off his armor. You rubbed his back with chia oil—although you were half-dead yourself and bleeding, too. He could not have asked for greater love, for a more devoted—" I almost said "lover," not because a demon was in me but because it was the truth and beautiful. But the word would have horrified him, even now, and I said, "Brother."

We sat quietly for a while, two ancient veterans who had shared days and adventures that are given to few men and never to women. But we could not speak now any more than we had been able to speak of our inner selves then. I wanted to touch his shoulder, to assure myself that we were both alive and substantial, but I could not for fear he would shudder and draw away. The Great Wall of Tlaxcala might as well have stood between us.

The shadow of the bell tower had grown longer; it shaded him now. I had not noticed this before and it seemed unnatural, odd. I felt something strange in the air, some faint sound that was not the trilling of insects.

"My son is in danger, Aguilar," I said, although I had not meant to confide in him. "I would not impose this on you, but he is the Captain's child also. You probably remember the boy better than I do. He was christened Martin, after the Captain's father. But I called him Tepi. We were parted when he was little more than a baby. He had learned to walk, he was speaking, almost enough to talk to me. We have not had a chance to talk since then. This time, when we finally meet, we will make up for it. I have much to tell him."

"Marina, Marina," he whispered, and I was sorry I had exposed myself to his pity.

"It was not as you think," I assured him. "I knew the boy could not stay at home with me. His future was first in Mexico City, as they call it now, and then in Spain. He went to school in Spain, as you probably know. He served in the king's army; he has been honored and decorated. It is time I heard about these matters not from others but from him."

I moved close to him, kneeled on the ground, and when I shut my eyes the air rang with the shouts of men, the clash of lances. My memory called up a battle with a soldier shouting, "Santiago!" and a thousand voices raised the war cry of Spain. We charged the heights amid singing arrows while cannon thundered. For a moment I felt alive once more.

Squealing and shrieking, three ragamuffin children, two little boys and a girl, raced into the monastery yard playing a roughneck game. The boys, seeing us, whispered together, then approached awkwardly and bowed. Then they began turning cartwheels on the bare ground near the tombs, not exactly a game, for their faces were solemn as sacrifice. They moaned as they performed, and one began to utter shrieks of pain.

"What are they doing, Aguilar?"

His hands, stumpy as turtle heads, shot out of the sleeves of his robe. He mumbled, "Blessed . . . blessed . . . In the hour of our death." The urchins stood, panting, and the little girl joined them, chanting.

> *"We turn the wheel of Catalina,*
> *She who died above the fire.*
> *Now give us alms for Catalina,*
> *Whose holy body burned with fire."*

Then I remembered that this was the Feast of Saint Catalina, some ancient lady who was roasted alive on a wheel, seared and cooked like a spitted goat. In other words, punishments then were much like they are now. They say she was three days broiling. Well, that is terrible, but the gods had been taking Aguilar nibble by nibble for twenty years, I supposed.

Still the youngsters had put on a lively show, and I have enjoyed religious acrobats since childhood. I tossed the boys some bits of copper, and the pious little performers began screaming and struggling, each trying to gouge out the other's eyes to claim the whole reward for himself alone. The girl began to throw rocks at her companions; her aim was bad, but I liked her spirit.

The howls of the smaller boy brought a monk running from the cloister, and brandishing his staff, he drove the children, thoroughly cursed, out of the yard, then paused to snatch up the coppers they had dropped in flight. He popped them deftly into the fold of his sleeve.

"I hope these Indian vermin have not disturbed you, my lady," he said, saluting me. Why do they always say Indian? We used to say Aztec or Mixtec or Otomi or whatever. We called people by their nationality.

The monk was a tall young Spaniard with an insolent face and full lips I found appealing. There was a time when I would have enjoyed unknotting the cord holding his robe shut. I might enjoy it still in different surroundings. Who knows what I might enjoy, given proper inspiration? I am old but not dead.

Keeping his distance, the monk poked Aguilar with the tip of his staff. "Your prayers are over! Time to return to the refectory for dinner, Brother Luis."

"Brother Luis?" I asked, astonished.

"Yes, lady. This is Brother Luis de Palos. Forgive my shouting, but the rot of the disease has reached deep in his ears and he hardly hears anything softer than thunder. Brother Luis!"

As the old monk struggled to his feet, the cowl fell back and I saw that I had been completely mistaken. Except for the hooked nose and the sharp chin that seemed to point at each other, he did not resemble Aguilar in the least. Now, as he mumbled, I realized he said "Maria," not "Marina," and I had misunderstood his *aves*. He had lost his rosary, but his benumbed fingers did not know it, so they went on twitching as they counted the beaded decades.

"Brother Luis has had a busy morning," said the young monk. "He has said the endowed prayers for the two ladies."

"Endowed prayers for which ladies?"

He gestured toward the crypts. "The two Catalinas who lie here, the daughter and the first wife. Captain General Cortes, I mean the marques de Valle, left money so a prayer would be said here every

Friday and the rosary told nine times on their saint's day—today, of course."

"And for Cortes himself—since he, too, lies here now. Do you pray for him?"

"We prayed yesterday. Of course, we have no endowment for him yet. I suppose there will be one." He considered this pleasant possibility, then said, "My lady, if you are here to see the new chapel the viceroy is building, it's on the far side of the cloister."

"Is it very grand?"

The monk swelled with un-Franciscan pride. "New Spain has not seen its like! Oh, it's not large, only room for His Excellency's family and their guests. But three hundred Indians have been impressed to work on it."

"Indeed?" It sounded familiar, like building a temple base in the old days. But then it would have been three thousand or thirty thousand workmen. How small scale Europeans are!

"His Excellency has ordered the foremen to mix five pounds of gold dust and a cask of Spanish sherry into the mortar. He says nothing is too good for God. What do you think of that?"

"I think the viceroy is trying to bribe the Almighty and get him drunk at the same time."

I had the pleasure of watching him blanch. No doubt he will report me to some authority when, back in the cloister, he gathers his wits to see I have blasphemed the whole Trinity: God, gold and the viceroy.

"Come, Brother Luis, come along!" He nudged the old man with the staff, prodding him toward the gate near the cloister.

As I watched them go, it occurred to me that I may have made no mistake in identity, that I had met, at least fleetingly, the ghost of Jeronimo de Aguilar in the guise of a priest—which, of course, was what he always wanted to become. So he got his wish, even if it was granted beyond the grave. How like Aguilar to return as a leprous Franciscan! For a moment we had been drawn by the gods into a vortex here: the Captain, the two Catalinas, Aguilar and I. Inevitable!

I rose to leave, intending to ignore the crypt that was the bone bin of Catalina Xuarez, the woman my lord foolishly married in Cuba before he was called to be a god. But I hesitated when a bit of color caught my eye, a handful of orange flowers that lay in the bird-stained niche beneath her epitaph. Who remembered or cared enough about

Catalina to leave her flowers—even on the day of her martyred patron saint? Probably the bouquet was paid for by the prayer endowment. Yes, that would be the case. My lord the Captain was thoughtful of protocol.

Leaving the yard and going toward the shore, I picked my way among cactus and fire thorns, keeping an eye to the ground for scorpions. Unwillingly I thought of Catalina. Even I, who had reason to study her, can now picture the creature only in fragments: a too-long white neck she craned and extended when she preened herself—an egret stretching its white throat to swallow. I see a thin nose and half-circles of thin brows above pale eyes, and a mass of faded brown hair teased into ringlets. When she smiled, she pursed her lips to hide a missing front tooth, but at times she forgot and the tip of her pink tongue would dart into the hole when her lips were parted. And I remember soft hands that constantly plucked at her curls, her long earlobes, the necklace of gold beads she loved.

I think she never saw me, although I secretly watched her often enough. I had to know everything. Of course she knew about me—was there anyone in the world who didn't? Each new scrap of knowledge she gleaned drove her to further rages, more torments. She sighed in public and screamed in private; she was a cramp in his guts from the first.

I never understood her. Why should it have driven her wild that we occasionally fucked? There were many other women besides me, of course. Why not? As soldiers say, there was gravy to go around. She was his *wife*! What else mattered?

Often she locked herself in the private chapel he had given her, and there she wept for hours. They said she withdrew because she suffered asthma. Asthma! Her pains were in a place other than her windpipe. Because of her haughty demeanor, few people suspected, as I did, that she lived in fear and bewilderment. She had been uprooted from her class, snatched from a life spent dodging bill collectors and mending old clothes; in a single day she went from nothing to become Empress of the Only World. She had to speak with great lords and chieftains, although her voice was more practiced at summoning swine or bawling at the two or three starved slaves in her cane field. Pathetic creature. But in those days I was too young to pity her.

Yet I think there was a trace of compassion mixed with my contempt. Looking at the stingy bouquet on her grave, I felt sorry her life had not been happier. Now her stone was crudely inscribed with her name and some unreadable, flattering lie in Latin. "Born 1499— Died 1522." Nonsense. She was at least four years older than that. Poor Catalina, consigned to eternity still lying about her age.

I was not among the guests the night of the famous dinner party when she went through the Narrow Passage. But I had spies among the servants, and I quickly learned about the events surrounding her death, a final departure that, to say the least, was most timely.

In the summer of 1522 when carrion crows still plied the skies above the ruins of Tenochtitlan, my lord the Captain kept his residence and headquarters in a palace that had once belonged to an Aztec prince. It stood in a wooded suburb called Place of the Wolf, Coyoacan, a name that frightened Doña Catalina, who thought it ill omened. But it was to the Place of the Wolf that Doña Catalina de Cortes came in July, freshly delivered from Cuba by her penniless brother. He arrived with several dubious Spanish ladies and his itching palm upturned.

Three months later on a night in the month of the Ending of the Rains, the Captain gave a banquet to celebrate the arrival of a letter from His Most Catholic Majesty, Carlos of Spain, Emperor. The letter recognized the Captain's conquest of the world. Twenty-six guests were present and seated at a single table improvised by laying boards over trestles; such a table had never been seen before; it resembled a sacrificial altar on which twin offerings could be made at once.

The Captain wore black velvet with white lace. Doña Catalina was decked in borrowed finery, imitation cloth of gold that did not flatter her complexion.

Lake whitefish, venison, jicama, chayote and honey cakes were served. The plates and mugs were Mixtec ware, the knives Cuban.

Doña Catalina appeared irritable and tense that evening. She chided the serving men, complained angrily about a pepper garnish and ordered the platters of chayote sent back to the kitchen, proclaiming in a shrill voice that it was "a barbaric vegetable, fit only for swine and dogs of Indians." The prince of Tlaxcala graciously pretended not to understand Spanish.

Captain Solis, the steward, was seated at Doña Catalina's left. During a lull in the talk, she turned to him and said, "Solis, you are forever taking away my Indians for some work of your own. The things I want done never get done, Solis!" Her tone was arrogant.

"Not my fault, lady," Solis replied. "It is His Lordship here who commands." He gestured toward Cortes.

Doña Catalina lifted her chin, stretching that long white neck. A demon prompted her to speak with the insolence of the Whore Goddess. "They are my own Indians! I assure you that within a few days I shall see to it that no one, absolutely no one, meddles with what belongs to me!"

Silence fell at the table. The shock could not have been greater if she had hurled a drinking gourd in the Captain's face. When at last Cortes spoke, his manner seemed not quite in jest, yet not quite serious. He smiled faintly, a look that a servant called his jaguar smile.

"Madam, I myself will have none of what belongs to you."

Two or three of the guests laughed aloud. They were soldiers; it was their kind of joke. The prince of Tlaxcala, not quite understanding, whispered too loudly in his broken Spanish, "Does he mean her tits and cunt?"

Doña Catalina's fish mouth opened and closed, color surged in her cheeks and she rose from the table. Spreading her full skirt, she bowed deeply to her husband, then swept from the room, leaving a pall behind her. A moment later the guests heard the doors of her private chapel slam shut.

The Captain seemed unaware of the disturbance. He offered rum newly brought from Cuba, talked about the plan for building a distillery in Veracruz; this led to a story of his youthful drinking bouts on the island of Hispaniola. He smiled often.

After the guests left at midnight, he went to the chapel and gently persuaded her to unlock the doors. Then he led her to her bedroom, entering the chamber with her while the servants were extinguishing the torches and candles in the banquet hall.

An hour later he cried out in a loud voice to the whole house, shouting that he believed his wife was dead—as indeed she was when the maids came running. They noticed bruises on her throat, and the gold necklace she wore was broken, the beads scattered among the bedclothes.

Everyone agreed she died of asthma.

Well, she angered a god. What did she expect?

7

Tenochtitlan, 1511

Never in all the sheaves of years have gods or men created another city such as Tenochtitlan, the capital of the world, the golden eagle's nest of the Aztecs, city of cities. Oh, but it was beautiful.

I first glimpsed it from the heights to the west at a stopping place almost at the end of our long and painful journey through the wilderness from Jalisco. Dawn was just breaking over the temples and palaces, the shafts of Our Lord Sun glancing off the waters of the lakes, shimmering. The courts and great stairways had just become luminescent. Behind the city rose the volcanoes, Sleeping Woman and her husband Smoking Man, white crowned against the brightening sky, the dark lower slopes veiled in mist.

And I, like Spanish soldiers who came years later, cried aloud that it could not be real, that it was an enchantment; it would dissolve in air like the green cities of ghosts seen by travelers in the northern deserts.

Lady Iztac stood beside me, quietly weeping. "We are home!" she whispered.

"The Place of the Cactus," said my father, putting his arm around my shoulders. "Look well, Mali. Always remember your first sight of it." I knew he meant not just Tenochtitlan but the whole panorama of cities, towns and lakes, the mountain-encircled world of Land Near the Waters.

I looked and remembered—as everyone not born there always did. I gazed down from the mountain meadow, marveling, seeing the darts of canoes plying the lakes and canals, the slow barges heavy with market goods. I saw the lines of tall cypresses—they looked no bigger than wands—living anchors for the soil of gardens that I thought floated, an illusion; but it was all an illusion, all magic.

We were at the end of our journey, no longer footsore from rocky trails, no longer mud covered from hiding in holes or bogs in daylight. In our long trek we had passed a score of villages but did not dare approach them, not knowing what side held their loyalty. Some, of course, felt loyalty toward neither Aztecs nor Tarascans and looked upon any defenseless traveler as fattened game, deer to be skinned, sacrificed and perhaps dined upon.

"We are far from the Tarascans," Lady Iztac protested one day. "These towns must be civilized."

Prince Chimal was adamant. "We will be mice a little longer. We do not know what war we were caught in, a Tarascan attack or a rebellion of the whole world against the Aztecs."

"Rebellion? Unthinkable!" said my mother.

"No. It has been thought of for a generation. Perhaps it has already happened."

Many days later we arrived safely in Tenochtitlan. We lived only four months in that vast and fascinating city, but I came to know its thousand streets and byways and canals like a native. Our home was a dilapidated palace my great-grandfather, or perhaps *his* great-grand-father, had built to house himself and his retinue when he came to pay state visits to the court at Tenochtitlan. In those days a Culhua prince was still that rich and that important. The neighborhood, once elegant, had declined and was now crowded with foreigners, mostly Mixtec craftsmen, who had converted noble residences into ground-floor factories with upstairs dormitories. Instead of cultivating flowers and blossoming shade trees on the roof, as genteel people did, they planted squashes and chilis in big wooden tubs, fertilizing their crops with nightsoil brought up each morning in pots from the dormitory. There was a stench; when Lady Iztac visited our own roof, she carried a nosegay of jasmine.

Her mortification at living next door to barbarians was hard to bear, but she found no alternative. My father was reduced to a state just above patrician poverty, having lost a fortune in the looting at the outpost—jades, pearls, quetzal feathers, great jars of cocoa beans and dyestuffs. Now he went to the court daily to petition for repayment, applying for any post that offered a chance to recoup his wealth. He had no influential relatives, unfortunately. Uncle Willow, his only blood relation, had secured a post among the royal tutors but had been promptly sent away on another search for exotic plants.

Prince Chimal gave orders that I was to learn about the city, partly, I think, because he felt all knowledge was valuable; mostly because he wanted me kept too busy to mourn Lady Flint Knife's death. His plan succeeded, and I was too occupied to think of my loss, although for months I suffered nightmares.

My mother had three ancient female cousins who all looked alike: leathery crones with liver spots and sour tongues. One or another of the cousins escorted me on my explorations of the city, hissing for me to lower my eyes, curb my laughter and take smaller, ladylike steps.

All three were obsessed by sex, especially the youngest, who muttered insults at passersby. "Indecent! An immoral costume! Oh, see what that vile man is trying to show off! Disgusting." I was warned and harangued about motherly-looking women and suave men who trafficked in boys and girls. "You are still a little young to catch their eyes, but tomorrow—watch out!"

What did I care for their railing? I was no longer the shy girl child of the outpost, always ready for flight like a doe. The city lay spread before me like an endless festival, and I was enchanted by the mysteries of winding arcades and courts within courts. I marveled at the royal aqueduct, the great canoe basin. The goose clucks and hisses of the chaperon at my heels went unheard.

I found a show at every corner: jugglers, acrobats, musicians, mimes and fire-eaters. I walked the length of the three stone causeways that connected the island city with the mainland, my chaperons following in litters, the youngest complaining that the bearers bounced the litter suggestively, trying to arouse her, and leered at her with smoky eyes.

The best days came when I went with nobody but my father's steward to the huge market at Tlatelolco where anything dreamed of in the world could be bought. Birds the color of flame dazzled me; others shone like living rainbows. We sniffed at woods that breathed perfume, inspected jars of potions and poisons; I clapped my hands at

the sight of giant radishes sculpted to look like penises with faces of
old men carved on their heads.

Tlatelolco, the City of the Mound, was the capital of the world
of commerce. It stood on marshy islands next door to Tenochtitlan;
you did not even have to cross water to reach it. Lady Flint Knife had
claimed that both Tenochtitlan and the City of the Mound were
founded by the same gang of thieves and riffraff, all fugitives from the
decent towns on the mainland. They became known as the twin
townships; they worked and warred together, yet had separate rulers
and much rivalry. The Tenocha Aztecs of Tenochtitlan were sons of
the war gods; the Tlatelolcan Aztecs seemed offspring of the Guiding
Lord who led merchant caravans.

The steward who took me to the City of the Mound almost every
week was a plump, affable man who loved to linger in the shade of
the market stalls, exchanging gossip while he sipped clover water. He
was a native of that neighborhood, born in a corner of the labyrinthine
bazaar "between the bolts of cotton and the sheets of bark cloth," he
said. "I am soft as the one and tough as the other." All the vendors
greeted him and enjoyed calling out his unusual name, Fierce Baby.

I wondered about the name, about what dream might have
inspired it. Then one day when we paused to sip honeyed tea, he told
me his story. I only understood later that this was a lesson in history.

"In my father's day these two cities were partners, called the
twins. But often with human twins one is a bully—" He gestured in
the direction of Tenochtitlan.

The year of Fierce Baby's birth, bands of wild youths from
Tenochtitlan, noble in family but not in behavior, took to marauding
in the markets. They would pinch and slap the bottoms of respectable
women; several rapes were committed. Meanwhile the nobles of Tenochtitlan were chafed with jealousy because a new temple in the City
of the Mound equaled their own great twin temples to Hummingbird
and Smoking Mirror. The Woman Snake, first minister and second
highest in the land, said in public, "These traders and market hagglers
are getting above themselves." Talk of war spread; both cities buzzed
like hornets' nests.

"Our ruler was King Mokiwix," Fierce Baby told me. "One day
while preparing for war, he walked through his palace kitchens. A pot
of small birds was boiling on the fire, and to the king's horror the birds
hopped from the caldron to dance on the bubbling surface. The king

let out a shriek. The omen told him defeat was at hand, so he planned an unusual defense.

"When the army of Tenochas advanced upon our city, they were confronted not by soldiers but by a regiment of naked women who danced forward, then turned to flaunt their bare asses at the troops. These women squeezed milk from their own nipples and sprinkled the enemy with it, mixing enchantment with contempt. A thousand children, naked except for feathers in their hair, danced beside the women."

"You were one of those?" I asked. "A child warrior?"

"I was too young, so my mother carried me on her shoulders. I already had a full set of sharp little teeth, and when an officer seized my mother by the hair, I bit the man's eye. Some say I bit it out, others that I merely blinded him. Several enemy soldiers fled at the unnatural sight." Fierce Baby sighed, shook his head. "Still, our city was lost, and we became subjects with no voice in our own government. The armed louts of Tenochtitlan can't forgive the wealth of our merchants."

Indeed, the rich traders always wore ragged clothes in public and groveled like penitents for fear of exciting the envy of the Tenocha nobles. They especially feared Moctezuma, who held merchants in contempt. He also despised craftsfolk and even artists unless they happened to be of high birth. At home one day I heard my father repeat what Uncle Willow had said about Moctezuma's Tenochtitlan: nowadays it was birth, not brains, that counted.

Of course these problems of politics and class rivalries, of bitter history, were too complicated to hold my attention; I had other concerns. At the royal zoo I gaped at Moctezuma's collection of rare creatures, caged humans and animals. Here, as in the market, the birds were creatures from paradise, godlings or noble souls. It seemed dangerous to keep them imprisoned—who could guess their power?

Listening to the birds, I thought of Lark Singer and wondered again why neither he nor Lord Lancer had paid a call. They were never mentioned at home, and I had been told sharply to hold my tongue the one time I ventured to speak of them. I could only hope Lark would appear at the house. I wished this on my rock crystal ring.

So the days passed, no two alike and never one with enough hours. I often thought: *Now I am alive.* The years at the outpost seemed like a journey through mist, unreal, a time of dreaming. The city had awakened me, aroused my blood. And while I had lost my old freedom of wandering alone, I had gained something more important: among the throngs of Tenochtitlan I was anonymous. No one knew my unlucky name or the omens at my birth. People could jostle me in crowded streets and not fear bad luck or contamination at my touch. They could sit next to me in a public boat without expecting the craft to capsize.

The three old cousins knew all about me, of course, and the eldest was especially wary, keeping a safe distance even while she harped on my uncouth deportment. Never would she so much as let her clothing brush mine, and she abhorred any mingling of our shadows on the pavement. Without saying so she made it clear that I was responsible for the disaster at the outpost, for my grandmother's death and my father's loss of fortune. I could have replied by asking why my parents and I were the only survivors, but it would have been futile. Nothing is more pointless than religious arguments between the old and the young. So I closed my ears and enjoyed the wonders of the city.

Then late one afternoon I was summoned to the roof where my father, when the wind was favorable, often spent the heat of the day resting or listening to music. Awnings gave cool shade, and the flowering shrubbery created the feeling of a rustic garden. He lay on a thick mat, naked and beautiful, one elbow propped on a pillow. To my surprise, Lady Iztac was kneeling beside him; usually she avoided the roof because of the Mixtec neighbors. Another person was present: a little way off, squatting near the parapet in the shade of a hibiscus, was the stout, middle-aged woman who served as Lady Iztac's housekeeper. I hardly knew her. She was called Water Lily but resembled that flower only in the silence in which she floated from room to room. The other servants feared her, saying she cast spells, which was why, I suppose, she could afford to encase her thick fingers in silver rings—the rewards of witchcraft.

As soon as I had paid my respects, Prince Chimal said, "I have called you here, daughter, to tell you about your cousin, Lark Singer."

"Lark? Yes?" I concealed my pleasure. Lady Iztac's disapproving stare showed me she had not forgotten my indiscreet conduct.

"A few months ago, just after his visit to us, Lark Singer was chosen by the priests of the city as the Unblemished Youth," said my father. "Do you know what that means, Mali?"

"No, father."

"Each year the priests of Smoking Mirror select the most beautiful boy in the city to represent the god-on-earth. During his reign he is honored above any earthly prince; he is worshiped as a godling, and his least desire is gratified."

"It is a great honor," said my mother. "The greatest earthly honor the world can bestow—except for being elected Revered Speaker, perhaps." The light of religion was in her eyes, yet she spoke in a tense voice and twisted her fingers nervously. What was wrong?

"How wonderful for Lark!" I exclaimed. "And for all of us, since we're his family."

"Yes," my father agreed without enthusiasm. "Of course, he has many duties as the Perfect One. We did not wish to disturb him with family obligations, so we did not tell him of our arrival here. But somehow he has learned of it, and he wishes you to call on him tomorrow morning in Texcoco."

To conceal my joy, I bowed my head deeply. "And am I to be allowed to go, my lord father?"

"Allowed?" Lady Iztac spoke sharply. "There is no refusal! It would be impious, even criminal, to refuse a god-on-earth. Do you understand that, girl?"

"Yes," I said happily.

"No," said Prince Chimal. "She does not understand at all. Water Lily will explain."

He clapped his hands, and Water Lily advanced upon me. I had never looked at her closely before. She was thick-lipped and heavy-jowled. Her face seemed expressionless except for her eyes, two glittering points of honed obsidian.

"Water Lily is a woman of wisdom and experience, daughter. She will instruct you and prepare you for tomorrow's visit. You are to obey her absolutely."

"Yes, my lord prince," I answered, suddenly uneasy.

Water Lily put a heavy hand on my arm and led me away as though she had just bought me as a new slave. "We will go to your chamber. I need to inspect you and choose your clothes."

It was on the tip of my tongue to tell her she was insolent, but I remembered my father's command—and his severity. Even without Prince Chimal's authority, Water Lily was overwhelming. Her voice was made to utter battle cries.

In my room she inspected me from head to foot, her eyes piercing my flesh. "You still have your maidenhead?" she demanded.

"Of course. I am not yet a woman."

"Ha! I know about outposts and soldiers! So we'd better learn the worst. Lie on your back and spread wide."

Obey her, Prince Chimal had said. So I did, feeling dirtied and invaded by her fingers, shamed by her peering.

"Still sealed tight," she said with a sigh. "Too bad. If you'd been popped, you'd be out of danger. He only takes virgins."

"Who only takes virgins? What are you talking about?" I struggled quickly to my feet, began putting on my clothes.

"The Unblemished Youth, the Perfect One. Your exalted cousin. He'll be given four virgin brides for the last twenty days. One bride for every direction except the center. He himself is center. That's why he wants to look you over."

"You're a fool! Lark Singer is my cousin and my friend. He only wants to see me, to talk with me, to—"

"He only wants to ram you with his unblemished *maquauhuitl*. That's what the Unblemished Youth has in mind and don't you forget it. Then what happens to you? After twenty days of ramming, you and the three others in turn, he's off to Smoking Mirror and you're just part of his leftovers. What's your father to do with you then? Sell you in Texcoco marked down as used cunt? Used, what's more, in public with the whole city knowing who and when and how. Most men will think twice about climbing on top of Smoking Mirror's widow. Well, it can't be helped."

I did not understand half of what she said, but I knew enough to realize my own ignorance. There was danger in the offing; I would do well to obey Water Lily and learn.

She held an unattractive garment to the light of the window. "This looks childish, which is good. And you'll bite your fingernails. Bite every one down to the quick, that's always nasty-looking."

Turning away from her, I stood at the window gazing down at the passersby and the Mixtec potters who were hawking their wares outside the factory.

"The whole city knew Lark Singer would be chosen as the god-on-earth," Water Lily went on, searching among my sandals for the scruffiest. "Lord Lancer was frantic because he's a widower with no other child to pass on his soul. So when the month for choosing came, Lancer whisked the boy out of the city, took him on a journey halfway across the world and didn't return until he knew another lad had been named and dressed in the holy robes."

She ran her tongue over her thick lips, almost smiling. "But nobody cheats Smoking Mirror! Only four days after Lord Lancer and the boy arrived back in the city, the Earth Monster gave a shudder, and when the ground ceased shaking, the lad who'd been named Perfect One lay dead with a cracked skull, killed by a falling roof beam! So they had to choose another youth for the rest of the reign. Of course, their eyes fell on your cousin. Prettier than ever and fresh from the country! Oh, you can't fool Smoking Mirror—he'll have his own." She chuckled, pleased by the god's subtle ways.

The next morning we took a boat to Texcoco, where Lark Singer and his retinue kept court in the old royal gardens. Water Lily sat beside me, nodding approval of my drab clothing, lank hair and ugly fingernails. My nose and eyes were red and puffy from sniffing a finely ground tobacco that made me sneeze and weep.

"Not exactly tempting, is she?" Water Lily remarked to Lady Iztac, who sat in the rear of the boat alternately remarking about how honored we were and how carefully I must proceed not to be honored *too* much.

"His brides of twenty days have great distinction and a hopeless future," she admonished me for the hundredth time. "Let us hope he still looks upon you as a child."

"He will," I answered. "And an ugly child at that." I was sure Lark Singer felt love for me; but it had nothing to do with marriage or mating. "What happens to Lark when his reign is over?"

"He goes to join Smoking Mirror, and the priests choose another god-on-earth," said Lady Iztac. "Did your grandmother give you no religious training at all?"

So Lark would become a sort of priest, I thought. I hated the thought of him garbed in black and with blood-matted hair. I imagined a special priesthood, more attractive.

At the landing dock Lady Iztac said, "Texcoco is full of people who resent Aztecs, Mali, so speak to no one. Also, it is a town rife with wanton women. Mostly foreigners, naturally! Do not flatter them by so much as a glance. Keep your eyes down and try not to overhear their obscene talk."

This made my ears sharp as a cat's as we entered Texcoco, town of gardens. There, indeed, were the pretty ladies with their painted teeth, their bells, flowers and embroidered parasols.

"What sorry creatures!" Lady Iztac said in an undertone. "These wretches are to be pitied."

Glancing covertly at them, I thought I had never seen happier women, all giggles and smiles. Doubtless there was a side I did not know about. We came to a low wall with a gate, and behind it rose a forest.

"You go alone from here," Water Lily told me. "Follow the path. When you see your cousin, greet him with a little smile, but do not touch him! Excuse yourself when you hear the midday Watch sung from the tower. Remember you are ill and exhausted, you cannot stay long. Don't forget to kiss the ground at his feet."

I nodded and started up the winding path, eyes downcast, concealing my excitement until I was out of sight. Then I hurried, almost running, through the cypresses and star trees. Ahead I could hear fountains splashing. A hummingbird sailed across my path bringing a blessing. No matter what terrible things Water Lily predicted, I knew I loved Lark Singer, and if he chose me as a twenty-day bride—which he would not do—what did it matter? No other husband was going to claim One Grass of Penance, a bride with disaster for a dowry.

I heard a flute playing silvery music, and at the end of the path I looked into a broad garden hedged by ferns and fruit trees. There I hesitated, spellbound; the scene might have been the great mural of Tlaloc come to life—this was the green heaven of the Rainbringer, the butterfly paradise where fountains bubble eternally and emerald birds skim their surfaces.

The astonishing trees made me think of the legends of Tollan: a dozen kinds of flowers and fruits all flourished on the same tree— magic. Then I realized that many of the blossoms were painted cotton and the luscious mangoes hanging from the branches were on strings, not stems.

In the center of the garden stood a pavilion woven of flowery vines and boughs. Lark Singer, playing a flute, sat on a cushion on the stone steps. Near him, listening and smiling, lolled several young men dressed in uniforms of a fine cloth I had never seen; I thought it was spun silver. One of the pretty Texcoco ladies kneeled at Lark's feet, keeping time to the music on a tiny drum. Two other ladies, just as lovely, sat nearby plaiting a necklace of orchids.

A slender girl danced to the tune Lark played, a dance celebrating birds, for she wore a crown of feathers and held plumes in her hands; a flock of birds of every color fluttered at her feet but did not take flight. The girl was naked, which seemed strange since this was not a religious dance.

A banquet had been spread on several low tables, platters and bowls heaped with delicacies. The air seemed sweet and heady with perfume and incense.

Lark Singer, half-reclining on his cushion, was the prince of this garden world. Dressed only in a loincloth of royal green and wearing no jewels but a jade necklace, Lark was surely the image of a god— if any god could be so beautiful.

Hesitating at the edge of this unearthly world, I felt shy. My arms were grotesquely long; my hands were two shapeless lumps. Mixed with my awe was resentment: the cotton flowers were really ugly and artificial, the scented air not decent to breathe. Worst of all were the wild birds that did not fly; they were ominous, contrary to nature.

One of the ladies saw me and pointed a delicate finger, laughing. "Look, some urchin has wandered in. Such clothing! Isn't she quaint?"

"Mali!" Lark Singer quickly handed the flute to one of his attendants and ran toward me, not godlike but boyish, arms wide. We embraced like two comrades—and I forgot to kiss the ground.

"How good to see you, Mali." He led me toward the pavilion. "You are still called Mali? No new name has found you?"

"I am still Mali. But what do I call you, Lark? My mother said Image of Smoking Mirror. Can that be so?"

"For you and for today I am Lark." He put his arm around me, gave me a hug. Despite Water Lily's fierce admonitions against touching the Perfect One and thus arousing him, I hugged Lark back.

"I am glad you're Lark. I've never liked statues of Smoking Mirror. You are as beautiful as he is ugly."

This caused a ripple of laughter among the pretty ladies. Lark made a gesture, and they and the attendants withdrew quickly but gracefully, making little bows. The young men, however, did not go far away. They took up stations beyond the shrubbery, where they played a quiet game with a ball. They seemed not to be watching, but I felt their eyes on us; I knew they listened like foxes.

"They never leave me," Lark said, sensing my thought. "Day and

night the Seven Companions are at my call. You could not have more
faithful servants."

Or *better jailers,* I thought. But I said, "You have learned to play
the flute. You play it well."

"Do you think so? Look." He opened a jeweled case and showed
me five different clay flutes of different sizes. "Each has its own tone,
and I have learned to play them all."

"Why five? Why so many?"

"For the five senses. A flute for sight and another for hearing, one
for touch and so on. Each flute must be played every day and none
neglected for love of another."

I understood he was quoting some teacher. The flutes stood not
just for the senses, which we know are servants of Pleasure, but for
other things as well, like virtue and wisdom.

"What beautiful instruments, Lark. I have never seen clay so
thin."

"Yes. Beautiful but fragile. When I started learning, I broke
several just by touching them too clumsily. I thought the priest musician who teaches me would be angry. Instead he only talked an hour
about the lightness with which we must touch life."

Sensing that we were on the path to theology, I changed
the subject. "How much longer will you be the Image of Smoking
Mirror?"

"Not long. I do not have the whole year that is usual." His eyes
wandered over the garden; he glanced again at the flutes. "I am told
that the end is better than the beginning; that the great joy is not in
taking everything, but in giving everything. Do you believe that,
Mali?"

He had become anxious, troubled. The dark eyes seemed darker,
and he ran a hand through his fine hair.

"Yes, Lark. Of course it is better!" I stammered the words
without the least understanding, much less belief. The beginning? The
end? The birds stirred near our feet, and I thought that for all their
bright plumage they were grotesque because they waddled instead of
flying. Their wings had been clipped; they had become fat and docile.
One of the Seven Companions, moving nearer, covertly watched us
while he pretended to tie the thong of his sandal.

"When I first came here I was uneasy because Smoking Mirror
is the Bringer of Darkness," Lark said. "But the priests have explained

that we only know light because we know the dark. We only have life because of death."

"You must be right. I am not educated in such matters." But I *did* know. For all the smooth words, I felt no need for death and darkness. I wanted only life, every second of it, and I could not think that dying would help my appreciation. Neither did I have to be blind at midnight to love the dawn. But, of course, I have always been shallow in matters of philosophy.

"You are wearing my ring!" he exclaimed. "I hoped you would like it. I had nothing else to leave you that morning."

"The best possible gift." I wanted to tell him that I had wept over the ring, touched it as a talisman when we crept through grasses and hid in swamps during the long flight from Jalisco. I had even washed it clean after it was stained by the blood of an enemy.

The words died in my mouth. One does not confide in the Image of Smoking Mirror or disturb his tranquillity.

He smiled gently, yet I knew his eyes were not on my face. I remembered how his presence had calmed the screaming man who had been caged for sacrifice at the outpost. Lark Singer and that prisoner had shared something unknowable to me, a glimpse of a kingdom whose password was "death." I could never share that vision.

The attendants and the ladies were drifting back, smiling and nodding to us. I sensed the hour was over. Taking my hand, Lark said, "You will see me only one more time, Mali. On that morning you must be happy for me. Promise me that."

I promised, speaking meaningless words while I gazed at him, thinking I had once drawn pictures in charcoal on his back and chest; I had held him up when he tried to swim. I marveled at my own innocence then.

I left awkwardly, clumsily accepting a basket of gifts from one of the companions. When I started down the path, flute music began once more. I supposed the nude girl had resumed her dance among the flightless birds. Which of the flutes was for her? Touch or sight or taste? Or all of them. I did not look back.

At the gate Lady Iztac and Water Lily waited anxiously. As we made our way back to the boat, they peppered me with questions. No, I answered, there was not an orgy in the garden; no, women were not copulating with beasts or reptiles; yes, I had been treated with respect. Lady Iztac seemed both relieved and disappointed.

Midway across the lake several vendors' barges hailed us, two old women peddling fried fish, men hawking herbs and dried blossoms. The aroma of hot grease was strong, and I enjoyed the smells of garlic and oregano. My lungs felt cleaner, rid of the thick fragrance of the garden.

I turned to Water Lily. "What exactly happens at the end of Lark Singer's reign? I know he joins Smoking Mirror, but *how* does he join him?"

"On the altar, of course. What did you think? The priests will offer his heart to the god." She nodded shrewdly. "And don't think Smoking Mirror won't take it. He's a hungry one; he gobbles anything!"

I had really known that, but I had not quite let myself believe it. Ahead, just beyond the boat basin, the twin temples of Hummingbird and Smoking Mirror rose majestically against the distant mountains. Here was the heart of the heart of the world. Twin wisps of smoke rose lazily from the high altars. Suddenly I hated this city I had found so beautiful. I would have wept, but my mother was watching.

I intended to put Smoking Mirror from my mind, but in the next days everyone was talking about the Dark Lord.

Two events alarmed the city. The first, which was to be repeated many times in many neighborhoods, came on a night when Lady Moon was hiding in her grave, beheaded, her child torn from her womb. It was during the Eighth Watch, the chill stretch of darkness when weak infants and men who have been wounded are most likely to slip quietly from life into the Narrow Passage. No one willingly ventures out at that hour.

I lay on my mat sleeping fitfully, fighting against a dream of fleeing down the endless corridors of a cave. A huge figure pursued me slowly but inexorably and I thought it might be Smoking Mirror himself, for the monster limped, dragging one leg like Smoking Mirror, whose foot had been gnawed away by his own sister. Again and again I shouted to my father for help, and it seemed that my own shouts awakened me. Then slowly I realized it was another voice I heard—a woman in the street was crying loudly and in terrible distress.

I sat upright, my arms gooseflesh, peering into the dark. The voice, human yet animal, a woman yet not quite a woman, cried again.

"My sons, we are destroyed! My sons, where can I hide you?"

In my life I have heard horrifying sounds made by human throats —the wailing of bereft women searching a battlefield at twilight, the shrieks of men under torture when white-hot irons seared their flesh, once a girl flayed alive. But never before or after did I hear a cry that so chilled my blood and the blood of all who listened.

And the voice, laden with terror and torment, compelled me and drew me through the darkness into the patio. Outside my chamber light flickered in the passageway as my father appeared carrying a torch; Water Lily, along with the rest of the servants and slaves, fumbled the wall searching for the door to the street. All the household was there except Lady Iztac, who doubtless kneeled on her mat praying.

Prince Chimal threw back the bar that held the door, and everyone ran into the street where torches now blazed as for a festival. The Mixtecs poured from their factory dwelling, a hundred of them of all ages, naked and babbling. Opposite us our neighbors the fat family had taken to their roof and leaned over the parapet, round faces pale with fright.

The cry came again, but distantly now. *"My sons! Oh, my beloved sons!"*

One of the Mixtec women began to scream hysterically and a man slapped her. Her shriek caused panic, and other Mixtec women wailed, beating their bosoms. Their men joined the outcry, raising trembling hands toward the black sky while they wept. Then we heard keening from another quarter, the clothmakers' streets nearby, then from the direction of the imperial college. A wind of wailing swept the city.

My father led us back into the house, barred the leather panels of the door, then went alone to the roof to try to read the stars. When he returned he said the heavens held no message; I suspected he held back something dreadful.

If the stars did not speak, everybody else did in the morning. Talk went from houses to markets to temples and across the lakes to neighboring towns, and with talk the mystery deepened. The Weeping Woman, as everyone now called the apparition, had been glimpsed by many. She wore funeral robes, crimson garments of death, and her figure was obscured by a cloud—some said a nimbus that flickered and glowed, pale as the blue fire of the Old God that hovers above marshes and bogs.

Strangest of all, every listener heard his own language in the Weeping Woman's lament. When she had cried aloud in our street, we understood her plainly. Yet the Mixtecs claimed her words were uttered in their language; Maya slaves understood her in Maya and so did the Zapotecs in the weavers' district. In all languages the message of destruction was the same, except some of the subject peoples claimed she cursed the Aztecs for greed of goods and victims, promising vengeance upon Tenochtitlan.

No one who heard her—and tens of thousands were awakened that night and on later nights—doubted the coming of disaster. Water Lily, indomitable before, moved in a trance for days; Lady Iztac, tight-lipped, spent the mornings visiting different temples. But which god was to be placated? There were so many, and they were all so spiteful and unpredictable. Smoking Mirror, the night ruler, had to be involved. So Lord Moctezuma, after three days of anguished uncertainty, ordered the sacrifice of three hundred and sixty Tlaxcalan hostages, one for each night of the sacred calendar. He released five other hostages to recognize the nights of the Unlucky Days.

Water Lily brightened at this news. "It will be all right."

Two hours later the steward returned from market with an alarming report. Lord Moctezuma had changed his mind; the five freed Tlaxcalans were seized on a causeway as they tried to flee the city, and now their hearts were to be offered on the altar of the Temple of the Unknown God near Texcoco.

Water Lily gasped. "The Unknown God is worshiped only with music! He eats nothing else. He accepts no other sacrifice."

"A female theologian! A cunt who knows more of religion than the Revered Speaker Moctezuma himself!" Fierce Baby sneered at her. There is always war between a steward and a housekeeper, but it was worse in our house because Water Lily was so haughtily a Tenocha and Fierce Baby knew she held Tlatelcans in contempt. It did not help that both were Aztecs.

Fierce Baby was as worried as Water Lily about Moctezuma's strange change of decision. The Unknown God, also called the Causer of Causes, had a beautiful temple erected by the old poet-king of Texcoco, Lord Fasting Coyote. At the top, in the holy of holies, was a collection of remarkable instruments for making music, but no altar. Lady Flint Knife had often spoken of this god with approval: he bothered no one, so nobody bothered about him—which Lady Flint

Knife said was ideal behavior between mortals and gods. Others claimed that the Unknown God was Plumed Serpent in disguise. Did Moctezuma think this? Was his offering of the hostages a sop to a god who, according to prophecy, would return in person and bring the destruction the Weeping Woman lamented?

During the days that followed, while the world waited for the omen to become clear, Prince Chimal ordered me to stay away from the precincts of the great temples. That area seemed dangerous, the spot where a lightning bolt would strike or the earth would split and belch flame. Any catastrophe would start there, in the heart of the heart of the world.

Meanwhile a different sort of excitement came to our household. Lady Flint Knife, not long before her death, had committed a new will to the Word Rememberers and the royal scribe of Lord Lancer's party. This will was officially recognized when Lancer returned to the capital. When her death became known, no action was taken because the Guardians of Inheritance supposed all her heirs were dead, slain at the outpost. Now the matter was sifting through the courts, and as usual, the Guardians were arguing the legality of the bequests. My father expected a decision daily, and I seldom went far from the door so I could be first to hear any news. Also, anticipating an unknown inheritance kept my mind off Lark Singer, whose reign, I knew, was nearing its close.

One morning nine days after the first visit of the Weeping Woman, Lady Iztac summoned me to her presence. "The steward is going to Tlatelolco today to buy new cooking pots. Go with him and supervise his purchases instead of standing about goggling, as I'm told you do. It is high time you learned the value of household goods, Mali. I doubt you even know the worth of that pitcher you carelessly dropped yesterday."

She was hardly bothering to reprove me; she knew me for a lost cause. Still she added, "I want you to stop looking mournful and afflicted. I know you are thinking of our cousin. It is impious for you to be sad about the glory that awaits him. Such feelings endanger our whole family. These are perilous times, so do not annoy any god with your long face and sighing."

So I accompanied Fierce Baby. Trips through the city did not enchant me these days. When I looked at the slim cypresses, row on row in military ranks holding the soil, I thought of the garden across the lake; the flower boats and incense vendors reminded me of its perfume.

Today instead of entering the maze of the great market we made our way through the crowds toward a pottery section a few streets away on a small plaza, a route that brought us near the foot of the Temple of Hummingbird on the Left, Bringer of Victory.

There are scores, perhaps several hundred, temples of Hummingbird, and they tend to be ugly because most are thrown together in haste just after some victory they commemorate. They are built with much pomp and self-congratulation, but no love is wasted for long on a war temple, and this quickly shows. The one in Tlatelolco was no exception other than it was larger than most. One hundred and four steps, twice the sacred number, led to a high stone platform on which stood a sanctum made of granite blocks with a roof of wood and thatch. Inside, I had been told, a huge statue of Hummingbird in battle garb presided. The god was flanked by various stone attendants, all carved from basalt and painted blue. Fierce Baby said they were now so coated with dried blood splattered and splashed from the altars that they seemed dressed in leather armor.

I disliked this temple as much for its history as for its ugliness. This was the spot where the soldiers of Lord Face in the Water won their contemptible victory over the naked women and children. The victors had pulled down the great temple, which had been dedicated to Plumed Serpent, and covered the site with garbage and shit. But soon he raised a new sanctuary, this one to Hummingbird, the only god who is completely Aztec.

As we passed the temple base, I noticed that no rites were being performed; the temple stood deserted except for two black-clad priests who squatted on guard halfway up the stairs. One was picking lice out of the other's caked hair, and it so resembled a sight I had seen among the monkeys in the royal zoo that I paused and laughed out loud— my first laughter in several days.

"Smoke," said Fierce Baby, glancing up at the temple.

I followed his eyes and saw a curl of smoke rising from the thatch of the temple roof. "Why are they burning torches in daylight?" I asked. "That can't be incense!"

"No, it's too thick, too dark."

At that moment one of the priests leapt to his feet and ran up the stairs, while the other, also alarmed, tried to follow but tripped on his ragged robe. Soon both were shouting and gesticulating to the passersby and vendors in the plaza below.

"Help! Bring water jars! Hummingbird is on fire!"

"Hummingbird on fire?" The steward lifted a cynical eyebrow. "Now solid stone is burning? There is nothing so absurd that a priest won't claim it."

But the smoke changed from a curl to a billow, and from gray to sooty black. A bright tongue of flame licked the eaves while men and women came running from all directions, bearing jugs and bowls and even gourd dippers. The two priests shrieked, then suddenly both leapt into the air and began hopping up and down, performing a mad dance. Then I saw that the stone platform on which they stood had —incredibly—also caught fire, and the flames darting over the surface gave a fiery tickle to the priests' bare feet. They retreated down a few steps and, seizing water intended for Hummingbird, started to bathe their own burns. They did not leave off exhorting people to double their efforts, to bring more water to quench the flames. Someone belatedly began to pound the great alarm drum but was driven away when the fire swept over the drum's wood and leather.

The temple roof crashed down, a shower of sparks scattering the water bearers, and now everyone could see in the open temple a marvel that was taking place: the flames were nourished by the stones themselves, the carved statues wrapped in shrouds of consuming fire, although all the wood and thatch of the temple had long since turned to ashes. Again the frightened men and women tried to hurl water, but the water seethed an instant, then hissed into scalding steam while the blaze roared, angry and ravenous.

Someone shouted that the fire had turned to liquid, that it was running like molten lava at Hummingbird's feet. I saw a thin stream of blue-red brilliance creep over the high platform and stood gaping, hypnotized by this miracle of blazing stone. Only the steward, who had come to his senses, saved me from being trampled.

"Run!" he shouted, seizing my arm. "Run now!"

"What—?" By the time I could speak he was dragging me away —only in the nick of time. The crowd on the temple steps suddenly saw that the fire was unearthly, devouring stone and water as ordinary fire gulps oil. Panic seized them.

As hundreds of screaming people fled down the temple steps to escape the flaming god, a thousand others poured into the narrow plaza below, drawn by the smoke and shouting, called by the drum beating. The plunging crowds met like two clashing armies, and no one knows how many fell and were crushed in the struggle. We managed to shelter in a doorway until it was safe to start for home.

"Plumed Serpent is coming," said Water Lily that night as she peered at the sunset. "Then there will not be just one woman wailing in the streets but ten thousand."

Whole families appeared at our door to hear Fierce Baby's account of the destruction of Hummingbird's house. I, too, would have been a celebrity had Lady Iztac not forbidden me to appear before strangers.

Everyone in every city of the valley knew the alarming story: No one had been in the temple when the fire started, and nothing had been left burning there earlier. The temple, of itself, simply burst into flame. Stone had fueled the fire—a hundred witnesses swore to it. And, of course, the ground on which the temple stood had been taken long ago from Plumed Serpent and given to Hummingbird of the Left. The sky god was reclaiming his property, obviously aided by the Old God of Fire.

"Oh, we will weep soon," said Water Lily. "All of us! We will weep blood."

My father, along with every sage and astrologer in the city, had been summoned into council. That night we waited for him in the patio—servants and slaves, Fierce Baby, Water Lily, the three elderly cousins clasping one another's thin hands. A little girl, an orphan who worked in the kitchen, could not hold back her sobbing. I took her in my arms, tried to comfort her.

"I have been good," she pleaded through her tears. "I never left stains on the pots, I never stole cakes or put my fingers in the honey. Why will Plumed Serpent kill me?"

"He will not hurt you, my darling," I said, patting her little shoulders. "Probably he will bring you gifts—sweet cakes and pretty yarn to tie in your hair." She did not believe me, and wept until she fell asleep exhausted.

Very late Prince Chimal arrived, escorted by two linkboys sent from the palace to carry torches. "Why are you not all asleep?" he asked, astonished at such a gathering in the patio. "There is no reason to fear."

"Is Plumed Serpent returning? What does the council say?" Fierce Baby's question was impertinent, but the worry was in all our minds.

My father sighed. "The council knows no more than any of you. If the god comes, we shall welcome him. History says that when he ruled the Only World before, he loved justice, was famed for his mercy. Why be afraid?"

This was not an answer his listeners wanted or believed. Justice and mercy from a god? They knew better. On every side they saw famine and slaughter and slavery. Drought parched the crops or floods came and drowned them. Volcanoes exploded into clouds of fire and burning ash. These were the usual gifts from the Rulers of the Universe. Everybody knew it.

"Please, Lord Prince," said Water Lily, for once strangely humble, "you are a reader of the stars. Give us a prophecy."

My father hesitated, then made a gesture of futility, lifting his hands and dropping them. "Very well. This is what is in the stars. The future will be as difficult and as hard to bear as the past has been— but you will bear it. Be satisfied with that. Leave the worry of returning gods and flaming temples to the priests. They are paid to worry, you are not. Now go to sleep, all of you."

They went slowly, wondering at his words, searching for some hidden magic in them. At least the little girl had stopped crying. Prince Chimal made a gesture for Lady Iztac and me to wait.

When we were alone, he said, "There is news that for us is more important than these mysteries. Early today, before the city lost its mind, the Guardians ruled that Lady Flint Knife's will is legal. I have heard its contents."

Lady Iztac caught her breath. I knew she hoped my father had gained a huge fortune, that his mother had been richer than anyone supposed.

Prince Chimal, aware of her ambitions, shook his head. "No, my lady mother did not secretly own the jade mountains. Long ago she invested much of her property in my political career—you know what return that has brought! But she still owned family lands to the south near the border of the Maya kingdoms. We will live comfortably on those plantations."

"We are to leave the capital, my lord?" Lady Iztac made an effort to conceal her disappointment, but her feelings were too bitter to hide.

Once more she faced exile. She looked as shaken as if Prince Chimal had struck her.

"We leave as soon as arrangements are completed. Provided, of course, that our daughter will welcome us to her estates."

"Welcome you?" I asked. "I do not understand."

"You must welcome us to your lands, Lady Ce Malinalli. You are the heiress, my daughter. Lady Flint Knife left all she owned to you. I am your guardian and administrator, but the lands are yours."

Too astonished to speak, I stood awkwardly as my father embraced me. In the silence I heard Lady Iztac's voice.

"Odd that she should pass over her own son. Especially to leave her property to a girl! I suppose some invading spirit prompted her." She gazed at me thoughtfully and said, "Some unnatural force."

On the second morning of the thirteenth month, called the Feast of the Mountains, we arose in the darkness of the unlucky Seventh Watch, dressed ourselves in robes whose colors mingled the green of life with the crimson of death and traveled across the lake to the temple at the Hill of the Locust. This was the morning of farewell to Lark Singer.

Afterward I banished all that happened from my mind, but when it seemed I had forgotten, the memories would stir again like a jaguar in a thicket, sleeping by day but rampant in darkness. Some god would make me live those events again, would send the dream again. So I never lost the anger I learned that morning, but drew strength from it.

I remember mist covering the face of the lake, gray fog shrouding the volcanoes and the towers of the city. A flare blazed on the prow of our boat, and the rowers cried and beat wooden clappers to warn off other craft moving invisibly nearby. The dawn wind stirred the mist. It billowed around us, barring our way. Far away I heard ocelots calling the approach of daybreak.

The mist lifted. I saw Lady Moon, big with child, and shining dimly in the west was Morning Star. A hundred boats were converging on the shore where the hill, Chapultepec, loomed in shadow, but blue fires gleamed on the temple steps—fallen stars. Flutes played the music I had heard in the Texcoco garden, and somewhere a woman was singing in a thin, crystalline voice a song that told of the flowing water, the passing of the winds. "We share this earth a little while. Only a short time here." The prow of our boat ground against the stone quay.

Lord Lancer, since this was a day of honor for him, was waiting to greet members of his family and clan. He wore a splendid robe, crimson and green like ours, and he bowed, nodding. He raised both hands in salute. His smile seemed false, ghastly. Lark had said, "Remember to be happy for me." I repeated this silently but it did not help.

Someone whispered, "Lord Moctezuma is here! The Revered Speaker has come!" I glimpsed a man in priestly black climbing the steps toward the altar. I did not see his face; he did not matter to me. The temple, I thought, was dingy. Perhaps it was chosen so that the greatest beauty would end in humiliation. Perhaps that seemed fitting, reassuring to those who gathered to watch.

With a cry of trumpets and a jingling of a thousand tiny bells, the flower boats arrived bearing the Exalted and his attendants, his musicians, his wives. They carried burning pine splinters, and sandalwood that sputtered and gave little showers of sparks. On the shore we formed a double line leading to the temple, up the steps to the platform, the altar, the final destination.

Lark Singer stepped ashore wearing not his beautiful tunic but a robe of cheap cotton, torn and faded. His face was marked with a black smudge of repentance and humility: he had been raised high above other men, had known what they would not know. Now he would be brought down, brought beneath their feet.

Turning back, he embraced each of the four young women who waited near him, a brief farewell. Then, his head high and his eyes shining, he mounted the stone steps to the first platform. The Companions followed, one offering the box that held the flutes Lark had played in the garden. He lifted one from the case, held it tenderly, then broke it in two, letting the pieces fall to shatter on the paving stones at his feet. A sigh, a low murmur of pain and recognition, passed through the worshipers.

When he moved past me, I forced myself not to cry out. His face was exultant, enraptured. He had never been so beautiful, and I closed my eyes, unable to watch the breaking of the second flute . . . or the third and fourth and fifth.

He reached the high altar at the moment when Lord Sun, a globe of red fire, burst above the city on the eastern shore, sending his rays across the water to strike the temple and bathe the door of the sanctuary in light.

Four priests held Lark upon the altar, a fifth raised high the
obsidian blade. I held my breath waiting for Lark to cry out, a wild
cry terrible and lovely raging from the temple to the sky. But in that
endless second while the blade flashed in light, there came no sound
but a boy's stifled sob. I thought he said, "Quickly." I am not sure.

The crowd shuddered when the knife swept down, some of the
women weeping in joy and passion. The priest displayed the heart,
holding it up in his outstretched hands; it was still beating.

Somewhere, I thought, far away, a silver waterfowl had burst
from the reeds, free into the light, sailing toward the clouds on great
wings, its voice ringing across the water. Lark had said, "I think when
the gods weep, they sound like that." The gods, I felt, were weeping
now. But here they wept in silence.

We turned from the temple and moved toward the boats. The
rite had ended—although for me it would never end. Over the waters
of Lake Texcoco the city glowed red in dawn, Lord Sun still a ball
of flame on the horizon. I thought of the temple I had watched
burning, fire licking the posts, the roof crashing down, shimmering
blue flame consuming the statues of the gods. For an instant it seemed
to me that the whole city across the lake was ablaze, smoke the color
of blood pouring from the palaces and sanctuaries. The flower boats,
the wooden stalls of the markets, the cages where men and women
awaited sacrifice—all of them were wreathed in fire. Then nothing
stood on the islands of Tenochtitlan but columns of flame and smoke
that drowned the sun.

"Come, Mali," said my father. "It is over now."

But I stood a moment longer, gazing at the far shore, until at last
the vision faded and the city of fire became once more a city of wood
and stone.

Ten days later we left Tenochtitlan, traveling south with an armed
caravan of merchants. Twenty hired bearers carried our supplies and
household goods. We had sold the few slaves we owned, discharged
such free employees as Water Lily and Fierce Baby. The Mixtec potters
next door had bought our house and so doubled their factory.

"I am happy to go," said Lady Iztac when she learned of the sale.
"The city is being taken over by foreigners." I had seldom seen her
so close to tears.

But she cheered up when she discovered that Lord Lancer was

making the southern journey with us. "Nothing keeps me here. I need to breathe different air, see new stars," he told my father. Prince Chimal accepted him graciously as a companion for the journey. But I overheard him tell Lord Lancer, in his gentlest voice, that he would find the stars were everywhere the same and grief walks in our own sandals.

Subdued now, Lord Lancer bore little resemblance to the man who had swaggered into our Jalisco outpost in his gaudy clothing, his fingers flashing gold. Of course, we were all much changed or at least seemed changed since that day.

We journeyed south, then east, skirting the volcanoes and avoiding the land of the hostile Tlaxcalans, a land of crags that our caravan leader described as a nest of scorpions. We followed streams in the valleys, through rocky land where deer stared at us from sparse forests above and wolves howled at night. This was a safe route, the path of runners who brought fresh fish from the sea to the table of Moctezuma almost daily, so the trail was dotted with relay stations and guard posts. We met caravans homeward bound to Tlatelolco, and twice we encountered trains of Moctezuma's tax collectors, the bearers staggering under the weight of tribute—cocoa beans, dyes, plumes, salt and honey.

One morning we quickly made way for a swift-messenger who bore the imperial crest that gave right of way on any narrow path and through the gates of way stations.

"What news?" the men shouted at him, as they always do, hoping for at least a brief answer such as, "War again in Tlaxcala" or "Uprising in the Red Land." This time there was no reply.

But two days later we learned the news he carried to Moctezuma. A small company of soldiers who had traveled all the way from the border of the Maya kingdoms joined our camp for the night, requesting provisions and hospitality, as was their right. They had been an escort for the swift-messenger who had passed us, guarding him on the unsafe southern stretch of the route, letting him race ahead when they approached civilization. Naturally they knew every detail of the courier's message, and they were eager to share it, to impress us with a remarkable story.

Their captain, young Lord Storm Arrow, was received as the guest of Prince Chimal and Lord Lancer, so I was called upon to serve the chocolate and pass the pipes of tobacco. Lady Iztac offered the perfumes and garlands. Neither of us missed a word that was said.

"The Maya lords have reported strange happenings. For once they are worried enough to share their knowledge."

Everyone knew how clannish and close-mouthed the Maya were. If an earthquake shook the whole world, they would try to keep it secret.

"The canoe people on the coast have again seen towers riding on the sea. Some say towers, others say palaces or temples, but everyone agrees they have wings."

"This is not the first time that wonder has been reported," said my father.

"Yes," said Lord Lancer with a faint smile. "Maya pulque can make any man rabbit-headed. They saw clouds."

The captain shook his head. "Not this time. They saw men or monsters resembling men. They wore strange shells for hats, or maybe their heads were made of shell. The towers were indeed as high as temples."

"Temples floating on the waves." My father looked thoughtful. "Surely that was a magnificent sight, a wonder."

"Like eagles in the sun!" exclaimed the captain. He did not mean that the towers resembled birds. But there was nothing in the world so fraught with power and omen as the sight of eagles, kings of the air, crossing the path of Lord Sun.

The captain lowered his voice. "Some say that Plumed Serpent is returning. They say the towers are his temples, that they are borne by his wings."

"Then we should rejoice," said my father. "Plumed Serpent, when he came to us before, was the wisest lord on earth. He would be so today."

"Wisest except for the Revered Speaker Moctezuma," Lord Lancer added quickly, giving my father an uneasy look.

"Yes," said Prince Chimal gravely. "There is always an exception, perhaps."

That night I fell asleep with my head full of visions of towers on the sea and eagles in the sun. But I did not sleep long. During the Fifth Watch the heavens were split with lightning, clouds rolling across the Star River bringing torrents of rain and winds that ripped branches from the trees. The thunder of Tlaloc made the ground tremble.

Violent as that storm was, I would have forgotten it except for other events. For in that year and in that same month far to the south, one of the winged towers I had just heard about was wrecked by a storm that may have been the same one that lashed us on the mountain trail. I have always thought so. The men aboard were swept into the sea, tossed and buffeted, at last sucked down through the Narrow Passage. Most perished in the waves; a few swimmers reached the beaches, where they were butchered alive by the Shell People who found them. One man fought his way to shore and stumbled inland through swamps and jungles. He evaded serpents, quicksand and arrows tipped with poison; he had an uncanny skill at staying alive—strange because he was thin and frail, with no strength at all except in his eyes. They burned with an odd, unflickering light.

His name was Jeronimo de Aguilar. I would meet him one day in the Spanish camp in Tabasco, and our meeting would change the world, for between us we were the speakers for the returning god.

I knew him in danger. We found ways to survive when death seemed sure, and our escapes were unlikely. Yet somehow Aguilar kept himself alive.

But the last time I saw him he was a ghost sitting under a tree keeping watch over my lord the Captain's tomb in the bleak graveyard of Texcoco. Unlike me, he must have lost his knack for survival.

8

The Lair of the
Serpent—1512

The estates I inherited from my grandmother, like other lands I would one day be given by His Most Catholic Majesty, lay near the great brown and green river that coils lazily through the country called Coatzacoalcos. That name, in the old tongue, means "Lair of the Serpent," but it is not called this because, as the Spaniards later supposed, its jungles are aswarm with snakes. Rather, it gained its lovely name and honor because this vast tract of forest was the first home on earth of Plumed Serpent, his refuge and sanctuary.

One day the goddess Serpent Skirt, a virgin, was gathering feathers at a place called Snake Hill. A lovely plume, soft and many-colored as a rainbow, drifted from the sky, and the goddess pressed it against her bosom, enchanted. From this union the god was born.

It was also from this land he fled in sorrow, accompanied by a few dear friends such as the hawks and gophers, when he fell from grace after committing incest with his divine younger sister. And here the loyal serpents wove themselves into a raft to bear him eastward across the sea, the Lord of the Dawn.

Later, when people assumed that I myself was born in the same country, I did not correct them. After all, it is fitting that the companion of a god should spring from the god's own homeland. So, for religious reasons, I encouraged this mistake and a few others. In matters of faith, poetry is superior to fact.

. .

We arrived in the Lair of the Serpent in a month when, by Aztec decree, four women and one man are sacrificed and eaten to honor the Rain Bringer. The rites took place two days before we reached the river boundary of the province, and Lady Iztac, annoyed at missing the festival, vented her irritation to Lord Lancer, who was walking beside us one morning.

"Oh, these useless delays! The day is over before we are even on our way."

I looked away in embarrassment, pretending not to hear. We started late each day because recently my father had become preoccupied with Morning Star. Since Morning Star is the temple and celestial embodiment of Plumed Serpent, Prince Chimal was watching for promises of the god's return. He believed he had observed two possible omens and was sending reports to the capital.

It was shameful enough that Lady Iztac did not appreciate his work, but inexcusable that she voiced disapproval. It especially pained me that Lord Lancer, who always looked so smug and knowing, heard her complaints.

Lancer should have rebuked her for unwifely impatience; instead he said, "Prince Chimal would do well to concern himself less with the stars and more with his own safety. Attracting Moctezuma's attention these days is like flirting with a jaguar. The beast purrs one minute and springs the next."

That, of course, was outright sedition, and it struck me that Lord Lancer had great confidence in my mother's loyalty to him. I felt relieved when he left us to urge on the porters who were struggling across a ravine.

Lady Iztac was mollified when we reached the town of Painala and discovered that the whole countryside had turned out to greet us. Musicians and acrobats escorted us to the plaza where a delegation of elders and priests, decked in their finery, waited.

Lord Lancer glanced at me in surprise. "The estates you inherited must be greater than we supposed. A reception like this is not given for the owner of three turkeys and a maize patch."

He was right about the unexpected size of my inheritance, but wrong about the cause of the ceremony. While the priests smothered us with fuming pots of incense and the elders kissed the earth, we were told that the cacique who ruled in Painala had recently died, and while we were making our slow journey, swift-messengers had reached the town to announce that Prince Chimal was the new cacique, Aztec overseer in the region.

It did not mean much. The office was mostly ceremonial, for the people really governed themselves according to local customs and religion. Except at tribute-paying time, Aztec rule was light here. Still, my father had been honored, and I dared shoot a triumphant glance at Lord Lancer. So much for his dismal predictions! I did not know what my father had said in the council meetings in the capital, but Moctezuma the jaguar, instead of springing, had purred and even given Prince Chimal a kiss. We were again in favor.

When I remember those first happy days in the Lair of the Serpent, a hundred shades of green undulate in my memory: ferns and palm fronds and still pools mirroring leafy branches that overhang the waters. I also think of fireflies that girls wore tied in their hair or in tiny cages at their wrists, living jewels twinkling in green shadows.

Once again we were on the frontier of Aztec dominions, so far away that the people had never seen Aztec women before, only a few males, merchants and soldiers and tax gatherers. But this frontier was like the shore of the endless ocean. To the south and west stretched an almost impenetrable jungle, the forest of the Rain Bringer, whose trees stood taller than the highest temples, god trees inhabited by hostile spirits. Few journeyers entered this leafy ocean, and of those who did, only the strongest returned. I had no suspicion then that I myself would cross it not once but twice and live to remember.

Beyond the forest barricades lived the Maya, a race old when Time itself was yet in the womb of heaven. They were the first humans formed of mud from the young earth. Perhaps the monkeys are even older, for Time has shrunk them, but no one knows for sure.

From time to time Maya traders would appear in Painala, the caravan owners fat and sleek even after traversing the jungle, but their porters and guards resembling skeletons. Their strong Maya noses jutted from starved faces, making them as beaked as the macaws Lady Iztac kept in bamboo cages.

The Maya brought salt, honey, slaves, perfume, pigments and quetzal feathers. Their language sounded strange, and it was supposed to be derived from the speech of birds. I doubt this, for I learned to speak Maya well, yet the birds never answered me as they used to answer Lark Singer.

From one of the first Maya parties we saw, Prince Chimal bought me a slave, a gentle girl whose masters called her Moju because they said she was as tall as a jungle tree of that name. Actually Moju and I were almost exactly the same height, taller than most women.

I began to learn her language, and that is how I discovered my gift for tongues. If I hear a foreign word twice, it seems mine forever. I am proud of this. I do not care that some people have said I could speak seven languages and tell the truth in none. Let them sneer. Languages have served me faithfully; truth I have found to be less reliable.

Usually the traders who emerged from the jungle with Maya trade goods were not themselves Maya. The commerce of the jungle paths was left mostly to men of mixed blood whose only loyalty was to a good bargain or an easy theft. Like respectable merchants, they carried the emblems of peaceful trade—feather fans and banners of the Guiding Lord of Aztecs, the North Star of Maya. But at heart the merchants from nowhere remained bandits, stealing when they could, trading when they had to.

Lady Iztac's favorite jungle trader was a one-eyed man from Xacalanco, town of two rivers. He had replaced his lost left eye with a leather patch on which was sewn a false eye made of white shell and black obsidian—yet this left eye was no colder than his right. He was called Hawk by the men who worked for him; it was appropriate since he dealt chiefly in captured birds and slave children. Both were kept in cages too small for them.

The day after Moju's purchase, Hawk approached my father, practically burying his face in the dust. "Exalted Lord, I beg you to examine a treasure I have brought, a rare creation for which I paid a fortune in the Land of the Shaking Earth."

"You dare to offer such merchandise in the presence of my daughter?" Prince Chimal frowned, assuming from the trader's lewd tone that he spoke of a female slave or some extraordinarily beautiful boy.

"Oh, no! Your Highness mistakes his servant. Here is the treasure I meant." He brought forth from a basket a true rarity, one of the beautiful painted books of the Maya, a folding book made of fig bark paper.

"You have desecrated some temple to get this," said the prince. But even as he scowled he reached for it eagerly, and soon a price was set.

Later I looked over my father's shoulder when he studied the pages, first being sure that Lady Iztac was occupied elsewhere, since it was doubtless blasphemous for a female to see the paintings and characters. Prince Chimal had tolerant views, and soon we were exclaiming together over the beauty of the writing. My father could even read the date glyphs; he had learned Maya numerals, since the Maya, being themselves as ancient as the stars, are naturally the world's greatest astronomers.

The book seemed to be a work of theology: a masked god fondled the ripe breasts of a woman while he explained the creation of the world to her. They drifted in a canoe while the god spoke of the fusing of land and sky to become heaven and earth; then he demonstrated heaven by mounting her and uniting their bodies in divine coitus. It was a breathtaking painting—the mighty sweep of the god's thighs, his great arm muscles. On the woman's face was a look of joy and holiness.

"Is such a union possible, Father?" I asked. "A god and a mortal woman?"

"Why not?" He smiled at me. "At moments like the one shown here I have felt myself to be a god. At least I have had a god's understanding of the power of life. And I have seen women no god could resist. This book, I think, is true and sacred."

We studied the picture a long time, the most beautiful painting either of us had ever seen. I would never forget the woman's face, although the features of the god's mask eventually blurred in my memory and became someone else.

The season for penance and weapon making came. Trappers, led by Lord Lancer, went into the forest and brought back live game in nets for autumn sacrifice. Lord Lancer seemed to have forgotten his grief. The handsome features again became proud and petulant; he now advised everyone about everything and was forever issuing obvious and unnecessary orders. Although he had no apparent reason to remain with us, he never spoke of leaving.

This was the mellow season in the Lair of the Serpent. Twice winds from the ocean brought deluges of rain, downpours so heavy you could not see your own outstretched hand. But most days were golden and serene. The weeks, like dry fronds floating in the sluggish river, drifted slowly one into the next.

A trader brought a third-hand report that Moctezuma had led a disastrous attack against the Tlaxcalans. Lord Lancer was concerned that old army comrades might have fallen, but the trader assured him that most of the lost were Texcocans. "Lord Moctezuma watched the battle from a hillside, and when he saw how matters lay, he withdrew the Aztec troops on the flank. The Texcocans were left to hold the field. They did not last long."

"What are you saying?" Lord Lancer demanded. "Are you accusing our army of betraying its allies? You look like a rotten Texcocan yourself!"

Blows would have been exchanged had my father not intervened. A week later the truth of Moctezuma's abandoning his allies was confirmed by a herald from the capital who had come to remind the people that tax collectors would arrive next month. "There has to be another side to the story," said Lancer.

"There always is," my father replied. "Any matter concerning the Revered Speaker seems to have endless sides."

Although few traders except jungle men passed our way, we were on a route often taken by pilgrims bound for the shrines of the Mixtecs and Zapotecs to the west. Prince Chimal built a house near the pilgrimage trail so no religious traveler would lack shelter from the rains. Gods often disguise themselves as pilgrims to their own shrines; to turn them away brings calamity. Yet we did not want visitors, immortal or otherwise, to become a nuisance, so the guest shelter stood a few bow shots from our own dwelling and beyond a mask of foliage.

One morning a servant came to me and said, "Prince Chimal wishes you to take food for three pilgrims to the shelter."

"Three? Very well. Help me carry it."

"No, he said you are to come alone. I don't know why. Some religious reason."

Prince Chimal was waiting in the doorway. "Does your mother know we have visitors?" he asked.

"No, my lord. She is in the village."

"Then come in. There is a surprise for you."

Inside was only one pilgrim, a man whose face was almost completely blackened with the soot of repentance. It was a moment before I recognized our visitor as Uncle Willow.

"He is leaving almost at once and you will not mention his being here," my father told me.

While I packed the food so Uncle Willow could carry it in a pilgrim's basket on his back, the brothers talked and I learned what had happened, although most of the story came later when Prince Chimal talked to me privately.

Not long after we left the capital, Uncle Willow returned from his expedition with more new plants for Moctezuma's gardens. He was congratulated by the first minister, Lord Woman Snake, and told to take up his duties as one of the twenty royal tutors.

"What a group had been chosen!" Willow said with pride. "All men with skill and learning. The best minds in the world, I truly believe. Only you were lacking, brother."

"Luckily for me, apparently."

"Also, you are too well born. We were all sons of second wives or concubines—even sons of slaves. There was not a royal idiot or a noble nitwit among us."

Moctezuma was apparently worried that a faculty of commoners was teaching his sons and nephews, but Lord Woman Snake soothed the First Speaker, assuring him that the teachers were men of unusual ability and loyalty.

This was the situation when Moctezuma set out on his ill-fated war. Then, on the mountain road, some impulse seized Moctezuma. Perhaps he had a vision, perhaps a voice spoke in a dream. He ordered Lord Woman Snake, who was with him, to return to the city and immediately put all the royal tutors to death. He gave no reason but was so deeply concerned lest Woman Snake falter in his mission that the next day he dispatched other officials to make sure no tutor escaped beheading. But Uncle Willow, somehow warned, disguised himself and fled the city.

"Why? Why such an order?" Uncle Willow, who had spoken quietly until now, suddenly struck his own palm with his fist. "We were devoted to our work, we respected Moctezuma as the Speaker and as a god. Why this?"

"The tutors were killed not for what they did but for what they were," said my father gently. "Long ago before he came to power and was crowned by the gods, I heard Moctezuma deliver a speech in a council. He told us that precious stones are out of place among ordinary pebbles. Onyx must not be mixed with gravel and beautiful plumes cannot be worn with the feathers of crows and sparrows. He meant, of course, that nobles cannot mix with common folk."

Willow sighed and nodded. "I know. Lord Woman Snake told me that every servant in the palace had to be discharged when Moctezuma took command. More than a hundred."

"Not just discharged. They were beheaded in secret. Not one lived to compare Moctezuma to his predecessor. And not just courtiers fell in that bloodletting. Many officials went to the altars even in the far provinces. Somehow I was spared." Lifting his right hand, Prince Chimal made the gesture of resignation to fate. "I think I will not be spared much longer."

I felt a chill at these words, and Uncle Willow, alarmed, declared he would return to Tenochtitlan at once and give himself up if it would ensure my father's safety.

"It has nothing to do with you, brother," said Prince Chimal. "I have told Moctezuma plainly what I have read in the stars. A god is returning to claim his kingdom—Plumed Serpent or some other. I am like an ambassador who delivers a declaration of war and so becomes the first casualty. But why expect the worst? The Revered Speaker is a god, so he is capricious and inscrutable."

Yes, he was a god. We did not judge his cruelty or unfairness in human terms any more than we judged the god of a volcano for spewing lava or the Rain Bringer for lightning. You did not judge such catastrophes; you merely tried to escape them.

Uncle Willow, after a night's rest, left at dawn for the Mixtec shrines on the far side of the mountains. He had friends there, men he had met on his last expedition who shared his love of plants and flowers. "I will return when Moctezuma dies," he told my father. To me it sounded like promising to come back a day after the end of eternity. My intuition was right; I never saw or heard of him again, and I do not know if his escape had anything to do with what happened soon afterward.

In the next weeks, as I entered my thirteenth year, I showed signs of womanhood, and I tried to keep this secret, although Lady Iztac must have guessed. However, she was occupied with organizing and dominating the other wives in the community, especially trying to convince them that they should cover their breasts in public, Aztec fashion, except at religious rites. Her Aztec prudishness did not win her many friends. Meanwhile, any spare hours she devoted to prayers and rituals for her own fertility, so she gave little thought to mine.

Then one morning the outer world invaded our lives. First we heard the faraway booming of drums and the groan of shell horns. Soon far-criers announced the arrival of emissaries, officials from the imperial court. In the town all work was abandoned as everyone rushed to the temple plaza where public events were held. This was an unexpected show.

The officials arrived an hour later, entering with pomp: fifty-two men, one for each year of the great sheaves of time. Their garments seemed woven of flowers, light flashing on golden pectorals and chains, while banners streamed in the morning sun. The towns-folk stood gaping; no one had expected such a splendid and obviously important caravan. No swift-messengers had preceded them, which was strange, so no one had had time to make arrangements for a proper reception.

I arrived late at the plaza, which did not matter since the women of Prince Chimal's family had no part in the public greeting. Our roles were to be played later at home, the offering of hospitality. I found a place near the rear of the crowd.

"What have they come for?" an old woman asked.

"Maybe it is about Plumed Serpent," said another man. "Maybe new omens have been seen."

People nearby caught part of his words and I heard a murmur of "Plumed Serpent . . . new omens."

My father, noble in his plain, straight tunic and wearing for adornment only the copper ornaments made in the town, met the Aztecs at the foot of the temple stairs. He was so tall and serene and lordly that my heart almost burst with pride and love.

The first formal greetings were exchanged, words I could not hear, then the elders of the town and the leaders of the Eagle and Jaguar orders, resplendent in feathered and furred uniforms, mounted the thirteen steps to the lowest platform, my father in the center. I was surprised that Lord Lancer was not among the dignitaries. Relishing public attention, he always tried to stand where the sun shone brightest. Why had he absented himself today?

What happened next must have taken a long time—such things are never done quickly—but for me it was over in the drawing of a breath. Or is my recollection playing a trick, sparing me too much pain?

An orator in royal green cried the praises of Moctezuma. "His power . . . his all-knowing wisdom . . . his divine justice." The listeners next to me began shifting their feet and exchanging puzzled looks. I still did not see Lord Lancer, but as the orator invoked the Revered Speaker's name for the hundredth time, Lancer's words about Moctezuma suddenly came back to me. "A jaguar . . . The beast purrs one minute and springs the next . . ."

Suddenly wary, I paid attention to the orator. "And let all the world know that the Revered Speaker, the great Moctezuma, will now reward the utterances of his subject, the star-reader Prince Chimal. This prince has reported grave omens to the councils. Moctezuma has heard Chimal's words; he has weighed them well."

Two stalwart men stepped forward carrying a thick wreath of orchids and jasmine, a decoration for my father. I started to cheer but stopped when I realized the crowd had fallen utterly silent. As the men placed the wreath around my father's shoulders, over his head, Prince Chimal gazed upward, lifting his chin as though to read the stars even though it was bright daylight. Then I thought I saw him close his eyes —but I was far away.

Surely I was the only one present who did not suspect what was about to take place; it was a common enough event. But, reared at an outpost, I was still ignorant of Aztec subtleties. I would learn quickly.

Some signal was given. The wreath bearers jerked the strong cord concealed beneath the orchids, turning the garland into a strangler's noose. For a moment Prince Chimal did not struggle but sank to his knees, meeting death calmly. But then his hands flew to the rope, tearing at the blossoms, fighting for air, for life. No one dies with dignity in a noose. His lids sprang open, the whites of his eyes rolling madly, while his mouth worked, the lips stretched back over his teeth. I watched frozen, unbelieving.

I thought: *The jaguar has sprung.* Or else that notion came later —I suppose I thought nothing, saw nothing but the horror of my father's murder.

The stillness of the crowd was broken by Lady Iztac's scream. She fought to break from the hands that held her, struggled to reach her husband, shrieking his name. Suddenly I, too, began fighting. I hurled myself helplessly against those barring my way. Then I realized Prince

Chimal had already crossed the Narrow Passage. No more sounds came from my throat.

The executioners tied the cord in a gaudy knot; they seized their victim by the ankles and dragged him from the platform down the steps. "Oh, please, no!" I pleaded in a whisper. "The stones will hurt his head! Please!" I could not realize that he was beyond pain.

The crowd began to disperse. An execution is not like a sacrifice: there is no celebration, no honor to the victim or the watchers, nothing is lifted to the hungry sun or fed to the thirsty earth. Death by the cord is as inglorious as the wringing of a fowl's neck. Afterward the corpse is dragged away for crows and vultures to devour, for coyotes to raven. Since there can be no mourning, no rites of departure, the victim's life is ended but unfinished. I found myself standing alone, and the most terrible thing was that there was nothing to be done.

Like a sleepwalker I made my way toward my mother. Lord Lancer had appeared and his arms were around her, supporting her as he tried to lead her home. Weeping, pounding her fists against her body, she sobbed out words about shame and ruin.

"Be strong, my dear," he said. "It will all be forgotten soon."

She looked up at him, nodding mutely. She was dazed, I thought, as I knew myself to be. But Lady Iztac was not dazed when she realized I was standing at her side. For an instant she appeared not to know me, but simply stared. Then I saw her dead eyes kindle, and she uttered a hoarse sound, hurling herself upon me. Her claws raked my face, drawing blood.

I must have shielded my eyes—I was not blinded—but I had no will to thrust her away. I deserved this pain and far worse. When Lord Lancer dragged her from me, she was still clawing like a cat, hissing and spitting.

"You and I will be next, my lord!" she cried, straining against him. "You will see her evil destroy us! My husband is dead, so is your son. So is every person who was near her in Jalisco. All except me, and she will bring my death, too!"

"Not now, be still," said Lord Lancer. "Let me take you home."

"I tell you she lives only that the rest of us may be destroyed."

People began to gather to listen and stare. They whispered among themselves, peering at me, and a man made the sign against evil. I did not care. Until this day a flame of life had burned strong and fierce in me, a torch—not a candle. I was born with a hawk's will to survive.

But at that moment I could have turned to the crowd and shouted, "Kill me before I kill you!" I would have welcomed the knife thrusts.

But it was not ordained that I should be torn to pieces in the plaza that day. The people were still more curious than alarmed, and soon Lord Lancer quieted my mother, soothed her with gentle words until she leaned her head against his chest, weeping softly. Then she allowed him to lead her home.

"You are kind, my lord," she murmured. "You have always been kind to me."

Realizing that the show had ended, the spectators drifted away. After a time I felt the sun beating down upon me. The stones of the temple seemed to waver before my eyes. I could not stay there. And so I followed Lady Iztac home. There was nowhere else to go.

Sometimes in dreams or in half-dreams when I am dozing in the sun, I remember their necks but not their faces. Doña Catalina stretching her white egret's neck, thrusting it out to tempt the hands that would choke her . . . My father's lifted chin, how he raised his head so the noose could do its work quickly . . . The twisted neck of an Aztec prince—he dangled from the branch of a jungle tree. I remember the soles of his feet had been burned off and the bones showed, charred . . . The white, unwashed necks of two men—were they brothers?— hanged on the beach at Veracruz. They were the first Spaniards I watched die, and it struck me as strange that godlings' necks should be snapped as easily as my father's.

Lord Lancer and Lady Iztac were married on the first favorable day after the new moon. I was aware of the marriage but saw none of the feasts or ceremonies, for I was too ill to care what was happening. Later, when I understood, I was told that their mantles were tied at the most expensive and shocking rite ever held in Painala.

Their haste to scamper under one blanket startled the neighbors mostly because such a display of eagerness was unseemly. Of course, when a man has been executed, no official mourning is allowed; Lady Iztac had no legal reason for waiting. Even so, their rush to mate caused scandal. Long afterward I heard two women gossiping about the affair.

"The woman was so hungry everyone thought she would devour the groom like a spider," said one. "And it almost happened. They say

Lord Lancer's ears and nipples were bitten until blood ran. Who knows what else was bleeding?"

The other woman grinned. "Oh, yes, she used the wedding bath to wash away her widow's tears. It hardly speaks well for her first husband! It sounds as though there were no rains all last year!"

They clucked and cackled. This was months after the disgrace, but I still burned with shame because my mother had made herself a laughingstock.

Lady Iztac also flouted custom in a more serious way. As a widow, her obligation was to marry a brother of her dead husband. Since no legitimate brother was living, she could unite with any male of Prince Chimal's clan—and a hundred of his Culhua clansmen would have taken her gladly had they known about her widowhood. Instead, she married into a clan allied with her own, so the union had an ugly taint of incest. Pious folk shuddered, especially when she flaunted her marriage ceremony at a public banquet, practically guaranteeing that the Dark Lords of Punishment would notice. Most people, wary of a curse, shunned the rites, and Lord Lancer's attendants had to importune utter strangers to join the feast so the guest mats would not look empty.

Such immorality might have caused a riot had not the couple obtained legal permission from some bribed priests. Also, in a most unusual way, they won consent of the new governor Moctezuma had sent to the town.

Since there were no male relatives of the bride to perform the sexual duties of the Early Nights, these chores went to this new cacique. When he pronounced the marriage legal, he also pronounced himself Lady Iztac's honorary uncle and claimed the Early Nights. So much for jurisprudence. Lechery defeats law every time.

The bridal bath was scented with perfumes and aphrodisiacs costly enough to have beggared the Jade God. I, unknowingly, paid for all this. The family estates were mine alone; I owned everything down to the last mango.

But prostrated by my father's death, I did not understand what was happening. Much of the time I lay in a stupor, but often nightmares came and I felt the touch of orchids and leather against my throat, a caress that made me awake screaming. I thought I was going mad. Certainly I seemed to be dying, hardly having enough strength to rise from my rush bed mats. I fell on the floor so often that Moju took to sleeping near me. I supposed that since she was close to me, she, too, would be destroyed in some violent way. Her only hope was that I might die quickly, before her—which seemed likely.

During this time someone, I cannot remember who, told me my father had been condemned for foretelling the coming of Plumed Serpent and the creation of a new kingdom. Moctezuma, hearing this once again, had alternated between anger and despair, then ordered Prince Chimal's death. The formal charge was inciting fear in the realm. Moctezuma was never able to accept fate or resist it; he chose to kill the owl that hooted doom.

Weeks passed; the nightmares ceased, but my strength did not return. The season of Gifts of the Rain Bringer came, awakening the land to new life, and Lady Iztac also felt life stirring in her womb. I would soon have a baby brother—at least that was what the diviners who swarmed to the house proclaimed. A strong male! They clapped their hands triumphantly, then took their fees and vanished. Although too weak to care deeply, I wished a girl upon Lord Lancer. Later, I could not imagine myself willing such tragedy upon any infant relative. What would have happened to a girl child who came as such a disappointment?

In the days after the announcement of pregnancy, I heard chopping and hammering nearby but paid no attention. Then one morning four male slaves entered my room, picked me up by the four corners of my bed mats and carried me to a small house that had just been built a bow shot away. They deposited me inside, then left, telling Moju to fetch my possessions. So, by Lady Iztac's orders, I had a home of my own. I preferred its quiet and supposed that my mother felt safer, although I knew a curse could fly much farther than an arrow.

Day after day I lay half-asleep, my brain fogged by the beating of rain on the woven roof. I watched rivulets trickle down the ridgepole to drip on the beaten floor. Some days I ate what Moju brought me, more often I refused it. She did her best to amuse me, singing Maya songs and reciting cradle verses that I hardly heard.

One dream returned so often that I realized it was a vision from some god. I relived the day of my father's execution, all exactly as in life, the gleam of sunlight on gold, the fluttering green banners. But just before the strangling was to take place, a man near me in the crowd cried loudly, "Who pays for those plumes the Aztecs wear? Who buys their jade? We do! The tax gatherers have squeezed everything from us. Now they will extract our teeth and toenails!"

An old woman shouted, "Whose children feed the altars of Tenochtitlan?" She pointed a bony finger at the royal orator. "Look how sleek he is, how fat! He has eaten the livers and roasted flesh of my grandchildren!"

The crowd surged forward, every man and woman screaming a different imprecation. Blades flashed in the air; the temple steps were crimson with a cascade of Aztec blood. My father, tall as a tower, led the massacre.

Lord Lancer visited me several times, calling me his own daughter, patting my hand and trying to comfort me although there was an uneasy look in his eyes.

"This demon will leave you soon, daughter. You must be strong for your new brother's birth celebrations." He wore a huge raincoat made of leaves daubed with rubber. Its bristles filled the room, and that night I dreamed I had talked with a gigantic beetle.

For several mornings no rain came, and I knew the season was changing. Moju helped me to the door, and for an hour I sat in the sunlight, drawing in its warmth and power. That same day I began to eat with appetite and managed to walk to where laborers were chopping down the jungle growth that invades all fields during the rains.

I had not fully recovered. Sometimes in the days that followed, despondency would fall upon me like a shadow obliterating the sun. But the shadow always faded soon, and I knew I would become whole again.

My brother knocked early at the gate, entering a month before the expected day, which caused terrible fright in Lord Lancer's household. The midwife came running, already shrieking that the infant's death was not her fault, some ritual must have been neglected by others, some warning ignored. She could have saved her lamenting. My brother popped from the womb shouting for life, as fleshy as a ripe calabash.

At the naming feast Lord Lancer said, "My son will be called Chimal Six Deer." My heart leapt. "Six Deer is his name as decreed by the calendar. And Chimal because that is an old name and a brave one. I had a great-uncle called Chimal, a warrior of great valor."

So Lord Lancer, in an act of graciousness, preserved my father's name without admitting this in public. Then the cacique, letting bygones be bygones, joined in applauding the name. He then sat through the feast leering at the curtain that screened Lady Iztac. He did not quite lick his chops in recollection.

Later that day, while Moju was heating stones to make steam for my bath, she gave me an odd look and said, mostly in Maya, "What a good thing for your father's spirit. His name reappears on earth much less than a year after his departure."

At least that was what I supposed she said—some words were unfamiliar. I nodded agreement, supposing there was some Maya belief about such matters. Afterward, as I sat hunched in a cloud of steam with my hands clasping my knees, I remembered how she had stressed *"much less than a year."*

Indeed it was less. The thought Moju had implanted now sprouted, and I counted the months. If my new brother had really entered early, he was Lord Lancer's son. But if he had lingered to full term, then Chimal Six Deer must be my father's child. The haste of the wedding had been such that no one would know for sure.

"Except Lord Lancer," I murmured. Oh, yes, he was certain; I had seen the pride in his face. Yet by now the whole town must be agog, whispering and speculating and counting on fingers.

I straightened up in the bath, bumping my head against the low ceiling. Chimal Six Deer, I knew at that instant, was my father's son, my full brother. Why else would a god have prompted Lord Lancer to choose the name Chimal? My father had been Lancer's rival, not his friend. So Prince Chimal lived on in this child; he had achieved immortality. For the first time since my father's death I felt content. I let go of the ghost I had clung to.

I left the bath, smiling at Moju as she poured cool water over me. From my mother's house I heard squalling, the imperious cries of little Lord Chimal Six Deer. What lungs he had!

I would watch over my new brother, I would protect and love him. And now, at last, Lady Iztac would feel safe and happy. She had a husband she worshiped, a beautiful son to adore. With such joy in her life she would have no time to notice me.

I was, of course, innocent and unsuspecting. A few years later I would have instantly detected the thoughts now simmering in Lady Iztac's head. When I looked at her I saw only a mother smiling as she nursed her baby. I could not then look behind the smile and see the fear. After all, I was the same girl who, less than a year before, had noticed only the orchids and not the noose offered by Moctezuma's messengers. I had remained blind and trusting; I would soon learn my lesson.

The first sign of the calamity came a few days after the Season of Serenity. The rites had been faithfully kept: the women—I was still a few weeks too young—had been beaten with straw-filled bags. They wailed, pretending that pain caused their tears to water the earth. This watering would invoke the Rain Bringer, who, even in the south, is stingy at the end of the year. When he saw the women's tears, could he then be heartless enough not to add a few of his own? Well, yes, he could be and often was.

The ceremonies finished, the women turned to the parching of maize while the men hunted, fished or were pleasantly idle. New crops had been planted.

One morning I was alone in my small house secretly examining the painted Maya books I had stolen from my father's chest. Suddenly a human shadow, so massive that I should have recognized it for an omen, fell across the doorway and a voice croaked, "Long life to all inside. I seek Lord Lancer."

"A moment," I answered, scrambling to hide the books under a mat, since my touching them might be sacrilegious. Then I stepped outside. A hag, warty and rheumy-eyed but attired in rich traveling clothes, awaited me. As I greeted her, she stepped close to peer at me. Perspiration beaded her forehead although the morning was cool.

"You are, I suppose, Ce Malinalli, cherished daughter of Lady Iztac?"

I nodded, growing uneasy under her scrutiny. "I am Malina, yes."

Her bejeweled hands made a little clap of delight. "Then you, my blossom, are the lucky girl who has caused me to journey to Painala. I am Tlahua the Matchmaker. A young lord of my own town, rich and handsome, saw you when his hunting party passed through here a month ago. He swears he will wed no maiden but you. I have journeyed here—three days' hard travel—to arrange this happy matter."

Two male slaves had been lingering in the background with bundles on their naked backs and tumplines across their foreheads. At her gesture, they came forward and unpacked pretty mats for us to sit on, two small fans and a gourd of honeyed clover water. Tlahua the Matchmaker, helped by the slaves, eased herself to a sitting position, then gave a deep groan of contentment.

"I hope, my flower, that you will not think me brazen for speaking to you before consulting your mother and guardian. Will you forgive my boldness?"

I nodded, still astonished by her errand. Had the time really come for me to think of marriage? I felt bewildered.

The year of anticipation is supposed to be the most exciting time of a girl's life. That is when girls whisper together, giggling over their water jugs. They sing at their looms, mooning about the future, and crush flowers in their armpits to sweeten their smell, even though there is no one but other girls to sniff them. I had always felt scorn for those dithery brides-to-be. Could they not see the end to which their whispering and coyness led? They had only to feel their mothers' callouses to know their own futures! Now, as Tlahua the Matchmaker gave me her best conspiratorial smirk, I suddenly envied those girls their blindness. I wanted to feel those fluttering hopes, the tingles of anticipation. Yet I knew these delights were not for me—not by fate or even by nature. I could not pretend to myself.

"I am not too wicked and forward?" she asked.

"No. I want to hear you."

Actually she was not being as daring as she suggested. Marriages were, of course, arranged between families and clan councils. But the wishes of the young, if they were reasonable, were seldom ignored. Tlahua would do well to enlist me on her side from the start, and that was what she attempted now.

"I am going to be very naughty," she confided with a wink and a titter. Unrolling a scroll, Tlahua the Matchmaker revealed a portrait of a handsome youth in festival clothes. His resemblance to the Young Maize God was remarkable, so close that the artist must have used a temple statue for a model; which meant the portrait also resembled Lark Singer. I looked away quickly, disturbed.

"What charming modesty!" exclaimed Tlahua, mistaking my feelings. "So rare in young people nowadays."

As she put the scroll away, a piece of bark paper fell from her basket to the ground, seemingly by accident. I glimpsed another portrait of the same youth, naked except for jewels. His erect cock was half as long as his arm and at least as thick.

With a cry of alarm, Tlahua snatched up the lewd picture, both of us pretending I had not seen it. I felt nothing but faint amusement at this ploy of matchmaking. Could girls be so easily deluded? I supposed they could be; they were trained for it. I thought of the book I had been examining before Tlahua came—a god mounting a woman as their boat drifted on lazy water. The scene was beautiful, holy.

Tlahua quaffed a long drink from the gourd, shaking her head as though to rid herself of drowsiness. Could she be a little drunk? There was an odd confusion in her gestures and smiles.

"The heat and the journey have taken their tolls," she said, again wiping her brow.

Then she went on to extol her client, a youth named Three Water Fox Paw. She praised his wealth, his daring, his kindness. "Such a fine family! His dear mother—who loves you already, my dear—is as sweet as orchid paste." I was growing bored with this catalog of virtues when suddenly the old woman leaned toward me, put her lips almost in my ear and whispered in a lecherous tone, "He has a bottom like a mango, my flower. Like two mangoes! Ravishing! Delectable! Why even at my age, I might—"

At that moment Lord Lancer arrived, so I never learned what she might have done with the delectable bottom of Three Water Fox Paw. Roasted it for the New Year, to judge from her tone.

On such occasions girls are supposed to spend the next hours in eager hope or in dread while their elders make the first decisions. Instead I passed the time in quiet calculation. I considered the lands I owned, their produce and their management. I recalled that Lord Lancer's best cloak was frayed around the neck clasp, and long ago Lady Flint Knife had described his jewelry as "glittering with cheapness." So I weighed my situation as I awaited a summons.

It came at sunset. Lord Lancer had me brought to a bower near his house, a place where my father had often retired to smoke alone or with one or two friends who enjoyed silence and the contemplation of Plumed Serpent as Evening Star. Lord Lancer now sat in my father's place, wearing the gold medallion entwined with dolphins my father used to wear. His green robe had also belonged to Prince Chimal. For a moment I hated him, silently naming him a thief. Then I reproached my own thoughts. What did I want? That the robe be burned, the gold melted? Why should I begrudge these gifts to Lady Iztac's husband and Lark Singer's father? I had been pointlessly resentful. Yet I also knew that Lord Lancer was unworthy of the clothes he wore.

Although he greeted me fondly, Lord Lancer seemed ill at ease. He talked of trivial matters and avoided the obvious reason for our interview. I waited, hands folded and eyes cast down, feeling no suspense since I had already determined his only possible answer to the marriage proposal. Dusk was gathering, the last quarrelsome grackles flapping, then settling into their accustomed trees; around me the air grew heavy with the aromas of tobacco and sweet-by-night. At last Lord Lancer came to the point.

"I have told this marriage broker that you are still too young for wifely responsibilities. The young lord may inquire again a year from today if he is still so minded and the omens are favorable."

Of course. I had weighed the changes that my marriage would make in Lord Lancer's life. He would no longer control the estates; those rights would pass to my husband, although ownership would still be mine. Lord Lancer could not delay this loss forever, but in the meantime he would convert all he could lay hands on for his own profit.

Even now as he talked gently about my youth and the glorious freedom of girlhood—hah!—I saw him thinking about the exchange of slaves for jade, leasing out fields for precious plumes. In two years all the wealth except the land itself would be portable and tucked into his baggage. The whole story was written in his fatherly smile.

I decided to test him. "I suppose my father's clansmen will be consulted about marriage offers. Of course, I am only a girl and ignorant of such things, but would it not be courteous to inform them of—well, of my affairs?" I let my voice trail off and looked innocent.

"Certainly! I have already seen to it," he said much too quickly, then fell silent. The bowl of his pipe glowed like a red jewel in the shadows. I felt his eyes examining me carefully. "I can see why this young man is so eager." His tone became soft as the hair of new maize. "Nowadays you are nothing like that boyish girl-child I first met in Jalisco. Many men will desire such beauty as yours. But we will avoid haște. Trust me, Mali."

He edged closer to me; his garland of ucuquiro blossoms had a pungent odor. "Looking at you makes me know how eager you must be to have a husband to share your nights, dear Mali."

I was kneeling beside him, and he gently rested his hand on my thigh. "Naturally I, too, look forward to your marriage. Count on me to do well by you, daughter. A marriage must begin with the right instruction."

For an instant I thought he meant he would choose wisely for me among proposals. Then I realized he was envisioning the Early Nights. He would claim them through marriage, as my only male relative present. Lord Lancer would become my "uncle" as the cacique had become Lady Iztac's. I managed to conceal my revulsion; I did not so much as flinch, and Lord Lancer did not suspect the shudder that passed through me.

I am not ashamed of my feelings. I do not think I was unnatural or unfamilial—although I admit the fear of coitus with Lady Iztac's husband was extreme. No passion should be so dominating. My feelings were too strong to be wise or moral.

Had Lord Lancer been my real uncle or real father, as he was suddenly pretending to be, I would have felt only the normal shyness and uncertainty all brides feel. But his suggestion was sinful. For the first time I really understood what Lady Iztac meant when she curled her lip, as she often did, and hissed, "Indecent."

My thought of Lady Iztac miraculously seemed to cause her to appear in the flesh. She emerged from the darkness, speaking as she moved, her tone agitated. I wondered afterward how much she had seen and heard. Had she been lingering nearby? Did Lord Lancer's desire for me arouse her to start planning my future? I think not— but I will always wonder.

"My lord, it is the old woman, the marriage broker," Lady Iztac said. "A demon has seized her. Should I send for a priest? A pulse doctor?"

I had not realized that Tlahua was our guest that night, although she had claim to our hospitality. Using this emergency as an excuse to escape Lord Lancer, I rose quickly and offered to go on any errand to the plaza since—unnaturally—I had no fear of darkness.

Lord Lancer looked annoyed. "No, we have not yet finished our discussion, daughter. But first I will see this woman. Bring torches."

Tlahua the Matchmaker lay on a mat in the guest quarters, groaning and shuddering, teeth clenched, her face ghastly. Could this be the same woman I had spoken with this morning? Then I remembered her unquenchable thirst, her sweating forehead, and knew the demon must have been inside her even then, gulping the water she swallowed.

A swarm of fireflies had entered the room through the open doorway, drawn by the demon that possessed Tlahua, for they hovered over her, a twinkling, luminous cloud. Although she saw and heard nothing else, the fireflies alarmed her. She thrashed and flailed, striking wildly at them, and we were terrified, for they are the Children of the Night, the luminous souls of infants who die in darkness. To harm them is like harming a butterfly; only savages would risk such a crime.

"Hold her arms, tie her hands together!" Lord Lancer shouted at her two slaves who hovered in a corner exchanging frightened glances.

While they bound Tlahua's wrists, Lord Lancer studied the inflamed face and gingerly touched her brow. "I think a spotted god has slipped inside her," he said, now looking as apprehensive as the slaves. "We will know in a day or two." So we left her with the servants watching and the fireflies swarming over her, excited by the god's presence.

Two days later Lord Lancer's suspicion proved right. The matchmaker had swallowed a spotted god who soon killed her after abusing her violently. Meanwhile other spotted gods had entered her slaves and they, too, perished, as do most of those who entertain this murderous guest. The victims burn as though fire courses through their veins, the god hammers on the inside of their skulls, then, after a few days, blue spots discolor the skin. The god himself is blue-spotted and uses his own markings to brand those he has seized as slaves.

Suddenly spotted gods appeared everywhere in Painala. As the end of the year and the five Unlucky Days approached, the cacique and both his wives were felled; most of his slaves became inhabited, but half of them expelled the demons. All seven of the temple priests lay fevered and moaning and speckled—we feared not one would be left alive to perform the rites of the New Year and rekindle the fires. But one of them finally escaped the god's clutches, surviving to conduct the funerals of his brethren.

In the midst of all this death and weeping, one thing pleased me. I heard men mutter that the Aztecs were to blame, that such horror never visited the Lair of the Serpent until the Aztecs conquered the land and made it a vassal province. I overheard a feather weaver say, "It was unlucky to kill the other cacique. He was familiar with the gods—that was in his face."

I could have both wept and cheered when he spoke thus of my father.

Lady Iztac, terrified for her little son, forbade the slaves to approach the house, ordering them to sleep in the fields or forest. Their sins and impieties, she declared, might draw more demons to the house, demons looking for the cradle of her beautiful child. Moju was banished with the others, and I stayed alone, longing to make myself invisible, not sure which was more dangerous, spotted gods or Lady Iztac in panic. My worry, it turned out, was a premonition.

A few nights after the banishing of the slaves, I sat alone in my doorway trying to hold serene thoughts in imitation of my father. I focused my attention on Lady Moon, now golden and swollen with child, the joy of her motherhood casting a lovely light. Despite my efforts to shut out disquieting thoughts, I kept hearing distant funeral music from the temple, the chants and threnodies that had continued for ten days and nights on end. I heard the names of the newly dead cried twice, as the priests always do. "Seven Reed Floating Blossom . . . Aaaayyy! Seven Reed Floating Blossom . . ." Then the keening of a woman, probably the girl's mother, dreadful to hear. The night wind carried not only the wailing but even the fumes of copal burning for the departed. Death drums boomed, whistles and trumpets wailed grief.

"Lady Moon, I think only of Lady Moon," I said aloud, pressing my hands against my ears.

Suddenly I saw a figure, tall and ghostly, emerge from the nearby trees, and I drew back into the doorway as it took several uncertain steps toward me, slowly lifting thin hands. I was making a sign against evil when I recognized Moju.

"Oh, my friend," I cried, running to her, holding her so she would not fall. Her skin was burning. I saw a blue mark on her throat, two more on her shoulder. She had returned to die.

I managed to help her to my mat and gave her water, remembering the gods' thirst and hoping water might placate this one. But she could swallow little. I was bathing Moju's face when someone carrying a torch approached the doorway.

"Daughter, is it you?" Lady Iztac called, not coming too close. "I thought I saw you come from the forest. Why were you there?"

"I have not been out," I told her, going to the door. "You saw Moju. You know we are the same height. She has come back."

"Come back?" Lady Iztac took an angry step as though to enter the house, then checked herself. In the torchlight I saw caked blood on her cheek and neck; she had been piercing herself with thorns for penance and prayer. "Send her away at once!"

"No, I cannot. She is here to die."

"To die? Of the blue ones?"

"Yes. I think he will kill her tomorrow. Perhaps the next day."

Lady Iztac stood in silence, looking at me, hearing the funeral music and the crying of names. At last she spoke. "Tell me when she passes through. I will arrange a funeral. I know you are fond of her."

"My mother is kind."

She left me then, gliding in the shadows, the torch high. Her words and her voice had not been what I had expected. Instead of anger there had been an unfamiliar sadness about Lady Iztac. Was it futility? Had she yielded all hope? I could not tell, and the puzzle disturbed me as I sat beside Moju through the night waiting for the god to kill her, wishing he would do it with merciful speed. But he was slow in taking his pleasures.

That morning, with Moju barely alive, I went out to fill the water gourds. This was the last day of the year, and the funeral services had halted long enough for people to gather food to last through the Unlucky Days that began tomorrow. I had gone only a little way on the path to the well when, to my surprise, I saw Lady Iztac standing under the tree where, in more favorable seasons, she tied her loom. She was arguing with a man, a stranger, whose back was toward me. Odd, since she had driven off her own slaves and warned friends to approach no closer than two bow shots of her door. Then the man turned slightly and I recognized the jungle trader Hawk, the one-eyed man from Xacalanco.

I continued to the well, unnoticed by them, wondering what treasures Hawk was offering to lure Lady Iztac from the house. Who was guarding my brother, since not one slave remained on the premises? Strange, too, that Hawk would be going about his usual business on the last day of the year. A few minutes later, when I returned with the filled gourds, no one was at the tree. Preoccupied with Moju, I supposed they had finished their bargaining and thought no more about it.

Moju died that afternoon, slipping through the Narrow Passage so silently that I was not aware she had gone until I happened to notice the glaze of her eyes. I quickly placed a bowl of herbs and water near the mat where she lay so the house would be protected from evil, then with a heavy heart went to tell Lady Iztac.

Keeping a safe distance, I called out the news. "Shall I fetch slaves to carry her?" I asked.

"No." Lady Iztac answered from the depths of the house. "Go back and wait with her. I have made arrangements." There was a long hesitation, so long that I was turning away when she spoke again. "You must not grieve too much, daughter."

"I am not grieving." It was a lie, but there was nothing else to say.

"We do not choose our fate. We only follow where the rabbit leads us."

She sounded quite moved by this little piety. Of course, she had reasons to be upset—the spotted gods, the Unlucky Days, the wails of mourning.

I returned to watch beside Moju's body. To keep from dwelling on her goodness to me, I tried to invent and say prayers for her in the Maya language, and was surprised at how many words I knew.

I grew restless, uneasy. Why didn't the bearers come for Moju's body? Three times I went to the door to look, reproaching myself for impatience and an uneasy mind.

They finally came in the dimming twilight in the First Watch of the Night, two swarthy, thickset men I had never seen before. One of them carried a litter made of saplings and deer-hide thongs. It was undecorated; no red ribbons of the dead fluttered from the poles, no garlands. They might have come to haul away the carcass of an animal.

"Who are you?" I asked, stepping quickly outside as they neared the door. I did not like their looks, and saw now that they did not wear pectorals of the Lord of the Underworld. Lady Iztac had ordered common slaves, I thought angrily, not ministers to the dead. "What signs do you bear? You may defile the body."

"Where's the dead girl? Show us. We have no time to waste. Four more corpses await us tonight."

I gestured for them to enter the house but did not follow, distrusting strangers in those dark, narrow quarters. I waited in the open, a safe distance from the door, and let the Maya prayers I had invented run through my head.

One of the men exclaimed loudly, "What's this? Breath on my hand! I feel breath!"

"She is still alive," cried the other. "This girl is alive. Quick, give her water."

"Alive?" I had been certain Moju breathed no more, but clearly I was mistaken. This happens with spotted gods; the victim seems dead as a stone, then can come back to life awake and even hungry.

"Moju!" I cried, plunging through the door into the unlighted house, eager to feel her breath on my own cheek.

Powerful hands seized my arms from behind and pinned them. When I opened my mouth to shout for help, a gag was thrust in. I kicked and struggled, tried vainly to bite, but now a rope held my wrists. A deer-hide bag was thrust over my head and shoulders, then tied tightly at my waist. I managed to kick the man who knotted it. My heel struck soft flesh and he yelped with pain. Then I was knocked to the floor, bound with more cords until I lay helpless as a trussed turkey and almost smothered. They rolled me onto the litter and lashed me to it.

I ceased struggling, lay too stunned to think, terrified that the stench of the deer hide would sicken me and I would choke to death behind the leather gag. A heavy blow struck my ribs, knocking the breath from me—the man I had kicked was taking his revenge. After that I heard a sound of something being dragged away, then only silence.

I felt sure my assailants had gone, taking Moju's body with them, and I realized dully that she had been dead all along. I had been lured into the house by a cruel, simple trick. Why had they now dragged away her body? And why had they left me behind in a place where, in time, Lord Lancer or Lady Iztac would surely find me?

But when? Panic seized me, fear of death by thirst or hunger or suffocation.

When a little time had passed, I grew calmer. I tried to assure myself that I lived by wiggling my fingers, but my pinioned hands had gone numb and would not obey. So I twisted my head, then tried to chew through the leather gag until I was exhausted and gasping for air.

Then, from Lord Lancer's house, I heard the solemn booming of a drum. With it, muffled but unmistakable, came Lady Iztac's strong, clear voice raised in the formal lament. "My child, my child! My treasure has been taken from me! Let the gods share my sorrow!"

Her child was dead? I tried to force my numb brain to understand. My brother must have died suddenly this afternoon, taken by a spotted god. Or the men who had seized and bound me might have entered the house and killed him in his cradle. It must be that! I tried to scream, but the gag choked me.

Lady Iztac cried out again, once more the death song for a lost child, but a different verse. "She is gone, gone! My blossom, my flowering branch withered by death. Oh, my daughter! Ce Malinalli, Ce Malinalli!"

Not my brother's name but mine. Yet I was not dead! My lips moved, trying to form words, to shout a denial. Why was she mourning me, telling the world that a spotted god had taken her daughter?

There was an unbearable hammering inside my head. I gave up trying to understand, struggled no more against the thongs that cut my ankles and wrists, closing my eyes, hoping the pain would leave me. I waited for the relief of death.

At some hour in the Watches of the Night, I suppose in the utter darkness after Lady Moon had fled, the litter to which I was bound was lifted and carried from the house into the forest. I learned in that short journey what it is to be a corpse, to lie absolutely powerless, trussed as in funeral bindings, blind in darkness like the grave. If it had not been for my hearing, surely I would have died of terror. In those hours I lived on sounds.

The men carried me roughly, letting the litter tilt and sway, and they were so silent they might have been Earth Monsters or Mud Men. But as we moved through the night, monkeys chattered and screamed, so I knew we were on a forest path, yet not far from town because I heard the funeral drums and horns sounding from the temple.

Suddenly my feet tilted upward, my head sank. We were ascending steps, several very steep steps. Then the bearers put down the litter and I felt cold dampness of stone under the ropes and matting. A tomb, I thought. Now they will leave the grave goods, the jar of corn kernels and a piece of jade, then seal me up forever.

Instead they simply left me, deciding that the corpse could wait awhile, I suppose, since it could not run away.

I was still close enough to the great temple to hear the funeral rites, faint and at a distance. I recognized the name of a neighbor being mourned; later came the obsequies for a small girl I knew, a niece of the dead cacique. I felt no surprise soon afterward at the crying of my own name. I heard afar the passing song of the priest for Ce Malinalli,

child of Lady Iztac, taken by a spotted god. In my mind I joined the
song, a prayer that my crossing would be easy and that the dead branch
I carried would burst to blossom in the Green Heaven. Let that girl
be dead, I thought. She was an unlucky creature, best to be rid of her.
Then I drifted into a half-sleep and knew no more.

My prison that night and the next day, I later realized, was a temple
just past the edge of the town, the House of Men, a small sanctuary
for purification where men came during certain festivals. Bride grooms
spent the Early Nights here. My female presence in the sanctuary was
an abomination, but I had been brought here by men who must be
godless. The Dark Lords' curse would strike them, not me.

Godless, yet none the less superstitious. Even they would not risk
travel on the First Unlucky Day, and that was why I lay stored like
a carcass in a place no one would dream of visiting until the New Year
had safely begun.

Sometime the next morning I faintly heard footsteps approach,
then hands fumbled with the cords holding the hateful bag. When it
was pulled off, I lay dazzled, blinded by the light in the dim temple.
At last I realized I was gazing into the face of one of the men who
had seized me the night before. His nose was flat and broad, his lips
thick as an Olmec statue's. Also, in the Olmec way, his head must have
been bound with sticks in infancy, for his skull was elongated, almost
gourd-shaped.

"Can you understand me?" he asked in a harsh accent. I nodded.
"I am going to take the gag out and give you water. But listen
carefully. You see this knife?" He held an evil-looking dagger of
quartz. "I will have this touching your throat, little turkey. Your first
gobble will be your last. Make no sound or . . . kkkkk!" He made a
noise of slashing, then pulled away the gag and I gulped great swallows
of air before drinking the water he held for me.

Even if the blade had not been poised to slit my throat, I could
not have shouted or even spoken. My voice had left me and would
not return for days. The water I managed to take, but my throat would
not open for the bits of food he offered. When I spat them out, he
shook his head at the waste, picked them up and ate them with quiet
enjoyment, chewing slowly with his few teeth.

My lips formed a question. "Who are you?"
He placed a thick finger across his mouth to show he would not

answer. Then, treating me as cautiously as a netted jaguar, he unbound one of my legs, gestured for me to move it for exercise. Blood poured into it with a thousand needles. Each limb was given the same treatment, then tied down again. Last of all he replaced the gag. I made no resistance, had no strength.

I supposed he would leave then, but he had other interests. When I had been seized, I wore only a thin cotton tunic that had been so ripped that now I was almost naked. I had not thought of this; I had worries more serious than modesty. But now, as he squatted beside me, his eyes studying my body, my nakedness frightened me. Like the cords and gag, it was part of my helplessness, my humiliation. He saw me press my thighs together, try to draw back my breasts, and shook his head.

"Ah, no, you are not made for a poor man like me. Not I but some rich lord will pierce the drumhead and enter heaven." He sighed at fate. "But I will take what I can while I have a chance."

Bending over me, he slowly and almost sadly bit first one of my nipples, then the other. I felt his gums and shuddered. For a long time he sat silently staring at me, fascinated yet showing no pleasure. A fly landed on my hip, crawled over my naked thigh toward the mound of my front portal. I moved as much as I could trying to shake it off, but I could no more resist the fly than the man. He watched the creature's progress, intent and unsmiling, then murmured softly, "He knows where the honey is."

Then, taking off my sandals and starting with the bottoms of my feet, with relentless slowness he moved his lips and tongue over my body, leaving not a pore untouched. He worked carefully but without the least sign of passion, gumming and licking while revulsion made my stomach writhe.

One night, years later, I was sleeping in the jungle and awoke in horror to find a tarantula crawling over my breast, the ten hairy legs as soft as feathers. Afterward, when I was safe but still shuddering, I remembered the soft probings of that Olmec mouth in the House of Men. It was the same feeling.

I will kill this man, I thought. *His torments will be as slow as mine now.*

When, after an eternity, he finished his joyless labor, he carefully replaced my sandals, covered me with a length of thin cloth and left. Long after he had gone I still felt his wet mouth on my throat, his tongue licking my eyelids. Slowly I came to realize what it meant to be a slave. This violation was the first, but not the last. Other experiences would no doubt be more painful, although I could not imagine any more repulsive.

I could not yet think clearly, could not even see what was so obvious—that Lady Iztac had connived with the trader Hawk to arrange my abduction and that Moju's corpse, wrapped in red ceremonial garments, had been passed off as mine. I did not realize I was dead, mourned in Painala.

But I knew from the first that slavery of some kind lay ahead. To survive I must learn submission, no matter how unnatural and degrading it seemed. I thought of Hawk as my first master; his face with its glossy eye patch loomed in my mind. If he had power over me, I would make myself yield without being broken. I would submit until the day came when I could cut his throat.

Part Three
THE GODS

9

The City of Mexico—The Feast of Ascension—May 2, 1564 A.D.

I have hired a spy, an Aztec hag as old as I am who empties and scrubs piss pots in the viceroy's palace. No one suspects she understands Spanish, so she overhears secrets. Three days ago we met at a place on a canal where women gather to gossip and wash clothes. Being toothless, she spits when she talks, and in five minutes my left ear was waterlogged.

"Servants and followers of the Avila brothers have confessed under torture," she confided. "They planned to rebel and set up a new kingdom. Martin Cortes, the Marques del Valle, would be our king."

She heard me sigh and added querulously, "Why not? He is the son of Plumed Serpent."

"What about the other son of Plumed Serpent?" I asked with pretended casualness. She does not suspect who I am, does not know my particular interest.

"The bastard has told nothing. They say he would have been a great noble, a duke perhaps, if the rebellion had succeeded. Besides the king, a council would rule the new kingdom. Sons and grandsons of the Spaniards who came with Plumed Serpent. Also descendants of the old rulers, Aztec princes."

Yes, I thought grimly. They would be allowed to carry messages and pour the wine. I have no illusions about the Avila brothers and their likes sharing power. After all, I knew their fathers, men hardly willing to share a turkey at a feast.

The hag and I met again yesterday at a different place. Her report, although irrelevant, was pleasant. The viceroy's hemorrhoids, which he pretends are saddle sores, have turned acute. His physician has ordered applications of ice brought daily from the volcanoes. When the freezing compresses are held to the viceregal anus, His Excellency howls like a coyote. The bloodstone I cursed and hid behind the altar is already working.

But what is happening in the dungeons where prisoners are howling louder than the viceroy? Has Tepi been put to the question, as they say? I imagine my son with a rope being slowly twisted tighter around his arm or leg or—God forbid—his skull. The rope is such a simple yet excruciating way of questioning. There is no need for racks or white-hot pincers. A rope and stick will do nicely.

It is useless to picture these scenes, and when I am awake I can banish them. Asleep I am helpless. Last night my lord the Captain came to me; he stood beside my bed. I kneeled, not in my chamber but among the ruins of Tenochtitlan, holding Tepi, newly born, in my arms. I lifted him up.

"Your son, Lord. Whole and perfect."

But he frowned. "Will you protect him when I am gone?"

I awoke trembling, filled with the panic of the helpless old. "What can I do?" No answer came in the darkness, neither my lord nor any other god spoke, and I almost wept, cursing myself for my weakness.

They recently made a pretty park on the site of an old Aztec market; it will be inviting when the saplings become shade trees. This morning I went there to watch an auto-da-fé staged by the Holy Office. The Inquisitors burned nine persons at the stake, one alive and eight others freshly killed by the iron collar. Sixty more convicts were lashed, clubbed and dragged at the tails of horses.

I found the show unimpressive. In my girlhood almost any town could have presented a more spectacular pageant. Such displays were called public sacrifice, and we have learned that they were very wicked. Today we watched a public purification, very holy. To the victims, of course, there was no difference at all, and I found the changes mostly in the size of the cast and the costuming. But I am no theologian.

I would not have attended today except I feared that Tepi and

even Lord Martin might unexpectedly be paraded out dressed in black
sanbenitos and consigned to the flames, since treason against the king
is also a crime against God. I was alarmed that the Inquisitors, to
prevent protest, might burn the two men anonymously. Who can
recognize a convict in those all-enveloping shrouds of St. Benedict
they call sanbenitos? I had to see with my own eyes.

Yesterday I haggled with a vulgar Spaniard who rents balconies
and roof space fronting the cremation corner of the park. "This bal-
cony is perfect," he assured me. "So close you can almost spit in the
flames, yet the wind carries smoke in the other direction. Close to the
judging scaffold, too."

Because of my nun's habit he added, "You are entitled to the
religious discount, Reverend Mother. Half-price and nothing extra for
chair cushions."

Then he tried to soak me double. I threatened him.

Lady Maria Monica, mother superior of the convent where I stay,
was delighted to accept my invitation for a choice seat.

"I will provide lunch," she said. "Roast pigeons and a cruse of
wine my brother the bishop sent from Cádiz." She cannot utter a dozen
words without mentioning that her brother is a bishop.

Her little pink nose quivered with anticipation. "What a day
we'll have! But remember, Señora Xamarillo, you must join us at early
mass." She has special plans for Ascension Day services in the convent's
public church. Some sort of show.

I lay awake most of the night, again tormented by what might
be taking place in the prisons the Holy Office has borrowed to house
its hapless guests. Were Lord Martin and Tepi even now being measured for tomorrow's death garments? I doubted it, and yet . . .

At last I slept, but my eyes had hardly closed when the convent
was aroused by a crash of falling masonry. An earthquake, I thought,
leaping toward the door. But in the corridor I heard Lady Maria
Monica screaming at the top of her lungs, not in fear but in rage. No
earthquake after all. The shouts echoed in the stone stairwell.

"Oh, you Indian devils," she cried. "Fiends, heretics!"

Then her voice, which was coming from the public church,
subsided into a long, unbroken wail. A servant who had reached the
church entrance before me turned and said, "A bit of the roof has
fallen. It is not serious."

I returned to bed, and soon wished the whole ceiling might

collapse on Mother Superior just to silence her complaints.

At early mass I learned what had happened. The church had been built without the usual windowed cupola above the altar. Today being Ascension Day, Lady Maria Monica wished to follow the custom of having a statue of Christ hoisted on a rope and pulled out through the roof.

Since there was no high window, she ordered a small hole to be cut, but the workmen are Aztec masons, builders who do not really understand Spanish engineering and what makes arches stay up. So part of the dome collapsed. A small price for seeing God whisked up to heaven.

The statue stood on a special pedestal in front of the altar, and the rope that would effect the miracle was dyed magenta to match the hangings behind it. Since Lady Maria Monica had spread word that Jesus would fly today, the church was packed with all sorts of people —Tlaxcalan nobles wearing secondhand Spanish hats, Mixtec women reeking of perfume and Otomi men just reeking. All of them were avid to witness a miracle before they adjourned to the park for the In-quisitorial carnival.

The human odors, the chanting and the flickering of candles dulled my senses, put me into a daze that was not quite sleep. I was aware that an old man across the aisle in the male section was mum-bling prayers in the old tongue, an invocation of the Lord of the Underworld, Mictlantecuhtli, god of death. Perhaps it was hearing those words that caused my mind to trick me. I cannot say. I only know what happened.

As my eyelids grew heavier, I seemed not to be in the church but in another dim, shadowy place. The walls, if there were walls, wav-ered, changed shape and at last became leaves intertwined with vines and branches.

A man lurked in the shadows, a vague figure that caught and held my attention although I could not discern his face. Was he Spanish? He seemed darker than a Spaniard, yet lighter than an Aztec. Somehow I knew his expression without seeing it, a look of resignation and calm. Yet his eyes burned into me, pronouncing judgment. I could not look away; he held me as a serpent holds a rabbit, by sheer power of its will.

Suddenly the man was snatched into the air, jerked by an invisible force. Then I saw a rope around his neck, a blood-covered rope, and I knew his long hair concealed the hangman's knot. Ghosts hovered near, moaning in my ears. I watched the body writhe and kick as he strangled.

He rose slowly inch by inch, and when his head reached the leaves, he joined other hanged men also dangling from the branches of the great tree, a ceiba, that stood alone in a jungle clearing, a tree adorned with corpses.

I knew the man who twisted at the rope's end. Rising, I screamed his name, screamed as though my voice could somehow call him back to life.

"*Cuauhtemoc, Cuauhtemoc! Lord Falling Eagle!*"

Two of the nuns, seeing my panic, led me quietly from the church. One of them patted my hand. "Your piety does you credit, dear lady. But you have led a sheltered life and are too innocent to watch this wonder."

He was the last ruler of the Aztecs, final successor to the divine Moctezuma, heir to humiliation and slaughter. *Falling Eagle.* The eagle is the Sun whose descent brings night, so his name fulfilled a prophecy just as my own did. We were both doomed at birth but in different ways.

He embodied all that was best in my mother's race, tolerating no weakness in himself or in others. When his city faced unbreakable siege, Falling Eagle defended it with such valor that he prolonged everyone's suffering long after hope was dead. In the end his fortitude was suicidal, his pride a love of self-torture. What else? He was an Aztec.

After the city fell, he and other nobles were questioned with fire about the hiding place of the Aztec treasure, that huge store of gold that had vanished. As flames roasted their feet, the Lord of Tacuba, chained next to Falling Eagle, groaned in agony. Falling Eagle reproached him quietly. "Do you think I am standing in a bed of flowers?"

I waited nearby, ordered to translate if one of the lords broke and revealed the secret. But no Aztec spoke. The Spaniards were fools to have kept Falling Eagle near the rest. What Aztec could yield in his presence? He taught them to scorn the fire.

I watched sweat run down his face, a plain face in no way handsome or heroic, yet his silent endurance, his more than human courage caused my mother's blood to speak to me, to accuse me of taking part in sacrilege. Falling Eagle was still Revered Speaker, chosen of the gods. To touch him, even to gaze upon him, was sinful. What I now saw filled me with revulsion and fear. I turned away, sick and ashamed, thankful that my lord the Captain had not approved of this torment and had refused to watch it.

I saw flint in Falling Eagle's eyes, I read his thoughts; he would never speak. As soon as I could leave, I hurried to my lord's headquarters, entering his private chamber unannounced. He lay on a bed of woven rushes, not sleeping but staring at the ceiling.

"Since you are here, the questioning must be over," he said.

"Yes, my lord. They are bandaging the nobles' feet."

"What did they learn?"

"Only that Aztecs can endure fire."

"Of course. I told them it was useless. You cannot mistreat princes even if they are captives! We are Spaniards, not Moors; we revere noble blood." He sighed and his head fell back on the pillow. "No one would listen to me."

Yesterday he had been jubilant, brimming with life as he always was after a victory. Now all joy had left him; he looked desolate.

"I could not stop them. I cannot always stand against all of them. I am tired of distracting them from their greed. So let them wallow like swine if that is their nature."

The men who overruled him, who demanded the torture of Falling Eagle, they owed him their very lives. Yet they would not listen to him or obey. Ingrates! He should have called on the Tlaxcalan swordsmen to enforce his will. My lord had only to lift his hand and ten thousand of them would have fallen on any Spaniard who opposed him. With a single word my lord the Captain could have—

But he did not.

Suddenly a doubt came to me, and I gazed at my lord's unreadable features. His face, always gaunt, was even more drawn after the long struggle for the city. He was exhausted; no wonder he could not resist the clamor of the gold hunters.

Yet this told me nothing; I felt unsure. When he opposed the torture, when he described it as a sin against a king, had he really known that he must finally yield and allow it? Had he, whatever his words, actually *wanted* it—or at least wanted its possible results? Could I ever know his true intentions?

We do not always know our own deepest wishes, and certainly

we cannot trust our fellow human beings. How much less then should we trust gods and men who resemble them. Knowing that a god is unfathomable, I put away my curiosity.

But I forced myself to say what had to be said. "My lord, tonight you must kill Prince Falling Eagle. While he lives you—and all Spaniards—are in danger."

The words were out. I had suggested the unthinkable and was now even guiltier than the torturers. I almost expected a serpent to slither into the room and strike me dead.

He smiled gently, almost sadly, then shook his head. "I could not stop the torture. But as for his life, I have granted him clemency."

Clemency! That senseless word men use when they wish to feel virtuous while shirking their duty. In the old tongue we had no such word because the idea of setting aside laws or consequences is not only foolish, it is immoral.

I spoke respectfully and avoided his eyes. "My lord, I know that what I am urging is blasphemous. I understand that you are disgusted and repelled. But I truly believe Falling Eagle must die. I beg you for your own safety."

He shook his head again. "No. Never."

That was the end of the matter for more than three years.

In October, 1524, Hernan Cortes, newly appointed Captain General and Governor of New Spain, led a punitive expedition against the traitor Cristobal de Olid, who had rebelled against Cortes in Honduras, a land at the far edge of the world. No army, and indeed hardly even merchants, had attempted this terrible journey overland. We forded or bridged a hundred rivers, hacked out paths in jungles so fever ridden and so infested with monsters that men healthy one day would drop dead in their own tracks the next. We scaled mountains where every rock was an obsidian blade sharp as a Spanish razor. Afterward, learned men of Europe said this was the most incredible march in the history of armies. They said only madmen or fools would have attempted it. Yes. Exactly so.

Why this deadly struggle through the swamps of nowhere? We did it, although no one suspected the truth, because my lord the Captain had gone mad.

His madness came and went like the chills and burnings of malaria. I learned to recognize it by small signs—the lifting of an eyelid, the set of his lips, a tenseness in his fingers. Others seemed not to notice the changes—or perhaps they took madness in a god simply as part of his essential nature.

A seizure came upon him after the start of the Christian new year when the army was resting at Xical, jungle city of the Third Sun. He was sleeping nights in the main temple, a practice he followed whenever he arrived in an unfamiliar town. Some of the Spaniards whispered that this was clever of him, a shrewd tactic. I thought it merely appropriate that he should occupy the sanctuary. Now I think all of us were right: the godhood in him demanded the temple at the same time that his human shrewdness suggested it.

One night I was sleeping beside the man to whom he had recently given me in marriage, when a soldier awakened me. "The Captain says come at once!"

The temple was lighted by a single torch, and two candles flickered near a crude, hastily made cross of wood set on the altar that, until a few days ago, had been sacred to Smoking Mirror. Despite scrubbing and scraping, the chamber still stank of dried blood of sacrifice, fetid in the hot, damp night.

Although he stood in shadow, I saw instantly that his madness was upon him. There was a certain tilt to his head, a stiffness of his shoulders.

Near the altar stood Lord Coztemexi, one of several deposed Aztec princes we had brought along because we dared not leave them behind where they might raise rebellion. He held a painted cloth, an illustrated indictment accusing four of his fellow princes of plotting the murder of the Captain and the Spanish officers.

"They speak treason, Malintzin," he told Cortes. "Lord Falling Eagle is their leader."

At another time my lord would have whispered to me, "What else would they be talking of? Has any defeated ruler ever done anything else? Should I be outraged by what is merely natural? Is a jaguar immoral if it claws me?" And he would have chuckled—while he took subtle precautions.

But tonight he said in a strange voice, "Seize them all and bring them to me one by one for questioning."

I knew then that Falling Eagle would die before night went and came again.

What does it matter if he was innocent or guilty—who knows

or cares? He died because a god had gone mad and demanded sacrifice.
I only know I grieved and pierced my own flesh that night for both
the god and the victim.

At dawn the sky is green at Xacalanco because waters on both
sides of the town turn green in the First Watch of the Day. I stood
in that ghostly dawn beside a priest who would hear the last confessions
of the condemned men. Falling Eagle was brought to us and forced
to kneel. I gazed down at him—the last emperor of the Aztecs, the
Chosen of God—kneeling now at my feet. I should have savored
triumph. But this degradation was obscene and sinful.

Falling Eagle spoke in a whisper, but instead of a Christian
confession, he prayed to the Keeper of the Narrow Passage. I said to
the priest, "This true believer hates his sins and hopes to be saved by
Our Lord." The priest made the sign of the cross, almost moved to
tears by Falling Eagle's piety in the face of death.

Then three soldiers held Falling Eagle so his neck was stretched
over a log, while another soldier chopped off his head with a battle-ax.
It took four strokes. After the head was severed, they set it in a fork
of the great ceiba tree and hauled Falling Eagle's body up by the ankles
so the headless corpse hung upside down. Every Aztec I had watched
die seemed to twist beside him.

But there was only one other victim that morning. First to go
to the ax had been the lord of Tacuba whom Falling Eagle had once
rebuked for groaning in the flames. He approached the headsman
without a murmur, pausing only to glance back at Falling Eagle. I
think he smiled. Perhaps I only hope he did.

I recovered quickly from the indisposition that had seized me in the
church, and an hour later we set out for the auto-da-fé. Mother
Superior took along a basket of delicacies, Spanish wine and the little
brown spaniel who is seldom out of her lap. Our party traveled in four
sedan chairs decorated with Ascension Day banners, and musicians led
the way singing hymns and ballads.

"Such an outing!" said Mother Superior. "How can I thank
you?"

But, as I have said, the proceedings were of small interest. As
usual, those convicted were lashed through the streets wearing sanbenitos with hoods covering their faces except for eyeholes. The hoods
tapered upward like tall, pointed hats; they resembled hats the Maya

used to put on persons to be sacrificed. Watching, I recalled religious rites I had seen long ago in Tabasco.

Petty heretics, those sentenced only to a few years in prison or servitude, came first, garbed in very pretty yellow. "Look, a dwarf!" cried one of the ladies in our party. The mob was jeering and beating a small, struggling figure. A blow with a stave knocked the victim's hood to one side and we saw it was not a dwarf but a golden-haired boy of eleven or twelve.

Those clubbing him drew back, astonished, and Mother Superior exclaimed, "Oh, he is lovely! Who *is* this child heretic?"

Then the prisoners were scourged off to dungeons or whipping posts or pillories, and the great sinners, those condemned to death, limped through the park in heavy chains. They wore black decorated with red imps and tongues of flame. The mob in the streets and the spectators gathered near the crematory stakes cheered the show wildly. Although the affair was crude, I admit it was dramatic.

I felt enormous relief when I saw that none of the seven black-clad convicts was tall enough to be Tepi or Lord Martin, although it is hard to be sure of a man's height under those hoods, especially if he has recently come from the rack.

Six of the seven had wisely confessed heresy, so they were mercifully strangled by the garrote before being burned. But the seventh heretic remained recalcitrant, and since he abjured confession would be burned alive. Pious folk in the crowd were horrified that he would die unrepentant, damned to hell, and they pushed past the guards to throw themselves on their knees, imploring the condemned man to admit his wickedness. Since he did not deign to answer, I could not hear his voice. But his haughty bearing gave him a disconcerting resemblance to Lord Martin Cortes.

Mother Superior claimed to know the convict's identity. "A notorious Lutheran and Jew from Hispaniola," she announced. Still, I waited impatiently for him to cry out, as he must do, after the flames were kindled. I knew I would recognize Lord Martin's voice even muffled by a hood.

The fire was lighted, flames began to scorch his feet and he struggled against his fetters to perform the grotesque dance victims do at that moment, a little jig that always amuses the crowd. He danced, he writhed as they all writhe, yet not a whimper escaped him. I thought

again of Falling Eagle and clutched my hands together so tightly that
my rosary cut the skin.

When the flames of all seven pyres spiraled upward, hysteria and
waves of exultation swept the crowd, just as in the old days when
invisible gods passed among celebrants at public sacrifices, inciting
frenzy. People wept and cheered and prayed and applauded, just as they
used to do. Mother Superior, quite unaware she was bleating like a
sheep, uttered, "Baa . . . baa . . ." her eyes round and watery. Fathers
hoisted their children high to see the spectacle. Somewhere nearby a
woman kept screaming. The wife of the man at the stake? His mother?

Words spoken long ago came back to me, words whispered in
the night. "We will build a new world on these ruins. Everything will
be changed, will be better." How often since our creation by the gods
has that been said? I stared again at the scene in the park. Its most
repellent aspect was its familiarity.

Meanwhile Mother Superior's little spaniel had become distraught, yelping and howling and trying to slip his jeweled collar.

"It is the wickedness of this heretic," the lady exclaimed, smoth-
ering the excited animal against her bosom. "My darling knows the
devil is near, he smells brimstone! See how his little nose quivers."

I nodded, suspecting the dog was aroused by the aroma of so
much roasting flesh. The air hung rich with it. Spanish ladies pressed
perfumed lace to their noses while elderly Aztec women sniffed
thoughtfully, recalling childhood holidays.

Suddenly the flames at the nearest burning stake surged, fanned
by a breeze. The living victim's cloth hood was consumed, and I saw
his face, his blazing hair, and I felt relieved that he was not Lord Martin
or anyone else I knew. I discovered my admiration for his silent
endurance had been misplaced. His lips had been sewn together, and
I suppose rags were stuffed in his mouth. Do they do this often to
prevent last-minute blasphemies from the stake?

At that moment the spaniel snapped Mother Superior's hand,
causing her to burst into tears from pain and affront, so we left, and
I was spared the rest of the entertainment. Mother Superior sniveled
all the way back to the convent, alternately reproaching and cuddling
the dog.

Upon arriving home, the lady was consoled to find a letter from
the Holy Office; the convent had been awarded the services of a

repentant child heretic. He was to serve three years, "emptying slops, scrubbing privies, and performing such tasks as become a penitent whose soul remains in grave danger."

"It must be the golden-haired boy!" Mother Superior clapped her hands in delight. "Where is he?"

The nun who served as doorkeeper, knowing the lad was a heretic, had stuffed him into a cupboard, locked it and hung a rosary on the door to keep any devils inside.

The child proved to be the boy we had seen earlier. He is called Juanito, is eleven years old and has spent the last two years in the dungeons of the Holy Office, which explains his pallor. Juanito, a cabin boy, was captured with a ship full of English pirates in the Bay of Veracruz. Being English, he was reared in abomination since England is Satan's Kingdom on Earth. He has the face of a starveling, which impresses Mother Superior as spiritual. With luck, he will replace the loathsome spaniel in her affections.

Mother Superior, her earlier distress forgotten, summoned musicians onto the patio and invited all the elderly gentlewomen to enjoy the music and take refreshments while they inspected the English curiosity.

I withdrew to my chamber to rest, but it did me little good, for the singers were just below my window, and I had no more than dozed off when they burst into that same annoying ballad, "Lady Malinche." There is no escape. Someone will sing it at my funeral, for surely it will follow me to my grave. No, worse, it will outlive me.

> *"What is her secret? Lady Malinche!*
> *What story hides behind her eyes? Lady Malinche!"*

What secret indeed? Let them guess.

10

Tabasco

All the world knows the story of my life from the time I was seized by the Xacalancan traders until the day I emerged as the voice of a god. Ask any market woman, ask any scruffy missionary and you will hear the story of those five years:

When my master, the one-eyed Hawk, saw my beauty and noble bearing, he fell on his knees and swore by all the gods that my purity should not be diminished by so much as a plucked hair while I was in his custody. He swore to take me to his home city, that I might be presented to the eldest son of its ruler, who would surely marry me, thus elevating the blood of that noble house.

While he was prowling the jungle, Hawk encountered a caravan led by a Maya lord of great fortune and position in Tabasco. When this lord saw me, beheld the perfection of my face, the beauty of my body, he knew he must carry me to Tabasco that I might become high priestess of a Temple of Love there, the only such temple in the world. (In a single, brief conversation with me, he learned I had an astounding grasp of theology.)

My master refused to sell me, even at the outrageous price of half my weight in jade, half in chocolate and enough quetzal plumes to cover my body. A battle ensued, and the Xacalancans, counting their lives well lost, fell to a man defending me.

I was borne by the victors to the Temple of Love, where I reigned as high priestess, meanwhile being taught amatory arts and all the techniques of the Flower Prince—not taught by demonstration, which would have been profane, but educated chastely through pictures, poems and songs.

When the great ships arrived with Cortes the Plumed Serpent and his godlings, I was brought forth, the world's most knowing virgin, the supreme offering for his divine return.

Everyone knows this is the true story of what happened to me. Or—

When my master, the one-eyed Hawk, saw my beauty, he fell upon me and raped me at once, if a creature as lecherous as I could be said to have been raped. Being of a generous nature, Hawk then passed me among his men, not omitting the porters and slaves. I was fucked by all and sundry, much to their satisfaction and my own.

This orgy was but a prelude to the coming years when I inhabited every whorehouse in the Maya dominions. I was a willing slave in one such establishment when the Spanish devils arrived. My master was delighted to send me to them because I had learned witchcraft and he was afraid of me. Besides, my cunt was so loosened by constant pummeling that none could enjoy me except freakish men with monstrous organs—men like Cortes. Or—

The trader Hawk recognized the value of the merchandise my mother had given him. My virginity was guarded day and night until he found a suitable buyer, a rich lord from Tabasco.

I remained in this lord's house for the next years. Naturally he used me for his pleasure and shared me with his friends in a decent way, never to excess. Meanwhile, as an expensive pet that should be improved, I was given rigorous training in speech, singing and dance— which accounts for my later accomplishments. In public this lord boasted of my beauty and lineage. Privately he complained that I was unresponsive.

Then came the Forerunners and afterward came the whole fleet of Temples on the Sea bearing the creatures who seemed to be men but might be gods. Or they seemed to be gods but might be men. Certainly they were merciless enough to be gods, so it was necessary to propitiate them. I, being beautiful and expensive yet not much valued, seemed an ideal offering.

That is the true story. Or—

None of the foregoing is true. Or—
All of the foregoing is true.

Everyone knows that Lord Moctezuma's sister died and had been buried for four days when she rose from her tomb, alive but stinking in her grave clothes, and prophesied the coming of gods who would destroy the Aztecs.

Later it became fashionable to say that the princess had never really been dead but was entombed by mistake while suffering a seizure. Perhaps so, but at the time no one questioned the story. Even people far beyond Aztec frontiers felt uneasy.

More omens were reported as the calendar turned toward the fateful year One-Reeds when, according to Aztec tradition, Plumed Serpent would return to claim his kingdom.

But ahead of him came the Forerunners.

I was living in Tabasco, town of the rivers, when they appeared off the coast. We expected them that day because a swift-messenger had arrived that morning bringing word about alien creatures resembling men who had made landings at two coastal towns where the inhabitants put up fierce resistance. The creatures took a terrible toll of lives before they vanished over the sea.

When this news was shouted from the steps of the great temple, the crowd in the plaza cried out in consternation. Soldiers ran for weapons while the slaves, men and women alike, were set to building barricades of tree trunks to fortify the town.

"Kill the invaders! Attack them on the beach!" a priest was shouting.

"No, we must bargain with them, we must parley," cried an elderly noble, trying to make himself heard above the tumult of argument.

In the midst of all the shouting and cursing and debating, no one uttered the name that now loomed like a volcano in my mind— Plumed Serpent. He was returning. It was a year ahead of time, but I had no doubt.

I was thinking this when I happened to glance at an old man standing near the edge of the crowd, a slave who had been brought from the highlands years ago. His native language was that of the Aztecs and he had been born to their traditions. He stood silently now, a look of awe and dread on his face while he fumbled with a medallion, an image of Plumed Serpent. Clearly he believed as I did.

I soon discovered that all the highland and northern people in town shared this conviction, and there were quite a few of us— merchants, slaves, concubines and half a dozen Cholulan whores who had come to straddle the jungle paths.

The Tabascans are not fully Maya, but like most of the peoples of Maya country, they revere Plumed Serpent whom they call Kukul-kan. Long ago he visited their lands. Some say he brought paradise, others that he was a bearer of war and slaughter. But the southern swamp and jungle dwellers do not really expect him to return, al-though they have heard the northern legend.

Now I watched them erecting their feeble defenses, marveling at their ignorance, and started for the beach. If a god was coming, I did not want to miss his arrival.

Others felt the same way, whether they expected gods or merely curiosities, and soon the shore was lined with watchers, most of them hiding in the mangroves, a few of us standing openly on the sand.

When they appeared, I first thought I was seeing nothing but oddly shaped clouds on the horizon. Then, with the first tingle of excitement, I thought, no, not clouds. Banners. Huge banners moved across the sea, banners that strained against the wind as they rode above something that resembled a gigantic canoe moving miraculously with-out paddles. Yet it was really no more like a canoe than a dove is like an eagle. I thought of the long wooden houses Tarascans build in the land of cloud forests.

The banners—which now did not seem to be banners at all— stood taut in the breeze, their centers billowing, seeming to catch and hold the wind itself. How fitting, I thought! How beautiful that Plumed Serpent, lord of the air, should return with the wind wrapped in cloth bundles! I felt so stirred by the wonder of it that to my astonishment I found tears running down my cheeks for the first time in years. I, who never wept. Neither did I laugh in those days, but now I laughed aloud and clapped my hands like a child. So wonderful!

Then a heavy hand tugged at my arm and a voice said, "Are you deaf? Didn't you hear the order to fall back to shelter? Move!"

It was a soldier in full paint and regalia, an officer, so I had no choice but to join the retreating throng. Around me I heard murmurs of fright, and a child began to wail. But instead of fear I felt only wonder and an eagerness for the turn in my path that I knew lay just ahead.

At that moment I glimpsed my first promise of fulfillment, bright as a torch, although I could not even dimly imagine what form the promise would take. Yet I knew my life, my world, would totally change. Had changed already.

Unlike the others, I left the beach against my will. Yet I knew a delay did not matter; I would see Plumed Serpent, it was fated. One could not flee the god any more than one could fight him, I thought as I moved past the silly wooden walls the slaves were rushing to build.

Then the outrageous happened. All the women and children of the town were rounded up like a flock of turkeys and sent upriver to supposed safety. We were so heavily guarded that there was no possible escape.

We waited—waited for news, for thunderclaps, for earthquakes. We waited for maimed men to come limping along the riverbanks. A night passed and a day. I became desperate to know what had happened, and so did the other women—although for quite different reasons.

"Our husbands have been eaten alive, devoured!" cried one poor lady. "There cannot be a single survivor to bring word."

"We are next to go," said another, weeping. "These creatures will smell us out."

Then the next day a fleet of canoes arrived manned by Tabascans. A priest famous for his loud voice cried the news.

"Rejoice! The creatures have left as they came! No blood was spilled. They saw our valor and were frightened away."

Gone? It could not be! My new world, still fragile, suddenly collapsed.

In the last few days I had awakened to life again after years of torpor. I had discovered a purpose in my life and it was somehow in the service of Plumed Serpent. Now he had vanished into the east again, as he had done ten sheaves of years ago, and I was left behind, marooned, disconsolate.

I would kill myself, I decided as I walked toward the waiting canoes. I would arrange for my own sacrifice as soon as possible. I knew exactly how to do it, for I had considered this step many times but had lacked the will or energy to complete my self-destruction.

Ironic, I thought in a wave of self-pity, to die when for the first time in years the promise of life was before me.

Then I noticed that the elderly slave, the highlander I had seen earlier who knew of Plumed Serpent, had been brought along to help pole the canoes down the shallow river. I pushed ahead, managed to sit next to him and spoke in his language. "Old Father, did you see these creatures? Are they men or gods?"

"Godlings who have taken forms rather like men, my lady," he replied with no hesitation. "Of course they are the Forerunners. In my country—and in yours, I suppose—everyone knows the prophecy. Plumed Serpent comes next year. *Ay-eh,* what a time it will be! May we both live to see and survive it, my lady."

Naturally. These had been the Forerunners. No human prince, much less a god, would arrive in a strange land without heralds. My alarm, my disappointment had been for nothing.

Now I made myself comfortable in the boat, tucking my knees up and resting my head on my arms. For the first time in almost three days I fell asleep. I was content.

In the months that followed people argued and speculated endlessly about the creatures. Beasts or demons or men? A combination of all? Two unmistakable humans had been with them, men who spoke a dialect similar to the Maya speech common in Tabasco. They seemed to be captives and they shouted over and over that the creatures were devils incarnate. Did they mean demons or merely evil men? No one was sure; it was hard to understand their accents.

One thing about the creatures was obvious: they ate gold. Of all offerings given to placate them on the beach, only gold trinkets had excited them. They almost ignored the finest featherwork and embroidery but at the sight of gold became avid and demanded more. Very strange. Gold, perhaps being distantly related to the sun, was not without value. But who could prefer gold to jade or silver, both so much harder to work with?

Then the mood of the people changed from puzzlement to irritation. Visitors from neighboring towns chided the local warriors for cowardice, for fighting battles with words and bribes. Were they not men enough to defy the creatures? This was especially galling because the people of Tabasco are notorious as voluptuaries and gluttons, bloated with riches won from trade and the rich exports of chocolate and rubber. They are reputed to spend half their time in such frivolous activities as designing flower beds. Besides, they are a mixture of races, which always makes people defensive. So in every house there was now mortification and a resolve to show the utmost ferocity if the creatures returned.

I listened, I smiled pleasantly and vacantly at those who had power over me, thinking to myself that their days were numbered, imagining them decked out in their own burial clothes.

Meanwhile, with every passing month, every change of Lady Moon, I grew surer that I was Plumed Serpent's instrument, one of his chosen. My life at last had meaning.

And then he came!

The day was Six Flower, the beginning of the year for which the Only World had held its breath—One Reeds, the ripening of the prophecy.

The temples on the water gleamed in the sun, their wings spread, a flock of great birds, herons or egrets, white plumes emblazoned with crosses of scarlet.

Again barricades were flung up around the town, again the women were whisked away, but this time I was not with them. Snatching a bundle of food and a jar of water I kept handy, I ran to a tall mangrove tree whose stilts were planted at the edge of the river. I scrambled up it and hid myself behind a curtain of leathery leaves. "Safe!" I told myself. This time I would miss nothing.

I had hardly reached my perch when a scene of wild confusion broke out below me—men racing this way and that, waving darts and arrows, brandishing wooden swords toothed with flint and obsidian. Many were still putting on war paint as they ran, smudging their cheeks and foreheads, bumping into each other, tripping over the tangled mangrove roots. Five thousand voices were yelling commands and battle cries.

From my treetop I could see the mouth of the river and a large island in the estuary. As I watched in fascination, the first boats filled with Forerunners rounded the headland. These boats were not the great birdlike temples on the water, but small craft, not even so large as Tabascan war paraguas, which hold forty men. Even at this distance I could see how closely the passengers and oarsmen resembled humans. Except one who stood tall in the second boat, as towering as a god, his hair and beard so golden that they seemed plucked from the sun.

Of course he was an eater of gold; he had to be! *Plumed Serpent,* I thought, and my heart leapt. He was more beautiful than I had imagined, and far more human-looking.

Then the boats disappeared from view, hidden by the palms fringing the riverbanks. Neither could I watch the scene that followed. I could only hear the clamor, but I knew what was happening. The Forerunners—I still thought of them as Forerunners, even though I had glimpsed the god himself among them—landed on the beach while the Tabascans formed among the palms and along the riverbanks, shouting threats and imprecations.

One Tabascan voice rose above the others. "We are not women this time! Approach and we'll hack your heads off!"

I could not hear the reply, but with every passing moment more Tabascans arrived from outlying villages, some running on foot through the jungle, more coming in canoes, every man fully armed and painted. They were beautiful—like rainbows or butterflies or garlands. I hated them and silently breathed a curse.

Yet not a blow had been struck or a spear hurled. As the heat of the day wore on, the deadlock continued, neither side willing to yield position. The Tabascans, for all their brave shouting, seemed hesitant and afraid to attack, while the Forerunners seemed undecided. I heard the words "We come in peace" shouted several times by a shrill voice and in a strange accent, Maya words yet not quite Maya tones.

At last I saw the boats again crossing the river mouth, moving toward an island there, but if Plumed Serpent was still with his retinue, he was seated now and his golden head was covered by a helmet. Most of the Forerunners wore helmets that were exactly the shape of the crown of Plumed Serpent that every child can recognize from pictures. But in pictures the crown is made of leather or ocelot fur. These were of gold or silver or something else that flashed in the sun. Not gold, I decided, or silver either. Then the boats vanished around the island, and I heard men on the beach shouting that the Forerunners had landed there and were making camp. Two war canoes sped down the river to reconnoiter.

I slept in the tree that night, secured by a heavy vine I tied around my waist. Once I was awakened by a swooping night bird, a great owl or night hawk hunting the children of monkeys, and once by the voices of Tabascans passing on the path below.

"What do the creatures call themselves?" a warrior asked.

"He said Spaniards. That was the word—or something strange like that," his companion replied.

So now I knew their names, and I repeated it—as closely as I could—several times. The servants of Plumed Serpent were called Spaniards.

At dawn I was awakened so violently that despite the vine I almost fell from my branch. Hundreds, perhaps thousands of drums were beating, hand drums, hollow log drums and the great, shuddering drums of the temple in the town. A cacophony of trumpets and shells blared war. Looking down, still dazed from sleep, I gasped to see the last of the Spanish boats passing almost under me as it moved upriver. Ahead of it were two other boats and the two smallest of the Temples-on-the-Water. All the vessels were crowded with Forerunners—Spaniards, I mean—and they bristled with swords, knives and axes.

My heart sank as I saw that their weapons had blades of metal —again, neither silver nor gold—and everyone knew that metal, though beautiful, is always too soft to stand against stone-toothed wood. As the boat moved away from the tree, I saw a black object I took to be a log drum. It was long and round and had a hole at one end as though it were hollow.

Meanwhile the din that preludes attack had reached a terrible pitch, booming, shrieking and moaning. Then suddenly Tabascan warriors leapt from hiding to wade into the river, while at the same instant the Spaniards sprang from their boats, and the battle was on. They clashed in the shallows, swords hammering on swords, shields of metal slamming into shields of leather, men screaming as they were stabbed and hacked. I saw axes flash in the dawn light while arrows and darts poured deadly rain.

Near me a Tabascan lord I recognized raised his sword to deliver a death blow to a Spaniard, but the Spaniard also swung his thinner, lighter blade and it sliced clean through the Tabascan's wooden weapon. The lord stood holding the useless handle, dumbfounded, swordless. Then the Spaniard's blade slashed again and the Tabascan lord collapsed to die in water reddened with his own blood.

The fierce lines wavered, toward the bank, toward the boats, men stumbling and splashing in the stream. Darts and even arrows bounced off the Spanish shields and armor, striking and skittering away like hail on boulders.

In my life I had seen murder many times. Twice I had stood on the edges of battles, but this was my first sight of true war, and my blood raced. I shouted, I pounded the tree trunk as I felt that I myself was standing in that line striking down my foes, thrusting toward victory, protected and exalted by the power of Plumed Serpent. My woman's arm was as strong as I had always wanted it to be. I lifted the blade, I slammed it down like a hammer, I feinted and slashed and parried. Hidden in the tree, I was invincible!

Below me again and again the wooden swords were broken, the leather shields split, the darts blunted. Still the Tabascans swarmed down the banks, wave after human wave, trying to push each other aside to be the next to die. The Spaniards, I realized, could kill them twenty to one and there would still be thousands left. Plumed Serpent's forces were doomed.

Then the miracle came—the thunder spoke. A roar such as I had never heard shattered the air, then another and another. I saw tongues of lightning flash from the mouth of what I had taken to be a drum. *Not a drum,* I thought as it roared again, *not even an object but a monster, a living demon.*

A cluster of Tabascans fell dead on the bank, dropping from some invisible cause as though frightened to death. A tree trunk split, branches crashing down. The Tabascans, awestruck and shaken, began to retreat. They fell back before the roaring demons, cautious and wary, yet they did not panic, did not flee. They intended, of course, to gather behind the wooden barricades at the edge of the town.

But from that direction suddenly there came strange, unnatural sounds, roars smaller and sharper than those of the black demons but of the same kind, as though the monsters had spawned offspring who were venting their rage.

A Tabascan priest came running down a jungle path shouting, "The invaders have seized the town! They have taken the temple!"

I realized then that other Spaniards must have landed on the northern beach. The town seemed to have fallen without a struggle while the whole Tabascan army was occupied here at the river.

When this news broke the retreat of the Tabascans became a rout. They fled through the jungle with Spaniards chasing them. The boats, bearing the black monsters, moved upriver toward the town and out of my view.

I started to untie the vine from my waist, intending to climb down and follow the battle, but then prudence overcame my curiosity.

The Tabascans had fled in every direction—I realized I could not move without risking capture and confinement with the women. And while I did not really fear Plumed Serpent and his followers, I felt very wary of the roaring monsters. Who knew their nature? They might not understand that I was chosen of the god. So I stayed where I was.

That night I heard signal drums and trumpets in the distance as more reinforcements arrived for the Tabascan army. But there was no movement on the path until very late, when Lady Moon was on the highest throne of the sky. I saw first a shadow, then a man emerging stealthily from the thicket. A Spaniard. I waited, holding my breath, wondering if he could catch my scent as a jaguar might do. And could Spaniards see in the dark like owls?

He halted where the path widened, and just as I decided he had detected me, he did an extraordinary thing. In the dim moonlight I had identified him as a Spaniard by his strange clothing. Now he began to strip those clothes off. I leaned forward, eager to discover if a Spaniard had the penis of a man, and sure enough he did. Then he lifted his face toward Lady Moon, and she showed me he was not a Spaniard at all but a Maya from the northeast with the usual high-bridged nose and almond eyes.

As he had taken off each garment, he had tossed it over the low limb of a sapling. Now he glanced at the clothing, raised his arm in a farewell salute, then ran down the path, vanishing in darkness. I remembered then that there had been two Maya men sighted among Plumed Serpent's servants. Captives, the Tabascans had said. Well, one of them was a captive no longer.

I slept then, and awoke at dawn to realize I could no longer stay on my perch if I was to see anything. Fields lay farther inland beyond the town, and sounds of action came from there.

I made my way cautiously toward the noise of drums, stiff from my hours cramped in the fork of the mangrove. I avoided all usual paths for fear of capture, so my progress was slow. When at last I reached the edge of the fields at the plain called Ceutla, the battle was already joined. Again I took to a tree, this time a low cacao palm.

The fields of Ceutla are crisscrossed by canals and drainage ditches, pocked with bogs and pools. This is difficult ground to walk on, and I marveled that the Spaniards had left the barricaded town to fight here in the open. Their arrogance was superb.

But the rest of the scene appalled me. The Tabascan army

stretched from the edge of the jungle to the far horizon. Ten thousand men? Twenty? Maybe even fifty thousand, as they themselves were now shouting. They shoved and pressed against each other to get a turn at attacking the handful of Spaniards. I noted one favorable sign: the Tabascans had assembled so quickly that many had not donned full regalia; their clothing was plain, poor. The Victory Bringer is known to punish ill-clad troops for their lack of respect to the war gods. This gave me a little hope.

The air rang with cries, then the ground shuddered at the roar of the black monsters, whose fire-breath took heavy toll, but today the warriors were not cowed by the thunder. The mass of men wavered, only to charge again.

"O, Plumed Serpent, grant a miracle!" I shouted, searching the skies for a sign. Then, as though my prayer had invoked it, the miracle occurred. From the rear of the Tabascan horde came cries of terrified men, and suddenly panic swept the field.

"Monsters!" someone screamed. "Monsters are coming! Monsters with two heads."

The Tabascans fled, floundering in the bogs, piling up in ditches, the upright trampling the bodies of the fallen. What could have put them to flight at the very moment of victory? Until I saw, I could not have imagined.

The monsters charged across the plain, half-man, half-beast, each with a human head and a demon head, all of them armed with long lances. Moving on four legs, they had no trouble overtaking the fleeing warriors. At such a sight my own courage failed me, and I behaved as I have never done before or since. Sliding down the tree trunk, I took to my heels in panic, plunging through the forest, wildly hoping that if I could cross the river, I might be safe. Yet even in my terror I suspected that the river offered no real protection, since the monsters would simply leap over it.

So I became part of the rout, and I did not stop running until I reached one of the upriver camps, where I collapsed on the ground gasping, and slowly my senses returned. Soon I could take consolation in seeing that the fiercest Tabascan fighting men, staggering in, were just as terrified as I had been.

There was no question of further resistance. Now the problem was how to placate the monsters and pacify the gods. After a quick council meeting the Tabascan lords decided that the first important step was to sacrifice the man who had urged today's attack, the man who had assured them that the Spaniards were nothing but ordinary men, weak and mortal.

When I saw the victim dragged to the altar, I stood astonished. He was the fugitive I had seen strip off Spanish clothes on the path the night before.

"But they are only men!" he was shouting. "I know, I was captured and lived among them! Not monsters—just men riding beasts!"

The mob jeered, cursing him as a liar and traitor. Men riding beasts? Preposterous! Could you ride a deer or a jaguar? The very word "ride" simply meant to be carried on another person's back.

"Men riding beasts, that's all!" He was still crying out this nonsense when the knife plunged into his breast.

Thus, on the twenty-fifth day of March, 1519, the Kingdom of Tabasco was overthrown by a god. And thirteen horses.

I had fled straight back into captivity, so I did not see the negotiations with the Spaniards the next day. But I watched the Tabascan lords set out, trembling, dressed in the gray robes of humility. Their courage in going at all was great, for they were certain they would be devoured alive by the two-headed monsters or burned to ashes by the lightning breath of the squat black demons. There were tearful farewells with their families. Like everyone else, I supposed some horrible fate awaited them; they had earned the worst from Plumed Serpent.

But a few hours later they returned to the astonished camp and announced that the lord of the Spaniards—they still would not admit he was Plumed Serpent—had promised peace and friendship. At the same time he had threatened to slay every man, woman and child in the kingdom of Tabasco.

What else? Promises and threats, choices between eternal bliss or hideous destruction. That is how gods have always expressed themselves; it is the very basis of religion.

Meanwhile people were scrambling to find suitable gifts to propitiate the Spaniards and their dangerous demons. Gold was what the invaders craved, but gold is scarce in Tabasco, where people produce and hoard things more valuable. Soldiers started a treasure hunt among the bundles people had brought from town. I was idly watching the search, having brought nothing of value with me, when an officer approached and called my name.

"You are to come with me," he said sternly.

"Where? What is it?" I supposed my long absence had at last been noticed, and as usual, some small but humiliating punishment awaited. I had never become inured to such treatment; pain I had learned to accept; pleasure was outside my experience, but my pride could still be injured.

"Come along. My orders are from the Council of Four," he announced, trying to impress everyone within earshot.

When he turned to lead the way, I moved quickly ahead so he, not I, became the follower. It is important to assert one's rank in small ways, especially in dealing with officials.

My destination was a large pen made of thorn branches where a group of young women was already confined under guard. I tensed, then decided we were in no immediate danger from priests. In Aztec dominions I would have started my death prayers, knowing we were here only for a little fattening up before we made a final meal on an obsidian blade. This could also happen in Tabasco but not, I thought, to such a large group of victims. It would be too expensive. Tabascans, born traders, are always trying to shortchange the gods.

I knew none of my fellow prisoners; they all came from the lowest ranks—slaves of commoners, second-rate concubines. It was a seedy collection, a few of them decked in threadbare finery, the rest in patched castoffs. One thing they had in common: every woman in the pen except me was cross-eyed.

To the Maya, crossed eyes are the ultimate mark of beauty, rivaled only by the glory of a sloping forehead. These improvements on nature are induced in babyhood, the forehead reshaped by tight binding, the eyes crossed by hanging a bead between them.

So it seemed to me that we had been assembled because of feminine beauty, although a high Tabascan lord would have kicked most of them off his sleeping mat with a shudder. Yet superficially they were all rather pretty.

The officer who had brought me here returned with three more women, counted us twice, then said, "Twenty, that's right. Come along, all of you."

The elders who made up the Council of Four were the agents of Chac the Rain Bringer, but their power extended far beyond presiding at baptisms and other such rites. The Rain Bringer is so important that Tabascans and Mayas believe him to be four different gods blended into one powerful force.

A structure of branches and vines had been built in the deep jungle, a shadowy place, and the women with me had gooseflesh at the sight of the Lord Chacs in full regalia. Hideous masks with noses as long and twisty as snakes covered the upper part of their faces, and their mouths below the masks were painted to resemble the jaws of earth monsters. They were so evil-looking that I, too, might have been unnerved except I knew the men behind the masks while the other women, being of low station, did not.

A dozen lord attendants, garbed as nature gods, stood nearby, their tall headdresses resembling the muzzles of ocelots and jaguars.

The Chac of the East, robed in the crimson of sunrise, was a nobleman who often called at the house where I lived, so I was rather well acquainted with him and had never liked him—he used to pinch my bottom whenever I had to pass him. Now I felt his eyes staring malevolently through the eye slits of the mask. After a long pause for dramatic effect, he rose from his throne and addressed us in a solemn tone.

"Daughters of Tabasco, daughters of the rivers, you have been chosen from all the women of this land for a great honor."

I braced myself for the worst. When an official speaks of honor, you know there is a dagger concealed in his girdle.

The Chac, after another impressive silence, resumed in a voice from the tomb. "The most precious treasures are now being collected as offerings for the creatures from the east, the lords who call themselves Spaniards. You, my lovely daughters, will be among those treasures."

"The monsters!" screamed one woman. "We are being fed to the monsters!"

Wailing broke out in the room; a soldier seized one woman by the hair as she fought to escape. Most of them wept without struggling. As women, they were born to be trade goods and had resigned themselves to their helplessness long ago. I was hardly aware of their weeping because I stood astonished, marveling at the working out of my own destiny, realizing once again that we have little choice; we follow where the rabbit leads.

Order was restored by the officers, and the Chac spoke again, sternly. "Foolish women! You are not being fed to monsters but given to creatures who are men in one way or another even if they do not quite look it. They are powerful warriors, cunning and skillful. I admit they are repulsive to look at and worse to smell, but they are delighted to receive you and have even offered to take all of you in marriage—although I do not know what marriage means among them. Count your good fortune! Tonight you will be bathed and perfumed and prepared for tomorrow. Go in joy and do your duties well!"

The Chac paused, but his mask continued glaring at us. When he raised a jeweled hand, I supposed it was to give a blessing. Instead he pointed straight at me and spoke my name.

"Why are you smiling? You are a foreigner, a captive, yet you've been well treated here. Now you openly rejoice to leave your lawful lord, your adopted country. You are an ingrate!"

I lowered my eyes, trying to appear submissive. It was a mask I wore often but badly. "I rejoice in my lord's wishes," I answered. "He must have agreed I be sent away or I would not be here."

I could tell by the clenching of his hand that my answer irritated him. "Yes, your lord and protector agreed. He is well rid of you, woman! Your beauty is an unkept promise. You are cold and unloving, unnatural in your lack of normal passion. An instinct—the most important quality in a woman—is lacking in you. You might better suffer blindness or deafness. They would be less shameful."

The reproof, spoken in the presence of inferiors, stung because it was true. No man had ever awakened a spark of passion in me; neither had any woman, although my lord had arranged such experiments. I felt guilty, incomplete. Even punishments, a few of them severe, had failed to make me an adequate pretender of lust; my pain and revulsion still showed. I was not even an actress, much less a lover.

"I know these things because we of the council can look into your heart and see your secrets," he said, leering behind the mask.

I longed to retort, "You know because you are my lord's uncle. He confides in you, he complains of me." But I held my tongue. Let him impress the other women with his powers of discernment.

Leaning forward, he pointed at me again, a gesture consigning me to damnation. "We also know your history and your horoscope. Disaster is your companion. We were foolish to harbor you. No wonder you smile now when misery strikes here!"

Was I smiling, thinking of my departure? I must have been. I made my face grave.

"Go now, Ce Malinalli. Go and take your love of evil with you!"

I bowed and turned away, hardly daring to believe that I had heard these familiar, damning words for the last time. What did horoscopes mean to Plumed Serpent? He could shift them with the flick of his tongue!

As we were herded from the chamber, a whimpering girl beside me said in a low tone, "Will you protect me, my lady? Even demons will treasure anyone as beautiful as you. You must not tremble!"

Tremble? Then I realized that my hands were indeed quivering, not from fear but from excitement, as each step I took carried me toward another world.

That afternoon we were bathed, perfumed, combed, plucked and painted. Every woman was given new clothes that were beautiful, and cheap jewelry that I scorned to wear. I made my opinion known and soon a slave came from the council and presented me with a jade pendant and a bracelet so lovely that it confirmed what I already suspected.

The council, in sending the other women, was offering shoddy tribute goods and hoped Plumed Serpent would be satisfied if I was included to sweeten the gift for the god himself. I was the slice of venison tossed into a pot of beans to make the dish company fare. Well, good enough. At least I would have no rivals for the eye of Plumed Serpent—whose name I had already learned from one of the lords who had gone to the Spanish camp to negotiate. In Spanish the word for Plumed Serpent was "Cortes."

The next morning four war canoes decked out as flower boats awaited us, and we were lifted in by slaves, so water would not fade the blossoms painted on our feet. Forty warriors, two for each woman, accompanied us, all of them gorgeously clad in wedding clothes and, like the women, so embellished with plumes and flowers and tethered birds that on the river the boats resembled floating gardens full of nesting egrets and flamingos and green-feathered quetzals.

The men attended on the pretext of being brothers or fathers who were giving us away to our new husbands. Actually they were guards to make sure none of the women panicked and escaped. It turned out the guards were needed, for this was one of those days when Lady

Moon, a pale ghost of herself, rides in the sky long after sunrise, unbeheaded and triumphant.

One of the women, glancing heavenward, saw her and cried out, "Our Mother is watching! Mother Lady Moon will save us from the monsters!" The women began sobbing and beating their breasts.

"Shut up, you idiot!" I said, boxing the ear of the girl next to me. "This is a disgusting spectacle!"

The guards, realizing I was right, began pinching and tweaking the disconsolate brides, and we were at last able to complete the journey in silence. Several times I saw heavy tears drop from well-crossed eyes.

The Spaniards, eager to get a look at us, crowded the shore at the water's edge. They were tall, strange in their heavy beards, their faces oddly pink and red, their hair of unearthly colors. Bizarre creatures, but they were waving, shouting and poking each other with their elbows as they laughed, and I knew at once they were, as the Chac had said, "men in one way or another." If there were gods among them, as no doubt there were, they had assumed human bodies.

The two warriors assigned to guard me lifted me to their shoulders and stepped ashore. For the next moments the Spanish camp was nothing but a blur and a din to me—banners were flying, light flashed from shields, a hundred voices shouted in a babble I could not understand and that seemed less human to me than the speech of the Monkey People or the language of birds. I felt dazed, unreal, as the men put me down.

Then in my memory I heard Lady Flint Knife speaking. "Lift your chin, girl! Eyes ahead! Walk like a queen and you will be treated like one."

I took a few steps, then paused and looked slowly around. There, almost beside me, stood a god! His hair was the gold of the sun, his eyes as blue and bright as a clear sky at noon. He was far too strange-looking to be called beautiful, although he was well made and taller than any human. His smile, although unsettling, seemed to welcome me.

I kneeled and kissed the ground—not in abasement, and one's lips do not actually touch the earth—but in a gesture of courtesy and esteem. I kneeled and rose in two single, flowing movements, doing it gracefully, for I was well taught. The god smiled and bowed in return, which I thought inappropriate, although graciousness can never be improper.

Just then someone standing behind me spoke my name in a strange accent, so hard to understand that I did not recognize the words. Then it was repeated, more or less in Maya, "Lady One Grass." Although startled, I managed to keep my dignity, turning slowly, letting my body follow the lead of my eyes and shoulders as one moves gracefully in ceremonies. I lowered my head in formal greeting, then slowly lifted it.

I looked into a strong, quiet face. He was tall, almost as tall as the other god, and he wore a short, pointed beard, dark and glossy like wet bark. His gray eyes were almost luminous, strangely intense and aware, so compelling I felt awesome power behind his gaze.

Yesterday the Chac of the East, peering through the slits of his mask, had claimed to look into my heart and discern all secrets. Pretense, of course. But if this man—this Spaniard, and I fleetingly wondered again if Spaniards really were men—had said, "Ce Malinalli, I can read your soul," I would have answered without the least doubt, "Yes, my lord, I know."

Yet his gaze was not disturbing but consoling, as though in knowing me totally, he also understood me. In his hand he held a hat, as though he had just taken it off. His hair, thick and dark like his beard, fell to his shoulders.

I started to kneel in courtesy, but he caught my hand, held it, his touch both frightening and pleasing. He bowed low, brushing my skin with his lips, a gesture so unexpected that I drew back, startled. He smiled at my surprise, as though we shared some joke.

"Did you speak my name, sir?" I asked. "I thought you did."

Still smiling, he gestured that he did not understand. Later I learned he had memorized my name because the Tabascans had exaggerated my rank and importance, passing me off as an exalted princess to inflate the value of their offering.

There seemed something familiar about him, which was, of course, impossible. Perhaps the long, dark coat he wore? As I was wondering about this, he put on the cloth hat he was holding. Then I knew. The hat, the coat, the beard, the grave yet kindly face: *Plumed Serpent.* I recognized him from a hundred paintings, from statues, from carvings and reliefs on temple walls. This was Plumed Serpent down to the very twist of the feather in his hat.

I was not a child to be fooled by priestly disguises, not one of the ignorant Tabascan women who trembled before the masks of Chac. I would have recognized Plumed Serpent by his appearance alone, but what struck me was more than that. A priest of Xipe Totec, clad from head to toe in the flayed skin of a human victim, is awesome, but you always know the priest is not the god himself. It was not like this with Plumed Serpent; I felt the god's presence. I *knew.*

The golden-haired god had been standing nearby, and now he spoke. I could not understand the words, but I recognized deference; he addressed the dark-bearded lord as a superior. And quite plainly he called him "Cortes," which I already knew meant Plumed Serpent.

Suddenly I realized I had been standing in the presence of the god and, shocked at my own temerity, I dropped to my knees, touched my lips, then touched the earth with my fingers. "Forgive me, Great Lord, I did not know you at first."

He gestured for me to rise, seeming quite disconcerted by my humility, which added to my confusion as I tried again to apologize.

At that instant the air was rent by shrieks. I turned to see the nineteen other brides and several of their escorts fleeing in panic. A great beast, almost as big as a jaguar, was running wildly down the beach, baring huge fangs and emitting noises that resembled the barking of a dog, but twenty times louder and fiercer. Unlike any actual dog, this creature was covered all over with hair.

Clenching my teeth, I stood firm, trusting I would not be devoured in the presence of Plumed Serpent, who was known to abhor the eating of human flesh.

"Come back! The creature will not harm you," a Spaniard shouted in execrable Maya. "Behave yourselves and it will not bite."

The brides were brought back by force, some of them dragged from the water, sopping and disheveled, their wedding paint running. The beast, we later learned, was a giant variety of dog called a lurcher. (But a dog with hair!) It was led away while the Spaniards laughed and slapped their thighs, which I thought was insensitive. I glanced at Plumed Serpent. He disapproved of the laughter; he understood our fear, as I knew he would. I did not realize I had learned an important truth: he would see our feelings when all his followers were blind to them.

His face, I now realized, was powerful and beautiful. Gazing at him, I remembered the painted book my father had shown me long ago, a picture of a god mounting a woman whose face was radiant with joy and holiness.

Cortes excused himself with a courteous bow and moved away to give orders to his lieutenants. As I watched him go, I felt a stirring I had never felt before in the presence of a male being, and I thought: *The god has become a man. Both as a man and as a god, he shall have me. I swear it.*

The first days in the Spanish camp were so filled with wonders that my eyes ached from staring. I discovered glass, an astonishing material that light could pass through but water could not. I saw and touched steel, the most powerful of metals, yet so light a woman could lift a rapier with one hand, and this caused me to ponder. There were guns and gunpowder, mirrors, silk, pulleys and wheels.

Years before I had seen wheels on a little clay dog, a toy for rich ladies, but I had never imagined such a thing as a wheel could be *useful.*

Sails were the symbols of this new world. The Spaniards tamed nature and made servants of the nature gods, tricking the air with sails, enslaving the wind just as they enslaved animals. In our world we had thought only of yielding to winds and fighting animals. All this made the Spaniards godlike, for gods control nature just as nature controls men.

While discovering these things, I watched the Spaniards for signs of divinity. Godhood is not always permanent. Moctezuma, for example, was simply a man before he was elevated to be a god. Cortes was a god because he was Plumed Serpent, but Plumed Serpent had at times in the past been mortal and fallible.

The golden-haired Spaniard I had first supposed was Plumed Serpent was called Alonzo Puertocarrero, a name I could not come close to pronouncing, full of impossible sounds. He was at least a godling; it showed in his looks and gestures and was revealed in the respect other Spaniards showed him; one could see he ranked above them. I studied the other officers and found their divinity doubtful. They were only attendants of the god and their power came through him.

On the third morning the interpreter, a Spaniard said to have been held captive by Maya in the northwest, arrived at the enclosure where I was staying with the other brides-to-be.

"Attention, ladies!" He gathered us, flapping about like a crow in his dark garments, blinking with beady eyes, cawing for silence. "I am Brother Aguilar. This morning Father Olmedo, a holy priest, will teach you true religion. Those who heed will earn paradise. Those who do not will be cast into the lake of fire."

He made us suppose that this lake blazed just past the horizon, and for all we knew that might well be true. Just the same, I was excited and hopeful that the hard questions perplexing me would at last be answered.

"You may not lie with Christian gentlemen until you yourselves are Christians," he said. This mystified everybody; we exchanged glances.

Aguilar led us to a shady place among the palms where two poles had been lashed together to form a cross. A picture hung from it. Since a cross is a sign of fertility both of the earth and the womb among the Maya, it was right that the picture showed a wistful woman with a baby. Both mother and child were albinos, a pity because otherwise they seemed attractive.

Pressing his hands together, Aguilar bowed to the image, greatly moved. His long, doleful face even at this moment of pious felicity was all ridges and hollows and poking bones, giving him the skeletal look of Aztec priests who do penance by fasting. I decided that Aguilar, like them, was starving himself. Hunger would explain the touch of frenzy in his eyes. But I could see no trace of divinity in him —a human, although perhaps a god had touched him with a little madness.

Father Olmedo, also ungodlike but stout, arrived sweating and puffing, madly wearing heavy robes in the heat of Tabasco. Another penance, I supposed. He mounted a fallen tree so its height would lend him authority.

"This is the Holy Mother of God." He pointed to the picture, and Aguilar interpreted in his dreadful dialect. As the priest harangued and sweated, it became clear that this lady was the goddess Serpent Skirt, but shown here in younger days before her breasts became flaccid from nursing all the gods.

"Our Lady gave birth to her divine Son although still a virgin," said the priest. Half of the women smiled knowingly, thinking how easily men are fooled. The rest nodded, remembering two virgin births in highland religion.

Olmedo spoke of the Holy Trinity. "You cannot comprehend this mystery," he concluded.

But the idea was familiar; most gods have multiple personalities, just as people have light and dark sides, male and female aspects. Slowly I realized that this man was not going to answer any of the vital religious questions that fascinated me. Which god taught men to catch the wind in sails? How did you gain power over animals? What was the nature of Cortes's divinity as Plumed Serpent—was he born so, or did it come to him?

I approved most of what Olmedo said. This woman in the picture, Maria the Virgin, seemed in charge of everything, a novel but good idea since male gods had so botched the universe. I agreed that sacrificing humans was abominable if overdone—followers of Plumed Serpent had always believed this.

I stopped paying attention to the cloudy religious talk and concentrated on the words, their sounds and the meanings Aguilar gave them. I would quickly master this language, I assured myself.

The priest said, "You now understand all that is needed. Tomorrow, during Palm Sunday rites, you will be baptized."

"Thank you, but that is not necessary," said a woman. "We were all baptized with holy water long ago." Others agreed.

Aguilar, not bothering to translate, shouted. "Your baptism was the devil's work! I know your filthy religion, your foulness!"

I was astonished at his rancor. This man was as flushed with hatred as a Singing Snake is flushed with venom. "Christian baptism will purge you of sin," he said in a calmer tone. "Purify you."

One of the woman, a slut named Flower Pouch, asked the question that was in every mind. "Will the Spaniards fuck us afterward?"

The women leaned forward, interested at last. Aguilar's face turned ashen, but he was saved from answering because Father Olmedo, smiling benignly, lifted his hand and inscribed the sign of the Maya fertility cross. The gesture seemed appropriately erotic.

As we were leaving, Flower Pouch sidled up to Aguilar and asked, "Will the Great Lord of the Spaniards also take a woman? Is that his nature?"

"Cortes? Yes, it is his nature." Aguilar's lips puckered in disapproval. "But he will not choose a woman tomorrow. There are not enough women for all the officers, and Cortes is not the kind who would eat while his men are still hungry."

Idiotic. We were hardly a dietary matter—at least I hoped not. If every officer could not have a woman for himself, then they must share as men always do in a shortage. Aguilar talked nonsense.

The next morning I went to a secluded spot among tall ferns at the riverbank—there were no guards now, the women had nowhere to run. It was a place I had sought before when life seemed difficult for me. I sat staring at the ripples, trying to overcome my fears. Regardless of what Aguilar said, I knew I was destined for Cortes. But how would I behave when the moment of coupling came?

The Chac of the East had accused me of being cold and unloving. He was right—although I felt I had not been born to be indifferent. Long ago I had felt drawn to Lark Singer's body in an innocent way. I had found my father's male embraces sweet to me.

Then came the day in the temple, the House of Men, when a mouth had crawled over me like a wet spider. After that I had relived the tarantula caress a thousand times—in memories, in nightmares and most of all when any man touched me for pleasure. The first time a man had taken me, hurling me down on a jungle path, I had fought like a netted wildcat, and when he forced his entrance, I felt talons rip my body. Later on, when other men took me, the remembered pain was less, but my revulsion did not change. I forced myself to bear what must be borne, but I pretended nothing.

Would it be the same with Cortes? I stared at the water and tried to fathom my own nature. I was powerfully drawn to the god; I felt both his gentleness and strength. But I had seen other males who were beautiful to look at, even beautiful to think about. Then, when they came close, when I felt breath on my skin, panic seized me and there was no concealing it.

"It will be different with Plumed Serpent," I told myself. He was a god; coupling with him would be as glorious as the scene in the painted book. And if not? What if I choked and shivered and even screamed? He would send me from his presence in shame. I would kill myself then, find Aguilar's lake of fire and plunge into it.

A trumpet sounded, the signal to assemble. I brushed back my hair, pinched color into my cheeks and went to find the flower crown I would wear for baptism and marriage.

. .

Cortes kneeled before the picture of Our Lady, devotion in his face. He knows her, I thought. She is his mother.

Father Olmedo had made Our Lady seem a fleshless spirit hovering in the distant sky. With Cortes she lived, she was present.

"The new Christians will move forward and kneel for baptism," said Aguilar, gesturing for me to come first, which I would have done anyway.

I kneeled as close to Cortes as I dared, my eyes modestly lowered. Father Olmedo muttered some magic words, then sprinkled me with water. The fragrance of my flower crown did not quite drown the odor of his sweat.

"Marina," he said. "Lady Marina."

"That is your new name in Christ," Aguilar, kneeling behind me, whispered. "You are now Lady Marina. Forever."

"Lady Marina." I repeated it softly, having a hard time with the strange sounds but liking the name, hoping it carried a favorable horoscope. I quickly realized that the other women were not being called lady, which was as it should be. I had kept my rank.

The religious ceremony ended abruptly. The Spaniards gave whoops of joy and excitement, they clapped their hands, they embraced each other and even hugged the women. Thankfully, none of them touched me.

"What are they yelling about, Brother Aguilar?" I asked.

"Nothing, Lady Marina." He looked quite pained and blushed. "They are soldiers, they talk loosely."

So they were shouting obscenities. I had to learn this language, I thought. Aguilar was good for nothing but pieties.

"The women will form a line," Aguilar announced. I stood still, head high, and let the line form behind me.

Cortes, smiling gravely but with a raised eyebrow, walked the length of the line inspecting the women, nodding his compliments. He moved, I thought, gracefully as a jaguar. No, not a jaguar, an ocelot. Moles and ocelots were the earth animals sacred to him.

He paused before Flower Pouch—who now had a new and unpronounceable name—then, beckoning her to come forward, he led her to one of his officers, a red-bearded man, and put Flower Pouch's hand in Red Beard's.

The Spaniards went mad with joy, and Red Beard, grinning like a weasel, hugged Cortes, then pounded him on the back so profanely that I could hardly believe my eyes. I hoped and expected Cortes would strike the man dead on the spot. Instead he simply laughed as he disengaged himself from the insolent embrace. I felt dazed—and there was still more to come.

Eighteen times the performance was repeated, complete with hugging, shouting and even some lewd gestures. At last I was the only woman left where the line had once stood. Somehow I had known it would be like this, that he would save his own choice for the last. The Spaniards apparently knew it, too, for suddenly there was silence.

Cortes approached me. He bowed; with the others he had merely inclined his head. For a moment we looked each other full in the face. He was noble, I thought, completely forgetting to drop to the ground in obeisance. His expression seemed one of courteous admiration. Then some other feeling came into his eyes, but vanished almost instantly. Desire, perhaps? Even pain? I stood bewildered, almost numb as he took my hand and led me forward. Where were we going? To his tent? To one of his boats? The men standing near us were quiet. Some of them nodded.

Cortes halted. I found myself standing before the tall god with hair spun of gold, the one I had mistaken for Plumed Serpent the first time. I had forgotten his difficult title but his familiar name, I now knew, was Lord Alonzo. Cortes spoke gently, then joined Lord Alonzo's hand and mine. I was so stunned that I hardly heard the cheering.

I think for an instant my face gave me away—but only for an instant; then my mask was again in place. This joining was the will of Plumed Serpent. I must accept it, I must even try to rejoice in it. "My lord Alonzo," I said, smiling as I gazed into his disconcerting, sky-colored eyes. He stared at me in astonishment and with open pleasure, never suspecting my shock and pain. Lady Flint Knife would have been proud of me.

We walked along the river in twilight. I understood none of his words except "Marina," but his voice was low and pleasant. He meant to be gentle, and for this I felt grateful. He whispered, and I imagined he said, "You are lovely, I am pleased with you."

"You honor me, you are kind, Lord Alonzo," I answered, just as if I had understood him or he could understand me.

He blushed suddenly and turned shy. I knew, without grasping a single word, that he was asking, "Do you like me? Are you happy with the choice?" Men, I knew, always ask that when a marriage has been arranged without the woman's consent. Even customers of prostitutes ask it!

I answered, "Lord Alonzo's happiness is my own happiness." This was not true, but what woman was ever expected to answer the question truthfully? He knew from the way I nodded and lowered my eyes like a village bride that I was pleased with him.

He halted, and gestured toward a place among the ferns where we could sit and be private. His eyes asked if I liked this spot.

"It is beautiful, my lord." He did not realize I had led him here.

So we sat and he talked softly, twisting a strand of my hair in his fingers. There were fine gold hairs on the back of his hand and on his lower arm. It was odd but very pretty, and suddenly I wanted to touch them with the tips of my fingers, but I did not know his customs and was afraid he might find this immodest.

Only a few hours before I had sat in this same place worrying about pleasing Cortes. Well, that was one problem I no longer had. Why had Cortes given me to another? I was certain I had seen desire in his eyes. Could he, with Plumed Serpent's vision, have read my fears, my self-doubting? And I knew at once that he had. He understood me, and suddenly I was thankful for his wisdom. Lord Alonzo was my teacher; Cortes would take me when I was ready. This was in keeping with the oldest customs of marriage among my people. How could I have been so slow to see that Cortes knew all this?

Turning to the gold-haired god, I said, "May we begin now? Show me what pleases you—what will please him."

But he did not understand, so I awkwardly tried to take off his shirt, but I had never touched buttons and did not know how to manage. He chuckled, not ridiculing my ignorance but delighted, as when one watches a child discover some new thing. The hair on his chest was much thicker and longer but only a little darker than that on his arms. In the fading light it seemed burnished, exotic and beautiful. The paleness of his skin under the shirt astonished me, so white it resembled the lime-chalked faces of funeral dancers, but when he turned toward the light I saw that his broad chest was not white but ivory, the lovely shade and texture of figurines from Jaina.

When his hands and then his lips touched my breasts, I held my breath, waiting for the revulsion or the talons to seize me, but I felt only an unfamiliar warmth and tenderness. Looking down at the light skin and gold hair, so unlike the skin and hair of men, I felt the awakening of desire. Gradually, slowly, my body responded of its own will to his caresses. I forgot to be frightened, I lost myself in the strangeness of him.

Then, without warning, he placed his mouth firmly against mine, and his tongue probed to open my lips. I did not know what he was doing—we had no such kisses in our world—and for a terrible moment I thought the worst I had heard was true, that he was an eater of living flesh about to devour me. But the gentleness of his caressing hands calmed me. I let myself respond to the taste of his mouth, his tongue, and it seemed strangely sweet and warming. I wanted the warmth to continue, to go on forever.

A tingling grew inside me. It became a longing, and then a compulsion. This, I thought dimly, was what girls whispered about, what wives in secret boasted of to each other. I had not imagined its power, not suspected it. When he entered me, there was no pain, only completion, but I still cried out as brides do, not from fear but joy and fulfillment, then clasped him to me, engulfing him, joined with the god.

11

To the Land of
Bounteous Beauty

Two days later, on a bright morning with a gusty wind, we sailed westward along the coast. As the mouth of the familiar river faded from view, I felt nothing but joy and freedom. My life had seldom been happy, but at least as a child in Jalisco I had been content enough. In the Lair of the Serpent I had found suffering; but suffering suggests an awareness of pain, a sense of being alive. Even that had deserted me in Tabasco. For me the Land of Damp Earth, of the Rivers, had been a way station to the tomb, and now resurrection had come. I was like the earth after the rains have returned, like a tiny bird bursting an egg, a butterfly escaping a cocoon. I had returned to life; I felt full of singing.

The ship flew on the wind's back, while overhead the sails cracked so loudly they seemed to hold thunder. I stood on deck, touching a mast to keep my balance, trying to get used to the sense of flying over the water. I knew how gods must feel when they ride eagles. That morning there was nothing I could not do, nothing I could not become.

I did not know where we were bound or why, although I supposed we would go west and then north for Cortes to reclaim his kingdoms as Plumed Serpent. Every sign assured me that we were on our way to fulfill the prophecies. Also our journey seemed connected with gold trinkets the Tabascans had given to the Spaniards as part of the tribute

payment. These cheap ornaments were merely baubles such as Lord
Lancer used to wear, but they caused great excitement among the
Spaniards, and I could not fathom why. Gold was probably sacred to
Lord Alonzo and some others who resembled him because of their hair;
that would be natural. But Spaniards, I quickly learned, did not eat gold.

I resolved to ask Aguilar about this at the first chance, but Aguilar
avoided me as he avoided all the women. Whenever possible he
hovered at Cortes's elbow, and I could not approach him then because
it seemed forward, although Cortes paid me courteous attention and
I took it as favorable that Lord Alonzo and I were on the *San Sebastian,*
largest of the eleven ships and the one Cortes chose for himself.

The next day, after a satisfying night with Lord Alonzo, I studied
Cortes at a little distance. He leaned against the rail watching the flat,
gray-green shore, which was never far away, and I supposed his eyes
saw a hundred times farther than mine did. Probably he looked past
the jungle, through the mountains I knew lay beyond, and even now
he surveyed the Aztec domains he would one day rule. Or would those
lands turn out to be the place where he would be destroyed attempting
to conquer? Plumed Serpent had not always been invincible, not even
when all the moles and ocelots and buzzards had joined him in alliance.
He could be driven away again. Eventually, of course, he would return
triumphant, but perhaps only after sheaves of years had passed. I would
be long dead then, my bones so vanished that not even his moles could
find them.

The thought was unbearable, and I forced it from my mind. It
was pleasanter to watch Cortes, to study the human aspects of the god,
the face and body Plumed Serpent had chosen for his incarnation.

He was towering by Aztec standards, and tall even among the
Spaniards. His hair and beard were dark but not black—a wise com-
promise of complexion because Aztecs would find his color unusual
but not impossible. Most pictures of Plumed Serpent show him as
dark-bearded, but a few suggested yellow hair. Perhaps the god had
compromised on deep brown. His shoulders were broader than almost
any man's and his chest deep as a ballplayer's. I thought the god had
chosen his earthly vessel shrewdly.

The gray eyes, startling, gave away the disguise. In them the god
looked out from the human face.

I watched him turn from the railing, casually give an order to
a sailor, relaxed and easy. Yet he brought the end of the world, a force

like an earthquake, like all volcanoes exploding at once. Suddenly it struck me that I had been preoccupied only with the hope of arousing his lust. I fretted that he might not find my breasts attractive, worried about the shape of my hips. I had become like women I had always despised, women who think of nothing but sex. This is natural, they are brought up for it, their whole success depends on it. A woman need never do anything else in life if she manages that one thing well. I wanted more; I was born to understand more.

Surely there were other services I could offer the god, yet so far the one thing I had thought of offering him was the most fleeting of pleasures, one that could be beautiful but in time would satisfy neither of us. I must be more than a receptacle, even for a god.

I brooded all that day. If battles came, I would not be afraid to fight for him. My memories of the clash in Tabasco were still vivid, exciting, and I felt that Spanish weapons would make me as powerful as most Aztec soldiers. But would I be allowed to fight? I doubted it. There were no warrior women among the Spaniards, and I could foresee a problem. If I fought badly, I would embarrass our cause; if I fought too well, I would embarrass everybody.

I considered offering him pain. I could make a sacrifice on his behalf, pierce myself with needles, perhaps. But there was no sign that he wanted or needed that. Indeed one of the most appealing things about Plumed Serpent had always been his rejection of sacrifice. So what else? I was baffled.

We turned northward when we passed the great river of the Lair of the Serpent. I saw people standing among the trees on the shore, shy as deer, and wondered if my brother might be among them. I was twenty years old now, so he would be almost six, and I thought of him with longing. I waved my arms, I shouted, but my voice died in the vastness of the sea.

Two or three mornings later the great snow-crowned mountains loomed into view. The Spaniards marveled at them, and the Tabascan women, who had never seen so much as a hill, stood dumbfounded: they had always supposed their own town temple was the highest thing in the world. Some Spaniards were now proudly recognizing coves and rivers; they had sailed this coast before among the earliest Forerunners. The mountains brought Aguilar to the deck rail alone, and I seized the chance to talk to him.

"May I speak to you, Brother Aguilar?"

"Certainly, Lady Marina." He gave me an uneasy smile. "But our talk must be brief. I have religious duties to perform."

"It is about religion I wanted to ask." Religion was the last thing on my mind, but the subject was bait he would take.

"I will try to enlighten you."

"Father Olmedo mentioned the cardinal virtues. If you could explain—"

"Of course." He launched into a sermon. I quickly learned that Christian views of goodness were roughly those of any civilized person. He spoke so vehemently about honesty that I concluded he had been brought up among thieves and liars.

"Chastity is a virtue especially important to me. The love of it saved my life and changed my condition."

"Tell me, Brother Aguilar."

"I was aboard a ship sailing between Cuba and Hispaniola when a storm drove us ashore and we were captured by heathens. We were held in the most brutal slavery. The women with us died from sheer toil, dropped dead while grinding corn. They worked under a lash in the infernal sun! Then I saw my friends sacrificed one by one. I myself was to be killed and my flesh eaten."

He spoke quietly but with terrible intensity, horror in his voice. "One chief took a liking for me. My strangeness amused him. He saved me, offered me a wife. I refused to marry because I had taken holy orders, and to lie with a woman would have been damnation. He did not believe me and decided on a test. I was forced to spend a night on the shore of a lake with the most tempting and lewd woman he could find."

"How terrible for you," I murmured, my interest in the story suddenly sharpening. Aguilar was staring at the shore, remembering.

"She did every vile thing to me she could imagine. I had to submit to her caresses, her filthy embrace. She performed foul acts I never dreamed humans could invent. Oh, yes, she tried to defile me in every way. I think Satan himself possessed her."

I remembered the House of Men. It had never occurred to me before that a man could be violated.

"I did not succumb! She could not arouse me to sin. The chief who arranged the test was moved by my strength of will. He was kind to me after that, and life was easier. I was well treated, but lonely.

Worst of all, I had lost track of the calendar. I never knew which day was Sunday and holy."

"Yes, a tragedy." So the woman on the lake shore had not aroused him. Neither, I supposed, had any woman before or since. The Maya chief must have been the most ignorant man in the Only World not to have understood Aguilar's nature. I felt irritated by this boasting of mastering temptation when he had not been tempted but repelled. Aguilar seemed to be a man who hated himself, so he could be counted on to hate others.

"Perhaps your future will be happier than your past," I said, wondering if the prospect of happiness would frighten him.

"Oh, yes. All will be well when we reach Culhua. In Culhua we will build a cathedral of solid gold."

"Culhua?" He meant Culhuacan, I supposed, and I was astonished to hear the name of my father's city. "We are going there?"

"Yes. The Tabascans told us about it—the Land of Gold. It lies just inland from this coast, across meadows full of plump game."

I almost choked. This fool believed lies the Tabascans had told to get rid of the Spaniards. I was about to tell him the truth, that the vassal city of Culhuacan had been rich long ago when the Aztecs still inhabited a squalid place called Mudtown. Even then it was no land of gold. And to go "just inland" meant scaling the world's highest mountains—unless one followed a trail where every step was guarded by Aztec archers and spearmen.

Then, before I could speak, I realized that the Tabascan lie was another tactic of destiny. To go to Culhuacan meant going to the heart of Aztec lands. Plumed Serpent was fulfilling the prophecies while Aguilar and the others thought this was a hunt for mere gold.

Just then there came a loud shout from the helm, a cry I could not understand, but it brought men running. The cause of the excitement was a small canoe with a single fisherman that rode on the sea hardly two bow shots ahead of us. The man must have been dozing at his lines, for he appeared to waken now, and when he saw a monster, our ship, bearing down upon him, he almost leapt from the canoe. Cortes and Aguilar ran to the prow, hailing him, and I ran after them.

"Don't be afraid," Aguilar shouted. "We mean you no harm."

Aguilar spoke in his dialect of Maya, speech almost no one could understand this far west and north. The fisherman, after some hesitation, called back, "What language is that? Are you men or demons?"

Aguilar seemed puzzled. "What is this gibberish?" he asked me. "Can you understand?"

"Of course. He speaks my own language."

I did not add that it was lucky to have encountered anyone who spoke the highland tongue in this backwater of the world. The man was probably the slave of some official.

Aguilar said something to Cortes in Spanish, and Cortes turned to me with a surprised look. He spoke Spanish to Aguilar, who in turn spoke to me in Maya. "Ask the fisherman if there is a large city near here."

It was an ignorant question. We were near the northern border of the land of the Rubber People, and Rubber People build no cities. Their ancestors were children of gods and jaguars, but nowadays they are as useless as fleas. But I asked the question and the man answered.

"No cities, only small villages. But who are your companions, lady? Where do they come from? Can they be human?"

I repeated the words in Maya, Aguilar spoke them in Spanish, then Cortes made a reply and Aguilar translated, saying, "Tell this fisherman to take word to his people that we are agents of the Christian king of Spain, His Most Catholic Majesty. We bring his gracious sovereignty and true religion to this land."

I stared at Aguilar, trying to comprehend. I thought I understood the actual words, but the idea escaped me. How could I tell this simple fisherman what I myself could not grasp? I also doubted that Cortes had uttered such murky nonsense. Aguilar, whose grasp of Maya was uncertain, could have mixed the words up.

I said instead, "Tell your people that the ancient omens are fulfilled. Plumed Serpent is now returning to his own lands!"

I heard my voice ring across the water as though I spoke not to one man but to ten thousand. "Look upon him standing here! You know him, you have seen his images in the temples. Go now and tell the people."

The fisherman cried out in astonishment. Then, almost spinning his canoe in the water, he paddled madly for the shore, the first living herald of Plumed Serpent.

"He's terribly excited. Did he understand?" Aguilar asked.

"He understands," I said. "He will spread the news."

Cortes nodded his thanks to me, and I bowed my head demurely in return. But pride and pleasure filled me as I saw how matters would stand in the future. I had found my service, my value. I would be closer, more needed by my lord the Captain than any consort. I would be his tongue.

We sailed northward, skirting the steamy coast of the hot lands. Lord Alonzo spent time on deck teaching me Spanish words. I was pleased by both the lessons and his attention, for I had already noticed that Spanish men were like Aztec men, shunning the company of women except when they wanted sex or some other service.

Excitement mounted among the Spaniards as we passed landmarks familiar to those who had been Forerunners. But as the men grew eager, the Tabascan women turned pale and apprehensive, muttering among themselves. They were ignorant of the world yet knew we were entering the realm of Moctezuma, and they decided his gods had already smelled our blood and were licking their stone lips. I knew we were on the edge of Aztec dominions when I saw Mountain of the Star, huge and omnipotent, looming on the western horizon.

Mountain of the Star is the highest peak in the world, loftier even than Smoking Man or Sleeping Woman. I had seen his western face, the inland side, years ago when my family journeyed to Lair of the Serpent. Although we had been much farther away than now, we had dropped to our knees to implore the spirit of the mountain to grant us safe passage and not shake us off his shoulders or send his boulders hurtling down to crush us. He is a beautiful mountain but notoriously short-tempered and capricious. He is also ungrateful; he will accept your offerings of perfume and spiced honey, only to gobble you up without an instant's hesitation.

If the mountain seemed awesome, the shore was equally menacing in a quiet way. It stretched flat, gray-green and scaly, as somnolent as a lurking crocodile. The line of the shore was so vague that usually I could not discern where the sea ended and the land began. I turned away from it, thinking of quicksand.

Each night we cast anchor, the ships like great egrets that fold their white wings at sunset. One day at twilight, as the sails were being furled, an omen came to me. We rode on shallow water off a shore lined by grotesque trees dwarfed and twisted by thirst, their roots clawing for water. In the fading light I suddenly saw the trees change to skeletons, and I recalled Jalisco villages of the Dog People and other barbarians who fence their settlements with bleached human bones and skulls stuck on cactus spikes to warn off robbers and tax gatherers. The skulls say, "Enter, friend, and join us."

Behind these skeletons Mountain of the Star towered black against the sky, its shadowy slopes concealing the eyes of Moctezuma. I knew then we would pass through fields of the dead to meet darkness and fire. The dead coaxed us onward.

At that moment Evening Star, who is also Plumed Serpent, appeared serene in the heaven. I could look from it to the human form of the god, Cortes, who stood near the helm chatting with the pilot, untroubled by the mountain or the forbidding shoreline. The pilot, also undaunted, appeared to be telling a ribald joke, for Cortes laughed, then clapped the man on the shoulder affectionately. I felt reassured to see such utterly different aspects of the same god at the same moment. His human presence gave me hope, although in that red sunset Cortes seemed alarmingly mortal and Evening Star very far away.

Next morning the omen echoed in my mind like a remembrance of thunder. Neither was it banished when lookouts on the masts shouted, "Ulua! The Island of San Juan!"

Ahead lay a dismal island poking up from the water like a brown sea turtle, hardly more than a sand spit sheltering a bay where red dunes stood like a giant anthill between the beach and the jungle marsh.

Lord Alonzo bounded across the deck and embraced me, laughing, which astonished me because he always behaved formally in public and even in private showed little emotion until lovemaking was underway—then he would give faint cries and whisper desperate words I could not fathom.

"The Island of San Juan de Ulua!" he said. "Gateway to the Land of Gold! At last!" I knew enough Spanish to guess the meaning. His arms felt strong and protecting around me. I was moved by the beauty and joy in his sky-color eyes, and I clung to him a moment, liking his body, grateful that Cortes had given me such a teacher.

Then, as he released me, I looked up toward Mountain of the Star, wondering if there would be some sign, a welcome or threat. To my amazement he had vanished, although the horizon seemed clear and he had not veiled himself in clouds. Yet he was gone, hidden.

As we rounded the island, the Spaniards prepared to furl the sails and cast anchor in the bay. All the while they were laughing and joking, I felt a powerful sense that Mountain of the Star, although invisible, was still watching, still in wait for us. And so, too, I thought was Moctezuma. He, with his sorcerers and curse-makers, wizards, owl men, priests and warriors countless as the leaves of the jungle, was waiting behind the horizon, as hidden as Mountain of the Star but no less present or formidable.

I fingered a strand of black beads Father Olmedo had given me for counting prayers and wondered if there was the least chance their magic would work.

Our arrival took place at noon, with Lord Sun on his highest throne, which is the Pinnacle of the Light Bringer. It was Holy Thursday in the year One-Reeds, also called A.D. 1519.

I was quickly proved right about our being watched. The anchors had hardly brushed bottom when two long canoes, red and shiny as funeral drums, shot from concealment among the low dunes on the shore. The rowers had no hesitation about which of the eleven vessels was the flagship, for they made straight for us. Our ship was the largest and carried the most banners, yet their choice was still more than a shrewd guess. They *knew* who commanded, they had studied us for days, maybe weeks. Possibly their scouts had sent details by relay runners all the way from Tabasco. It also crossed my mind that Moctezuma might be told by demons.

The deck was so packed with Spaniards that Aguilar had to shove them aside to stand next to me with Cortes next to him. The three of us stood close together so Aguilar, who did not know the language of the Aztecs, could translate Cortes's Spanish into Maya; then I would interpret the Maya words. When the leader of the Aztecs climbed aboard with several of his men, Aguilar whispered, "What magnificent clothes! A prince has come to meet us."

Of course he had never before seen Aztecs so he did not know the splendor a prince would have shown, had not the least idea of what magnificence was. This officer was no more than a regular brigade commander, a knight of middle rank, who had slipped on an embroidered cloak with some quite ordinary feather work. The men of his squad, in workday tunics and loincloths, were even less impressive.

The knight, with typical Aztec composure and panache, did not gawk at the ship or the Spaniards but tried to make it appear that this was, for him, a routine visit, although in truth he might just as well have found himself square in the lap of Lady Moon for strangeness. His men gazed straight ahead, eyes carefully unfocused, faces so deliberately blank that a Toltec sculptor might have carved them. Obviously they had been given stern orders to reveal no reactions at all. They could have had their noses bitten off without blinking.

"Kindly present me to your Lord Commander," the knight said, after a symbolic kissing of the deck as equivalent to the ground. He had stayed down an unusual length of time, and I suspected he was covertly inspecting the Spaniards' shoes.

I gestured toward Cortes, although it was obvious the Aztec already knew who was in charge; he had been well briefed.

"I bid you welcome in the name of my lord the great Moctezuma, revered First Speaker of the Triple Alliance. Tell me, sir, what sort of men are you?"

"Friendly men." Aguilar translated Cortes's words.

"Friendly," I said, without adding "men." There was no point in confusing matters.

"What is it you seek here?" the knight asked, reciting memorized lines. "We will be pleased to supply anything you need to aid your journey."

Not precisely gracious, I thought. The arriving guests were being offered a lunch for the road before they even had time to catch their breath.

While I was translating this, the knight suddenly lost his studied composure for a moment. He had steeled himself to the sight of pale men and hairy men, but unexpectedly he caught sight of one of the black male slaves brought from Cuba. There were several in the company, belonging to various Spaniards. Whitish skin had been hard enough for this knight to accept; black skin caught him completely off guard.

Cortes covered the awkward moment with smoothness and courtesy, ordering food and wine brought, passing out some strings of blue glass beads to the guests—lovely necklaces, I thought. The knight, recovered from his shock, remained self-possessed, but his men were gawking almost openly now.

"We are interested in trade," said Cortes, but I doubt that my translation was heard because several Spaniards began talking at once.

"Which way to the land of gold?" one asked.

"Isn't that a silver pin that fellow is wearing? Will he trade it?"

"We bring true religion and salvation," Father Olmedo interjected. "The blessing of the cross."

At least I think that is what they said—Aguilar's interpreting could not keep up with the questions, and I understood only a word here and there of the Spanish. But I caught the gist of it, and suddenly I saw the whole preposterous scene as from a distance, as Lord Sun must have looked down upon it, and everything was idiotic, grotesque, *wrong*.

Plumed Serpent, not the greatest of gods but surely the most beautiful and nearly human, had returned from the Cloud World after sheaves of years to reclaim his kingdoms. Life as we had known it would soon be utterly changed, maybe even obliterated as it had been in the times of the Wood People and the Men of Mud.

And how were the universes greeting each other? One of humanity's junior officers, in his second-best clothes, was trying to understand banal questions about gold and silver baubles.

The Spaniards sat for the food and drink, the Aztecs squatted, and the knight smacked his lips to show appreciation of the wine. He was, I thought inconsequentially, the first man of the Only World to taste this beverage. He praised it, but with a suspicious look in his eyes. Intoxication is a terrible sin among Aztecs, although old folks may get honorably drunk to forget their arthritis.

"What are you called?" the knight asked me, allowing himself to betray a trace of curiosity.

"Lady Marina, servant to my lord here," I replied, bowing my head to Cortes.

But the knight could not say Marina—it came out Malina, and Cortes was instantly named Malintzin, an absolutely safe title meaning simply "Malina's lord." It neither affirmed nor denied his godhood. The knight had a gift for the meaningless; he was a better diplomat than I had supposed.

Yet I had by now realized that this man was not a direct envoy from Moctezuma. He had his special orders, of course, but there must have been others like him stationed at every possible landing place on the coast. True, he was the tip of Moctezuma's feelers; but the feelers had not yet begun to probe us.

The knight rose and took his leave, repeating welcoming words and offers of quick provisions for our departure. Cortes assured him again of Spanish honor and friendship.

"Our coming here is fortunate for you and your people," Cortes called to the departing canoes. "Fortunate!"

I translated from Aguilar. "Fortunate," in the old tongue, meant "favored of the gods," and perhaps that was why the granite-faced knight actually smiled as he waved farewell. More likely he simply responded to the warmth and charm of Cortes's voice and manner. Most people did; he had a magic that often transcended language.

Long after the canoes had gone, I realized that for the first time in years I had heard my native language properly spoken, not garbled by slaves or traders. The Aztec knight could well have been one of my own cousins. But I felt no pleasure, no awakening of a response. These men with their blank faces and empty eyes were not my people. They were merely enemies who had not yet unsheathed their weapons.

The next day, Friday, was the anniversary of God's death, although at the time I was not sure which god. Father Olmedo solemnly explained that this was the first of the only two days of the year when Christians could not swallow the wine-soaked wafer that was really God's flesh sopped in blood. It was very puzzling. In the old religion, gods always ate men; in the new one, men always ate God, except on two days of the year when they couldn't. My lifelong despair of learning theology had begun.

That day during the hours we were not on our knees, we waded hip deep unloading supplies to make camp on the beach. Aguilar clucked and cautioned me that manual labor was beneath my rank—and his rank, too, of course. But I found pleasure in hard work after such a long confinement on the ship. I especially enjoyed carrying weapons—I liked the feel and heft of them, the feeling of their coiled power.

Since there was not a patch of flatland here, an armed camp was set up on the dunes. Several times that day I caught glimpses of people peering at us from among the scrubby trees of the savanna. Since they were mostly women and children, they could not be Aztec spies; they wore clothing, so they were not Huastecs who are shameless, and we were too far north for Rubber People. I decided we must be in an old kingdom straight east of the great valley, a kingdom now a vassal state of the Aztecs. This place was called Land of Bounteous Beauty, a name more patriotic than true, for it was bountiful only in mosquitoes, sand fleas and scorpions. Perhaps the natives called it Bounteous Beauty in hope of attracting traders. Later the Spaniards renamed the wretched spot Rich Town of the True Cross, which was equally misleading.

Sometimes I found myself listening for the distant drums of an Aztec army, or perhaps an embassy or even a welcoming religious procession. Whatever the attitude, Aztecs should be arriving soon. A journey from the capital to the coast meant many days' hard walking for ordinary travelers, but Moctezuma had a corps of specially trained runners called swift-messengers. They were stationed in relays and sped over the mountain trails so fast that the Revered Speaker enjoyed at breakfast fish that had been swimming in seawater only the morning before. Yesterday's news would certainly travel as swiftly as yesterday's catch. Tomorrow, I felt sure, we could learn Moctezuma's intentions.

I watched Cortes kneeling in front of the great wooden cross that leaned in the sand. His face, transformed by devotion, was so moving that I repeated my new Christian prayers again. But before I had counted a dozen beads, my mind strayed. I started to wonder how gunpowder was made and exactly how you fired a harquebus.

On Easter Sunday, just as I expected, Moctezuma's emissaries arrived, provincial officials decked out in such splendor as they could muster at a moment's notice. These men were not, of course, from the capital. There had been no time for that—court dignitaries cannot run like swift-messengers. What seemed important and encouraging was how quickly the Revered Speaker had sent a response.

Before dawn that morning I had gently released myself from Lord Alonzo's arms and hurried through the darkness and silence of the Ninth Watch, knowing the day was crucial and I should be at my lord the Captain's service. He, too, must have sensed that crucial events were impending, because he soon emerged alone from his shelter before it was quite light. Since Father Olmedo had proclaimed this a feast day, Cortes was dressed in a dark red coat, which I supposed was a memorial color for the tomb from which the Christian god had arisen. I thought it remarkable the god had emerged exactly as Moctezuma's sister had done not long ago and wondered if there was a connection. I bowed deeply and from beneath lowered eyes noticed how handsome he looked today. He gestured toward the coat and asked a question that must have been, "Do you like it?"

"Yes, my lord," I replied. "And right that it should be tomb-colored today."

He recognized this as a compliment, for he touched my arm lightly, but to me it felt as though a spark had jumped between his fingers and my skin. I suppose I flinched at his touch, and I tried to cover my confusion with another obeisance. At the same instant it came to me that something was wrong. I looked at him again, trying not to stare rudely, slowly realizing what disturbed me.

"Forgive me, my lord, but you should wear your dark suit and hat. The clothing you wore in Tabasco. That is appropriate for Plumed Serpent."

He could not make out a word, but realized I spoke something important. "Aguilar!" he shouted. "Come here!"

Aguilar, dressed in a rumpled cassock in which he slept, and still rubbing sleep from his eyes, arrived. "What is wrong?" he asked me after Cortes had spoken to him.

"The clothing the lord Captain wears. Moctezuma's ambassadors would be confused by it, even disappointed. An official delegation may arrive today, and the lord Captain must look—"

I cut off my words. What I was about to say, that Cortes should look more like the usual images of Plumed Serpent, not only sounded impertinent but would be incomprehensible to Aguilar, who was utterly ignorant of religion except in its most crude and superstitious forms.

"Must look like *what*?" Aguilar demanded. "Why are you so concerned?"

"He should look like a priest," I said quickly. "This is a holy day—Father Olmedo said so—and our priests wear black just as yours do."

"But why a priest?"

"The lord Moctezuma is a priest. He studied religion in his youth before anyone knew his destiny. So a black suit, a black hat would be —would be courteous."

After Aguilar had explained in Spanish, Cortes nodded and touched my arm again, this time a gesture of appreciation. I felt no spark, only the pleasant warmth of his hand.

A little later, as Lord Sun burst up in the red ball of birth, his light seeming almost to split the eastern waters, Cortes emerged in his proper attire. He was Plumed Serpent again; it was unmistakable.

· ·

Rumor sped faster than even Moctezuma's swift-messengers. Long before the official party arrived at the beach, throngs of people had gathered in anticipation of the spectacle. The inhabitants of the Land of Bounteous Beauty were like crumb-seeking birds; they would venture impulsively from the protection of the thin foliage, blink, cock their heads and peer at us, only to skitter away in alarm at the first sudden movement in their direction. When the horses were brought from their corral to try their footing on the wet sand—the hardest surface nearby—everyone vanished, only to slip back later, drawn by an irresistible curiosity: it is not in everyone's lifetime that gods arrive next door. They expected to tell their grandchildren one day. As it turned out, many of them lived to do it.

Little cries of excitement, again like the chirping of birds, arose from the bushes when the first heralds of the Aztecs appeared shaking great wooden clappers while others waved standards of royal green. Several guardsmen followed, lifting their decorated spears in saluta-tion, then two speaking heralds who cried in unison, "Lord Tendile, Aztec Governor, Keeper of the Peace in this Land of Bounteous Beauty, now comes! He greets Malina's Lord, newly arrived from the sunrise lands."

I translated everything except the title "Malina's Lord" to Agui-lar. For that I said only "Malintzin."

Lord Tendile moved toward us with a measured pace, attended by two slaves with fly whisks and two small boys, twins, bearing smoldering cups of copal incense. Tendile, severe and shrewd-looking, wore not only badges of office but a brooch showing the toothy god of trading and merchandising. So he was a businessman turned envoy. I knew the type; they used to pay court to my father. This embassy was just what I might have expected, highly respectable yet not ex-traordinary. But then an astonishing figure appeared.

Except for the skimpiest loincloth and the most elaborate jew-elry, the man was as naked as a Huastec. His great paunch, adorned with a pearl in his navel, bulged like a pregnant woman eleven months gone; he might well have had a herald carrying it ahead of him. All this girth plodded with surprising solemnity under a canopy bedecked by ribbons and borne by slaves.

"Lord Big Belly! Eminent in the realm, beloved of the Revered Speaker! Lord Big Belly!"

I could hardly believe my ears. Aztec commoners and slaves sometimes are given unflattering names. But a lord called Big Belly? If this had taken place among Maya people, I would have suspected a subtle joke. But these were Aztecs, heavy-handed.

"Lord Tendile and Lord Big Belly," the heralds repeated, and the whole party moved forward in greeting, dropping to the ground, symbolically kissing the earth three times. Lord Big Belly, who had trouble rising, looked terribly mournful and somewhat dazed. Tobacco was being offered, but I wondered if Big Belly had been smoking something else. Hemp, for instance.

Cortes welcomed them courteously but gravely, explaining that the Spaniards were just starting a religious ceremony and hoped every-one present would join them. When I translated the words "religious ceremony," Lord Big Belly positively blanched, and his canopy bearers put their hands on his shoulders, a gesture that struck me as downright insolent.

While Father Olmedo intoned mass, I tried to figure out the significance of this peculiar envoy, Lord Big Belly. Why should he be sent here displaying his un-Aztec corpulence, bejeweled and berib-boned like a bride, his hair festooned with coriander and laurel leaves like a prize haunch of venison?

Then it dawned on me—that is exactly what he was. *A prize haunch.* The Revered Speaker was offering Cortes a walking banquet, fresher even than his own seafood breakfast, especially fattened for the feast, thoroughly garnished.

Astonishment arose in me that Moctezuma, who had studied for the priesthood, would ignore that Plumed Serpent shunned the eating of human flesh. (Except, as I had recently learned, in the form of Christian magic wafers.) Was this an insult, a denial? And no wonder Lord Big Belly, who was certainly no real lord, appeared nervous. Also no wonder that Lord Tendile and the slaves kept a sharp watch on him. How embarrassing if the main course bolted for the jungle.

Mass being finished, Cortes invited the Aztecs to join the Span-iards for a meal. Again the Aztecs exchanged uncertain glances, while Big Belly tried to suppress a groan, thinking his last hour had come. He brightened when he saw the Tabascan women begin to pass baskets of fruit.

Lord Tendile spoke in the smooth tone of a practiced salesman. "Malintzin, may we offer you some special treat? We bring the finest edible delicacies in the world." He did not gesture at Big Belly, but rolled his eyes in that direction. Tendile was a trader unrolling his prized cotton cloth or parading his concubines.

As I translated, I tried to add a warning by my tone, but Aguilar, unaware of any oddity, repeated the words, uncomprehending as a macaw. Courtesy forbade my pinching him. Neither did I dare presume that none of the Aztecs present understood Maya. How could I tell Cortes that some test was being made?

"Thank you, but we will provide the food today," Cortes said, to my great relief. Was he wondering about poison? His face was so smilingly innocent, so guileless that I suspected something.

Tendile's own smile did not falter, but I caught the slight narrowing of his eyes. "At least permit us to offer some special savories. They come by order of our beloved and revered Lord Moctezuma."

Tendile clapped his hands, cueing the musicians to play. Then three young men, their hair clipped short, moved forward with slow and sensual steps, a ritual dance I had never seen. They held great platters above their heads. A suspicion came to me that they were youthful priests disguised as slaves. A priest's hair becomes so matted with dried blood that it is impossible to comb or wash it. That explained the haircuts. Moctezuma, for his own devious reasons, wanted Cortes to be unaware he was being served by priests.

"Well-trained waiters," I said pleasantly to Aguilar. "They appear to have the same skills and training as our friend Olmedo."

Aguilar blinked at the priest's name, then understood I spoke a veiled warning. He said something to Cortes, whose face still revealed nothing.

The platters the priests offered might have been created by mosaic makers. Every fruit and vegetable in the world had been blended into a rainbow on one tray, a flower garden on another, a flock of songbirds on the third. All three platters were sprinkled with a reddish brown sauce I supposed to be a sort of *mole* with chili. I was about to help myself when I realized this was the same sauce I had seen flecked or stippled on stairways of temples everywhere. Blood sauce. Human blood sauce.

At that same moment Lord Alonzo made a gagging noise and dropped the fruit he held in his hand; Cortes turned pale, then the pallor was replaced by a look of revulsion.

"The smell of this food is the breath of hell," Aguilar exclaimed in Maya. "Brimstone! Tell these devils that."

I did no such thing. What was to be gained by crude insults? "My lord and his companions cannot partake of this," I told Lord Tendile politely. "Eating human flesh and blood is contrary to their natures."

Lord Tendile betrayed no surprise. "I see. But what of you yourself? You look to me like an Aztec, you sound Aztec."

"Do I? I am a servant of Plumed Serpent. Your lordship knows our religious traditions." And, I thought, has done everything to violate them.

Lord Tendile waved away the disguised priests and their offerings. "Tell me, who is this hairy lord we are calling Malintzin? Why does he honor us with his presence?"

Instead of answering, I translated the question, and Cortes replied something about King Carlos, greatest sovereign on earth and guardian of religion. I could make little sense of Aguilar's Maya translation, but I tried to explain, privately supposing that King Carlos was some incarnation of Ometeotl, god-goddess creator of the universe. That would account for the reverence in Cortes's voice. I guessed Lord Tendile was weighing this same possibility. He toyed thoughtfully with the carved serpentine ornament he wore through the pierced septum of his nose.

Meanwhile two scribes were busily working, one squatting nearby making memory symbols of our words, the other standing at a little distance sketching the scene, doubtless for the eyes of Moctezuma.

"My great king has heard much of the Aztecs and of Moctezuma," said Cortes. "He wishes to trade with him in peace and friendship. Also he wishes to offer Moctezuma the blessings of true religion. When and where may I meet Lord Moctezuma in person? We must talk of these matters."

Clearly Lord Tendile had been expecting these words and he instantly brought forth his rehearsed answer. "You have hardly arrived here and already you request a royal audience!"

"Any errand I do for my king cannot be delayed," said Cortes. His tone was light, but there was no mistaking his determination.

To change the subject, Lord Tendile gestured and the slaves brought a beautiful chest bound with deer hide. "I bring a few more small gifts from the Revered Speaker. Our offerings of food you rejected. I hope these trifles will be more pleasing."

He deftly displayed several elaborate ornaments of gold and worked feathers. Meanwhile the slaves were unrolling bolts of cotton cloth as white as the snows on Mountain of the Star. At the same time the heralds presented baskets of fruit, smoked turkey and fish, this time not sauced in sacrificial blood.

A murmur of "gold" arose among the soldiers. It was a Spanish word I had learned quickly.

Cortes in turn offered gifts for Moctezuma, a crimson cap and a magic medal. More impressive was a carved wooden throne matching the one my lord himself sat on, an impressive seat, but I thought its height must be dizzying. Cortes said, "Lord Moctezuma may sit on this when he meets me in the near future."

Lord Tendile bowed and murmured, "Ah, yes. Yes, of course."

Another artist I had not noticed before was sketching the ships, and one of the young priests, who apparently doubled as a scribe, had taken out brushes and bark paper.

Cortes also noticed the artists and suddenly gave commands. A moment later horses galloped across the beach, raising flurries of wet sand. The dogs were brought, barking and snapping. Just as I thought Lord Tendile would never lose his Aztec composure, the cannons were fired and he leapt straight into the air in alarm. Lord Big Belly pounded his fists into the sand, although I could not tell if in terror or delight.

Lord Tendile, hardly controlling his trembling, suddenly pointed to a helmet one of the Spaniards—I think it was Lord Pedro Alvarado —was wearing.

"That crown, I must borrow it!" he exclaimed. "The Speaker will be most interested."

I don't know why I had never before noticed that the helmet was exactly like the war crown that the god Hummingbird of the Left is always shown wearing in battle. I suppose I had begun to take miracles for granted; Lord Tendile saw this new world with fresh eyes.

Pedro Alvarado, when he understood what was wanted, promptly doffed the helmet and offered it. But he smiled and a certain light came into his eyes. I thought of a weasel contemplating a plump turkey as he whispered something to Cortes, who then spoke to Aguilar and I translated.

"Do us the favor of returning the helmet filled with grains of gold. We want our king to compare your lord's gold with his own."

Cortes saw Lord Tendile's astonishment at this brash request and instantly realized the error of having repeated a puerile suggestion from one of his lieutenants. My lord was never gauche, and now it embarrassed him. With a wry smile he added, "Spaniards suffer from a terrible disease and gold is the only cure. Or if not quite a cure, it brings temporary relief."

My lord the Captain had made this remark before and would repeat it later. Since then he has been bitterly denounced for the obvious lie, although he was simply uttering the truth with grim humor. No one understood the painful symptoms and eventual fatality of greed better than he did. He was surrounded constantly by men dying from it.

Lord Tendile, making his farewell, covertly inspected our camp again. "I will return with orders from my master," he said, then departed, his wonder at this odd collection of creatures and objects barely concealed. What a report he would have to make!

Big Belly was left behind to supervise slave women in preparing roast birds and fish for us daily. Moctezuma seemed inclined to hospitality. At least I hoped that was why he fed us so well.

I quickly learned that Big Belly was no lord but an ordinary workman who had gambled himself into slavery playing *patolli,* a game played on a board with beans or even jewels for counters. The goddess Five Flower presides over the game, punishing cheating and soon humbling the proud or reckless. Gamblers often lose their valuables down to the last shred of clothes and even their own persons when Five Flower scowls at them. So it was with Big Belly.

Much of his corpulence, he told me, was newly acquired. Some soldiers at a nearby military post had been fattening him for sacrifice at a regimental feast honoring the month of Desire for Rain. This was illegal, he had only two more years to finish his slavery for debt, but the soldiers were unimpressed by his pleas. Then Moctezuma's messengers had preempted him for Cortes; if Cortes ate humans, they wanted to present a succulent offering.

"Then you were a test of his godhood?" I asked.

Big Belly shrugged massively. "Well, Plumed Serpent does not take men's flesh or blood, and Moctezuma wanted to learn everything possible."

During the next days I saw my lord only at a distance when I watched him consult with his officers. Often the discussions were angry; I saw men turn from Cortes with insolent faces, rebellious, forgetting their positions as his followers. Why did Cortes tolerate this? My father, a paragon of patience, would not have endured their insubordination for an hour. But I saw Cortes cajole his lieutenants, flatter them with attention. Any other ruler, human or divine, would have stretched them across an altar and had their hearts out before sunset.

Every night clouds of mosquitoes with the beaks of vultures swarmed over the camp. While they kept me awake, I occupied my mind by repeating new Spanish words, yet often I found myself dwelling on worries. I worried that Cortes was so careless of his dignity; I worried that Moctezuma might be sending not a gift-bearing embassy but an army.

I worried that Lord Alonzo, although satisfying and often exciting, had nothing new to teach me. If my lessons were done, why did not my lord take me? What was wrong with me? Was I too tall, too strong for a woman? Lord Alonzo did not seem to find me so. I lay awake, swatting mosquitoes and cursing the Land of Bounteous Beauty.

Then one morning I noticed a stir among the shy folk who lived in the neighborhood of our camp. They appeared among the scrub trees, they searched for vantage points. It told me as clearly as signal drums that Lord Tendile was returning.

"Another embassy," I told Aguilar. "Not an army, or these people would be hiding."

"Coming from Culhua," said Aguilar smugly.

I saw he was envisioning gold. He did not picture the shining lakes and great cities, not the markets with all the goods of the world, not the flower boats or even the temples and palaces. He dreamed only of a land whose mountains were made of yellow metal. So did almost everyone around me, even the Tabascan women.

How could the Spaniards have so little vision? Long ago Plumed Serpent had chosen to be served by an army of moles, and it seemed the same today. The god had a penchant for blind retainers.

"An embassy, not an army," Aguilar announced to everybody, and I understood the Spanish words. But Cortes, despite my assurances, quickly had every man armed and ready for battle. Even the lord horses were prepared to charge if needed.

I was pleased that Cortes changed into the clothing of Plumed

Serpent; it is warming to have your advice appreciated.

The Aztec procession arrived during the Third Watch, approaching in magnificence, the deep-voiced drums sounding, horns and flutes singing. The attendants bore flowers and incense, braziers of smoldering fire that misted the air with the sweetness of copal. Watching, I relived my childhood: Lord Lancer's arrival in Jalisco, my father's welcome to the Lair of the Serpent, the great pageants in Tenochtitlan.

After the censer and flower bearers came marchers resembling a flock of huge birds winging toward us, beautiful but predatory. These were magicians, warlocks and curse-makers, fantastically arrayed in feathers, armed with claws and beaks. Owl men were first, then other sorcerers garbed as vultures, hawks, ravens and shrikes.

"Are they dancers?" Aguilar gaped, not knowing whether to be frightened or simply dazzled.

"Wizards of the Air," I told him. "There must be other magicians, too. Wizards of earth and water."

Aguilar paled and made the sign of the cross.

"They cast spells and cause misfortune," I explained, which was true. Then I added a small, malicious lie. "I understand they transmit their curses through gold. It's their familiar substance."

He looked at me in alarm.

Suddenly a gasp went up from the Spaniards, then came mutterings of amusement and even chuckles. I thought they were delighted by the sight of Lord Tendile, who was wonderfully garbed in orange and yellow with a headdress of scarlet plumes. Then I saw another figure, dark clad, walking behind Tendile where he had been hidden from me.

At a glance it appeared to be Cortes himself, brown-haired and thick-bearded, with a strong, straight nose and powerful brows. The man was also narrow-hipped, broad-shouldered and remarkably tall. I did not realize then that his sandals were triple-soled and the jacket padded. It was as though a statue of my lord the Captain had come to life.

"Viva Cortes!" some soldiers yelled. "Both of them!"

Moctezuma, after studying the drawings the artists had made, had found a double for Cortes—I realized this but did not yet understand why. Great Aztec lords often employed men who resembled themselves or who were adroit at disguise, using these look-alikes for unpleasant or wearisome errands. I had heard of a prince who kept a slave to be his impersonator at boring public ceremonies, an imitation so skillful that the slave was executed by royal order one day in his master's stead.

This use I understood. But why had Moctezuma sought out a double for Cortes and gone to such great pains to disguise him? It was unfathomable.

"More devil's work," Aguilar said. He wrinkled his long, thin nose, and I suppose he smelled the fumes of hell as he had claimed to do with the blood-sprinkled food. "Witchcraft!"

The elaborate rituals of greeting came next: the perfuming, ground-kissing and blessing. Cortes saluted his double, whose name was Quintalbor, with good humor. "Sit here beside me and no one can tell us apart." He slapped Quintalbor on the back with a casual friendliness that confused the Aztecs. Surely a god would not behave this way! But even less would a man pretending to be a god. To me the gesture was painful—and quite incomprehensible.

Quintalbor's face had been heavily powdered, perhaps painted with lime, which up close gave him the look of a corpse whose burial cosmetics have worn thin. The whiskers seemed made of dyed cotton or fur, yet at a distance the resemblance to Cortes was uncanny.

When they sat next to each other, the illusion collapsed. Two candles may be of the same beeswax, but there is no mistaking them when only one is lighted. Quintalbor's disguise conveyed something of the strength of Cortes's features, but Plumed Serpent's flame did not flicker in his face. Besides, the superficial likeness they had in repose vanished utterly in motion. Cortes in gesture and expression—the turning of his head, the lifting of a hand—had the power to fascinate, an ability given to only a few creatures such as hummingbirds, ocelots and dragonflies. You felt compelled to watch him. Quintalbor, once the first surprise was over, could be ignored.

I wondered if Moctezuma, subtle as a mantis, might be sending a message through Quintalbor. "See, we have at least one man who is Plumed Serpent's twin. You are not unique, we are used to imposture." If that was the intent, it failed. The god remained unmistakable.

After the necessary courtesies were over came the moment for which the Spaniards were holding their breath, the time for gift giving. One hundred and four heavily laden porters, their number representing a double sheaf of years, were summoned, and after covering the sand with straw mats, they spread out the treasures they carried. Around me

I heard deep and heartfelt Spanish sighs, murmurs not unlike those Lord Alonzo made at the height of passion. I understood, for I too stood rapt, and I thought, if there is a market in paradise where purified souls do their shopping, it resembles this.

Seven bolts of finest cotton cloth, each as heavy as a man could carry, were unrolled to show the seven colors of the rainbow crown shared by Tlaloc the Rain and Tonatiuh the Sun. Soon that rainbow was studded with vessels, statues and masks in wood, clay and stone. I stared at paintings made of ten thousand feathers, mosaics in turquoise and onyx, images of gods with fire opals for eyes—opals brought from the edge of the Dead World in the land of the Chichimecas. The stones glowed like milky stars. With a flourish Lord Tendile lifted a tapestry woven of flowers to reveal hearts of jade, Mixtec and Maya work, jade badges and medals, some carvings tinted with the blood-red cinnabar of graves.

The Spaniards gasped when the porters brought forth a shining silver Lady Moon, big and round with child. Then the gasps became a shout when next came a pure gold image of Lord Sun, a disc broader than my arms could span. Lady Moon they kept half a bow shot away —she dies too close to her brother Sun—but the great gold disc was placed on the sand before Cortes, as though to make the throne of heaven his footstool. He nodded and with the toe of his boot touched it rather gingerly, as though testing to see if it might miraculously vanish, conjured away perhaps by the sorcerers who were chanting at the edge of the crowd.

It was beautiful and appropriate, almost as wonderful as the tiny ornaments of exquisitely carved jade. It contained enough gold, I mistakenly supposed, to cure the diseases of a thousand shiploads of Spaniards. I did not understand then that the disease is as insatiable as a Spotted God; after eating everything else, it devours its host.

While everyone was exclaiming and marveling and measuring, I wondered how many cities had been reduced to slavery, how many clans impoverished and murdered to gather this array of riches. The world for the last three generations had been ransacked at Aztec knifepoint. I looked at an amethyst necklace sparkling in the sun and thought of my father.

Then I happened to notice an elderly man in simple, unadorned clothing. He was obviously an important member of the official party, yet his plain tunic, lack of jewels and the spirituality of his face set him apart. He carefully kept a little distance between himself and the givers of treasure as he kneeled to unpack a bag made of ixtle fibers, a coarse bag such as a common peddler might carry. As he turned, I saw the imperial crest of Moctezuma tattooed to his thin shoulder; so he was from the great household, Moctezuma's personal messenger.

Scorning the woven mats, the old man placed his few gifts on the uncovered sand. There was a medallion, nothing more than a leather thong with an ornament woven of quetzal and hummingbird feathers; it was old, the plumes had long ago lost their green brilliance. When I stepped closer I saw that the offering was not only old but second-hand, the feathers frayed from wearing. Next to it he put a clay flute and a conch shell that had been cut in half so it resembled a star, then added a single bead of unpolished jade, a few colored maize grains, then encircled his gifts with a belt of bark paper whose only decoration was a few flowers, violets and heliotrope, some blossoms living, others dead and pressed.

He lengthened the circle of the belt. It became an oval, the shape of all temples of Plumed Serpent as the Wind Lord, gently curved so the wind may go where it wills, passing in freedom as Plumed Serpent is freedom of the soul. The maize was His nourishment of the body and the spirit, the flute His music that rests the senses and fills the heart; in the star-shape shell was Evening Star, which sinks in beauty below the horizon as Plumed Serpent himself once descended into the underworld only to rise again in the flight of birds, riding the wind which is Himself, showing that we must fly from darkness toward the sun, toward light. The jade was not what He is but what He is to become, for Plumed Serpent is not a fixed god like Ometeotl or the Flower Prince. He dies and returns like the violets, he is a god-in-the-making, moving toward the set hardness of jade even as our own souls, so soft and elusive and perishable in form, move through the Narrow Passage toward the land where dead branches blossom and dead eyes see eternal light.

The Aztec embassy had given the riches of the world; Moctezuma's own messenger had offered Plumed Serpent himself. And who had worn the old medallion, the wings of the god in flight? No one had to tell me it was Moctezuma's own, his necklace from boyhood when he had studied to become a priest. The First Speaker was the most exalted lord of the Only World who could present great suns of gold and moons of silver, but Moctezuma the man chose humble objects precious to his own heart for his own offering to his god.

As I turned toward Cortes, I felt tears in my eye. I understood Moctezuma's devotion and I forgave him everything, at least for that moment—perhaps for all that single day.

My lord the Captain followed my gaze, saw that the old man's gifts were different, that they were special, and he gave me an inquiring look. I nodded slightly, almost imperceptibly. Cortes left the golden footstool, strode quickly to the little, symbolic wind temple and kneeled to put the medallion around his neck, the belt over his shoulders like a scarf. Seeing this, the old man began to weep, and when Cortes turned away, he prostrated himself, kissing the footprints Plumed Serpent had left in the sand.

The more elegant envoys, awed by what had happened, produced another treasure, a turquoise mask whose features were ingeniously formed by the undulations of a serpent. With it they presented a crown of quetzal plumes and a magnificent feather cape—the official regalia of the high priest of Plumed Serpent, and hence the clothing of the god himself.

Cortes permitted himself to be decked in these only for a moment, and I was relieved when he put them aside. Somehow they diminished him, diminished his godhood. Aguilar must have felt the same way, for he sighed in audible relief when the cape and crown were politely put aside. Cortes said, "My thanks to the great lord."

"The Revered Moctezuma bids us say he gives you only what is already yours," Lord Tendile replied. There was a murmur of agreement among the other Aztec nobles.

But while this was happening—at the very moment they were hailing Cortes as a god—the owl men and other enchanters executed sinister gestures with their hands and wands. A wizard shook a rattle made of human bones while puffs of yellow smoke rose, making the very air seem evil. My lord was being hailed and cursed at the same time, simultaneously welcomed and exorcised! It was my first glimpse of the mind of Moctezuma.

Cortes gestured, and the babel died away. He said, "These gifts have touched us. Now it only remains to journey to the capital and thank the great ruler in person."

Silence fell, the taut silence of a hot summer night before the lightning flashes. "No!" Lord Tendile replied, drawing himself up. "The journey would exhaust you. And it would be dangerous." He had rehearsed not only the words but the stern tone and gestures.

"No worry!" Cortes smiled confidently. "King Carlos expects me to meet Lord Moctezuma, since I have come so far."

I did not translate exactly because I myself did not yet understand about King Carlos. I said "Our high lord," which might have meant Ometeotl, Mover of the Universe. Nobody objected.

"Impossible! The Revered Speaker will not have you attempt such a perilous trip." There was no mistaking the threat. Lord Tendile made a farewell obeisance. "I wish you a safe return to your own land."

"We will meet in the presence of Moctezuma." Cortes gave a jaunty salute. When I translated, I did not conceal my pride in his defiance of Moctezuma.

Tendile, starting to withdraw, suddenly glared at me, dropping his guise of ceremony. "Whoever you are, woman, you are a traitor! Warn your master to leave before it is too late."

Anger heated by years of humiliations boiled up in me. "Warn your own master, Lord Lickspittle! I serve a god."

Tendile left in confusion and indignation. No woman had ever spoken to him so bluntly, and I suppose he regarded me as yet another creature from the weird beyond—like the cannons and dogs.

"What were you saying?" asked Aguilar, surprised.

"A religious quibble," I replied. Although there had been no more than a quick exchange of insults, I felt as though I had demolished the whole Aztec army. In girlhood I had been often cautioned that a woman must conceal the plumage of pride under the leaves of humility. Well, I had been buried too long under those dead leaves. I wanted to stretch the plumes, to discover if they were real, if they would become wings.

The Aztecs were hardly off the beach before the Spaniards swarmed upon the offerings like bees on a papaya, buzzing and sniffing and probing. For a moment I could believe the nonsense about gold being medicine, for I saw several soldiers biting on golden ornaments. Then I realized they were checking the metal's purity, testing its softness.

Beautiful cloth was trampled under boots, the great cotton rainbow ripped by spurs. From their hiding places the Tabascan women emerged—they had gone to ground at sight of the Aztecs—and they quickly salvaged the material, holding it before themselves like clothing, preening and cooing and quacking. Both Spaniards and women

were so thrilled that they instantly forgot the Aztec givers and the
distant treasure house from which all this wealth came. In their greed
they ignored the skill and cleverness of artisans who wrought wonders
in Tenochtitlan; the art they pawed had been handed down from the
Toltecs through a sheaf of generations. But dazzled by baubles, everyone ignored the greatest marvel of all, the Cities of the Aztecs.

No, not everyone.

My lord the Captain stood with the golden sun at his feet but
did not glance at it. Instead he gazed at the western horizon, and I
caught my breath to see that Mountain of the Star now rose against
the sky, shining and magnificent, an omen. At that moment I think my
lord and I shared the same vision: that all things were possible, no
dream too unlikely.

The next morning all the embassy except Quintalbor the impersonator
had vanished. They left behind an assortment of wizards, especially owl
men who peered at us from behind bushes and sand dunes. Big Belly
and his crew of provisioners also stayed. They had orders not to speak
to us, but Quintalbor wandered our camp aping Cortes and delivering
commands in gibberish he thought resembled Spanish.

"Your similarity to Plumed Serpent is astonishing," I told him,
flattery that warmed him like sunlight. "Moctezuma must have
searched the world to find you."

"Not at all. I was present when the portraits of Malintzin were
first shown. Lord Moctezuma noticed the resemblance at once. I am
a court official, keeper of the Special Cages."

"Ah! The Royal Zoo is justly famous."

"Zoo? I am not at the zoo!" His glare would have withered a
cactus. "The Special Cages line the hall outside Lord Moctezuma's own
chamber. The prisoners in them are all young and exceptionally beautiful. At any hour day or night the Speaker can have at hand a perfect
offering worthy of his own blade and altar."

He launched into shop talk of his profession. "Three selectors
help me inspect every new captive arriving with the tribute gatherers.
Only the finest are chosen for the palace sacrifices."

Quintalbor, full of self-importance, soon told me a story that
should have been a state secret.

After their first visit to us, Lord Tendile and the other emissaries
hurried back to the capital to report, arriving at the palace in the dead

of night during the Fifth Watch. Their business was so urgent they
had Moctezuma awakened to receive them. He had just retired to his
mat after waiting anxiously for news until he despaired of their
coming.

The emissaries were ushered into his bedroom, and one glance at
their stricken faces told him that Plumed Serpent had undoubtedly
arrived, that the world faced the gravest crisis in history.

"Do not speak until holy rites have been observed," he commanded.

They adjourned to a nearby room of state furnished with Moctezuma's private sacrificial stone.

"I was ordered to bring five offerings," Quintalbor told me.
"One handsome youth for each cardinal point and a girl to be the
Blessed Center. I happened to have on hand five Zapotec youngsters,
so the sacrifices matched. They had those lovely clear eyes you seldom
see except in the south." The memory pleased him; he was proud of
his office. "Moctezuma was delighted we could begin the rites at once."

One by one the captives were stretched across the stone with four
priests pinioning their wrists and ankles while a fifth collared their
throats with a wooden fork. Moctezuma cut out the hearts and offered
them, still beating, to the Points of Ometeotl. The emissaries hovered
close to the altar so they might be splashed with the spurting blood.

"They had talked with gods," said Quintalbor. "They needed
special baptism."

Moctezuma had to be mad—or at least religiously deranged. This
was his welcome for Plumed Serpent, a god known to abhor human
sacrifice! If some other deity had been returning incarnate—like Xipe
Totec who dresses in skin flayed from living humans—I would have
understood the Speaker's action; he would have had no choice. But to
propitiate the Lord of Gentle Wisdom? It was waste and madness.

"After the sacrifices the Revered Speaker looked at the pictures
the artists had drawn and saw my resemblance to your lord. Of course
I am a little darker and have no natural whiskers. But I was enough
like the pictures that Moctezuma summoned Lord Two Vulture
Wolf's Paw for advice."

"Who is he?"

"A great magician, the head of Moctezuma's owl men. You have
seen Lord Wolf's Paw. He came with the ambassadors and is still here.
The tall lord with a withered left hand."

I had seen this man near the camp several times, and his deformed hand certainly resembled a paw. He did not dress like the wizards he commanded, but there was still something sinister about him. Once I had watched him gathering herbs and berries.

"Moctezuma and Lord Wolf's Paw conferred, and I was sent on this mission."

Quintalbor did not know what purpose had been served by the impersonation or why he was to remain in our camp and copy Cortes's every gesture. He had been dismissed from the council hall before the plans were made. But he felt his role was of vital importance.

After this conversation I wandered in the thin shade at the edge of the beach trying to fathom the mind of Moctezuma. The Revered Speaker seemed like a god who has a bright face and a dark one. His brightness glowed in the lavish gifts and greetings, in the rich food he served us daily.

Then there were hints of darkness: the refusal to allow us to travel to the capital, the malevolent presence of the wizards and curse-makers.

Just as I was thinking this, I almost stumbled over an arrangement of feathers and tanned human skin placed in the middle of the path, a Spirit Guard set there to halt the passage of witches and demons. Although I was neither, I did not tempt any power by stepping around it —curses drip from such objects like water from a sponge. Kneeling, I looked closely without touching the thing. It had been arranged on a bed of leaves, berries and roots. I recognized nightshade and greenish gila berries whose juice burns the fingers; if swallowed, they guarantee a swift but painful trip through the Narrow Passage. So these were the spices Lord Wolf's Paw had been collecting. I turned back to the camp.

Here, too, I found mysteries. While gold might not be a sovereign cure for disease, its stimulating effect on Spaniards was amazing. Yesterday they had leapt for joy at getting it, kicking their heels like dancers at a harvest festival. This morning the Tabascan women had giggled about a startling improvement in the Spaniards' prowess as lovers—another result of this strange medicine. But today the pleasure had turned into suspicion and hostility. The gold fragmented them, divided them into distrustful factions. Small groups of men now gathered in whatever shade they could find. They whispered and cast narrow glances at other groups.

Everyone kept a watchful eye on an officer named Cristobal Olid, a huge puma of a man all tawny and with a puma muzzle. His task today was a sensitive one, commanding a crew that moved the gold and other treasure from the beach to the flagship. As I passed nearby, the heavy image of Lord Sun was almost swamping two boats that had been lashed together.

"Is the ship to take the gifts away?" I asked Aguilar.

"No. Aboard ship it is easier to guard against theft."

"Theft? You think the Aztecs might take the gold back?"

He turned away, and I realized he did not want to confess it was his countrymen he distrusted.

Walking along the edge of the water, I nodded politely to several clusters of soldiers. Now I could connect various Spaniards with their names and personalities. At first most of them had looked alike—pink skinned, bearded and beaked, hawks with hair for plumage. Some differed yet had all appeared so strange that they blended, and I noticed their common oddity more than their differences one from another. Now they appeared as individual as humans.

Now, at the edge of the camp, I saw the four Spaniards I liked the least, the Alvarado brothers. Today, as often, they were a faction of their own, holding a secret family conclave with Pedro, the biggest and boldest, presiding. Their hair and pointed beards were yellow as Sun, yellower yet paler than the metal disc Olid and his crew now struggled with. They squatted on the sand in a line, four Golden Condors—as I called them—perched on a branch with Great Condor dominating. Their thin noses swooped toward chins made more pointed by beards shaped like arrowheads. Everyone feared them; everyone was right.

Today the Condors seemed to be hatching mischief. But Cortes, I had noticed, put great trust in these four, so whatever mischief they were plotting was probably not against him. They always treated me with respect, yet I noted how contemptuously they behaved toward the Tabascan women. Certainly they had a touch of divinity—that was obvious as they sat reflecting the sunlight—but it was a malevolent godhood, what Aguilar called being a demon.

"Good afternoon, gentlemen," I said, trying out Spanish words I had learned from Lord Alonzo.

They looked at me, as astounded as if a coyote had spoken. The Great Condor, Pedro, recovered first. "Good afternoon, my lady." He stumbled to his feet, bowed and added something polite that I pretended to understand.

"Good afternoon," I repeated, and walked on, marveling that my uttering just three words in their own language had so elevated my position in their eyes.

Leaving the Spanish camp, I found shelter from the heat among the scrubby palms where Big Belly had hung up woven mats to shade the women and three or four male slaves who prepared our food. By now I was a familiar enough visitor that no one paid attention to me. I noticed that new cotton canopies were stretched between the trees and set on stakes a little distance away, covered nests for the owl men with leafy curtains protecting them from view while they forged their curses. So here, on this wretched beach in the Land of Bounteous Beauty, were two encampments only a few bow shots apart, one Spanish and the other Aztec, but both filled to the brim with plotters. I wondered when the talking and cursing would end and the fighting start.

Yet the scene around me also gave an impression of serenity, three women gossiping quietly as they peeled fruit, an old man building a fire to cook fish, Big Belly himself looking like an embodiment of the God of Gluttonous Pleasure as he dozed on a mat, a child with a fly whisk attending his rest.

Just as my worries were lulled and my own eyelids growing heavy, I was startled by a cry, half a sob and half a scream. Quintalbor, still dressed like my lord the Captain but wearing a vulture mask for a headdress, stumbled from one of the huts of the magicians, clutching and tearing the vine curtains as he reeled forward. He dropped to his knees, broken vines tangled around his neck and shoulders, his fists now beating his own stomach. With a long, terrible howl of pain Quintalbor collapsed on the sand, his whole body shuddering and writhing.

The women cooks, recovering from their shock, rushed to aid him, and I rose to do the same thing, but something held me back—perhaps memory of the Spotted Gods and how they leapt from one victim to another. I knew Quintalbor was dying even though he had been healthy and strutting only an hour ago.

Then from the shelters appeared a whole convocation of wizards, emerging so suddenly that they must have been awaiting Quintalbor's first groan. The whole feathered and clawed host of the supernatural now danced and chanted around the dying man, drawing out obsidian blades to cut away his mock Spanish garments, piercing and rending them, then at last trampling them underfoot. As the clothing was destroyed, so was my brief illusion that it was my lord the Captain who lay moaning and choking.

I did not know what poison they had used—I had not yet had my lessons in that art—neither could I fully understand the rites they performed, but I had no doubt I was watching the murder of my lord the Captain by sorcery. Quintalbor had become Cortes; now both could die together.

I slipped away, first moving slowly not to attract attention, then running and plunging through the sand, stumbling toward the Spanish camp, hoping desperately that I might not be too late, that my lord the Captain would still be alive long enough for me to kneel beside him and whisper words to ease his way through the Narrow Passage.

I had no doubt that the owl men's spell was invincible, that I had lost Plumed Serpent, and it seemed that around me the world was dying forever; there would be nothing but desolation. The god could not perish, but his form of flesh and blood could be swallowed up by time, eaten by eternity, and when after sheaves of years he returned again, I would be nothing but brittle bones and grave rags.

Then when I was ready to scream and pull out my hair and claw my own flesh like a Tabascan widow, I saw him.

He sat on a low stool in the doorway of his tent, smiling and unperturbed, several of his lieutenants gathered around him, listening and nodding, all of them oblivious to the horrible spell that had just been forged.

"Lady Marina." He rose, bowed slightly to acknowledge my presence. Then, seeing my distress, his face became grave and his voice gentle. He said, and I understood him, "What is wrong? Please sit down. Shall I summon Brother Aguilar?"

"No. All is well, my lord," I answered, the first time I had spoken to him in his own language. Silently I added, "Forgive me for doubting your power. I know better now."

I kneeled beside him, my face composed although my heart was still pounding, and I tried to understand as they continued talking, catching many words, missing many more. Gradually I became calmer and began to realize the importance of what I had seen. Now there was no doubt that Moctezuma had ordered his wizards to destroy Cortes and had gone to great trouble to achieve this, personally choosing the right impersonator from his own household, having the impersonator become Cortes, who would then be slain by proxy. In spite

of the gold and silver he gave, in spite of the sweet words, Moctezuma's intentions were evil, murderous.

Still, at the same time that he dispatched sorcerers, the First
Speaker sent things more valuable than gold, gifts to a beloved god.
I thought of the worn medallion, the clay flute. Was Moctezuma the
emperor struggling with Moctezuma the priest?

I pondered the problem, at last realizing I must think of Moctezuma as both a man and a god. Once he had been merely human,
simply General Courageous Lord, a celebrated soldier and priest, but
not divine. When he gained the highest office in the world seventeen
years ago he became a god or at least a godling. Like all gods, he was
half-light and half-darkness, half-day and half-night. Yesterday we had
seen the face that shone with gold, silver and turquoise; today I had
seen the other countenance, the Moctezuma who had killed my father.
I would remember both faces.

I wondered then what poison had been used to murder Quintalbor and if Lord Two Vulture Wolf's Paw had concocted it. There
might come a day when such knowledge would be useful. I could
probably not learn more about the deadly potion—that would be a
secret belonging to the owl men. But I could remember the name of
the man who brewed it. It is always prudent to know the names of
experts.

The next day we saw more of the scowling face of Moctezuma.

In the morning Big Belly arrived at the camp requesting a
meeting with Cortes, Aguilar and me. For once his usually cheerful
countenance was as long as it was wide and he delivered a message
instead of provisions. The Aztecs, for special religious reasons, could
light no fires and prepare no food today. He deeply regretted our
deprivation and would make up for it with future feasts—would we
like turkey and venison roasted with calabash flowers tomorrow? Wild
honey and mangos for dessert?

I listened coldly. The religious bosh was simply an excuse for not
feeding us, while politeness demanded the blatantly false promise of
banquets to come. Refusal must be made palatable with hope, like
beans with chili.

Ignoring Aguilar, I translated directly into Spanish for Cortes.
"This is a lie," I explained. "The month is still Desire for Rains. There
are no fasts."

Aguilar, ruffled, corrected me about the word "fasts" but he understood it. Cortes smiled at my Spanish, and I felt he wanted to clasp my shoulder as he did when congratulating soldiers on jobs well done. Formality forbade the touch, but his smile achieved the same result.

"Very well, a lie." He spoke to me, not Aguilar. "Is it also an order from Moctezuma?"

Big Belly, refusing to be questioned, waddled toward the Aztec encampment. I did not want his reply, I knew the answer, but this time I needed help with the words.

"Not an order. Even the swift-messengers could not yet have reported to Lord Moctezuma and returned here—although they should arrive tonight and then we will know for sure. But Lord Tendile, who is lurking somewhere not far away, expects a command to cut off our supplies, and there is always credit in anticipating a sovereign's wishes. I am sure no more food will come. They will try to starve us off the beach, force us to take to the ships."

"Why? They were so friendly yesterday." I felt he was testing his judgment against mine, that he had already found an answer.

"Only until my lord said he would go to meet Moctezuma. Not friendly after that."

"Thank you, Lady Marina." He dismissed us graciously, and as we left, he was gazing toward Mountain of the Star. I knew if we were forced to leave the beach, we would sail eastward, and I was exultant. Also I felt the glow of my lord's pleasure in hearing my Spanish, feeble as it was.

That night, warmed by Cortes's smile, I imagined that Lord Alonzo was Plumed Serpent. Suddenly the lessons I had been learning, the ways to give and take pleasure, seemed to fall into place. I worshiped the god with my lips and mouth and tongue, then arched my body to his. At moments I was the instrument a musician plays, then I became the musician and he the instrument. Afterward we clung together in quiet pleasure, both of us surprised and content.

Fortunately we had such distraction, because the early Watches were dreadful and nerve-racking, haunted with the cries and shrieks of Moctezuma's sorcerers. The noises echoing around the camp seemed so eerie and inhuman that I wondered if the owl men had actually changed into demon birds—I could almost hear the flap of giant wings.

Many soldiers gathered around a fire where Father Olmedo chanted quavering prayers.

At last Lord Alonzo fell asleep and then so did I, only to be awakened a little later by a sudden silence. Nothing rustled in the darkness; not a cricket sang. Rising quietly, I stepped out onto the sand, which lay silvery under Lady Moon. The silence was consoling now that the owl men had spent themselves and delivered what I hoped were their last-ditch farewell curses. Father Olmedo's fire had dwindled to smoking embers, his nervous congregation dispersed for sleep, but another fire glowed farther down the beach and curiosity drew me toward it.

I approached cautiously, then stood watching unseen in the shadow of a tent. Cortes, head bowed, kneeled near the edge of the sea where high tide brushed the shore. Beside him, also kneeling, was Pedro Alvarado, greatest of the Golden Condor brood, his whiskers white in the moonlight. There were two soldiers whose names I did not know, and all four were gathered around the unmoving, stretched-out body of one of the lord horses.

At sight of the horse, I drew deeper into the shadows. Horses still made me uneasy, although I now understood many things about them and even dared think of mounting one one day. At first I had assumed, naturally enough, that the riders belonged to the horses, but learned the opposite was true.

"They are not men or gods," Aguilar had explained to me. "Merely animals." Merely? As if a presence as magnificent as a horse could ever be *merely* anything!

But Aguilar's words and slightly scornful tone put me on to an important discovery. He looked upon men, animals and gods—he would have said demons—as inhabitants of three distinct islands with an uncrossable gulf between them. I had been brought up to believe that all beings shared a single mainland, or perhaps we were all members of a single, huge family with close cousins and distant ones, varied and often quarrelsome. Gods and humans were very close, sometimes almost indistinguishable. Other creatures were kin to both, even though they might look very different, and a few—jaguars and butterflies, for instance—were certainly superior to humans, although lower than gods. No Spaniard ever understood this, which meant that no Aztec ever understood a Spaniard.

The nearby fire flared a little and I saw that the horse lying on the sand was the fierce one that belonged to Cortes himself—I could recognize it by its lovely piñon nut color. At the same instant I realized that the horse was not sleeping but dead—a startling and terrible thought, for I had never considered the idea of such lordly creatures dying. They seemed too powerful, too majestic to be felled by death.

So this was how the owl men's spell had worked out; Quintalbor's murder had brought down not Cortes but the creature closest to him.

"Babieca!" said Cortes, and there was pain in his voice. "Ay, Babieca!" The horse's name? It had to be. Strange, because although I did not know the word, I had heard soldiers use it to each other as an insult, I thought.

Pedro Alvarado put his arm around Cortes's shoulders, a brazenly familiar gesture even though he meant only to console him. Alvarado shared his master's loss, his sympathy was genuine, and I knew that much as I might dislike the Condor, he was Cortes's faithful follower. In a camp rife with mutterings and false smiles it was important to keep track of loyalties.

"Babieca!" When Cortes lifted his face, I saw tears glint on his cheeks. Then I slipped away silently, not wishing to intrude upon my lord's sorrow, knowing I had already seen a tenderness he could not let the world see, for Spaniards are ashamed of their own tears. In one of his former lives, as a priest in the City of Tula, Plumed Serpent had often wept openly for his own grief and for the afflictions of others. We still hear his sorrow in the sighing of the wind.

The remaining Aztecs departed at the first hint of light, vanishing like the dawn mist. Moctezuma showed his royal displeasure and the end of his hospitality by taking away all the cooks, hunters and Big Belly. I have wondered if he ended as a regimental banquet.

Hunger came soon upon us. The Tabascan women scoured the shore for crabs, searched the bushes for berries while the soldiers brought down a few birds with their crossbows. These scanty rations were filled out with chunks of gluey starch brought from the damp holds of the ships. The stuff was neither dough nor bread but moldy paste made from some root that grows on the far islands. Globs of it were served up rancid and full of maggots.

One soldier, a man named Bernal Diaz, grinned at me and said, "Careful of your dinner, my lady. Mine walked right off my plate."

It was the oldest army joke, but the first joke I understood in Spanish, so I was delighted. And I liked this plain, honest man. He had a good face with no touch of divinity to arouse my suspicions.

Within a few days I began to fear that Moctezuma would really force us to take to the sea. We could neither remain on the beach nor venture into unknown mountains without provisions. There were too many hungry mouths—more than six hundred Spaniards plus the Tabascan women and a scattering of dark slaves from Cuba, most of them so black-skinned that they looked like Maya bachelors who paint themselves with soot and pitch when they go courting.

Hunger made me gloomy. I recalled that at one time Plumed Serpent had caused squashes to grow so big that a whole family could feast off a single one for a week. But Cortes did not possess that aspect of the god's power. Neither could he call birds to alight on his shoulder or rabbits to congregate at his feet. How complex are the different incarnations of the god! Plumed Serpent might return to the world a score of times and never be twice alike.

Some hungry Tabascan women came to me in tears. "Will we starve? Will the Aztecs come back and eat us?"

Flower Pouch, always insolent, challenged me. "You claim Cortes is a god! Why doesn't he change this sand to a garden?"

"You talk like Father Olmedo," I told her sharply. "Because *his* god is all-powerful, would one of ours be? People of the Only World have never had such a god—not even Ometeotl or Itzamna. Gods have their powers and their limits."

"So far we are seeing only the limits," she muttered.

I leaned close to Flower Pouch. "Maybe I will ask him for a special miracle. How would you like your breasts to turn to cactus? Nice little round ones with plenty of spikes!"

They fled and it was a long time before Flower Pouch bothered me again.

The Spaniards disagreed and hesitated. One night after a long session of arguments and protests, two soldiers passed the shelter where I was sitting and I caught enough of their words to understand the meaning.

"You have to admit Cortes lets every man speak," said one.

The other sneered. "Yes. He keeps you talking until you agree with what he's had in mind all along. Then you think it's your own idea."

Next day I lingered close to a conference Cortes held with his officers, hoping to learn new words. But I only heard the same ones over and over.

"Return to Cuba!"

"No, build a fort here."

"This is illegal!"

"Not at all. We made things legal yesterday!"

This squabble of crows went on and on. The Captain appeared to listen closely to every word, nodding in agreement even when they all contradicted each other. But twice I saw his eyes wander toward Mountain of the Star. Why did he not simply give these men an order? No, that was not his way. It slowly dawned on me that he waited for them to hear some command from Fate itself. His will, in unknown ways, must become theirs.

Even as I was thinking this, events made the decision. Bernal Diaz came running from his sentry post shouting that important messengers had arrived to see Cortes.

"Different people," he said. "Not Aztecs."

The messengers approached, five men whose bearing was more impressive than their simple clothes. They were barefoot, wore un-decorated white loincloths and cotton capes as protection against the sun. One—I supposed he was the leader—had a beautiful polished jade ornament in his nose.

They were all short and stocky as lowland people are, but carried themselves with the dignity of high rank. All except the leader wore identical jewelry, a sort of national badge. Their earlobes had been pierced and stretched to an unusual length, almost brushing their shoulders, and they had perforated lower lips. The ear and lip holes held some of the loveliest turquoise pieces I had ever seen, shining blue stars. They were Totonacs, people who in ancient times had lived in mountains now occupied by allies of the Aztecs. They had been driven into the hot country sheaves of years ago, and here the heat had shrunk them. The men were hardly taller than the Tabascan women.

Their leader saluted Cortes, then began to talk rapidly in a language I could not understand, as strange as the speech of the Monkey People. But two of them had dealt with the Aztecs and knew enough of their language that I could at least fathom their meanings. They were impressed that the Aztecs had brought gifts.

"Moctezuma has sent tribute," said one. "Strange. Tribute always goes the other way, as surely as rivers run downhill."

"Moctezuma fears us," I answered, which seemed to please them.

"The Aztecs have withdrawn your food."

"They were frightened; they ran away."

The leader, who spoke only his own language, suddenly exclaimed and pointed at a parrot-feather necklace a soldier was wearing. It had been part of the Aztec tribute, but Spaniards did not value feather work.

"Does he want the necklace?" Cortes asked. "Give it to him."

But the Totonac, after examining the feathers, shook his head and refused the gift. He had been mistaken, one of the interpreters explained. His grandson, the man's favorite, had been wearing a similar necklace when, at nine years old, he was snatched and carried away by Aztec tax gatherers for sacrifice in Tenochtitlan. But no, this was not the boy's necklace.

"Are many children taken this way?" Cortes asked, seeing the man's pain and anger.

The question brought a storm of replies and curses. The Aztecs had only recently conquered the Totonac nation, so the rage was new and blazing. I could not understand or translate more than the gist of their outrage.

"Then Moctezuma has enemies within his own empire," Cortes said softly.

"More enemies than friends, lord," I said. "Not just Totonacs. There are the Tlaxcalans, and no Tlaxcalan dies content unless two Aztecs die with him. Also, the Cloud People called Mixtec dream of rebellion; so does the City of the Reeds. There are others—so many others!"

"Will the Spaniards visit our city?" The Totonacs were almost unseemly in their eagerness. "Our chief lord urges you to come. He promises you gifts and women and feasting."

I translated as loudly as I could, hoping that I got the words right in Spanish and that the men would hear and become united about leaving this miserable beach.

"Only a day's journey north, then a little inland," they said, and I told Cortes.

"Inland?" He looked uncertain. He glanced at his lieutenants and the soldiers.

Just then I realized that some of the Spaniards were edging

forward, whispering excitedly among themselves. One of them pushed forward and rudely seized a Totonac by the earlobe, squinting at the ornament of turquoise he wore there.

"Gold, by the balls of Saint Joseph!" the Spaniard shouted. "This blue pebble is set in gold!" A band of gold so thin I had not noticed it rimmed the ornament.

"This fellow comes from a country that has gold!" the Spaniard announced. At least he said something close to that, for word was passed through the ranks and suddenly the whole army was excited.

"Yes, gold," I cried. "You can all go there." I knew I would not offend Cortes by taking the decision out of his hands. After all, Totonac country was on the way to Plumed Serpent's kingdom.

"Gold!" the men were shouting.

We left the beach the next morning.

The Spaniards struck camp with a speed that would have astonished the Aztecs. We marched northward, the ships with the treasure and heavy guns pacing us just offshore.

The Land of Bounteous Beauty had been wretched to remain in, and now it seemed even worse in departing. We stumbled in pebbly sand, the horses often floundering. This was wasteland where nothing lived but sand crabs and little brown scorpions who are the crabs' evil cousins. The scorpions, whose dagger stings can cripple you for a day or two, so worried me that I accepted Lord Alonzo's offer to ride behind him on his horse, clenching my teeth to keep them from chattering with fear. Soon I found it safe and almost pleasant, but as the sun rose higher, the heat from clinging to both him and the horse became unbearable. I took my chances walking among the scorpions.

Cortes constantly moved up and down the line, encouraging and urging. Moving back and forth, he must have covered double the set distance for the day, yet he remained fresh and cheerful at sunset.

He was always a marvel of endurance on the march. Partly because of him and partly because of their own unusual natures, the Spaniards seemed to enjoy themselves when pushing ahead, despite their cursing and grumbling.

Late that first afternoon a thorn pierced my foot above the sole of my sandal. As I kneeled to pull it out, Cortes was suddenly there, kneeling beside me.

"Allow me, Lady Marina," he said. When he grasped my ankle,

I decided it was worth the small pain. "This is too hard a journey for a noble lady. I apologize."

"No, my lord. I am as strong as any soldier here, yourself excepted." Did he understand me? "I have walked in harder country than this."

Most of the Spanish words must have been wrong. We were so close I could imagine his breath on my cheek. When he pulled out the thorn, I did not have sense enough to pretend to fall against him or utter a pretty little cry of pain. The most stupid girl would have performed such coquetry by instinct. I sat unflinching, trying to impress him as a good soldier when what I really wanted to be was one of the pretty ladies in the Garden of Texcoco, fluttering and mincing and exuding perfume.

"I hope that was not too painful," he said.

"There is no pain in my lord's presence." Too solemn a remark, not what one of the pretty ladies would have said. But he held my ankle a moment longer and his eyes said to me, *Soon now. Wait for me.*

The next morning we forded a shallow river. Soon the land changed, became green and fertile. Trees shading the beach were not ghosts or skeletons but flourishing palms and sea grapes. Taller forests rose on our left; the officers warned everyone about possible ambush.

Before noon the Alvarado brothers, who had ridden ahead as scouts, galloped back shouting that a town lay just ahead. I hurried forward, hobbling a little from yesterday's thorn.

The village proved glum and impoverished—a squat temple, garbage heaps swarming with flies and a few sagging pens that until recently had held turkeys. The inhabitants had fled.

Pedro Alvarado wrinkled his nose, and his golden mustache bobbed. "I smell cooked meat. They have just had dinner." Today he seemed not a condor but a beautiful yellow wolf. He started toward the temple, which seemed to be the source of the aroma. Cortes followed him; so did Aguilar and I.

The temple was a shabby hut of straw and bamboo on top of a stepped stone platform. It housed some religious sculpture, gods so crudely carved that I could not recognize them. Three carcasses, headless, limbless and eviscerated, were stretched on the altars.

"Are those human?" Pedro Alvarado demanded. Aguilar nodded and crossed himself.

"Where are their arms and legs?"

"Carried away for food," I answered. Alvarado did not understand my attempt at Spanish. I made gestures. "Food. To eat."

He turned pale, then hurried down the outside steps to vomit. "Cannibals! A nest of cannibals! I wish they'd return! I'd slaughter every last rotten one of them."

I would hear him say this several times in the future. It seemed strange that the Spaniards held human life so cheap and human meat so precious. Lady Flint Knife had taught me that cannibalism, except in dire emergency and with religious moderation, is unwise. It makes every living person the likely prey of everybody else; even wolves are more civilized. But it is the killing, not the eating, that is wicked. What does dead flesh really matter? Yet, of course, the fate of my own corpse concerns me.

(I have made arrangements for my own body when life has left it. After my required Christian burial, paid servants will dig me up and place my remains in a tree as the Toltecs used to do, so my flesh may be eaten by birds. I will return as part of them, a plumed companion of the Wind God. I think of myself as a lark or a flashing tanager. Probably I will come back as a crow or squawking macaw. My enemies predict that.)

We left this dismal village after eating a few half-ripe fruits the inhabitants had not bothered to pick, then soon turned inland following a swift stream. A deer flashed through the trees. Someone fired at it but missed, and Pedro Alvarado failed to catch it, swift though his horse was. Where deer can graze, maize can grow, so I knew we would soon reach settlements.

A party of men, beating drums and blowing shell horns, appeared on the opposite bank, brushing aside willow fronds to make their way along a narrow path. Seeing us, they made gestures of welcome and waded into the river, which looked deep but they knew was shallow.

"We have been waiting, hoping for you to come!" called one of the men who had been at our camp.

The lords who greeted us carried great bouquets of roses and presented a sheaf to Cortes, a sheaf to each horseman and one to me. On the far bank warriors, women and children arrived bearing so many bundles of flowers that the willow trees around us resembled an arbor made of blossoming vines. We crossed the stream, moving into a cloud of perfume and singing. Our vanguard, riding ahead, suddenly wheeled and raced back to us shouting, "A city of silver! Just ahead! Silver walls and roofs!"

The Spaniards almost stampeded toward this marvel, but Aguilar and I exchanged a smile, then laughed, for we knew that in many hot lands the roofs and walls are covered with white stucco, then painted glossy white. I had never heard Aguilar laugh before. His long, thin face unfolded and he looked almost friendly.

We entered Zempoala, the place of twenty waters, and I never would have believed that hot-land people, notorious for sloth and sexual dalliance, could have built such a city. Thousands of thatched houses sprang from the jungle floor, gathered around white palaces and temples of white and pink. I had heard of the town's lush gardens and its famed Temple of Little Faces, but still did not expect such beauty.

We paraded through a rejoicing crowd, were perfumed and garlanded. The soldiers were offered honeyed pineapples and plums, which they almost snatched out of the hands of the givers. This, I thought, is right, the way it should be: Plumed Serpent enters his kingdom in triumph and joy. I was exalted to be near him, a player in the greatest scene in history, yet knew even greater scenes would follow.

My lord the Captain, gravely smiling and saluting, asked under his breath, "Why such a welcome?"

I could not explain in Spanish that Plumed Serpent should expect no less. Besides, I was ignorant of Totonac religion and did not know my lord's place in it. I gave another reason, also true.

"They hate the Aztecs, lord. You come as a liberator." I got the word "liberator" wrong and Aguilar had to supply it.

"I thought so," said Cortes. He stood taller, his smile broadened.

The official reception was in the great plaza, a courtyard at least four bow shots wide surrounded on three sides by temples and on the fourth by the palace. My lord glanced at the sanctuaries atop the high platforms. His smile hardly changed, but I thought he suppressed a shudder. He spoke to Aguilar in Spanish too rapid for me.

"What did he say?" I asked.

"The temples are like buzzards perched on cliffs."

Their jutting bamboo and thatch roofs did faintly resemble wings, and I knew that the insides of the temples were indeed like the insides of buzzards: full of carrion. My lord spoke like an Aztec poet, although no Aztec would have shared his feeling.

A nobleman bearing the crook of royal office made obeisance. His face was painted with chalk to show he was a king's surrogate. White rods pierced his lobes and septum, and he carried a white ceremonial shield with silver chasings. He was magnificent.

"A death's-head," whispered Aguilar. "God save us!" There is no explaining taste.

"Welcome! Share what few luxuries we can offer guests now that the Aztecs have despoiled this land." So he came straight to the point of our invitation—Aztecs. The surrogate spoke such perfect highland speech that I suspected he might once have been a hostage in Tenochtitlan. "Our ruler, Lord Three Rabbit Thunderclap, begs forgiveness. He is too heavy of body to stand through a formal greeting, but will receive you soon. He suggests you dine first since you might be hungry."

Hungry? We were famished! It was hard not to plunge headlong toward the nearby mats heaped with delicacies. The soldiers tore into venison and turkey, tossing bones and gristle to the dogs that leapt to catch the treats, then fought over them. After we had gorged ourselves, a troop of pretty young women appeared with gourds of flowered water, cotton towels and pieces of expensive soaptree root to bathe the men's hands. Although they were not whores, they showed none of the modesty of Maya women or the reserve of Aztecs. Giggling, they made monkey eyes, flaunting their tits and flashing their thighs in the soldiers' faces, all but presenting themselves as dessert. One of them fingered Lord Alonzo's golden hair, then squealed with delight.

I decided rumors about hot-land sensuality were true, especially when my own finger bath was performed not by a woman but by a handsome youth whose navel was the heart of a tattooed rose. Vines running from the blossom down into his loincloth promised a whole bouquet of roses below. The host had given thought to my pleasure! I felt pleased when Lord Alonzo glared at the boy.

Horns blew, a herald shouted, "Now comes Lord Three Rabbit Thunderclap, ruler of Zempoala and the Thirty Towns of our nation."

His standard bearers swept before him, waving long poles with shields decorated with tufts of feathers and dyed puffs of cotton. Then Chief Thunderclap waddled toward us, leaning heavily on thick canes while two young boys held and propelled him from behind, one boy for each haunch. He was not only obese but gigantic, legs like mahogany trunks, drums for arms and breasts so bulging that prostitutes would have envied them. The cascade of flesh dwarfed his head and hands: I remembered a monster turtle god washed ashore at Tabasco. The Spaniards were unable to think of him as anything but the Fat Chief; his name was totally forgotten.

"Welcome!" he cried, and Cortes came forward to embrace him, but his arms could not reach halfway around the girth.

"Accept these small gifts," said the Fat Chief through interpreters. Pedro Alvarado accepted a wicker basket and pawed rudely through it, exclaiming as he found a few gold trinkets.

The Fat Chief, scenting disappointment, said, "I can give no more because I have been robbed by the Aztecs. Even my personal jewelry has been stolen. I beg you to accept these trifles they have overlooked."

Cortes nodded graciously. "We will repay these gifts with services. We come here to punish evildoers and serve justice." My lord the Captain then spoke of the Spanish king and matters of religion, condemning human sacrifice. With Aguilar, I translated, omitting the Spanish king and skimming lightly over religion. Some problems are too complex for a first meeting. "Human sacrifices should end," I repeated.

The Fat Chief sighed; he expected this and knew it would be troublesome. "You are our hope, Malintzin," said the Fat Chief, using that odd title for Cortes. I was not used to the idea that he was "Malina's lord," although of course he was.

After the chief had left, Cortes gave orders to the army. "Keep your hands off plump fowls and plump maidens. No offense is to be given these people! I am serious. I hope nobody learns how serious."

For two days I prowled the town, learning all I could about the people. They hated Aztecs bitterly, but I found them cowed by past defeats. I reported to my lord, who asked, "Will they fight?"

"Against Aztecs? I doubt it. They have been whipped badly."

Totonac leaders, chiefs of outlying towns, arrived daily, each bringing a mingy gift and a new grievance against the Aztecs. Lord Cuesco, the Fat Chief's surrogate and interpreter, gathered them in the plaza. A clamor rose as they shouted their charges: a daughter raped then killed by Aztec soldiers, a favorite wife carried off, sons dragged to the altars of sacrifice. An old man from a village of vanilla growers told how the Aztecs, who prize vanilla because it clears the head of vapors and the stomach of gas, sent tax gatherers every harvest to seize half the crop—and some of the growers.

In the middle of one of these meetings the Fat Chief arrived in a litter and spoke so eloquently that we almost understood his sorrow without translation. Fat men should be jolly as Olmec gods who seem to laugh even with jaguar mouths. The Fat Chief with tears coursing down his cheeks was more moving because pain did not fit him.

Cortes said quietly, "Do not be afraid. We will set things straight. We will protect you."

But just then sentries from nearby posts ran into the plaza shouting, "Aztec collectors! At the edge of town!"

The Totonacs scattered in panic, and the Fat Chief was trundled off shouting, "We must prepare clean quarters—food, chocolate—"

The Spaniards expected an army—at least a regiment. Instead five Aztec businessmen strolled into the plaza. They carried wands of office, and their cloaks and loincloths were embroidered with imperial seals, opulent but overdone to impress the provincial natives. Hairdressers had teased their locks into swirled heaps, inserting feathers and gold pins. All five carried nosegays of roses pressed to their faces—perfume to drown the stench of Zempoala. The Totonacs were to be robbed and insulted at the same time.

The Aztec party crossed within spear touch of the Captain, staring straight ahead and sniffing their posies.

"Fuck them," said a soldier, and made the sound of a fart.

The Aztecs, sniffing assiduously, moved toward the palace of the Fat Chief, followed by slaves with fly whisks and parasols. Trailing far behind was a captive retinue of Totonac lords who wore not a scrap of jewelry or plumage. Plucked turkeys, I thought, just waiting for the roasting spit.

The Aztecs, installed in rooms that had been made into bowers, summoned the main lords of Zempoala one by one. Halfway across the plaza I heard them berate the Totonacs for inviting Spaniards to the city, for welcoming and regaling us. When the Fat Chief was hauled before them, I moved close to spy through the open work of the rear wall.

An Aztec pointed at the Fat Chief with his little finger, the ultimate gesture of contempt. "You are hereby fined twenty of your subjects. Not slaves, mind you, but youths and girls of good family. Have them bound and ready for departure tomorrow." The chief moaned, and his wattles trembled.

"Be quiet, you emperor of gnats and worms! Perhaps you yourself would enjoy a walk to Tenochtitlan?" As the chief crawled away, a tax collector shouted after him, "Your wretched people are going to a good cause. Moctezuma will offer their hearts to the great Hummingbird to give us victory over the Spaniards."

They left the Fat Chief howling with grief. Some of his own children or grandchildren were sure to be among the victims. Nothing less would satisfy the Aztecs.

I hurried to report all this to Cortes, who considered the situation a moment, then asked, "You think the Totonacs will not resist this?"

I had to tell him the bitter truth. "Not yet, lord. Their fear is still greater than their pain."

He nodded, then a little smile came to his lips. "Then we must change that, Lady Marina."

An hour later, in the heat of the day when the Aztecs were napping, seven Spaniards and seven youthful Totonacs slipped into the flower-decked headquarters, and fell upon the sleeping tax collectors. The Aztecs, spluttering and raging, were tethered to long poles and marched through the plaza while a thousand Totonacs jeered and shouted. Three of the Aztecs were imprisoned in one room between the palace and the Spanish barracks, and two put in a courtyard not far from Cortes's private room.

My lord the Captain mounted a platform in the plaza and addressed the excited populace. Lord Cuesco, the royal interpreter, helped Aguilar and me in translating from Spanish to Maya to Aztec to Totonac. Actually I was only half-translating from Maya, for I understood most of my lord's Spanish words.

"The Aztecs will not dare rob you again," said Cortes. "You will send no more captives to them. You will no longer obey the underlings of Moctezuma!"

The Aztec officials, safely secured in heavy collars, must have heard the cheering but could not know who was speaking or what was said.

"Let all leaders return to their own towns and proclaim that this land is free of the Aztecs forever!" cried Cortes, and the messengers were on their way before he finished speaking.

After the public meeting a conclave of chiefs was held with Cortes presiding beside the Fat Chief. The Totonac nobles stared at Cortes and whispered among themselves. They knew no mere man would dare do what he had done, and they were accepting his godhood —some reluctantly, others eagerly, and even the most skeptical were shaken.

"Let the altars be prepared for sacrifice," said the Fat Chief. "None of these officials must return to Tenochtitlan to report what has happened here."

Cortes frowned at the general murmur of assent. "No. I will keep them. They have much to tell me." Cortes rose, gesturing that his word was final.

At midnight I was awakened and summoned to Cortes's chamber. Two of the Aztec officials were there, unbound but closely guarded by the Golden Condors and Bernal Diaz. A torch burned behind my lord the Captain so neither I nor the prisoners could see his face.

"Lady Marina, can you understand my words without help from Aguilar?"

"I will try, lord. Speak slowly."

"Good. I want no one, not even Brother Aguilar, to know about this." I nodded, understanding and proud. He said, "Ask these men why they are prisoners and what country they come from."

I asked, and the Aztecs were at first astonished that Cortes should pretend ignorance.

"Your lord knows exactly why we are captives and ill treated," the older man said. "He himself arranged it—and will pay for it, too!"

"I am hurt that you should believe such a thing," Cortes replied with a sincere tone that I did my best to imitate. "I suspect you are servants of the great Moctezuma, a lord who has been most generous to me. I expect to befriend Moctezuma, not insult him."

"But several of your turkey-skinned Spaniards were among those who seized us. We saw them!"

"Then they are rebels against me and will know no mercy!"

A soldier entered with cups of chocolate and a dish of plums for the Aztecs. "Refresh yourselves, my poor friends," said Cortes, offering the chocolate with his own hands. "It pains me to see such high lords brought to such miserable condition. As soon as you have eaten, you must leave here secretly. Go at once to Moctezuma and tell him what has happened. Assure him that I am at his service. I will release your companions as soon as I can."

"Leave? But we are surrounded by Totonacs. Every path will be guarded!" the older man protested.

"With my help it can be done," said Cortes. Then he disguised them in Spanish hoods and capes and dispatched six sailors to accompany them downstream to the beach, where a boat would take them south beyond the Totonac frontier.

"Go with God, my friends," he said, embracing each in turn. "Trust me to deal harshly with your enemies."

After they were gone, Cortes turned to us and said sadly, "Poor fellows! How they have suffered." Then, without changing his solemn tone or expression, he winked. "That should give the great Moctezuma something to chew over."

At dawn there was a great flap about the mysterious escape of the two Aztecs. Cortes raged at the Fat Chief. "This is insufferable! Were all your guards asleep? Well, the remaining three collectors will not get off so easily."

He ordered them fettered to a great chain from the ship, then, seeming to change his mind, actually had them taken aboard. "To watch them more closely," he explained. Meanwhile I assured the Aztecs of Cortes's goodwill and friendship.

"You will soon be on your way home," I said.

"We will soon be back with an army," one of them replied. Then all three began to bluster, but I could see they were shaken men, far different from the arrogant snobs who had entered town yesterday sniffing their roses, looking as if they had arrows up their asses.

They were not only shaken but confused. Why were they to be released, not sacrificed or at best enslaved? Cortes's behavior was so foreign that they could not comprehend it.

That afternoon Cortes assured a disturbed meeting of Totonac chiefs that he would protect them against any army the Aztecs might send. "And now, good friends," said Cortes, "in the presence of our scribe, Diego de Godoy, you will all swear fidelity to our Most Catholic King. Now the Spaniards and Totonacs are allies against tyranny!" Everyone cheered and swore.

So, in a daring stroke, my lord the Captain enlisted the frightened Totonacs in a war against the most powerful people in the world. At the same time he made a gesture of loyalty and gratitude to Moctezuma, who surely could not have known what to think. A god, I decided, is as subtle as a serpent. Also, gods love confusion and thrive on it. I had never seen Cortes look so happy.

Moctezuma responded quickly. A few days later, traveling under flags of safe conduct, two of Moctezuma's own nephews arrived accompanied by four elderly, distinguished noblemen who had nearly crippled themselves making the long journey so fast. Each noble was dressed in a different color—white, yellow, red and black—so each represented one of the four cardinal directions. The nephews, in green cloaks and loincloths, symbolized the center, the earth and Tenochtitlan. So the embassy presented the universe as a tribute to Plumed Serpent.

"You see!" I exclaimed to Aguilar. "Moctezuma again recognizes the god. Now he can do nothing but yield."

But they brought no offer of surrender. The older nephew, still only a boy with a cracking voice, recited the Revered Speaker's complaints against us. We had incited the Totonac towns to rebellion, to break their allegiance.

"My uncle and master does not understand this, for he knows who you are," said the boy, and suddenly I held my breath. Now the capitulation to Plumed Serpent must come. "Your coming here was foretold and you are of the same lineage as himself. So as his relative and clansman, why do you live now in the houses of traitors?"

The question was asked with such threat as a thirteen-year-old could put in his uncertain voice, and even that touch of menace vanished when the porters brought out gifts of gold and cotton cloth.

I was alarmed that the gold might distract Cortes from the importance of Moctezuma's words, but I need not have worried. My lord the Captain understood instantly and immediately pressed matters home, seeming to address the two nephews but actually speaking for the elderly men.

"Tell my kinsman Moctezuma that his servants, without his knowing, have mistreated and offended me. They deserted their posts of service on the beach, so we have taken shelter here." Cortes smiled and said in a gentle tone, "The Revered Speaker must forgive these people any accidental disrespect to him. I and all my friends and brethren are even now on the way to visit Moctezuma. We will explain in person and devote ourselves to his service."

I did not translate the last few words, which might have puzzled the Aztecs.

Cortes had the three tax collectors, well fed and clothed, brought from the ship and presented them to the Aztec party, along with some wonderful glass beads for the nephews. Pedro Alvarado led his horsemen in a mock skirmish in a nearby meadow, and then the Aztecs departed, eyes bulging.

Unable to keep my excitement to myself, I turned to Aguilar and exclaimed, "Did you see how they dressed? Did you hear their words about the same lineage? Moctezuma has recognized Plumed Serpent! He believes in Cortes!"

I spoke to Aguilar in Maya and used the word "Kukulcan" for Plumed Serpent. In both languages it means a god and a snake with feathers, but the Maya have their own legends so probably Aguilar did not understand exactly what I meant. I supposed that was why he gave me such a strange look.

The unfriendly glance did not surprise me. Somehow Aguilar learned that I had acted as a midnight interpreter for my lord the Captain without any help. He resented being left out and could see that my rapid progress in Spanish would soon make his own services unnecessary, a prospect he found intolerable. In the last three days he had not spoken to me, but when I was near him I felt the air was full of hornets.

After the Aztecs left, I walked by myself in the forest near the town, my head full of wonders and possibilities. I was unaware anyone had followed me when a voice said, "Lady Marina!" and a hand suddenly touched my shoulder. I whirled, my hand going instinctively to the blade I kept hidden in my hair.

"I must speak with you, you must listen!" It was Aguilar, his lips so pale, his face and voice so agitated that although I did not draw the blade, I held myself ready.

"What have you been telling these people about Cortes?" he demanded. "Are you saying he is some kind of heathen god? Some devil?"

"Your tone is rude, Brother Aguilar," I told him. "Speak to me when you are calmer." I started to turn away, but he would not allow it.

"I will have the truth! In your ignorance you are going to destroy him. What is this blasphemy about a plumed serpent? Do you realize this is damnable?"

I hesitated. When an enemy says you are wicked, you can simply walk away. When he says you are ignorant, it pays to listen.

"Perhaps you have something to teach me, dear friend," I said, trying to assume the tone of sympathy my lord the Captain used so effectively. I smiled, but when I touched Aguilar's arm, he flinched. "Let us sit down and you will explain matters to me." I led him to a nearby flat stone, an abandoned altar. He sat on it, not suspecting it was sacred to the Totonacs and therefore abominable.

At any rate the power of the altar or maybe my quiet tone seemed to soothe him. He spoke almost reasonably. "I suspect you are claiming that Cortes is some sort of god or demon. Some demon connected with a flying snake—horrible idea! Worse, I think you are encouraging him to make that claim or at least not deny the idea."

I answered cautiously, aware of Christian superstition. "If people mistakenly accept Cortes as a god, what harm is done?"

"The most terrible harm! Oh, can't you understand?" He was agitated again. "If they believe in Cortes, they do not believe in Christ or the Trinity or the Blessed Mother! They will all be damned."

"But they did not believe in any of that before, so—"

"No, no! You cannot change one hideous error for another. Besides, think of the danger to Cortes if he made such a claim or let it go unchallenged. It would make him a witch or some kind of devil. Such a confession, no matter how false, would damn Cortes's own soul for eternity—and he himself knows this." Aguilar suddenly lowered his voice. "Lady Marina, you and I can understand how such a pretense, although wicked, might be useful when we are in this barbarous land surrounded by savages. But what would the Holy Office do if such reports reached their ears? And believe me, the inquisitors' ears are long and sharp."

"I do not understand. Is the Holy Office another group of gods, like the Trinity? Or is it more like Recording Angel?"

"Lady Marina, I speak of the inquisitors of the Church. For the last forty years they have been rooting out heretics and witches, destroying enemies of God and the king. Their wrath would fall heavily on Cortes—he would be doomed—if they had the least suspicion that he passed himself off as a demon or claimed such power!"

Aguilar was so truly frightened for Cortes that I forgave his ignorance. It was sad that every day he was near a god he loved, Cortes, yet could not acknowledge the power by so much as a word. Pitiable!

I could not understand what Aguilar was talking about, but I grasped the main fact: there were Forces who hated Plumed Serpent.

So, speaking in a kindly and sincere tone, I lied to Aguilar and made him feel better. I ended by saying, "You agree that Cortes is most remarkable. Has he always been so?"

"I'm told in Cuba he was not thought extraordinary. A fine horseman and fighter—intelligent, of course. Maybe a leader. It is hard to judge a man in a place where nobles of higher rank claim all opportunity and honor. That's how it was with Cortes there."

"Higher rank?" I asked, indignant at the idea.

"Cortes is of respectable but common birth, hardly noble. Several men here outrank him by blood. Especially Lord Alonzo."

"Lord Alonzo is of higher rank?" It seemed impossible.

"Of course. You must have noticed how Cortes defers to him, pampers him?" Aguilar raised an eyebrow, gave me a meaningful look. "You yourself are of higher rank than Cortes, Lady Marina."

"But he is—" I stopped myself from saying "a god."

"Cortes demands that rank be respected in these lands just as it is in Spain. He is pious, and to affront nobility is to affront God who gives kings their power."

I nodded, thinking of what Uncle Willow had once said about Moctezuma's belief in the nobility of blood, the divine nature of rank. Cortes and Moctezuma shared this view, it seemed, but my lord was of common birth. It might be better, more appropriate. Father Olmedo said that the greatest god of the Spaniards was born a carpenter's son in a vassal nation.

"In Cuba no one noticed the great talents that you and I see in Cortes, Lady Marina." It was clear to me then that godhood had come to him late in life. Again, he was like Moctezuma.

Aguilar frowned. "They say he was always too fond of women. He not only has a wife but also a—" He started to use the Maya word for concubine, then rejected it. "Well, he supports another lady as well and has children by both. Not to mention his love affairs all over the island of Cuba. But these are venial sins, not mortal. Yet there have been too many of them."

He watched me for any reaction. But what did I care if my lord had a thousand women as long as I could take my proper place among them? Later I might find I wanted a man of my own for every night —Lord Alonzo had taught me pleasure. But what did it matter now?

Aguilar and I returned to headquarters, he easier in his mind about heresy and I a good deal wiser. I would be cautious.

. .

The seizing of the tax collectors followed by Moctezuma's sending gifts excited the Totonacs, and word spread beyond their borders. Olmecs arrived to see the liberator, bringing rubber balls and jadite carvings. The jadite was ignored, but the Spaniards, never having seen rubber, were delighted as children by its liveliness and bounce. Naked Huastecs with their personal histories tattooed on their bodies arrived from the north to gape at the Spaniards while the Spaniards gaped at them. Several Huastec men had honeybees tattooed on their penises; I thought this was a pretty notion, but the Spaniards guffawed. I still do not understand why; the pictures were charming.

Cortes explored outlying villages, promising the people justice and safety. Now he rode a tall horse the color of mahogany. Its name was Mule Driver, but when Cortes praised and patted it he murmured, "Babieca."

One afternoon we were returning to Zempoala, Cortes and Lord Alonzo riding with the column, Aguilar and I walking beside them. "These men are good fellows you can depend on," said Cortes. I had noticed that when he praised the troops, which was often, he always made sure his words were overheard.

Lord Alonzo answered in a lower tone. "I would call most of them cutthroats and gallows birds."

"They have shown they can be trusted in these villages." Again the loud voice.

The god Five Flower, who brings down the proud, must have been listening, for at that instant Cortes and Lord Alonzo both caught sight of a Spanish soldier sneaking out of a Totonac hut with a young fowl tucked under each arm.

Cortes shouted, "Seize that man and assemble the troops."

As men and officers came up from the rear, Cortes eyed the culprit in silence. When the army had gathered, Cortes said, "I will hang this thief. Put a halter around his neck."

The prisoner mumbled, shame-faced, then looked up and giggled, not believing Cortes's threat any more than I did.

"Why do you wait?" Cortes demanded of the sergeant holding the noose. "Let him make his confession on the rope. Hoist him up!"

Three men threw themselves on the rope, jerking the victim into the air kicking. That would have been the end, but Pedro Alvarado spurred his horse forward and slashed the rope with his sword, severing it at a stroke, saving the culprit's life.

There was silence; time seemed to have stopped. Then my lord the Captain flicked his reins and rode on alone toward Zempoala, never glancing back.

Such a penalty for a petty crime caused talk afterward when the men recovered their voices. Some of the soldiers suspected Cortes and Alvarado had contrived a drama to make an example of the first thief caught, a powerful lesson in discipline, yet it cost the army not a single man.

That was the sort of game Cortes could play. But I saw the Captain's face at the moment he ordered the hanging. I saw winter come into his eyes, how the smiling man vanished and the god emerged, merciless. The god was implacable, and I never forgot it.

During the next days Plumed Serpent was powerfully present in Cortes and filled with anger. The god would peer from Cortes's eyes like a priest glaring through the slits of a mask. He was silent as he watched the Totonacs prepare a feast in honor of their new alliance with the Spaniards. Haze hung over Zempoala, smoke from fires where women prepared fish and game for the banquet, from other fires that heated stones for steambaths of purification. Still more smoke curled from temples where priests made extra sacrifices to ensure good weather and good luck for the days ahead. Cortes watched with a deepening frown. I felt a volcano simmering toward eruption.

The festival began on the morning of the new moon, and the Spaniards seemed more prepared for battle than celebration. They wore helmets, carried weapons, and some had put on breastplates.

"Did Cortes order an alert?" I asked Aguilar.

"No. But the men feel uneasy. They sense trouble."

So, apparently, did the Totonacs. The Fat Chief had at least a thousand archers scattered around the great plaza, their holiday garlands making them no less formidable.

Yet the feast began cheerfully. The Fat Chief, beaming goodwill, was hoisted and shoved onto a platform in front of the temple. To warm up the crowd he told some ribald jokes that must have been hilarious in Totonac but did not translate well. Father Olmedo and Aguilar looked scandalized; Cortes sat stiffly on Mule Driver, stone-faced.

"Spaniards and Totonacs are brothers!" the chief announced.

Then a military band played on shell and horn instruments, and some knights of the dolphin order sang enthusiastically but off key. A local dignitary presented Cortes with a ridiculous little drum and the assurance that "he has only to tap it with his finger to bring the whole Totonac nation to his service."

It was such a routine civic ceremony, so dull and pompous, that I lost my sense of foreboding. Then the Fat Chief sprang his surprise.

"Spaniards and Totonacs must unite in blood forever. So now we present our fairest daughters as wives for your officers. Let us, through the children that will be born of these marriages, become one people!"

Seven pretty young women trotted out from a tent of flowers, all of them adorned with golden collars and earrings.

"These for your officers, lord," the Fat Chief told Cortes. Then he clapped his hands twice and the fattest girl I had ever seen waddled out to join the maidenly line. "My niece, the heiress to towns and plantations! She is yours, lord!"

The Fat Princess did her best to scamper to Cortes, her huge breasts trembling like hills in an earthquake. Cortes managed his only smile of the week, but the horse, showing excellent judgment, snorted and pawed, making the bride-to-be squeal and retreat.

Cortes soothed Mule Driver, then gestured for me to mount the platform so the throng in the plaza could hear me. He was about to deliver a speech and he wanted it understood by everyone. Aguilar stationed himself on the platform steps to prompt me if necessary.

"Our thanks for your generosity and affection. But before we can accept these lovely girls, before we can become brothers, the girls must be baptized as Christians."

The Fat Chief nodded agreeably. A little water would do no harm.

Suddenly Cortes's voice changed, grew stern. "You and your people must renounce the worship of these damnable idols!" He gestured toward the temple that rose behind the platform. "Stone devils! Let them be pulled down and smashed!"

The Spaniards began to cheer. They lifted their arms in salute. "Every day this week we have seen innocent men and women murdered in the worship of these monsters!"

So that was it. Because of the festival the priests had more than doubled the sacrificial ceremonies, and naturally Plumed Serpent was enraged.

"We have seen too much horror!" cried Cortes, and now he was really speaking to the Spaniards, although he addressed the Fat Chief. "How can we do anything for the glory of God if we let this continue? These idols must come down now. If it costs our lives, the price is small."

I stood stunned, unbelieving, not wanting to translate these wild words. With the Aztecs and with his own obstreperous men, Cortes had proved himself the master of subtlety—he delayed, cajoled and shifted. Now he stood ready to throw everything away in one burst of passion.

"Day after day we have seen murder—and worse—committed in these stinking temples. Will we stand for this? We are Christians and Spaniards!"

The army replied with a roar. Had it really been so terrible? The Totonacs could not have been sacrificing more than five or six victims a day at most—not unreasonable at a momentous time in history. I had not noticed it.

I started to translate, muddling everything, and Aguilar was too excited to help. But the Fat Chief, understanding instantly, began to rage against Cortes.

"You are mad! To destroy our gods is to destroy ourselves. We will die for our religion!"

"Die then!" Cortes shouted back. "Your bloody monster gods will be smashed today!"

When the Fat Chief gestured, a thousand warriors lifted their spears and another thousand nocked their arrows. Now there was nothing more to say, nothing left but the dying. Crossbows and harquebuses were shouldered, swords drawn. The Fat Chief raised his hand; he had only to drop it for the slaughter to start.

Suddenly I found myself speaking into the silence. I did not intend it or plan it, but neither the words nor the voice seemed my own. "People of Zempoala, how dare you reject the wisdom of Plumed Serpent? For sheaves of years you have waited for his return. Now you point your spears at him! I will tell you who dies tomorrow. All of you! When Moctezuma learns that the Totonacs are enemies of the Spaniards, when he knows the Totonacs have no protectors, he will spring from the mountains like a jaguar to rip out your guts and eat them."

Some unknown power had taken possession of me. The voice that rang so strong in my ears was mine, yet not mine. With this power came an elation I had never known. I stood tall as the great trees behind the temple; my voice sounded to the peaks of Mountain of the Star.

Slowly I turned to face the Fat Chief. "You know which Aztec holiday comes next—the Festival of the Furnace. For insulting Moctezuma's officials, you will be hurled into the fire pit, bound but alive and screaming. When your flesh is seared, when you have no more voice left for shrieks, they will drag you from the flames with their wooden hooks and rip out your beating heart. How you will welcome death then!"

I lifted my hands to the crowd. "You will all perish the same way. Moctezuma's dogs will lick up your blood. Only Plumed Serpent can save you. Obey him now, or you and your children will wail before Lady Moon returns full once more!"

It was finished. I felt the power ebb from me and I shrank again into my own body, exhausted. Silence gripped the plaza, Spaniards and Totonacs staring at me, incredulous. I heard the name "Moctezuma" rustle through the crowd like wind in a dry thicket. Near me a warrior lowered his sword. The archers hesitated, confused. People whispered, "Aztecs . . . Yes, the Aztecs will come."

I sensed the presence of a goddess, hovering near me, and I knew I had stood for those moments in her radiant shadow.

The Fat Chief turned to face the temple, weeping and praying. Slowly his body sank and he collapsed on the stone platform sobbing, his arms still reaching toward the temple. Then thousands of people, warriors and priests and women, wept with him. I thought: we have won. Plumed Serpent has won.

Lord Cuesco, recovering himself, spoke to Cortes. "Our gods have been good to us. We love them and cannot profane their temples. But we are helpless and you, of course, can do as you will."

When the Spaniards understood this, half a hundred of them swarmed up the temple steps, whooping and yelling, flinging aside priests who tried to stop them. Father Olmedo was in the forefront, and Aguilar scrambled up, invoking the Spanish war god. "Santiago! Santiago the Moor killer!"

Then the ancient stone gods came hurtling down the stairways. Rain Bringer crashed and rolled and at last shattered; Serpent Skirt and Maize Mother followed him to destruction while I stood quietly weeping, foolish as any Totonac. These gods had served me ill, blighted my life, and I hated them. Yet, unaccountably, tears streamed down my cheeks.

I cried aloud when I saw the Old Lord of Fire wrenched from his sanctuary, his beautiful brazier crown still smoking, filled with burning coals that were now spilled and scattered as Old Lord toppled from the high platform. Sparks and glowing coals showered down, striking the Fat Chief, searing his back and burning some of his hair. He screamed in pain but would neither shake off the live coals nor let others help him as he repaid Old Lord with his own suffering—and no doubt thought of the agony I had promised him in the Aztec fire pits.

As the thatched roof of the high temple burst into a cloud of flame, the Totonac mob surged forward, yelling, spears lifted. Cortes sprang to the platform, seized the Fat Chief by the hair and held a dagger to his throat, while soldiers on the steps pinioned the nobles and priests trying to defend the temple.

The Fat Chief made himself heard above the tumult, commanding the people to cease resisting. They obeyed unwillingly.

"The fat fellow is less pious with a knife at his throat," said Pedro Alvarado. But he was mistaken—the Fat Chief took sacrilege on his soul not to save his life but to preserve his people from the Aztecs. He was braver than the Spaniards realized; after all, I saw him unflinching under the burning coals.

When the mob was quiet, Cortes released the Fat Chief and made apologies. He said to Pedro Alvarado, "Thank God we did not have to harm him."

Alvarado shrugged. "Why not?"

Cortes looked shocked. "He is a king!"

A few hours later, well before the end of the day, the Festival of Brotherhood was resumed where it had been broken off. At any rate the Totonacs, if not pacified, put on smiling masks.

The brides were presented; Father Olmedo sprinkled water on their heads and pronounced them Christians. Cortes accepted the Fat Princess graciously, scowling when several soldiers made coarse jokes behind their hands.

Lord Cuesco's daughter, a pretty girl called Sweet Twin Pineapples, was paraded out next, and Cortes announced that she would be given to his "friend and comrade Alonzo Puertocarrero." Giving Lord Alonzo a second woman was not quite such blatant favoritism as it seems; three other officers were also given second bedmates. Still, I remembered what Aguilar had said about Cortes defering to rank and lineage.

I felt I had a glimpse of the future. The Fat Princess would be given her pleasure and honor, then quickly discarded. Without her golden collar, of course, which would remain in a Spanish treasure chest. Then, in some painless manner, Lord Alonzo would be left with only this new bride and I would be with Cortes.

Today I had served my lord the Captain well. Now he would take steps to bind me closer to him; such was his way. How would he do it? The game would be fascinating.

I threw a rose to Sweet Twin Pineapples, smiling my genuine goodwill and congratulations. She would like Lord Alonzo—he was sweet and beautiful.

The Spaniards and Totonacs made a formal alliance, agreeing to be brothers. The Spaniards would provide justice, true religion and protection from the Aztecs. In turn, the Totonacs promised to scrub and whitewash their temples, to put up pictures of Our Lady and build crosses. They would lend bearers, warriors and guides as well as provisions when called upon.

The Totonac priests were to cut their blood-matted hair. (In fact, it had to be sawed off, since the gore of years had hardened into a sort of sandstone.) They would don new white clothing as acolytes of the Virgin and would daily decorate her shrine with fresh blossoms and candles that the Spaniards would teach them to make from beeswax. This seemed a remarkable change for these men, to go from butchers of humans to florists and candle-dippers in a single day. But no one else found this odd—unless the Virgin herself did.

After much complaining, the Totonac nobles agreed to banish their male lovers and concubines.

"You must renounce sodomy," Father Olmedo told them.

Lord Cuesco looked puzzled. "The Almighty Mover of the Universe cares about this?" he asked.

"Deeply," said Father Olmedo.

The Spaniards, if not the Almighty, did abhor sodomy except when they enjoyed it secretly among themselves—as anyone who ever strolled at night near the bushes along the beach could affirm. Of course there were many more women available now in Zempoala so it was easier to be pious.

The Fat Princess proved to have a sullen nature. Cortes quickly but politely got rid of her, not before he had her baptized as Doña Catalina, which was the name of his Spanish wife in Cuba. I found that curious, but later I would understand.

I took little part in the feasting and celebration that night, although my lord the Captain gave me a place of honor, praising the speech I had made before the temple. I thanked him, I smiled at the Totonacs and applauded the torch dancers. But all the while I was trying to recall the least vestige of what I had felt, what I had been. In memory I could recall the thousands of faces looking up at me, staring and transfixed. I could hear a faint echo of a powerful voice that was a little like my own. For a few minutes I had been . . . extraordinary.

12

Towers of the Gods

My lord the Captain, without killing a single Totonac or losing one Spanish soldier, had made his first great alliance and secured the city of Zempoala. He had moved as slowly and cautiously as a hawk circling the sky; now he was ready to act with speed and sureness. I discovered one of his plans through Lord Alonzo.

Since the feast Lord Alonzo had been sharing his sleeping mat with his new partner, since he naturally wanted to discover what novelties she offered. We did not, as my enemies have claimed, all climb into the same hammock like three wildcats in a bag. Lord Alonzo would have been mortified by the idea. After all, he was a well-brought-up Catholic and suspicious of elaborate pleasures.

Late one afternoon he asked me to stroll along the river path. He was full of suppressed excitement, as though he had just won a fortune at dice or learned about an inheritance. He did not deceive me when he pulled a long face and spoke in a mournful tone. "My love, I have sad news. You must be brave."

"My lord, I will try."

"Cortes plans to send a messenger to Spain, a person of rank and honor, to be his spokesman. This messenger will deliver a letter to the king himself and will take to the king the treasure we have won so far. My love, I am the man chosen for this mission."

"Then we must part." I concealed my soaring hope. "When will you go, my lord?"

"As soon as the soldiers can hold a council. Cortes explained to me that he wants the men to feel that sending the treasure is their own idea. I will go tomorrow or the next day, I suppose, in the *San Sebastian*."

The *San Sebastian* was Cortes's flagship. He would never send it away if he expected to explore the coast or return to Cuba. So the god within him had finally given the order: we would march inland; Plumed Serpent would return to his kingdom.

I looked away as though to conceal tears. "When will my lord return?"

"Well, not for two years at least," he replied, pretending gloom. "Who knows? And I cannot bear leaving you alone here. A frail woman in a dangerous country!"

What could he mean? Surely he was not mad enough to dream of taking me with him? Now Cortes would need his interpreter more than ever. Going to Spain was like going through the Narrow Passage —there was no return and who knew for sure what lay at the far end?

"My lord is kind, but must not concern himself. Think only of higher duty." I spoke every Spanish word slowly so I would get it right.

"I *am* concerned. What gentleman would not be? So I have planned your future. Cortes is my dear friend. I think I can persuade him to—er—take you under his protection. He has even hinted he finds you quite useful. Er—just until I return, of course." He stammered and blushed, unused to pimping.

"How kind you are, how clever!" I clasped him in my arms, disguising my joy as ardor. Cortes was crafty as a badger! How had he introduced the idea into Lord Alonzo's unsuspecting mind?

We went to a private place—he had discovered a willow whose drooping fronds made a tent, and in that tent he was loving and golden. I remembered our first joining in Tabasco, when I had been so afraid and he so reassuring. He had seemed so experienced and godlike to me then. Now I thought him less of both, but still beautiful. In Tabasco our lovemaking had begun near a river where foliage brushed the water. It was romantic of him to have found a spot so similar for our farewell.

When he took me, I was pleased by his hunger. Apparently Sweet

Twin Pineapples had not cooked up and served him a Totonac dish so exotic that he could now be pleased by no other fare. No, she had not outdone me. I found that reassuring.

Afterward we both wept a little at the prospect of separation. He shed a few tears to flatter me, and I showed him the moist eyes his pride needed.

"I love you, Marina," he said. "Will you remember me when I am far away in Spain?"

"Oh, yes, my lord."

Two days later Lord Alonzo sailed on the *San Sebastian*. I never saw him again.

I had no part in what my lord the Captain did after the *San Sebastian* departed, but his decision has become so famous that it is part of the language. Today the most ordinary person is said to have burned his boats if he embarks on some petty course from which there seems no turning back. Nonsense. It is not the same thing at all.

The story is still dramatically repeated and embellished in those piss-on-the-floor taverns where paunchy veterans gather to complain about their low pensions and listen to each other's lies.

The truth is more sensible. Cortes disabled his ships—no, he did not burn them—after he learned that some men were planning to desert by sea to Cuba. This had to be stopped; he needed every blade and bullet. Besides, the governor of Cuba, who understood nothing of Plumed Serpent's mission, would have caused terrible problems if his followers in Cortes's army could have reached him just then. He caused trouble enough as it was, being covetous of gold and glory.

So the ships were run aground and important instruments were hidden. Hidden, too, were sails and tackle. The ships could have been made seaworthy in a few days, of course. My lord the Captain was too wise to indulge in silly heroics. But only a handful of the professional sailors suspected this. The soldiers were fooled then just as everybody is fooled today.

In the month of Falling of the Ripe Fruits, a day the Spaniards called August 16, 1519, we left Zempoala, pressing inland and upward on the northern flanks of Mountain of the Star. His crown of snow blended with the mists that morning, obscuring him, which seemed an unwelcoming sign. I whispered, "Tall lord, we will soon be perched on your shoulder. Be kind to us."

The Totonacs had proposed a roundabout route through wild

country, not the trails any swift-messenger or trading party would have chosen. But these obscure paths would lead us far from Aztec outposts and to the borders of the mountain-hemmed Republic of Tlaxcala, a fiercely independent nation the Aztecs had often tried to swallow. It had always proved to be a scorpion in their mouths.

We were a noble-looking company that morning. First went an advance guard, heavily armed; then came forty Totonac warriors, rich lords in their most brilliant regalia. They were followed by Father Olmedo and the chaplain Juan Diaz, who carried a great cross studded with turquoises he had somehow extracted from the ears and noses of new Zempoalan converts. Behind him fluttered the banners of San Diego where the sun gleamed on armor, muskets and the brass-studded trappings of horses. We were shining and fit to be a god's escorting servants in liveries of steel.

I tried to explain this to Bernal Diaz, who walked beside me for a while. When he at last understood my Spanish, he grinned, a broad grin that made his plain face charming. He said, "Not noble, my lady. I wear shoes made of rope. My clothes are so mended and patched that I'm a scarecrow."

Then he explained what a scarecrow was, and I added it to my catalog of marvelous inventions.

Cortes, sometimes riding and sometimes leading Mule Driver, moved back and forth along the line. Zempoala is the Place of Twenty Waters, where mountain streams rush down slopes toward the city, and now these creeks were in summer spate. At one crossing Cortes lifted me up beside him, and the horse splashed through the foamy water. I caught my breath at the touch of his hands. Then he put me down, turned back and performed the same kindness for a toothless old Totonac woman, a slave of one of the new brides.

"Cold water is bad for your bones, mother," he said, and she squealed in delight, not understanding, terrified of the horse but thrilled by the touch of the god. It was the great moment of her life. My lord the Captain was like that; he enjoyed performing small gallantries, especially unexpected or inappropriate ones.

We passed several villages, but in every case the inhabitants had fled, taking all their worldly goods and even hauling away the stone gods from their little temples. Word had run before us from Zempoala; no one was taking chances.

When cool air flowed down from the peaks, the Spaniards became boisterous. Heat oppressed them, and I marveled that they endured armor in the jungles. To them cool air was like swallowing a gourd of pulque—they were a bit tipsy for the first hour. Someone began to sing; soon four hundred men were singing ballads about rivers and rich lands. I loved the laughter, the deep male voices.

I sat for a while in the shade of some bellflower bushes, letting the column pass, because at the rear would come several hundred Totonac bearers carrying supplies and baggage. Lord Alonzo had given me a bolt of cotton cloth and I wanted to make sure it was safe. Also, I wanted to see the foal again.

The foal, an amazing creature all legs and eyes, was the first horse born in the Only World. I thought its birth a favorable sign, an omen that Spanish horses would flourish and new creatures would populate the land. Her owner, Juan Sedeño, named her Canela for her dark cinnamon color, but I called her Citli, a star, because of a white decoration on her forehead. This seemed a clever and original name until I learned that half the mares and most of the whores in Cuba are called Star.

Citli's mother developed an unnatural aversion to the foal, usually thrusting her away when she tried to suckle. Lord Alonzo said the mare had sore nipples and soon all would be well.

As I waited, the women who had boarded the ships in Tabasco —a lifetime ago—approached. Far from home, they now clung together and moved along the trail in a fixed pecking order like a flock of grackles. Flower Pouch, the most aggressive, naturally led the flock, whose number was diminished by half. A few had stayed behind in Zempoala; others, who had been whores before they cut their second teeth, had slipped into the jungle hoping to prosper along the trade routes. None had willingly joined this march toward Tenochtitlan. They knew the dangers.

When they passed, Flower Pouch was pretending to cover her ears to shut out the singing. "Terrible! Like a thousand macaws. Who but Spaniards would sing as they prance toward Moctezuma's altars and fire pits!"

"They are even stranger than usual today," said one woman.

"Madder," said Flower Pouch. "They will laugh when they march over the brink at the end of the world."

Hearing this, I hated her and was tempted to leap from cover and teach her respect. But I kept still and wished her a bad end. I really

thought of no worse a fate than I supposed would be hers anyway—
she would slip away from the trail soon and end up with some village
farmer who wore dyed corncobs in his hair. She would spend the rest
of her life spreading her legs to receive his seed or deliver its fruit. I
was angry but I meant nothing horrible for her.

But it is dangerous to ill wish a person's life. You never know
how potent the curse may be. I remembered my curse later when
Flower Pouch came to a grisly end.

I found my bundle of cloth being carefully handled. Just as I was
thanking the porter, I heard sounds of consternation at the end of the
column where Citli's owner, Juan Sedeño, and two other horsemen
were bringing up the rear. I rushed to see what was happening.

Sedeño's mare, the loveless mother, was balking and neighing
angrily while Sedeño himself tried to spur her up the ridge beside the
trail. I could not understand his curses and gesticulations, but one of
the bearers, a slave from the south, told me in Maya what had happened.

The foal had been wobbling docilely beside her mother where
the trail snaked along the base of a low cliff. Suddenly three deer poked
their heads through foliage above, and the foal, catching sight of them,
bolted. She scrambled up the nearest slope, fast as a kinkajou, to join
the deer and then disappeared with them, her mother and the other
horses refusing the climb.

Much later that day, while we followed the bank of Red Throat
River, I saw the foal grazing with the herd of deer in a meadow across
the stream. She heard the whinny of other horses but scampered away
with her new family. The Totonacs predicted that monsters would be
spawned by the foal, fierce offspring with the valor and strength of
horses, the horns of a stag. It seemed possible.

Before the afternoon rain we camped in a broad valley rich with
vanilla and cochineal. Passion fruit, whose flowers are holy, flourished
wild here, and nearby some of the trees blazed with flame vine. Five
Totonac bearers, who seemed to be acting on orders from Cortes,
appeared and built a large shelter of woven mats, then gestured that
it was for me. The shelter was so elaborate for a one-night encampment
that I immediately thought, *He has arranged this and will spend the night
here.*

I was surprised; I had expected to be summoned, not visited.
Several days had passed since Lord Alonzo's departure, and Cortes had

not spoken a word to me in private. For the sake of the Totonac alliance he had had to provide a few nights' entertainment for the Fat Princess. She had been left in Zempoala, so now, I decided, I should prepare myself.

I decorated the roof poles with sweet-by-night, hoping the fragrance would not be too heavy. (Perfume excited Lord Alonzo, but afterward he complained the smell was unhealthful.) I sang to myself, something I had not done since childhood, as I strung bougainvillea to make an arch at the door. A very simple arch. I did not want the room to be a bridal chamber—not quite. But he would be pleased by it. How could he not be?

At dusk the Spaniards posted guards and I noticed that the men who were off duty did not remove their steel breastplates. Would Cortes? It was an alarming thought. How could I possibly do all I had planned if he would not take off his armor! Of course he would. I tied a loop to one of the poles so he could hang it up quickly and easily —no awkward moments.

While the Spaniards were posting their sentries, the Totonacs sent out four sky-scanners to watch for sunset omens, and these men soon rushed back to report that a great white heron had slowly circled the camp three times, then vanished into the western sky. The Aztecs are the Heron People; their sorcerers are on close terms with herons and egrets. So the bird might be a spy dispatched by Moctezuma.

I bathed quickly in the river, wishing I could use the steam hut the Totonacs had already constructed, but it was only for men. Then I made two garlands of flame vine and sat down in the shelter to wait.

Near the end of the First Watch a party began on the far side of the camp, the Spaniards celebrating, singing the same songs they had sung this morning and just as loudly. There was moonlight but I lit a candle, which made the room beautiful. Candles were still new, still almost magical to me. I thought I should have one burning when he arrived.

By the end of the Second Watch the Spaniards had become a little drunk, the music slurred and sentimental. Cortes had to be with them, of course. In fact, only Cortes could have organized this celebration since it broke all the regulations about late hours and drinking. I hoped he would not be kept there too long.

I blew out the candle, worried about his delay, wanting to save some of the gentle light for him—he would like it; it would show his welcome was special.

Listening to the revelry, I realized there had been a marked change in the Spaniards during the last few days. They had always seemed full of eagerness and afraid of nothing, but now they walked and sang as if they owned the world. Yes, that was it: they owned the world. When my lord the Captain ran the ships aground, he had left these men with no world but the one they now inhabited. They had to claim it or perish. Cortes had turned them to steel.

Even as I thought this, I realized that Cortes would not come to me tonight. This celebration was the end of their first day's march on their journey into the unknown. He belonged to the soldiers tonight.

Not only tonight. He was theirs first and last forever. "Know that and remember it," I said aloud.

I lit the candle again—not for him but for myself, because I needed something beautiful to look at, but although I forced myself to sit quietly gazing at the flame, I found no composure, for there was a storm inside me and I knew that I had followed the god but also longed desperately for the man who contained him. I wanted to be carried to his door on the back of a matchmaker, as all brides are carried. I longed to share the ritual marriage bath with him; I would manage his household and see that he was happy by day, blissfully fulfilled at night. I wanted all the ordinary things I had always scorned.

Yet I wanted to go with the god to the end of the world, to climb mountains, to stand in battle. I needed to feel again the presence of the goddess who had stood beside me when I addressed the crowd in Zempoala. The goddess was not the companion of contented wives who sit all day nursing babies while they embroider their husband's tunics.

The candle had burned low. I glanced at my almost-bridal chamber, seeing the wilting garlands, the jasmine that now made the air heavy and cloying. I felt humiliated. I had behaved like a foolish spinster who paints and bedecks herself each day to sit in her front door, hoping against hope that a handsome youth will smile at her, will be lured.

I seized the garlands and hurled them outside. I tore down the arch of vines. Expect nothing, I told myself, and you will never be disappointed! Surely life had taught me this lesson by now. But how could I live with nothing to look forward to? If disappointment was the price of hoping, then there was no choice but to pay it.

I lay down on my mat and tried to ignore the dying sounds of the Spaniards' party. An Aztec woman such as my mother would have known exactly what to do in the turmoil I now felt. She would have jabbed some cactus needles through the thick of her palm and the physical pain would have blotted out everything else. It was not, perhaps, such a senseless custom as my grandmother claimed.

At last I fell asleep, and when I suddenly awoke enough time had passed that the camp was completely silent except for the soft footsteps of a roving sentry. I was not aware that I had dreamed but I knew that somehow the goddess had come to me in sleep. She had not spoken; neither could I see her face, which was hooded, but with one scornful gesture she told me I had been a fool.

I had done what I had always sworn never to do—behaved like an Aztec wife. No wonder I had felt as miserable as they did. I had put out my perfumes and petals, then waited like a flower that traps insects. Waited as women always wait for men who come and go at their pleasure.

Why had I not simply put on my garlands and gone to the Spanish celebration? I was as much a part of the army as any soldier there, and far more important to Cortes's success than most of them.

If a man would have helped in an hour of loneliness—and I did not think it was that simple—I could take a stroll in any direction. There were some fine Totonacs nearby and some even better Spaniards. Or if it was only Cortes who could have appeased my longing, I should have gone to him and made that plain. Any man—Aztec, Maya or Spanish—would have attacked the problem directly. I, instead, had sat disconsolate among the flowers.

I lay back on the mat, perhaps not content but at least calm, aware that I had been a fool but knowing I would not again be foolish in the same way. I had learned something I would use for the rest of my life: if you let yourself think like a wife and act like a wife, you are in great danger of being treated like one.

Late the next afternoon we reached the most beautiful spot in the world, the town of Sand River, which the Spaniards call Jalapa. Its stucco buildings nestle on a shelf of meadow and forest greener than quetzal plumes. To the east the land cascades down to the jungle and sea, while westward it surges up into peaks and crags, the white towers of the gods. When I remember Sand River, I think of orchids and snow.

We entered the town in a triumphant formation we would often use, my lord the Captain mounted and in armor at the head of the column. I walked beside him carrying his standard, the proud companion of the god. Then came other horsemen, other flags and the priests displaying crosses. Spanish soldiers were followed by our regiment of Totonac warriors, now grown to more than a thousand—perhaps two thousand—as men from the allied towns joined us at every crossing of the trail.

The Spaniards were so delighted by the Totonac numbers and eagerness they seemed not to notice their allies' childishness about war. How pathetically proud they were of their silly weapons—tasseled clubs, sharpened bones, the decorated shells of sea turtles for shields, so fragile that an Aztec swordsman would have laughed. The Totonacs flaunted their ribbons and paint, while I wondered grimly how long they would have lasted on the Jalisco frontier.

Yet their enthusiasm and bravado were touching. I had grown up among the world's fiercest, most professional soldiers; it was charming—but maybe a little sad—to see young men who thought they could bring down Moctezuma's empire with a pointed stick hardened in some village bonfire.

A cheering crowd welcomed us to Sand River. I translated the formal greetings, the mandatory words about the Virgin and the king. They knew what I was going to repeat. I could tell from the townspeople's faces that swift-messengers had already relayed every detail, and I would have wagered all my possessions, down to the very clothes I stood in, that there was not one stone god left in the temples. All of them had, of course, been hidden nearby and would be brought home as soon as we were safely gone.

"We will put the Virgin's portrait in the highest temple," said Aguilar happily.

I wondered how the Virgin would enjoy sharing a temple with She-of-the-Serpent-Skirt starting tomorrow. Probably they would like each other. Their resemblance was so great that they had to be sisters, even twins.

My quarters were set up as they had been the night before, but now I had the sense not to bother with special scents and floral arches, although I scattered a few flowers on the mats as any civilized person would do.

In the morning I overheard tearful farewells, probably false, as the Spaniards sent most of the women back to Zempoala. The trails would be harder now, and we had only one more day in friendly territory. Other women, new women, would no doubt be offered along the way.

Today's destination was the stronghold town of Xico, a Totonac aerie perched just below the rim of the world. Above Xico there are no villages or farms; only lizards live in the gray rocks among trees gnarled by the bitter wind. The trail to Xico is so steep, so blocked by landslides and rushing waters, that even tax collectors shun it.

The horses struggled for footing, sliding and stumbling until they were almost carried up the last ridge. We entered the town panting and disheveled, and I felt a sense of familiarity, a stirring of childhood memories; then I realized that this was a frontier outpost, the last stop before the wilderness.

Here, as in Sand River, word had run ahead of us. The temples were empty of gods, and the priests had been so scrubbed and barbered that their skins looked burnished. The noblest families of the town were sleeping in straw huts tonight so their houses could be used by Spanish officers.

My own shelter was as usual, and I felt grateful for the tightly woven walls when after sunset a chill wind swept down from Mountain of the Star, a cold omen as the mountain warned us away. He need not have bothered sending his icy breath; our route tomorrow led us away from him toward his smaller brother, Mountain of the Tower. I shivered on my mat, curling myself into a ball like a caterpillar, and at last fell into troubled sleep, aware that this was our last night among allies. Tomorrow we entered Aztec preserves where Moctezuma lay in wait, claws sharpened. I could not have been sleeping long when a Spanish soldier awakened me, calling my name outside the door.

"Sorry to disturb you, Lady Marina. The Captain needs an interpreter."

"Yes, I'll come at once."

The soldier had kept his voice low, almost a whisper, suggesting some intrigue or emergency. I remembered the midnight talks with the Aztec tax collectors and decided something unexpected must have happened.

Cortes had set up his headquarters in the most imposing house in town. The sentry gestured silently for me to enter, and I moved quickly through a dark hall, then across a patio of beaten earth toward a curtained door. Streaks of light showed around the curtains as the wind stirred them. The house smelled powerfully of vanilla, and baskets of dry pods were stacked against the walls.

I entered quietly and found my lord the Captain alone, seated at a table in his wooden chair, which I considered a throne because the seat was so high. He sat in it when receiving dignitaries. The chair was a marvel; its heavy wooden legs, seat and arms had somehow been bent into curves, then the whole thing was hinged so it folded into a bundle of sticks for a porter to carry on his back. An identical chair had been placed on the opposite side of the table. The little altar where he said his prayers twinkled with candles in ruby cups, and his armor hung on the wall near the sleeping mats. I knew he expected important visitors because he wore his favorite doublet, dark velvet with little gold knots.

Unaware of me, he sat bent over a leather-bound book, reading by the light of a hanging lamp brought from one of the ships. The shadows softened his features, made his brows less severe. He would never be beautiful as Lord Alonzo was beautiful, yet looking at him, I again understood why Plumed Serpent had chosen to inhabit Cortes. My lord the Captain conveyed power even in repose, even when the god was not strongly present in him—tonight I did not sense Plumed Serpent in the room.

Cortes glanced up, seemed startled to find me there. "Lady Marina, forgive me. I did not hear you enter."

I made a small reverence. He rose and bowed to me, something he did not do in public. I felt uncomfortable causing him to stand. It was a Spanish custom I would never get used to. "A messenger said you need an interpreter, my lord," I said, wishing he would sit down.

"Interpreter? No, he misunderstood. I asked you to come for two reasons. First, I wanted to talk with you about the Dalcalans."

Another new Spanish word, Dalcalans. When would I master this impossible language? "I do not understand 'Dalcalans,' my lord."

"These people whose land is ahead of us. The enemies of the Aztecs."

Then I realized what he meant. "Oh, the Tlaxcalans. That is how we say it, my lord. *Tlaxcalans.*" I had corrected him before I thought of my rudeness. I could have bitten off my tongue.

He was not disturbed; he chuckled. "I have no head for languages.

I was the despair of the monks who pounded Latin into me. Let me try again." He said, exactly as before, "Dalcalans. Is that better?"

"It is perfect, my lord."

He repeated it several times, quite pleased, then moved to stand behind the chair near me. "Please sit down, Lady Marina. I've been with soldiers so long my manners are rusted."

In total confusion I tried to obey him, wondering what would happen to me. In his presence I always tried to appear graceful and poised—like a queen, Lady Flint Knife would have said. But how could I be queenly when I had never sat in a chair before? As far as I knew, there were no chairs anywhere in the Only World. Our heels were our chairs. There were thrones for high officials, but these were low stools safely near the ground, like the little stools more pretentious Maya men used when they dined. Well, there was nothing for it but to try.

Cautiously I lowered myself onto the high seat, sure that the thing would tip over, perhaps fold up with me inside. If it was really safe, why did Cortes hold the back to steady it? I perched on the edge, feeling ungainly, then slid back. I tried to relax, but the seat was so deep that my heels did not touch the floor, and this was unnerving. I took a firm grip on the wooden arms. Somehow I made myself look as if I had been sitting in chairs all my life.

Cortes sat in the other chair, leaned toward the table, smiling. I tried to smile back.

"Besides asking about the Dalcalans, I wanted to thank you for your help. Especially for the speech you made in Zempoala. That day you were worth more than all my cannons and cavalry."

"My lord is kind." I lowered my eyes. If only I could plant my heels firmly on the floor!

"Until now I've had no chance to thank you. Tonight I thought we might have supper together here."

Supper? I nearly did fall from the chair. So this was the night I had waited for, the night for which Lord Alonzo had prepared me. I had come rushing to the occasion in rumpled clothes with my hair loose and not even a touch of cinnabar on my lips and eyelids. I was hopeless!

Cortes called at the door for an orderly, who brought a tray of food and lighted candles for the table. There was a cup with some crudely arranged flowers—a touch Spaniards did not ordinarily think of except for the Virgin's altar. The night's intentions were clear enough.

But while we ate roast rabbit—flavorless without chili—Cortes questioned me keenly and it seemed endlessly about Tlaxcala.

"Four states make up the Republic of Tlaxcala, so the land is ruled by a Council of Four. The great lords rule, but lesser nobles have a vote and give advice," I said, sounding like an Aztec tutor in a clan school. I struggled to explain, often not finding the Spanish words, that Tlaxcalans live severe and admirable lives dedicated to health, strength and service to the state. The boys and youths compete fiercely in public games to strengthen their bodies for later army duties.

"They are proud. They have never paid tribute to anyone and boast they will give their lives before they give one kernel of maize to the Aztecs. They drink in hatred of the Aztecs with their mothers' milk."

Cortes looked thoughtful. "They sound like Romans during the Republic, or maybe even Spartans," he said, which meant nothing to me. "I will like the Dalcalans."

If so, he would be the only outsider who did. Tlaxcalans were notoriously boorish and boastful, suspicious of the arts and immune to poetry. Their only songs were battle shrieks or tedious ballads recalling their victories. They speak the same language as the Aztecs, but in Tlaxcalan throats it turns into the growling of bears. In religion they were like the Aztecs but less extreme: bloodstained, not blood-soaked, but I suspected this was merely lack of opportunity.

"They distrust comfort and forbid luxury, but they are rich," I told him, dredging up the last fact I knew. " 'Tlaxcala' means 'Land of Bread.' "

He sat considering and digesting all I had said. Hoping to forestall more difficult questions, I touched the small book on the table and asked, "What is this, my lord? I know it is a Spanish book, like Father Olmedo's missal. Is it the same?"

"No. This book is not holy like a missal, but in its way it is almost as wonderful." When he touched the cover, his fingers were gentle, loving.

"Is it stories of the gods? I mean, the saints, of course."

"It tells about a great warrior. He was called El Cid."

"El Cid? I have heard his name."

"You have?" He leaned toward me, eager. "Where? Tell me."

"The soldiers sing ballads about him."

"Oh, yes." He looked disappointed. "You have heard of him only from Spaniards, not from your own people."

"Only from Spaniards," I answered and regretted the reply at once. Why did I tell him the truth when it was something else he wished to hear?

"I had hoped legends of him might have come this far. They are beautiful stories."

"I would like to know them."

"Would you, Lady Marina? Every Spanish schoolboy grows up with them. Not all the stories are in the book, of course. Many are not written down but always told or sung. El Cid teaches us honor and duty. Every boy longs to grow up to be El Cid."

Did you, I wondered? Something in his voice as he began telling me the stories made me think he loved and admired El Cid yet his own dreams had been different.

I understood most of what he told me about this Spanish champion, the greatest swordsman in the world. It had been El Cid's duty to kill people who were not Christians and he had done this with matchless success. By deceit and trickery he captured a great city for his king, and another time after a city had surrendered to him he broke all his promises, letting his men indulge in an orgy of murder and rape and robbery. He sounded rather like Moctezuma's predecessor, King Ahuizotl the Wrathful, but the ruler to whom El Cid was so loyal was even worse than Ahuizotl, accepting the vilest slanders against his faithful knight.

"But El Cid never wavered in his devotion to his sovereign," said Cortes.

"Why not? He had been badly treated. Unfairly, too."

Cortes looked startled. "But the king is appointed by God. God rules through him."

"Aztecs believe that, too," I said, thinking of Ahuizotl and Moctezuma. But it was not the same. In the Only World we had never claimed that our gods were good or kind or even likable. The one attribute all gods shared was power, nothing else. We did not expect their appointees to be better than they were. One had a right to ask for more from the benevolent God of the Christians.

"Listen to this," he said, and rose to pace the room as he read. Squirming on the chair, I longed to pace with him or, better still, sit quietly on the floor at his side.

He read a passage where El Cid bids farewell to his wife and daughter, quite beautiful as far as I could tell. But I knew Cortes would never have such feelings, speak such words. He would be kind and courteous—but what was a wife to Plumed Serpent? My lord the Captain was greater than El Cid and not much like him.

"He was all that a man could be," said Cortes, putting down the book. "The sword of his God and king."

"Does my lord have other books?"

"Only this and a book of prayers. But I have another in Cuba, a wonderful work about a knight named Amadis. Sometime I would like to talk to you about Amadis." Again he stroked the leather binding. "My father gave me this when I went away to school in Salamanca. A generous gift. Books are rare and expensive, and my father is only a country squire—not a great nobleman like your father, Princess."

I suspected that the title elevated me a little, but he seemed pleased at having used it.

"We, too, have books, although they do not look like this," I told him. "There is a library in Tenochtitlan, one in Mani and many others. But I have looked at only one book closely. It belonged to my father."

"A story? A tale of adventures?"

"Well . . . yes." I could hardly tell him about the god and the woman tenderly copulating while drifting on the river. Instead I repeated a tale Lady Flint Knife had told me, about a warrior princess who destroyed her enemies and claimed a throne.

"A warrior princess? Are there many such?" he asked.

"No. But a great queen ruled the city of Palenque, a warrior."

"Amazons," he said, pleased. I did not understand.

"Are there no warrior women in other lands, my lord?"

"Not anymore. I heard of a woman in France who wore armor, led troops and won great victories. She was called the Maid."

I savored the idea briefly, feeling the armor, imagining myself on a horse. I charged with a thousand knights behind me. But I asked him cautiously, "After her victories, did she rule as queen?"

"The Maid of France?" He shook his head. "No. She won the

country for her king, which was her duty. Then she claimed to hear voices from God and the angels, so she was burned at the stake as a heretic, a witch. By the Inquisition, I suppose. Of course, what she claimed was satanic—damnable."

"Yes." I considered this and took warning. I also recalled what Aguilar had told me about the Inquisition. Never would I mention the goddess who spoke through me to the Totonacs at Zempoala. Besides, I did not think a woman who wore armor and led armies and won victories would last very long whether she heard angels or not.

The lamp had burned low and smoked. Cortes rose and extinguished it. His eyes seemed luminous in the flicker of candles, and when he looked down at me, I caught a glimpse of the god behind them. The god was smiling, mischievous.

His rising gave me a chance to escape the chair. I stood, lowering my glance respectfully and folding my hands. The silence seemed endless. Wind rustled the door curtains and a spatter of rain swept across the roof.

"I have kept you late with my talk, Lady Marina. Forgive me. You must be tired."

"No, my lord."

Why did he keep the table between us and speak with such deference? It was, I supposed, his respect for rank. He was treating me like a lady, even a princess, and would not impose himself. It was gracious and frustrating.

I moved around the table, lifted my head to look directly into his eyes and, yes, the god was there. I said, "Tomorrow we go into Aztec country. I will not be afraid because my lord is leading us. I wanted to say this, wanted you to know."

He took me gently by the shoulders, not smiling, and although he spoke softly there was fierceness in his voice. "We will conquer this land! We will triumph over cities and kingdoms because God wills it and we are his servants. Do you know that, Marina?"

"I know. I have always known."

He drew me close and my body, against my will, trembled. "Do you want me?" he whispered. "You deserve more than I can give you. I belong to the king, I have God's work to do. And I have other promises. Do you understand me?"

"I understand." Did he mean he could not be my husband as my father had been husband to my mother? Of course he could not be.

Who would have expected such a thing? We were meant, as in the book, only to drift awhile on the river. His hand found my breast, his lips pressed against my hair. I trembled. My breath came too rapidly in little gasps, like a frightened but eager village bride. I forced myself to be calm, to be clearheaded. Now I must recall not only all that Lord Alonzo had taught me of Spanish ways, but all the lore of the Flower Prince and his arts that I had heard from older women.

Releasing me, he turned to blow out the candles on the table, which gave me a moment to compose myself. At the altar other candles still flickered ruby red, the shadows softening his cheekbones. Yet in the dimness he loomed immense, a giant, the gray eyes so luminous and compelling that I lowered my own, afraid to meet his gaze, afraid I could not control my trembling. He was so much larger than any man, so much more powerful.

When he took my arm to lead me to the sleeping mats, I stifled a small, involuntary gasp. Now the time had come, the hour my whole life had prepared me for. I would be perfect for him. I would perform as skillfully as a temple dancer whose body is trained as an instrument of pleasure.

I shed my clothes quickly, doing it well and smoothly, I thought. I did not let his nearness confuse me, so my hands were steady as I reached to undo the fastenings of his shirt. Once, with Lord Alonzo, I had been fumbling at this task; now I would be deft, would sigh lovingly as my fingertips revealed and caressed his chest. I knew just how.

But suddenly he took me into his arms. I felt his face press against mine—downy, the feathery softness of the god. I felt his breath, then his lips which did not burn as I had imagined, but were warmly sweet and gentle. My memory blurred, but I realized I must now part my own lips moistly, only a little at first, then more fully to welcome him and then—

But he engulfed me, covering my body with his own, dissolving me into him, and my skills were swept away as before a flood. I *was* the village bride crying out in joy and pain and fulfillment. I clung to him wildly, not knowing or caring what I did, not even wondering what he must think of me or if I pleased him. I had thought of myself as the instrument of his pleasure, but instead he became mine; I had hoped to serve him, awakening him to desire, then even rapture. Never had I thought of being lost myself in a whirlpool.

Yet when at last we were quiet and my senses returned, I knew from his touch, from his gentle kisses, that whatever I had done was somehow right, that in spite of my madness, perhaps even because of it, my lord was content.

Years later a young woman asked me, "How does a god make love?"

Because she was sincere, I tried to answer. "As a man does," I said. "Only better."

Yet that was only a poor part of the truth. The rest I could not have explained to her even if I had been willing.

I fell asleep beside him at the Ninth Watch, the last hours of the night, and it should have been the deepest, most contented slumber of my life. But I awoke in the ruins of a flaming city where the streets were piled with corpses whose hair and flesh crackled with fire. On every side walls of houses crashed down in clouds of dust to show rooms turned to furnaces. The corpses, though dead, still shrieked and sobbed, and trying to escape them, I fled, my sandals splashing blood. I ran up the steps of a temple, stumbling, tearing my hands on the stone stairs, but when I reached the top I found the sanctuary ablaze like the city below. From here I saw a vast landscape, mountains and broad lakes, desolate, forests turned to smoking embers. Although it was night, vultures wheeled in the sky and they were the only things that lived.

Part Four
THE RETURN TO HIS KINGDOM

13

The City of Mexico—
The Feast of Pentecost—1564

Eight days ago a bolt of lightning slashed across a clear sky and struck down the wooden cross on Tepayac Hill, sacred to the Virgin. People crossed themselves or made the ancient gesture against evil, wondering what would come next. Then, only hours later in the dead of night, the Weeping Woman was heard sobbing in the streets, as chilling as when she came in my childhood to warn the Aztecs.

I was asleep when she approached the convent. I dreamed I was young again; my own baby was crying, and I awoke murmuring his name to console him.

"Tepi, Tepi. Go to sleep, dear."

Strange, because I nursed him so short a time and heard him cry so seldom.

I came fully awake, remembering that Tepi had indeed cried, and I had crooned to him, giving him my breast. I imagined him now, fettered in a dungeon, and shuddered, wondering if the Weeping Woman foretold his execution.

I did not pray. I repeated all the curses that have become a nightly litany, although sometimes I change the words as I think of new evils to befall my enemies: the viceroy is some nights buggered by a porcupine instead of a cactus, the archbishop's mistress grows fangs in her cunt, the High Inquisitor drowns in pig shit.

Before the Weeper vanished at dawn, she may have slit the throat of a twelve-year-old boy—not the first time she has committed murder. The victim, an acolyte at the cathedral, lay stretched on the pavement outside the closed doors of the church. He was the grandson of a Tlaxcalan prince who had retained his rank through a decree my lord the Captain signed a generation ago. This youth had recently won a prize for Latin, so some people say he was slain by men still loyal to the old gods. Others believe the opposite, that he was a victim of Spaniards who think that a person not born in Spain can master Latin only with the devil's help.

"Mexicans have little natural intelligence," Mother Superior told some ladies who were playing at making lace in the garden. "So Satan lends them skill to invent heresies."

Nowadays I hear this word "Mexican" from the mouths of Spaniards and always with a tinge of contempt. It comes from an old word we used meaning Aztec, but now refers to anybody not pure Spanish although they may be Zapotec or Otomi or Maya. Well, why not? A new race is springing up here. Let us be Mexicans.

Each day at sunset I meet the hag who spies for me at the fountain where we pretend to draw water.

"My lady, I have learned a great secret!" she hissed at me through toothless gums. "The Marques del Valle has been released!"

"Impossible! There would be mobs in the street."

"He was taken secretly from the city. He was chained and disguised in a Franciscan robe and cowl. Fifty horsemen are escorting him to Veracruz, where he sails for Spain. He is exiled for life."

Exiled for life? He was legitimate heir to the conqueror who delivered a world to Spain. Yet why should I be surprised? I had expected worse for him. If only he had struck boldly months ago, as his father would have done! The whole country would have risen with him and we would now be . . . what? The Kingdom of Mexico? But the marques is not his father.

Keeping my voice calm, I asked, "What of his half-brother?"

"He is still chained in a dungeon." She leaned close and whispered, "Everywhere people are saying prayers for the son of Plumed Serpent."

I slipped her two coins instead of one and we parted, I to my desolate room in the convent to try to understand what was happening.

Why would they release the more dangerous son and hold the other? I supposed they dared not murder a true noble. But what of *my* son? I sat staring at the ugly crucifix, the image with its blue glass eyes, and felt I had earned better treatment than this.

The next morning I ordered a sedan chair for a tour of the city, since soon, dead or alive, I will leave it not to return. I have a hunger to revisit places that seem landmarks in my life, though I know such visits are futile and disappointing. I am really ghost hunting, somehow hoping to see not merely streets and buildings but to meet miraculously people who once inhabited them. Will I encounter some vision of myself forty years younger, full of hope and foolishness? Oh, I could tell that girl a thing or two!

I hired three husky Otomis, two to carry the chair, another armed with a club to clear the way, driving off beggars and vendors. Often vendors are actually thieves who lean through the window pretending to display merchandise; then they will snatch earrings or a brooch from the astonished passenger. I long for Aztec honesty. Besides having my guard, I borrowed a cleaver from the convent kitchen and keep it on the cushion under my silk fan.

"To the Hospital of Jesus the Nazarene," I told the bearers. But we had gone only three or four blocks when I glanced out and shouted to the men, "Stop!"

"Here, Reverend Mother?" They sat the chair down in a dusty open space that once had been a park. I recognized it only because a canal, now dry and filled with garbage, divided the field. Two charcoal burners, black-faced and sooty, were chopping down the trunks of the last dead trees.

One of the men helped me from the chair—my joints seemed to have rusted in a sitting position—and I stood surveying the dead landscape, which was full of memories but without ghosts. Here, long ago, my lord the Captain planted mulberry trees, and that year he sent half across the world for marvelous worms that spin silk thread.

During the few years when the rulers of Spain let him have his way, he performed miracles, planting orchards of fruits no one had ever seen or tasted: apples, cherries, plums. He gave us such crops as wheat and sugarcane; he built mills, foundries, shipyards, bridges. I watched the world change and in a little while it might have become the fabled Tula when the first Plumed Serpent ruled there: the land of plenty where tortillas grew in wild orchards and spiders spun not webs but fine cloth of a hundred colors.

Nowadays the Spanish nobles and Aztec survivors agree about

only one matter: both sneer at my lord as a pirate itching for gold. But he was the greatest builder and planter our world ever knew. No wonder people still worship him; no wonder his name is still so magical that it makes that shit of a viceroy tremble! Cortes would have turned the world into the Gardens of Texcoco.

We had once stood together on this spot, admiring the mulberry saplings, newly planted, and the rich earth was wet around them. I remember the sunlight flashing on the canal. My lord was full of the future that day.

"We will have more silk than Cathay," he said. "It will be as important as the sugar mills. Did I tell you about the vineyards I am planning?" Then his face changed, and although he spoke aloud it was to himself, not to me. "Where else have men ever had a chance to begin everything afresh? We can make a new world here. Who knows? It might even be a little like Paradise."

Now the mulberry trees are dead; the gardeners who tended them have been herded off to toil in the new silver mines. Today's greed starves tomorrow's riches. Each month more ravenous Spaniards debark at Veracruz, usually second sons of bankrupt knights with holes in their stockings. The lucky ones will soon acquire tracts of land worked by men and women who are slaves in all but name.

This is what we have inherited from my lord's dream of paradise, this swill trough for high-born pigs. I curse their unborn children. Leeches, maggots, stuck-up snots.

At least the blood-caked priests are gone, and the garbage stinks less than the old temples of Hummingbird and Smoking Mirror. The world is better than it was, even if it is less beautiful.

My bearers could not approach within two bow shots of the Hospital of Jesus the Nazarene because the pavement was so heaped with plague victims dead or dying. They were piled up row after row, some on mats or blankets, the rest on the cobblestones.

They call this a plague year—as most years are. Aztecs say this curse called smallpox is Smoking Mirror's vengeance on those who have displaced him. Christians say it is punishment for sin. If either belief is true, why have I of all people survived? I suspect these smallpox devils are akin to the Spotted Demons who decimated the Lair of the Serpent when I was a girl. They must be relatives—Spanish cousins, you might say.

A gnarled Franciscan friar, more antique than I am, was hobbling about with a big dipper, sprinkling holy water on the dead and dying. When he saw my sedan chair halt, he came creaking over to peer through the window with rheumy eyes. Seeing my black-shrouded figure, he croaked to the bearers, "Take this corpse directly to a church for burial. We have no room here."

Then, before I could protest, he doused me with cold water. *"In nomine Patri et—"*

"Thy mother's hole, you piece of goat shit!" I screamed at him. Arthritis and all, he jumped knee-high in the air.

It is intolerable to be thought a corpse *twice* in one lifetime!

The bearers retreated with the chair, and by the time I had brushed off the water I repented the insult and made the sign of the cross. After all, I respect Franciscans. When the first large shipment of them arrived at Veracruz, twelve of these missionaries trudged barefoot over the mountains three hundred miles to the City of Mexico with nothing between their thin bodies and the rain except the cheapest robes of coarse cotton.

My lord the Captain greeted them on the spot where my chair now stood, falling to his knees, kissing the ragged hems of their habits. Prince Falling Eagle and other Aztec nobles stood in the huge crowd that watched this, and they were astonished because the Franciscans were scrawny as crows, yet Plumed Serpent humbled himself in the dirt to pay homage with tears in his eyes. So the lords kneeled, too, and so did the soldiers. Soon thousands of worshipers were on their knees before men who looked no stronger than dry twigs. The friars proved themselves worthy of the welcome; the lives of the people are better because of them.

But why, when I look around at this new world, do I always see fops and not Franciscans?

Telling the bearers to wait, I hobbled back to the corner where I could see again a part of the city that had meant much to me. The squat hospital is graceless, ugly enough that Aztecs call it an insult to the Lord of Beauty. But inside are noble rooms with cedar beams; orange trees in the patio give fragrance and dappled shade, while fountains pour over lovely stone. It is so serene I would believe it was a reflection of the Green Heaven, except I know it is only a small copy of the courtyards of Moctezuma.

. .

Smoke still rose from the shattered walls of Tenochtitlan when my lord the Captain began a new city on the ruins. The force that made him invincible in war did not yet weaken in peace. From dawn until dark and sometimes even until moonset, he worked. He urged on the masons and carpenters, praising and correcting, using a stick to sketch the outlines of new structures in the dust. He could have built a new city from the rubble with his own hands.

God Almighty, he said, had given him custody of this world for the king, so churches and shrines had to be erected quickly, waiting only for the completion of forts.

One day Aguilar drew me aside and said in a worried tone, "Cortes is restless. Peace cannot contain him for long. He looks unhappy, discontented."

"Naturally. He's newly a widower, he's expected to appear mournful." As if anyone could regret getting rid of that bitch!

But I knew Aguilar was right. Some nights Cortes rose from our bed and paced in the moonlight like a caged ocelot. Often, after drinking wine, he told me again the stories of the knight Amadis who visited lands inhabited by dwarfs and giants who remained young forever after bathing in magic fountains. I heard longing in his voice.

Sometimes, even in candlelight, I was shocked to see how much he had aged in a year. His beard was flecked with white, his eyes hollow. I felt pain and surprise. It had never occurred to me that you could glance away from one you loved, then look back to find him young no longer. I suspected then that Plumed Serpent had gone from him and would not return. I rebuked this idea; I drove it from my mind.

No, peace could not contain him. He assigned the building to others, then marched off to explore the ends of the earth, making his doomed expedition through the jungle of Honduras, and it was on the way there that I admitted to myself that the god had totally deserted him and left madness behind.

During most of the time of Cortes's wandering, I slept next to the husband he had given me, a good enough man, but I often lay awake wondering where Cortes might be. I longed to be with him. Not for power, certainly not for sex as singers would claim, but because I was like him: peace could not contain me, at least not easily.

I wondered what Cortes searched for. The lands found by Amadis in legends? He himself had already discovered kingdoms more marvelous. Maybe he only wanted to put himself beyond the reach of jealous nobles and royal ingrates.

Whenever he returned to the capital, the dream of a great new city stirred in him. Then new walls, higher towers arose. During those interludes he founded the first hospitals in our world, the one dedicated to Jesus the Nazarene among them.

The afflicted were taken to this building to be prayed over, sprinkled with holy water and have a little blood drawn from their veins before they expired. The idea of setting apart a special building where people could die had never occurred to us, so it was a great novelty.

Later I learned that the purpose of a hospital was the opposite of its results, that they were places for recovery, not death. But even though no one carried into one of these charnel houses was likely to walk out, the intentions were kind, and it was better to perish on the floor of the hospital, out of the rain and wind, than to lie on a rubble heap somewhere.

Newcomers are now told that Cortes chose this site for his charity because he first met Moctezuma here. Actually my lord built here for a private reason, the same reason that brought me back to visit this spot once more.

When I realized that the birth of my child was fast approaching, I went to the place called Huitzilan near the heart of the devastated city that had been destroyed only a few months before. A famous temple of the Goddess of Childbirth had stood in Huitzilan since the beginning of the world. The mother of the first incarnation of Plumed Serpent, who was All-in-One and a sister of Lady Moon, came to this island shrine when she felt the first stirring in her womb. I could only hope the temple had survived the siege.

Those days I was filled with mixed fear and elation, not knowing if I was pregnant by the man or the god. Long ago an Olmec woman entered a sacred cave where she mated with a god, and later she birthed a baby whose mouth was a jaguar's fanged muzzle and whose tiny feet were armed with claws. Another woman, a Maya, coupled with a god and spawned a race of web-toed river dwarfs. I felt my own baby would be whole and human, probably beautified by the god. Yet I was afraid.

I found the temple had been razed, the priestesses fled. But under the fallen roof lay the most beautiful statue I had ever seen, a goddess whose child was just coming forth, her face shown at an instant when exultation triumphs over pain, life over death.

My servants retrieved her broken altar from the ash heap and, since she was small, it was easy to hide her behind a banner of the Blessed Virgin in the shelter I had built. For more than a week I lived there, gently guarded by the goddess and the Virgin.

I posted guards so no tethered bird or animal came within bow shot lest the baby strangle on its own cord. I kept a scarlet cloth and a broken knife nearby as custom demands. Two loops of rope dangled from the roof poles for me to grip when the time came, but I ordered that these be brought in already knotted, not tied in my presence, which could cause disaster.

One day when I was fretting about some neglected safeguard, I suddenly thought of my mother, of how desperate she had been for the safety of my brother before his birth. Now I knew her feelings, and looked into her soul. A burden of anger I had forgotten I still carried seemed lighter.

Our son was born, perfect and beautiful. Cortes lifted him from the basket cradle and said, "We will call him Martin for my father." The baby's tiny hand gripped Cortes's finger. "A strong fellow for one so little!"

I was proud that my lord named him for his own father— an acknowledgment, a recognition. A few years later, when my lord had another son by his Spanish wife, he called that boy Martin, too, showing once more it was the name nearest his heart. But to myself I would always think of our son as Tepi, which means "the little one."

My lord glanced at the woven walls, the floor of beaten earth. "Why did you come here? Why was my son not born in our house in Coyoacan?"

I had prepared my answer carefully. "Near here, my lord, you and Moctezuma greeted each other the first time, the meeting of two great races, two peoples. Our son is the meeting of two races also, but in him the peoples have become one."

"We will make the world remember this spot," he said, then kneeled, crossed himself and made a silent prayer to the Virgin and the Goddess of Childbirth concealed behind her.

He kissed his son; he embraced me, brushing his lips across my forehead. Then, with a joyous yell, he ran from the hut. I heard him gallop away, shouting as he went.

Minutes later every cannon in the Valley of Mexico roared, thundering again and again, while the new bronze bells clanged. Neither were all the voices raised in celebration Spanish. Earthen and log drums beat their joy, and trumpets of shell and horn joined them.

I cradled Tepi to my breast, and in his tiny body, in the beating of his heart, I felt my own completion.

He was the first Mexican.

I returned to the sedan chair. "Go. Take me anywhere." As we turned the corner, it occurred to me that my lord's bones should rest in the Hospital of Jesus, birthplace of his son. But that is so reasonable nobody will ever think of it. No, he will molder forever in Texcoco, where wild dogs howl at night.

The bearers halted without orders and came around to help me dismount. They had delivered me to still another hospital, perhaps assuming I was on a tour of pesthouses. Or did they assume I needed the care of this particular infirmary? It is devoted to the treatment of what delicate folk call illnesses sent by Venus. Pox and clap. These are two more Spanish cousins, but some say they are native demons who went to Spain and returned strengthened.

The infirmary has a delicious name: Hospital of the Love of God. Lifting my veil, I winked at the bearer, who was a husky fellow. "So you think I'm not too old to have caught a dose? Shall I pass the devil on to you, my boy?"

He blushed and stammered, the best compliment I've had in years.

"No, I won't get out, and you needn't get in. Take me to a less loving neighborhood."

A moment later I found myself in the most loveless district of the city, the square fronted by government palaces, the dens of lawyers and bureaucrats. Safer to have lingered at the pesthouses!

At that moment the municipal councilors, who must have gathered to concoct a new swindle, filed across the street, barring my passage. I glared at the parade of marching vultures: black feathered, white ruffed, hook beaked and balding. They swung their wattles and paunches.

Suddenly a fire of old anger flared in me and I shouted, "How dare you be alive? To live on? Vermin! Monkshit!"

. .

My lord the Captain died in Spain during his second long sojourn there. He had tried, as vainly as his hero El Cid, to get justice from a king who ignored him. Who was this upstart Cortes? An adventurer without a drop of royal blood. Cortes was an example that could produce menaces.

Then Cortes died, sixty-two years old, younger than I am now. He was elderly in years, of course—most men do not live so long. But in him was a power that should have preserved him. They say he was weakened by despondency, that he died of failure. Cortes despondent? Not likely! Not for more than two days.

Rumor traveled six months ahead of him; new hope arose: human leeches would be plucked from the people's flesh; mass murderers, some of them true fiends, would be brought to justice. Cortes's former lieutenants and many of his common soldiers had turned into the worst oppressors. These would be punished.

But instead of a triumphant homecoming, my lord found the Narrow Passage.

When news of his death reached me in the spring of the next year, I mourned less for Cortes than for the world that needed him, the work that would not be finished. My private sorrow had been spent long ago when I knew I would not see him again.

I felt anger more than sadness. Soon I was casting a baleful eye at everyone who had unjustly survived my lord. I saw men whose sole profession was smoking their pipes. By what right did they still puff when Cortes breathed no more? I found myself condemning not only scoundrels but decent people simply for outliving a man so much greater, more useful, more needed. In time I recovered; I accepted that survival is a lottery and it is no good protesting that it is rigged and crooked. Yet I still think there are persons whose longevity should be added to the list of their faults.

Now, watching the vile counselors cross the street, my old rage blazed again and only half-cooled when the last of them vanished into some hole or other. An elderly *lepero* squatted against the palace wall. I tossed him a coin and called, "What mischief has the council been up to?"

"They confirmed the Precious Metal Law," he answered.

This law makes it illegal for anyone except Spaniards to handle silver or gold; it strikes at the craftsmen who for a hundred generations have created beautiful jewelry. The archbishop has pronounced that handling such metals might corrupt the souls of the "Indians."

So our souls are too pure to be endangered by wealth, yet so wicked that the devil prompts us in learning. I have just decided something: a soul is worth exactly what somebody else gains by saving it.

The council's action, long expected, had quick effects. My chair was hardly out of the shadow of the palace when a young man thrust his head and arm through the window.

"Lady, a bargain!" My hand touched the cleaver. "Look at this beautiful pendant! Pure gold."

He dangled a lovely medal, not hung on a chain in Spanish style but with a delicate thong.

"Whose portrait is carved on it?" I asked.

"The Blessed Virgin's. What else?"

A lie. I recognized the shadowed face of the Unknown Goddess who first spoke through me in Zempoala. "How much?"

I bought it and returned to the convent. There I opened my dress and hung the pendant around my neck, then rebuttoned. I now wore a crucifix on the outside of the black cloth, a goddess within. It felt comfortable and accustomed, like hiding She-of-Childbirth behind the banner of the Virgin. And I think my people will always do this, even if in the passing of centuries the goddess becomes invisible.

I ordered chocolate brought to my room and it was delivered by the pretty blond boy, the English child heretic. He has already been promoted from slop pots to serving trays and has replaced the spaniel in Mother Superior's affections although not, I hope, in her bed. He is too young for such a shock.

We chatted; he knows all about the inquisitional jail from his own experience. "What about the rats?" I asked. "Are they not terrible?"

"Not really," he said, looking thoughtful. "In fact they are quite tasty if you have a fire to roast them. But raw they are disgusting."

He still worries about friends of his in prison. I said, "If I buy food, could you take it to your friends?"

"Oh, yes. With a small bribe to the guards."

So it was settled. I have another spy in the enemy camp.

. .

I should have slept well, but my mind kept returning to the streets I had just visited, peopling them not with today's drunks and counselors but yesterday's soldiers, camp followers and Aztec lords. To be old is to be better acquainted with the dead than the living.

At the same time the English boy's pale face kept disturbing me, reminding me of a boy the same age but far more childish. Time has blurred my memory of that face, but I see parts of it—the sulky set of his lips, the eyes unchildlike and full of hate. Time has dimmed his image, thank God. But I still see him.

It was that year, 1524, when my lord tossed away his conquest, deserted his kingdom and went south, supposedly to punish the traitor Olid in faraway Honduras. But who knows what he really sought?

We were on the threshold of that vast quagmire, a land that reminded me of a gigantic green spider web spun of creepers and strangler vines. Yet the fringes of that vast trap are so pleasant, so inviting.

We followed the windings of a river that some said was the stream of Lair of the Serpent, passing orchards of papaya, almond and banana trees.

One day in a village I asked if we were near Painala, for the frangipani and hibiscus aroused memories.

"There is no longer such a town," a woman told me. "Spotted Demons visited it years ago. In time everyone died."

So they were all gone—my mother, my brother, Lord Lancer. At times I had thought fleetingly of them. I assumed they had heard of me—was there anybody in the Only World who had not? But they could not guess who I was. I had imagined confrontations with my mother, a reunion with my brother. But none of these imagined meetings had seemed real to me, and now they would never take place.

Before leaving the village, I had a mass said for my brother's soul and paid a local priest of the goddess Twisted Flower Branch to sing funeral rites for my mother after the Christians had left. It was appropriate for Lady Iztac: that goddess used to send scorpions and venomous spiders to sting her enemies. Like Lady Iztac, she was implacable.

Long ago my mother had ceased to be my enemy when I realized she had played her role in life and sent me to Plumed Serpent. That was neither her fault nor to her credit.

But news of my brother's death left me empty. Tepi had been left behind with a wet nurse. I would be a mother again when I returned, but Tepi was not mine to keep. Cortes's son would be reared in Spain, and I had made peace with the hard wisdom of this. I had considered bringing my brother to live with me, a possibility that had now ended.

We moved on to another village, then another. I had much to occupy my mind. Cortes had arranged for my marriage to Don Juan Xamarillo, a Spanish sea captain who could give me respectability and the gift of his own absence much of the time. He would allow me great freedom, he would even be an exciting husband; but I could not yet imagine my future as any man's wife.

I was also concerned by the alarming moods afflicting my lord the Captain, and afraid of what would happen when he left this gentle edge of the jungle.

We arrived in a prosperous town called Jaltipan, an obscure village of my father's old domain that had grown into a small center of government. Cortes had sent word that lords of estates and village chieftains were to gather for Christian baptism. After that he would confirm their titles, as he did everywhere.

He slept alone that night in the newly scrubbed temple. Then in the morning we assembled for mass in the public square. After that we received oaths of allegiance while priests baptized the overnight converts, dipping water with a seashell, which is sacred to San Diego—he sailed across a sea in one.

Two lines formed, one religious and the other civil, with notaries recording baptisms and deeds. There were other interpreters now, but I stood at my lord's chair. The morning had worn on when I happened to turn toward the line of civil claimants and found myself looking squarely into the face of Lady Iztac.

She stared at me unbelieving, mouth open and eyes wide, then shook her head as though to banish an illusion. I recovered my wits and lifted my hands in formal greeting. "God is pleased to have us meet again, Mother."

Still unbelieving, she uttered my name. She had lost several teeth, which made her look older than she was. In fact, she appeared so frail, so helpless that suddenly I pitied her—the last emotion I had expected to feel. But she soon disabused me about her weakness.

"So it is you! You are the one they have talked of so much. La

Malinche, Doña Marina. So you turned out to be the destroyer, as we knew you would. Why am I surprised to find you here among the Spaniards? I should have guessed!"

Pushing past me, she began to rail at Cortes, who could not understand a word she uttered.

"I was tricked into coming here today, lured here by my lying daughter. She has trapped me and hopes to take vengeance." Throwing herself on her knees, she kissed the ground. "Do not believe my daughter, Malintzin! She was born cursed. It was not my fault she was kidnapped."

Then she thought of an explanation—you could see it enter her head. "My husband arranged it. Yes, my husband. I did not know."

Cortes stared in astonishment and distaste. Tragedy moved him, but he detested melodrama. "Who the devil is this hag?"

I felt no shame; Lady Iztac had nothing to do with me. "My mother. She is not quite herself. The shock of our reunion."

"Your mother? I heard only the other day that your mother—"

"Was dead? Yes, my lord. A false report, God be praised."

"I am happy for you," he said doubtfully, trying to smile at Lady Iztac.

Drawing encouragement, she slowly rose. I saw her putting on her dignity like an unfamiliar robe, and a semblance of Aztec pride appeared.

"So you return in triumph, Ce Malinalli," she said. "You have done well by the pain of others. The whole world talks of it. Well, that was fate."

She stood tall in her threadbare finery, almost handsome. I realized Lord Lancer was dead or she would not have been here representing whatever property was left—not much, to judge by her clothes. Naturally Lord Lancer would have left her impoverished. He had a magic touch with money—he could make it vanish.

Her head rose higher as she displayed herself to Cortes as a person of importance. It was Lord Lancer's style, not her own. To me she said, "Whatever vengeance you take on me will also harm your brother. He is your own flesh."

"He is alive? Where is he?"

"Of course he is alive. I protected him, guarded him." A flicker of hope entered her eyes. "Chimal! Come at once!"

A boy in the patched outfit of an eaglet junior soldier inched forward in the crowd, then suddenly raced to Lady Iztac and buried his face in her bosom.

"This is your sister, darling. We thought she was dead, but she is alive and very famous, very powerful. Greet her properly like a little man." When he did not respond, her voice changed, turned hard as flint. I remembered that tone. "Chimal!"

The face he unwillingly turned toward me was not one I recognized, had nothing of my father or grandmother. His lips were thick and pouting, his chin weak. He was no more the brother of my dreams than Lady Iztac was the mother of my memories.

The boy stared at me without speaking. In his look I read the stories of his wicked sister who had mercifully died. And later stories, not of his sister, but of a whore called La Malinche, a monster of treachery. I was both these women to him; I would never be anything else.

I became aware of applause, of cheering, and looking around, I saw that a dozen soldiers had gathered. Murillo, Bernal Diaz and Lopez stood near, smiling at me. They had heard the joyful news of my family's survival, had come to join me in thanksgiving. This was the stuff of their romances: the wicked mother, the princess sold to bandits. Now they awaited the last scene: forgiveness and reconciliation. I would not disappoint them.

Lifting my arms in prayer, I looked heavenward. Softly, so others could not hear, I spoke to Lady Iztac. "I mean you no harm. Our meeting was an unlucky accident, not a trap. Let us forget it as quickly as we can."

My smile was just a little tearful as I took a gold chain from my neck and draped it around hers. I pulled off my rings to press them into her hands—except for the jade one my lord had given me. I tore off ornaments sewn to my skirt and gave them to my brother, who looked apprehensive, as if the silver might be unclean. Oh, he was indeed Lady Iztac's son, stuffed with pieties from the cradle. I was presenting him a small fortune and he could only cringe and look sanctimonious.

I said softly but very clearly, "If you think I am handing you turkey shit, you have only to refuse it." He lost no time accepting. He even managed a smirk.

I gave my silver combs, the opal pendant, the turquoise brooch. Lady Iztac and Chimal had enough to keep them in comfort for years.

Everyone watching was appropriately moved; the romantic tale had ended as they hoped.

Three days later, when we were far from Jaltipan, I sent a swift-messenger to Lady Iztac. He carried two clay stamps, my father's crest and my own, and the name of a merchant in the capital, a man who served as my agent. He would give Chimal money if need ever arose. Chimal had only to present a paper marked with the stamps.

Although for years we lived within four days' journey of each other, I did not meet Lady Iztac or my brother again. Three times, at long intervals, papers were presented to my agent, who gave them money. There was no message from Chimal. I did not expect one.

Now, as the bell softly tolled three in the Convent of the Holy Child, I imagined Lady Iztac still alive. She was not a harridan scarred by deceit and hardship as I had last seen her, but as queenly as when she danced naked in Jalisco.

I imagined a messenger from Mexico City arriving. He greets her, then says, "Tragic news! Your grandson Martin faces torture and death at the hands of Spanish judges."

She nods; her face does not change, does not betray the satisfaction she feels. "Spanish judges? It was bound to happen. He is his mother's son. Ah, those gold-hungry Spaniards!" Her noble profile, chin high, looks very Aztec.

Then she withers and shrinks, becomes the woman I met in the jungle village. "Tell me, if he dies, will there be an inheritance?"

The next morning I hired a boat to view the city from the lakes and canals, the way I first explored it when I was a child. I took along the heretic boy, whose name is Juanito, to wield a fly whisk and carry an umbrella. At the nearest canal, the only available boat was a flower-decked, gaudy craft that had just returned from a bridal celebration. When we stepped in, our feet crushed roses.

As we moved into the lake traffic, Juanito and I made a curious sight—a crow of a nun and a boy in penitential garb seated together under a nuptial arch. But no one looked askance, since no Spaniards saw us. One of the many things I love in my own people is their easy acceptance of oddity. They find amusement, not offense.

This was a feast day, Pentecost, when tongues of fire danced at the supper table of the apostles, so fire-eaters and fire-jugglers were out in force in holiday paper costumes. Matthew, Mark, Luke and John paddled by us wearing outrageous false whiskers, streams of flame issuing from their mouths. I marveled that the fake beards did not catch fire.

Families had rented cheap holiday boats, little craft nearly swamped by a dozen adults and uncountable children. Other families, less prosperous, milled about on the shore, not playing games or criticizing spectacles as Spaniards must do when they celebrate, but merely being part of the crowd. In gathering together we reach beyond ourselves, we join with a larger being, and so the people live as much on holidays as on corn—fortunate these days when corn is scarce.

They also live on flowers. One night before we made love and fell asleep, my lord the Captain told me about a hero—was it Amadis? —who visited a distant land where the folk had no mouths and were sustained entirely by the perfume of flowers. I thought, *By their color, too. We drink them through our eyes.* He said, "People here could almost do that. I never expected to see warriors—fierce fighters, too—go into battle with a spear in one hand, a bouquet in the other."

Yes, we live by flowers. There is hardly a hut in the city so mean that it does not have at least a few marigolds struggling for life in a cracked jar.

The boatman turned into a narrow canal leading to the center of the city, a waterway lined with sober mansions. Juanito, although I had not been paying attention, was recounting his life story. The boy and I have something in common; the very young have nothing but their life stories to tell and the very old wish to tell nothing else.

He said, "So the black men, the slaves, were chained and put in the hold where there wasn't room for them. They were stacked on top of each other like bricks in a wall."

Juanito had been cabin boy on a ship commanded by the English pirate Sir John Hawkins, a monster who brought African slaves to the Indies, flouting Spanish and divine law. He had been driven ashore at Veracruz, victim of a wind raised by God.

"The black men were sold at an island before we reached Veracruz. All except those who were too sick. We threw them overboard."

"You drowned them?" His pleased tone, not the drowning, startled me.

"Oh, it is all right. Black men have no souls. And they are not the only ones who look human but aren't. On the ship I heard about lands to the north full of redmen who also have no souls and cannot even be made to work, so they are useless. When I grow up I will sail north and kill all those redmen and take their gold and furs."

I knew little about the people across the northern deserts, the cousins of the Chichimecas or Yaquis. God help them when they are visited by the English! Perhaps we have been lucky.

The canal ahead was blocked by a long line of barges being prepared for tonight's fiery spectacle on the lake. These pyres will roar up from the water like volcanoes.

"They say it will be the greatest show of fire the city has ever seen," said Juanito.

"Not quite."

How my mind wanders! I remembered the greatest celebration I ever saw here, although that night I had little chance to watch it. I was occupied by a more serious matter.

It was the year the world came to believe that my lord the Captain had perished in the jungles of Honduras. Usurpers had seized his offices and estates; new crimes against the people were devised every week.

Then my lord reappeared, landing on the coast by night. I was one of the first to know, for then I had spies everywhere, messengers at my command. I journeyed to the capital to meet my lord, thinking he might need me.

The country was in a fever. Common people, who had already mourned his dying, believed Plumed Serpent had returned through the Narrow Passage, like Jesus Christ, or Saint Lazarus or Moctezuma's sister.

He arrived at the city before me, so I sent word to the Monastery of San Francisco, where he was in seclusion for a religious retreat, that I would call on him tomorrow.

His withdrawing to a monastery surprised me, although it was said he would remain there only a week. I knew he would give thanks to God for deliverance from the jungles, but a monastic retreat? Huge public masses were more his style.

He sent no answer, and while I waited I heard alarming news. Luis Ponce de Leon, a Spanish nobleman who had the ear of the king, was now on the road to the capital, having landed at Veracruz a few days ago. He bore documents signed by the king himself; he was a Royal Visitor whose mission was to bring my lord the Captain to trial for crimes and treacheries. Now the vipers of the Spanish court would have the day they had so long prayed and intrigued for. Their jealousy of Cortes, son of nobody, gnawed at them.

On a street I met an old friend, the soldier Pablo Suarez. I asked, "Why is Cortes in seclusion? Some illness?"

"No. Unless it's an attack of religion. He's always been pious as a bishop and just as horny. What a salute we'll give him when he comes out, Lady Marina. I'm in charge of two batteries of cannon, new guns from Flanders. Satan himself can't fart louder."

Soldiers honored me by talking to me as they talked to each other.

I felt danger; the air crackled with it: the ominous presence of the Royal Visitor, Cortes's failure to answer my message.

Late that morning, without waiting for an invitation, I went straight to the monastery and entered through the unlocked gate and door. I had found out where the visitor's suite was, so I went swiftly down a stone corridor, passing the domestic chapel where three men, penitants, kneeled with their backs bare, lashing themselves with the painful little whips called disciplines. They were too busy flogging themselves to notice me. Nothing, it seemed, had changed with the years.

In the antechamber two pimply-faced acolytes stood guard. "You cannot go in," said one.

"No," said the other. "The Captain General is with Friar Ortiz."

I knew about this Friar Tomas Ortiz. My comrade Bernal Diaz had warned me. "Beware of this priest. He came on the ship with Ponce de Leon and does more meddling in politics than work at saving souls. By the way, some passengers from that ship have come down with cholera. If Ortiz gets it, small loss."

I waited impatiently. A few minutes later Ortiz was ushered out, sweeping past me, my dark-complexioned face not worth noticing, I suppose. His Augustinian habit was made of special, rich cloth that rustled like a feathered cape; a jeweled crucifix dangled from his neck. I noticed his smirk about the errand he had just completed. While the guards fawned on Ortiz, I slipped into the reception room unannounced.

The long hall was dim even at midday, a forbidding chamber, just the place to contemplate doom and repentance. My lord stood in shadow, his back toward me. He was contemplating a cross that hung on a wall where a window should have been. When I could bear the silence no longer, I said, "My lord, I could not wait another day. Forgive my eagerness to see you."

He turned slowly, unsurprised by my presence, and I thought he smiled, although it was hard to tell in the shadows. Two candles in red cups flickered on a table. I remembered that first night in Xico, two candles glowing red on the altar.

We did not say the things friends or lovers say after a long separation.

"It is over, finished," Cortes told me. "Friar Ortiz has told me the worst. He took a great risk for my sake."

A risk? Not likely. What was this monk up to? We sat in chairs on opposite sides of the table and again I thought of Xico. I think he did, too. What a long way we had come since then.

"Friar Ortiz told me what is planned, my future. He broke a vow to do this. He could be hanged for it."

I wondered. Countless men have been hanged, drawn and quartered for *keeping* their vows, not for breaking them.

"Ponce de Leon has letters from the king. He is to take command of the country, to bring me to trial, to confiscate my lands. And, yes, one thing more."

"What is that?"

"To execute me for high treason." My lord looked away from me. "So the conquest of Mexico ends on a gibbet—or with my neck crushed in a garrote. The friar says I will be given a choice." I stood frozen, for a moment unable to take in what I had heard.

"Any trial will show your innocence," I said, struggling to sound calm.

"The trial will be mere ceremony. The decision has already been made in Spain." His face was gaunt, not just from this news but from nights with no sleep wondering when the blow would fall. I saw in him something I had not known before—resignation, an acceptance of fate. I thought of Moctezuma and tried not to shudder.

"Seize this Ponce de Leon," I told him, giving my voice strength to counter his weakness. "Try him for forgery of royal letters and hang him ten minutes later."

"The letters are real. The king—"

"No, forgeries. Anyway, the king will change his mind. He has done so often enough before."

"Oh, my dear!" He came around the table, leaned against it, putting his hands on my shoulders. "You show courage, as I expect. But less wisdom. Friar Ortiz gave me much the same advice, but not as clever as yours—he did not think of forgeries. He says I should seize Ponce de Leon, raise an army and force the king to terms. Of course, I made no reply." Cortes sighed. "What does Ortiz want? To be archbishop of Mexico?"

I said, "He is right, my lord. Act now; strike as you once did."

In the silence I felt a storm gathering. Now, for the first time, my lord spoke to me in anger. He did not raise his voice; he did not need to. But I felt that force that had caused men to cower. "How could you hold such an opinion of me? Do you believe I would defy my king? Think of your own soul, Marina, before you urge me to treason. Ask God to forgive you."

I felt convicted—guilty and ashamed. Yet I believed him wrong and foolish. Why accept the judgment of a king deluded by liars? But his rebuke condemned me and I bowed my head. I thought of my father proudly mounting the death platform. He had known that the flowery wreath hid a strangler's cord, yet he did not denounce the injustice of Moctezuma. Like my father, Cortes could question the whole universe, but not the word of the king.

Moctezuma was God. So was Holy Carlos of Spain. I had seen countless people die for such allegiance. Mysteriously, they died at least willingly if not always happily.

Why was I different? As the question crossed my mind, I knew the answer. I had given myself to Plumed Serpent. So I was exactly like those I professed not to understand. Except I knew the truth and they, of course, were mistaken.

"Forgive me, my lord," I said. "I spoke rashly."

"Let us forget what you mentioned." But he turned away from me. "Excuse me now. Tomorrow morning I return to the city; there is an official welcome. Later I give the staff of office to the Royal Visitor."

"Will my lord need me later?" How could I put this delicately? On such matters he could not endure bluntness. "I could return to-night. Or perhaps tomorrow after the ceremonies . . ." I did not finish the question; his silence had answered me.

"Perhaps it is not as bad as Ortiz says or believes." My lord spoke almost to himself. "This trial could be a blessing, a chance to clear my name forever. Why should I doubt the king?"

It was prudent not to answer this question. "When shall I return, my lord?"

"I cannot say. I must be alone now." Even in the shadows he must have seen the desolation in my face, for he smiled and said, "Come to me when this is over. After it ends."

I almost fled from the monastery. What did he mean, *after it ends*? Was I to join him only in death?

On the shore of the lake I hesitated, striving to calm myself. I had learned much about this divine King Carlos. His mother had been an imbecile unable to count her own fingers or tie her own shoes. The king had a fat belly and a fatter behind, a slave to gluttony. He had bribed the pope to exempt him from fasting, so even on Fridays and before taking Holy Communion, he gorged himself on meat and eel pasties, slobbering his rosary between gulps and belches. While this pig swilled, Cortes had starved on the beaches and in jungles.

I knew King Carlos played at death, enacting his own obsequies, complete with mourners and chants and hundreds of wax lights. He lay stretched in a coffin, wrapped in a shroud, thus becoming the saddest but least scandalized mourner at his own funeral. Every Aztec ruler, even the blood-guzzler known as the Wrathful, had been better.

I climbed into my boat, shaking off my servant's helping arm, knowing one thing clearly: Cortes would make no move to save himself. I must act for him, act swiftly and boldly. I whispered a prayer to the goddess to lend me wisdom or at least craftiness, but I did not expect her to answer—she had been silent so long.

In the sunlight, with my boat moving smoothly toward the city, I saw matters plainly. Friar Ortiz was a conniving man bought by my lord's enemies. Why believe what he so generously revealed? Perhaps he was only inciting Cortes to rebellion; and, if so, he had already warned Ponce de Leon. In scorning such bait, my lord might be right for mistaken reasons.

My mind turned to Ponce de Leon. I had learned little about him, only things the world knew. His father had sailed with Columbus, later conquered Puerto Rico, then died in some savage northern land searching for a magic fountain of youth. Another Spaniard enraptured by romances.

Ponce de Leon was a lawyer, in itself enough to arouse mistrust.

Before the boat touched shore at Coyoacan I knew what I must do.

Two Vulture Wolf's Paw squatted on the muddy floor of his hovel and glared at me with his remaining eye. The other had been gouged out since last I had seen him, probably in the futile defense of Moctezuma's palace.

In the shack copal smoke almost stifled me, and there was no light except where a thin Lady Moon touched a yawning hole in the roof. In darkness the wizard's single eye gleamed like an owl's as he studied me—with hatred. I had done much to bring him to this poverty. But he had to pretend graciousness to any client who would pay for his skills. He lived in hiding from the Christian priests, furtive as a lizard in a rock pile.

His wife, a slattern with hunger written on her face, would have turned me away at the door except for the rattle of coins. Now she lurked behind a torn curtain, listening. I could dimly see her bare, bunioned feet below the cloth.

Outside the city was going mad with celebration, hailing the return of Cortes, although a few Spaniards claimed some of the yells greeted the Royal Visitor, Ponce de Leon.

Lord Wolf's Paw and I ignored the tumult, although I was grateful that the confusion would make my visit unnoticed. I did not like to rely only on my disguise, a mask with a crane's beak such as Spaniards wear to fend off plague.

The wizard pressed bony fingers against his temples. A whisper came from behind the curtain, "How much can she pay?"

He said, "Let me understand. You wish me to invoke a curse upon this Ponce de Leon. A spell that is swift and deadly."

"Yes, swift. I will not pay to watch him wither from age." The Royal Visitor had already announced that the trial of Cortes would begin in five days.

"You wish a particular demon invoked? I know many. The fiend Rotten Bone, Devil Lord Carrion—"

"Lord Carrion costs more," said the whisperer urgently.

"I want a certain demon, but I do not know his name," I answered. "He was aboard the ship that brought Ponce de Leon. He has already attacked several other passengers. Why not Ponce de Leon?"

"A Spanish demon?" Wolf's Paw shuddered. "That is hard and dangerous. You must pay extra."

"Double!" came the whisper.

"I will pay double."

He concealed his joy. "Wise of you. Better to invoke a demon already known to be stalking the neighborhood. Otherwise people might imagine crude things, like poisons."

His bluntness disappointed me; I had supposed him too wily ever to mention that word. We were to speak only on a high plane of spiritual afflictions.

"This is how the devil behaves," I said. "The victim complains of fever and headache . . ." I went on to detail every effect of the plague that came aboard the ship bearing Ponce de Leon, a sickness called cholera. I wondered what concoction Wolf's Paw would brew to duplicate the symptoms.

"I recognize this devil." His eye closed; its glow seemed snuffed. Did the eye gleam naturally or was there a potion for this, too? "Tell me about this Spaniard so I may use the right chants."

"He takes chocolate for breakfast, not made by his cook but delivered from a market stall. While he dresses and privately perfumes himself—he abhors bathing—the chocolate cools in a cup on the terrace. Each night before sleep he enjoys sherry from a decanter that stands all day on a table beside his bed."

The eye blinked like a firefly. "Beside his bed? My lady knows this Spaniard well."

I did not bother to rebuke his insolence; it was cheap revenge for his sufferings. Neither did I mention the spies who served me.

Wolf's Paw nodded, made a sign with his warped fingers. The interview was over.

"The money," said the whisperer. "Get the money!"

Some gold changed hands. Lord Wolf's Paw said, "May I offer you refreshment? A cup of whatever my poor house affords?"

I thought: nightshade, perhaps? Rat's bane? No, old friend, you are too late. You should have done that to me long ago.

Our boat moved forward, jarring me from my reverie. Juanito said, "I beg pardon, señora. I did not understand—my bad Spanish, I think."

"Understand? What?" I was unaware I had spoken aloud.

"You said Ponce de Leon. You said it twice."

So I now mumble my thoughts. I must buy myself a muzzle.

"Who is he?" Juanito persisted. "Another saint?"

"Well, he was a little like a saint. Very wise and righteous. He came to judge a trial to disprove lies about a man named Cortes."

"How did the trial come out?"

"It was never held. Ponce de Leon died suddenly of cholera. Cortes always mourned the loss of a chance to defend himself. Because there was no trial, some wicked people doubted Cortes."

"What a shame."

"Yes, unfortunate. But we cannot question God's decisions." That was what I said to Cortes at the time. In my opinion it is safer to be doubted than risk hanging.

And who knows? Maybe it really was cholera. I have sometimes wondered if my money was wasted, if he would have died anyway.

I visited half a dozen more places, becoming bitter against the world for changing, angry with myself for trying to recapture old sorrows, as though I could somehow defeat them in a second engagement. The disappointment of visiting scenes of the past was not that they evoked tragedy but that they evoked nothing.

"To the convent landing," I ordered the boatman.

"Are you angry?" Juanito asked, his face apprehensive.

"No, boy, of course not."

Soon I would leave this city, I decided. For Tepi I could gain nothing by staying, so why did I wish to remain close to his prison? Most of his life, ever since our early separation, I had heard about him only from infrequent visitors, reports so delayed that time had tempered them. Now it would still be best to hear what happened long after the worst was over. Bad news is one of the few things that softens with age.

Besides, I was needed at home. New grindstones were to be installed in my sugar mill, a factory built from a model of the first one my lord the Captain designed long ago. If the stones were not ready by harvesttime, a hundred families would face bad times. Also, we had six new looms, Spanish style but my own carpenters made them, marvels for weaving damask when we have solved a few problems. When I remember women in my childhood I usually picture them harnessed to a backstrap loom. What a cost of aching bones and strained eyesight. But now . . . machinery is a glorious thing.

One year a young Franciscan lived at my hacienda, a scholar. At supper he told of pagan gods, Greek and Roman, for he loved them less than the saints but liked them much better. One night he talked of Prometheus, who stole fire from the smithy of heaven to give to earth.

"It does not mean fire alone, but all the arts that use fire as well," he explained eagerly. "He taught men to tame horses, build chariots. Even to plant crops." He sighed, and there was love in his tone. "Ah, Prometheus!"

I glanced at flaming candles in iron holders, the damask table-cloth, wine in glass goblets. Outside in the stable where the wheeled wagons were kept, a horse neighed. Beyond the stable lime trees stretched near fields of sugarcane, and two windmills pumped water day and night. I smiled at the priest, remembering my lord the Captain, and said, "Ah, Prometheus."

Beside me Juanito exclaimed, "Look, señora. How beautiful."

A market barge was passing, loaded with delicacies for the festival—cakes, fruits and candies. I hailed it and bought a generous selection to take back to the nuns—a farewell gift. Suddenly I felt cheerful.

I gave Juanito two oranges, and he tried to eat the first one like an apple, peel and all, so I showed him how. "I saw this fruit once before," he said. "When I was a little boy on the ship. The captain had some."

"I was much older than you when I saw my first one," I told him. "They are becoming common here now. Last year, just before the summer rains, I planted an orange grove near my house. Fifteen little seedling trees."

"Is their fruit as sweet as this?" He sucked loudly.

"Clearly you are a sailor, not a farmer. My trees will not bear fruit worth eating for six years. They grow as slowly as boys do."

Six years. I think I will never taste those oranges. My astrologer gives me only three more summers, although he hedges with talk about a comet. Yet while I have been away I have worried about drought or that someone might leave a gate ajar and goats would eat the seedlings, depriving me of admiring those fine, fat oranges—that I probably shall not live to see anyway. Last year I also set three little olive trees, also brought from Spain. I am warned they may not survive in a warm, wet climate—no one has tried before—and in any case they will not bear for twenty years or more. Still, I imagine tasting the cured fruit. Feckless optimism.

But perhaps planting the oranges I will not taste, the olives I will not nibble, are two of the important things I have done during my time in the Only World. Most of my life has been spent not as servant of Plumed Serpent or lover of Cortes, not on a glorious road of adventure, but in running a farm where subduing the jungle is harder than defeating nations. Perhaps, in the long run, that is the important and lasting work I did.

Juanito, perhaps trying to repay the gift of the oranges, decided to entertain me by reciting his newly learned catechism. Mother Superior has been teaching him; his voice begins to sound like hers and both sound like parrots.

After rattling off words awhile, he came to, "What must I do to be saved? First, I must hope to be saved. We are saved in hope." He hesitated, looking perplexed. "What does that mean? Wouldn't anybody hope?"

"You need not know the meaning; in fact, it is better not to. Just know the words and ask no questions," I said, which was probably the best advice on any subject he ever had.

But he made me think. Is hope a savior? It seemed more like a jailer. Certainly I was a prisoner of my own hope for Tepi. Hope kept me here in the city. Probably, despite my new resolution, hope would hold me captive again tomorrow morning and I will not break its shackles and leave.

Our boat bumped the lower step of the landing. As Juanito helped me out, I glanced up at an imposing house, almost a palace, that faced the quay. Above the entrance was a Spanish coat of arms carved in stone, as always an eagle to squawk of high rank, a helmet to brag that a number of Moors had been slain. Below were other squiggles of heraldry, among them two joined peaks that I supposed represented the distant volcanoes. A conqueror of Mexico? What old acquaintance had built this? Then I remembered and chuckled.

Before dying of cholera, which evil tongues called poison, Ponce de Leon dictated a will giving his legal authority to an aged attorney, Marcos de Aguilar, a blunder that should have proved his brains were fried with plague.

Don Marcos was a relic, not only decrepit but so ravaged by syphilis that even the Hospital of the Love of God would have rejected him. The demon was devouring him alive. When the Royal Visitor's will was read, consternation erupted. A walking corpse had been named ruler of New Spain!

The corpse refused to take full command without a letter from the king. Neither would Cortes, wary of royal displeasure, take charge except to proclaim some laws for protection of the people, who were now called Indians and being exterminated or enslaved—yes, the new world we had all bled for had come to this so quickly! It was as though we had been conquered by Aztecs all over again, but these Aztecs had white skins.

When the new decrees against slavery were challenged, my lord withdrew to private life, resigned all offices and wrote his beautiful Fifth Letter to the king. He read it to me, the words so simple yet so noble that El Cid himself might have spoken them.

Don Marcos de Aguilar, now high lord of New Spain, had a peculiarity. Because disease had eaten away his innards, he renounced all food except human milk, which he sucked from the breasts of women. He kept three wet-nurses, one Spanish and two Aztecs, as a self-replenishing larder. All three were ripe and swollen. Everyone felt disgust, but there was no hushing up the matter, for Don Marcos, in a manner of speaking, frequently dined in public.

The common people Don Marcos so despised took a more tolerant view, saying that everyone starts life on the same staple.

Meanwhile, pacing in the garden of my house in Coyoacan, I decided that this state of affairs could not continue, that someone must act to save the country, and it would not be my lord the Captain.

Don Marcos's diet made the service of Wolf's Paw useless, so I considered the chances of an accident. Don Marcos, in lawyerly fashion, had taken charge of the public treasury, so now he was building himself an expensive new residence. Perhaps Wolf's Paw would arrange a curse to cause bricks or beams to fall at an opportune moment. I needed to inspect the scene.

I waited until the Feast of the Holy Cross, a day when no masons or stonecutters work except to build altars at construction sites and then have a party. I would call at the new house to present a wreath for the holiday altar, a gracious gesture. I would wear my best jewels, since no arrival is untimely if you look rich enough.

That afternoon as I stepped out of my boat at the new quay, I heard a shrill, querulous voice cry, "Careful, you fiends! Oh, I'll tear your eyes out, I swear it."

At the top of the steps there was no festival, no altar. A score of men were toiling on the walls of a half-built house, and since the foreman carried a leather whip, I knew the laborers were slaves. I saw fresh weals on the back of an old man working as a stonecarver. No wonder Don Marcos had just vetoed my lord's decree against slavery. He had labor costs to worry about.

A big canopied bed, so dripping with tassels and fringe it could have been a Floating Gardens pleasure boat, stood in an open space. Sitting in it, propped on lacy pillows, was Don Marcos.

"Every brick is counted! Remember that, thieves!"

A woman of mixed blood stood nearby, her bulging breasts like calabashes. So he had brought lunch with him.

Don Carlos squinted at me with hooded eyes. "Who the devil are you? Why do you bring flowers? I'm not dead yet, whatever people may wish."

I introduced myself. "The roses are a blessing for your new house. May you dwell here in health."

"I know you. You're Cortes's Indian whore. Is there a way to poison flowers? If so, he'll know it."

I looked into his ravaged face, and a death's-head leered back at me. I felt the chill of the Narrow Passage. No need for curses or poisons or accidents. The Dark Lords had seized him; he was in their claws and already as good as gone.

"What are you staring at?" His rouged cheeks trembled. "You've come to put the evil eye on me."

"No, my lord," I replied softly. "It is too late for that."

As I turned away, he shouted at the foreman, "Whip this whore off my property."

But the man, who of course recognized me, pretended not to hear. I paused beside the old stonecarver with the marked back.

"What beautiful work, grandfather," I said. He was engraving a coat of arms. We spoke in the old tongue.

"Thank you, lady. I have carved the Spanish eagle so it looks like our old god Lord Vulture. The Spaniard wants these pointed shapes to show the volcanoes. But I have fashioned a lovely mouth mask of the Rain Bringer. He will not know the difference."

The Rain Bringer? I thought the two peaks looked more like two fat breasts, flowing mountains that kept their lord alive today but not for much longer.

I chuckled, and the old carver, thinking I laughed at his Rain Bringer trick, joined me. "Everywhere artists are making such jokes. The eye of the Flower Prince is in the faces of cherubs, the Holy Cross becomes the Blessed Cardinal Points."

Behind us Don Marcos harangued his slaves in a voice that rattled from the tomb. "Faster! The roof must be done before the summer rains! Faster!" He choked, then summoned failing strength. "I will move in soon. I shall be living here next fall."

Hope dies last.

14

The Rim of the World—
August, 1519

We were by no means the first to cross the rugged shoulder of Mountain of the Tower, that peak both Aztecs and Spaniards call the Coffer because of its shape. Fleeing slaves and other fugitives have tried this route for centuries because the trail is so hazardous that no one bothers to pursue. The mountain gives its own punishment.

We paraded from Xico, drums beating, horses prancing and our banners snapping in the breeze. Some of the natives cheered; others simply shook their heads as they watched us march toward the wilderness at the rim of the world. Thunderheads lurked above Mountain of the Star.

"We take the harder route, but one free of enemies," Cortes said, lightly touching my hair. He smiled, remembering last night, I thought, and I tried to say with my eyes things I could not yet put into Spanish words—no, not ever into any words. Someone approached; he dropped his hand and looked military. Like most Spaniards, he was strangely embarrassed at showing tenderness in public and quite proud of showing hostility.

The Totonacs, who knew a little of what lay ahead, had bought or stolen every blanket in Xico. The trail, they said, lay just below impassable snowcaps, skirting their white edge. Gradually, as we climbed, the scrawny trees became even sparser, and at last we left them behind altogether. Spiked grass clung to crevices, but nothing else lived, not even ants, except for two buzzards circling the somber sky, patiently watching our advance, an omen so obvious it took no seer to recognize the birds as familiars of Lord Two Vulture Wolf's Paw.

We reached an ancient lava bed, a waste studded with cinders frozen into stone. There rain struck, icy needles stinging my face like nopal spines. The Totonacs, never having felt true cold in their lives, began to groan. Then hundreds of them wailed in unison, making the Spaniards glower and quietly curse their new allies as weaklings, not realizing that people of the hot lands express all feelings aloud, as naturally as crows.

My teeth were chattering when a young soldier approached and put a heavy cape around my shoulders. "Cortes said you are his voice, and his voice must not grow hoarse with cold. He has assigned me to take care of you."

I could hardly see the youth because of the blinding rain and the cowl he wore above his armor, but I knew his voice. He was the one with strange red-yellow hair and green eyes like a cat's. He played the lute and often sang in a sweet, sorrowful tenor.

"Thank you." He took my arm to help me over rough places, which slowed down both of us. But he was proud of his duty, probably the first responsibility he had ever been given. Later on, as the rain whipped us and the wind howled, I found his touch comforting. When it seemed the gale might sweep us down the slope, we halted and clung together.

Cortes moved along the line, cajoling and urging stragglers ahead. It was risky to lag; jaguars live in caves near the peaks.

That night we did not try to set up shelters but shivered under the flat cloth of the tents. My lord held me close to him, slept briefly, then left to see to the welfare of others. The next day the rain turned to sleet and pelting hail. My escort, the same youth as yesterday, finally had courage to introduce himself. He was Jaime Garay, and he explained he was a Basque, which was very different, and much better, than being a Spaniard.

"This cold is nothing. My country is far worse." He was proud of the wretched climate of his native land. "At least there can be no ambush here. Who would suspect we would cross this way?"

I knew the answer: Moctezuma. Twice today I had noticed fine, broken threads on the path, curse-threads wizards stretch to bar the way of enemies. Breaking them might bring landslides or falling timber. The owl men, I thought, had been here ahead of us. I was relieved that horses led our column so they broke the threads. It would be hard to devise curses against horses, since they were unknown creatures.

Jaime Garay, after maintaining silent fortitude for hours, spoke almost in despair. "It will be warm when we reach Culhua."

"Culhua?" Then I remembered he meant Tenochtitlan.

"In Culhua a dozen different fruits grow on the same tree. You can pick opals and emeralds from the bushes."

Where had he heard these old tales of the Gardens of Tula? I said gently, "The land is quite rich, that is true."

"Rich and warm! The lilies have blossoms of pure gold."

He looked so chilled, so hungry, that I said nothing.

The mountain turned his evil face to us, sending avalanches of ice and boulders. Here and there in this hateful land we saw clusters of huts, villages too poor to give us even scraps of food. I wondered why anyone would remain here to endure such a life when Jaime said, "My own village is larger but not much better than these. We have our Holy Church, but not much else."

"You left because it was so cold, so hard?"

"No. I would have stayed and been a woodcutter like my father. But I have five sisters. They must have dowries or no decent man will marry them."

With some trouble he made all this clear to me, that fathers in his country bought husbands for their daughters, the opposite of what I had always known.

"In Culhua I will pick an opal or even an emerald for each of my sisters." This hope gave him strength to walk faster and I had a hard time breathing, for the mountain draws the goodness from the air. "Culhua," he said, panting. "It cannot be far."

I was beginning to understand about the desire for gold. Most of these Spaniards had known nothing but poverty. They simply hoped to live as well as most Aztecs did.

Again when darkness fell we made no attempt to make a real camp—there was hardly enough earth to hold tent pegs. Neither was there anything to burn except the little fuel we carried to cook food. We used that; there was no food anyhow.

The next morning we reached a narrow defile between the two great mountains, ground that might have belonged to either mountain god, so neither the Totonacs nor I knew which to pray to. We invoked both.

Pedro Alvarado exclaimed, "In God's name, this is the coldest pass in the world." So it was instantly named Gate of the Name of God. Sheer cliffs loomed on both sides, and had Moctezuma chosen, he could have buried us under an avalanche of rocks. But I understood why he did not halt us in that manner a moment later, when I saw another broken thread. His first line of resistance was magical.

Beyond the pass lay a desert even more hostile than the one we had already crossed. The horses and cannon became mired in bogs of saltwater and were hardly rescued before they stumbled in a vast field of ashes that became grit in my eyes and under my clothes. I chewed and spat the dust of cinders. This was ground sacred to the Old Fire God whose holy image the Spaniards had destroyed in Zempoala. Now he took revenge, raising choking clouds, concealing pits and precipices.

Cortes appeared beside me, and to my astonishment, he was chuckling. "Your lovely hair has turned gray, my dear," he said. "Yet you are beautiful even in old age."

His tongue was dry from ashes and I had a hard time understanding the words, but I knew the meaning of the smile, the reassuring touch. During those hours, when we were freezing and tried to pretend death was not near, Cortes laughed at hardship and made others laugh. The soldiers drew strength from him; the Totonacs felt the power in his voice.

He kept saying, "Only a little farther. Just over the next rise!" He repeated it so many times that the words could have become a joke; instead we believed him, thought he was stronger than the Fire God. Totonac men about to die of cold and exhaustion felt until the end that their lives, held in Plumed Serpent's hands, were eternal.

That night, when many of the ill-clad Totonacs fell asleep never to awaken, only my faith in Cortes, my being able to cling to him, saved me. The wind shrieked; nearby I heard the roar of snowslides plunging down the mountain; I wondered when we, too, would be swept away.

The next day the trail narrowed, became only a wrinkle on the cliff, and with no warning Cortes's horse stumbled. Jaime Garay and Aguilar both leapt forward and steadied Mule Driver, holding her against the rock wall, risking their lives without a thought.

Afterward, when I tried to thank them, Aguilar turned away,

sounding almost angry. "It was nothing! Only my duty." Yet I thought his brusqueness concealed pride; I thought he wanted to say, "You saw what I did for him, and I would do even more!"

Jaime Garay shrugged and murmured, "Well, if Cortes dies, we all die." A moment later he said, "I hope Mule Driver doesn't go lame. Cortes must not walk."

"Easier than riding on these paths."

"Walking is undignified, common." When we huddled behind some rocks to escape the wind a moment, he tried to explain that a certain class of men walked and were forbidden to ride animals; others, a little above them, rode animals called mules. Noblemen rode horses and did not walk. At least that was the foolishness he seemed to be telling me. I supposed it was magical; it had to do with power over other creatures.

"If the horse goes lame, Cortes could take one from a lesser man," I said.

Jaime looked shocked. "Steal a horse? Oh, no! Impossible even for the commander. You don't understand."

No, and I never would. We faced the wind and the mountain god again. "You call the horse Mule Driver." I almost shouted to be heard above the gale. "Cortes says Babieca."

"A joke about El Cid's horse." A moment later when the wind paused, Jaime said, "Babieca is an unlucky name. El Cid was treated badly by his king. Cortes will be treated the same. We Basques know the signs of things to come; we have second sight."

When he said "king," I supposed he meant Moctezuma. I did not realize that Jaime Garay had another monarch in mind.

Gradually the mountain became less cruel, the spirits of the air less angry. We approached a few stunted pine trees, then suddenly a warm breeze from the west cleared the sky. We had escaped the mountain —most of us. The Totonacs fell on their knees to thank the unknown gods of the land we had entered, and Father Olmedo ran to fetch a cross to place before them while they were in a kneeling position.

Before sunset we approached a few fruit trees and corn patches, and now there were huts scattered along the trail. The Totonacs said we were near Xocotlan, Town of Orchards, and soon we glimpsed its polished buildings far below, at the foot of a dizzying cliff, in greener, richer land.

I knew a little about Xocotlan, which is a holy spot. Pilgrims from all over the world came here to venerate its great skull rack, said to be the finest in the world, and to be inspired by the shrine's remarkable collection of human thigh bones.

Oh, it was good to be off the mountain and back in civilization.

We did not enter Xocotlan that day. We looked too exhausted, too bedraggled and footsore to make an impression. After pitching camp at a prudent distance, we picked fruit for supper and gathered pale lavender flowers that the Totonacs wove into garlands.

Cortes sent messengers to herald our arrival and explain our friendly intentions to the king, a ruler always male but always called Orchard Mother. Meanwhile Xocotlans in watchtowers surveyed a Totonac army and a band of hairy goblins, some four-footed and others metal-skinned, poised on their doorstep.

The Totonacs were worried because the City of Orchards had been an Aztec vassal for a sheaf of years, and they suspected that custom had made the yoke seem lighter.

Lord Dolphin Crest, the chief Totonac interpreter and a military leader as well, said, "After a generation the people become used to the Aztecs seizing their children, taking half their food. They begin to see the tax collectors as hurricanes or droughts—terrible, but part of nature."

I doubted this. I remembered the anger of Jaliscans, the resentments of farmers in the Lair of the Serpent, the rebellious boasting of traders and pilgrims. Their hate was endless; the world longed for destruction of the Aztecs.

At sunset a swift-messenger with a royal seal on his headband was seen entering the city, coming from the direction of Tenochtitlan, doubtless bringing orders from Moctezuma.

While the Totonacs fretted and performed rites, the Spaniards built campfires even though the night was mild, then lounged around them, joking, relaxing after the hard journey. Now that the numbing chill of the mountain had faded, my own spirits rose. When I joined the soldiers, they greeted me politely, even warmly, and seemed not at all surprised that I should be with them; the hardships of the trail had made me a comrade. When Cortes took my hand and held it, no one gave so much as a glance.

The next morning the army marched in close order, firearms

loaded, bolts nocked in crossbows. As usual, Cortes led the column, looking grave and godlike on Mule Driver. I walked beside him, just a few steps ahead of Aguilar, Father Olmedo and the chaplain, all three of them bearing crosses. Next came a group of horsemen, chosen because they had the most spirited mounts; then drummers and trumpeters, all heavily armed and armored. So we advanced with rattles, blasts and neighing, an astonishing entrance. Behind us marched foot soldiers guarding the cannons, then more cavalry. The Totonacs, singing hymns to Plumed Serpent, brought up the rear.

Arriving at the broad avenue leading to the plaza and temples, I felt again a tingle of power and pride. But as I studied the scene without appearing to look, my excitement changed to wariness.

Every inhabitant, all twenty-five thousand of them, had turned out, crowding the right-hand side of the main street and lining the flat roofs of the houses. But while the right side was packed, the left remained deserted except for a few tethered Xolo dogs who barked at us from doorways, then retreated when they caught sight and scent of our big lurchers. For the Xolos, it was like men meeting giants.

The faces of the people were solemn, even hostile, although they had dressed themselves in festival costumes, men in orange and green cloaks, dyed loincloths and tassled sandals. The women wore embroidered skirts and capes. Here and there I saw painted palm leaf fans and whisks, but no weapons were visible; spears must have been leaning just inside doors. It struck me as strange and ominous that the crowd, bright as a rainbow against the whitewashed walls, remained utterly silent.

Halfway to the plaza I heard a few cautious cheers from lovers of Plumed Serpent, then the halfhearted shouts of a claque hired the previous night by the Totonacs. More important, I saw people quietly making the sign of Plumed Serpent with curled fingers. Mostly they were women and they did it furtively.

Leaning down, Cortes spoke to me. "So it is a welcome after all. Silent, but still a welcome."

"Half a welcome, my lord. Only half."

He looked again, then nodded, although he did not fully understand the meaning of the deserted left side of the street, the side sacred to the Aztec Hummingbird. I doubt he noticed that the flowers of greeting a few people waved were stale and wilted, showing that our welcome might wither quickly.

King Orchard Mother had chosen to keep Xocotlan neutral for the moment. We were to be hailed on one hand, ignored on the other. It was like the ancient custom of carrying a lighted torch in broad daylight to show that for you it is still night, you choose to be blind to what takes place before your eyes. Such are the delicate signals of diplomacy.

We formed up in the main plaza, Spaniards in front, Totonacs behind. We waited while the sun rose higher, began to grow warm. Orchard Mother was delaying his entrance to show unconcern and superiority. I could picture him groveling before Moctezuma and whining, "Revered Speaker, I kept those demons baking in the sun for two hours. They were dry as adobe."

Finally Cortes grew annoyed. The Temple of Smoking Mirror had four tiers, each with a platform thirteen steps above the one below it. Worshipers were expected to kneel on the landings to purify themselves before they reached the holy-of-holies at the top. Cortes, uttering an angry exclamation, suddenly spurred Mule Driver up the steps to the first landing, where the horse reared, then turned as though to defy the crowd. Three other horsemen, taking their cue, followed, and iron-shod hooves flashed fire on the stairs. Aguilar and the priests ran to join them and so did I.

Cortes hesitated, looked around as though seeking the king, then charged up the next flight, where we again followed. By now the whole army was gathered at the temple base.

The swarm of Xocotlans began to buzz, their anger mixed with fear. In a few minutes Cortes would mount to the sanctuary of Smoking Mirror, and certainly the Xocotlans had heard about what had happened to stone gods in other cities.

A priest poked his raven's head through the curtains of the high sanctuary and shouted, "Beg the king to hurry! These fiends will desecrate the shrine!"

Others took up the shout, warriors moving closer to the doorways, to their weapons. I suddenly felt the presence of shed blood so powerfully that I took it for an omen; then I recognized the smell and saw that real blood was trickling down a sluice cut into the temple balustrade. The Spaniards had not yet noticed this.

A commotion arose on one side of the plaza—the right side, naturally, not the Hummingbird side—and heralds rushed to proclaim the king's imminent arrival. Cortes's ploy had worked; the delaying monarch had been flushed from hiding. When the crowd parted to let the royal palanquin pass, we stood astonished. The platform, borne by a dozen porters, had no side curtains, and sitting cross-legged was the Fat Chief of Zempoala who seemed magically to have reached Xocot-lan ahead of us and now, decked in an elaborate new cape and head-dress, moved toward us.

Pedro Alvarado exclaimed, "By Satan's ass, it's Fatty himself! How did he get here? What trick is this?"

Then, when the palanquin came closer, I realized that this was not the Fat Chief after all but a king younger but even more obese than the Totonac ruler, a blubbery mound of flesh so rotund I doubt he could have risen without a crew to hoist him up. He resembled a huge Olmec god carved from a single boulder, one that could roll downhill like a ball.

"King Olintetl the Fierce approaches!" intoned a herald. He did not say Orchard Mother, so doubtless there was a snub involved.

"Olintetl approaches!" But instead of approaching, the king ordered the bearers to halt a bow shot from the temple steps, where he waited, glaring up at Cortes, as solid as a mountain. His attendant priests shook rattles and blew bone whistles.

When Cortes spurred Mule Driver down the steps, I caught my breath and so did Aguilar. If Mule Driver balked or stumbled now, Cortes would suffer a terrible loss of face.

But Mule Driver managed as though trained to the steps of temples, and the other horses followed without much hesitation. I hurried after them and found a position on the stone balustrade where I could stand with my head a little lower than Cortes's helmet but a little higher than the king; we needed every advantage. Blood flowing in the sluice almost touched the sole of my sandal.

The king began speaking loudly.

"Lord Moctezuma, the all-wise and all-powerful, has bidden me to greet you properly, strangers. I see that you and your—" He hesitated, not knowing how to refer to the horses. "Four-footed com-panions have already been drawn toward the high temple. This is just as I expected." What a smooth liar he was! "You were attracted by the blood of new sacrifices. Only this morning as you approached, we sacrificed fifty youths and maidens in your honor. Their blood is still fresh for your drinking, if you and your"—he glanced again at the horses—"friends feel thirst."

"Plumed Serpent rejects blood sacrifice!" I answered without waiting for Cortes to speak.

When Cortes understood what had happened, he kept his outward composure. His voice was soft but cold as the wind on the mountain peaks.

"Tell this monster that only savages and wild beasts drink human blood. He sickens me!"

The Spaniards looked uneasy at hearing this bluntness. I softened the words in translation and added a quotation many of the Xocotlans would know, Plumed Serpent's famed warning about the sacrilege of taking life. "For even the cricket is sacred, and the lowly ant not to be despised. How much more precious are the lives of your brothers and sisters, the children of Ometeotl!"

Orchard Mother had the grace to look reproached and instantly decided to move the Spaniards away from the temple. "Food awaits you if you will follow me. Poor fare, but the best we have." He made a gesture of gracious offering. Then his tone changed and he added, "Our women and children will go hungry that we may show you hospitality."

Again the half-welcome, the contradiction, the double mask.

We moved toward a secondary plaza, passing temples and palaces that the Spaniards thought more magnificent than I did. The architecture of Xocotlan is handsome but monotonous.

The meal, served by ugly hags and codgers, was scant and unflavored. While we ate, the king lectured about the glories of Tenochtitlan and Moctezuma, sounding like one of the public praise shouters that Tabascan suitors hire to impress the families of prospective brides.

"Tenochtitlan, the greatest city in the world, is built on deep water and can be entered only by causeways. These three causeways are broken by drawbridges, five or six for every one. All the houses —tens of thousands of them—have flat roofs so they can be turned into fortresses faster than a heron can fly over the city. Tenochtitlan is magnificent, unapproachable, invincible."

After we finished our meager dinner, the king's own feast and that of his courtiers was served—great, steaming platters of meat adorned with corn cakes dyed and shaped into blossoms. No one had the least doubt about where the meat came from—this butchering had been done at the temple. Cortes turned ashen; all the Spaniards looked ill.

To make matters worse for Cortes, many of the courtiers were couples, male lovers, a custom usual enough anywhere but especially common and encouraged in Xocotlan. Now these lovers were holding hands affectionately, proud to show off their partners to newcomers. They fondled each other, but I saw nothing unseemly.

Cortes stared at the scene for a moment, then slammed down his drinking gourd so hard he shattered it. He rose to his feet.

"Tell them that all this is abominable to God! They must leave off cannibalism and sodomy and the worship of devils."

King Orchard Mother considered the jumble of admonitions, then deliberately put his thick arm around the waist of the nearest young man.

"We will think about this. Sacrifice and the drawing of strength from the flesh of offerings is a religious question. We will consult priests. But the feelings of young men toward one another are matters of nature. If the Spaniards wish to change nature then they, not I, must perform a miracle. Personally I think this view is silly and unnatural."

I tried to translate and failed. Aguilar was no help since now all he could do was sputter and blush. But my lord understood that his demands had been rejected.

I said to Orchard Mother, "In time you will see the wisdom of what has been said. We have no quarrel."

Orchard Mother nodded graciously, but Cortes turned away, troubled. I knew his conscience, his godhood, was offended.

Before we left Xocotlan the king, impressed by Spanish prowess and the stories of the Totonacs, requested a meeting, a private conclave with only himself and Cortes with their chief lords. We gathered at sunset in a court near the royal palace, a beautiful place where carved beams of cedar lent a subtle perfume to the air. The king, as usual, arranged to be late.

When he was borne in on his litter, I noticed that with every step the bearers took, his rolls of flesh quivered and trembled. "I warn you again about approaching Tenochtitlan," he said. "Moctezuma has the greatest army in the world ready to tear you to shreds. In the city alone he has one hundred thousand men! Twice as many are stationed at frontier outposts and can reach the city fast as charging jaguars."

I was sure this was a lie. Of course the Triple Alliance could call up a huge army, but most of the time there were very few men under arms.

"Also, wealth is power, and Moctezuma has a thousand times the riches of any ruler on earth. His vaults are heaped with jade and emeralds. Gold to him is like clay to us."

As I translated, Pedro Alvarado's eyes gleamed. His head was thrust forward not to miss a word, and his ears pricked up. Cristobal de Olid and Alonzo de Avila suddenly strained like lurchers on chains. Orchard Mother had concocted just the relish to whet their appetites; at that moment not all the fires of hell could have discouraged them from leaving here and going forward. I suspected the king was like the captain of a team in the sacred ball game; he was guarding opposite courts at the same time. He wanted the Spaniards destroyed but the Aztecs bloodied. Or perhaps the other way around—who could tell?

While the king was lecturing us, I noticed a tall man enter accompanied by a secretary who carried paper, brushes and pens. They took an unobtrusive position, the secretary making notes and sketches, his master directing or prompting him. The tall man was dressed as a Xocotlan, but his bearing and his chiseled features proclaimed him an Aztec. King Orchard Mother became aware of the newcomer and grew even more lavish in his praise of Moctezuma. Cortes glanced at the stranger, looked at me, and I whispered, "Aztec."

My lord said, "We may visit your neighbors in the Republic of Tlaxcala. Tell us about them. Are you friends?"

"Friends!" Orchard Mother feigned outrage. "The stinking Paper-Wearers?"

Tlaxcalans had become known as Paper-Wearers because Moctezuma had blockaded their land, cutting off the cotton supply. They made do with clothes of bark paper and animal skins. There was a lot of smuggling, of course, and as Orchard Mother detailed Tlaxcalan poverty, the necessities they lacked, I wondered if he was himself growing rich on contraband.

"They have no quetzal plumes, no murex for dyes, no cotton. Their food is tasteless because they lack salt . . ." Then he came to more important information. "The Tlaxcalans are such cowards they do not fight in the open like men but cringe behind a high wall they have built on this side of their miserable valley. There is only one entrance, not a gate but a trap they have devised. I will show you."

Commanding a servant to bring him bark paper and a piece of

charcoal, Orchard Mother sketched a plan of the entrance through the great wall of Tlaxcala, which in truth was less an entry than a death trap.

"The defenders hide behind the second high wall," said the king. "They stand on parapets and platforms, ready with boiling pitch, with stones and arrows. An invading army is funneled in between the narrow walls, an aisle so narrow that only three or four men abreast can pass through. They are slaughtered as they run this gauntlet. Any survivors are killed in the field beyond."

"If I go that way, I will simply knock down the walls with cannon first." Cortes dismissed the problem. But I felt he was impressed by the design of the trap. I was not sure he saw something that struck me at once: it was a two-way trap; it made retreat as dangerous as advancing.

Orchard Mother assumed a mask of wisdom and conspiracy. "The roar of your fire monsters would announce your arrival. Better to try to slip in when the entrance in unguarded. The Tlaxcalans are careless and so cowardly that once you pass their walls, they will surrender with no more than a show of a fight. If their army assembles, do not worry. It will be a bluff, not a battle."

I was watching the Aztec agent, and when he heard these words, the ghost of a smile flitted over his face. So Orchard Mother was lying. What a pompous fool to flatter himself that he could trick Plumed Serpent. But even fools can be dangerous. I was happy that we would leave in the morning and soon be out of reach of his pudgy hand.

After the sullen silence of the Xocotlans and the deceit of their king, it was a joyful change to march through the towns and settlements nearer the Tlaxcalan frontier. These hill towns and riverbank villages hailed Plumed Serpent, heaping flowers on the Totonac heralds who hurried ahead telling of the liberation of Zempoala from the Aztecs.

The Only World stood poised for the return of Plumed Serpent. The clear purpose of my life shone before me.

We moved through a great corridor between the eagle crags, following a stream that would lead us to the Wall of Tlaxcala. At night we made protected camps, my lord sleeping with me in the big tent he had given me. When finally he had his private altar set up in it, I knew he considered the tent home. The night before we reached the border of the Republic of Tlaxcala we sat up late, talking by the light of a candle.

"Do you believe what the fat king said?" he asked. "Will these people, the Tal—"

"Tlaxcalans."

"Yes. If we breach the wall, will they surrender?"

I had thought carefully about this matter. "No, my lord. They are the bravest soldiers in the world. Their male babies are cradled in the hollows of shields. But I think when we reach the Tlaxcalan entrance, it will be unguarded."

"They will welcome us?"

"Only as a waiting jaguar welcomes a deer. The glory of war, the whole purpose of this endless war between Tlaxcalans and Aztecs, is not killing enemies on the field but capturing them for sacrifice."

He considered this. "Then they will be surprised by our manner of fighting." He closed and tied the flaps of the tent. I caught a glimpse of a sky of burnished silver; Lady Moon was thick and swollen. "Tell me about war, my dear. I know it is not a woman's business, but tell me what you have heard about its customs, its rules."

I began to talk at random and soon found myself astonished at how much I knew and had half-forgotten. I grew up in an army outpost. I listened to the shop talk of soldiers, of officers and royal inspectors who visited my father. Aztecs believe that women are ignorant of the strategies of battle, but that could be true only of a woman deaf and blind. War was life. We overheard talk of the hail-of-arrows opening charge as we served the appetizers, boasting of final victory as we offered chocolate at dessert. It had been much the same in the Maya country. My duty had been to please men, usually military men, and of the two things most pleasing to men, listening to them is the easier.

"You are a marvel, my dear," he said at last. "You talk like a general who has led a hundred campaigns."

"No, my lord. Like a general's daughter."

"Come to bed."

Village storytellers and market balladeers have told a thousand versions of those nights my lord and I spent together on the march to Tenochtitlan. Always we are locked together in passion hot enough to singe the listener's earlobes. Or, if there are ladies present, we tenderly hold hands or our lips brush. The touch, though sweet, of course, is described as a tide, a volcano, a surging river—it all depends on the hazards of the land where the story is told. For some reason the beauty of passion is usually put in terms of catastrophes.

A tiny truth gleams like a firefly in those tales. We knew passion, we knew tenderness; we were even playful—which no one seems to suppose at all. But instead of spending our time in rapture that shook the earth and rent the heavens, we were more likely talking tactics and politics. That was our work, our lives.

Those were the hours I cherished most, and I supposed myself peculiar. Then, years afterward, I heard an old farmer's widow lamenting at the wake held for her newly dead husband. She did not wail for the lost kisses of courtship or the embraces of the marriage bed. Instead tears ran down her leathery cheeks and she sobbed, saying, "We planted the corn together every spring for forty years. We pulled the weeds and drove away the crows. When one field turned barren, we burned it off and cleared another." It had been work and hope that united them, not passion—although they must have enjoyed that, too. So it was with me.

We talked of war, of government, of tomorrow. Less often we spoke of the past, of his life. Although I had learned most of the words I seldom understood him—Spain was too remote to comprehend. But I recognized the position of his family; impoverished gentry struggling to hold a little prestige are the same everywhere.

"We ate stew without meat three times a week, ham and eggs on Sunday. My father had to spend too much for his horse and clothes."

He was sent to a school called University of Salamanca when he was fourteen years old. "I lived with an aunt even poorer than my father—eggs on Sunday but no ham. It was miserable to be in patched trousers when your companions are all rich. I lasted two years."

After talking of his family's poverty, he would urge me to speak of my father, of high offices and lands in the south, the house in Tenochtitlan.

"A palace," he said, nodding. "Of course. How many servants?"

I exaggerated, making everything grander. He needed to have a princess, a woman of wealth and rank. It repaid his boyhood.

"I was nineteen when I sailed for the Indies. I wanted to find the magic kingdoms of Amadis. Instead I landed on a boring island called

Hispaniola." It was there he first saw slavery and decided in the long run it did not pay, although later he owned slaves in Cuba.

"Slavery here is almost never for life," I told him. "And all children are born free."

"That is right and Christian," he said. Then his thoughts returned to his eight years in Cuba. "I did well. I found a little gold, I ran a plantation, men respected me. Yet now it seems that all that time I was not really alive, not quite awake. It is hard to describe. Can you understand?"

"Yes, my lord." Who knew better than I? From the day I had been seized in Painala until the coming of the ships I had been numb, stifled by a mist. Only the coming of Plumed Serpent awakened me. Both men and women find full life only when a god touches them.

"I moved only from day to day," he said, and he drew me close to him on a pillow made of a rolled blanket. "I became secretary to the governor of Cuba. I married a woman of gentility. It was a wise move to marry above myself."

Then he chuckled. "No, let me be truthful. I had to marry Catalina because I seduced her. Do you know the word 'seduced'?"

"Yes, the soldiers use it often."

"Yes, and try it often enough, too. So I married Catalina. She is always ill and complaining."

He quickly dismissed his wife from his thoughts. One sigh and she was banished.

"Two expeditions went out by ship to find and conquer new lands, but I stayed behind. Somehow I was not ready. When those attempts failed, I was secretly pleased. My future was still waiting.

"One afternoon I fell asleep, a sleep like death. I had a dream more real than anything I have seen on earth."

My lord sat up. He stared into the shadows as though the images of the dream formed again in the darkness. When he spoke, I too lived what had come to him in the vision.

"I was dressed in rich cloth, a cloak of samite, a shirt of Damascus linen. Strangers bowed to me like servants. They spoke words of praise and honor. I saw a banquet hall set with silver and fine crystal. Liveried footmen bowed me through the doorway, and as I entered, heralds blew a fanfare of trumpets as they do for the king. But this was for me alone."

He leaned back on the pillow, smiling at the shadows. "When

I awoke, the dream stayed with me more powerfully than any memory. I told no one—I did not want to be locked up as a madman or ridiculed for having ambitions above my station. Yet I had changed; I had become another man. That dream was a glimpse of my future. I knew I would either dine with trumpets or die on the gallows trying."

So it was that Plumed Serpent took possession of Cortes and he became a god.

15

The Land of Bread

The Republic of Tlaxcala is a broad valley so fertile for corn that it is called the Land of Bread. Long before we reached the actual boundary, the famed wall, we passed mountain fields where corn grew thick as a Spaniard's whiskers.

The Council of Four that rules the country had sent out wizards to impede us or frighten us off. Their strips of paper, painted with magic grotesqueries, hung from the pine boughs or were stretched across the trail on threads.

The farmers who tilled the nearby fields and gardens had vanished, called up into the Tlaxcalan army probably, but we were none the less carefully watched. Animals of the mountains and forests peered from almost every copse. I saw two foxes gaze at me, then dart into a thicket. Deer lingered in the clearings, strangely bold, curious to watch Plumed Serpent pass, a sign that the gods of the land welcomed us; even the crows gave no challenge, which reassured the Totonacs who know much of bird gods.

We halted at a friendly town near the border, and my lord sent four Totonac ambassadors to Tlaxcala. Dolphin Crest would lead them, instructed to assure the council that we sought only friendship and peaceful passage through the republic.

"We must send a gift, something impressive," Cortes said.

At that moment one of the lieutenants, Andres Tapia, passed by, scowling as he always did. He was a powerful man, clearly favored by some demon, but he usually looked as pained as a mask of the Lord of Indigestion.

"The red hat Tapia wears is the right gift," I said, pointing. Tapia halted at the sound of his name, turned back to frown. Who was complaining about him now?

"That Flemish cap? Only that?" Cortes asked.

"It is the best thing." The fluffy cloth hat resembled crowns carved on statues of gods and was almost exactly the hat Plumed Serpent wore when he was shown as the Hunter of Wisdom.

"I'll not give my hat to heathens!" Tapia protested when he understood. "These people ahead are not worth it. My woman tells me the Aztecs only let this country live to give their troops some practice now and then."

His woman was the slut Flower Pouch, and if she made this clear she must be learning some Spanish. No wonder Tapia always scowled. The Aztec boast about tolerating Tlaxcala was laughable. Tlaxcala survived only because of its army of sixty thousand men. They were staunch patriots and allied with ignorant but brave Otomi warriors ready to sell their lives dearly defending the mountain passes. Seizing Tlaxcala was like picking up a hot coal—possible but painful.

Tapia reluctantly surrendered his fancy cap. Cortes said, "We will also send them a long letter with official seals."

"My lord, no Tlaxcalan can read Spanish. I am not sure they can read in any language."

"So much the better." Cortes smiled.

The letter and hat were given to Lord Dolphin Crest, who was donning the clothes of a diplomat—a double-knotted cloak covering his navel, a special cotton wrap and an official buckler. This uniform was recognized in all civilized countries, and he assured us that Tlaxcalans were friendly to Totonacs. I think he was less than certain; I saw him slip a tiny carved heart of jade into his plaited hair, so he would have a handy token for passage to the netherworld if the Tlaxcalans were less friendly or less civilized than he claimed.

For two days we awaited Dolphin Crest's return, Cortes chafing at the delay. At last he became certain the embassy had fared badly and ordered the troops to march.

From the east, the narrow neck of the long valley of Tlaxcala slopes upward steeply. Ramparts of cliffs tower on both sides. The land is beautiful, rich and yet forbidding; the crags seem overwhelming, a world of granite.

We reached the crest of a wooded ridge, where Cortes ordered a halt. Just a few bow shots ahead rose the famous wall, gray as the cliffs themselves. From here we could see the top—at least ten paces wide and fortified with a low parapet. The wall reached from mountain to mountain and was so high that a horseman standing in the stirrups could not reach the top.

Aguilar, standing beside me, said one word. "Formidable."

I nodded. Everyone felt the same way. But not a single guard kneeled behind the parapet, and the narrow entrance, exactly in the middle of the valley, appeared unwatched. Yet the absence of guardians at the gate seemed to make the scene more menacing because it was strange.

Bernal Diaz had moved to the front of the column to study the rampart. His face was full of wonder. "The stone almost speaks," he said.

"What does it say to you?"

"It says, Pass if you dare, stranger. Will you be able to come back out again?"

"Yes," I said. "I hear it, too."

All the army seemed to hear the same message as they gathered on the ridge, staring and whispering. A moment more and their courage might have failed them, but my lord the Captain touched his spurs to Mule Driver and the chestnut mare reared, pawing the air, neighing fiercely.

"Forward, soldiers!" he shouted, then pointed to the banner Aguilar carried. "Forward in the name of the Holy Cross! By this sign we conquer!"

Mule Driver trotted briskly down the slope and the army followed, many of the soldiers singing as we entered Tlaxcala, moving through that curving gray corridor in the wall. I thought, *This is indeed the Narrow Passage. From here, no return.*

Cortes paused in the meadows beyond the wall only until all the troops and baggage porters had cleared the entrance. Then, taking six horsemen with him, he rode ahead as vanguard, ordering me sharply not to hurry after him but to stay with the army.

"I cannot risk you," he said. "You are too valuable to me." It was a commander's remark, not a lover's.

So I moved along with the infantry at what seemed a snail's pace, guarded by the zealous Jaime Garay, who was so ebullient that I decided the silence of the countryside had actually unnerved him.

"What a stroke of luck—perhaps a miracle," he said. "We caught them off guard, came through their damned wall without drawing a blade. God is on our side!"

"Yes. Let us hope He stays there," I answered, having no illusions about the easy entrance into the republic. We had been graciously allowed to enter the hunter's net. I needed no gift of prophecy to predict what would happen next; they would try a tactic learned long ago from the Aztecs, a ruse my father had employed against the Tarascans. Our army would suddenly "surprise" a small troop, perhaps ten or fifteen warriors who would shout defiance, then flee. The pursuers, lured on, would swipe at a fly and hit a jaguar: the enemy would be massed in ambush just ahead. I knew it. The silence of the birds told me.

It happened as I expected, although I did not see the skirmish that would lead to the first of the three great battles in Tlaxcala.

Cortes and his six-man cavalry vanguard soon came upon fifteen or twenty warriors who were dressed in full battle regalia and armed to the earbones. The warriors, of course, retreated according to plan, after making the appropriate obscene gestures. Naturally the Spaniards pursued, Cortes shouting and gesturing to the Tlaxcalans to come back and talk. He wanted a parley, not a battle. But the warriors kept going and so did the Spaniards.

Up to this point it followed the classic plan. But the Tlaxcalans had not made allowance for the speed of horses; the little band of warriors, offered as a gambit, had expected to escape, not be swallowed like live bait. A horseman named Martin Lares, who could outride the devil himself, caught up with the warriors and ran two of them through with his lance. To his surprise and to the surprise of the other Spaniards who were now catching up, the warriors turned and gave battle—an event not included in the master plan.

The Spaniards did not know, of course, that the bodies of the dead are sacred in Tlaxcala. A soldier who abandons the corpse of a fallen comrade is cursed by the Lords of the Night who will torment him to his grave and doubtless long afterward. The lords are unforgiving about such sins, especially in Tlaxcala.

The Tlaxcalans, forgetting they were merely decoys, attacked so fiercely that three horses were killed and three wounded along with two of their riders. Just as the fight was turning fatal, a few more horsemen arrived. Cortes, suddenly discerning the Tlaxcalan scheme, sent Lares galloping to summon the infantry and cannons.

The call for help was in the nick of time. Suddenly several thousand Tlaxcalans burst from the concealment of a stand of pines farther up the valley and rushed to join the battle. A long and exhausting charge was the opposite of what the Tlaxcalan leaders had planned. They had expected to pounce from ambush and destroy the Spanish vanguard in two strokes of a sword. The power of Plumed Serpent had upset their timing, the battle was lost, and they retreated even before the cannon could be brought up and fired.

When the field was cleared of the living, we counted seventeen Tlaxcalan dead. I supposed that at least as many more had been carried away by their fellow soldiers. No Spaniards were killed, but four had been wounded so seriously that their slashes had to be cauterized.

The wounded, both men and horses, were still being treated when leaders of nearby villages arrived carrying the blue feathers of peace. With them were two of our four Totonac ambassadors, but not Lord Dolphin Crest.

Our envoys had no useful report. After addressing the council they had been separated from their two companions, taken to a nearby village by forest trails and closely confined. They knew nothing of Dolphin Crest's fate or of our victory.

The spokesman for the villages, a bumpkin decked out in fancy official clothes too small for him, was so unnerved by the outcome of the battle, so scared of Cortes's possible divinity, that he could do nothing but pour out pleas and abject excuses.

"The attackers were not Tlaxcalans! No, no! We are kindly, hospitable people. How we regret what has happened!"

"I'm sure you do," said Cortes, and I made sure his irony was not weakened in translation. "Unfortunate for you."

"This terrible assault was by Otomis. They are a wild and uncontrollable people. We must tolerate them as allies because the Aztecs give us no peace. So in a way this attack on you was the Aztecs' fault."

"I will mention it to Moctezuma," Cortes remarked, and the man looked even more distressed.

"We apologize for killing your wolf-deer." He meant the horses. "We will pay any damages you ask."

"Their value is nothing to us." With a wave of his hand Cortes dismissed the matter. "Many more are on the way here. A hundred will arrive before morning. I suppose they will feel vengeful about the killing of their fellows, thirsty for blood. But payment to us will not save you in that matter."

The chieftains blanched, then took leave awkwardly, stumbling over their own feet as they tried to imitate royal manners by backing away from the Presence. I would have felt more sympathetic to these warrior-farmers and might have put a little credence in the Otomi excuse if the east wind had not brought an unmistakable smell of boiling pine sap. Behind us smoke rose in the air where pitch was being heated to give us a farewell bath if we tried to retreat. The Wall of Tlaxcala had been reoccupied. The passage through it had turned into a jaguar's mouth.

The grand gesture of refusing payment for the horses was strategic, but it did not fill our bellies that night. The inhabitants of the abandoned village where we camped had, as always, carried away everything down to the last scrap. A few of their Xolo dogs wandered back home at nightfall and were promptly stewed for supper, the fate they were bred for anyway.

The next morning, just as the camp began to stir in the false dawn, Lord Dolphin Crest and his companion stumbled into our lines bedraggled and weeping. Being Totonacs, they expressed all emotion, and Dolphin Crest felt humiliation.

"We were received by the council in the community house. They showed all the courtesy a diplomat should expect—at first." Lord Dolphin Crest described how the four lords were seated on the low stools of office, the *ycpallis*, which are thrones.

"We behaved perfectly. We kept our eyes down, our bodies covered. I explained about the Spaniards and their power, about the white-skinned, blue-eyed servants of Plumed Serpent who had freed us from Moctezuma."

The lords had listened in silence, their heads bowed so their mouths touched their knees. After Dolphin Crest's speech, the council had sat quiet and unmoving, appearing to give the matter the reflection great questions deserve. Then the envoys were dismissed so the council might deliberate.

"We were separated on a pretext." Dolphin Crest's voice was unsteady. "Then I was seized and bound. The diplomatic badges were torn off me and they put me in a cage. We were to be sacrificed to Smoking Mirror today, but my friend and I managed to pry loose the bars and escape. I warn you, the Tlaxcalans will attack at any moment."

"Yes," cried the other envoy. "They are just beyond those hills. Five thousand men, six thousand—who can count them?"

The general alarm was sounded on the trumpets. Cortes mounted the stump of a lightning-struck tree and addressed the men, giving not one of those grandiloquent speeches romancers later put in his mouth but plain instructions about handling a lance.

"Do not thrust; charge and aim for their faces. Hold the weapon thus, under your arm so they can't wrest it from you. Above all, stay close together. To become separated is to die."

We moved forward then, abandoning the village; there were four hundred Spaniards, perhaps two thousand Totonacs and several hundred hill men. No, fewer Totonacs. Some stayed behind to guard baggage hidden in a pine copse. The few women still with us lingered there, too, preparing for battle in their own way: Flower Pouch was tinting her cheeks with cinnabar and showing a girl from Xico how to shade the eyelids with murex powder. Each to his own weapons, I thought, and rummaged in the supply baskets until I found a short, light cutlass one of the sailors must have left behind. I draped a scarf over it; I would have the advantage of surprise. Camouflage, the soft cotton disguising the sharp steel—exactly what Flower Pouch was doing in a different way. I did not search for a shield but carried the top of one of the rattan baskets, no use against swords or axes, yet offering protection from darts and arrows. It looked quite innocent.

I did not think of myself as preparing for battle or doing anything unusual. Plumed Serpent's cause was endangered; I was coming to defend it, not grimly but with joy. Cortes, on Mule Driver, was only a bow shot away.

The Tlaxcalan vanguard advanced from the woods ahead, perhaps a thousand men but a token of what was to come. Cortes shouted my name, and I rushed to his side.

"Send interpreters ahead quickly. Say we want no blood shed, only peaceful passage. Tell them that."

Lord Dolphin Crest understood instantly and ran boldly ahead, crying the message, his bravery kindled by Tlaxcalan mistreatment.

But before he could finish his message, almost before he could start it, a shower of arrows, darts and stones pelted us. The Tlaxcalans, yelling for our flesh and blood, shook their javelins and charged.

"*Santiago!* Have at them!" Cortes shouted, lifting his lance, and his voice echoed from the cliffs.

The horses thundered past me. Then I brushed shoulders with foot soldiers pounding behind. I had never imagined everything would happen so fast. I felt dazed, bewildered, and suddenly realized I was being left behind.

By the time I caught up, the Tlaxcalans had given ground, seemed almost to be retreating, and as I splashed through a shallow stream, I wondered if this was yesterday's ruse repeated today, a small vanguard to lure us into the maw of a monster army. It did not matter. We would sweep over them like a hurricane, we were invincible—we were gods. I heard my own voice shout, "Santiago!" I could hear the pounding of my own heart and it was like drum music.

We reached the spot where the neck of the valley curves and opens into the great plain beyond. There before us stood the Tlaxcalan host, and again I paused, this time in sheer wonder.

I have heard there were a hundred thousand warriors swarming in the fields that day. Some have said thirty thousand or fifty thousand. How do you number the drops in a cataract, the blades of grass in a meadow? I saw the famous yellow standards of the proud house of Titcala surrounded by thousands of warriors whose bodies were striped with white and yellow. Next to them the banners of the Rock Heron Clan waved and dipped in the wind. A clamor of whistles, a din of woodblocks and drums shook the valley like the roar of the Thunder Snake. Then the tide of men surged forward, beautiful and deadly.

Above it all the voice of Cortes rang out. "The more the enemy the greater the triumph! Cut them down! God and Santiago!"

Suddenly there was only silence around me—or so it seemed afterward. My ears shut out the din, or its very force had deafened me. I moved like a dancer in a pantomime, making the gestures I knew were needed yet not knowing what I did. A warrior, a Tlaxcalan lord in feathered armor of white and yellow, had somehow entered our ranks. I stared at him dumbly as he lifted his heavy sword, toothed with obsidian razors, and brought it down with both hands on the neck of a mare ridden by Pedro Moron. The horse was beheaded at a stroke. The warrior, raising a shout of victory, paid no attention to me, a woman, but lunged forward to capture the fallen rider. He could have killed Moron where he lay with one more sword stroke, but capture, not death, was his object. I made a quick thrust with the cutlass, using it like a dagger. The point pierced the quilted armor with no resistance and the blade sank deep—it was so easy. Spaniards rushing to save Moron from other Tlaxcalans pushed me aside. On my left, from the corner of my eye, I glimpsed a white and yellow figure. I whirled, slashing with the steel, and a second warrior fell. In the confusion I had lost my housewifely shield, the basket top. But I did not need it now. The goddess was beside me, deflecting arrows, turning the spears aside, making me invisible at perilous moments while she sang her death song in my ears. All that I saw and felt was intensified, made brilliant, like the time in the south when I had eaten a certain plant at a women's ceremony and the world had become as vivid as heaven. I was lifted from my body, exalted.

A Tlaxcalan knight, an eagle warrior, seized me by the hair to take me captive, but, astonished to see I was but a woman, released me with a sound of disgust and turned to find a worthier prisoner for sacrifice. I struck. It was the last mistake he ever made.

At an hour when Lord Sun stood in the west, the silence around me became real, no longer a failure of my hearing. I was among only Spaniards and Totonacs, all of us dazed. The Tlaxcalan horde had melted into the woods and hills, retreating down the ravines where we did not dare follow. Today's fight was over; we had won.

We camped at a place called Hill of the Tower, a village stocked with provisions, so the soldiers held a feast that night. Totonacs danced and improvised songs reviling the courage of the Tlaxcalans, but in truth we respected them. I understood why Moctezuma had never successfully invaded the republic. The Revered Speaker had lost his favorite son in one attempt to crush these Rock Heron people; he still could do no better than blockade them.

"How many did we kill?" Pedro Alvarado asked. "The harquebuses brought down a lot. Did the cannons bring down a thousand?"

Harquebuses and cannons? I had not even heard them firing. War was a confusing experience. In battle everyone saw and heard different things.

"They carry away the dead and the badly wounded so we can't count their losses," said Bernal Diaz, who misunderstood entirely. "It costs much. How many fell trying to haul away corpses?" He could not appreciate that a comrade's corpse was sacred here and if left behind would be eaten—not cleanly by birds, but by human enemies who would absorb the strength and valor of the dead.

Alvarado cocked his head. "Listen!" From far away came the rumble of the great temple drum. "What's going on?" His freckled hand touched the hilt of his sword.

"Not a battle; a religious rite," I said. "They are sacrificing the Totonacs they captured today."

The soldiers relaxed. Alvarado said, "They fought well, too. For heathens, they have guts."

On the far side of the camp Totonac voices now rose in lamentation, the threnody for lost warriors. Later I learned that about three hundred Totonacs had died on the field or been taken, which was the same thing. No one, not even my lord, bothered to count them.

No army appeared on the morning horizon. The Tlaxcalans, occupied with the debates that are the plague of republics, foolishly gave us time to repair our weapons, to treat our wounded and, most important, to rest. Cortes also took advantage of the respite to lead a war party against the outlying villages and farms. At the same time he sent several Totonac knights to renew efforts for peace with the enemy. Lord Dolphin Crest led them; he said his honor demanded he return to the council. My lord always sought peace while attacking. He reminded me of stone gods the Maya set on the corners of buildings: his eyes always looked in opposite directions at once.

Pedro Alvarado was left in command at the camp, and I waited with him to translate when our embassy to the Tlaxcalans returned— if they ever did.

The reply came about noon. Lord Dolphin Crest and his fellow knights arrived with a Tlaxcalan delegation who would pronounce the official message—and what a delegation it was! The three messengers were dressed in stinking rags of paper and carried a few bedraggled plumes as symbols of mock diplomacy—a crude insult. Naturally they mistook Alvarado for Cortes and were utterly astounded by his golden divinity. The leader, disguised as an old man, recovered from shock and croaked out a message.

"Come to the City of Tlaxcala! There we shall make peace by giving your blood and hearts to our gods. We hope you enjoy the feast we have planned, for you are the main course."

Having insulted both our eyes and ears, the strange delegation hobbled away, bent over so their bare bottoms pointed at us.

"What is happening in the city?" I asked Dolphin Crest.

"More troops have arrived from the western frontier. The whole army will attack tomorrow, about fifty thousand men."

When Cortes returned with provisions and several hundred captives, he confirmed this. He had heard the same report everywhere; no language had been needed to make the deadly news clear.

Father Olmedo and the chaplain, Juan Diaz, got no sleep that night. They were up until dawn hearing confessions of men who were taking no chances of dying unshriven on the plains of Tlaxcala. I do not mean they expected death even though they knew the odds. They were willing to risk their lives, unwilling to take a chance on hell.

For me the next day's battle was nothing like the first one; I was in the midst of hand-to-hand combat only briefly. Cortes said nothing about the part I played in the initial fight, but just before dawn, as I was helping him buckle his armor, he glanced at the shawl under which I had hidden the cutlass. I was afraid someone else would claim it.

"Today you will stay among the cannoneers, dear Marina. Do not leave them and charge down the hill. They can use some extra protection." He made the remark in the grave tone he used when he lightened a serious order by joking.

"I will help as I can, my lord." I looked away, not sure if I was hurt or humiliated, uncertain if he took what I had done lightly. The men I had killed did not die as a jest.

"I know you will." He gave me a quick embrace. "I only ask that all my soldiers are as brave as you."

His lips touched my hair, a gesture that meant much to me this morning. Last night he had been unusually ardent; I wondered if he tried to give me a child, if this had to do with premonitions of death, and it alarmed me.

The artillery was entrenched on the hillside, commanding the level plain below. It would fire above the heads of our army in its first charge, then strike at the Tlaxcalan flanks where it could mow down the enemy without killing our own troops.

Cortes stood before the soldiers. He bowed his head a moment, then crossed himself and said only, "Remember what Spaniards have done in our own times and in the times of our fathers. The world has not seen our like before. God and Saint James!" He swung into the saddle.

The Totonacs and hill men stood expectantly, waiting to learn the meaning of their leader's words, not suspecting that at that moment he had forgotten them. Appearing to translate, I addressed them. "Plumed Serpent reclaims the Land of Bread today. His mother, the Blessed Virgin of the Serpent Skirt, will lend you strength. God and Saint James!"

The Tlaxcalans did not move into view as one mass of warriors but appeared gradually on the field, small groups arriving from all directions, clusters and then mobs, several thousand gathering when the east was hardly more than streaked with light. New clans of the republic appeared today bristling with weapons; strange green uniforms now almost outnumbered the white and yellow of the Rock Heron clan. The red sun gleamed on obsidian blades and on arrow tips of copper the Tlaxcalans were now learning to use. Stretched across the fields, brilliant and glittering, was a gigantic and deadly rainbow that soon would become a flood.

The meager company of Spaniards and their thirteen horsemen —even wounded horses fought today—looked less like an army than a troupe of performers about to entertain a vast, gaudy audience. But the plumes and flowers of the Totonacs who enforced the Spanish flanks made a brave show.

Spanish trumpets and Tlaxcalan horns blared at the same moment, with whistles and yells of the enemy rending the air. Then the cannons roared beside me, spreading death across the valley. The first ranks of Tlaxcalans dropped as by magic, as if the Cold Lord had breathed upon them, turning their blood to pitch. When the cannons and harquebuses thundered again, hurling shot above the charging Spaniards and Totonacs, I thought the sound would burst my skull. An aging artilleryman —how did such a grandfather come from Cuba?—handed me two wads of damp cotton, gesturing for me to plug my ears. I did not do it. I would miss nothing today, not even the pain.

Watching the plain two bow shots below, I learned to my amazement that after a certain point numbers do not matter in battle. Thousands, probably tens of thousands, of the enemy were waiting on the distant edges of the horde, useless. Others tried to elbow through the crush of warriors to have a chance to kill. They fought among themselves for possible glory. Many were wounded accidentally by the weapons their companions carried; others were trampled to death when the mob grew uncontrollable.

The Tlaxcalans had learned nothing from the first battle. They still fought to capture, not to kill; they paid a terrible price for trying to rescue the dead and dying. It takes more than one disaster to change a man's religion, so they fought as before, piously and foolishly.

A small force of white-and-yellows broke through the Totonac defense at the foot of the hill and surged upward, hurling themselves upon the cannons, attacking the guns instead of the men who fed them. One warrior howled in frustration as he shattered his stone and wood sword across a cannon barrel, confounded that he could not chop the thick, headless, fire-breathing snake in two. Someone had left a loaded crossbow nearby; I snatched it up and fired the bolt into his chest. As he dropped, the old artilleryman pulled the weapon from my hands and shouted above the din, "You mustn't do such things, my lady!" as though I had been guilty of a breach of manners. Was a crossbow sacred and warped by a woman's touch? I retrieved my cutlass from its place near the cannon and stood ready. I did not have long to wait, and twice more I proved that when it is steel against wood, a woman's strength equals a warrior's.

Above the rage of battle I heard Cortes's voice, clear as a trumpet. "God wills it! In His name!" In ancient days the call of Plumed Serpent could be heard ten leagues distant when he summoned his followers, both men and animals, to the sacred hill in Tula. Hearing Cortes speak like the god, I knew victory was ours, although at that moment we seemed doomed.

For another hour the enemy encircled and outflanked us. Just as it seemed we could hold no longer, a great drum boomed a signal from the woods across the river, then shell whistles repeated the call. Half the Tlaxcalan army, all those who fought under the sign of the Rock Heron, abruptly left the field. They did not flee; they simply walked away from the battle at the moment when it seemed they must win. I shouted to the Totonacs, "Plumed Serpent struck the drum. It is a miracle!"

That was the end. The rest of the army, a force that still outnumbered us by many to one, lost heart at the defection of their comrades. At last they fled in disorder, and the horsemen might have cut down another thousand in retreat, but the horses were too exhausted to follow.

Later I learned that one of the Tlaxcalan leaders, a hot-blooded young fool, had grown peeved over some personal matter and withdrawn his men from the field, and that was the cause of the Tlaxcalan debacle.

That night my lord looked haggard and drawn even in the softness of candlelight. I saw bloodstains on his collar, his sleeve. He said, in a voice no more than a whisper, "Our Lord wished to help us." Then he kneeled in silence at his altar, remaining longer than ever before, and although his back was to me and he did not pray aloud, I felt power filling the room, radiating from him. At last he rose, turned toward me, and I saw his face. The god was with him; he looked rested, serene. As he stood in the shadows, I almost expected a radiance to appear around him, he seemed so beautiful.

That victory should have ended our troubles in the republic, but there seemed no end to Tlaxcalan stubbornness. After all, they had suffered defeats as terrible at the hands of the Aztecs, yet survived to taste victory.

They believed their wizards who advised them that Spaniards were children of Lord Sun: their power would wane as daylight did. So a night attack was planned that would have been disastrous for us if they had delayed until Lady Moon was beheaded. But her light was clear when they struck, and they were slashed down along with the dry stalks in the cornfields where they tried to hide themselves.

Cortes raided more villages, one of them a town of a thousand houses. As always, he sent the noblest prisoners to the capital with messages of peace. Spies entered our camp on what we now called Victory Hill, spies passing themselves off as traders and vendors. Since I spoke the highland language, which they did not realize, and by now had learned quite a bit of the Totonac tongue, I easily detected the Tlaxcalan agents. They were punished in the usual manner, the slashing of their hands or thumbs, and sent back to Tlaxcala in mourning.

Meanwhile an even greater danger surfaced; a faction of the army that demanded to return to Cuba. A meeting was called; I stood on the edges, for this was a Spanish matter, silently giving thanks to the Earth Mother that our Totonac allies could not understand what was said: the army was worn out, fifty Spaniards had died and been buried secretly lest the Tlaxcalans learn that Spaniards were mortal; even if the republic surrendered, which seemed unlikely, the city they marched toward, Tenochtitlan, would prove to be a death trap. Some of the Spaniards, I gathered, were becoming linguists. They knew more than I had repeated to them.

Cortes was patient. He made no mention of his divine mission, but warned them that retreat would look like weakness, the Tlaxcalans would harry them all the way to the sea; they would die in retreat. At last, losing his temper, my lord rebuked their weakness. In the voice of the god he said, "Let those who would rather die in glory than live in disgrace stand fast with me!"

That ended the argument, but I think the discontent would not have stayed suppressed if a Tlaxcalan embassy had not arrived the next morning.

This time they approached with dignity, bearing the blue feathers and white badges of peace. The mission brought five plump Chichimeca warriors, bound captives marked with the stripes of sacrifice, and other gifts of corn, cherries, bread and turkeys.

Their leader kneeled, before Cortes but did not kiss the earth. He rose and said, "If you are a fierce god, eat these Chichimeca and we will bring more as your appetite requires. If you are a gentle god, we bring you incense and plumes. If you are a man, here is the food a man requires."

I held my breath as Cortes considered an answer. At last he replied, "I and my companions are men like yourselves. That is the truth. I will speak truth to you; you must speak it to me. And in plain truth, we must not fight again. Let us be friends."

I did not know quite what to say. Not only were the Tlaxcalans listening eagerly, but our Totonac allies as well. The moment was crucial, and I decided to answer with the truth as Cortes intended rather than confuse everyone with words that could only be misunderstood. "Plumed Serpent returns in the form of a man only a little different from yourselves . . ." From then on I repeated Cortes's words exactly, but at the end I added, "We accept your gifts except for the Chichimeca sacrifices. Are your priests so ignorant they do not know Plumed Serpent loathes the shedding of blood, he gags at the taste of human flesh? You have lived next door to the Aztecs so long that you have become like them!"

The Tlaxcalans left in confusion, impressed but uncertain, and the fighting did not end. Like my lord the Captain, they talked peace while waging war.

Then, a few mornings later, a splendid procession marched up the valley—Aztecs approaching from the eastern route, the trail we had in fact secured for them. I counted two hundred soldiers and six nobles gorgeously arrayed. I had never supposed that a day would come when an Aztec army would be a welcome sight, but it was. Now the republic might see what it was up against.

The message was simple, the gifts elaborate. Moctezuma, alarmed by our success against the Tlaxcalans, was renewing his attempt to bribe us.

"He will honor the king you have mentioned," said their leader, Lord Two House Atempanecatl. His manner was generous, but somehow he kept a threatening edge in his tone. "He will send a yearly offering of gems, slaves and gold. You, in turn, will advance no closer to his capital. This is a sad condition he must make, for he longs to see you, but the populace is so fierce and unruly that the danger to you would be intolerable to him."

A fortune in gold and beautiful cotton clothing was spread upon the ground, and the gold did not glitter more than the eyes of some soldiers. Even the wrathful Tapia smiled.

"Tribute and honor for the king!" Cortes exclaimed. "Then Moctezuma has agreed to become a vassal."

I had to consult with Aguilar. The exact meaning of the words was difficult, and I suspected Moctezuma and his councillors had purposely made matters cloudy. I thought the Aztecs were offering continuing bribes and nothing more except courtesy; Aguilar insisted this was a greater surrender. Lord Two House would do nothing but confuse things further with ambiguous words. The gold, at least, was solid.

My lord the Captain behaved as graciously as the Flower Prince himself, welcoming his guests with dignity, insisting they remain a few days in our camp to rest while he considered their words. His real wish, of course, was to display them to the Tlaxcalans.

Lord Two House accepted with a courteous, self-deprecating flutter of his bejeweled hands. He was stout and stolid; he seemed unusually tall until you realized his sandals were triple-soled to give him height. I decided he was vain, and behaving so obsequiously must have pained him.

While the Aztecs were in camp, the Tlaxcalan commander, Lord Xicoten, launched a three-pronged attack on Victory Hill, hoping to destroy Spaniards and Aztecs together. It was folly; Xicoten must have felt desperate to gamble so.

Two days before my lord the Captain had been attacked by a Shivering Demon; he burned and trembled with chill at the same time. To cure this he had taken a powerful purge that would blow the monster out through his anus. He lay on his mat, sweating in the cold morning, waiting for the purge to work, when the trumpet sounded attack. He jumped up, staggered, but managed to stay on his feet. "Tell someone to saddle Mule Driver. I must lead the troops. Hurry!"

I was horrified. "My lord, you can't! You have taken—"

"I know damn well what I have taken! Tell them!"

He spent the whole day in the saddle, and struck the enemy down quick and strong as a jaguar, both warrior and leader. Not until the following morning did nature and the purge take their course and expel the demon.

I did not think this very remarkable, although I was grateful that his performance did not disappoint the watching Aztecs. Long afterward learned doctors of the Church debated whether this staying of my lord's bowels might be a miracle, sounding much like certain Maya priests who are passionately concerned with entrails. A Franciscan named Torquemada, an erudite scholar, hailed my lord's constipation as the Work of God that "the Conquest might be carried out and many souls saved." Well, maybe so. Personally I think my lord was like a ball player who races back and forth defending his court until the game is won, and only discovers afterward that he has played with a broken ankle.

At any rate, Moctezuma's envoys, gazing from the tower on Victory Hill, saw Cortes lead triumphant soldiers against the Tlaxca-lans both by day and night. Meanwhile the guardians of the republic, knowing well who observed the war, decided it was the last chance to make peace. A delegation, headed by Lord Demon Caller, arrived in rustic pomp. Wearing their best clothes and their tallest although moth-eaten plumes, they presented themselves to Cortes. In Tlaxcala even magnificence tends to be threadbare.

Certainly they looked shabby compared to the Aztecs who stood nearby, looking down their straight noses at these hostile country cousins. Lord Two House's plump face was disdainful as the Tlaxcalan party assembled in the little plaza in front of the tower on Victory Hill. Demon Caller was lean and as tall as Lord Two House pretended to be. His left cheek and neck were stamped with a cherry-colored mark some god had given him at birth. It vaguely resembled the sign of the patron of wizards, Howler Monkey; I suppose that explained Demon Caller's unusual name. Some would have said his name was perfect for his present mission.

Demon Caller had not quite finished his salutations when Lord Two House, seething and unable to wear the mask of diplomacy longer, interrupted angrily.

"What are you doing here, savage? I know what you have been up to lately! You have incited revolts in eleven places. All the way from your own miserable valley to Cholula—eleven different places. Your agents visited Tepatlaxco to cause trouble, then it was Ocotepec and Texmolocan." Two House went on naming crimes and locations until he ran out of breath.

When he paused, Demon Caller, grinning like a kinkajou, added to the list of rebellious towns. "Don't forget Callamaya, your perfumed highness. And remember the folk in Tecalco who skinned two of your tax collectors alive. I was there, too."

"What mischief are you making today? I will not stir from this spot until I hear every word you say to the fair-skinned lord."

Then the two ambassadors of peace, who had both made such dignified entrances, were spitting and snarling accusations. I have seen wildcats behave better. Finally, at a nod from Cortes, I called them to order and gave the Tlaxcalans leave to speak.

Lord Demon Caller delivered a formal speech, sometimes being prompted by a Word Rememberer who hovered behind him. "We had no part in the first attack upon you. That was the mistake of our allies, the Otomi, who are good people but impulsive."

Lord Two House snorted. "Skunk shit. That is what Otomis smell of. So do Tlaxcalans, for that matter. Why don't you leave and clear the air?"

Cortes silenced him with a glance. I had not translated the insult. I did not know the Spanish word for "skunk."

Demon Caller explained that the Council of Four had later opposed the Spaniards only because of the Aztecs. "Since they are cowardly fighters, they try to win by cunning. We heard that Aztec wizards caused the sea to cast you up and you were their creatures."

When Demon Caller finished with a ringing declaration of friendship between Spaniards and the republic, the Tlaxcalans threw themselves on the ground, palms down in the dirt. I pitied their wives trying to scrub those ceremonial clothes clean.

I read joy in my lord's face, joy and triumph and relief, but his scowl was so black that nobody else would have suspected the truth.

"When I offered my friendship before, you spurned me. I am angry. If you are sincere, let your people send me another embassy, lords of greater importance. Perhaps I will take that as an earnest sign of your goodwill. For now, go away and think over your past mistakes."

As the dejected Tlaxcalans departed, Lord Two House first looked pleased, then puzzled. Was Cortes really so powerful that he could toss the bouquet of friendship back into the faces of the Tlaxcalans? That, of course, was precisely the effect my lord the Captain intended. I bowed gravely to Lord Two House while inside I shook with laughter.

The Council of Four wasted no time in placating Cortes. I thought they would wait a few days; pride required it. But the next afternoon their delegation appeared. Since they arrived in the Fifth Watch of the day, they must have left the capital at dawn. Xicoten the Young, the general who had caused us so much trouble and the fifth most important personage in the republic, led them, and this time their dress would have passed muster in Tenochtitlan itself. It should have; most of their wardrobe had been stolen from Aztecs.

Not that Tlaxcalans were born thieves—they were honest by nature. But Moctezuma's blockade deprived them of cotton—as well as chocolate, rubber and all other exports of the hot lands—so they wore stiff cloaks made of cured maguay pulp and uncomfortable paper loincloths.

All fifty of the Tlaxcalan senate appeared, and Xicoten made a fine impression. He was broad-shouldered, tall as a Spaniard, and his face was interestingly dotted with pockmarks of some disease demon, spots so regular they might have been placed there as beauty marks by a Tarascan skin artist. The young general's bearing was so dignified that Lord Two House thought it more prudent to withdraw to the tower where he could eavesdrop.

Xicoten made no foolish excuses. "We thought you allies of Moctezuma so we attacked you with all our power. You defeated us by courage and because you are blessed by the gods or, indeed, are gods yourselves. We ask you to come now to our city, to live among us, to share what we have."

I was convinced of the young general's sincerity, but Cortes said coolly that he would ponder the invitation.

Xicoten was not a bow shot from camp when Lord Two House left the tower and approached Cortes, laughing loudly. "What frauds! Who could believe such blatant deceit?"

"He seemed straightforward to me," I said. Two House looked annoyed that I presumed to speak to him on my own.

"The greater the lie, the more innocent the mask," he quoted solemnly, and at the same moment his own mask was changing from confidence to irritation. "I have sent a messenger to Tenochtitlan. Ask your master to wait until word comes back from the Revered Speaker."

Cortes listened and nodded. For an instant our eyes met in understanding, and I knew he was quietly raising the price of his friendship, whether with Aztecs or Tlaxcalans or both.

My lord kept his word and waited. Meanwhile the Tlaxcalans courted him daily, lords appearing with gifts, always modest produce of the country, a turkey or a basket of avocados. These were the most precious things the beleagured republic could provide, trifles compared to the bribe that soon arrived from Moctezuma: gold and two hundred more garments, featherwork and opals.

Lord Two House presented the tribute and gave us a warning. "The Revered Speaker, the wisest of rulers, hopes you will guard these treasures against the Tlaxcalans, for they are liars and robbers, so poor they cannot afford even one of these cotton cloaks my lord now gives you with such an unstinting hand."

"Who should know their poverty better than Moctezuma?" Cortes asked. "After all, he himself causes it." But a little shake of his head indicated I was not to translate.

"The honesty of the Tlaxcalans does not concern Plumed Serpent," I said. "If they are scoundrels, he will simply destroy them and have done with it."

Two House received this information with mixed emotions.

At that exact moment and certainly not by accident, horns sounded in the valley. Not a delegation but the entire government of the republic was approaching the Hill of Victory.

"An attack!" Two House shouted.

"Nonsense," said Cortes. "They are merely coming for lunch."

And Lord Two House, apprehensive that he himself might be on the luncheon menu, fled to the tower where he had hidden his weapons. They were gone, of course; my Totonac servants had removed them the day before.

The Tlaxcalan senate and the council itself arrived. Old Xicoten, too feeble to stand, addressed Cortes from his litter.

"Oh, Malintzin, we know you have delayed coming to us because of Aztec lies. We confess again we first thought you were allied with the wicked Moctezuma. If we had known then what we know now, we would have swept the trails ahead of your footsteps, we would have carried you on our backs from the shore of the sea. Come with us now, Malintzin! We are your servants and friends."

Cortes, who seldom believed anything spoken, believed this. "We would have gone to your city before, old father, but had no way to transport our thunder monsters." He meant the guns.

"Five hundred bearers will be here before Lord Sun goes one hand span down the sky."

Cortes suddenly smiled. He had chosen the good faith of the Tlaxcalans over the gold of the Aztecs; it was settled. To me he said, "Go tell Lord Two House to send his escort back to Moctezuma. But he and the other Aztec ambassadors are to pack their things and wait. Tomorrow they will join us on a journey to a place Aztecs have wanted to enter for a long time, but have always failed."

I, too, was smiling. "Do you mean heaven, my lord?"

"No, you insolent wench! I mean Tlaxcala."

They welcomed us with roses, with songs and the drums of thanksgiving. Woven garlands of marigolds, the blossoms of immortality, were heaped over the necks of the horses, chains of flowers entwined around their riders. Pedro Alvarado, resembling a gigantic bouquet, disentangled his beard from a flower necklace that matched it and said, "I feel like a fool." Then he laughed, pounding his own thigh, and could not seem to stop. One of his brothers began beating him on the back in alarm and nearly got knocked down for it.

Tens of thousands of people were singing and cheering; children darted from the throngs in the streets to touch the flower-laden cannons or put a frightened yet delighted hand on the flank of a horse.

Jaime Garay wept with joy at the reception; so did Francisco Montejo and some of the other younger men, although they tried to conceal it. We had been clenched in death combat with these people for nearly a month, but now they gave themselves to friendship as full-heartedly as they had thrown themselves into war. The generosity of their love was a moving thing. Here, at last, was the full reception of the god, the opening of arms and souls for Plumed Serpent.

He did not disappoint them. With his own sword he slashed open the doors of great wooden cages and freed men and women who were trapped there awaiting death on the bloody altars. These rescued captives became our devoted servants, ready to give back their saved lives had this been asked of them.

The great temple of Plumed Serpent had been readied as a dwelling for Cortes; I stayed there as his consort.

Only one danger suddenly loomed before us. We were in the midst of peace and friendship, we had found allies as brave and devoted as any in the world. Cortes the man, always shrewd and practical, would have done nothing to disturb this happy state. But Plumed Serpent, stirring within him, demanded the destruction of Smoking Mirror and Hummingbird, the banning of sacrifice and flesh eating forever. Again it was Father Olmedo and Father Juan Diaz who persuaded him to have patience. For the moment Plumed Serpent was stilled, and the Christian God consented, unwillingly, to let Cortes hold back his hand.

When I recall the three weeks we spent in the City of Tlaxcala, I think of a place I know in the Zapotec country of Oaxaca, land of forests. There is a long stretch of winding trail that traverses a rise of ground that seems too long and gradual to be called a hill, much less a mountain. You are not aware you are climbing until your breath feels short, and if you happen to look around, you can see a great distance behind but little ahead. You are unaware of passing the summit; the beauty of the forest draws your eyes from the road; there is a stream with stepping-stones where you must lower your eyes and be careful. Besides, the route is winding, and you are not mindful that the climb and the crest are behind you until the descent is almost over.

So it was with the road I followed with my lord the Captain; so it is with most people. We do not know that the rabbit of fate has guided us to the highest peak we ever reach until the trail is downward.

We did not suspect a turning point had come, or that these were the best days of all, the best nights. We talked much of the future, of the adventure that lay ahead, without suspecting its horrors. He had not for an hour lost his vision of the valley beyond the mountains.

Since his godhood was at rest, he could admire much in Tlaxcala. "It is far bigger than Granada," he said in wonder.

"A hundred and fifty thousand people, Lord Demon Caller tells me."

"Not richer than Granada," he added, as though making up for a small blasphemy. Then, because he was honest, he said, "But the people eat better. In their way they are better dressed. I have not seen one beggar. Have you noticed the sewers and the water supply system?"

I had not, but pretended I had. We took public sewers for granted.

"We could learn from them. And they could learn from us about building aqueducts with arches."

He respected the authority of the judges, warning his troops against offending them in the least way. This was not because of diplomacy; Cortes respected anything that ran well and quietly, including societies.

"There are few slaves here," he remarked one morning while on an official tour. "Almost none compared to Zempoala and certainly none compared to Cuba."

The Aztec ambassador sneered. "No, they cannot even afford to own each other."

"Then they are a safe people," Cortes retorted. "No men are as dangerous as slaves, for slaves have nothing to lose."

That night he told me that one day the African slaves in the Indies would rise up and murder all their Spanish masters. "Horrible! But blame it on stupidity, blind greed. We will not let that happen here."

"No," I said, imagining old Tula reborn and flowering. How big were the ears of corn in those days? As tall as a man, they said. Yet I was thinking less of corn than of justice. Often now my lord spoke as though he had already reclaimed his kingdom.

Those who hate me and long for the wonderful old days when we devoured one another's flesh say that Spanish wheels spin in my head, driving out thought, that the glint of Spanish steel blinds me to beauty, that I care for nothing but things and gadgets.

Only the rich who never spent their days grinding corn by hand, stone on stone, can enjoy such snobbery. People who think an aqueduct is less beautiful than a temple to the Rain Bringer have probably never carried water or gone without it.

The Aztec ambassadors, especially Lord Two House, were constantly trying to persuade my lord not to think of approaching Moctezuma's stronghold. When they realized he was determined, they urged him to travel by way of Cholula, the sacred city, a venerable nation half-republic, half-theocracy, but unfortunately allied with Moctezuma.

"Allied?" exclaimed old Xicoten. "As allied as your hand is to your arm! Moctezuma rules Cholula, which is a snake's nest. The Cholulans talk piety, then shoot arrows into our backs. Stay away!"

He suggested a different route, a road through lands friendly to Tlaxcala.

The next day at a meeting Lord Two House addressed Cortes formally. "Cholula, city sacred to Plumed Serpent, awaits your arrival, Malintzin." He had decided that "Malintzin," which simply means "Malina's lord," was the safest form of address.

"It awaits you indeed," said Demon Caller, bristling. "Our spies report that Moctezuma has dispatched fifty thousand troops as a greeting committee."

"More lies!" Two House, after restraining his rage, turned to Cortes. "Of course, if the Spaniards are afraid to enter Cholula, a center of great religious force, we understand."

"Afraid? Who says we are afraid?" Cortes demanded. At that second he was committed to the Cholula route. Lord Two House had outfoxed the fox himself. I glared at him in annoyance and admiration.

I think not in all history, not since the World of Ocelots, has a greater army marched through land more magnificent. We moved toward the great volcanoes, the plumed Smoking Man and his sleeping consort the White Woman in her blanket of snow. We crossed a country of frothy streams and eagle cliffs. The entire Tlaxcalan army, one hundred thousand strong, Cortes said, was on the move, along with half a thousand Totonacs and almost as many Spaniards. The tread of our feet must have shaken the earth down to the thirteenth step of hell.

Most of the Totonacs had returned home, bidding us sad and affectionate farewells, striping their faces with black and white of mourning, for they predicted our death when we entered Aztec lands. They tolled drums for a mournful last good-bye. Once again I witnessed my own funeral.

In the craggy ramparts that make the west wall of the republic, we caught sight of the panorama of the Valley of Anahuac, the two huge lakes and the thirty cities, far below, gleaming like Spanish glass and magical in the distance. My lord dismounted, gazed in awe, then said to me, almost in a whisper, "I have seen this before. In dreams."

The god was stirring in him, reminding him. "Amadis himself did not discover a world so enchanted."

At the edge of the stream that marks the beginning of the Sacred Lands, Cortes dismissed all but six thousand of the Tlaxcalan troops. The rest of us, seven thousand marchers, might pass as a triumphal procession; more than that was clearly an invasion.

As we were making camp and the Totonacs were paying homage to the god of the stream, a Cholulan delegation arrived to greet us. Cholula is holy, consecrated to Plumed Serpent, but so many other gods dwell there that it boasts a temple for every day of the year except the five unlucky ones. These shrines have been built by twenty-six different nations; priests and pious folk from every one of them come on pilgrimages, often making long visits, so Cholula is always thronged with foreigners. Naturally their politicians and priests are skilled in courtesy and the arts of hospitality.

Such was the delegation that greeted us on the bank of the stream —gracious, suave and so poised that they concealed their curiosity about Spanish strangeness. Even so, they could not fully hide dismay at the sight of six thousand Tlaxcalan warriors, who might as well have been that many wolves.

They perfumed Cortes, his lieutenants and the lord horses, leaving a peculiar mixture of aromas in the air above the smoking braziers; the fragrance of copal I recognized as the sign of welcome and honor. I suspected the other scents were to purify intruders and perhaps render them harmless. I felt no insult. We were entering the holy precinct of Plumed Serpent and the Thousand Gods; its guardians had to be careful.

When the rites were finished, the chief of the delegation, a handsome senator who was also a priest but not dressed as one, said to me, "You are Lady Malina also called Malinche?"

"Lady Marina," I corrected him, turning my name into Spanish. "I am the servant of Plumed Serpent."

"As I am. As we all are in his own city, Cholula." He made the sign of the god. "I am Lord Four Motion Deer Racer. Since you are of our own flesh, a cousin, perhaps of Aztec birth . . . ?"

I smiled without answering, and after the question had hung midair for a moment, his breeding forced him to continue speaking. "You can present our case to this lord from the sea—Malintzin?— better than I. These Tlaxcalans are not enemies—holy Cholula has no enemies!—yet they are not really our friends nor are they pilgrims. Please ask your lord, with tact, to keep the Tlaxcalans outside the city. So many guests, especially armed guests, might alarm other pilgrims. The hospitality we offer you, humble but our best, should not be strained by distractions."

Like all diplomats, his talk tended to be bubbles of flatulence, yet I was charmed by Lord Deer Racer. His knowing smile, his twinkle, suggested he was amused by his own game and knew I understood what he was really saying: get those thieving, murdering Tlaxcalans away from us.

"He wants the Tlaxcalans to stay out of town," I told Cortes, who appreciated frank speech although he seldom used it.

"No wonder." Cortes had noticed the Tlaxcalans admiring the cotton clothes worn by the envoys. One lout, dressed in spun cactus, had even fingered an ambassadorial cloak to check the material. Again I saw how Moctezuma's spiteful trade embargo had created bandits, not vassals.

Cortes inclined his head to Deer Racer, gestured to show the Tlaxcalans would stay where they were. The pleased ambassadors left then, Deer Racer giving a last baleful look at the Tlaxcalan troops. His glare was not a slip of the diplomatic mask; he meant to show us his suspicions.

Afterward I walked alone along the stream, perplexed, trying to fathom the intentions of the Cholulans or the secret promptings of Moctezuma. Earlier we had passed several roads, routes that avoided the city and led directly to Tenochtitlan. They had been blocked recently by trunks of giant cottonwoods. Moctezuma was dictating our route, sending us into Cholula.

Cholula was devoted to Plumed Serpent. His temple there, a

man-made mountain, was the biggest structure in the world, even greater than the buildings of the People Who Have Become Gods. This marvel, visited by armies of pilgrims, belonged to Plumed Serpent. Yet I heard talk that the Cholulans planned our destruction.

Could they deny Cortes godhood? He had arrived exactly as the prophecies announced. To deny him was denying that two and two are four. It went against reason.

But the city made a fine business of Plumed Serpent, selling food and lodging and Plumed Serpent rings. Also, a terrible god allied with Plumed Serpent lived inside the base of the main temple. He was the Water Monster and on the least provocation would open the stones of the temple and sweep invaders away in an avalanche of water. Whenever a crack appeared in the temple, the priests, fearing floods, mortared it with a mixture of lime, cement and the blood of children freshly sacrificed. Only that sealer would keep Water Monster captive.

More children and unblemished youths were offered when the stargazers discerned that Plumed Serpent's position in the sky was weak. These rites also generated trade, pilgrims, money in the form of chocolate, plumes, jade and gold.

In Plumed Serpent the Cholulans had a fountain of wealth that had nothing to do with the gentle god of my ancestors, a god who could hardly bear to pick a flower because it meant taking life, and so righteous that even the moles and disagreeable badgers formed an alliance to recover their father's desecrated bones.

I had heard my grandmother inveigh against Cholulans as hypocrites. Now I understood her charges against them.

How could people with a religion and a business so debased recognize Plumed Serpent tomorrow? We should expect anything.

I reached a spot where a rivulet plunged down the hill to meet the stream, foaming like pulque. A path wound upward to some ancient buildings almost hidden among the rocks. A woman, probably a farmer's wife, kneeled on the bank washing clothes.

"What place is that?" I asked, pointing up the hillside.

"The Shrine of Skull, lady. Once a town, now only a few altars and an old priestess."

I had heard of this shrine as a child. This was where the Warrior Princess had come long ago. Here the priestess had told her to take up arms and reclaim her kingdom.

"May a stranger approach the shrine?"

"Only by moonlight. The priestess awakens with the owls and goes to sleep with them. She is mad, lady. Do not go there."

I thanked her and returned to camp, hoping my lord had news to ease my worry. There was only more gloom from the Tlaxcalans.

In the morning as we formed up to enter the city, everyone was jittery. Then an omen came. I heard the call of a lark although this was not the season, a call so close and sweet that I knew something strange was taking place. An image of Lark Singer came powerfully, and I stood still, awaiting a message. A yellow butterfly, a departed soul the color of a lark, appeared almost within arm's reach, its wings like gold, too heavy for flight, and it dropped dead at my feet. I understood that Lark Singer had sent a warning.

As the trumpet sounded, I saw other butterflies, white ones, dead on the ground and suspected it betokened the destruction of the Spaniards. I clutched the bouquet of marigolds I carried, glad I had concealed a stiletto among the blossoms. I would not die cheaply.

Singers and dancers met us at the edge of the city, dancers who were also acrobats, walking on their hands, performing somersaults to the beat of woodblocks. Then a hundred voices joined in a chorus, a hymn of welcome, I supposed. But the words of the old song were inappropriate, even ironic today. They sang:

> *"Where is the house of quetzal plumes?*
> *Where is the turquoise house?*
> *Where is the house of precious shells?*
> *In Tula, lost Tula.*
>
> *Our lord Plumed Serpent has fled,*
> *He has gone to the land of the east,*
> *To the red and black country,*
> *Gone from Tula, lost Tula."*

You do not sing a dirge for a returning god. The choirmaster should have been dragged to the nearest altar. But, of course, he had his orders.

Something cold stirred in me and I shivered in the sunlight. I gazed ahead at the huge temple of Plumed Serpent, magnificent against the blue Cholulan sky. On the horizon shone the white, jeweled gleam of the volcanoes. I should have felt exultant; instead I felt threats and the warning of some clouded memory.

We were quartered in four long buildings facing an open square. "Easy to defend," said Pedro Alvarado, and his brothers nodded sagely. They were tense; a little bloodletting might relax them.

Cortes addressed several thousand people in the plaza, among them pilgrims from every corner of the world. I translated the familiar words about the king and the cross but without eloquence. The goddess did not come to inspire me. Politely the Cholulan senators promised allegiance to "this king you have mentioned." But a change of religion? Well, they would think about it. Their nervous eyes made me suspect they were more preoccupied with the Tlaxcalan army that was camped on the edge of town.

We retired to a smaller courtyard for a brief reception with scanty refreshments. The chief wives of the dignitaries were there, clustered in a little knot. I had no time to pay attention to the women beyond a few smiles and glances, but one smile accidentally struck a target and in doing so changed the history of Cholula.

I learned this the next morning when a slave announced that his mistress, a prominent matron of Cholula, waited outside to call on me. A bouquet of orchids was presented and a name given—Princess Totolin. More titles were strewn ahead of her like petals at a feast: she was wife of the Third Speaker of the Cholulan senate, niece of the Cholulan ambassador to Moctezuma and several other remarkable things calculated to impress me.

I received her in a little private garden, where she swept in like an avalanche of jasmine, the tide of perfume rolling ahead of her. "Lady Totolin, princess of Amozoc," the slave intoned.

She embraced me like a lost sister, exclaiming, "Oh, my dear, my dear!" and emitting little clucks of delight. Her name, Totolin, meant turkey hen, which was remarkably appropriate.

A froth of questions whirled in the air. Was I related to the distinguished such-and-such clan of so-and-so? No? Well, I looked it. Was I the missing daughter of Lord Four Rabbit Sky Arrow? Well, I looked like her, too. How did I endure my captivity among these demi-human creatures called Spaniards? Regardless of my misery, I must not even *think* of suicide. Deliverance was at hand!

From all this gobble and cluck I gleaned certain information. She had been encouraged to offer friendship by the warmth of my smile yesterday—in the crowd I had seemed to single her out, to appeal for rescue. My speech and bearing revealed a noble background like her own—refined. We even shared a taste in jewelry. "That opal pendant you wore, exquisite!" She had inventoried every ornament from a bow shot away. The lady had an eye for wealth.

Why had she come here? Her calling on me was presumptuous, and the reasons she gave did not convince me. Yet she seemed too giddy and dithering to be a spy sent to pump me. I was ready to dismiss her with some excuse when, after a wary glance around, she edged close, lowered her voice and turned confidential—no, conspiratorial.

"My dear, you are in danger. These evil creatures from the sea who have captured you are soon to be destroyed, along with their filthy Tlaxcalan slaves. Those who survive here will be scourged to the capital to feed the altars of Hummingbird. Sweet child, you might perish with them!"

"How ghastly! Tell me more. What will happen and how can I save myself?" I prayed my reactions seemed genuine.

Her husband the senator was also an army captain, she told me. A few days before he had received a splendid gift from Moctezuma, a golden drum, and orders to join action to wipe out the Spaniards. Cholulans who opposed this would be killed, too.

"I'll be free then!" I exclaimed, clapping my hands softly in joy. "I'll no longer be the servant of these demons!"

"Yes, the demons will die. But you must find a safe refuge or you might be mistaken for their friend. Luckily I can offer you shelter in my own house. One of the best and safest in the city!"

She gave me a look so flirtatious and filled with intimations that I suddenly decided she was a woman who loved other women, which, of course, explained her extraordinary visit. She was here sniffing for passion, not information. I felt relieved.

Then she dispelled my notion. "My second son, a young man as beautiful as the Flower Prince himself, has seen you twice. First in the procession when you entered the city—how lovely you looked, like a queen! Then he was near you while attending his father at the official reception. He was again struck by your beauty and marveled at the way you changed that Spanish growling and barking into real language. He is overcome with passion for you and begged me to make this visit, to speak for him."

So that was it. As she rambled on, touting the charms of her son like a madam extolling her whores, I thought of Tlahua the Matchmaker who had also been a harbinger of death. "My flower, you could be safe with us. Your mantles would be tied, and you locked in my son's loving arms when the massacre comes."

I made little sounds, feigning maidenly hope and fear. "How much time do I have to escape? When does the killing start?"

"The time will be planned tonight. My son—oh, wait till you see him!—and I will come here after dark when we know the plan, the details." She smiled benignly while searching for a polite way to get to the business matter looming in her mind. "I will bring my own servants as porters. No doubt you will have much to carry. You must conceal your jewelry carefully, since those cutthroat Tlaxcalans may be roaming the streets." For a second the turkey hen's eyes were a hawk's; she was already pricing the dowry.

"I will pace away the hours," I said, ushering her out. "You are delivering me from demons, kind lady."

"Call me mother," she said and waddled out, trailing perfume.

I hurried to Cortes and told him the story. He was not surprised. "This jibes with everything I've seen," he said. "Aztec messengers arrived in the city but did not come to me. From the roof here you can see that a section of town, several blocks, is walled off. The whole Aztec army could be hiding there."

Again, as yesterday morning, something cold and terrible stirred in me, but I could not name it.

Cortes looked at me sharply. "You are trembling, and I know it cannot be from fear. What troubles you? Is this old lady imagining things or lying?"

"Why would she lie, my lord?"

He smiled. "Her son loves you—why wouldn't he, my dear? She wants you as a daughter-in-law, so she might frighten you into hiding in her house."

I had thought of this, too, and it had not seemed impossible, but now I found myself saying firmly, "No, she spoke the truth. I am positive!" The coldness inside me was doing some of the speaking, or at least the prompting. An oracle, but not one like the goddess, whispered that the Aztecs were concealed nearby, waiting to slaughter us.

Cortes nodded slowly. "Then we will be ready. I am sorry these people swore allegiance to the king yesterday. Now they are not just enemies but traitors."

"Traitor" was the foulest word he knew. Other crimes might be forgiven or countenanced, but treason to the king meant death. He considered the Cholulans' vague promise binding; I had regarded it as mere politeness.

Nothing happened that night, but the soldiers slept in their armor. The next day some Totonacs who had been out exploring brought reports of deep pits planted with sharp stakes and covered with mats. Lady Totolin sent a slave who recited a message. "In the sixth misfortune the jaws unclamp for Serpent Skirt." A child could have deciphered the code: I would be rescued from the monsters during the Sixth Watch of the Night. The riddle referred to the Queen of Love imprisoned in the mouth of Earth Demon, a familiar legend. The turkey hen was being clever, playing at intrigue. So nothing would happen until after midnight. We relaxed.

More ominous signs were observed that afternoon. Several thousand women and children had left the city and were being escorted to a camp in some mountain fastness—Tabasco over again, I thought. Cortes announced we would depart for Tenochtitlan in the morning, requesting baggage porters and extra rations for the journey. The Cholulans replied that several hundred men would be ready to assist us at dawn, but no food was delivered. At last night came.

Cortes called a conference of officers, and they met over a meager supper. I heard Diego de Ordas shout, "Sir, these people are giving us murderous looks and I am not mistaken!" A rumble of voices arose in agreement; never, not even in the worst days on the beach or in Tlaxcala, had I seen the Spaniards so keyed up.

Cortes hammered on the table for silence. "Don't worry about them—just be ready for them."

I had been waiting outside the hall for a message from Lady Totolin. Now I was summoned by Cortes because three Totonac warriors had just come to him babbling with excitement.

"Malintzin, the town is seething," they told him. "Seven people, five of them children with long lives to live, have been sacrificed to the war god. A priest read the omens afterward and said the god is pleased, he will give them victory if they promise to offer twenty of your soldiers after the battle."

"Oh, my God," said Diego de Ordas. "What did I tell you?" Cortes looked at him coldly. "What did you expect?"

Lady Totolin and her son arrived as she had said, very late in the Sixth Watch while the city was sleeping and the Spanish barracks pretending to sleep.

"My son, Lord Three Wind Spring Finder," she said in a whisper, lifting a torch high that I might admire his beauty.

Spring Finder, blushing, drew in his stomach and stood tall, his heels not quite touching the beaten earth of the courtyard. He was younger than I expected, my own age, and his face was what you might have expected his mother to produce—a turkey egg, dark and oval and innocent. Since he was courting he wore a garland of zinnias in his hair and rather awkwardly presented one of the blossoms to me.

"What news?" I asked urgently. I was not paying enough attention to Spring Finder, not acting like a prospective bride. But I suppose that was natural under the circumstances.

"The attack will be made when the Spaniards leave the city. Come at once, there is no time to lose," Lady Totolin replied. Now I knew all that was needed.

"Wait here while I gather my valuables." I showed them into a small room. A sentry in the shadows was already watching the door.

"A moment, my lady." Spring Finder stopped me with a timid touch. "I believe my mother has explained my love for you. I would have you come with me for that alone and not from fear. I do not understand. What attack?"

"Be quiet!" Lady Totolin snapped. "Why should you know? Do you think your father tells you everything?"

I felt sorry for Spring Finder, who looked hurt and puzzled. He must be quite ineffectual for his father to have left him out of a matter so important.

Spring Finder dropped to one knee, and his hands, surprisingly strong, gripped my waist. "My mother says you will come because you want a loving husband, children and a quiet home where your own language is spoken. Is this true?"

"Of course!" I managed to pull free of him. Why did he insist on delaying me, on confusing matters?

"Would you rather wait? Perhaps know me better? I do not like this sneaking here in darkness like a thief stealing a slave."

"Give me a moment to get my things," I said, leaving before he muddied a stream that had been so clear before. A stupid young man to have been kept in such ignorance—yet winsome in his silly garland of zinnias.

Aguilar, who had been told about the elopement ruse, was waiting in the corridor, his dark cassock black in the shadows. "Yes, it is treachery," I told him in Maya—I could not think of the Spanish words. "Have the mother and son held in a more secure place." I hesitated. "Tell the guards to be gentle with them. They are well-meaning people—at least, the young man is."

I hurried to inform my lord the Captain. All the while the coldness I had first felt entering the city was welling up, stronger than ever. Fear I had not known since childhood came upon me. It was the Sacred City, I told myself; the silent temples that ringed us were full of ghosts.

The rest of the night, the few hours of blackness after the death of Lady Moon, passed like a fever dream. I translated numbly, needing Aguilar's help with every other word. Several Cholulan senators had been captured quietly and brought in for questioning, a knife held at their throats. More Tlaxcalans arrived to report discovering heaps of stones behind the roof parapets of houses. Siege defense. But for all this activity the city remained calm and sleeping; no one seemed to guess our suspicions.

I did not go near the wooden cages where Totonacs were guarding Lady Totolin and her son.

Dawn found two thousand armed Cholulans gathered in the broad plaza outside our compound. Lord Deer Racer appeared in ceremonial battle dress as their commander, his face wreathed by the fanged helmet of the Ocelot Order. "Please tell your lord that his honor guard is ready," he said to me, sounding proud of his treachery. Even in preparation for slaughter he was perfectly groomed.

"What honor guard?" I demanded. "He asked for no such troop."

"But he did—during the reception. Did I misunderstand? Oh, the confusion of languages!"

Our artillery was already in place, ready to rake the plaza; the cavalry mounted to charge the mob.

Cortes, on Mule Driver, addressed the Spaniards. "Look at these traitors eager to butcher us in the ravines, waiting to gorge themselves on our flesh! But the Lord has other plans!"

Then he wheeled upon the Cholulans, eyes blazing, voice ringing, the angry incarnation of the returned god.

"I know the plot. I know your vows to your bloody idol. He is a false god, a devil who cannot save you now."

Lord Deer Racer tried to approach Cortes but was hurled back by guards alert for assassination. "No, Malintzin," he cried. "We have only sacrificed at Moctezuma's orders. No treachery was meant. But there are the Tlaxcalans and Moctezuma, so—"

Around him a hundred Cholulans took up the cry. "Yes, Moctezuma!" Others were babbling about Tlaxcalans; I could not understand their words.

Cortes's face was flint. "You swore an oath. Your crimes now come home to you."

As I repeated his words, a flock of screaming grackles, black as curses, swept through the dawn sky above the courtyard. They flapped and seemed to shriek death. I felt panic. I stumbled over the words.

Cortes said, "Treason, by royal law, cannot be unpunished."

He paused, and his eyes met mine. I read a question in his face, and a dozen confused images whirled in my mind: Spring Finder's bafflement about an attack, the guilty look of Lady Totolin, as though caught in a scheme. Then in my mind's eye I saw the walled-off section of town where thousands of Aztecs might be waiting—I almost saw the flash of their obsidian blades. My lord was still questioning me silently, and I nodded assent, pleading with him to strike now, to have an end to this fear.

He shouted, "You must die!" When his hand dropped, a musket fired, the signal for attack.

The cannons spat iron and stone across the plaza, hewing down the Cholulans where they stood. They were only a mob, not an army, and when they tried to flee in panic they faced harquebuses and crossbows secretly set up at the narrow portals to the streets. They trampled each other, they fell dying across their own dead companions while the mounted lancers charged among them doing their terrible work. Three hundred of us on foot struck them from behind, and their terror was so great they did not seem to realize the enemy was at their backs.

Wading through the fallen enemy, we broke free into the street beyond the plaza where the city, aroused by the cannon fire, was still trying to wake up. Confused faces peered from doorways. Then I heard shouts: "The Tlaxcalans are attacking! Tlaxcalans!" Figures of men and women in nightclothes appeared on the roofs. Stones were hoisted, then hurled, most of them crushing the heads of Cholulans who were running from the horses. Why had the roofs not been manned earlier? I could not understand why these people, bent on destroying us, were so unprepared.

A familiar figure confronted me: Lord Deer Racer, weaponless, his helmet ripped from his head and dangling half-severed on his chest. The ocelot shirt was blood-drenched.

"No plot!" he gasped at me. "No plot. We did not . . . deserve . . . We feared the Tlaxcalans." I thought he was going to drop dead at my feet, but he managed a last gesture, pointing toward the plaza where the Cholulans lay strewn in their riddled finery. My eyes fastened for an instant on a bodiless arm, the wrist encircled by a gold and feather bracelet. I saw one of our Tlaxcalan spies dart from a doorway, quick as a weasel, and tear the bracelet off. He flourished the arm in the air, a souvenir of victory, and uttered a cry of triumph, a howl.

Lord Deer Racer had sunk to his knees, blood trickling from his lips. He mumbled, "Plumed Serpent? This is the work of the Gentle God?" Then he fell dead, a crossbow bolt sticking in his back.

I gazed at the carnage, a smeared red handprint on the wall, a sandal with part of a foot still in it—the work of cannon shot. Across the street another Tlaxcalan, a scout I had spoken to last night, staggered from a house, bent under a heavy wicker chest he was stealing. His arms were draped with women's clothing. I heard more cries. "Tlaxcalans! The Tlaxcalans have come!"

Too late I knew why stones were piled on the roofs, barricades flung up to wall off the temples like a citadel. The people had prepared for the Tlaxcalans to attack them; they knew their neighbors better than we did. I understood Spring Finder's questions, Lord Deer Racer's protests.

And now, after the first massacre, the attack Cholula had actually expected began. From far away I heard a battle paean I had learned to dread during those weeks we were surrounded on the Hill of the Tower. The Tlaxcalans, announced by their blood warble, were moving in to enjoy the slaughter—and the looting.

I ran then. I raced down the broad avenue we had followed entering the city. I would meet the Tlaxcalan army, I would stop them, pretending Cortes had given a command. That was what I intended, although nothing was clear in my head except a horror of watching. I had to escape.

I ran, pursued by the curse of what I had done—or at least had helped do. Behind me I heard screams, wailing. I again saw my lord's face as he asked me to cast the final vote: life or death for the city? I had chosen death—the choice that is irreversible.

When I could run no farther, I stumbled on, losing a sandal somewhere. At the stream beyond the town I paused, my lungs bursting and my heart drumming. Then I went slowly along the stream following a path I vaguely remembered. The shrine of Skull was nearby; I had been led to this place.

Although it was full daylight and the owls were sleeping, the old priestess was awake, lingering in a shadowed doorway. "Welcome, daughter. I have been waiting for you." I believed she had.

She looked dry and wrinkled as a mountain leaf, as though she would crumple to dust at a touch, but her arm, encased in a black sleeve, felt strong and comforting when she helped me enter the purifying chamber beside the temple.

"Is that a weapon you carry?" she asked.

I glanced down and saw I still held the cutlass in my hand, and its blade was brown with dried blood. When I dropped it on the floor, the clatter echoed on the stone walls. Had the blood defiled the shrine? Or was this a place where blood was welcomed, savored? The priestess said nothing.

"Drink this, daughter." She offered me an earthen mug, its contents frothy, steaming. The taste was bitter; rue had been steeped with other herbs to brew it. "Drink it all."

In the shadows I could see only enough of her face to know it was seamed and leathery as a mask of the Woman of Ashes, ancient consort of Fire. Her voice was like the rustle of wind in a dead field. "You came armed. It is a long time since such a woman has visited here." She pushed back her cowl and I saw that her hair was plaited into two white cones above her temples. I wondered if she could be ageless, if she had known the Warrior Princess sheaves of years ago.

A tall clay brazier stood in a corner holding a banked fire. She fanned the coals, and a harsh incense pervaded the chamber, but when

I breathed in the smoke, it soothed me. Slowly the edges of the morning were blunted, the cries stopped ringing in my head.

I began to talk, rambling, telling of the destruction in Cholula. In the darkness her pale eyes seemed to grow, at last became so enormous that they were two burnished shields, glowing, brighter than Spanish steel, brighter than silver, and in them I saw my own reflection, but the image was not of a tall, strong woman but of a girl slender and shy as a fawn. The girl ran lightly across a hillside, skimming through tall grass to join her parents who awaited her. Prince Chimal smiled at me; Lady Iztac chided me for something, but I was too full of youth and the freshness of morning to mind her. I turned and looked down on a village sleeping peacefully. The town wavered in the last morning mist. Then armed men, painted and plumed for war, poured into the streets from hiding. Where had they come from? A temple? A granary? Then, in confusion, I saw they rushed from behind the walls newly built across the streets of Cholula.

Cholula blended with the Jaliscan village where I had watched my father's men slaughtered on the day the first of my lives had ended. I cried out at what I was watching, and the coldness, the dread I had struggled against for three days now burst from me as I recounted that morning of butchery long ago. The ghosts I had lived with so long did not emerge gently from their cavern—they clawed and shrieked to stay concealed, fought not to show their faces, then at last the flock of specters charred and withered in erupting flame of the brazier.

The priestess was speaking. "You saw evil, you believed evil because you carried it within you. These ghosts will not come back again."

I lay exhausted on the straw mat, not knowing if an hour or a day had passed. The incense had faded. I smelled the dampness of old stone. A lizard darted across the floor.

The priestess bathed my shoulders, my throat and temples. She held something precious in her dark-veined hand—a blue bead or a turquoise, I thought, then realized it was the egg of a robin. Slowly she passed it over my body, touching me here and there, pressing and whispering a conjuration to summon all evil from me. Gradually and with hushed prayers she drew the illness of the past into the purity of the egg. I saw the pale shell darken, turn cinder black.

She chanted in the tongue of the Old Ones, the long-dead temple builders who became gods. When she had finished and the egg flamed in the brazier, I murmured the prayer of contrition.

"Mother of Earth, mother of the Waters,
   Old mother of Fire,
Look upon thy daughter.
Smile upon her, turn not thine eyes away . . ."

The priestess whispered, "Tell the goddess of the sin that brought you here."

"A god asked my counsel, and I answered a lie. I brought death and terror on a city."

"You are as strong as that?" Her voice was gentle; I wondered if she smiled. "Cities suffer only from gods they themselves have created."

"What do you mean? I do not understand, mother."

"You will know in time when you need to know. Rest now. You have come a long way and still have much farther to travel."

I slept then, tasting the bitterness of the cup she had given me.

When I awoke, Lord Sun stood near the last Watch of the Day, but for a moment I was confused, thinking, because I was so refreshed, that it was morning, not evening, that I faced east instead of west. My skirt was torn, my legs and arms scratched by brambles, and there was a closed wound in my foot where I had stepped on a sharp pebble.

"Mother!" I called, but the priestess had vanished.

I wandered through the ruined outbuildings, finding them deserted. Ants had made a castle in a roofless chamber where, according to worn carvings, the Flower Princess had once kept her court, held her voluptuous revels. In the crumbling temple a great horned owl perched in the darkest corner, challenging me with round, luminous eyes. I thought of burnished shields, wondering if the priestess had hidden herself inside this bird.

"My thanks, Mother of Skull!" The owl did not blink, but she ruffled her feathers as a token of acceptance when I placed an opal on the altar—small payment for what I had been given. On a rock outside I found my cutlass, polished and gleaming in the late-afternoon sun. It had been cleaned, then left so the hilt pointed toward my hand, the blade toward Tenochtitlan. I understood and felt strong again, free of old fears and ready to go on.

Cholula lay red in sunset when I passed the outer markers of the Sacred Precinct, averting my eyes from corpses where the Tlaxcalans had done their gory work, the payment of old feuds and treacheries.

In the center of town there was a chilling silence near the temples where barricades had been smashed by cannon fire. No Aztec army had waited in ambush behind them. I nodded greeting to the sentries at headquarters. They seemed listless, numbed by killing.

Lady Totolin and Lord Spring Finder must have escaped from the wooden cage only to be slain by someone in the courtyard, for I found them there among the dead, lying side by side. She seemed surprised by death, her eyes wide; the onyx jewelry and garnets she had worn were gone, her fingers torn where rings had been ripped from them. Spring Finder lay facedown, the zinnia garland still in his hair. I broke a strand of a jade necklace I wore and slipped a bead into each dead mouth, toll for the yellow beast guarding the Narrow Passage. It was all I could do; it was nothing.

My lord the Captain had fought house to house for more than six hours, then was occupied with securing the streets. He had not noticed my absence.

Long after midnight grisly reports were still coming in. I translated for the notary who was taking everything down for a later accounting. We thought at first there were only three thousand Cholulans dead and we told my lord that. Later it seemed twice as many, then twice that again. Who could know? The Tlaxcalans had utterly sacked the city, spreading murder and mayhem down street after street. They stole slaves and women, youths for pleasure, they rounded up more than a thousand prisoners to take back home for sacrifice. Pedro Alvarado managed to free the captives, then went on to do work just as deadly himself.

While the killing was still in progress, stone gods were hurled down the steps of temples and crosses were hastily set up near altars still rank with gore.

"A victory for God," Aguilar proclaimed.

During the next days, while the dead were being hauled away and blood scrubbed from the stones, my lord the Captain installed new rulers. They were chosen from the first nobles who came to offer surrender and they claimed, to a man, that they were of a party long opposed to Moctezuma. Carefully they explained that there were wicked Cholulans and good Cholulans; these were the good ones. Of course.

Ever since, men have argued bitterly about Cholula. Some Spanish priests and many Aztecs accuse my lord of a pointless massacre. I, naturally, was his evil genius.

As soon as Cortes had expelled the newly rich Tlaxcalans from the city, women, children and elderly folk began returning even though roof beams were still smoking. The survivors were sorrowful but resigned; there was no murmur of revenge. What use is it to curse the Earthquake Monster?

Cortes summoned all the Cholulans to the main plaza, the court in front of the temple. He spoke of religion, of the king and loyalty. He gestured toward a cross made of two tree trunks that now stood atop the temple. "This lifts its arms to protect your city," he said. My lord's face shone with faith, and the Spaniards were deeply moved, especially Aguilar, who loved the man as much as the message. He whispered, "What a churchman he would have made! A veritable Saint James!"

"Saint James slept alone," I whispered back in Maya. "Not his style at all." It was an unkind remark. Aguilar blushed and looked hurt and angry. I should not have said it.

I did my best to make Cortes's sermon clear. When he asked if they had questions, an old man in deep mourning with crow feathers in his hair cried out, "We honored Plumed Serpent above all gods. Why has he punished us so?" He began sobbing.

An angry murmur arose. Someone called, "Old fool! The gods always demand blood and he has taken it. What did you expect?"

I am not sure what Cortes said in answer—a long speech about the king and the saints. He had not really understood the question.

Suddenly, as I began to translate my lord's words, I felt myself warmed by sunlight although the sky was overcast, the clouds unbroken. I appeared only to be translating, but the goddess, answering my prayers, had entered me and now spoke with my voice, using the words of the priestess of Skull.

"Cities suffer from gods they have created." I hesitated, gazing up at the mighty temple, the very Presence of the god on earth, and the eyes of the crowd followed mine. In the silence the goddess spoke again.

"People of Cholula, you have made Plumed Serpent into a monster of blood and death. So he has returned to you in the form you created and worshiped. So it is with all cities everywhere. They are given back what they themselves have valued."

When I, or the goddess, lifted my arms, they were wings. "Remember now Plumed Serpent's justice. Worship him as the Gentle God who reveres life, and in that manner he will deal with you."

The goddess left me then, but above the temple the whole sky was clearing as a portent.

"Amen!" cried Aguilar, thinking I had just spoken the prayer that ended Cortes's speech. Actually, I had, but in a way the people could grasp. Ten thousand voices, taking new hope, rose to answer.

My lord the Captain, fierce and beautiful in triumph, touched Mule Driver's flanks, and the horse wheeled to lead the procession of victory. In Cholula, high on its plateau and close to the clouds, one thinks it is possible to touch the sky. My lord, raising his hand to greet the throng of mourners who were at the same time celebrants, seemed to touch it then.

But once he looked away from the crowd, only a glance, but it was a glance I knew. He looked toward the white-crowned volcanoes that guard the lakes and valley beyond. He was thinking of Moctezuma.

Part Five
THE VALLEY
OF AMADIS

16

The City of Mexico—The Feast of St. Cosme—September 26, 1564

In three days I leave this city forever, thank God; I am done with illusions. All my life I have been contemptuous of people who blinded themselves with hope, yet in my own case it took no less an event than a double beheading to make me see the truth.

I should have gone months ago. Here I have been useless, while at home my orchards and gardens need me—no, more honestly, I need them. Even last spring I suspected I could do nothing for Tepi. Yet I lingered until the summer rains began, then deceived myself that the roads were too flooded for travel. Ten days ago, when the beheading of the Avila brothers was announced, I was still hoping.

It seems too grotesque to be true that one of Cortes's sons has been violently exiled and another languishes in a dungeon facing death. Such ingratitude was impossible to believe. How foolish of me! I learned long ago that gratitude is the most unnatural of emotions. Besides, the royal court took what Cortes gave but resented him for being able to give it. What is more galling than the success of an upstart? The god should have chosen them, not him.

Now I look back with disgust at the months I have spent uttering prayers, pronouncing curses and planting spies.

Several times I tried more direct action, searching out acquaintances I had not seen for thirty years, warriors now even more wheezy and decrepit than I am. I rehearsed pleas, assuming my friends were not too deaf to hear me. And if they could not help Tepi, which officials could be bribed or blackmailed?

The first address I tried was in a wretched slum. My old acquaintance had fallen on such hard times that his two spinster daughters kept a shop in the entrance, displaying scented candles. I noticed burns on the women's fingers; they dipped the candles themselves. Since no help could be found here, I hurried away without leaving a name, carrying a bundle of sweetish-smelling tapers. Maybe the nuns will like them.

The next two prospects proved to be men long deceased, the third was senile, the fourth himself in prison. At another house, my last possibility, I found myself an unexpected guest at the wake of the man I sought.

I spent the next weeks watching rains turn the streets to rivers. I hung the pendant of the Unknown Goddess on the wall near my prie-dieu and beseeched her.

"I served you, I was your voice. Help me now, give a sign!"

The tiny face gazed past me at the crucifix on the wall opposite, so I took down the offending cross and put it under my cot. "Tepi is Plumed Serpent's son! Call up an army even if it is only moles and coyotes!"

Again silence. "You ingrate! You demon cunt!" I put the cross back in place to spite her.

So my days have passed, waiting for nothing and watching the bad omens of spring hatch during summer. A new royal judge, Alonso Munoz, arrived and he is the king's evil half. Like Hummingbird, Munoz thrives on blood, giving the headsman and hangman no rest. He has enriched the language with two words: his last name has come to mean a foul dungeon, his first a gibbet.

Eleven days ago the Avila brothers were paraded to the civil chopping block in that same pretty park where the Inquisition holds its rites. It was the Feast of Our Lady of Sorrows, which was appropriate, a day for sacrifice.

These brothers had somehow brought Tepi into the royal net, and their father, long dead, was no friend of mine. Yet he was my comrade in arms; I attended the elder son's christening and seem to remember holding the younger boy in my arms as a baby. So I attended the executions. When sons of a comrade are beheaded, I suppose it is only decent to be present. I went swathed in mourning, sorrowful-looking as the Lady whose Day we celebrated.

I did not think I would be affected by the killing of Alonso Avila's sons—what are two more among so many? But then the muffled beat of the death march filled me with dread, a fear that something unexpected was about to happen. When the procession, robed in black and magenta, moved into view, I was shaken by apprehension.

The condemned men, wearing collarless shirts, mounted the platform. While a notary read the charges and a chaplain intoned prayers, I thought of Lord Moctezuma. I saw his solemn features, the great eyes that were always beseeching phantoms or demons. I knew his ghost hovered near, and I put my hand on my breast to touch the Unknown Goddess. The little lump of stone under the cloth did not give comfort or dispel the eerie presence.

"Lord, why return to me now?" I whispered. I knew there was a reason, but I could not remember what it was.

The first victim, the older son, kneeled with his head stretched on the block. Then Moctezuma's face before my eyes obscured the scene, making the figures on the scaffold waver and fuse like images in water.

Drums crashed, the ax flashed in the sun. I felt myself carried backward in time, I saw a glint of armor, light striking Alonso Avila's helmet. It was a morning a lifetime ago when he sprang forward, seized Moctezuma's arm and clutched his hair. Now, as on that morning, I stifled a scream.

The head of Avila's elder son plopped into the basket.

Ten of us went that morning to Moctezuma's palace. We laughed and talked cheerfully, showing friendliness that hid our intentions. No one would have suspected that two hours earlier we had received alarming news, a report of murder and rebellion by Moctezuma's allies on the coast far behind us. The Spaniards disguised their fear well, although we were only a handful in this swarming city. If revolt on the coast sparked revolt here, the Aztecs might rip our flesh from our bones while we were still living.

In the hall leading to the royal quarters, we passed the cages holding victims for special sacrifice, and every one of us felt as caged as they were. I remembered Quintalbor, poisoned by wizards on the coast for his resemblance to my lord; these had been his cages, his charges, his pets. The memory hardened my heart for what we were about to do.

My lord the Captain had chosen five officers and two soldiers for the task. Aguilar had come to help translate, not really needed, but my lord was tactful.

"How good to see you!" exclaimed Moctezuma, uttering his shrill, birdlike laugh, a sound that always unnerved me. If he noticed that every man was armed, he gave no sign. Neither did I feel he was communicating with the spirits that hovered in any room when he was present. Today he was only a richly dressed lord receiving welcome callers. He was like my father. This, too, was disconcerting.

"I dedicate this day to the Lord of Gifts," he said, offering Cortes a bowl of opals from which he could take a handful as one might take kernels of parched corn. Opals for my lord, silver rings for everybody else. "And you, my dear, must have something special," he told me.

Moctezuma glanced around the room, then smiled. Each morning his chamberlains brought him fresh decorations, newly cut flowers and a cage of birds chosen from the royal aviary—scarlet tanagers for the Feasts of the Dead, canaries and larks for Days of Lord Sun, a rainbow of birds for special celebrations. Today, honoring the Lords of the Night, the cage held a flock of grackles, black and glossy as onyx.

"Accept one of these," he said. "I will give you a silver cage for it."

I remembered the same dark birds wheeling and screaming against the sky in Cholula. Was that why he now offered me this strange gift? His smile was innocent as a clear spring. But what did he really mean? Full of dread, I stammered.

Then my lord turned to business, saving me from accepting a gift from Moctezuma at a moment when the Dark Lords were watching my deceit. Cortes mentioned the trial of a traitor, and the affair was settled at once.

So Cortes brought up the real concern of the morning. "Lord Moctezuma, you must come with us. For the present you will be a guest at our headquarters."

He was being made a prisoner, but time and much talk passed before he grasped this impossible idea. Then his face altered; I had seen the same expression in the eyes of wild creatures caught in traps. Invisible wings were beating at invisible bars.

"Take my eldest son as hostage, take my daughter!" His voice became painful to hear as he searched Cortes's face trying to discover whether he dealt with the man or the god today. I think he saw the god and the god was implacable. "I cannot go! The palace is sacred, the people will not consent."

The argument went on four unbearable hours, my lord the Captain cajoling, pleading, explaining. Finally the officers lost patience.

"We've heard enough!" Alonso Avila touched the hilt of his sword. "He will come now. If he calls for help, I'll kill him."

The others moved to surround Moctezuma, Velasquez de Leon leaning close to him. "Kill him and be done with it. This devil should eat a few inches of steel."

Moctezuma, bewildered, turned to me. "What do they say? To force me to go insults me and dishonors them before the people. They are my guests, sacred, and I fear for them. Beg them not to demand this of me."

Amid the shouting of the officers I spoke quietly but urgently. I dared not translate the threats the officers spoke; my mouth would have rotted from uttering filth.

"Leave now, Revered Lord. If you delay or cry out, they will harm you where you stand."

"Harm? They want to kill me?" At least he had said it, I had not.

"What would happen to the people?" I asked. "Have you the right to die uselessly?" It was fear, not courage, that allowed me to speak so to Moctezuma.

For a moment he debated, deaf to the anger around him. Then he said, "I will go. My servants can prepare an apartment for my brief visit with friends. Your headquarters is my father's old palace. I am merely returning home."

He clapped his hands to summon servants, but Alonso Avila leapt forward and seized Moctezuma by the hair. Sunlight flashed on armor. I thought a sword had been drawn, and I gasped. I would have screamed if I had had breath.

"No!" Cortes's voice brought Avila to his senses a second before the servants entered, so no one else saw the desecration. The caged grackles, alarmed by the violence against Moctezuma's godhood, shrieked warnings.

Moctezuma gazed at the man who had assailed him, and I know

he read his own future in Avila's eyes: chains and fetters, shame before his people and ignoble death.

But he smiled at Avila, knowing something else we could not foresee, looking past his own fate. Without a word, without lifting his hand in the usual gesture, he invoked the Dark Lords, silently pronouncing Avila's punishment. I felt it; a chill went down my spine.

He said only, "If we must go, let us go serenely."

The second head missed the basket, rolled off the scaffold and an urchin retrieved it, holding it up by the hair for the crowd to applaud. A guard snatched the thing back, boxing the brat's ear.

The ceremony was over except for public display of the executed. The heads would hang for a year in iron cages, food for crows—and for grackles. The image of the pecking birds so disconcerted me that I stood still, catching my breath. Then I spoke to Moctezuma. "Leave now, Revered Lord. You have had your revenge—at least this much of it."

I no longer felt his presence, but I was not fool enough to think he was gone or that he was satisfied.

At one side of the scaffold I saw a cluster of elderly Aztec gentlemen, threadbare but aristocratic. They had cheered both executions, and now they smiled and chatted. Near them were two aged Spaniards I recognized from old days, Hernandez and Morales. They had not been with us at Zempoala or Cholula but had arrived later, in time for the last battle at Tenochtitlan. I did not know them well, but remembered both had married Aztec women and had families. Good men, I thought. But now they nodded approval as the first iron cage was raised to its hook on a pillar. I did not know what their quarrel with the Avilas might be; I had paid little attention to the scramble for spoils in New Spain. My life was spent far away from the centers of power. Yet it disturbed me that they, who could know nothing of the curse on the Avilas, should approve the executions when my son was still held as an accomplice. What was wrong with them? I felt more alone than ever.

I walked slowly toward my waiting chair, at last admitting to myself that my son's fate had doubtless been sealed long ago. I could not change the future because I could not change the past.

Hope died then—and freed me. That afternoon my Maya astrologer found a favorable date for my departure.

• •

The next morning in the convent I lighted thirteen pure beeswax candles on the altar of the domestic chapel in gratitude for the decision I had finally made. Extravagant, but I wanted a holy number and thirteen is the lowest—except for Sacred Four, and four candles seemed stingy. At the same time I burned special Maya incense as an offering to Ometeotl.

I kneeled alone, breathing the sharp fragrance, and it brought visions of the south, remembered jasmine and jungle dahlia vines and the tree-that-weeps-blood. Then, without warning, Mother Superior intruded upon my privacy. Since the nuns here are a discalced order, shoeless, she sneaks through the halls on bare feet, and you never hear her until she has pounced. I am told she secretly and wickedly wears slippers in winter.

"Heaven save us!" she exclaimed, wrinkling her pink pug nose. "What is that nauseating smell?"

I did not flinch at this insult to a hundred generations of perfume makers.

She clucked and shook her head. "Do you suppose a mouse has died behind the wainscoting?"

I smiled sweetly. "More likely it is the stink of a live snake. Snakes creep in when the seasons change, and they love the darkness behind woodwork."

That afternoon I saw carpenters rip out the chapel panels, searching, and felt satisfaction.

I made my final purchases in the markets: four mules, eight donkeys and seven men. The price of donkeys is outrageous, but I made up for it by driving hard bargains for the men. Since outright slavery has been legally abolished, I bought the men by paying off their debts, just as in the days of my parents. All the men look strong except two who are stamped with branding irons, showing they once worked in the mines. They seem robust, but men who bear that mark, known as the Spanish kiss, usually have little life in them. Once we are home, I will free all the men. They can then stay and work for me or go their way. Usually such men stay and find wives.

African slaves I could have bought outright; that is still lawful. But I will not own humans; I remember my lord's warnings about people who are desperate and have nothing to lose.

With the men and animals I can carry home all the things I bought: exotic seeds and seedlings from the Orient and Europe; quicksilver, steel blades and needles; Spanish wine for visitors and for communion; an astonishing invention called a spinning wheel, a marvel that my chief carpenter can easily copy over and over again.

Everything for my journey now waits in Texcoco, my place of departure. It is a little out of the way, but I must pay last reverence to my lord's bones. They will expect me.

Returning from a market across the lake, I sat in the public boat near two flossy matrons, perhaps half-Spanish but their skin so whitened with cornstarch powder that they looked three days dead.

"I adore that new gown you're wearing," one gushed to the other.

"Oh? My Mixtec seamstress made it, but it's Spanish down to the last button—except the lace is Flemish." Her clothes were more truly Spanish than her accent.

"Everything you wear comes from Europe! You're a Malinche!"

"I confess it."

A Malinche is one who prizes all things foreign—and prizes them to excess. I have heard the word a thousand times yet it always startles me. It is unjust; I prized the best and hated the worst of both worlds.

It is better to be insulted than forgotten, yet I cannot complain on either count. Until this summer I had not suspected how large I still loom in the minds of the people. There is the great mountain peak that bears either my name or my lord's—it pleases me that our names are blended and confused in a volcano. And I have heard women in the convent whisper salacious stories about my adventures over their embroidery, passionate fictions I wish I had lived. (The truth was good but not *that* spectacular.)

Market women invoke me along with saints or goddesses or Virgins. Grizzled soldiers, not quite old enough to have known me, drop my name and claim acquaintance. A cult of dancers has formed in my memory, although I am not quite dead.

I was packing the few possessions in my chamber for tomorrow's departure when Mother Superior Lady Maria Monica tapped on the door.

"Señora, I have arranged for us to take refreshments together this afternoon before rosary. A farewell chat. You are really leaving tomorrow? I cannot persuade you to stay longer?"

The rent I pay is substantial. "Not unless some deliveries I am expecting do not arrive. I have told the gatekeeper to expect a messenger tonight." The hag who spies for me in the palace will come if there is last-minute news of Tepi. Also the English boy, Juanito, will keep watch for me near the prison and the council hall. This, as always, will prove useless, but it is a final gesture.

"Then I shall bid you good-bye later this afternoon," said Mother Superior. "Come to my Moorish garden. A special guest will be there, a most important person."

From her tone, it would be the Almighty; perhaps the whole Trinity. "How kind," I murmured. "I shall look forward to it."

There is a roof terrace above the convent chapel, an open space with a parapet to give privacy from the public square below. Lady Maria Monica has put out a few potted plants, had a fountain painted on the wall, and thus created her Moorish garden, whatever that may be.

I wore a veil that afternoon in case the unnamed guest should be some old antagonist. At the roof garden I hesitated in the doorway in case Mother Superior's spaniel was at large, nipping ankles and pissing on skirts. The terrace was empty except for a very old priest lounging on a cushion on the floor shaded by a bamboo awning. I decided he could not be the guest of honor since his hands were gnarled by labor and his bunioned feet stuck out from under an Augustinian robe that was mud spattered and patched in a dozen places.

Making a small reverence, I mumbled my name unintelligibly. The friar nodded. His weathered and craggy face made me think of a Maya river dwarf, as gnarled as a root at the water's edge. "Good afternoon, señora. I am your servant Friar Andres de Urdaneta. The Lady Mother is taking a friend of mine on a tour of the convent's public rooms. She will return in a moment."

Friar Andres? As he handed me honey cake and a cup of clover water, I suddenly realized that this gnome was none other than Urdaneta, the world's greatest sailor. He was the first pilot to sail across the Pacific from east to west, discovering what is known as the Great

Circle of Winds—a matter that has to do with Plumed Serpent as god of the air. In his youth he had been a sailor in the East, and twenty years after his retirement was routed out of a monastery outside the city to make his amazing voyage because he was the only man in New Spain who knew the oriental seas.

He sailed for more than a year, crossing the vast unknown ocean in both directions, yet he was still standing at the helm when his leaky, battered ship arrived home in Acapulco. All the rest of the crew lay disabled, most of them dead.

Looking at him now, I felt uncomfortable that I had allowed age to intimidate me. He had been far past seventy when he started his trip. Well, he was special, god-touched, I told myself, but the excuse did not quite absolve me.

"Tell me, what did you think of the beheadings?" he asked abruptly.

"I beg your pardon?" His bluntness took me aback.

"The beheadings," he repeated with a touch of impatience. "I saw you standing near the scaffold in those same clothes and noticed your height. I hope you enjoyed the affair as much as I did. I live in a hermitage in the Desert of the Lions, but I walked all the way into the city, three hours' hiking, to see the Avilas chopped. Worth every step of the way! A good day's work."

I kept silent, wondering if I had fallen into some sort of ambush. Perhaps, as the soldiers used to say, I had landed on a coast full of Moors. The old man could be a political spy, and caution was in order. "You did not approve of the Avilas?" I asked.

He snorted. "Approve? They were a plague of locusts in the land, they and their kind. So were their fathers before them, piss on their graves. Their sons will probably be locusts in the future. Too bad Cortes isn't still living. He'd have made short work and good examples of those traitors. We'd have seen a burning, not a beheading."

"He had no mercy for treachery," I said, remembering a day of execution long ago at Moctezuma's palace.

"Right. God puts traitors at the very bottom of hell."

He was too blunt to be a spy; I felt easier. Yet I chose my words carefully. "I have lived forty years in a remote place, out of touch most of that time. I do not understand today's politics. What was happening with the Avilas?"

"This is only the latest battle in an old war," he replied. "But maybe it will be the last for a while. The struggle goes back to the Conquest—which you, dear lady, are too young to remember."

His sight was failing or he had not noticed my aged hands. I said nothing.

"The men who came here with Cortes were magnificent soldiers, God knows, and did a noble work. But really they were a crew of pirates. They only wanted loot, treasure, slaves. I hope the truth doesn't shock you."

I hid my surge of anger. "Are you speaking of the Captain General himself? Of Cortes?"

"Oh, no. Cortes was different, God knows why. He forestalled his own army at every turn. Those who didn't get rich, and that was most of them, never forgave him. And every last one of them wanted him to rape and pillage the whole country. But he respected the natives here. Even admired them."

Yes, that was mostly true. But all the soldiers were not mere bandits. They "sought their fortune," which meant they intended to steal it. Ironically they enlisted in the service of a god. What an unlucky surprise for so many of them!

"Cortes never mastered the greed of the strongest ones," said Friar Andres. "Naturally—since he never mastered his own. But Cortes was a reasonable robber. I suspect he took a lot less from the people than the native rulers always had. Can we ask for better?"

All that this ancient dwarf said was blasphemy, and mostly it was the truth. After all, my lord the Captain was a god, not a saint. "Now Cortes's sons seem to be on the other side, the side you condemn. Why is that?"

Friar Andres shrugged. "I suppose they're greedy, too. I've met both of them a few times. A friend of mine, a brother Augustinian, is a chaplain in the prison."

"Greedy? That was all your impression?"

"Oh, no. The heir, the Marques del Valle, strikes me as another courtier—unsure and wavering, an easy dupe for scoundrels like the Avilas. What does he know of the people of this country? What does he care?"

"What of the other son—I forget his name—the one still in prison?" I hoped for a good opinion, but did not now expect one.

"The bastard?"

"He is not a bastard!" I retorted before I thought. "Cortes paid the pope well to legitimize his children. It was all done properly in Rome."

"What is *not* done in Rome these days?" The friar gave me a glance, shrewdly suspicious. Then he went on. "I think Martin Cortes is a good man. He's handsome—after all, his mother was the most beautiful woman in the world—but not vain. I suspect he simply followed his titled brother into this wicked cause."

"*What* wicked cause? That is the matter I do not understand."

"You women are much too sheltered. You should be more aware of the world," he said, and nothing could have annoyed me more. Then he explained slowly, as though talking to a dull child. "The Spanish crown, in its fumbling way, has been trying to stop the seizing of lands and enslaving of common people—Indians, if you will. The church has demanded this. But men like the Avila brothers still want to live by the sword. No, not so much the sword as the whip and branding iron. They say they are fighting for liberty, and of course they are—their *own* liberty to enslave everybody else. Most people who talk a lot about freedom mean freedom to pick your pocket."

"Cortes's sons are like that?"

"I didn't say that and I don't think so." He gave me a glance that despaired of the logic of women. "The marques simply thinks he should be king of New Spain because his father should have been. Who knows? Maybe it would have been better if Cortes had been king."

Maybe? How could anybody doubt it? Now I despaired of the logic of men. "And the other son?"

"The bastard—forgive me, Don Martin—is mostly loyal to his brother. Cortes would have liked that. You know, he hasn't confessed or uttered one word against anybody else. The questioning has been severe, quite painful, I'm told. Yet they've pried nothing from him. I admire his strength."

I tried not to picture the questioning. But I thought of Falling Eagle silent in the fire; I thought of my father, of Lady Flint Knife, of Lady Iztac. Tepi could face his questioners without flinching; he could endure. Endurance was in his blood. Perhaps that was the most powerful thing the new race had inherited from the old. I saw it on the streets, in villages, at mines and mills—a people who could last.

"Martin Cortes is completely ignorant of this country," the friar continued. "He doesn't care about it. He was taken to Spain as a child."

Five years old, I thought. No, he did not care, had been taught not to care. He did not think of this as his country or of me as his mother. I had only pretended it might be otherwise. And, as always, recognizing truth was better: I could not lose what I had never really possessed.

"Thank you for explaining." I did not show my feelings; I, too, could endure silently. "I understand now why some Aztecs looked on the beheadings as a victory. I was puzzled. Also, Friar Andres, may I say I admire what you have done? Mother Superior told me there would be a special guest today, but I had no idea it would be so great a person as yourself. I—"

The old man laughed. "Dear lady, I am *not* the special guest. This high and mighty nun thinks all sailors are flea shit, even if they've taken holy orders. The honored guest is coming to join us right now—a decent enough fellow in spite of his title."

Lady Maria Monica fluttered in, ushering a Franciscan priest even older than Friar Andres and just as threadbare. He wore a long fringe of snowy hair around his sunburned tonsure. Lean and tall, he walked as erectly as arthritis would allow—just as I tried to do, but I think he did it better.

Friar Andres, imitating a herald, announced loudly, "Make way for His Grace Vasco de Quiroga, bishop of the howling wilderness of Michoacan!"

I had heard much of Quiroga, even in my distant part of the world. After the king decided he would not allow Cortes to rule the world he had conquered, he sent a council to govern. Five murderers, two of them true monsters. When these thugs were deposed, a second council came and Vasco de Quiroga, a lawyer, was among them. At this time my lord was imploring the court to stop attorneys from emigrating. "Spain's foulest exports," he said. "Lawyers and pox."

By then I was living in the south and Cortes was pondering a return to Spain. Cortes did leave, but Quiroga remained, at last became a missionary priest and then a bishop, reaching this office despite his goodness and Christianity. He was sent far to the west, near the land where I was born. His domain was remote from the center of power, a place where his saintliness could embarrass nobody, and in a land where the worst Spaniards had destroyed much.

He won the love of the people. The Tarascans, whose religious lord he was, called him Tata, which means grandfather. It is not easy to become grandfather to thousands of Tarascan warriors.

Mother Superior replenished our cups, offered a chair to the bishop, who waved it away and sat on the floor cross-legged like a Tarascan.

"His Grace has been telling me of his work among the savages," she said.

Savages? I held my tongue. Strange that I should find myself ready to defend the civilization of the Fisher Folk.

"Only as savage as some Spaniards have forced them to be," said the bishop.

"Of course he has been talking about his Utopia." Friar Andres sighed. "He can't stay off Utopia for ten minutes."

"Utopia?" I asked. "Is that a new city in the Lake Country?"

"It is the name of an imaginary country and of a book by the English martyr Thomas More," the bishop answered.

"English?" Mother Superior turned wary.

"He pictures an ideal society on earth. It is rather 'on earth as it is in heaven.' We are trying to create such communities in the west."

"My brother, also a bishop, mentioned this book in a letter." Lady Maria Monica looked stern. "One matter shocked me deeply. It is suggested that couples, before marriage, should be allowed to examine each other's bodies. Naked, Your Grace! Surely you do not encourage such gross immodesty as—"

The bishop chuckled. "No, the Tarascans do not need Thomas More to tell them about that precaution. They anticipated him by centuries." Then his blue eyes, bright and clear as a child's, became serious. "We put importance on other matters. There are no locks on our doors, for there can be no thievery when all property is held in common. You cannot steal what is already your own."

"Property in common?" Mother Superior was upset. She glanced at *her* flower pots, *her* chairs, *her* cups from China. I suspect she saw Tarascans carrying them off.

"Your rule is like that of the early Christians," remarked Friar Andres with a touch of malice, pleased at Mother Superior's discomfort.

"Food is dispensed from public storehouses. We have no luxuries, but no one works more than six hours a day."

The nun clucked her disapproval, knowing that the devil finds use for all leisure time except her own.

"Everyone is given education, and those of high intelligence

continue their studies longer." The bishop continued serenely, unaware
or uncaring about disapproval. "We reward virtue with material gifts,
and there is never forced servitude except as punishment for crime."

"Just like the Republic of Tlaxcala used to be," I murmured. No
one heard me.

"Such communities actually exist, Your Grace?" Lady Maria
Monica asked.

"Oh, yes. There are sixty of them already. We have classes in
reading, in the useful arts, in agriculture. Even in canoe building."

Canoe building? Teaching the Fisher Folk to build canoes is like
teaching accountants to steal or bees to make honey.

"If you want to see these ideal villages, you'd better hurry," said
Friar Andres. "In Greek the word 'utopia' means 'nowhere.' And
nowhere is where they will be tomorrow. Just let men like the late
Avila brothers get near them, and you'll have cats in your dovecotes."

"I know that." Vasco de Quiroga was untroubled. "But our
impossible ideal has worked for quite a few years already, so we have
proved something. Such proof cannot ever be quite lost to the world."

"This book *Utopia* sounds very dangerous," said Mother Superior, at last daring to contradict a bishop directly.

"It's only dangerous to the poor, sweet souls who believe it,"
Friar Andres replied, smiling tenderly and sadly at the bishop.

"My brother holds that all books are dangerous to ordinary
people," Lady Maria Monica continued boldly.

"Oh, no. Only a few, only the very best." Vasco de Quiroga was
thoughtful a moment, then said, "I once talked to an old conquistador,
a discerning man. He claimed that three generals actually conquered
Mexico. Captain General Cortes, he said, along with General El Cid
and General Amadis. The legends, the dreams of heros put down in
books inspired the army just as much as Cortes did."

Yes, they all dreamed and believed in romances—which was why
they could do the impossible. My lord the Captain believed in miracles
as part of his godhood.

Then, indiscreetly, I blurted something that has gnawed at me for
years. "Your Grace used the word 'conquistador.' We always hear of
the Spanish Conquest, never of the rebellion of the world against the
Aztecs. I realize there was Divine Intervention—" I meant Plumed
Serpent, but they could take it as they chose. "Yes, the Spaniards gave
weapons, horses, leadership. But with them the country rose in a civil

war that was bound to happen soon. Most of the people were not conquered; they simply joined a new world."

"Whatever can you mean?" Mother Superior asked, puzzled.

"Later on, thousands of people were robbed and enslaved by Spanish brigands. Every thief in Spain arrived. But it did not start out like that! No book will ever say these things, because all the books, all the records are written by Spaniards who do not even know what happened. They only know what they saw, which is not the same thing."

"Señora, this makes no sense at all," said Lady Maria Monica.

But the bishop smiled. "Yes, the real conquest was by lawyers and priests and settlers. Not to mention imported bandits—you are right about that. Only now are we seeing the end of it."

"With Judge Muñoz in power, we may see the end of everything," said Friar Andres.

"You are mistaken, friend," the bishop replied. "Muñoz, I think, has already been ordered back to Spain to answer for his cruelty. Right now he is a frightened man, and the bloodletting is over."

"It never ends," murmured Friar Andres. "But maybe it will abate."

"We may see a truly new world emerge here." The bishop spoke softly, yet there was a strange power in his voice. "I will tell you my vision. I am close enough to death to see the future, and I see two centuries—even three—of peace for this oppressed land. Do you realize how great an achievement that would be?" He raised a hand to keep Friar Andres from interrupting. "Let me finish, you old cynic. Such a time of peace has never happened before in any country we know, and I realize that peace does not always mean justice or happiness. But I think my villages near the lakes will endure while most of the world suffers war and famine. That vision shines before me like the Grail, and I believe it will come to pass."

Mother Superior laughed for no reason. "Sherry? Who will take sherry?" Her party had turned serious; she had to rescue it.

Friar Andres squinted at the lowering sun, preparing to leave. I turned to the bishop. "You knew Cortes, Your Grace?"

"Not well. When I came here, he had been ordered to withdraw from the government. Still, we called on him once to put down a rebellion. He was the only man the common people loved enough to obey. He had their trust—that speaks well for him."

"Now they love you the same way," said Friar Andres. "Bishop Tata, everybody's grandfather. They think of you as partly man but mostly god. Unchristian, Your Grace! Yet you and Cortes are the only ones the people have trusted."

"Oh, no, there have been many good priests," said the bishop quickly. "And don't forget La Malinche. Doña Marina was one of the most remarkable women the world has known. Even today she is second only to the Virgin of Guadalupe and some folk even think she is the same personage."

"Horrifying!" exclaimed Mother Superior. "The woman was a harlot."

I folded my hands so no one could see their trembling.

Friar Andres rose, touched the bishop's shoulder. "The sun is low, old comrade. You begin a long journey tomorrow."

"Ah, yes, your journey," said Mother Superior. "Are you prepared, Your Grace? Do you have your horses and bearers?"

Vasco de Quiroga chuckled. "I have a burro and a servant. I would not need the servant, but he helps me celebrate the Holy Mass. We will reach the lake country in a week, God willing. There is nothing to fuss about."

I thought of my own caravan, my horses, mules and porters, some of them armed, and envied his simplicity.

Mother Superior put her hand on my shoulder. "My friend travels tomorrow, too, and I can see she is upset at the prospect. I have never seen her agitated before. Your Grace must bless her for the journey."

As I knelt before him, I felt the presence of Plumed Serpent. The bishop had conquered a corner of the world through his own radiant goodness. Since goodness by itself so seldom wins, I knew the god walked with him.

I did not really listen to the Latin he spoke, although I knew his power was flowing into me. The sky turning crimson, the dark line of mountains that rose between us and Cholula turned my mind to a different journey, our march down the great slopes toward Tenochtitlan.

That morning the Tlaxcalans had also blessed each other, invoking the long-toothed Guiding Lord to smooth their way and sweep the trails of evil. That morning, knowing they faced a road that might lead to the high altars of Tenochtitlan, they prayed for strength and swiftness, anointing their feet with the blood of hawks.

17

The Month of the Flamingo—November, 1519

The time of year that follows the Feast of the Mountains is an unlucky season, but sacred to lovers, especially men who love other men, propitious for any lovemaking—maybe because it is a time when you cannot safely do much else. During these weeks old whores, too spent to make a living anymore, offer themselves for public sacrifice, a holy ending for a career of service. Pious maidens, some of them panicked by the first flow of menstrual blood, also present themselves for death at the temples, purely for devotion to the Flower Prince. It always seemed sad to me, since they had never enjoyed his rites except in dreams.

This time is favorable for certain birds—the quail and, of course, the flamingo who returns to the world after hiding half the year beneath the waters of the sea. But all other creatures must watch out. Only the Nameless Days at the year's end are riskier.

Yet the Month of the Flamingo was almost upon us when my lord the Captain announced that our work in Cholula was finished. We had made the inhabitants Christian or silent (or dead); we had built a cross on top of the Temple of Plumed Serpent, the largest structure in the world, and my lord was pleased that thousands of people came, as he said, to marvel at it. I did not tell him that most of them came to stare at the great holes in the temple base where priests had split open the walls expecting to let loose a flood and destroy the invaders—the avenging deluge they had threatened for generations. When not a drop of water burst from the stones, everyone realized that Cortes, an incarnation of Plumed Serpent, was in league with the Water Monster who lived under the temple. Naturally people afterward fell to the ground and worshiped.

Now citizens were frightened because the priests had no way of sealing up the holes. No fresh blood of youthful sacrifices was available for mixing the mortar, and who could know when the Water Monster might change his mind and open the spouts from the depths of the earth? Then one morning I noticed that the mending had been done in the dark, and knew what else must have quietly taken place the night before.

We had remained in Cholula almost two weeks, and privately my lord was tormented by indecision. The final step was at hand, the move into the Valley of Anahuac and then its impregnable capital. Cortes could not determine how to proceed, and the god dwelling within him was silent or absent, perhaps offended by the slaughter that had taken place in His sacred city.

Some nights after we had made love and Cortes seemed at last quiet and content, he would suddenly leave me to walk the corridors of the palace headquarters. I was seeing for the first time what I would know too well later—that my lord was a driven spirit who could endure anything but rest.

Lately Pedro Alvarado had become more important than ever, commander during the days when Cortes was withdrawn and silent. One morning just after dawn he strode unannounced into our quarters, bold and rude as a Chichimeca. I think he was drunk. He was sleeping with Flower Pouch now, and gossip claimed that their mats were awash in pulque. I was angry at the intrusion, not just because I was naked and he eyed me as a cook might inspect a haunch of venison, but because Cortes had at last fallen into a fitful sleep after a restless night.

"What is it? What's happened?" Cortes, alarmed, leapt up although he, too, was naked. Before Alvarado could answer, he was across the room reaching for clothes and armor.

"Nothing, Cortes. I just want to talk to you."

"The devil you do!" My lord covered himself with a blanket—
he hated being seen naked by his men. I had already snatched up a big
shawl from the floor.

"Cortes, we cannot stay here much longer," said Alvarado, reciting a speech he had rehearsed. "There are rumors that this Moctezuma
devil has moved an army into the passes behind us. He is cutting us
off from the coast. It is time to retreat."

"Or to advance." My lord looked at him steadily. "Did you
break in here to offer military advice?"

"To advance, then. But one or the other soon. The army is
worried, Cortes. Men talk of getting back to Cuba. It is the trouble
we had on the Veracruz beach all over again."

"What is your advice?" Cortes was icily courteous. "Advance or
flee?"

Alvarado shook his head. "I want gold—that's why we came. But
I also want my heart to stay in my chest awhile. I'll do what you
decide, Cortes. Only decide something soon."

His bluntness was insufferable; an Aztec commander would have
had him flayed alive for the next festival. But Cortes listened patiently.

"Very well. I will decide soon." Cortes would say no more, so
Alvarado went to report to everyone that he had jogged Cortes into
action and their joint decision would soon be announced. Flower
Pouch bragged about this.

For the next two days my lord pondered, and I waited for the
god to prompt him. His destiny was to march ahead, but there were
many ways to do it and perhaps long detours. Besides, this was an
unlucky season.

Meanwhile, Cholula was rife with "crickets," which was our
word for spies, since crickets are silent, hard to detect, but will sing
loudly once near home fires. Spies are also called mice. Moctezuma's
crickets eyed every move we made, but now I had crickets of my own,
spies the Tlaxcalans had planted among the Aztecs, and there were
other men of many countries who wished to serve Plumed Serpent and
came to me secretly.

One day at dusk Lord Demon Caller, the Tlaxcalan general,
called on Cortes, bristling with intrigue and importance.

"Our best cricket in Moctezuma's palace has sent a report. Two
baskets the size of big squashes were sent to Moctezuma from the coast.
They were marked with holy signs and brought by swift-messengers.

Moctezuma spent half a morning with the baskets, then went to the great temple. He pierced himself with seven thorns. Smoking Mirror himself was overheard speaking to Moctezuma."

"Smoking Mirror is the chief devil?" Cortes asked me.

"He and Hummingbird," I answered. By now I knew that a devil is a god not in your service.

"What did the devil say?"

Lord Demon Caller lowered his voice. "The god told Moctezuma not to fear the Spaniards but to keep faith and please the gods with new sacrifices. That is now being done."

"So the devil grows brave," said Cortes. He dismissed Lord Demon Caller, then paced a moment, frowning, before he spoke to me.

"Is this good news or bad? Who knows? Is this bloody idol ordering an attack?"

"No, my lord. I am sure he said no more or less than you have heard."

Cortes sprawled in his chair, stretching his legs. I always marveled that the contraption did not turn over. He looked at me gravely. "You have been eager to press ahead, to go on to Tenot—"

He could not pronounce "Tenochtitlan." I said, "Call it Mexico. That is also its name and easier to say."

"Yes, Mej— Well, does this message about Moctezuma's idol change your mind? Is it discouraging news?"

I stepped behind his chair, rested my hands on his shoulders. "It changes nothing. My lord is more powerful than Smoking Mirror."

I did not say all that I felt—that I might lose my life in helping the god return to his city, but I could not live on without trying. Cortes covered my hands with his own, a sure touch, and I knew my feelings were also his. In the long run we had no choice.

But the next morning, in spite of what our cricket had sung, another embassy arrived from Moctezuma urging Cortes not to advance. "Ours is a poor city built on water, so there is no food," said an elderly noble who lied with dignity. "The roads are dangerous. The Revered Speaker regrets you cannot visit him, but sends you these gifts."

Cortes accepted the offerings, then sent the officials away telling them he still must meet Moctezuma face to face. But I thought he sounded less determined.

That night one of my crickets brought more news. The god Hummingbird had told Moctezuma to allow Cortes to enter the capital. But why? Was it a trap? One spy claimed it was a better way to destroy the Spaniards, to pen them up in the city. But another cricket argued that Moctezuma longed to see and to worship Plumed Serpent. Aztec agents, meanwhile, spread rumors that the city was a huge quagmire awaiting Spanish boots. The troops became more nervous; Cortes still said nothing.

But the next morning a small party of Spaniards returned from an expedition, the kind of risky adventure Spaniards love. They had tried to climb to the crest of the mountain giant, the volcano Smoking Man. His gray column of smoke had beckoned them for weeks, ever since they first saw it in Tlaxcala. So they climbed. But Smoking Man would not let them touch his crown; he rumbled and shook the ground under their feet and let loose an avalanche. But they went high enough to bring back ice and snow. When Cortes pressed a ball of white coldness into my hand, laughing, I remembered the bitter chill of Mountain of the Star, but he was delighted. "Fields of snow, and we are south of Cuba! The tales journeyers have told are true!"

"Marvels lay beyond," one climber said. "We could see it all. Green fields, blue water and cities of silver!"

The men murmured; they had learned nothing from the false gleam of Zempoala. Jaime Garay, awed and enchanted, said, "I have never imagined such a country. Perhaps it is a mirage, like dreams in stories the Moors tell."

Cortes again turned his face toward the mountains; I knew a spirit was stirring in him.

That night when we were alone, my lord talked once more of the hero god Amadis, recounting how he defied sorcerers and giants to search out the Forbidden Chamber. "Life without risk is life in a dungeon. Amadis knew this."

Later, when we embraced and our bodies joined, I suddenly knew from the ardor of his lovemaking that he had reached a decision and he was full of joy.

So the matter was settled not by arguments or embassies or reports from spies, but by the beckoning god of the mountain, by the Smoking Man.

The next morning, full of life and with his face glowing, he assembled the Spanish troops in the plaza outside headquarters.

Mounted on Mule Driver and looking splendid in his dark suit, he addressed them. "I waited and prayed over this matter because of the dangers ahead. But you yourselves urged me on, and I can no longer refuse you, no longer stand between you and your fortunes, your wealth. Day after tomorrow we march to the rich cities beyond the mountains. God and Saint James!"

I could remember no delegations of men urging him to press ahead, but that was always the god's way, making men believe he only obeyed them when actually he commanded. Now a cheer broke out in the ranks; more than half the men, their blood up from tales of gold, applauded. Others stood white-faced and angry, and one man said, too loudly, "Onward to the lion's den, you poor fools!"

Lord Dolphin Crest, leader of the Totonac allies, soon appeared at headquarters, bowing deeply. "Explain to our father, Lady Malinche, that the Totonacs will return to their own land now."

Cortes had become "father" since the victory at Cholula. I asked, "Are you afraid of the unlucky season?"

"Perhaps. We were first to rebel against the Aztecs, so we will be the first slain."

"Plumed Serpent will protect you," I assured him, wondering if he really had so much power against Hummingbird and Smoking Mirror. Besides, gods are fickle. Plumed Serpent might do well to trade some rebellious Totonacs for Aztec surrender.

"Just tell our father that we are homesick," said Dolphin Crest. "He has already promised us wealth if we go on, but we do not choose to make our wives rich widows just yet."

Cortes bade them good-bye with lavish gifts of feather mantles that Spaniards did not value. I thought their departure was a small loss. They had fought bravely against the Tlaxcalans but had a terror of the Aztecs, a panic that Moctezuma would smell instantly. I said to Dolphin Crest, "Your father wishes you to leave twenty men with us, a symbol of Totonac loyalty." Moctezuma, I thought, should see clearly our alliance with other nations. I decided to ask for such an honor guard in every town we passed through.

The Tlaxcalans proved to be the opposite of the Totonacs. Cortes was meeting with Pedro Alvarado about the condition of the horses when Xicoten the Elder, blind and led by his fierce son, appeared along with three other Tlaxcalan commanders, all of them arrayed in gorgeous battle plumage stolen from dead Cholulan aristocrats, a sight that made me even more eager to leave this city of bad memories.

"The sons of the republic, ten thousand of us, will march beside you to Tenochtitlan," the old man announced, tossing his head to display new jade earrings.

Cortes, who had not counted on this offer, rose impulsively and embraced both Xicotens, older and younger. "True courage!" he said. Nothing moved him so much as loyalty; it was, he said, so rare.

"Thank God and the Virgin," said Alvarado, grinning, looking golden and wolfish. He had admired the Tlaxcalans' efficient slaughter in Cholula.

Suddenly I felt cold, frightened, so alarmed that I knew the goddess was whispering to me that Cortes was about to do something foolish, even fatal. "I must speak to my lord in private," I said. At that moment Aguilar rushed in, delighted by the news about the Tlaxcalans.

Cortes excused himself and moved with me toward the adjoining room. Alvarado said loudly to Aguilar, "Your business must wait, Brother. That cunt has to be alone with Cortes this minute. She's too horny to last the morning."

The insult surprised me; then I remembered he slept with Flower Pouch. But this was not the time to worry about insolence.

In the next room I hesitated, studying Cortes's face, hoping the god was present. I knew now what had alarmed me. Plumed Serpent would never hammer at the gates of Tenochtitlan with a Tlaxcalan army massed behind him. Such was not the god's way. Plumed Serpent must enter simply as himself, a divine king reclaiming his rightful crown; he could not come as an invader.

"The Tlaxcalans, my lord, will draw the arrows of the Aztecs. Ten thousand men are enough to enrage Moctezuma, but not enough to win the battle that will follow."

Was I getting the Spanish words right? I could not tell him bluntly about the god. I knew his fears, his horror of his own divinity.

"What use can this army be?" I went on quickly, seeing his astonishment. "The Aztecs may pretend to welcome them to their city, but they have learned the lesson of Cholula. They will block the causeways behind us, then weapons and stones and boiling pitch will rain from every roof. Arrive there, my lord, only as Moctezuma's friend and savior, not as leader of his blood enemies."

"Marina, you are asking me to give up the Tlaxcalan army, the bravest—"

"They killed Moctezuma's favorite son. Almost every Aztec family has lost a son to the republic. Could Moctezuma hold back their rage—even if he chose to?"

He gazed at me, uncertainty in his face. I had urged him to refuse ten thousand warriors, and my reasons were only a small part of the truth. I had not said, Be a god, not a human invader. But I thought I saw understanding of this come into his eyes; I thought he divined my real meaning.

Cortes turned away silently, as he always did when weighing a decision. I sent out a prayer for the god to guide him; there was no more I could do. Then Cortes returned quickly to the waiting Tlaxcalans, and I followed, trembling.

He addressed Xicoten the Elder. "Dear friend, I must refuse your loyal offer of your army." I breathed again.

Pedro Alvarado jumped up, exclaiming. "Cortes, you can't—"

Cortes silenced him with a sharp gesture and continued speaking. "Give me only one thousand warriors. Let them seem to be porters for my supplies, and keep their weapons well hidden."

"Cortes, this is madness!" Alvarado's face was flushed. The two Spaniards faced each other, Alvarado a giant, yet my lord was the more powerful.

"Who commands here?" Cortes's voice was soft, but it was the god speaking.

"You do, Cortes." Alvarado turned away, baffled. Then he scowled at me. "At least I hope you are still commander."

Xicoten made only a formal protest. The old man was relieved at saving nine thousand men while satisfying the honor of the republic with the sacrifice of only a thousand. Yet he had loyally offered everything. I would never be attracted to the folk of the republic. Their dreary religion condemned almost everybody to hell except politicians and generals, all of whom went to heaven—which is the exact opposite of what other people expect and hope for. I deplored the Tlaxcalan lack of music and painted books; I detested their cold baths and exhortations to virtue. But there was no denying their loyalty and courage.

Cortes escorted the Tlaxcalans into the courtyard, his arm around Xicoten the Elder.

"This must be your idea!" Pedro Alvarado was suddenly looming over me, the tallest man in the world, gripping my shoulder. "You persuaded him to give up an army. How? Witchcraft?"

Aguilar gasped. "Careful, sir. That word is—"

"I know the word, priest, and I think it is the right one."

Alvarado's fingers threatened to crush my shoulder bones, but I kept my pain from showing. I spoke to Aguilar in Maya. "Tell this Spanish lord not to put his hands on me. Cortes would think it improper, insulting."

I was too dazed and angry to understand Aguilar's Spanish words, but when Alvarado did not release me, I raked my finger-nails across the back of his left hand hard enough to draw blood. He let go as though he had seized a porcupine. His hand flew to his mouth.

"Why, you bitch!" He was astonished that a woman should defy him, and passed it off with a false chuckle. "Are you a wildcat in bed, too? I'll find out after Cortes finishes with you." Spurs clanking, he strode from the room.

Aguilar turned on me, furious. "Have you no respect? No female humility?"

He spoke Maya, and I answered in the same tongue. "None. If his anger upsets you, go smooth his feathers. Show your own humility."

"You have caused trouble for Cortes! It is unforgivable!"

Aguilar rushed out, clucking and flapping, to console Pedro Alvarado, although his only worry was for Cortes.

I had made a powerful enemy. But as usual, there was no helping it; the goddess had given me no choice.

Later the flower of the Tlaxcalan army reported, more than the thousand men Cortes had asked for. Their ranks were also swelled by hill men and farmers who refused to leave Plumed Serpent; they were on a holy pilgrimage. More than a hundred Totonacs and twice as many Otomis presented themselves, so our company was larger than a retinue, smaller than an army. Still, two thousand men would not seem a threat to the Aztecs.

Lord Demon Caller, after presenting the Tlaxcalans as baggage carriers, drew my lord aside. "The crickets are singing again. Moctezuma has again pierced himself and consulted Smoking Mirror. The god said to let the Spaniards enter the city."

The cricket's message proved true. The next morning six Aztec lords arrived to present offerings of gold and cloth. With the gifts came Moctezuma's welcome.

"Thank your gracious king," said Cortes. "And tell him that coming to his city was what I always intended."

So on the first day of the Month of the Flamingo, Father Olmedo celebrated mass at dawn in the great square of Cholula, and the Tlaxcalans prayed to their somber gods while anointing their own feet and weapons with hawk's blood. Then, with pale light shimmering on the snows of Smoking Man, the company of Plumed Serpent set out on the final marches. Moving along the road, raising a great cloud of dust, were four hundred and fifty Spaniards and four thousand allies, a strange collection of men and a few women, most of us full of joy and fear at the same time.

Cortes had kept three Aztec officials as guides and escorts. They were eager to do the guiding—too eager, he felt, suspecting an ambush. The Aztecs looked annoyed when people from every mountain village we passed lined the way to do reverence. Each time we paused, some country chieftain would cautiously approach me to mutter complaints of Aztec oppression. Would I explain their suffering to Malintzin? Would I intercede for them with the god? They could bear Aztec tyranny no longer.

Since childhood I had known the hatred much of the world felt for the Aztecs, but I had supposed it lessened in their own neighborhood. The opposite was true, and that night when we camped in Calpan, I could have spent all the Nine Watches listening to tales of Aztec injustice, kidnapping, rape of young daughters and sons, wanton murder.

When I repeated all this to my lord, he said, "My mother used to tell such stories about the days when the Moors ruled Spain. Then the kings and El Cid brought justice to the people. That is the work we will do here." Later he kneeled as usual at the altar, but as he prayed with the candles flickering on his features, he looked young and so full of visions that I, too, almost saw the bright future of his imagining.

In the morning outside Calpan we reached the meeting of two different roads to Tenochtitlan; one was barricaded with trunks of great trees, the other well swept and inviting. "This way, lords," said one of the Aztec guides. "The way is smoothed and ready."

"No," Cortes replied. "The other way." He called the troops together. "March in close formation, so close that every man's beard is on the shoulder of the man ahead of him."

Just as we moved forward, I heard a rustling in the dry grass and saw a serpent slide quickly down the closed trail Cortes had chosen, and I knew it was leading the way for us.

It was a hard trail. The air grew cold; so did the ground, and I felt a chill through my sandals as we moved upward, panting as the mountain drew the goodness from the air. We crossed the high shoulder where Smoking Man leans toward Sleeping Woman; there was snow under our feet, and the Totonacs began wailing. But they forgot their misery when, from the heights, the full view of the valley lay spread before us, the gleaming lakes, the thirty cities of the shore bathed in light.

Bernal Diaz, standing near me, sighed and said, "The Valley of Amadis. The legend has come true."

Cortes spoke, almost in a whisper. "The promised land—we have reached it. This is what Columbus dreamed of."

Then, seeing that many of the men were awed and frightened by the spectacle, the size of the towns, he laughed loudly and quoted a proverb, "The thicker the Moors, the richer the spoils." The others joined his laughter, yet on the brink of the cliff, with the teeming valley of the Aztecs below, our voices seemed hollow.

Cortes moved among the soldiers, talking to some of spoils, to others of God and glory. Even as he spoke, wind swept down from the two mountains, whipping our pinched faces with sleet. We pressed ahead, fingers numb, and before the day was over two Spaniards died of the cold, and everyone cursed the mountains while I silently prayed that the volcano gods could not understand Spanish and take vengeance for the insults.

Yet even as we shivered, everyone talked of the gleaming promise that lay ahead, of what they had seen below. Hearing them marvel, I felt tall with pride. They had known the world beyond the seas, the world of gods who tamed animals and winds, yet they had seen nothing so great as this valley where my people had lived and built for a hundred sheaves of years, the cities of my father's forebears, ancient and beautiful when the first Aztecs crept bloodstained from the swamps to slash out an empire.

We camped that night at Merchants Meeting, a stopping place for caravans bound to or from the capital. We were unrolling bed mats, pitching tents and lighting cook fires, when sudden excitement swept through the camp. Some Cholulans shouted that Moctezuma himself was approaching, would arrive in a few minutes.

There was consternation among the Tlaxcalans. Moctezuma arriving? The First Speaker, a god, had journeyed more than two days to meet us on the road? No ruler in all Aztec history had so lowered his dignity before. I was stunned, then unbelieving as a hundred Aztecs, with full pomp and fanfare, entered Merchants Meeting and moved toward the wide square.

"Can it really be Moctezuma?" Cortes asked sharply. "I remember that man they dressed to look like me."

I nodded, recalling not only Quintalbor the impersonator of Cortes, but also the story of a king of Texcoco who, suspecting treachery, had sent his own son disguised as himself to keep an appointment with an Aztec ruler. The son, successful in his imitation, was promptly flayed alive and his skin stretched on a rock. Moctezuma knew this bit of history, too. Probably now he was testing the waters by sending a double.

The imperial party drew near, a male chorus intoning an anthem. Moctezuma, if this was indeed the Speaker himself, was carried in a litter adorned with dyed plumes, not natural ones. Cheap, I thought, my doubts growing.

Lord Demon Caller, now disguised as the foreman of the porters, hurried to my side. "I recognize this false Moctezuma. He is an unimportant noble."

"Order him away," said Cortes, gesturing angrily toward the impersonator. "Are you Lord Moctezuma?" he called.

"I am," the man replied.

Cortes waved a disdainful hand, then walked away.

I approached the heralds. "My lord is disappointed that his friend Moctezuma could imagine Cortes would not recognize him. Now leave here at once."

At that moment Alvarado's cavalry staged a mock charge, and the bogus royal party scrambled down the trail frightened out of what wits they had. I was glad to see them put distance between us. Besides being a test of Cortes's intentions, I suspected that the impersonator carried magic.

To our astonishment, still another embassy from Moctezuma appeared in the morning as we broke camp. They had nothing new to say except that if Cortes refrained from visiting the capital an annual tribute would be paid him each year. Paid in gold and on the coast. Cortes shook his head and gave me a sardonic smile. "Day before yesterday I am invited. This morning I am bribed to stay away. Lord Moctezuma is as fickle as a courtesan." But for the ambassadors he said, "Much as I would like to please Moctezuma, I am forced to enter his city. I have orders from my own great king."

I translated the word "king" as "ruler," so it might have meant Ometeotl, greatest of gods and lord of the universe.

We pressed on, descending sharply now toward Amecameca, which is perched on the mountain's knee. The inhabitants received us graciously, offering their best food and housing, but Cortes was suspicious. He had noticed large numbers of men moving in the woods that afternoon, shadowy men skulking on both sides of the trail.

"Explain to these people that Spaniards do not sleep at night," he told me. "We are mountain cats who see in darkness. We also hunt in darkness, so let them keep their distance."

I told the townsfolk, who were astonished, then received more secret deputations from villages who renounced Moctezuma and swore loyalty to Cortes.

Cortes, after sunset, went to check the posting of sentries. "Whatever these people say, they are plotting treachery. I can feel it. Well, they will find me standing in front of their thoughts."

While he was gone, there was a stir at one of the guard posts, and Jaime Garay came running.

"Lady Marina, some sort of madman has come along the road from the valley. I think he is demanding to see you."

"Bring him to me," I answered, "but not by yourself. We will need two more guards." I had long suspected that Moctezuma might try to destroy me before Cortes had other interpreters; I was taking no risks.

A moment later three sentries came, escorting a distraught man dressed in the torn robe of an Aztec priest. But his hair was not a priest's hardened mat of blood; instead it foamed from his head, a wild mane, grayish white with ashes of repentance. He staggered, and one of the guards caught his arm to keep him from falling. The other two held pine torches high so I could see the Aztec's face, which was bruised and bloody. I did not recognize him until I noticed his withered hand. This was the haughty Lord Wolf's Paw, Moctezuma's chief sorcerer and poisoner.

"Watch him closely," I told the guards. "Be careful. He is more dangerous than a singing snake."

Wolf's Paw flung himself down before me, almost eating earth as he kissed the ground. "Help us! Help us, Malinche." He burst into such spasms of weeping that I could not understand his words. I ordered pulque to be brought, and after a long drink he managed to stammer out his story.

Moctezuma, learning that Cortes was pressing on toward the capital, had summoned his trusted priests and necromancers. "Go meet the invaders," he commanded. "Stop them by any power of earth or hell."

An array of magicians set out on the road, armed with all the hideous appurtenances of their art. But halfway along the trail, as they climbed a hill at the edge of the valley, there appeared to them a vision as horrifying as they themselves.

"A figure came toward us, Malinche," said Wolf's Paw, trembling. "At first he seemed to be a peasant from Chalco by the Lake. Then, as he came closer, we saw he was possessed by the four hundred rabbits."

In other words the peasant was drunk. Four hundred rabbits are the spirits of strong drink. They bring both truth and destruction, peace and violence.

"Possessed! They overran his arms, his hands and mouth, his face and hair. Eight ropes were wrapped around his chest for enchantment, and he barred our way. Then, as he raised his hands, rabbits clinging to them, we knew this was Smoking Mirror himself."

Now I listened in alarm, knowing Wolf's Paw spoke the truth; this was no trick of Moctezuma's, no deception.

The rabbits vanished, said Wolf's Paw, and the god spoke in a terrible voice of judgment and doom. "Why do you come? What is in Moctezuma's mind that he only now awakes? Too late!"

The wizards pierced their own flesh with thorns; their blood trickled on the ground; they built a mound of earth and covered it with grass as a throne for Smoking Mirror, but the god refused them and spoke again in a roar of thunder. "You need not have come! I will not heed you, not ever again. Turn now and look toward your city, then weep for what you see."

Wolf's Paw groaned and ran his twisted fingers through his hair. "Malinche, all the city was afire! We saw the temples and palaces in

flames, and the lake turned to lava. The causeways melted; they sank
into the fire, while we heard shrieks of the dying. Silence came only
when none was left to cry. I turned away from the horror, sickened.
We all turned away to find the god had vanished."

For a moment neither of us spoke. I stood numb, trying to
interpret the vision, while Wolf 's Paw, still stretched on the ground,
quietly wept.

"Why have you come here?" I asked when I felt my voice was
steady.

"The others returned to Moctezuma. They will tell him to swal-
low death, to wait with honor for the fate that is his—no, ours. But
I remembered you, that you must be one of our own people. Now
I beg you to help us."

I remembered the death agony of Quintalbor, and that, given the
chance, Wolf 's Paw would rather have poisoned the god than the
imitator. I had no pity for him now.

"Go to the city, wizard," I said. "I cannot help you any more
than Smoking Mirror could. Accept Plumed Serpent and perhaps your
vision will not come true. You have no other hope."

I gestured to the guards, and they led him away, sobbing. Then,
pulse pounding, I ran to talk with my lord the Captain, realizing that
the vision of the priests was the same as one I had suffered in sleep.
There had to be truth in it. But who burned with the city—Moctezuma or ourselves? Or all of us?

He was in the tent we shared. His altar had been set in the corner
as usual, and he had just finished his prayers. He seemed serene after
praying, and his calm did not change as I poured out the story.

He considered the news. "So these devil gods are deserting Moctezuma. I always knew they would."

"Yes, my lord." His quietness calmed me; I felt some of his
assurance. Yet I could not put from my mind the horror of the flaming
city. Strange that I, born to bring destruction, destined to be its
conveyor, should be so appalled.

"Why would I raze their city?" he asked, seeing how troubled
I was. "I must claim it for God and the king, not destroy it." Cortes
smiled at me. "Come and sit with me, close to me. You say that it is
the most beautiful city in the world. I wish only to make it better—
to bring it gentle religion and justice. You've heard the people in every
town we have passed. Could we do worse than Moctezuma?"

"Oh, no, my lord."

I turned to unbuckle his armor as I usually did. "No, not to-night," he said. "I will sleep in this. We are too near the lion's den."

Later, after I had put out all the candles except the two on the altar, he spoke in the shadows. "How could there be four hundred rabbits? Did they count them? Did they cling to the man's arms the way this wizard said?"

"It means drunkenness, my lord. The rabbits are the spirits trapped in the pulque."

"But were they *really* there? Rabbits—real animals?"

I hesitated, unsure. "I suppose so. I don't know. Does it matter?" To me it came to the same thing whether there were actual rabbits or spectral ones.

After a time he said, "Day after tomorrow, God willing, I will meet Moctezuma face to face. Tell me about him. What was he like as a young man?"

"A soldier who wanted to be a priest. Devout and pious. He was famous for bravery."

"And as a king?"

"He has been fierce and merciless. Once, when he subdued a rebel city, he ordered all the older people killed because he thought they must have incited their children to revolt."

I told of other punishments and executions, but I did not mention my father or the slaying of the royal tutors. Those matters were too close to me.

"Then he is not weak," said Cortes. "I had supposed him so. One day he offers me friendship and the next morning sends poisoners. He changes from moment to moment."

"Yes, he changes almost daily because the gods change, my lord. He is their instrument." I did not think my lord was understanding. "What Smoking Mirror decrees yesterday, he may revoke tomorrow. Even great rulers, even gods like Moctezuma, are at the mercy of the winds, of the flights of birds. A butterfly crossing their path may show a different way. How can men stay the same when they are turned by the whim of any god?"

"Can Moctezuma not follow his own reasoning?"

I could not answer, and I would not mention the mountain god Smoking Man who summoned my lord on the journey we were now making.

The minds of Spaniards were not like our minds. Their thoughts shot out like bolts from crossbows, while ours fluttered and glimmered like fireflies; we heard voices Spaniards did not hear, saw visions they were blind to. Our bodies might meet and join, we might learn each other's language, but our minds would be separate until, perhaps, some new generation we created together would bring a union.

I envied those unborn children, imagining their wholeness, never suspecting that some would not be two natures blended but two at war within themselves, enemies till death.

18

City of the Sun

In the morning we left Amecameca, child of volcanoes, and then we paused to regroup in close formation at the edge of the town, for here was a place of likely ambush, the ruined quarries and brickyards that could conceal an Aztec army.

They were deserted, but I gazed for a moment at the ancient pits and trenches, remembering that a dozen generations ago, when the Cholulans decided to build their huge temple to Plumed Serpent, they captured and enslaved all the folk on this slope of the mountains, more than twenty thousand. These victims made the bricks for the temple, then, lining the trail to the pass, they passed them hand to hand till a new mountain was made on the volcano's shoulder. Then, under Cholulan lash, they moved this new mountain to the place where it stands today, the temple of Plumed Serpent. Half the slaves perished in the cold. So the temple to the Gentle God had been defiled and cursed from the beginning.

I knew the god had brought me here to remind me of this, and I turned away, full of new strength.

We moved through tall timber, down into the warm meadows. I walked at the head of the procession, beside my lord, carrying my banner proudly. Jaime Garay began to sing; others joined him, and far back in the column I heard the strumming of a lute.

But their singing faded as the day wore on. Now at every break in the forest we saw the cities and lakes, the proud Hill of Locusts rising from the water. Overawed at the size and number of the towns, the Spaniards fell silent. Cristobal Olid moved up beside Cortes and said, "My God, what are we walking into?"

"Our future," said Cortes with a faint smile.

"A short trip, then," Olid muttered, then went back along the line of march to spread more gloom and fear.

"He should have more faith," said Aguilar, who had been white as cotton for the last two hours and whose lips seldom stopped mouthing prayers.

Jaime Garay offered to take the banner I carried, saying I must be tired, but I would not part with it. Today it seemed more than a sign of triumph; it seemed a weapon.

"Today I keep thinking of the Children's Crusade," Jaime told me, then explained how long ago thousands of children, too small to hold weapons even if they had had them, marched against a savage army to capture something called Holy Sepulcher. "That is what we are. Children going into the dragon's cave."

"The crusading children are now hailed as martyrs in heaven," remarked Aguilar, trying to cover his fear with piety.

"Yes," said Garay. "That is what worries me."

But I glanced at my lord, who smiled back at me, and I knew he was no child leading children but a king returning to claim his own. I was suddenly as buoyant as the flag I carried streaming in the wind.

Then the trail straightened. We left the forest, and the waters of Lake Chalco shimmered just ahead. Ahead was our last stop before the Heart of the World, the town of Ayotzinco, child of Lake Chalco, whose houses are built on stilts and stand in the shallows like long-legged waterfowl. While the soldiers were exclaiming about this, I happened to glance backward at the road we had followed and saw an astonishing sight. People, thousands upon thousands of them, mostly men but some women, had joined our procession. Twenty thousand? Thirty? The column crowded the trail, wound upward on the slope and vanished without ending in the woods far away; not an army, but simply farmers and townsfolk following their lord toward some unknown miracle. Surprisingly, many of these pilgrims were Aztecs, and the sight filled not only my eyes but my soul. They knew the prophecies; they had seen the truth.

The next morning, at the end of the First Watch while we were preparing to leave Ayotzinco, our Tlaxcalan scouts came running with news that a large number of Aztecs, not an army but still another embassy, was approaching. "I think it is young King Cacama of Texcoco," said a scout, round-eyed.

Texcoco was now the second most important city of the lakes, and my crickets had told me that Cacama was a likely successor for Moctezuma one day. I could not quite believe so exalted a prince would come to us in person.

My doubts vanished when I saw the party enter our camp. Cacama was borne in a litter exquisitely decorated in green feather mosaic with silver, gold and turquoise chasings. Eight lords, all of them splendid, carried this litter, and when Cacama descended, they stooped to sweep the ground before him with whisks of precious plumes. He strolled toward Cortes, proud and casual, full of indolent grace. My spies had also told me that of all the Aztec princes, Cacama was the one who had most strongly urged the destruction of the Spaniards on the coast, then in the mountains.

"Malintzin, I and my attendants have come to accompany you to Tenochtitlan. We do this at the command of Moctezuma."

Before my lord could reply, before I had even finished translating, his gracious tone suddenly changed. "But I also urge you to turn back now and save everyone grief. Moctezuma cannot provide you what you wish."

All the other lords were now speaking at once, imploring Cortes not to accept the invitation they themselves were offering. Then there was silence. Nothing remained for them but to give way or defend the road against us. A murmur arose among the Spanish troops. The splendor of the Aztec deputation aroused both their greed and fear. I was thankful that a peninsula in the lake hides Tenochtitlan from Ayotzinco; this was not a good moment for the Spaniards to look upon the greatness of the city or see the smoke of its high altars.

Cortes's voice rang out. "We accept the invitation of Lord Moctezuma. We will enter your city as friends, as agents of our king and servants of God."

My lord then presented Cacama with strands of glass beads, especially lovely in the morning sunlight.

Cacama hesitated, then turned away in obedience to his ruler's command. I heard some of the Aztecs sigh as they followed him to the green litter. These, we all knew, were the final words of diplomacy; the way to the city was open.

But as we began this last day's march, I remembered the words Bernal Diaz had spoken outside the Wall of Tlaxcala. "Pass if you dare. Will you come out again?"

Someone else had the same thought. As we took the first steps forward, Jaime Garay glanced at the crucifix Aguilar carried and said, "The Children's Crusade marches on. God and Saint James."

The road skirted the shore, passing through lovely little towns, then becoming a causeway that leads to the Place of Precious Black Stones, the town called Iztapalapa. Crowds lined the road, some cheering, others scowling, most simply gazing in wonder. Children too young to know fear tried to touch the horses and had to be thrust back forcefully, their ears boxed. We moved through orchards where other children, and sometimes their parents, climbed the fruit trees to see us. Since it was early November, roses bloomed in profusion.

Despite orders, soldiers would dart from the column to enter roadside houses, take a quick look, then run out, exclaiming about the embroidered cotton cloth that covered the walls, the carved cedar beams and brilliant murals on stucco.

Cortes paused at one residence, a lakeside summer house with flocks of waterfowl painted and carved at the entrance. He said to Aguilar, "Can there be another such land in the world?"

"No. If so, it is not yet discovered."

"And will not be, I think. It could only be heaven."

But even as he said this, I knew that as long as he lived, he would always imagine other lands beyond other mountains.

At Iztapalapa, on the shore of the salt-colored water, we were lodged in a palace fragrant with sandalwood and cedar, where sculptured terraces held lily ponds and arbors, so beautiful that Aguilar whispered that it must be the prelude to some enchantment. I remembered the garden where I spoke for the last time with Lark Singer.

My lord asked, a touch of awe in his voice, "Was your father's house like this, my dear?"

I lied because it was a lie he wished to hear. "Oh, yes. Perhaps not quite so large, but more beautiful, I think."

That evening from the terraces we looked across the lake two leagues to where the white temples and palaces of Tenochtitlan shimmered and floated on water like huge Spanish ships at anchor. They softened to pink in early sunset, then deepened to the cinnabar red of temple altars, ominous against the darkening sky. Tonight no torches flamed in sanctuaries; tomorrow was the Day of Ehecatl, bringer of whirlwinds, so no rites would be performed. The sign was right—as had been all signs for years—for my lord's entrance into his city. Yet standing near Cortes at the parapet, I was frightened, overawed by the panorama of Tenochtitlan.

"Even as late as yesterday, I could have turned back," he said.

I nodded, knowing it was true in a way. If our whole lives, the trails of our rabbits, had been different, yesterday we could have halted. But I doubted even that.

Suddenly he held me close against him, clinging as though he might be embracing a woman for the last time, trying to lose himself and his uncertainty in me. So we drew strength from each other.

In the Second Watch of the day, with arrogance masking our fear, we marched in procession as befitted companions of a god. Our glances were quick and uneasy; soldiers' hands rested on sword hilts. I grew aware of a strange, unnatural silence. No lurchers barked, no horse neighed, no breeze rustled our banners. A triumphal march should be made to music, or I had imagined war cries and the clash of arms. Instead we moved in silence.

Moctezuma's prime minister, the redoubtable and cunning Lord Woman Snake, had been named our guide, and gorgeously dressed in a seasonal cape of flamingo feathers, he led a party of nobles to escort us to the causeways, intersecting roads of stone running through the lakes, the only passages between the mainland and the city islands, wide enough for four men to march abreast. Woman Snake commanded our horde of followers to camp far from the approaches to the city. "There is no room for so many on the islands," he said.

"No room?" Pedro Alvarado jeered. "It is as big as Toledo and Sevilla together."

"Bigger by far," whispered Jaime Garay, awed.

"The house prepared for you will hold two or three thousand, but no more." Lord Woman Snake, plump but elegant, was unyielding. He eyed us warily, as frightened as we were and as pretending of confidence.

So our company, without the pilgrims, moved on, four hundred

Spaniards and two thousand men of other races. I do not know how many women were still with us—perhaps a hundred.

Now we were watched by tens of thousands of eyes as the lake on either side of the causeway swarmed with canoes. The world had turned out to see Plumed Serpent, their faces grim or suspicious or resigned, all of them knowing that in some way their world would change this morning. I, too, felt the approaching miracle or catastrophe, and my blood pounded.

We passed between the two fortress towers that guarded the junction of causeways. I marched as usual beside my lord, who rode Mule Driver. Behind him came eleven other horsemen, and on his right walked Aguilar and Father Olmedo, brandishing crosses and chanting rosaries, their unsteady voices praising the Virgin. Aguilar's head was lifted, his eyes half-closed in the elation of faith. I envied him. My faith in Plumed Serpent was no less, but I knew the fallibility and weakness of gods.

Mule Driver's iron-shod hooves echoed hollowly when we touched the first wooden bridge, one of several that could be pulled from the causeways to halt entrance to the city—or make the islands a prison for enemies already inside. Every Spaniard measured the removable bridges with his eyes and knew the openings would be too wide for leaping.

Suddenly horns and drums sounded. A thousand Aztec lords emerged from the city, advancing with measured steps to meet us, the throne of Moctezuma held high on a carpeted platform, the Speaker himself seated there. Dwarfs strew flowers ahead, covering the royal path with petals.

Our own Aztec escorts hurried to greet the Speaker, and when Cortes saw the crowd part and the throne being lowered, he dismounted. I glimpsed Moctezuma before he was again surrounded by attendant princes and I saw a man of middle age dressed in a pure white robe like a priest of Plumed Serpent. He had left behind his gold crown of the Sun, but wore sandals with golden soles so he would walk, as we said, on sunbeams. He had put on a single necklace of jade and opals.

But my lord appeared even more regal, his armor glinting, a sight new to the Aztecs, his helmet bright as a polished mirror. On it he wore five curling feathers I had chosen and arranged, the clean white of Plumed Serpent's wind clouds, one for each direction and a fifth for the holy center. The white feathers also recalled his virgin birth. His armor seemed part of him; he appeared to be a creature sheathed in silver like the beautiful Shell Prince of legend who emerged from the sea encrusted in pearl, gleaming and magical.

I hoped that Cortes would simply stand and let Moctezuma approach to kneel and kiss the earth—I had advised this. But when my lord saw Moctezuma advancing on foot with two princes supporting each arm, he strode forward impulsively, opening his arms wide to embrace Moctezuma, a gesture that encompassed the whole city, the world and all its people.

Two of the princes—Falling Eagle was one of them—rushed to prevent this greeting. One exclaimed, "Sacrilege! No!" Yet it was more than sacrilege they dreaded; they were terrified for Moctezuma. Cortes hesitated, and I hurried to be at my lord's side when the two gods spoke to each other.

It seemed that two worlds were meeting: the world of the present, embodied in Moctezuma and in his lords, in the temples rising behind them; in Cortes was the world of the past reborn, Plumed Serpent's world of Tula, whose gardens were long dead but seemed to bloom again today. Moctezuma felt as I did and spoke my own thoughts when he greeted Cortes.

"With great trouble, O Lord, you have arrived here in your own land, your own city, to take your throne. I have guarded that throne for you."

I kept my eyes from Moctezuma's face, as was proper, but when he spoke I saw his hands trembled, and at last he had to clasp them to have control. He was terrified, yet despite the panic inside him, he kept his dignity before the people.

I expected Cortes to reply, but instead he shook his head slightly and gazed silently at Moctezuma, who continued the greeting, haltingly now.

"Your departed servants, the kings who were my ancestors, also preserved your city. I only wish, Lord, they could rise from their graves to behold your face as I do, most welcome Lord."

As I said these words in Spanish, words I had longed to hear, my lord seemed disconcerted, although no one else noticed it.

"Now you must rest with your companions, these lords from the mists and oceans. You must take your ease in the home I have prepared for you."

I waited for my lord to accept his kingdom, but he only said, "I have come with love for Moctezuma and no harm will come to him. Later we will speak of important matters."

Then we moved forward, Cortes following, pausing a moment for my lord to place a necklace of lovely glass beads around Moctezuma's neck. Moctezuma touched the glass tentatively, then his fingers ceased to tremble. He had won favor.

A messenger arrived breathless with a gift Moctezuma had just sent for, also a necklace, but this one of gold wrought in symbols of Plumed Serpent. As the First Speaker reverently placed it around Cortes's neck, I heard sighs and muffled exclamations from the crowd. "Plumed Serpent," they whispered. "Plumed Serpent."

Moctezuma, after meeting Cortes face to face, had recognized the god. He believed. In my relief and happiness at his believing I wanted to say that he had no reason for fear, he should rejoice in the new world of justice my lord had often spoken of. I even forgot that Moctezuma was my enemy—which was in itself a beginning of that better world.

We advanced slowly into the city, and with every step I felt more lightheaded with victory. It was as though I had eaten peyote for a rite—the colors of the flowers and banners blazed like fire.

The great canoe basin near the palaces and the main temple was packed with boats filled with silent spectators. They watched gravely as we passed the serpent wall, and I heard a vast sigh when we turned into the entrance of the palace of King Face of the Water Lord, Moctezuma's father, ruler two generations ago. This had been appointed our headquarters, the largest residence in the world, and by giving Cortes his father's house, Moctezuma further announced his subjugation. Cortes was his father, his lord.

I remembered the building from childhood. It had housed a convent of temple priestesses, for it stood almost in the shadow of the shrines of Smoking Mirror and Hummingbird. Somewhere in its vast recesses the imperial treasure was kept, and several hundred men of Moctezuma's honor guard, young bachelors or male lovers, had lived here. Now it was empty except for a swarm of servants who bustled about the countless rooms, lighting braziers of charcoal and perfume in every chamber. The old palace was chill and shadowy in November.

In the central courtyard Moctezuma ushered Cortes to a throne covered with beaten gold set with jewels. "Your true place is waiting," Moctezuma said, and Cortes, again after a hesitation, took his seat. For me it was a triumphal moment; but my lord seemed to have no pleasure in it.

"This is your home." Moctezuma seemed to grant Cortes not just this residence but the whole city. "Eat and take rest. I shall return soon."

The First Speaker and his retinue of five hundred nobles withdrew. For a moment the Spaniards said nothing; they looked at the splendor around them, the cedar beams and fine carpets, still unbelieving. They stared at the magnificence, then at each other. At last someone—I think it was Cristobal Olid, who had been so frightened earlier—burst out laughing. Then everyone laughed, relief passing from one to another like a torch in darkness. The serving slaves must have thought these gods from the ocean were utterly demented.

"I smell food," Pedro Alvarado shouted.

"Smell but don't touch a bite until this building is secure," said Cortes. He seemed to be the only one who was not giddy with relief. Unsmiling, he gave orders. The palace was searched for hidden entrances; the cannons were mounted on the roof and sentry posts designated. Quickly the house of King Face of the Water Lord became a Spanish fortress, but even then Cortes would not permit the men to eat until Father Olmedo and the chaplain had celebrated mass in thanks for our safe entrance.

"Only Our Lord Jesus Christ could have performed this miracle for us," Cortes announced, his voice ringing in the courtyard. I knew he was also thinking of another god, although he would not name him.

Cortes kept the men and himself so busy checking the guns, supplies and defenses that not a moment was given to rejoicing in the day's success. Twice I tried to approach him to praise his success, then I realized he did not wish to speak of it. I could not understand why he should be troubled, even angry, only a few hours after his greatest victory, the entrance into Tenochtitlan.

I wandered through the immense palace, exploring the patios, admiring the pools and flowers although the building had the grim style of two generations ago. I heard excited voices coming from a room near the royal banquet hall and found Jaime Garay and the officer Gonzolo Sandoval. The chamber was small, probably designed for smoking and intimate conversations, and standing on either side of a doorway were the corpses of two young men in royal attire, the bodies carefully tanned and dried to preserve them and painted with cosmetics. Each held an unlighted torch in a propped-up hand.

"Statues or corpses?" Jaime asked, but his ashen face showed he knew the answer. I thought the figures powerful and beautiful, almost alive. I liked the idea that although they were dead, the two princes could hold torches to give light in darkness. I had seen similar works, but none so beautiful.

"They were sons of the ruler of a city the Aztecs conquered," I explained. "Now they serve as Moctezuma's torchbearers. They are famous everywhere."

Garay muttered about savagery and satanism, two words I had come to know well lately. Sandoval, my age and so no older than the princes, exclaimed, "Moctezuma seems civilized, yet he keeps these grisly things. Disgusting!"

Again I marveled that the Spaniards, who held life cheap and in battle killed almost as sport, were so concerned about the dead. To me they seemed perverse and superstitious. My lord would have a hard time welding these two worlds into one as he spoke of doing.

I had still not talked with Cortes when Moctezuma returned in the afternoon with a group of nobles, all of them dazzling in their jewels and finery. Another golden throne was brought, so now the Speaker and my lord occupied equal seats. This I thought represented a subtle shift in the last few hours. Moctezuma had been changed from servant and supplicant to fellow king. He was no longer dressed in priestly white but wore royal green and carried the staff of a monarch. I wondered which nobles had been advising him, cautioning him not to surrender but to negotiate. All the Aztec faces were averted, and I could guess nothing. In the crowd I saw Lord Wolf's Paw, a ghost of himself. Certainly this haggard man had not advised Moctezuma to make a show of equality. When I caught his eye, he looked quickly away and cringed as though we shared an indecent secret.

I managed to look straight into Moctezuma's face, hard for me although I was servant of a far more powerful god-in-man. Moctezuma, who had lived almost a full sheaf of fifty-two years, did not seem an old man at all. A thin beard lengthened a face already long, and his eyes were disconcerting—too clear and penetrating, uneasy with the burden of godhood. His gaze was constantly wary and shifting, as though he watched invisible specters. But otherwise his manner conveyed power and assurance.

After a ceremony of greeting, Moctezuma began. "Long before you came here, Malintzin, I knew of your forerunners who landed on the coast of the eastern sea." He went on to give dates and details. He was in closer touch with the Maya than I had thought possible. "I followed the prophecies of your arrival. My own sister returned from her grave as your herald—if it was of you she spoke. Was it, Malintzin?"

Cortes bowed—which could have meant anything. Why would he not simply say yes and end the matter?

"I watched your journey from the coast with admiration, applauding your victories as I saw them in pictures my artists drew."

Cortes thanked him. "My friends do come from lands where the sun rises," he said. "I have been sent here by King Carlos to urge you to become a Christian."

My lord glanced at me and said in a low tone, but sharply, "Are you translating my exact words? Be careful. Perhaps you need Brother Aguilar's help."

"Yes, my lord." Probably I did. When Cortes began to talk of King Carlos, I always found it difficult. This lord was more than an earthly ruler, it seemed; maybe part of the Trinity. I suspected from overhearing talk in camp that he had not sent Cortes here, that he had never even heard of Cortes any more than the almighty Ometeotl, Lord-Lady of the Universe, had heard of me.

Aguilar stepped forward eagerly, and Cortes said, "Ask the great Moctezuma if he will become a vassal of King Carlos."

We asked this, although Aguilar's Maya dialect did not help much. I suspected Moctezuma took King Carlos for yet another, more powerful aspect of Plumed Serpent.

"Oh, yes, I will be his vassal," Moctezuma replied so quickly that Cortes was taken aback. He was not used to instant victories.

Moctezuma, still smiling, asked, "Are you and all your companions vassals of the same ruler? You are brothers and united?"

It was a shrewd question. Could he know of the quarrels, the dissension in our ranks?

"We are all brothers in love and friendship," Cortes replied blandly, for it was the type of deception he was used to. "We are closely bound together in service to our king." Cortes paused, then added strongly, "Bound as you are now by your own words."

"Yes." Moctezuma nodded in relief and content. "I am one with you now. Brothers in love and friendship."

Suddenly Moctezuma seemed weary, as though he had managed to survive an ordeal but it had left him exhausted. He ordered gifts presented to everyone—a diversion, I thought—then left, courteously but in haste.

"My lord," I exclaimed, keeping myself from embracing Cortes. "He has become the king's vassal. You have won another victory."

"Perhaps. We will speak of it later." He turned away abruptly and went to inspect, for the fifth time, the placement of the cannons on the roof.

That night I placed flowers and incense in the chamber we were to occupy. I had dishes of sweetmeats for our celebration, and I set out half a flagon of Spanish wine I found among the provisions for saying mass. Guards were posted outside against intruders, and the altar candles burned to ward off evil.

But my lord came in late and ill tempered, complaining of the sentries. I waited until at last he spoke of what really troubled him, his voice agitated. He almost whispered, as though he were afraid of being overheard, although no one could have crept within bow shot.

"As you know so well, Marina, Moctezuma thinks I am a god or demon. He said as much this morning and tried to make me claim it. You understand this is impossible for me. No matter what the consequences, it is impossible!"

I looked away, answering carefully. "Who knows what Moctezuma thinks? And if he is not hostile, does it matter?"

He took my arms, gazed into my face, and I saw torment in his eyes. "Can you not understand that it matters if I lose my soul? Is that a small thing?" Then he sighed and released me, running his hand across his forehead. "No, you cannot know. You probably do not know what sin is. In religion, you are an innocent."

I said nothing. It would have been sinful to contradict him when he believed this so completely.

"Apart from damnation—which I suppose you cannot understand—do you know what would happen if such a report reached the king? What if he heard that I claimed to be a demon or a wizard? A Christian who spread such heresy would probably not be allowed to live, much less rule as viceroy of this land. And what is the use of conquest if I cannot rule?"

"My lord, let me worry about these matters for you." I tried to move into his arms, but he turned away. "If I tell Moctezuma what I truly believe, it can be no lie—and no fault of yours."

A doorway led to a terrace overlooking the city. He leaned in it, gazing at the night, at the streets and canals gleaming under the fullness of Lady Moon who was great with child. In the temples fires were being rekindled for the end of the Unlucky Day. Sacrifice would resume tomorrow; the sun would be fed.

"I thought it was my destiny to bring this land to God," he said. "To build His kingdom on earth here. No man in history has had such a chance before. Who am I? Nothing! Less than nothing, except I am a Spaniard and a Christian. Yet God has given me this opportunity. I told you of the vision I had in Cuba—it was so real that I can still hear the trumpets. To achieve that dream I would be more than willing to seize this city by deceit. But not by the single lie that is loathsome and fatal to me."

He moved from the window into the shadows where I could not see his face, but I knew his pain and his anger from his voice. "Today Father Olmedo and the chaplain heard Moctezuma take me for a pagan god, a devil, and had not the courage to deny it. Much worse, I did not deny it either."

"But you have never made such a claim, my lord!"

He gave a small, bitter laugh. "No. But *you* have, my dear. And I have let you be believed. Today it went past this. I was offered the kingdom as a gift to a devil. Even my own priests are happy to accept this!"

He stepped into the moonlight again. The shadows of the room's hundred columns wavered and swayed in torchlight. Cortes sank onto the bed of mats, weary and desolate. The god was far away tonight, leaving him only a man, human and filled with uncertainty. I loved him now simply as a woman loves a man. Such times were brief and precious.

I kneeled near him and spoke gently. "You are disturbed by the frailness of language, my lord. You always say that what you have done so far has been by the power of God."

"Yes, and that is true. How else could we have survived?"

"Then God is with you. That is what Moctezuma means. He also speaks of legends, but still he means the god within."

"No, not so simple." Cortes sighed. "I do not understand these gods and demons. For you, they are everywhere. We cannot take a step without treading on a god."

Or moving through one in the air, I thought. "Try to understand, my lord," I was almost pleading now, something I had sworn to myself never to do. "If one tree in a forest towers above all others, we say it is a god—greater, more powerful. We do not mean its bark and wood and sap, but its spirit. We feel its presence. We feel the same with rivers and mountains. When you look upon Smoking Man or Mountain of the Star, you feel their godhood. So it is with certain men, too. They have spirits like mountains or tall trees. You know a god is in them. Is that not the same as being blessed by Saint James or Virgin Mary—which is good, not evil. That is what Moctezuma feels in you, and what I feel. You are not deceiving either of us."

He shook his head. "You have caught me in a web of words, and I would like to surrender. Partly I believe you. But there is more. Aguilar has mentioned a certain demon, a snake with feathers. A snake, God save us! The devil's own body. You and Moctezuma, I suspect, would both like to have me be this serpent come back in human form. No, my dear, it is not as simple as high mountains and tall trees or the blessing of Saint James."

I could see what was coming and felt panic. Tomorrow, if this mad reasoning continued, he would behave like Moctezuma, pulling up his sleeves to show the human flesh of his arms, proving nothing but giving weapons to Moctezuma's nephews who were already looking at us with hate that went beyond the doubting of godhood. They wanted our hearts and blood—and I knew it.

Aguilar, I supposed, had caused this trouble. Aguilar, whose head was an empty cave with bats of theology flapping about in the darkness. Thinking of Aguilar gave me an idea, perhaps hopeless, but anything was worth trying to assure Cortes and stop him from some wild denial of his godhood. Gods, even Plumed Serpent, are easily offended and once openly denied might leave Cortes and not return again. I had to make an attempt even if I sounded like a fool.

"Father Olmedo tells us that with God and Christ all things are possible, my lord. Could it not be that long ago Christ gave my people this legend of a divine power coming from the eastern sea? Could not this be His design to pave the way for the coming of Christians and God's kingdom here?"

I shuddered a little, knowing the Lords of Darkness and even

Plumed Serpent himself might be listening to my blasphemy. If so, let them inflict their torments. I had caught my lord's interest, so I went on quickly.

"Surely it would be wicked of you, my lord, not to take advantage of what God has created for you—short of any sinful lie, of course."

At last my lord the Captain smiled. "You can argue like a whole council of bishops—but I believe you may be right. At least it is worth thinking on." Taking my hand, he drew me beside him. "In war or even in love—yes, in love, my dear—I can lie like a Muslim, then fall asleep with a clear conscience. But lies that offend God I cannot tell. And you, my dear, must never tell them for me."

"No, my lord. Believe me, no!" Tomorrow, I thought, the god would return and he would cease to worry.

"You have found some Spanish wine," he exclaimed. "I'll have some now."

As I poured it for him, I knew all would be well.

Just before morning in the false dawn, the Spaniards were aroused by alarming noises. Each day in Tenochtitlan began with the sacrifice of captives and of cock quails at the temple next door to the palace. Quails are speckled white on black so they are the thousand stars of the Sky Serpent; they are the night that must be killed before Lord Sun can rise. The Sun drinks their blood and breakfasts on the hearts of morning victims. The humans usually die quietly, but the quails set up a terrible squawk.

Also, the palace and temple were near the Royal Zoo, whose meat-eating inmates were fed the leftovers of sacrifice. So when the quail cocks screamed, an animal chorus raised a hungry clamor, anticipating the daily feast. Jaguars and pumas roared, ocelots yowled, coyotes and wolves joined with howling and barking. This uproar frightened the Monkey People, who screamed loudest of all.

Spaniards leapt from their mats and snatched up arms. Then calm was restored when they learned the racket came from penned animals. But minutes later it grew light enough for them to see blood trickling down the sluices of the nearby temple, which unnerved them. Yesterday's relief at having entered the city unopposed suddenly changed to dismay.

Alonzo Avila, commander of the guard that morning, leaned

over a parapet better to see the flowing blood and said bitterly, "We are trapped in this hell pit. They have probably cut the causeways." His remark instantly became a rumor, and Cortes himself had to reassure the men that all was well.

The alarm, although it was a false one, did him good; yesterday's doubts were gone; the god resumed leadership. "Send word to the Emperor Moctezuma that I shall repay his visit this morning."

Cortes chose four captains and five ordinary soldiers to accompany him. The soldiers did not go along as guards but as representatives of the army; my lord was careful that the men felt they had a say in things even when they did not.

Moctezuma's palace, which had been completed only a few years ago, was smaller than his father's but far more beautiful. Twenty large doors opened onto the streets that bounded it, and inside were three garden courtyards luxuriant with flowering shrubs, many of them exotic and unknown to me. I thought of my Uncle Willow and his badly paid quest. Which of these had he discovered?

The Spaniards gaped at walls built of alabaster, jasper and marble, young Gonzolo Sandoval uttering an involuntary, "God! This must be heaven!" when we entered Moctezuma's inner apartments where a hundred carved animal gods seemed to race across the ceilings.

Moctezuma, seeming delighted by the visit, took Cortes's hand in a practiced imitation of the handshake he had discovered only yesterday. He seated Cortes on his right, on his own couch, and insisted that all the Spaniards sit down on little, low stools that Spaniards so hated and complained of.

"Welcome, my brothers in love and friendship!" he said, and it was more than a greeting. He believed the words; it gave him pleasure to speak them. I wondered how a ruler so fierce could give himself over so completely, with such happiness. But I remembered how many years he had lived in fear of Plumed Serpent's coming, of the dread day of the prophecies. Now that day had passed and he himself was still safe and honored. Perhaps his joy was relief at deliverance from a fate unimaginable.

So that the interview might be intimate, he had dismissed all the servants, the musicians and dwarfs. Only four of his nephews attended him, and they remained discreetly in the background, turned away and pretending invisibility. I stood behind the couch between the two lords and also tried to be invisible.

Today it was Cortes who began the conversation, speaking the words of religion I knew so well from so many repetitions. My task was easy. He spoke of Jesus Christ who suffered death to save the world, was buried and rose on the third day.

"Like my sister," said Moctezuma. I did not translate.

Cortes suddenly leaned forward and used words I had not heard before, although the ideas were not unfamiliar. "He made the sky and the earth and the sea and the sands. He created everything in the world and gives us the waters and dews. Those creatures your priests hold as gods are only devils. Their looks are horrible and their deeds worse. What use are they? My Lord Moctezuma, wherever we have raised our crosses, these demons flee and dare not come back."

Several of the Spaniards murmured, "Amen." They were moved by the plain words and so was I—for it was the god who spoke them.

"In time the king will send saintly men to explain all this to you, far better men than we are."

Better men? He and his companions had just taken the greatest city in the world. What men could be better? I did not understand, and I did not think my lord would waste time with the ugliness of humility.

Moctezuma toyed for a moment with his jade necklace, touching the ornaments of Hummingbird and Smoking Mirror. "Malintzin, your words are not new to me, for my messengers heard you speak these things to other peoples. I know about the three gods and a cross." He drew in his breath, then looked directly into Cortes's face. For once his eyes did not waver. "We hold our own gods to be good. No doubt you feel the same way about yours. So we need not talk of this again." It was final; he had drawn a line.

In the silence that followed, the birds singing outside near a fountain sounded unnaturally loud. The Spaniards, perched uncomfortably on the low stools, glanced at each other and shifted their feet.

Then Moctezuma laughed, seeming relieved that this challenge, too, was safely passed. "Before we leave this talk of gods forever, there are some things I should say. I tried to prevent your coming here because I heard that you unleashed thunder and lightning. Also that the lord horses devoured whole towns full of people. I did not really believe this nonsense, of course. Still, one must be careful."

Moctezuma stood up. I noticed he was tall for an Aztec, although not tall for a Spaniard. "I know you have been told that I am a god as you are supposed to be." He was wearing a plumed mantle, and suddenly he thrust his arms from it, raising them high, baring them, turning them this way and that like a dancer that all might see. "Look! They are flesh and blood. I can be touched."

He touched himself, throwing off the mantle, clasping his own arms and then his chest and shoulders, gripping and pinching his coppery skin. "And like all men I must one day die."

His nephews seemed to shrink into the corners, cringing in mortification, and I wished the Earth Monster would open his jaws and gulp me down. Of course his arms were flesh! What had that to do with the holiness and godhood of his office? I knew in youth he had tried to escape his fate, to reject all power and live a humble life. Had his reign been so lonely that now he longed to embrace the first equal who had ever presented himself?

These confused thoughts were tumbling in my head, and I stumbled on the translation, repeating, "Like all men I must one day die."

"Not for many years, I trust, great emperor," said Cortes, laughing also, but uneasily. To the Spaniards, who were his witnesses, he said, "We have tried to bring him the Word of God. We have done our best."

When I did not translate this, Moctezuma suddenly leaned toward me, and his strength made me draw back. Whatever he might say, there was a special power in him. "What did Malintzin say just now, daughter?"

"Only that you are a great and wise emperor, my lord."

Moctezuma did not quite smile. "Let us hope the coming days will prove him right."

We left then, pausing to accept still more gifts from Moctezuma, offerings sullenly presented by the shamefaced nephews.

"You overwhelm us with kindness," said Cortes.

"No, it is you who are kind to me, brothers." The emperor pressed his own turquoise ring into Cortes's hand with the eagerness of a debtor paying a long overdue obligation. But I suspected no gifts could ease the burden of Moctezuma, he so completely believed Cortes's godhood and doubted his own.

For four days no Spaniard left the palace where we were fortified. Cortes paced and chafed and slept little. Early the fifth morning he slammed his fist on a table and said, "We cannot stay penned here forever. They will grow used to us, and that will make them bold."

He decided to study the city and make plans, but there was only one spot from which every street could be viewed, the high sanctuary of Hummingbird built in the adjoining town by the merchants of Tlaltelolco. So I was sent with Aguilar to inform Lord Moctezuma of our intended visit to the temple. With us went the youngest Spaniard in the army, a boy named Ortega, who was quick with languages and knew many Aztec words.

Moctezuma was having breakfast behind a golden screen, since no one was allowed to see him doing so human an act as eating. The boy Ortega was old enough to ogle the four lovely girls who presented the royal food. While we waited I counted fifty jars of foaming chocolate being offered and either rejected outright or turned back after a sip had been taken. The leftover chocolate, worth the price of two or three slaves, was given to the emperor's dwarfs and hunchbacks, who hung about like dogs at a feast.

I explained our errand in a loud voice, and after a long hesitation Moctezuma replied. He sounded upset, even annoyed.

"This I have not prepared for. Must the visit to the temple be today?"

"Today, great lord. That is Malintzin's will."

"Then make sure his servants do nothing to outrage the gods or the people. But you have my permission."

Permission, of course, had not been asked, which he well knew. As we left, Ortega, who surprisingly had understood it all, whispered in Spanish, "He consents but does not like it. He is only turning a good face to bad weather."

The boy liked to talk in sailor's expressions, but this time he spoke a larger truth. Moctezuma, in this and in all matters, had decided he could not change the storm winds, so he smiled into them.

Before we could assemble our party to leave, Moctezuma himself was already on his way to the temple, carried in state, his three heralds preceding him with their golden wands of office. Our procession had no less dignity, for Cortes and all the horsemen led two hundred soldiers marching in close order.

But that order proved hard to keep. When we moved into the teeming, overflowing market, the Spaniards paused to gape and exclaim and even broke ranks in their astonishment at the abundance of rare merchandise. Heaped high were tobacco, cochineal, jaguar and fox skins, cocoa, amber, cloth of cotton and feathers, work in gold and silver and every other treasure the world had to offer. Vendors haggled over prices and buyers offered payment in shells or jade or cocoa beans and often with goose quills filled with gold dust.

Bernal Diaz exclaimed, "My hometown has the biggest annual fair in all Spain and it is not half so grand as this—which happens every day."

He was also astonished that there were watchmen to keep order and judges to check weights and measures. His town, I thought, must be a backward place, rather like Jalisco.

We reformed ranks and moved from the market into the temple yard, a great plaza paved with polished white stones. A flock of old women kept busy all day scrubbing and sweeping so that not so much as a mote of dust sullied the holy precinct. The temple itself, whose grandeur had once brought grief and slaughter upon its builders, loomed before us like a mountain. Gazing at it, I thought suddenly of Lady Iztac. She used to tell the women at the outpost of the wonders she knew in the city, vividly recalling twenty days in her childhood when each day a thousand captives were offered up to Hummingbird, half of them at this shrine. Here in this plaza she had stood to watch, hour after hour, day after day, ". . . until the priests' arms almost dropped off from the labor of wielding the blades."

Moctezuma waited for us at the top of the temple's famous stairway of a hundred and fourteen steps, so high and steep that no one could approach the gods easily and with a haughty bearing. Nobles were usually carried up to the high sanctuaries by special servants, practiced climbers, around whose shoulders they crooked their jeweled arms. Moctezuma had already sent down his own bearers to assist Cortes, but he waved them away. No Spaniard would be helped for fear of showing weakness. But I was pleased to be whisked to the top by strong, surefooted men and glad to arrive on the great platform without gasping and panting.

"Malintzin, my beloved brother, you must be tired from such a climb!" exclaimed Moctezuma, offering Cortes his hand.

"Not at all. Neither I nor my friends ever tire from effort." It was as close as he came to admitting the strength of Plumed Serpent.

From this height the city and lake and far towns lay spread like a carpet, broad squares of white, blue and yellow. Moctezuma led Cortes to a vantage point and displayed the world he owned with a sweep of the imperial arm, a gesture at once proud and casual, like a Maya prince exhibiting his concubines. My lord the Captain studied the bridges and the six causeways spanning the water; he watched the fleets of canoes and barges plying the lake, then smiled with courteous admiration while, I knew, he made his war plans.

"It is too big," said Pedro Alvarado sharply. "We have entered the biggest net on earth."

My lord turned and spoke quietly, not just to Alvarado but to all the officers and men who stood nearby awed and uneasy. "Gentlemen, what a favor God has granted us. We stand here in the very throne room of the devil. When this city falls—as it soon will—this great world we see is ours for the taking."

Staring down at the vastness of the city, I had faith, because only a god could have had such a vision of conquest. Otherwise the dream would have been madness.

Father Olmedo had been the last to arrive at the top, and he was still puffing when Cortes said to him, "Now might be a good time to suggest that a church be built here. Shall we ask Moctezuma?"

Olmedo glanced around nervously, saw the bloodstained attendants with their knives. "Perhaps not quite yet, my son. We should not be hasty."

My lord nodded. By now he was unsurprised at lack of zeal in everyone but himself. Yet he seemed compelled to act; I knew the god was urging him on. "If we cannot have a church yet, then we should see what is already here. Marina, ask Moctezuma to show us his gods."

I asked, concealing alarm. The Spaniards looked wary, and Cortes's smile faded when Moctezuma, after consulting the priests, agreed to lead us into the sanctuary. "Ask my brothers to be reverent and seemly," he said.

Parting leather curtains, leather of human skin that in life had been decorated with tattooing, we came into the dim presence of Hummingbird of the Left. The god-in-stone crouched silently, awesome and beautiful, girdled with serpents. In the shadows he seemed gigantic, and his entire body was encrusted with pearls and opals.

"He is the Decider of Wars and ruler in the Seventh House of Heaven, so the color blue is sacred to him." Moctezuma spoke softly, reverently. His voice was much like the voice of Cortes when he mentioned the Blessed Virgin. "We Aztecs are his chosen people. He elected us above all others to rule the world."

"That is quite a necklace he wears," murmured Pedro Alvarado, greed in his eyes—which were so blue that Hummingbird must have admired them. I translated, knowing the praise would please Moctezuma.

"The necklace was my gift to him. It is made of the heads and hearts of conquered kings wrought in silver."

Three fresh hearts roasted on a nearby brazier, and the air was heavy with copal incense. Some of the Spaniards coughed.

Smoking Mirror's shrine, separated only by more curtains, was almost as impressive. I avoided the flat stare of the god's luminous eyes, feeling I was in the presence of enchantment. We were old enemies, he and I. Despite that, I gave grudging admiration to the lovely obsidian mirror he wore for a leg in place of the one that the Earth Monster had bitten off.

Smoking Mirror stared through the thin haze at Cortes, hateful and fierce, seeing through the human flesh to the spirit of Plumed Serpent within.

"Lord of hell, lord of darkness, king of wizards and enchanters, ruler of eagles, the sacred one-in-four." Moctezuma intoned the hymn like a man telling the rosary. The Spaniards near me paled, trembled and tried not to retch. They hurried outside in the middle of the next prayer.

Cortes lingered a moment to show he was not disturbed, but he took deep breaths once we were in the sunshine. He turned to Moctezuma and laughed, falsely, I thought. "Why, sir, you are too wise not to know these idols are devils and evil. Let me set a cross here."

Father Olmedo blanched and whispered, "No, my son, not yet!"

When the temple priests, standing near, understood the request, they buzzed like singing snakes. "Blasphemy!" one cried, and another began a whole litany of curses.

I thought Cortes, seeing Moctezuma's shocked expression, would leave off, but he was determined to test the Speaker's limits. "If not a cross, then we will clean one of these rooms and install an image of the Blessed Virgin."

The priests were in consternation. A young one shook his stiff, matted locks in my face, as though I and not Cortes had proposed this desecration. "You would put a woman in the place of Hummingbird? A woman! Vileness, filth!"

Moctezuma, struggling to hide his shock, said, "Malintzin, if I had known you would speak such an insult, I would not have showed you our sacred gods."

Cortes seemed satisfied by the upset he had caused; he had achieved some aim—although I could not tell what it was. "Time we were going, I think," he said, glancing at the sun. "Will you accompany us, sir?"

Moctezuma shook his head, almost weeping, and said to me, "Explain that I must stay and make atonement to the gods for any insult."

We descended the stairs, and this time no help was offered. I supposed that Moctezuma had pierced himself with the seven thorns of penance long before we reached the bottom.

As we crossed the sacred plaza fronting the temple, the Spaniards muttered nervously about the horrors of the shrines and the vastness of the cities surrounding us. Even Pedro Alvarado, so often given to boisterous but uneasy laughter these days, seemed subdued. "The den of Satan," he said.

But my lord the Captain, speaking more to himself than to anyone else, said softly, "Those demons escaped us only for today. The devil's reign is ending here soon, I swear it."

I felt new power in his voice and turned toward him, startled, and saw the god gazing calmly from his eyes. My own apprehension dissolved.

I had earlier sensed that Cortes was coming to believe what I had told him, that his mission here was preordained and blessed, that the legends were stratagems of Jesus Christ and Virgin Mary. Accepting this, he had shed fears of blasphemy and grown in strength. Meanwhile the god was stirring fitfully within him. Now meeting Hummingbird and Smoking Mirror face to face had fully awakened Plumed Serpent; the divine enemies had seen each other, taken each other's measure.

Now the gods were ready. They would bring the whirlwind.

19

The Clash of Gods

The first miracle that showed Plumed Serpent was at work came only hours after my lord had visited the temple. Some Spanish soldiers who for two days had been searching the palace for a proper place to build an altar noticed faint marks that might conceal a hidden doorway. That night in secret the plaster was chipped away, the door unsealed, and behind it lay the fabled treasure hall of King Face of the Water Lord, a chamber heaped floor to ceiling with gold, silver and jade. The beam of a hooded lantern flashed on opals, pearls, necklaces, bracelets, gold in ingots, slabs and sun discs.

The officer Juan Velazquez whispered in awe, "It is the storehouse of King Midas." And I, not understanding, corrected him. "King Axayacatl," I said.

The officers were eager to remove everything, even the feather mantles they despised as effeminate, and actually had necklaces in their hands when Cortes halted the plundering.

"We are guests here and must behave like gentlemen, sirs. In time all this will be ours—but properly and legally."

I supposed my lord would swear all the finders to secrecy, but instead he summoned every Spanish soldier, quietly and in groups of three or four, to view the splendor. Then he ordered the door resealed and plastered over as before.

Later in our chamber, lying on our mat in the darkness, he

chuckled. "That should whet their appetites. Did you see their eyes? Hungry as pelicans, all of them. Now I will be free to do as I will. For the sake of what is in that room they will follow me straight through the gates of hell if I command them."

So Moctezuma himself gave Cortes the means to press forward.

The next day Pedro Alvarado said with a guffaw, "What a fool this great Moctezuma is! Who but a fool would leave his hens behind when he's renting his house to foxes?"

The soldiers he spoke to, including his own brothers, did not answer, for they had already come to respect Moctezuma's generosity and kingly demeanor. The real fool, I thought, was Alvarado, who could not understand simple logic. Moctezuma was not lending the palace to foxes but to gods; and the treasure, down to the last topaz, belonged to the gods anyhow. He did not take it away—which would have been simple—nor did he make it easy for the Spaniards to find. Scenting out the hiding place was another test of godhood, one the Spaniards easily passed. Moctezuma behaved sensibly. What could have been plainer?

As on the beach at Veracruz, the presence of gold changed the atmosphere and the palace became as taut as the air on a hillside before a thunderstorm. Cortes watched the men thoughtfully. He quietly put in a word here and there; he arranged discreet conversations. That evening, as I suspected, the officers and certain key soldiers asked him to meet with them; they had urgent matters to discuss. I wondered what idea he had implanted in them that they would now insist he adopt as their own inspiration.

The meeting was held in the hall that had been selected as a chapel. I was asked to wait outside, beyond earshot, in case my knowledge of Aztec customs and religion was needed. Time went by; Lady Moon moved heavily and sluggishly over the open courtyard, devouring the Star Lords as she passed them. I could hear a murmur of tense, insistent voices in the closed and guarded meeting room. Then Gonzolo Sandoval appeared in the doorway and gestured for me to enter.

There were more than a dozen men inside gathered in the shadows, a cluster of tension and conspiracy. My lord the Captain asked me to repeat what the Tlaxcalan crickets had chirped about Moctezuma and some baskets, a report I had heard at the time we were leaving Cholula. Only a week had passed, but a week so extraordinary that it took a moment for me to recall the baskets.

"There were two, about the size of big squashes. Lord Moctezuma let no one see their contents but took them to his private quarters and later to a temple, I think. They seemed to contain magical objects."

Cortes, sitting behind the single candle, was masklike in the strange light. He held a letter up for all to see. "Those baskets, gentlemen, held the heads of two of our comrades who were murdered outside the fort at Veracruz. Moctezuma ordered the heads that he might study them."

There was a shudder in the room, then an angry clamor. "Who? Who was killed?"

Cortes said a name I did not recognize and added, "Also Arguello, poor fellow." I remembered Arguello's great head wreathed and enlarged by a thick, curly beard; an alarming example for Moctezuma to take as a typical Spaniard.

While the men in the room were cursing Moctezuma and quarreling about what should be done, it dawned on me that Cortes had known of these slayings even before we left Cholula. Of course he had kept silent—the army was worried enough already. Now I better understood my lord's private apprehensions.

No one else seemed to notice this matter. Cortes at last silenced the angry clamor, then resumed speaking. "Juan Escalante, our commander at Veracruz, also wrote me that a horse was slain, and by now its head is doubtless in this city."

Again their voices rose. Someone said, "The servants have lately turned sullen. There is a plot afoot. We should have this murdering Moctezuma where we can get our hands on him if they attack."

Bernal Diaz, usually calm, exclaimed, "They could put arsenic in the food. We should act quickly, at once."

Cortes nodded to dismiss me, but as I was leaving, I heard a little more. Alonso Avila, always brash, leaned toward my lord, his black, pointed beard glinting in the light, his nose thin as the rain god's. "I say we arrest this filthy savage and keep him on a tight chain. If he resists, make him pay."

Cortes answered calmly, "Gentlemen, I have heard your suggestion that we take the Emperor Moctezuma into our custody. It is a serious, dangerous venture. I must think about it."

Then I was outside the room, wondering if they could really mean what I thought. Avila and others were actually proposing to seize the sacred person of Moctezuma—which was unthinkable. In six generations no one had so much as frowned at the Revered Speaker. Yet Cortes had just agreed to consider the idea.

I was crossing the courtyard, telling myself that I had misunderstood, when a sudden picture loomed in my memory. I saw Cortes on the steps of the temple in Zempoala, hand on his sheathed sword, shouting to his men to seize the Fat Chief and kill him first if the Totonacs resisted. Seize the king. That had been his thought then. Clearly it was his thought now.

Later I lay on the mats, covered by a blanket against the November cold, but I slept little and my lord did not sleep at all. Always before when he called a meeting and listened to the opinions of others it meant he had made up his own mind. Tonight he paced the room, the terrace; he leaned against the parapet overlooking the plaza, dark except for the street torches now that Lady Moon had fled. He kneeled at the altar, whispering his prayers in a language I now knew to be Latin.

The prayers seemed to give him no relief, and once I heard him speak aloud with anguish in his voice. "What shall I do? Give me the answer." Then, after silence, he prayed again in Latin.

When I did fall asleep for a few minutes, he soon shook my shoulder. My eyes flew open, and he was leaning over me. "Forgive me for waking you. Where is the Aztec army now?"

I managed to pull my wits together. "What Aztec army, my lord?"

"The one they talk about. A hundred thousand men or twice that many. We have never seen these troops. Where are they garrisoned?"

I finally understood what he meant. It was the word "army" that I had not grasped; we had no such thing.

"Everywhere and nowhere, my lord. Almost all men are soldiers when they are called to fight. The rest of the time they are farmers or merchants or scribes or—"

"No army! There is no real army!" He slammed his fist into his palm, excited.

"There are soldiers at outposts, but not many. Tax gatherers also have a few hundred soldiers under arms at all times."

He said gently, "Thank you, my dear. Go back to sleep."

Of course I did not; neither did he. When dawn came he had still made no decision. Then another miracle occurred, a miracle of timing.

The captain of the night guard rushed in, calling out that two Tlaxcalan messengers had arrived in disguise carrying urgent despatches from
the coast. He handed my lord some papers.

Cortes scanned them, nodding as though the news they conveyed
was not surprising. He said, "Summon all officers to the chapel. Order
the men on immediate alert, all under full arms and ready for attack.
Do this quietly! Let everything seem as usual."

As soon as the officer had left, my lord turned to me. "Our
commander at Veracruz and six of his men have been killed, murdered
by Moctezuma's orders apparently on the day he was pledging fidelity
to me." Cortes seemed not angry but pleased by the news and the
treachery. "The whole coast and the hill towns have rebelled."

He folded the papers, thrust them into his belt. This news had
made his decision for him, forced him to make a bold stroke. So the
god, not the man, had finally settled matters and relieved Cortes of
uncertainty. In only a moment he had changed, become certain of
himself and even eager.

I was still kneeling on the mats, wrapped in a blanket and with
my hair loosened for sleep. "My dear Marina, dress yourself quickly
but carefully," he said with a slight smile. "We are calling on Moctezuma this morning. Who knows? He may return here as our guest.
Let us try to persuade him."

Three hours later, after a scene I recall only in nightmares,
Moctezuma yielded and became a captive although he was called a
guest. Afterward many of his own people and even some Spaniards
scoffed at his surrender. I wonder how King Carlos would have
behaved with a god giving him orders and a blade at his throat.

That day in the Fourth Watch when the sun stood high, Moctezuma
left his own palace to enter luxurious imprisonment in the Spanish
quarters, which were, of course, in his own father's palace only a
hundred paces down the street. He made the short move under heavy
guard, but everything was done subtly. There were only two oddities:
he was carried like a man in mourning, in a plain litter his chamberlain
ordinarily used for visiting markets; and the nobles who shouldered the
poles wept openly, keeping silent while tears streaked their faces.

A small crowd quickly gathered, and rumors flew. Moctezuma,
to prevent any disturbance, called out, "My dear people, I am happy
to spend a short time with my friends. I am safe and well; have no

worry." He saluted them graciously; then the litter was brought inside the walls and the gates closed behind him.

I waited in the courtyard, bowing as I watched him dismount. He had put on a robe of plain cotton, the kind worn for saying prayers, yet when he rose from the litter with his head high and his gaze steady, he seemed splendid, his new nobility unneedful of quetzal plumes and jade. When I saw his changed bearing, the serenity of his face, I unwillingly thought of my father and I turned away.

I had expected a defeated man full of pleas and self-pity. But in accepting captivity, an astonishing change came over him; he shed his fears and indecisions. He wore the mantle of victory, not humiliation.

A suite of apartments was being prepared for him, flustered servants running back and forth between the two palaces, bringing carpets, screens, hangings, even his favorite statues. Soon clerks and scribes arrived with tribute records, for this was more than a change of quarters by Moctezuma—the center of the world's government was being shifted.

Late the next morning, when things were still not quite arranged in the royal apartments, callers began to arrive: the princes of the Triple Alliance and the cities of the lakes to wait on Moctezuma. In the midst of this I was summoned to his presence, supposing he wished me to convey some message to my lord the Captain. I entered the reception hall under the glares of a dozen of the most powerful Aztec lords. His two daughters and his son were also there, and they averted their eyes from me, as though avoiding some vile sight.

I paused just inside the entrance, but Moctezuma waved for me to approach close to him. A servant presented me with a golden pendant, an image of the young corn goddess.

"A token of my gratitude, daughter," he said, and I felt uneasy that he should address me so. "You gave me good advice yesterday."

Behind me Prince Cacama, Lord of Texcoco and Moctezuma's nephew, spoke, his voice sharp with resentment. "What advice, Revered Speaker? Let this lady share her wisdom with all of us." There was a murmur of agreement in the room. I knew the Aztec lords would have been pleased to rip my heart from my chest.

Ignoring them, Moctezuma spoke to me. "You are the servant and consort of my friend and brother Malintzin. Yet I know you are of our people by birth and speech. You will understand what I am about to say."

I bowed my head, keeping silent, aware that I was but an excuse for what he wished to convey to the lords and princes; the message was for them, not me. I kneeled near his low stool when he gestured for me to do so. Moctezuma had been educated as a priest, and now as he spoke of religious matters, his voice took on the pitch and a trace of the singsong lilt of priests who instruct youths in temple courtyards.

"The god Plumed Serpent has appeared among the people many times, no doubt, but we know details of only two visits before the present one. The first great visit happened so long ago that it is past memory even of the Rubber People to whom he gave the secrets of fire, the growing of corn and making of cloth. He taught them the first writing and first poems, then he vanished."

Moctezuma gave us a moment to absorb this well-known bit of history, then continued, his tone louder and more intense. "The god returned as a priest in Tula long afterward to bring those people blessings. But his presence also caused war among the gods, war among peoples. Beautiful Tula was destroyed, its splendor burned to ashes. Now coyotes prowl those ruins."

A few of the listeners nodded in agreement, but the room was tense with hostility and suspicion. Lord Woman Snake wore a mask of acceptance, but a vein in his temple throbbed angrily. I also saw sorrow in the faces of some lords who were ready to weep for the fate that had overtaken the king and the kingdom.

"Plumed Serpent has now arrived as the prophecies foretold. Or you may say his agents and servants are here—it is idle to quibble about the form in which the god shows himself. As you all know, I resisted at first. Now I see matters clearly and will not defy the gods or rage at the inevitable."

Moctezuma rose, strong as a stone god in a temple, an emperor addressing his subjects. "My lords, we shall stand like the great trees near the ocean, bending to this wind from the sunrise, yet be unbroken. Plumed Serpent has come and gone before. Why should he not do so this time? Let us placate him, give him all he seeks and speed him on his way. Yet we must not offend Hummingbird or Smoking Mirror. Smoking Mirror crushed Plumed Serpent in the war that destroyed Tula, drove him to the sea and forced him to flee on his raft of serpents. This could happen again, and we must not be on the losing side of a clash between gods. Our course is clear; we have only to follow it."

He had finished; the future, both the world's and his own, was settled. Moctezuma resumed his seat, motioning for a servant to hand him a pipe of tobacco that had been waiting in a brazier.

After a long pause Prince Cacama spoke. "Lord Speaker, we know you are versed in religion. The rest of us are simple men without the advantages of a priestly background, so we—"

"Since you are untrained in such affairs, you have leave to obey without questioning," said Moctezuma. "Now you are all dismissed to continue the duties of government."

The chamberlain struck twice on a drum to end the council. As the lords withdrew in silent consternation, Moctezuma sat quietly, drawing deeply on his pipe, at peace with himself and imperturbable.

Making the awkward exit without turning my back toward the Speaker yet keeping my eyes downcast, I almost collided with Prince Cacama. For an instant I looked full into his face and saw that he was an ill-favored man, his features too broad, his mouth petulant. He scowled at me, as I expected, and I thought: he resents me in part because I, a woman, am taller than he is. It was irrelevant, even frivolous. But the revelation proved true in time: Prince Cacama could not abide having *anyone* stand above him.

I left Moctezuma's quarters joyful at the decision he had made. The new kingdom—the changed world—could begin at once and without war. Cortes, in all things except religion, had suddenly become emperor of the world; I even felt happy that Moctezuma had somehow achieved a victory in surrendering.

But I did not talk of this with my lord the Captain. That part of him that was Plumed Serpent already knew of Moctezuma's submission, and the affair was too complicated for the human side of Cortes to grasp without misunderstanding. Besides there was little time for questions and answers. The next days were filled with affairs of government as Cortes, acting through the mask of Moctezuma, took command of the state. We were busy every daylight hour, and I did not have the night hours with him for Moctezuma gave him first one, then another, and then a third young woman to lie with, all girls Moctezuma had fathered on court beauties, so he did honor to Cortes, which pleased me. My lord spent several nights with them, then returned to me as I had expected. I wondered if these women would teach him exotic secrets of the royal bed mats; they did not.

At the beginning of the new month the commander who had

attacked and slain the Spaniards on the coast returned to the capital for punishment by order of Moctezuma, and with his officers was executed in public for murder and treason. Both Moctezuma and the victims looked upon this as a holy sacrifice, not a criminal affair, but I did not tell Cortes this for fear of causing confusion. The day of the execution my lord tested his power to the ultimate by fastening Moctezuma's feet in shackles, saying it was because the Speaker might try to interfere with the punishment. This was hardly the real reason: my lord simply wished to demonstrate his power.

Moctezuma, breaking his usual serenity, wept in the shackles, not from pain or from humiliation of his high office, but because Cortes did not trust him. Afterward my lord himself kneeled and undid the fetters, apologizing. "My friend," he said, "if you wish to return to your own palace now, you may."

"No, Malintzin," Moctezuma answered after only a second's hesitation. "I am happier here."

Both these gods were lying, as is the way of gods. And each pretended to believe the other, in the way of humans.

There was never an hour of understanding. Cortes posted guards to make sure Moctezuma did not escape—which, at this time, was the last thing the emperor wished to do. But Moctezuma believed them to be his protectors, not his warders. He gave the guards and all other Spaniards who passed his way presents of gold, silver, cloth and girls. So the Spaniards praised his generosity, never suspecting these were offerings to gods or the servants of gods, not gifts to men. Each day Cortes gave Moctezuma lessons in the Christian religion, which fortunately had no effect. No one appeared to realize that the Speaker's conversion would have meant utter catastrophe for Plumed Serpent.

Meanwhile, Cortes sent out small parties of Spaniards to find the royal gold mines, to search for harbors and make maps, all this with Moctezuma's help. The Speaker, eager to satisfy the Spaniards so they might soon be on their way, suggested that tribute be collected from the cities on the lake. The Spanish officers, needless to say, were quick to accept such assignments and, unluckily, Pedro Alvarado was chosen to lead a party to Texcoco, the proud city ruled by the proud Cacama.

Alvarado returned that day at sunset, having been rowed fifteen miles across the lake with a group of several Spaniards and a score of

Tlaxcalans. The valuables he had extracted from the Texcocans were spread in the courtyard for Cortes to inspect.

"You did well, Pedro. This is more than we asked."

Alvarado chuckled. "All it needed was sweet persuasion—and a little hot tar."

Then the story came out—Alvarado was quite proud of it—that when Cacama proved reluctant to give, he had been stripped naked, bound, and Alvarado had dripped hot tar on his body. "It is a powerful argument, hot tar. The savage squealed awhile, then learned generosity."

My lord paled but concealed his anger. Alvarado was popular with the troops, who liked his bluff manner and crude jokes. Now the men found this story of gall and extortion funny. But I knew Prince Cacama's pride would not brook such treatment, and the next day my crickets told me that Texcoco was seething with rebellion.

Soon Moctezuma's spies brought word of a plot against him hatched by Cacama and four other rulers of lake towns. One of the rebels was Moctezuma's own brother. They were secretly raising an army and would strike in eight days when Plumed Serpent, as the Evening Star, would be weakest.

My lord fell upon the plotters like a plunging hawk. Prince Cacama was lured into a building that stood on stilts above the lake on the Texcoco shore. One of the rooms had a trapdoor, and under it three canoes full of armed men waited in secret. Cacama was seized and netted, then delivered across the lake to Cortes and Moctezuma. He screamed obscenities at his uncle.

"When will Prince Cacama be executed?" I asked.

My lord appeared shocked. "He is of royal blood! One does not slay a prince."

Instead, Cacama's neck was fastened into a link of a huge chain that had been brought from one of the ships. Soon he had four close companions in iron links, the other rebellious princes. Later on people said that execution would have been kinder; it is always easy to choose that particular kindness for someone else. When I imagined the death Cacama would have designed for me, the chain seemed less severe.

As Evening Star waxed in the next days, my lord's power also grew. Moctezuma suddenly decided to swear allegiance to King Carlos —perhaps that was what Cortes wanted, perhaps then he would go away. A public ceremony was held, complete with a Spanish notary. During the swearing of fidelity many of the Aztec nobles wept, and Lord Woman Snake could hardly contain himself. Usually, because I was a woman, he pretended I did not exist, but now he hissed at me, "People should embrace a new ruler with joy, not sorrow."

"Yes, great lord, that would be better," I answered, wondering how many of the subject peoples had joyfully embraced the rule of any Aztec emperor.

The ink was no more than dry on the oath of allegiance when Moctezuma announced that he was giving all the treasure in the vault of King Face of the Water Lord to King Carlos. (Was *that* what Cortes was waiting for? *Now* would he leave?)

"I know you have opened the door of the strong room, so you realize this is no petty offering."

My lord was deeply moved by Moctezuma's gesture, and the other Spaniards were overwhelmed at being given what they had already resolved to steal. All this seemed like quibbling to me, except it confirmed Cortes's power to the people, plainly showing Moctezuma's love.

In the month that followed, the Feast of the Flags, when the Spaniards eyed the naked women dancing and turned from the sacrifices, my lord the Captain seemed to possess everything: immense wealth, the obedience of the god-ruler and safety from his most apparent enemies who remained helpless in his great iron necklace. The people, occupied with their festivals, seemed uninterested.

Now was the time for my lord to be prudent, to gather strength and move warily. This is what the human side, the practical nature of Cortes, would have done; it was what I expected. But I reckoned without his godhood and without Smoking Mirror.

Twice each night at changing hours my lord would wake and quietly go to check the sentry posts. One night in a late watch he gently awakened me, holding a finger to my lips for silence. "Come quickly," he whispered.

We moved without a torch through the maze of palace corridors to the apartments of Moctezuma. A side entrance to a room he used as a chapel was closed off with leather curtains that laced tightly for warmth and privacy. Two sentries stood outside these, leaning and craning their necks to hear what went on inside. Even in the shadows

I could see that their faces were pale with alarm. Cortes gestured for me to listen.

High-pitched, eerie sounds came from the chapel, twitterings and moanings that were neither birdlike nor human. For a moment I did not suspect that any of this was speech; then I caught distorted words. ". . . Not answer . . . I will not speak."

With a sharp blade one of the sentries made a slit near the bottom of a curtain and, kneeling, I peered inside. There was a hazy glow of burning twigs, pitch pine or sandalwood, and I could make out the figures of Moctezuma and his chief priest, both prostrate before an altar above which stood a big stone mirror, a mosaic of obsidian. Another person, a child or a small woman, lay stretched on the altar, arms and legs dangling lifelessly over the edges, a fresh sacrifice. The priest writhed and moaned in a trance as he struggled to his knees, lifting his bloodstained face until it was faintly illuminated by a reflection from the mirror, which I thought was propped to catch the gleam of Lady Moon. Then I realized Lady Moon was dead tonight; the mirror had been turned toward a window so I was seeing a pale flicker of firelight from a platform of the great temple across the way. The fire must have been kindled for this purpose; it was as though the gods crossed from the temple and had entered the chapel, moving through air on the ray of light.

The priest clawed his own cheeks, drawing blood, then uttered again in his strange, nightbird voice. "I will not tell you now . . . not yet." Then his words changed to shrill cries, inhuman noises although they came from the priest's mouth. This was the voice of Smoking Mirror himself, and I had never heard anything so awesome and powerful. I rose and stepped back so my lord could see, my arms covered with goose flesh.

Crouching, he peered into the room, then shuddered. After a moment he stood, leaned against one of the pillars. His face was drained of color; I had never seen him like this, ashen and ill, except at the worst times of his suffering in Tlaxcala. "We have seen the devil," he said so softly that the guards, already terrified, did not hear.

In our own chamber, still shaken, he asked, "Who spoke?"

"Smoking Mirror, my lord. Moctezuma consulted the god, and the god spoke through the priest but would not answer."

"What was that glow of light? I have never seen anything so hellish."

I explained about the mirror and the temple fire. "So if Moctezuma cannot go to the temple, the power of the temple is brought here like witchcraft." He rubbed his hands over his eyes. "That was a corpse on the altar. How could this have happened? I have forbidden it; I have given orders!"

I said nothing. Let my lord learn for himself that Moctezuma bribed the guards daily.

My lord moved to the terrace door. From here only a corner of the great temple was visible, but the flames of the sacrificial fire cast dancing shadows on the stone stairs. Some wild creature, perhaps a caged ocelot in the menagerie, shrieked and another answered. A nightbird cried in a voice like Smoking Mirror's.

"Satan is there and we cannot live beside him. He must be destroyed. Whatever we do here is useless until that is done."

For the first time, the only time, I saw Cortes show fear, and what frightened him was not anything earthly but the gods he often said were powerless.

Although he slept little that night, in the morning Cortes rose brisk and eager. The shadows had gone. He called on Moctezuma earlier than usual, and after the briefest preliminaries courtesy would allow, he bluntly demanded that the great twin shrines of Smoking Mirror and Hummingbird be changed today to a Christian church. "You have lived too long on the edge of evil, Lord Moctezuma."

This was the moment Moctezuma had dreaded, planned against; the confrontation he had given everything to avoid. "It cannot be, Malintzin. The people would never allow it, and the gods themselves would destroy the city."

Like Moctezuma, I too feared this clash of gods, and as I translated the words, I denied to myself that I had any part in the quarrel. Soon I realized that Cortes, like a market vendor, had begun by asking the highest price, one he knew would not be paid. Now that the fears of the night were behind him, he would settle for much less than destruction of the temple.

At last he and Moctezuma, both unwillingly, agreed that one chamber of the temple might be set aside as a shrine for Our Lady. "You will see, Lord Moctezuma!" Cortes exclaimed. "Her pure presence will drive this fiend out."

I would not have translated the words exactly that way, but the page Ortega was listening and I had no choice. Upon hearing them, Moctezuma blanched. "I have only agreed to ask permission from the priests," he said, but Cortes was not listening.

That same afternoon several Spanish soldiers with Father Olmedo, Aguilar and the chaplain climbed to the twin shrines. Cortes himself carried a picture of Our Lady, and Father Olmedo bore a statute of a minor Christian god, a giant named Saint Christopher. No one would have chosen this Christopher but there was no other statue and Our Lady could not be left alone without a holy companion nearby. Christopher would protect her. My lord the Captain was in high spirits, climbing the steep stairs two at a time, pausing for the rest of us to catch up.

Aguilar was exultant but nervous, afraid of the priests who watched us from above like perched vultures. "We really have permission?" he asked Cortes.

"Not only permission, but this, too." Cortes slapped the hilt of his sword.

A moment later Aguilar said to me in a low tone, "I think Father Olmedo is right. Conversion cannot be done by force. It must be by understanding and universal love."

That, I think, is what he meant, but he spoke in Maya and it came out, "Loving everybody in the world." His face was doleful.

"Do you love everybody, Brother Aguilar?" I asked.

"Of course I do." Which, of course, was the same as loving nobody at all.

I stopped at the platform thirteen steps below the top and the shrines. They did not need an interpreter for this task, and I had no wish to confront Smoking Mirror in his own house. I sat quietly on a step, trying to follow my father's way of achieving serenity. I gazed at the magnificent volcanoes, hoping to draw composure from Sleeping Woman, strength from Smoking Man. I contemplated the white purity of their snow crowns.

Above me were sounds of heavy objects being pulled this way and that, a swish of mopping. Father Olmedo sang a hymn, Aguilar's reedy voice joining in uncertainly. Time passed. I had almost achieved harmony with the mountains when I heard angry shouts from one of the shrines. There came a terrible crash, and then a priest was shrieking

Aztec curses. A Spanish soldier raced down the steps with the officer Andres Tapia shouting after him, "Cortes says bring forty men. And double the guard on Moctezuma!"

I scrambled toward the top, hearing more imprecations and yells. Four priests of Smoking Mirror were flapping about the entrance to the god's shrine, one of them brandishing a sacrificial knife, while several Holy Women in gray robes, pilgrims to the temple, wailed and wept. Two Spanish soldiers confronted them, swords drawn. The sanctuary of Smoking Mirror, the god's throne room, had a wide entrance with curtains studded with a hundred bells, copper and silver. I had almost reached this doorway when from the inside a steel blade slashed the curtains, rending them, bringing them down with an ear-splitting clangor on the stone floor. My lord the Captain stood for an instant in the entrance, sword in hand, then vanished into the dark interior.

I was delayed by one of the Holy Women who, mistaking me for a worshiper, seized my arm. "Do not go in, daughter! There is sacrilege."

A priest screamed, "Filth, filth, filth!"

I shook off the woman, reached the open doorway, stumbling over the heap of leather and bells. Blinded by the sun, I saw only shapes of figures inside. Andres Tapia had pinioned the arms of the chief priest as he tried to attack Cortes, who at that second swung a heavy iron bar at the head of Smoking Mirror. The god's golden mask clattered on the altar base. I shielded my eyes from the exposed face lest the sight turn my blood to fire. The mask was broken. The chief priest ceased struggling and began to sob.

I turned away, frightened, as my lord moved to the lesser gods, raised the bar and struck and struck.

"Enough, my son!" cried Father Olmedo. "This will do no good. Think of the danger."

My lord threw down the bar, his work finished. He had grown in power and stature; he was exalted. But when he spoke his voice was soft and gently chiding. "Should we not risk something for God?"

In the next days it appeared that we had risked everything. The city began to stir. The streets were often emptied of men as councils were held in neighborhoods and military orders had conclaves. News of the violation of Smoking Mirror, the sacrilege, raced across the lakes and into the mountains.

The Spaniards nervously applauded Cortes's act but could not understand why he had chosen such a risky time. "What happened up there?" Bernal Diaz asked, scratching his head and frowning. Apparently nothing unusual, no new outrage, had taken place. Cortes had simply tossed caution to the winds in a moment of religious passion.

"It's not like him," said Jaime Garay. "He's always so shrewd, so calculating. He won't even roll dice without considering the odds and wagers."

Only I understood the outrage of the god as he gazed upon his ancient enemy Smoking Mirror. In the time I was with my lord the Captain I knew many remarkable days, saw much that seemed miraculous. But his greatest moment, his purest act, was when, against all prudence, he swung an iron bar and struck the mask from Smoking Mirror. That picture I remember above all others—the god surprised by his own passion.

At this time no rain fell, which was not strange in this season, but the priests fomented rumors that the Rain Bringer had abandoned the land forever, shocked by the presence of a woman's picture in the high temple. A delegation of farmers approached Cortes, their leader displaying some dry, dead corn cobs. "You offended our old gods and brought drought. Now let the new woman god give rain!" It was a challenge, and I suspected that the cobs were actually culls from an old harvest; this was a trick by the priests. But my lord accepted the dare.

The Spanish soldiers were ordered to pray for rain, working in shifts like guard duty. They showed little enthusiasm.

Pedro Alvarado bellowed at the troops. "Down on your knees and pray, you fuckers! Put your backs into it!"

The praying grew louder, but no cloud appeared. "Bring out the women," Cortes ordered. "Get them off their backs and on their knees. Let them pray in any language they know."

For the first time in weeks I saw Flower Pouch and her coterie of harlots, who had all taken to powdering their faces heavily with chalk to look Spanish. They resembled dust dancers at a village festival. The women prayed and chanted, Flower Pouch twirled her rosary at God, but no rain fell.

The next day, desperate, we climbed to the high temple where

Father Olmedo, sweating, celebrated a special mass in view of the Virgin and under a cloudless sky. As we descended the stairs, thunderheads rolled in from the mountains, and such a deluge poured down that we waded ankle-deep back to the palace.

Cortes lifted his face to the sky and laughed, water pelting his helmet, streaming down his rough cheeks and through his pointed beard. He shouted at invisible Aztec priests, "Now, you blood-soaked bastards! What do you say now?" Thunder rumbled across the valley, and he laughed louder, slapping the shoulders of the men near him so hard they staggered. "You spawn of Cuban whores! You pray even better than you fight. I'm changing headquarters into a convent!"

This victory for Plumed Serpent caused consternation. Apparently the Aztec priests and Smoking Mirror decided they had no alternative but suicide or murder, and the latter seemed more desirable. Along with certain nobles, they met with Moctezuma, so I expected the worst when the Speaker sent word he had to speak to Cortes at once.

We found Moctezuma recovered from his distress about the temple. He was quietly smoking and seemed to have laid his worries upon the gods once more, for his smile was serene, his eyes clear and innocent. But he said, "Malintzin, all Spaniards must quit the city at once. The gods have at last spoken and told us to kill all of you, to drive you to the sea and beyond."

He did not say that the Battle of Tula between Smoking Mirror and Plumed Serpent was to be fought again with Plumed Serpent doomed to defeat. But that was what he meant. "So I have warned you."

My lord's manner revealed nothing. The two opponents smiled at each other, and a servant poured friendly cups of chocolate. A Spanish orderly was attending Cortes, and my lord addressed him pleasantly. "Go calmly with a smile and put the army on alert to repel an attack." He turned back to Moctezuma. "I am afraid we cannot leave without ships. I trust you will restrain your people from any rash act until we can build vessels."

Moctezuma considered this, then nodded. "I shall try to give you time. My carpenters are at your service."

We were dealing with a side of Moctezuma we had not encountered before, serene and hard as jade. Smoking Mirror and Hummingbird had at last reassured him. He might delay to avert a divine civil war, but threats would win us nothing today.

Yet my lord tried. "One other matter. You yourself must accompany us to our own land beyond the sunrise. My lord King Carlos will insist on meeting a ruler who has already pledged loyalty to him."

Moctezuma flinched, for an instant thinking not of the gods or his people, but of himself. The idea of the world beyond the ocean was as alarming to him as it was to me. Then he recovered. "I suspect my removal would not be permitted. Meanwhile I urge you not to delay building your ships." He gestured to show the conversation had ended, and his chamberlain presented me with a jasper bracelet.

As we moved across the courtyard, Cortes murmured, "This may not be serious. He changes with every puff of wind."

Yet that same day my lord gave orders for Martin Lopez, a shipwright, to leave for Veracruz with some Aztec carpenters. They were to build three ships.

I found this ominous. If Cortes abandoned the task of Plumed Serpent and sailed away, what would become of me? He would not leave me to the mercy of the Aztecs, yet he could hardly take me to Cuba to be his consort, since he already had at least two wives there. I knew from the soldiers about the lives of women in Cuba. I could not even become a whore there, had I been able to play that role, for unlike our pretty ladies, the women who gave pleasure there were despised and degraded. Spain was unimaginable. In Spain I would be displayed like a creature in the royal zoo. I was frightened.

My lord held me close that night; he covered me with his body and his kisses, whispering urgently of my beauty and his own undying love—all so magical that I lost myself in the illusion that this joy would last forever, that there would be no other life: he would not change and I would not change. So I fell asleep content, believing this delicious dream.

Then a different dream came to me. I was climbing a mountain trail, and looking down I saw the foal Citla, the little horse who left her mother to run with the deer. Now she searched in vain to return, to find the other horses. A cold wind swept down from the mountain and she fell, dying.

I awoke sitting upright on the mats, knowing that if we failed and my lord took ship for the east, there would be nothing for me but death.

. .

For twelve days life in the palace continued as before. Each morning my lord called on Moctezuma to deal with affairs of the empire. Now I accompanied him only when there were translations of delicacy. I was not happy visiting the Speaker daily. Something in his new tranquillity upset my own; his knowing stare left me uneasy as he seemed to gaze into my future and found the view tragic.

One morning my lord returned puzzled. "He is strange today. You must see for yourself this afternoon."

When we called on the Speaker, he almost chuckled. "I expected you back. Why did you not tell me the amazing news this morning? Did you not trust the boy's translation?"

I answered for Cortes. "Exactly so, my lord." What news?

Moctezuma waved to his attendants, who unrolled a long sheet of cotton painted with pictures. "This was delivered just now. But I knew the main facts early this morning."

The painted letter showed palm trees and sand, with waves in the background—the coast at Veracruz. Thirteen Spanish ships rode at anchor; five others were aground and broken. The beaches teemed with men, horses, supplies and guns. "These newcomers are in the harbor where you first landed, Malintzin. You should not have kept this news from me." He gave Cortes a sharp look, and a note of severity crept into his voice. "I share your gladness at the arrival of your brothers. Now you will not need to build ships for your departure. They have been provided."

Cortes, showing no surprise, examined the pictures. "Until now I knew of the landing only by intuition. So it is confirmed."

Cortes stepped quickly to the door and called to the guards. "Spread word that reinforcements have landed on the coast—ships full of men and horses. Give thanks to God!"

There was a cheer outside, and a moment later, as we excused ourselves from Moctezuma, a loud celebration began. A harquebus was fired into the air; horsemen galloped in the courtyard, yelling and flourishing banners. But I knew from my lord's face that this news was anything but good.

"So those gold-hungry bastards from Cuba are here," he said.

The army soon realized that the celebration was a pretense; not comrades but voracious rivals had debarked. I did not understand the details. I knew my lord had jealous enemies in Cuba, including a governor who knew nothing of Cortes's mission. I realized we were in jeopardy from two sides now.

Most men would have despaired, but my lord drew strength from adversity, not yielding to fate but shaping it.

Before sunset he sent the officer Andres Tapia to Veracruz to learn what was happening. Tapia walked by day and at night was carried on the back of a Tlaxcalan bearer. Meanwhile my lord began distributing gold taken from the royal treasure. He bought and cajoled and promised. We soon learned that the newcomers had indeed arrived to destroy Cortes and were well prepared. There were eight hundred soldiers, eighty horses and at least ten cannons.

"Your brothers on the coast disappoint me," Moctezuma said, not quite concealing a smile. "They insult you, Malintzin. They call you a fugitive and an outlaw. But I have made them welcome with a few gifts of food. And gold, of course."

"You are kind," Cortes answered, bowing.

"I try. I find the joy of life lies in being kind to friends." Moctezuma smiled. "And ruthless to enemies."

"I agree," replied Cortes, also smiling.

Days passed with the hurrying of messengers. One morning three Spaniards, one a priest, arrived in an odd manner. They had been netted in Veracruz and carried all the way to Tenochtitlan laced into hammocks flung across the backs of strong porters. My lord received them sympathetically, saw to their quick unwrapping and soothed the spluttering clergyman.

Cortes decided to march swiftly to the coast and settle with his enemies, leaving behind Pedro Alvarado in command of eighty Spanish soldiers and four hundred Tlaxcalan warriors to hold the palace and the city. I was to remain with them, since there would be no need of me in Veracruz. For once all the enemies spoke the same language.

"I have cautioned Pedro to be discreet," my lord told me. "You may have to remind him."

"I will," I said. It would be like asking Smoking Man not to erupt.

Cortes asked the Tlaxcalans for five thousand men. A swift-messenger, still out of breath, recited Xicoten the Elder's reply. "Great Lord, our armies are at your command for war on Aztecs or other humans. But we cannot fight demons like yourselves. We will supply you with twenty loads of hens."

"Hens!" Cortes sneered. "How appropriate."

My lord the Captain marched from the city on the fifth day of May. As the troops moved away, Moctezuma glanced at me and said, "He is leaving you behind. I am surprised any man would do that. Or any god."

"My lord, it is only until he returns."

"Of course. Until he returns." He knew Cortes's troops were outnumbered ten to one, and the smile he gave me was not without sympathy.

20

On the Rampart

Before my lord left he gave permission for the people to celebrate the festivals of Smoking Mirror. "No humans are to be sacrificed." My lord had to say this to avoid trouble with the Virgin Mary; Moctezuma had to agree to avoid an open battle. Both knew the sacrifices would take place as usual.

During the days before the celebration I had much time to think. Pedro Alvarado had relieved me as translator, making it clear he did not trust me. "Only a Spaniard can understand the lies of another Spaniard," he said, clapping the boy Ortega on the back. "This lad will do."

So I slipped out to listen to talk in the city. This season many people of rank wore masks, so I went unrecognized in a lovely mask of a vixen with hawk's plumes. The Aztecs would have said it was not a disguise at all, but the face my soul deserved.

From market vendors I learned that Smoking Mirror had not changed his mind about slaughtering the Spaniards, and in the canoe basin the boatmen talked of war and the great sacrifice after the festivals ended. I now felt an attack would come only after word arrived that Cortes had been defeated by the new invaders.

Swallowing my distaste, I went to Pedro Alvarado to report, finding him in a courtyard where some Tlaxcalans were polishing his armor.

"Ah, it is the lady with the wildcat claws," he said, holding up his huge red hand as though it still hurt from my fingernails in Cholula. Wounded pride heals slowly.

Ignoring this, I tried to explain the situation in the city. "What are you saying?" he asked, winking at a crony who was lounging nearby. "I cannot understand you."

I repeated slowly, but again he interrupted, scratching his head in mock perplexity—although he could have been attacking his fleas; he did that, too. "Your attempt at Spanish, Doña Marina, is hard to make out. I suppose you speak more clearly under a blanket."

"You will never know," I said. My instinct was to leave, to endure no insolence, but I felt duty to my lord. "I am saying there will be no war until the festival ends. Even after that the Aztecs will not try to storm the palace until they hear that Cortes has been defeated."

"So you savages are counting on Cortes losing, are you?" The misunderstanding now was obviously deliberate.

I kept my control. "My lord will win a great victory. I only say we need not fear rebellion soon."

"How reassuring. Now I will not need any extra sentries—just as you once felt we would not need an extra Tlaxcalan army. And look at us now!"

There was no possible reply to such stupidity, but I was compelled to finish. "You must send a message to Cortes. After his victory he must not reenter this city except by attack. The Aztecs will be waiting like spiders in a web. We must fight from the inside, Cortes from the out."

For a moment he was speechless. Then he laughed and spoke with contempt. "It is interesting to have a woman's view of the military situation. Tonight I'll ask my woman Flower Pouch if she agrees with you. Thank you and that will be all, Doña Marina."

I left looking proud, showing neither my anger nor my despair for him, knowing I would have to find another way to get a message to Cortes.

On the first morning of the festival I went at dawn to the terrace overlooking the great plaza. As the women and children gathered for the early pageants, I studied the walls and parapets of King Face of the Water Lord's palace, trying to think of its defenses as Cortes might have thought. Most of the palace was one story, but a high upper floor rose in the middle and this design created the terraces on all four sides. There were no windows on the outside, only into the courtyards, and the front and rear entrances were blocked by heavy gates the Spanish carpenters had made. Even a few soldiers should be able to hold the building a long time.

Today Alvarado had decided to send out small patrols, eight men at a time, to scout the neighborhood and make sure the celebrants were not carrying arms. At least that was what he said, but he was so rattled no one could know what lurked in his mind.

About noon I went down and lingered just outside the gates to watch the entrance of the festival statue. Alvarado and several men were also there in armor and looking fierce. The boy Ortega stood beside Alvarado, full of importance, hoping to be asked to translate.

As usual at public rites, some arrangements had been neglected, and near us a young priest of Hummingbird supervised a gang of slaves who were embedding tall poles in the pavement. Later on torches would be attached to these to light the Dance of the Men tonight after moonrise. Alvarado glanced suspiciously at the poles, and I wondered if he thought they might be converted into scaling ladders to attack the palace. He suspected everything today.

The plaza was not even half-filled, only two or three thousand celebrants had arrived, when the big drum of the temple rumbled to announce the entrance of the festival statue. The people, shouting praises, dropped to their knees and waved streamers tied to their wrists.

The statue, borne on a litter so wide it would hardly pass between the buildings, was a gigantic sculpture three times as tall as a man and fashioned from dough, a mixture of amaranth seeds and blood. The image was encrusted with jewels and wore a headdress of tree branches painted to resemble plumes. His obsidian leg flashed in the sun.

The watching Spaniards whispered uneasily among themselves. Then Pedro Alvarado, still worried about the poles, shouted to the priest in charge of the work. "What are those things for?"

Ortega translated with a dreadful accent, but the priest, on the second try, understood. He glared at the Spaniards, made an obscene gesture and gave an insolent answer Ortega did not understand.

Alvarado turned to me. "What's all this?"

I did not want to add to the tension by repeating what the priest foolishly said. "The poles are to hold torches tonight."

Ortega, hearing me say this, jerked excitedly on Alvarado's sleeve and whispered to him. Alvarado paled and whirled on me, his fists clenched. "Doña Marina, I am told your words are false. You have lied to me about these poles."

I sighed but answered politely. "No, my lord. I told you their purpose. I did not try to translate the priest's words. But since the boy understood a little and you insist on knowing, he said the poles were to stick Spanish heads on after the dance tonight."

"By the Virgin!"

"He added that yours, my lord, would be especially pretty up there." After all, I thought, he had demanded a translation.

Alvarado stared at the nearest pole, his lip curling as though his own head were there gazing back at him. He looked around for the priest, who had wisely vanished into the crowd.

"Get inside the palace," he ordered the men who were with him. "Cancel the patrols for today and call a meeting of all officers."

I followed them through the gates, astonished that Alvarado could take such an outrageous retort seriously. As I started up the stairs to my own quarters, Alvarado shouted after me, "Any more lying translations, lady, and you will pay for it!" For a second I wondered if he might hang me from sheer fright; and I wondered what my lord would do about it.

I stayed by myself the rest of the day, not actually afraid, yet not wanting to test Alvarado's rashness. At sunset the beat of the drums quickened. I knew that the male dancers, men in the first flower of manhood, were now entering the holy precinct, the plaza before the temple where the god presided. One youth had been chosen from each noble family, the most graceful and beautiful son. There were about six hundred of them.

I heard whispering and a clank of armor in the courtyard below, where, I supposed, the Spanish guard was changing. Alvarado seemed very nervous, apparently turning out every man and actually sending pickets outside. I lay down on my mats, trying to ignore the drumming, considering how I might send a message to my lord warning him not to return to the capital except with a besieging army. This was only the fourth day of a festival that lasted twenty days; there was plenty of time.

Suddenly the whole room shook as the cannons on the roof exploded. My ears were still ringing when I heard screams from the temple plaza, and I ran to the terrace. I could see only one corner of the precinct near the temple steps, and that part dimly through a haze of smoky torches and incense. I knew more from hearing than sight that a slaughter was taking place, that Spanish soldiers were hewing down the unarmed dancers. I saw young men in bright plumage run this way and that, turning and dodging to escape. But they were trapped; the attack had been planned carefully. I watched frozen, unbelieving.

The massacre was over in only a few minutes and the plaza left to the dead and the corpse pickers, Spaniards who were tearing rings and brooches from the murdered Aztecs. I saw one soldier rip a silver bracelet from an arm and wave his prize proudly. This was Cholula over again, but now the vultures were Spaniards. They stole sandals and capes; they stripped the dead naked and left them lying uncovered and bloody in the moonlight.

Some of the victors had already returned to the palace, laughing and comparing plunder. I heard Pedro Alvarado shout, "That will teach the fuckers! Put my head on a pole, would they?"

From Moctezuma's apartments came a shrill cry of grief that changed to a sound like the howling of a wounded animal. I covered my ears, sickened, but when I wept, it was not for Moctezuma or even for the fallen dancers, but for the dream of Plumed Serpent. If someone had told me that Evening Star had died and would never again appear in the sky, I would have believed him.

The attack on the palace began before dawn, although most of the city was still numb with shock. Every dancer in the holy precinct had been slain, so not one leading family had escaped tragedy. Most of them postponed their vengeance, delaying to mourn and make plans. Others, hysterical with grief, attacked the palace with stones, clubs and their bare hands. Moctezuma was led out on a terrace to try to calm the people. They dispersed, but I knew they would come back with renewed fury.

The Spaniards, despite their elation the night before, were not unscathed. Eight soldiers had been killed in attacking the dancers, a tenth of our force, and some others were wounded. Pedro Alvarado seemed genuinely surprised that the palace was being almost besieged. He had mistaken Aztecs for Cholulans; he had expected them to grovel, not fight.

I kept to myself, emerging from my quarters only when I heard loud cheering in the courtyard and went out to learn that Cortes had won a great victory in Veracruz; messengers had just brought the good news.

"A miracle! The troops from Cuba have all joined Cortes!" someone shouted, causing louder cheers, my own voice joining.

Another soldier called out, "Cortes will soon march in here and settle with these savages."

I turned away; that, of course, was exactly what I feared. The cheers had hardly died before Alvarado was sending a messenger to Cortes saying that our plight here was desperate.

That night I bribed a Tlaxcalan runner to try to slip out of the city and warn Cortes that the streets of Tenochtitlan had become a death trap.

The attack on the palace was renewed in the Second Watch of the morning. The mob hurled rocks and blazing pitch against the walls. Twice they tried to storm the entrance. Looking cautiously over the parapet, I saw that perhaps a thousand people surrounded the palace, and many of them were elderly men and women—probably parents of Alvarado's victims. So, despite all the yelling and drum-beating, this assault was only a gesture. The Aztec army was still waiting.

But after three hours of noisy threats, Pedro Alvarado lost his head and had Moctezuma almost dragged to the roof. I was summoned to translate because, under pressure, Ortega could not really be trusted.

Moctezuma stood at the parapet of the main roof terrace and raised his arms to the crowd. Alvarado, looming behind him, growled orders to me. "He is to tell them to go home peacefully. Let him say the gods command it."

But Moctezuma was already speaking. "My people, war has broken out between the servants of Plumed Serpent and the servants of Smoking Mirror. Plumed Serpent has taken a terrible toll of victims among those who danced for his enemy. Now let the gods of our temple take their vengeance in their own time. You cannot do it today. Go home now. Listen to your leaders and your priests."

Cries of protest and anguish rose from below. One voice was lifted above the rest, and I looked down to see Moctezuma's son, child of his royal wife, in the forefront of the throng. "My father, let us tear down the gates," he cried. "Let us rescue you from these devils."

"No, not now! Go away, my son!"

Alvarado, not understanding and not trusting me, saw only the anger of the crowd and their reluctance to obey. Suddenly he drew his dagger and held the blade to Moctezuma's heart, letting the people see that with one thrust he would kill the Speaker. There was a gasp, then murmurs and cries of outrage. I could hardly believe what I was seeing—Alvarado must have gone utterly mad.

At that moment it would have been so easy, so simple for Lord Moctezuma. He had only to throw his body against the knife and end his struggle. His life had been spent in the service of Death; the Narrow Passage was a familiar corridor to him. But his own death was a luxury he could not yet afford. Had he died then on Alvarado's dagger, nothing could have held back the Aztecs. Moctezuma could not have delayed the people until Cortes returned, and all the Spaniards were gathered into a great cage, his father's palace.

"Go back to your mourning, and do not fear for me. Our hour of justice will come, but it is not yet."

They moved away then, shocked and weeping, many of them believing Moctezuma merely feared for his own life. So did Pedro Alvarado, who said smugly, "Now we know how to handle them." The fool did not realize that in showing the Aztecs how lightly he held the life of the Revered Speaker, he had also shown them how little they had to lose.

Before leaving the rampart, I knelt in front of Moctezuma and made the ancient reverence. One must salute courage even in an enemy.

We waited then. We waited through the Month of the Desire for Rains, through the swelling and delivery of Lady Moon. The Aztecs kept a cordon of warriors around the palace; sometimes javelins or darts landed on the roof or rocks thudded against the walls. There were alarms, but no real attack.

Meanwhile, just out of crossbow shot, the solemn ritual year of the Aztecs wound on. Standing on the rampart, I watched the priests fill a canoe with the hearts of human offerings to Tlaloc. Then a boy and a girl, bound and weighted with stones, were placed on the bed of hearts. Crowned with flowers, the couple was then joyfully taken to the deepest part of the lake, where the canoe was sent to the bottom, to the green world of the Water Goddess.

Often I gazed across the lake trying to see the trails on the far shores, hoping to see the banners of my lord the Captain, yet fearing I would, wondering if he would arrive with a vast army to storm the city or a thin column of Spaniards to march into the den of knives. During those days I had a frightening sense of being trapped on an island within an island—as, of course, we were. It was what newly caught birds feel in nets and what I had felt only a few times in clearings in the southern jungle.

Then on the Robing of Lord Sun, which Spaniards called Midsummer's Day, silence fell on the city. There had been unusual sounds the night before: the coming and going of priests at the temple, the assembling of men. I had thought it part of the ritual. But in the Second Watch a sentry cried out that he saw flashes of metal across the water, the glint of sun on steel.

Soon I knew that my lord had received my message of warning, even if he had not entirely believed it, for he was entering the city not by the nearest route, a long causeway that required two hours' exposed marching to cross. He took a more protected road.

The city seemed deserted; nothing stirred, the Xolo dogs were silent, even the birds had forsaken the plazas and courts, not a canoe bobbed in the harbor. Then we heard a Spanish trumpet followed by the distant rattle of a drum. In the palace the soldiers began cheering. Alvarado ordered a cannon fired as a salute and to show we still lived. Soon, down the broadest avenue, marched the Spanish column. I saw a force with twice as many men and ten times as many horses as our army had when it first entered the city more than seven months ago. I knew that Cortes, by victory in battle and subtle dealing, now commanded the whole force that had invaded to destroy him. They were so clean, so well dressed, and their boots had no holes; the horses were plump! It was a sight so heartening that for a moment I let myself believe that numbers, not gods, counted.

My lord the Captain, proud and splendid, halted Mule Driver at the palace gates. Behind him these Spaniards, most of them new and unbelieving that a city so magnificent could exist, gaped at the palaces and temples as the veterans had once done. Yet I saw they were uncertain, apprehensive. The silence around them, the absence of people in the streets, was unnerving.

Cortes entered the courtyard amid welcoming shouts of the garrison troops, and the great gates closed heavily behind the Spaniards.

Now all the demons, as the Aztecs would have said, were gathered in one place, on the island within an island.

My lord greeted me graciously, holding my hand a moment too long for mere courtesy, and there was pleasure in his eyes. "I have looked forward to our reunion," he said.

But everything else displeased him—the hushed city, the deserted avenues when he had expected cheering and worshipful crowds. Also, he was embarrassed before the newcomers because he had assured them of a triumphal entry into a city he ruled, showers of golden gifts. None of this had happened.

I did not hear my lord's harsh interview with Pedro Alvarado, but I knew the rebuke was searing. Alvarado deserved hanging, which did not happen. I had hoped for this and said some prayers, knowing very well it was too good to expect.

He sent a curt message to Moctezuma refusing to call on the Speaker, accusing him of bad faith in dealing with his enemies, and demanding that the food markets of the city be opened to supply rations for the Spaniards or serious steps would be taken.

I delivered this ultimatum, my first call on Moctezuma since the terrible day when Alvarado had held the knife at his heart. I was shocked by the change in the Speaker. His eyes were dull, his cheeks without color. He seemed shrunken by the failure of his plans and hopes.

"Tell Malintzin I will try; I will think about this. But I have not the power I once had. My Spanish page Ortega will bring word."

I did not join my lord and his officers for their afternoon meal, although he had invited me. It seemed wiser to keep a distance between myself and my lord's ill temper. I watched quietly from the stairs, and noticed a change in Cortes. He had always been proud, but now he seemed haughty, disdainful. He talked much of his success in Veracruz, and I found it strange that he should think outwitting a few hundred Spaniards, apparently men of the worst sort, a greater achievement than defeating the whole Republic of Tlaxcala in open war or entering without battle the capital of the world. Always before he had attributed his victories to God or the Virgin, even though most of them belonged to Plumed Serpent. Now all gods were forgotten and the success was his alone. I decided to be wary of this new Cortes.

During the meal Ortega came from Moctezuma's quarters, approached Cortes and spoke in a low voice. My lord shook his head as though refusing some request, then as Ortega was leaving, he called after him, "Oh, very well. Let it be done if it will open the markets faster. Also, this will please the scoundrel."

The scoundrel could be only Moctezuma, but I had no idea what request had been granted.

I went to our quarters and made arrangements for the night, wanting to make my lord feel welcomed and cared for. It was a warm day, hot for that usually cool city, so I had our mats moved onto the roof terrace, where I arranged flowers and sprinkled perfume. I brought out Cortes's altar and put new candles on it to protect us from night spirits; the parapet would protect us from any Aztec archers, although I felt sure no arrows would be fired tonight. Those would wait for tomorrow.

On my way to find a jar of Cuban wine for tonight, I passed Moctezuma's door. The leather curtains were parted to catch any cool breeze, and I glanced in, then halted in surprise. Moctezuma was seated not on his low throne chair, not even on a mat, but on the floor. He had changed his green robe for the coarse clothing of a priest and sprinkled ashes in his hair, the sign of humility. He had stripped off all jewelry, and the clay seal of office, which he usually wore on a thong around his neck, lay broken on the floor in front of him. Softly he sang a hymn to Smoking Mirror, one every child learned.

> *"Lord of the shining stone,*
> *King of the nine Dark Houses . . ."*

I moved on, puzzled, and came upon Ortega, who was chatting with a sentry.

"What was the favor you asked for Moctezuma earlier?"

"At dinner? Lord Moctezuma suggested that his brother, Lord Cuitlahuac, be freed from the great chain and released. He said it would speed the opening of the food markets."

"Cortes granted this favor?" I suddenly felt uneasy.

"Oh, yes," the boy answered. "It was no important matter."

I could have struck him in the face. Why had he not come to me before asking Cortes? Cuitlahuac was Moctezuma's eldest brother, the natural successor who was always head of the Aztec council during the Speaker's absence. "Was this done? Was the lord released?"

"He left the palace half an hour ago." Ortega smiled. "I suppose food will be delivered soon. Moctezuma said his brother would have the power to do it."

No doubt. Power to deliver other things, too. Arrows and fire. By tonight the Aztec council would have met, and the empire would have a new ruler.

I decided not to tell my lord; there was nothing to be gained. Besides, he was in a proud mood and it would be humiliating to learn that Moctezuma had outwitted him so easily.

That evening would be the last quiet night my lord and I would spend together in Tenochtitlan; we both knew this, and I was glad Cortes had let go his anger, his disappointment in returning. We both also knew that war would wait until tomorrow. He unbuckled his breast plate and took off his helmet. He made himself easy with the wine jar and lit two more candles.

He wanted to talk even more of his victories, of his cleverness in dealings on the coast. He had done all this with his men, but it was important he say these things to a woman, and that a woman praise him.

I listened attentively, understanding little of what had happened but realizing he had done remarkable things. "El Cid would have boasted of such a victory!" I assured him, hoping it was so. "Amadis in those wonderful tales never achieved such things."

He chuckled happily, then became serious when he said, "I think they did not do better than I have done. Strange that I should live to make such a comparison! I am impudent! Anyone but you, my dear, would think me mad to do such bragging."

He drank deeply from the jar of wine. "Two weeks ago I defeated proud men who would not have deigned to speak to me on a street in Spain—or even in Cuba, where rank is held lighter. I bent them to my will, Marina!"

For a moment he savored what had happened, how he had made his enemies his servants. "Yes, I have already made a mark for a man who was born a nobody. I told you my father is a knight, and in a way he is. But when I was a boy, we were so poor that on wash days my mother's petticoats had to be dried inside the house. They were so

patched we were ashamed for the neighbors to see them. Yes, I was
born a nobody, and people who are somebodies will hate me forever
because I put five princes on a chain!"

The great drum of the temple sounded softly in the night. One
stroke, then another. A signal for tomorrow, I thought.

I took a sip of the wine he offered me; it stung my lips. "You
should not have returned, my lord, except with a Tlaxcalan army to
camp outside the city. I tried to warn you that matters had changed
here—and now they have changed even more. Yet I knew you would
come back no matter what I said."

"Of course. I could not leave you behind, my dear. A princess
trapped in a besieged castle! What sort of knight would I be if I did
not rescue you?"

He kissed me lightly as he spoke this lover's lie that I understood
as such. "You are wiser than Amadis, my lord. You do not offer your
life to save bloodless princesses. Besides, we were not in great danger
here, not for a while yet. We were the bait. What fisherman kills live
bait?"

He rose, turning away from the temple, looking toward the
palace of Moctezuma, empty now except for a few servants and
concubines, but torches flared at the corners of the dark building. "If
not for a beautiful princess, then why did I return?" he asked.

"For your men," I answered. "I have seen you with the soldiers.
I know your love for them, for your comrades."

He shook his head and sighed. "You think I love that gang of
pirates? You are as foolish as they are. Is it for love of them that I push
and drag their carcasses over mountains and through swamps? Why
should I offer my life to save their unwashed necks? I command a herd
of swine, and they are gold-eating swine. I rule them by promises of
greater swill." He moved to the parapet. Fires burned on the opposite
shore, where armies were gathering. "When I look across this lake I
can see not just tomorrow's war but the kingdom of the future, my
world of dreams. These men you think I love see nothing but a great
trough to stick their snouts in."

"Yes, they are greedy. Who is not?" I said. "The Aztecs accuse
the Spaniards of being ravenous for gold. But the Aztecs themselves
want not only gold but everything else—even the living hearts of their
neighbors. You have seen their storehouses stacked to the beams with
stolen goods, tribute wrung from weaker people. What is the differ-

ence? Is it more wicked to steal gold than to steal everything else as well?"

"What is the difference?" he said wearily. "And how different am I myself? I need gold if I am to buy the world I imagine, and for that I am greedy. But at the same time I want something better than what I can snatch and run with. I can build a new world here, God and the king willing. When has a common man, born a nobody like me, had such a chance?"

My lord kneeled near the wine jar, took a deep swallow. He looked drawn and tired in the pale yellow light. He spoke in a puzzled voice, the tone of a man who does not understand his own actions. "You warned me that this city is a trap, and others also said that. I agreed a week ago but kept marching toward it. This morning I felt certain when I saw the deserted countryside, the causeways open and unguarded. Yet I kept on, I came back!" He finished the wine, then hurled the clay jar, smashing it against the parapet.

"This is *my* city, my capital. Here I am king, and I cannot be a king without this place. Elsewhere I am nothing."

So Plumed Serpent had commanded his return, and Cortes had no more choices than I had ever had. We sat in silence watching the candles. The great drum of the temple sounded softly again. I was about to ask him what swine were and did they resemble Pedro Alvarado. But then, with a cry that was almost a sob, he took me in his arms, pressed his lips against mine and I forgot the question.

His hunger for me seemed desperate, fierce, and my own desire rose to match his as though we both knew that death waited outside the room, that this might be our final time. Then gradually I sensed a change in his body, his passion. As a lover, he was accustomed more to giving than to taking; he seemed always to put my pleasure above his own. But tonight, after our first embraces, I felt he needed something from me he had not asked before—he longed to be comforted, to draw strength and assurance from me. He wanted, almost, to cling to me and weep for the dream that might be lost tomorrow.

But although he could not weep, could not quite surrender himself, he let me comfort him, trembling a little under my kisses and caresses, then resting on my bosom. I held him as tenderly as a child, whispering of his greatness and of his certain victory. I think he came near to believing me.

But whether he believed or not, I knew that at last I had returned a little of the strength he had so often given me. I looked down at his worn, lined face, and never had he seemed so beautiful.

The next morning my lord sent the officer Diego Ordaz with four hundred soldiers to make a show of strength in the streets and to test the city. He was hardly out of sight when the deserted avenues swarmed with warriors, squadron after squadron pouring down the alleys, the empty roofs suddenly coming alive with thousands of screaming men shooting arrows from the house tops. Ordaz fought a step-by-step retreat that left eighteen men dead and all the rest wounded.

At the same time another Aztec army hurled itself against the palace, flinging rocks, spears and fire. The building quaked with the firing of our cannons and muskets. I fought on the parapet, stabbing and striking with a long lance tipped in copper, sometimes almost face to face with eagle knights as they climbed over the bodies of dead comrades trying to scale the walls.

We battled all day, and even darkness did not bring much respite. When dawn came Cortes decided to counterattack, suddenly sallying out toward the temple precinct. The Aztecs had chosen the same moment for a new assault, and the two armies clashed within bow shot of the palace. The Spaniards advanced half a block, meaning to burn some houses, but a drawbridge had been removed, and they could not wade or swim the canal because an avalanche of rocks poured from the roofs. All over the city bridges had been pulled up and carried away.

When the Spaniards retreated—actually fled—to the palace, ten thousand jeers and whistles rose from the Aztecs. A noble with a voice loud as a temple drum shouted that not one Spaniard would be spared from the altars. "We are hungry for your flesh!" he cried. "This fighting whets our appetites." The Tlaxcalans with us, he said, would live a little longer in cages while they were fattened up.

I learned to shoot a crossbow that day, and I fired it with good aim even though javelins were striking the wall near me. I was too exhilarated to be afraid; I fought with a strange joy. Afterward, when I came down from the wall for a little rest, I could hardly stop trembling. But neither could many soldiers.

My lord began building what the Spaniards called battle chariots, wheeled fortresses made of wood with loopholes for aiming muskets and crossbows. There were to be three of these monsters, and hopes ran high that they might turn the overwhelming tide.

"These chariots and lots of prayer," said an elderly soldier lately come from Cuba. In his youth he had fought a tribe called the French and later a host of true demons called Turks. "But I never saw men so fierce or willing to die as these Aztecs," he said, wincing as I tightened a bandage on his arm. Of course he had not faced the likes of Aztecs—their courage had conquered the world. But even as I thought this, I heard the Tlaxcalans who were defending the walls burst into one of their wild songs, harsh singing full of the cries of hawks and eagles. No, the Aztecs had not enslaved quite everybody, and it was good to have three thousand undefeated Tlaxcalans fighting shoulder to shoulder with the Spaniards here. The Tlaxcalans had made the difference; without them Cortes could not have survived even the first assault.

Meanwhile Lord Moctezuma had confined himself to a room of his apartments and, still clothed as a priest, he recited prayers and spent the days in meditation, oblivious of the battle. He refused to speak with Cortes but received a visit from Father Olmedo and some officers. I did not hear what was said, but that same afternoon in the midst of a furious attack I heard a trumpet blast and was astonished to see Lord Moctezuma appear on the roof terrace a bow shot away, flanked by his recent visitors. Suddenly the din of battle ceased; Moctezuma stood alone in the silence.

Both his royal crowns, the gold panache of the sun and the silver crown of Lady Moon, had somehow vanished from the palace. Now, in a foolish attempt to restore his power, he appeared in a makeshift headdress some slave had fashioned from bark paper and painted yellow. It sat askew on his head, like the grotesque crown of a mime at a festival. Yet nothing—not the ludicrous hat or the shabby robe—could lessen the dignity of his face. It was useless, even mad, to have brought him here. Even so, he remained godlike and imperial, the king. He had grown taller in casting off his burdens. Except for the low parapet, he stood unshielded before the people.

"Sons of the Herons and of the Seven Caves!" He addressed them by their ancient name and lifted his arms in blessing. A hostile murmur rose as he began to speak of their gods. Near the palace, in the forefront of the line of battle, stood young Prince Falling Eagle, and I saw murder in a face that otherwise was almost boyish. His veneration of Moctezuma had turned to hate.

Falling Eagle shouted, "Who is this woman who speaks? Who is this disgusting wife of a Spaniard?" Then, as jeering voices shouted at Moctezuma, Falling Eagle nocked an arrow in his bow.

Moctezuma saw him, turned a little so he faced Falling Eagle squarely and let his robe fall open to offer his chest as a plain target. He said, "Those who attack will bring down wrath and destruction on our people. Let the gods judge between us, young prince."

The arrow struck his shoulder. He staggered, refusing to drop behind the wall to safety. Then came a deadly shower of stones flung by the mob, striking him in the chest, the arm, the head, breaking his bones, Moctezuma fell, and three Spanish soldiers carried him to shelter, his hair brushing the tiles of the roof.

Moctezuma lingered three days more, then died of grief and of his wounds.

Now there was no hope except to escape this deathtrap of a city. Until that chance came we hung on desperately, clinging by our very fingernails. The battle chariots sallied forth and briefly scattered the enemy, Tlaxcalans and Spanish soldiers capturing the high temples of Hummingbird and Smoking Mirror before the defenders could regroup. The shrines were quickly lost again, and now the Aztecs garrisoned the temple with five hundred of their best fighters.

"Drive them out of there!" Cortes ordered the officer Juan Escobar, giving him a hundred men for the task. My lord would have led the charge himself, but his right hand was wounded.

Three times we watched Escobar attack and fall back, his men reeling under the avalanche of stones and arrows. Cortes bit his lip and groaned. "They cannot fail! It is the shrine of the Virgin, too!" Then he whirled to me. "Strap my buckler on my arm!" he ordered.

"But you are wounded! Your hand—"

"Strap it on!"

I fixed the small shield on his arm and a moment later he was out through the gates and running toward the temple steps, a few men following him. Among those was Aguilar.

Above the clamor of battle on all sides, I could not hear what Cortes shouted that gave new spirit to the defeated men, but I saw them rally. They fought their way upward, step by bloodied step, taking terrible punishment yet pressing on. Aguilar, without armor or a shield, was at Cortes's back, defending him, and twice he saved my lord's life by risking his own. He threw himself like a jaguar upon a warrior who one second later would have beheaded Cortes, and when three priests armed with daggers slipped behind Cortes, it was Aguilar who drove them off with a spear he had found on the steps. A few weeks ago I had thought Aguilar loved no one. I was wrong; he loved Cortes and was ready to die for him.

They captured the temple, hurling down the stone gods the Aztecs had replaced, seizing stocks of provisions we needed badly. Since the shrine could not be held against thousands of warriors who were massing in the plaza, my lord set fire to the twin towers and left them behind flaming like a pyre for the gods he had destroyed there.

When Aguilar returned, I threw my arms around him and tried to kiss his cheek, but he pushed me away and fled, finding me far more alarming than the Aztec warriors.

For three more days we held the beleaguered palace, managing to capture and hold four bridges in the neighborhood. Meanwhile the carpenters built a platform to serve as a portable bridge for our flight from the city.

We planned to leave under cover of darkness as soon as Lady Moon was dead and shrouded. But a Spanish astrologer named Botello, a necromancer rather like Lord Wolf's Paw, caused terrible alarm among the soldiers by saying that the stars doomed us if we remained past the month of June. The men demanded we depart that same night, so the stars, not Cortes, chose the unlucky hour.

Mist hung over the lakes that night with just enough soft rain to make the pavements slippery—my lord feared for the horses. We gathered in the courtyard, silently forming ourselves into a long procession. Then confusion and a dangerous amount of noise broke out when my lord announced that the men might help themselves to the Aztec treasure, the king's portion having already been removed and packed.

They stampeded wildly toward the heap of gold and jewels that glittered in the torchlight, stumbling over each other, wounded men fighting off starved men in a desperate scramble. They pushed and pulled and kicked, tearing at bandages, wielding crutches. Some men threw themselves prostrate upon the pile, stuffing their shirts, trousers and armor with ingots and bracelets. A few seemed to be eating gold just as the Aztecs claimed they did, cramming their mouths with rings and beads when their pockets overflowed. A few wiser men took only a few opals or pieces of carved jade, treasures they could safely carry, but most of them clawed and snatched and cursed, unmindful that they might now face the last hour of their lives.

It was nearly midnight when the vanguard slipped into the misty street. Then came one hundred younger men commanded by Cortes himself—my lord would hold the center. Some Tlaxcalans and older men followed, and I went with them. Near me were the chained and gagged prisoners: the captive lords of the cities, a son of Moctezuma's and two royal daughters as hostages. Pedro Alvarado with thirty soldiers, some mounted, brought up the rear. Half a hundred Tlaxcalans carried the portable bridge.

We reached the first gap at the edge of the causeway with no alarm raised; the city lay sleeping, so silent that I was worried by the muffled hooves of Alvarado's mare. The gap was quickly bridged, we crossed, and the platform was taken up behind us and carried ahead. Now there was no retreat.

Just as the vanguard reached the second gap where our bridge now spanned the water, the silence was shattered by a blast of trumpets. Then drums boomed, whistles blew; the Aztec sentries had discovered us. Suddenly the city and the lake swarmed to life like a nest of deadly hornets. Warriors loomed up in the night ahead of us on both sides as canoes full of armed men sped across the water.

The battle, waged in fog and darkness, was three miles long and six paces wide. I pushed forward, dodging right then left, snatching a sword from the hand of a Spaniard dying of arrow wounds. His neck was hung with golden pectorals. Helped by two Tlaxcalans, I drove off a canoe trying to land and cut our column in two. A horse reared and kicked, driving the line of chained prisoners over the edge of the causeway where they drowned soundlessly, gagged and weighted with iron fetters.

The terrified horse, struck by fire arrows, also plunged into the lake, taking his rider with him. It was the astrologer Botello who sank in his armor, unsaved by his own prediction. I saw Jaime Garay dragged into a canoe alive, and I struggled to reach him, to help, but was blocked by a wall of bodies. The canoe edged from the causeway, then capsized as Jaime fought. The Aztecs clung to the craft, then swam away, but Jaime sank like a stone. The gold he had crammed into his pockets and armor went not to his sisters in Spain but to the Water

Goddess who grew rich that night glutting herself on Aztec treasure.

I inched ahead, thrusting and jabbing; then, seeing myself trapped ahead and behind, I dropped the sword and leapt into the water. I swam among the canoes, expecting to be seized by the hair and dragged to captivity. My lungs seemed to be bursting. My shoulders throbbed when at last my feet touched bottom near the last unbridged break in the causeway before the shore. Standing up, my chin just above water, I saw that the gap was almost filled by cannons, baggage and corpses. Then I heard Cortes's voice, powerful and ringing, utter a battle cry as Mule Driver leapt the gap and carried her rider to safety. My lord had survived.

Half-wading, half-swimming, I reached solid ground near Tacuba, staggered across a gravel beach, then collapsed in grass, gasping and choking. I lay trying to summon strength to go on, to move farther from the shore because I could hear Aztecs in canoes shouting "Death to the invaders!" only a few bow shots away. I heard no one approach, but suddenly a hand shook my shoulder. I rolled onto my back, searching wildly for a dagger I could not find, then saw a Spanish face gazing into mine, a young soldier without armor in a torn shirt.

"Come. You must not stay here, they will catch you." The voice was soft like a woman's, and I realized the ripped shirt revealed a woman's breasts. A demon, I thought, or a goddess.

"What are you?" I whispered. "Who are you?"

"I am Maria Estrada." She laughed, a little madly. "I came from Cuba a month ago. I was dressed in a boy's clothes, no one knew for a while. I am the only woman in this country."

She moved away, gesturing for me to follow, laughing shrilly. The only woman? I closed my eyes again, believing she was part of a nightmare, a fever dream. Yet I knew she was real, and vaguely I remembered some mention of a warrior woman who had come from Cuba in disguise. I had supposed it was a Spanish joke.

I found the remnants of the army huddled in the plaza of Tacuba. Cortes rounded up a few more men who were wandering in the night half-demented, and led us to a refuge a little distance away at a temple on a hilltop. A few warriors from the town tried to defend this stronghold, but my lord himself, though almost exhausted, led a charge and drove them off. There the army, not quite dead, lay down and slept in its own gore.

My lord kneeled and prayed to Our Lady. I heard him whispering to her in the dark, and this was no longer the proud victor who had ridden into Tenochtitlan a week ago, fresh from victory on the coast. His prayer was hoarse and desperate as he beseeched her almost in tears.

"You have brought me this far, you have saved me. Now only you can help. Lady, I must have a miracle."

Silently I made the same prayer to the Unknown Goddess.

At dawn a company of warriors from Tacuba attacked us but were easily driven off by the Tlaxcalans, who, although they had lost half their forces, seemed stronger than the Spaniards.

When full daylight came Cortes counted his losses. Six hundred Spaniards had been killed or captured—which meant death. Only twenty-four horses had survived, and all were lame. Most of the soldiers could hardly lift a hand, and some seemed to be living in nightmares, crying out in fear for no reason.

I offered a jade bead to the Water Goddess for the spirit of Jaime Garay; but most of the Spaniards I knew well had escaped, though every one of them was wounded. Most of the newcomers from Cuba had died because they had crammed gold into their clothes and armor. Pedro Alvarado, whose stupidity had caused the Aztec uprising, proved the injustice of God by surviving. Alvarado's chief consort, although not his favorite, was the Tlaxcalan princess called Doe Eyes who now went by the Christian name Doña Luisa. She had somehow managed to escape and this was important because her father was Xicoten the Elder, whose goodwill we needed. Alvarado's favorite woman, Flower Pouch, had disappeared, and I thought we were better off without her. The woman from Cuba, Maria Estrada, never talked to me again, but I saw her several times dressed in light armor, sprawling and swaggering like a sergeant. No other women escaped the causeway.

That night I sat on a step of the temple we had fortified and watched the flicker of light on the horizon toward Tenochtitlan. My lord, after making his round of sentries, climbed the stairs and joined me, trying to conceal a limp.

"I cannot understand this," he said wearily. "Where is the Aztec army? They could have destroyed us so easily today. Where are they?"

"Over there." I pointed toward the distant glow. "Sacrificing and feasting. They must honor Smoking Mirror and Hummingbird."

He looked incredulous. "They are taking time to celebrate? They let us escape while they hold a feast? Madness!"

I was too tired to explain, but it was not mad at all. The captives had to be offered quickly to the Victory Bringer, and the soldiers who had captured them had to be present at the temples for the sacrifices. What use in pursuing us if they offended Hummingbird by neglect? He would deprive them of their next victory. But if they pleased him and Smoking Mirror, they would destroy us no matter how long the delay. The Aztecs were behaving logically. It was Cortes who did not understand.

He nodded slowly. "Then God has given us another chance."

Not God, I thought. Gods. Hummingbird and Smoking Mirror.

The next morning we limped northeast, skirting the lake, the men with the sorest wounds hanging over the backs of the weary horses, a ghost army in tattered, blood-begrimed shrouds. Our only hope lay in reaching Tlaxcala, and even there we were unsure of a welcome. But we were the defeated; we had no choice. I walked with my eyes on the ground, dragging one aching foot after the other, resisting despair.

At a fork in the trail we paused in the shade of an orchard, and nearby rose a tall outcropping of rock like an upthrust wing. We were dangerously close to Texcoco but had to have rest, and from here we could see the lake and any activity on it without being easily seen ourselves; the rocks and trees screened us.

At the foot of the rock stood a little shrine, an altar with a statute of Xilonen, mother of the young corn and lady of prophecy. I had heard of this place; the little goddess was famed for offering glimpses of the future. She knew everything—when the Earth Monster would next shake the ground, when cities would fall, even how many kernels would grow on every ear of newly planted corn. But at this moment I did not want to see the future; the present was painful enough.

I sank to the dirt near the stump of a burned tree, wondering if I would ever rise again, and closed my eyes. In spite of myself I began to pray to both the Unknown Goddess and to Xilonen, who suddenly seemed near. "Give me a sign. Give me hope to go on."

The goddess came as a soft, cool breeze, and I held my breath awaiting the omen. Perhaps a lark would call, or Lady Flint Knife would appear to touch my brow and ease my fever. Expectant and fearful, I opened my eyes.

There was nothing. No bird, no apparition—only rocks and spiky cactus and half-dead men sprawled in the dust. Across the lake, hazy in the distance, Tenochtitlan rose like a city of tombs. Yet the goddess had felt so near, had almost whispered to me. My desolation seemed unbearable.

I felt a small but burning pain on the soft skin above my sandal. I forgot the goddess and the omens when I saw several large, red-brown ants whose bites are like fire making their way across my foot. Rising with more strength than I thought I had, I brushed them off.

I leaned against the rock, resigned that no sign would come, and idly watched a thin line of ants march toward the dead tree stump, tiny soldiers armored in hardy, glossy skin. Then I heard buzzing, and taking a wary step or two closer, I saw that the stump held a hive of bees who were rich with honey. A thick, golden syrup had trickled down the bark, where the ants had found it. A few ants managed to eat their fill and carry the sweet stuff away. But many more, so many they were uncountable, were mired in the honey as in quicksand. They struggled, kicking and twisting, some of them living a long time before they sank and drowned. The bees, gentle creatures, went on with their work, unmindful that their home had been invaded, heedless that part of their dwelling was now a graveyard.

I called out, "I have found honey." One of the men built a smudge and drove the bees away; then we dipped our fingers. I relented in my feelings toward the goddess who had mocked me with her presence and promised me an omen. At least she had given me something sweet to taste, probably the last sweetness I would ever know.

We moved on, passing fields where farmers had just left, then through a village whose inhabitants were gone, taking every crumb of food with them. Aguilar said, "They fear us. They have fled." I had not the heart to tell him they had simply gone off to Tenochtitlan to celebrate and savor a morsel of Spanish flesh.

We found wild cherries, then pressed on to Star Hill, an abandoned town but with food in its gardens, where we rested two days, then went to Xoloc, fighting off a few allies of the Aztecs. My lord laughed about being wounded twice in the head, but wept over the killing of Mule Driver.

Soon we reached country where the very ground holds power. I saw in the distance the ancient city of Those Who Became Gods, deserted twenty sheaves of years ago, the oldest city in the world, with giant temples, to Lord Sun and Lady Moon, who were born there.

Aztecs always felt awe of this vast ruin, knowing its dead avenues were paths for ghosts. I think they gazed on its fallen majesty and thought of Tenochtitlan, realizing that nations are as frail and transient as are men themselves.

We paused for water at the sacred springs. I remembered the war canoes beside the causeway, the warriors shouting, "Death to the invaders." Which invaders? We had invaded just as they themselves had once done, and Plumed Serpent's Toltecs had done long before them. How many others before the Toltecs? How many yet to come through fields where conquerors lay buried? No one owns the earth for long.

Since Aztecs avoided the haunted ruins, for an hour or two we were unmolested by the skirmishers who had begun to harass our flanks. Cortes ordered the wounded removed from the horses. "God and the horses are our only hope. The horses must rest."

Far on the horizon I glimpsed the high sanctuary at Otumba, and hope surged in me. If we could safely pass that town, we could reach the mountains that barricade Tlaxcala. For the first time in days I could imagine myself alive tomorrow. Then, mounting a low ridge, we saw spread before us the fertile Plain of Apam—and the Aztec army.

It seemed for a moment to be a dream, and I foolishly said aloud, "Oh, how beautiful." I could not have imagined that Death could come in such gorgeous array.

Waiting for us were thirty thousand warriors—or twice that, or half that many. Who could know? Their ranks stretched like a rainbow across the plain between foothills and the forest. Their tall panaches of green and crimson plumage swayed like cornfields in the wind. The spotted host of Jaguar Knights and the silver-gray Eagles were there, as were cohorts from the Cities of the Lakes, brilliant in the mantles of their own towns and clans—blue, purple, black and orange—while a thousand banners fluttered above them. Here was spread a vast garden of dazzling and lethal blossoms. On a little knoll in the center and toward the rear I saw a royal litter shaded by a canopy, and near it stood the gold net standard of Lord Woman Snake. "He commands today," I told Cortes.

Cortes addressed the troops, briefly but stirringly recalling Spanish glory and commending them to God. I spoke to the Tlaxcalans, seeming to translate, reminding them of their honor, of the Land of

Bread, and that they were sons of the Eagle Crags.

We gathered in close order. I was wearing the helmet and breast-plate of a soldier who had died the day before. The armor seemed light and comfortable, somehow familiar. My lord glanced at me and gave me a smile that was a parting gift; he nodded to say, "What better way to die than this?" I nodded back, but in the moment just before the battle, I felt angry and cheated that the long road from Jalisco should end this way. I deserved more; I was not yet reconciled to joining the Dark Lords.

Then with shouts and whistles we charged down the slope toward that waiting Aztec garden, and its flowers gave way, yielding in the center to welcome us, then to encircle and envelope like a snake's embrace. The cutlass felt light in my hand. It was the willow wand of a dancer, and I performed a dance as in a fantastic dream, weaving and thrusting and striking while my heart pounded. I lifted the buckler to ward off a blow, then struck back to bring the enemy down. An arrow glanced off my chest, deflected by the armor, and I knew that I was impervious, magical; and if not, my lord was right: there was no better, no easier way to die. Now I understood him.

A man like a giant towered before me and could have crushed me with a blow of his stone-toothed sword. Instead he reached to seize me, to take me alive, and an instant later he fell although I seemed only to have touched him with my blade.

I fought near my lord, back to back with Aguilar, and we might have been killed a dozen times, but the Aztecs wanted prisoners, not corpses. They would pay dearly to take living captives back to the altars. Otherwise there was no honor.

My lord fought as only a god could do, wielding his sword so powerfully that a hundred men who faced him toppled like dry stalks before a scythe. The Aztecs knew he was the god; they dared not touch him with a spear or ax, dared not risk shedding a drop of his blood, for it belonged to Smoking Mirror. Cortes must be brought to the temple intact, heart still beating strongly when he was offered on the high altar. But he slashed through their nets to kill the snarers, cut the nooses, chopped the hands that tried to hold him. Yet still they came on, one upon the next, rushing into the deadly harvest to fall upon fallen comrades.

Then, when no one expected it, suddenly, miraculously, a path opened through the Aztec horde, and with a fierce shout Cortes hacked aside a few defenders to reach the top of the little knoll and the litter of Lord Woman Snake. When he struck, wounding the Aztec commander, that haughty lord sank to his knees, yielding his gold net standard. Cortes brandished it high, shouting to the field, "It is victory! God and Santiago!"

Juan Salamanca, fighting on Cortes's left, seized Woman Snake's golden crown, wrenching it from the Aztec's head and giving it to Cortes, who put it on, standing now on top of the royal litter with the standard aloft and his boot on the chest of Lord Woman Snake, god of the battle.

The Aztecs, seeing who had triumphed, cried out to each other, and despair swept through their ranks. They broke and fled the field in confusion. Dazed by our salvation, we stood alone in the reddening sunset among the dead and dying. The road to Tlaxcala was now open and we took it, leaving behind many good men and a lost treasure that would cause anguish long afterward.

We also left behind an unknown guest with the Aztecs, though no one realized it at the time. This guest was brought from Cuba by an African slave whose name no one remembers, even though this black man turned out, by accident, to be the most powerful of Cortes's followers, the greatest conquistador. Neither could anyone at first find a name for the invisible guest. He seemed to be a cousin of the Spotted Gods, but no one in the Only World had encountered him before.

Soon he had a title: he was Lord Smallpox.

Part Six
RESURGENCE

21

Tlaxcala—Tenochtitlan—
July 12, 1520–August 13, 1521

All the world knows what happened in that year after we emerged alive and victorious from the battle on the Plain of Apam. What we achieved next has been celebrated—or cursed—in a thousand tales and songs. Even stolid Tlaxcalans have made epic poems about those days, poems that clink on the ear like the chiming of a cracked bell. Tlaxcalans are steadfast but tone deaf.

We were welcomed back to their republic in a shower of blossoms; Cortes was hailed not just as friend and ally but as the god he had proved himself to be. I hid my astonishment with a mask of pride. We had fled ingloriously from Tenochtitlan, dodging arrows and javelins; we had lost most of the treasure, most of the horses, all the guns and powder, half our soldiers. The survivors looked even worse today than yesterday, still tattered skeletons.

But the cheering Tlaxcalans saw us as the only army that had ever penetrated the Aztec capital. Cortes, for half a year, had ruled the Aztec empire as master of Moctezuma, then escaped the city and routed the Aztecs. Plumed Serpent was not vanquished; he had simply withdrawn to gather strength.

Soon the Aztecs sent emissaries inviting the men of the Land of Bread to join them. "Together we will drive the foul-smelling, hairy-faced, worm-skinned invaders back into the sea!" the Aztec ambassador declared.

Both Xicotens, father and son, denounced them for impiety, and the old man shouted into the ambassador's face, "For fifty years you have drunk our blood. Now you offer us the privilege of dying beside you. Make no mistake, the death of Tenochtitlan is ordained. Now perish alone as you have ruled alone. We will help in your destruction, not share it!"

The ambassadors fled, pelted by children hurling garbage and dung.

I thought my great usefulness was ending, since many men were mastering a new language now. But while my lord rebuilt his army, drawing men and guns from ships that came to Veracruz, I discovered a new form of warfare, the battles of politics and diplomacy. I sent messengers to thirty different cities saying, "Rise now against the Aztecs and you will be favored after their empire falls. Drive out their tax gatherers, harass their caravans. Death to the tyrants!"

My messenger to the Tarascans gave the Fisher Folk news that the Aztecs were preparing an incursion into Tarascan lands. So a thousand guards went to the frontier, forcing a thousand Aztecs to go out to face them, weakening the capital. My "secret information" was not totally a lie. After all, the Aztecs were always planning such incursions; it was their history.

My mice in Tenochtitlan, mostly foreign slaves, reported that the Aztecs themselves were far from united. Some were horrified by the slaying of Moctezuma, others recalled the old religion of Plumed Serpent, still others nurtured private hatred against the nobles. For instance, relatives of the slain royal tutors, victims like Uncle Willow, resented all of Moctezuma's family. Thousands more rankled at the nobility's contempt for men of lesser birth. In Texcoco, where Aztec puppets had usurped the throne, my spies found especially fertile soil for seeds of rebellion.

A talented emissary I sent to Xochimilco, town of the Flower Gardens, moved the people to tears as he reminded them of how the Aztecs, a generation ago, had dragged away women and children to be slaves. I had hopes for an alliance there.

Not all my messengers were successful, and a few were sacrificed and eaten, a traditional fate of diplomats. Yet every day I was wounding the Aztec jaguar, drawing a new trickle of blood, and I felt content to do this alone, without commands or advice from Cortes. I had begun to feel strong in my own right, and it was a good feeling.

I had importance outside Cortes's shadow, which I needed now that he spent more nights with "wives" presented to him by men who hoped for favors or to become grandfathers of gods. The women arrived like gifts at a funeral, too many at a busy time. Still, some were beautiful and my lord enjoyed them.

Usually I was sensible about this, but one morning I heard two plump, soft new concubines giggling about how youthful and handsome Cortes was, "Even with gray in his hair." Jealousy or rivalry seized me, and I went to gaze in my Spanish mirror.

No wonder my lord was finding pleasure elsewhere! I was worn and sinewy from the last months. I thought with malice, "It was in Cortes's service. I will recover, but he will soon be more grizzled."

Then I admitted that I had struggled for Plumed Serpent the god, not Cortes the man, and the god was unchanging. In time, if I survived, I would enjoy other men as he enjoyed other women now. I chased the hornets from my head and went back to work.

That same day an omen came. A Spanish scout brought a new horse in, a pretty young filly. I would have paid no special attention, but a lark sailed over her calling my name, and I looked sharply. It was the colt I had named Citla, the one who had deserted her own kind to run with the deer. Now she had returned willingly and happily to her own clan. I knew why the lark called me: I, too, would one day return to my own people.

I went with some Tlaxcalan leaders to greet new Spaniards arriving from Veracruz. We were to meet at the wall, that barrier whose entrance had once seemed like the Narrow Passage to me. While we were waiting on the rampart, a hundred men appeared in the meadow, not Spaniards but warriors wearing the yellow crescent of Chinantla, a town past the Cholulan border. They carried spears tipped with copper, a new trick they must have learned from Spanish lancers.

"We have come to join you," their leader shouted. "A sheaf of spears against the Aztecs. We follow Plumed Serpent!"

The Tlaxcalans eyed them, wary and confused by such words from old rivals. So I called out, "Welcome, brothers!" They were ushered through the entrance, and suddenly Chinantlans and Tlaxcalans were embracing each other, united by a common enemy. The world had indeed changed.

Meanwhile, Prince Cuitlahuac, Moctezuma's brother, reigned

eighty days as First Speaker and died of smallpox, which was now called Divine Spot, a curse from the Lords of Darkness. Prince Falling Eagle became Speaker. It seemed odd to me that no one thought of the wisdom of the astrologers who had given him an unlucky name, a name that spelled failure as surely as mine spelled destruction. Moctezuma had left one surviving legitimate son, a pitiable youth who had been made half-witted and crippled by some demon in childhood. There was also one living royal daughter, ten years old. Falling Eagle secured his throne by promptly marrying the girl and killing the boy. So, besides an unlucky name, he began his reign with the blood of his brother-in-law on his impious hands.

Foreigners living in Tenochtitlan began quietly to leave—Mixtec jewelers, Zapotec potters, merchants from Zacatlan. All these might have stayed to defend the place where they had prospered, but now they smelled death in the air. They blamed the Aztecs for rejecting Moctezuma's warnings and antagonizing Plumed Serpent. I wondered what had happened to the Mixtecs who lived next door in my childhood. They would have fought well for their home.

In the forests of Tlaxcala, a place without lakes or even real rivers, my lord began to build a navy. There were to be thirteen brigantines. Some would carry cannon, and when assembled on the shores of the Aztecs' lake, they would sweep the waters clear of war canoes, control the causeways and cut off the city from food and drinkable water, since the lake was salty near their islands.

No Tlaxcalan could understand what was being done, and most of the Spaniards scoffed at the idea as impossible. But my lord smiled and urged the Spanish shipwrights and Tlaxcalan carpenters to harder effort. He had metal fittings brought from their hiding places in Veracruz, where they had been cached ever since he "burned" his ships.

It was in such things as this, plans no man would have considered worth dreaming about, that my lord showed his godhood. Who else in a mountain-locked valley would have envisioned an armada? Who else would have turned the waters, which were the Aztecs' friend and defense, into their enemy?

Knowing that my lord would need a place to launch his ships, I sent messages to Texcoco, reminding the jealous Texcocans of their past glory and of Aztec insults. I made secret promises in the name of the god.

Yet at the same time that I was using the god's name freely, I

had a small fear about Plumed Serpent—tiny but as gnawing as a
mouse. These days my lord talked less of the new world he had
imagined and more of matters in Spain. King Carlos overshadowed
Amadis and El Cid in his thoughts. Also, the new men arriving from
the Spanish islands talked of nothing but spoils. So did the Tlaxcalans.
All swine, I suspected.

I was distracted by this worry at the time I tried to conduct
delicate negotiations with Texcoco, intriguing to get a safe shipyard
and launching place for us. My fears nagged until one night my
grandmother appeared to me.

She was at her favorite tree, her backstrap loom lashed to the
trunk. Looking up from her work, she frowned at me, quite out of
patience.

"Ce Malinalli, your hopes are too high! A fool's dreams!" she
warned me. "It is enough to try to make a *better* world. Do not hope
for a *good* one at a single stroke."

"Lady Grandmother, that is the promise of Plumed Serpent."

"For the time being it is enough to destroy the Aztec abomina-
tions, to avenge your father and his people. Plumed Serpent may have
to return a hundred times in a hundred forms before the earth becomes
the Gardens of Tula."

"Yes, Lady Grandmother."

"Be happy with small gains or you will be forever miserable."

She and her loom and the tree vanished then, leaving me joyless
but with a little more wisdom.

Near the end of the month of Falling Waters we celebrated the
anniversary of the birth of Jesus Christ in Spain—a day called Christ-
mas. The next morning Cortes inspected his new army, riding a big
horse new from the Island of Jamaica. My lord, always handsomer
riding than walking, seemed magnificent, his face strong and fierce as
an eagle's, yet when he smiled the men felt his warmth and comrade-
ship. I could have believed he loved them that morning; perhaps he
did. He nodded gravely at forty horsemen, at five hundred and fifty
Spanish soldiers on foot, many with crossbows and muskets.

Behind the Spaniards, filling a broad meadow, stood thousands
upon thousands of Tlaxcalans and other allies now trained to fight in
the Spanish manner by two of Cortes's officers. "Now they fight to
kill, not capture," one of their commanders boasted. "They attack in

close order. By the Virgin, I could even have taught them to march with their beards on the next man's shoulder, except they haven't any beards, most of them!" He roared with laughter, but there was pride in his voice.

To me the Tlaxcalans seemed glittering and splendid. For a moment I did not realize they wore clothes and jewels and plumage looted in Cholula.

At the end of the inspection I heard Pedro Alvarado say to young Sandoval, "Now it's all luck and the Virgin. We have a bigger army than when we first entered that cursed city. But only half as many men as when they drove us out."

He had not noticed fifteen thousand Tlaxcalans! But that blindness was not unusual among Spaniards.

Two days later we left Tlaxcala, marching with nine cannons but leaving the unassembled ships to be brought later when we knew the high mountain passes were secure. Three different roads lead from the Land of Bread to the great valley of the lakes, and Cortes, following my advice, chose the hardest route, the trail my spies had said would be unguarded although blocked with felled trees.

These were harrowing hours, for the Aztecs could have crushed us several times by setting loose avalanches. They did not try; again, Smoking Mirror and Hummingbird gave them no counsel.

We camped that night on the Aztec side of the frontier, shivering in the cold heights, and on the second morning looked down once more on the cities and waters. Cortes halted the army on a broad promontory where the towns below lay spread in glittering temptation.

"Let us now kneel and thank God, brothers," Cortes commanded. The army knelt, Aguilar standing before them with a cross made of pine branches.

When their prayers were finished, but before the men had risen, a newly arrived priest, a certain Friar Pedro who had just come with an official party from Spain, mounted a fallen tree trunk and addressed the Spaniards. He waved a clutch of papers at them and held scrolls bundled under his arm.

"Good news!" he cried. "From the Holy Father in Rome I have brought forgiveness of any sins Christians may commit while bringing religion to these wicked lands. For only a small price, payable in the heathens' gold, you may have a dispensation or an indulgence in advance of doing what would otherwise be crime. God's blessing on your good work."

I did not translate for the Tlaxcalans or other allies. Long ago they had heard much the same thing, although their dispensations, of course, came from Smoking Mirror.

We started down the slope and the Spaniards, suddenly cheerful, began to sing, a song so old and familiar that they all knew it. I understood the words but not the meaning as their strong voices rang out in the clear air of the morning.

> *"Nero watched from Tarpey Rock*
> *Rome at his feet aflare.*
> *Children, women, screamed and died,*
> *But he did not care."*

On the plains outside Texcoco we paused a moment to see what sort of reception awaited us in the first large city of the Triple Alliance.

My lord said to me, "If you are right, if your spies have gained this city for me without a fight, how can I reward you? I will give you any gift you name."

From the tales of romance and chivalry my lord had told me, I knew what my reply should be. I was supposed to say, "One kiss from you, my lord, is the greatest prize." I considered replying like this—which I think he expected—but it seemed foolish and a lie.

I said, "When the fighting is over, when victory is ours and you can afford this gift, I would like a horse."

He stared at me in astonishment. "Woman, there are not fifty horses in this half of the world!" Then he roared with laughter. "Very well. A horse for the City of Texcoco. But you must be patient about collecting."

We moved on then, the men still singing, and at the outskirts of Texcoco a delegation of elders met us, carrying sheaves of roses and smoking jars of incense.

"Welcome, Malintzin, welcome Malinche! Our city is yours. Enter in peace and happiness."

Later, safely inside the city, Pedro Alvarado complained that the peace was a ruse to gain time, that the women had fled with their children, and so had the king, taking his treasure and best arms. Of course they fled. Alvarado had his own reputation to thank for that.

But by words alone, and words spoken at a great distance, I had gained for my lord the place where he could soon launch his ships— the first navy that ever crossed mountains.

We climbed the high temple in Texcoco to implant a cross there. Although it seemed deserted, Cortes suspected that armed priests might be lurking in ambush, so he swept aside the belled curtain of the Holy of Holies with his sword . . . then gasped.

Inside the sanctum entrance, stationed like guardian statues, were five horses, seeming at a glance to be alive. They were only heads and stuffed skins, yet I expected them to toss their manes and neigh. My lord's face paled, then became set in stone.

Farther inside, in the dimness where gods had been taken from altars, the faces of five Spaniards hung on the wall like bearded masks. They had been tanned, then painted to make the skin living. I recognized the men but had not known them; Cortes spoke their names and crossed himself. Near the door hung still another face, this one a woman's, topped with hair dyed a hideous yellow and the skin chalked white, a death's-head. This was all that remained of the once pretty countenance of Flower Pouch, left here like the Spaniards as a warning and promise. I turned away, regretful I had cursed her and wished her an evil end. Flower Pouch was the one the Aztecs caught; I was the one they longed for.

22

The Shrine of Xilonen—
August 13, 1521

Let storytellers in the markets and plazas recount the fall of Tenochtit-
lan. Poets still mourn it as the most beautiful city the world has known.
Except for Tula, I suppose it was; at least the Spaniards thought so.
But memories of its beauty and terror are best left to poets.

I saw only a little of its death throes, although my enemies have
claimed I was a vulture wheeling in the skies every day during those
seven months of agony as, wall by wall and house by house, the city
crumbled.

My lord warned me to stay away except when summoned to the
siege lines. Smallpox, the Divine Spot, had slain half the Aztecs before
we ever fired a cannon on their city. God knows how many more
sickened and died in the days that followed. The Spaniards had grown
up with this demon; those destined for him perished in childhood or
fought him and survived and were safe afterward. In their world,
where he was familiar, he had lost strength; in ours he became a giant
stalking the valleys like Death himself. His strides were longest in the
crowded streets of Tenochtitlan.

"It is the Almighty God's punishment on them for sin. Especially
for sodomy," Father Olmedo announced in a sermon. When I translated this for the Tlaxcalans, they were astounded that the Lord of the
Universe would take time from moving the stars and changing the
seasons to be concerned with such small matters. Others asked why so

many women and children also suffered. With Father Olmedo's God anything was possible, just as with Smoking Mirror.

While the Divine Spot was doing its work, the Spanish fleet cleared the waters of canoes, claimed the causeways, and after savage fighting Lake Texcoco became a Spanish pond.

Meanwhile warriors from twenty nations, from a hundred cities, were joining us. Soon the city was ringed by Spanish steel and one hundred thousand fighting men: Chichimecas from the north wearing hairless dog skin, tattooed Huastecs, Otomis, Chalcans, Otumbans . . . The whole world, led by Spaniards, united to raze Tenochtitlan. Moctezuma's ghost should have been appeased—the truth was as grim as the prophecies.

When I recall those months—and I try not to remember them often—they do not come like most memories, unfolding before me like a painted book. I see only swift pictures emerging from darkness, flashing before my closed eyes and vanishing in dark again.

. . . I remember meeting Bernal Diaz at the foot of a causeway after a skirmish. He was gaunt and bloodstained; there was no trace of the elegance that had caused him to be nicknamed The Gallant. He no longer bothered to put a flower in his helmet.

He gestured toward a group of Chichimeca warriors lounging nearby. "They are beasts, wolves. I have never seen such horror as they have done today against helpless women and children. Why are they here except for spoils and feasts on human flesh? I have heard stories of the wars in Italy, how armies on the march are followed by flocks of crows and kites who gorge themselves on the corpses when a battle is over. These savages are worse than those birds."

I nodded, smiling in sympathy, and plucked a straw flower for him to wear. Yes, he was right; there were many here for spoils. I did not ask, "And why are *you* on this spot today, Bernal?"

. . . One afternoon I saw a fleet of canoes from Xochimilco dart between the Spanish ships and safely reach an Aztec landing. Until now Xochimilco had been a neutral town, and I had flattered myself it was because of my diplomacy in reminding them of old scores against the Aztecs. Now I felt defeat, for they were joining the enemy.

The Aztecs thought so, too, and they welcomed them through the defenses, embracing them as allies. But that same night the Xochimilcans were caught trying to slip away, loading their canoes with bound and gagged women and children they were stealing as slaves, repaying the ancient debt I had counted on. Most of the Xochimilcans were slaughtered in the canoes but a few reached the shore, where they were cut to pieces by their pursuers. That night coyotes came down from the hills and licked their blood from the stones.

. . . I stood with the Spaniards after a struggle when the Aztecs managed to carry off half a dozen soldiers. The day was bright and we were so close to the great temple that we could watch the rites. The Spanish captives were painted and decked in costumes of Hummingbird's chosen. They wore feathers on their heads in the shape of fans, and were forced to dance wildly for the god, prodded by spears and flaming torches. We watched helpless, groaning, as the offerings were stretched alive on the altar, their hearts torn out, their entrails thrown to beasts that waited below. A young soldier beside me pounded his fists on his thighs and screamed, "Oh, let me kill them! Let me kill them all!" Three days later he himself was caught and met the same fate as those comrades he dreamed of avenging.

In August, when the city lay in its last convulsions and every day and night smoke hung over it as above a pyre, I had my tent set up on the hillside near Texcoco. I would take no risks now; I realized I was carrying my lord's child, and suddenly my own life became precious in a way I had not known before.

Each day I thought the futile struggle would end—the city was the Land of Death, without food or water or hope, defended only by Falling Eagle and the skeletons of priests. Yet at dawn I heard the beating of the great snakeskin drum. The fowls were sacrificed; the sun could rise on another day of horror.

Then one morning there was silence. Watching from the slope, I saw four canoes attempting to escape from the smoking ruins, and as they came nearer, I realized that one bore the royal awning and the crest of Falling Eagle. A Spanish ship swept down upon it. There was no escape except by death spat from a cannon's mouth. I watched Falling Eagle, who had taunted Moctezuma for holding his own life too precious, rise and surrender and save his, that proud young man's wisest and most pathetic act. So I saw the end of the World of the Fifth Sun; I gazed on victory and did not rejoice.

Soon I would be called to translate the first interview between Falling Eagle and my lord. Cortes would want me there; others might have learned the language, but I was his own tongue.

Not long ago I would have rushed to the meeting. But now I had a different sense of time and importance. I must be alone to welcome the new world, alone with the goddess and the child I carried.

I spoke to a Tlaxcalan guard. "I am going to the Shrine of Xilonen. If Malintzin sends a messenger for me, he will find me there."

"Should we not go with you, Lady Malinche?"

"We are safe today. Besides, I have the goddess."

The crossroad where the shrine stood was not far away. I followed the trail near the shore, passing fields where farmers and their wives and children were toiling patiently in the sun, bent to their work, the fall of Tenochtitlan as remote to them as the falling of a star.

One of the farm women gave me a shy, polite smile. I remembered that on all our marches such people had quietly greeted us, watched a moment, then returned to their labor, our splendor meaning no more to them than a momentary amusement.

Today in the fields and orchards the families worked amid a cloud of butterflies, the spirits of their own ancestors who had broken this same soil before them and whose bones lay beneath it, beyond the reach of conquerors and kings.

I found the shrine and the gap in the rocks where I could see both the altar and the lake. Here I had kneeled a year ago—a lifetime ago—and implored the silent goddess who had given me no better an answer than the sting of ants. Today she looked smaller and even shabbier, the winds and rains having torn away all but the last threads of her mantle. Even the dead flowers were gone.

A cactus grew among the rocks, and breaking off a single thorn, I pierced the lobe of my ear and let a tiny drop of blood fall on the altar. Lady Iztac would have approved, but I did not do it for her. It was for all that had vanished.

Closing my eyes in prayer, with my right hand I made the sign of mystic invitation. Around me the glen sang with voices. A locust whirred, thrushes called, and soon I felt spirits close to me—Lady Flint Knife, my father, Lark Singer—although neither they nor the goddess spoke. Yet meaning hovered in the silence, a whispering that was more than the drone of bees.

But at last with my left hand I made the gesture of return to the world and opened my eyes. There was only the blue lake with distant sails and down the trail the farmers in their fields. But now the hum of bees I had ignored grew so strong it demanded my attention. The swarm, I now saw, had long ago returned to the stump we had charred last summer. They had rebuilt the hive, comb by yellow comb, raising again their labyrinthine city of halls and tunnels, chambers and throne room.

The red-brown ants had also returned, although in depleted numbers. In companies of five and six they advanced, tested and struggled, a few to leave triumphant from the comb where others drowned.

I supposed that the Lords among the ant survivors were speaking to their followers. "We have conquered," they said, lifting their crippled feelers high. "We have mastered the hive!"

I knew now that this was the message of the goddess, and I looked from the bees down the trail to where the brown-skinned farmers quietly repaired their gardens, binding up branches soldiers had broken in the orchards. Gently my child stirred within me.

A clatter of hooves sounded on the trail, and in a dusty cloud three horsemen rode into view. Two men were riding the biggest horse, Brother Aguilar clinging behind the horseman.

"So here you are," he said, climbing down breathless. "Cortes wants you at once. And I have important news, wonderful news. The Aztec king has been captured! By God's grace the siege is over!"

"I know," I said.

He looked annoyed, cheated. "Cortes wants you to translate at the first interview. I could do it, of course. I know this language now. But Cortes insisted. Everything must be exact for his report to the king."

"Ah, yes. The king who owns this world now. I had forgotten."

"Well, there's much less to own than a year ago, I'd say." Aguilar, in his patched and dusty habit, lingered beside me, shading his eyes from the sun, peering over the waters toward the ravaged islands. Smoke still curled from the smoldering roof beams, but it was thinner now.

"Finished for good," he said happily. "It will never rise again. Satan's capital demolished for all time."

I remembered the words of the priestess at the shrine near Cholula. I said, "The gods give back what cities themselves have most valued."

Aguilar did not hear me. "The fighting is not quite over. Our men are still digging, hunting down the last holdouts. Still, the city is finished. In a few years not even a rubble heap will mark it."

I gazed across the lake, where white sails with crimson crosses billowed in the wind, and because we stood in a place of prophecy, I knew the sails foretold the ship that would one day take my lord the Captain back to Spain forever. Of course he would go—Plumed Serpent always did.

To the south the great volcano gods stood watch over the valley and the blackening skeletons of the Cities of the Lakes. But I felt not death but rising life, my child and my lord's, strong and clear as the music of flutes. I saw the fallen domes and towers standing again lofty in the sun, as eternal as anything can be upon this fragile earth.

"Lady Marina, you really must hurry now."

But for a moment more I hesitated, watching the men and women toiling along the shore, yet my mind was drawn beyond them and held in an unfathomable future. Across the fields and waters I looked again toward that desolated city where, among the ruins, the ants were still conquering the hive.

"Please, my lady." Aguilar had grown impatient. "We have won a victory, but you must not feel your work is over now. In a sense, it is just beginning."

"Yes," I said, turning away. "I know."

23

The City of Mexico—Eve of St. Judith—September 27, 1564

My last night at the convent I slept little, and the sleep I did manage was broken by dreams. I watched the death of Pedro Alvarado, although he had actually given up the ghost more than twenty years ago in Jalisco when I was far away. He had slashed his way through the valley of Oaxaca, brought blood and fire to Guatemala, and at length he himself believed he was what the Aztecs named him, "The Sun," and all-conquering.

Then, in the wilds of Jalisco trying to slaughter some warriors he despised, Alvarado made one foolhardy charge too many. The Sun and his soldiers were routed. While fleeing ingloriously on foot, a horse fell on him as they both tried to scramble up a steep ravine. Something inside Alvarado was crushed, but he was eleven days dying, and in my dream I stood at the bedside the whole time praying he would get on with it.

Near the end he opened his eyes and glared at me. "What are you doing here, you Indian cunt?"

"Waiting for sunset," I said. Then he shuddered and died, and I seemed to hear the whole world sigh with relief.

A moment later the corpse suddenly sat up, uttering a shriek so blood-curdling that it awoke me. I shivered on my mat, knowing that Alvarado burned in hell.

Rising, I put on a robe and went to the window, hoping the cool night breeze would banish the dream, clear my head. Considering he had been a man once touched by a god, Alvarado had died so ordinarily. What poet could sing of a hero squashed by a horse while running from a battlefield?

The true gods who came to live among men were like my lord the Captain. Or, in a different way, the two old friars I had met that afternoon, a sailor who had unlocked the gates of the East for us, and a missionary who did something even harder: he opened the hearts of men. We had need of such saving gods now, just as we had needed Plumed Serpent.

Across the street lay a compound of crumbling adobe houses that were rife with smallpox. Each night brought another wake for the newly dead. I heard weeping now. Leaning against the sill, I said a prayer. "Return, my lord! Come soon."

A bell tolled midnight, marking the end of the Feast of Saint Cosme, the start of the Day of Saint Judith, the woman with a sword. At almost the same time I heard knocking at the convent gate, and I knew the summons was for me.

I hurried down the outside stairs, using my hand to shield a candle against the wind. In the courtyard my two strange spies awaited me, the old woman and the boy Juanito, both breathless from running. She was wheezing and gasping and could not yet speak, but words tumbled from Juanito.

"Señora, the council is meeting now. Don Martin has been questioned for hours. As soon as his confession is recorded, they will pass sentence."

Then the old woman spoke pantingly in the Aztec tongue. "Yes, lady. They tortured him in the prison; they twisted a rope tighter and tighter first around his arm, then his chest, and at last his forehead."

I knew about the use of the cord. A skull could burst from the pressure.

"And he confessed?" I felt hollow, dead. What did it matter if he confessed or not? I could only hope that the torture was over.

"Oh, no! I heard the guards say he spoke not a word, made no sound at all."

So he had not been broken. I thought of the scars of the lash on Lady Iztac's back, of Falling Eagle standing in the fire yet managing to speak of roses. We were a people who could endure. We might not win, but we endured—yes, we did that well.

The boy said, "The council will soon sentence this lord to death. When they meet so late at night, they always do."

A gust of wind blew out the candle. I stood almost in darkness, bewildered, not knowing what to do. But there was a faint light from Lady Moon among the broken clouds. Then I felt more than heard a stirring among the shadows.

"Who is it? Who's there?" I asked sharply. No answer came, but suddenly I felt the presence of the goddess all around me, whispering in the laurel tree near the gate, hovering invisibly in the deserted colonnade. She had returned—after so many years of absence. I knew then what I must do and I had the power.

"Wait for me here," I said. The voice seemed stronger than my own. "Juanito, my bearers are sleeping outside the wall. Wake them up, have my chair ready. Light torches—all of you will carry torches!"

I moved swiftly, easily up the steep stairs that until now had been a punishment to my bones. In my chamber I dressed quickly but carefully, putting on the special gown I had brought with me but never worn. I ripped the linings of old clothes where I had sewn jewels to conceal them, opals set in silver, gifts from my lord; it was right I should wear them now. I arranged my hair so it fell upon my shoulders as it does in the painted books that tell of Malinche. Last I fastened around my shoulders the royal green cape, brocaded cotton with quetzal plumes. The featherwork was old and a little faded, but tonight would seem regal. The medallion of the goddess felt warm, alive against my breast.

Downstairs five torches blazed near the gate. As I came into the light, I heard Juanito gasp. I felt calm and purposeful, yet intensely alive. I felt young.

"Take me to the palace where the viceroy's council meets." The bearers gaped and bowed as I entered the chair.

Tonight the way was lit by torches, but we made our way as silently as long ago when I crept through these same hushed streets with the soldiers and my lord trying to reach the causeway of escape. I felt the same quickening, the same mixture of hope and fear that I knew then. But now I was stronger.

At the great plaza the nightwatch waved us past, not questioning the occupant of so rich a chair. Juanito through the open window asked, "Which entrance, señora? I know a side door that is sometimes not locked or guarded. We might—"

"The main portal."

"Yes, señora."

"You and two bearers with torches will follow me and wait outside the chamber where the council meets."

At the arched entrance I dismounted from the chair, and two guards stepped quickly together to bar my way with crossed spears. "Your business here?" The sentry's voice was gruff, yet I heard a trace of awe in it.

"It is I, Malinche. The Lady Marina of Cortes. I will speak to the council now. You may announce me."

He hesitated only a second, then turned and scurried ahead. I followed slowly, unhurriedly, motioning to Juanito and the bearers to trail behind. I would not have needed a guide; candles burned only in one chamber, the great hall on the arcaded upper floor. Except for those gleaming doors, the palace stretched as dark and silent as a tomb. I mounted the stairs—easier, I thought, than climbing temple steps to address throngs in Cholula or Tlaxcala or in a score of other cities. It seemed only yesterday I had spoken to those hostile mobs; and I had moved them, tamed them—sometimes with the Captain's words, more often with my own.

Ahead of me in the council chamber my arrival had been announced. I heard voices raised in questions and confusion. My own name was spoken, and someone exclaimed, "Didn't she die?" Another voice said, "She must be seized as a witch!" A witch? Yes, they might decide that. It was a chance I must take.

The hall fell silent as I entered, moving slowly to the center of the room, strong with the power of the goddess. Two tapers burned on tall pedestals, and I stationed myself between them. This must be where prisoners stood awaiting judgment; there would be bloodstains on the floor, but I did not glance down. I said, "It is I, Malinche."

The score of candles burning in the room seemed faint, feeble against the dark, leaving the long hall dim and shadowed. A dais ran the width of the hall and on it, seated behind a narrow table, were the lord councillors, five solemn figures. Hunched at a nearby desk with a lamp was the official scribe.

The viceroy had enthroned himself in a carved chair at the center of the table, Don Luis de Velasco, with a spade-shape beard below the features of an ancient hawk. Here was the enemy I had ill wished and cursed, yet I felt no emanations of evil from him now. On his right were two monks, heads shrouded in black Dominican hoods; and on the left were two magistrates, their bloodless faces almost as white as the lace ruffs they wore with their black velvet jackets. I recognized the one at the end; he was Muñoz, the royal judge, a hangman and headsman. I was surprised that the face of cruelty should be so soft and flabby.

I stared up at them in silence, a row of death's-heads—remembering the masked council of Chacs that had condemned me in Tabasco a lifetime ago. I had been judged before, I thought. I know this charade.

The viceroy leaned forward, curious, peering. To oblige him, I lifted my face to the light that he might more easily inspect me. "You are Malinche?" His voice was thin, papery. Suddenly I sensed the nearness of his own death.

"I am she." The Dominican at the end crossed himself; the other, nodding, whispered in the viceroy's ear; I had been recognized.

Don Luis said, "I have heard much of you, my lady."

"And I of you, my lord."

"It seems you are well loved in this land." He paused, then added with a faint smile, "Well hated, too, I think."

"Even as yourself, Excellency."

The Dominican made a growling noise, but Don Luis's smile warmed a little. "I regret we meet in such circumstances. I know your errand. You have come to plead—"

I raised my head again and stared at him, looking like anything but a suppliant, and he hesitated. Then no one spoke until Judge Muñoz, unable to contain himself, began to bluster. "We respect a mother's feelings, we are merciful men. Why I myself—"

"Your mercy is famous, sir," I said. "The whole land rings with tales of it." The viceroy's brows lifted.

"We are the king's highest court. If we listened to every mother of every accused—"

"I am not every mother," I said quietly. "I am Malinche."

It was not my words but the goddess that rebuked him. He stopped speaking and lowered his eyes to the table while the others glanced at him, counting his cruelties.

The goddess had taken command; it was her voice, not mine, that spoke her own words. "I have not come to beg or plead or even to remind you of gratitude. I come only to ask a question. My lords, how will you be remembered?"

I looked slowly from one to another, then my gaze rested on the viceroy. "You are outstanding men, persons of high achievement, or you would not be in this room tonight. But no matter what you have done in your lives, no matter what great works you do in the future, if you commit the error you are now pondering, that act alone will be remembered after your own deaths. Men will say: *He killed Cortes's son.* Those words will blot out all else."

My voice rose, filled the room as in old days it rang across plazas. Now the goddess and I were one. "Killed Cortes's son! Killed him in the capital of the land Cortes gave the king. Killed him in the presence of his mother, Malinche! Know, my lords, that if my son goes to the scaffold, I shall be at the scene so all the world can see my grief and share it. I believe I can promise you a crowd. Is this your wish, my lords?"

The viceroy leaned forward, now seeing me not as a curiosity but an embarrassment, even a threat. Judge Muñoz glared, perhaps wondering if he could safely have me murdered on the spot. And still the hall was silent; the councillors did not look at each other; Don Luis folded his long fingers and studied them. He, too, I thought, sensed the nearness of his own dying. Finally he spoke, his face drawn, his eyes half-closed, and he spoke not to me or the council but to the scribe.

"Write this for the official record, one copy to be kept here, the other to be sent to Spain." The scribe dripped his quill, then wrote quickly while Don Luis dictated.

"Don Martin Cortes was questioned scrupulously, first with the cord, then after forcing six pitchers of cold water down his throat."

I shuddered, but all eyes were on the viceroy. "The prisoner made no statement. In this condition, the said Martin being ill and somewhat fatigued by the torture, the said torture was ordered suspended."

Somewhat fatigued? Those were his words put into the official record and I heard no tone of irony. Then the viceroy spoke to me. "We will let the whole matter of this conspiracy end here. Your son will be fined and banished at once from New Spain." Tepi would live, then! "His release will take an hour or so. Do you wish to wait at the prison?"

Before I could reply, the Dominican who had recognized me

spoke urgently. His face was still shadowed, and a bodiless voice seemed to come from the cowl. "Forgive me, Excellency, but the lady should return home at once and quietly. Her appearance here—although it had no real effect on the council's decision—might cause unnecessary talk. My agents investigated this case thoroughly, and I know she has had no contact with her son since he was an infant. In fact, her disappearance has been so complete that Don Martin believes her dead. He told me so himself."

I stood stunned, trying not to show confusion. The priest went on softly, smoothly. "Any sudden, new association, between them now might have the odor of still another conspiracy."

Judge Muñoz broke in. "Yes. These are not mere private persons. Both are political figures who bear watching. They must avoid contact, avoid any appearance of scheming together."

The Dominican cowl turned toward me; I saw a pinched, ascetic face unknown to me before. "Since Don Martin goes into exile, what difference can it make? The Lady Malinche has a subtle mind and will take my meaning."

Yes, I understood. I was not to meet with Tepi—this was the price of his release. I was about to protest, but the goddess checked me, whispering, "I have given you a victory. Do not complain of the cost." I yielded then. I had given Tepi to another life long ago; then, in the last months, I had in my mind many times buried, mourned him and become reconciled.

The councillors, now glancing at each other, awaited my agreement. I said, "I understand. It will be as you say. Besides, my lords, I am too old to have a new son, and he is too old to endure a new mother."

I almost managed to smile at these men I hated, this devil's spawn who had dared torture my lord's son. "By your leave, I now bid you good night. To use His Excellency's words, I, too, am somewhat fatigued."

I did not bow, but inclined my head. To my surprise, Don Luis rose. Then the others followed his lead. They all stood as I left the chamber.

Outside, descending the stairs, I felt relief but no exultation of victory. The matter was simply concluded; I could move on now to other things. I gripped the railing with my right hand, and the boy Juanito steadied my left. Strange, when such a little while before I had mounted the steps so easily. Of course, the goddess had been with me then. Now she had gone—forever, I suspected.

At the convent I bundled together my possessions, resewed the jewels into their hiding places, then kneeled to give thanks to the goddess, although I felt she paid no attention, even when I said, "I will not trouble you again."

For a time I remained kneeling, not in prayer but in meditation, as I forced from my heart a small idol that had subtly become enshrined there. Tepi would not go with me to my lands in the south, would not live there now or later. All summer I had dimly entertained this illusion. Now I destroyed it, not only because of the council's orders but because it was a foolish dream. The trail of the rabbit I followed led another way. Why should I wish to change a path that had been, all in all, a good one? It was still good and might yet run a long way.

My bearers and I started across the lake toward Texcoco in darkness, the barge moving toward the pallor of false dawn. We were long delayed at the canal that connects the town with the water, then delayed again at the tax collector's roost where the viceroy's bandits tried to pick me clean.

Merchants and departing travelers were milling about, a priest blessing pilgrims, sprinkling holy water and calling upon St. Christopher the Giant. Some older men, Mixtec pottery sellers, were covertly invoking the Guiding Lord.

I gathered my men and goods and animals, checking everything, giving orders to repack one load, seeing that all the knots were tight and the coverings proper. I set an order of march and examined weapons. Absorbed in my tasks, I did not think about my most important duty until it was full daylight. Then, assigning others to take care of the last details, I made my way alone toward my lord's tomb at the Monastery of St. Francis.

I felt weary from the night before; every bone and joint complained of my abusing them. The trail was muddy and puddled, so I moved with great care not to soil the somber black cape I wore for my visit; later I would change to something suitable for travel.

I had almost reached the churchyard gate when I heard horses approaching at a fast trot behind the wall. They were coming toward me. The trail was narrow. I tried to leap aside, but the ground sloped.

Five horsemen rode out of the gate, almost riding me down, the hooves splattering me with mud from hem to collar.

"Goat fuckers!" I screamed at them, shaking my cane. "Whore sons!"

They laughed, and I supposed they would ride on, as such piss pots always do, but the man in front halted them. "Apologies, my lady." He spoke to one of the others. "Pablo, help her clean off the mud. I am in no condition to dismount."

"Don't touch me with your leper's hands. Just unblock the gate, you sons of mongrel bitches!"

They rode on then. I was struggling to brush away the mud when I looked up to shout a parting curse. A breeze had lifted a banner one rider carried, and I saw the flag of Cortes. I also saw that the first rider, the man I had insulted, was hunched in the saddle, not holding the reins but clinging to the horse's neck and mane. The next rider reached out to steady him, but he shook his head.

I had only a glimpse of his face—as dark as my own although he wore the beard and clothes of a Spanish officer. As they moved beyond my vision, I thought the rider was in pain. A possibility crossed my mind, but I banished it as unlikely and entered the churchyard.

The burial ground stretched as raw and ugly as it had been last spring; the rains had not softened this bleak place. But then it had been a shrine for pilgrims, strewn with litter. Now it seemed unvisited; the worshipers had forgotten.

But at my lord's tomb lay a sheaf of Castillian roses, newly cut. I caught my breath, realizing that the rider who was in pain had indeed been Tepi—no, Don Martin. I must always think of him by that name now. Why had I not known at once? I remembered his father clinging to his horse all day at the worst battle in Tlaxcala. The son had come to his father's grave as quickly as he could, no matter what he had suffered yesterday. Endurance, I thought. Yes, that was his heritage.

I felt proud of him, yet grateful I had not looked into his face.

My own offering for Cortes's ghost was only a single blossom, one of the dark marigolds of autumn that our people have always given the dead, the flowers that line the paths on special days so the souls can find their way back home.

I hesitated, gazing at the great volcanoes whose shoulders we had once crossed, and I pictured beyond them that long passage of eagles that winds to the sea, the corridor through which gods have always come and departed, gods who have changed the land violently, yet somehow never made their own best dreams come to pass. I closed my eyes, remembering how my grandmother had once spoken to me in a vision, telling me not to hope that the world would be good, only that it might be better. "Ce Malinalli, be happy with small gains or you will be forever miserable."

It was time to go. I had composed a long farewell to say at this moment, but now it seemed pointless. Plumed Serpent, glowing and beautiful, was not present in this graveyard. He waited elsewhere, as he always did—in the wind, in the morning star, in the hearts of those who longed for him.

Turning away, I whispered the prayer I had spoken last night. "Return, my lord! Come soon!"

The Conquest of Mexico

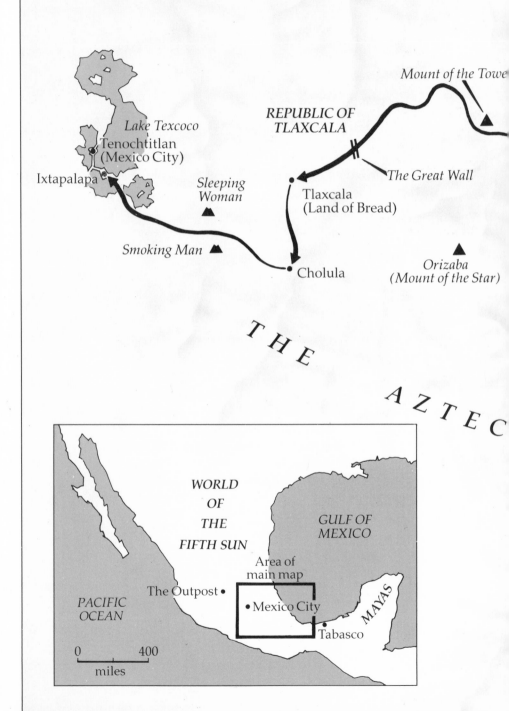

Mount of the Tower

REPUBLIC OF
TLAXCALA

Lake Texcoco

Tenochtitlan
(Mexico City)

The Great Wall

Ixtapalapa

Sleeping
Woman

Tlaxcala
(Land of Bread)

Smoking Man

Orizaba
(Mount of the Star)

Cholula

T H E

A Z T E C

WORLD
OF
THE
FIFTH SUN

GULF OF
MEXICO

Area of
main map

The Outpost

PACIFIC
OCEAN

Mexico City

MAYAS

Tabasco

0   400
miles